P9-DEV-503

THE
CRIPPLE LIBERATION FRONT
MARCHING BAND BLUES

OTHER BOOKS BY LORENZO W. MILAM

Sex and Broadcasting: A Handbook on Building a Radio Station for the Community

The Myrkin Papers

The Petition Against God: The Full Story Behind the Lansman-Milam Petition RM-2493, by Rev. A. W. Allworthy

Under a Bed of Poses

The Radio Papers: From KRAB to KCHU

K. M. POST

Lorenzo W. Milam

THE

CRIPPLE LIBERATION FRONT

MARCHING BAND BLUES

MHO & MHO WORKS   1984   SAN DIEGO, CALIFORNIA

This book is published by Mho & Mho Works and was manufactured in the United States of America.

Designed by Douglas Cruickshank.

Quotes for Parts I, II, IV, and V are from *The Sound and The Fury* by William Faulkner, © 1946 Random House.

The first part of this book appeared in "The Sky's No Limit." Excerpts also appeared in #89, #91, #92, and #93 of "The Sun," 412 West Rosemary Street, Chapel Hill, North Carolina 27514.

Copyright © 1984 Mho & Mho Works.

Names have been changed to honor the innocent.

This Book is distributed by Bookpeople, 2940 7th St., Berkeley, California 94710. Orders of less than five copies may be sent directly to the publisher:

    Mho & Mho Works
    Box 33135
    San Diego, California 92103
  Include $1.00 for postage.

Mail a stamped, self-addressed envelope to the above address for a complete catalogue of other books being offered by Mho & Mho Works.

Library of Congress Cataloging in Publication Data
Milam, Lorenzo W. (1933-   )
    The Cripple Liberation Front Marching Band Blues
    1. Handicapped—Psychology
    2. Handicapped—Sexual behavior
    3. Roosevelt, Franklin D.—Warm Springs Foundation
    4. Basketcases—Care & Feeding of
      I. Title
    HQ 30.5.M55   362.104 2   LC# 83-62347
ISBN #0-917320-09-3 Paperback

1 2 3 4 5 6 7 8 9 10 J Q K A

PART I

was the saddest word of all
there is nothing else in the world
its not despair until time its not
even time until it was

— The Sound and The Fury

I have so much to tell you of the new life that grew out of a windy fall day, half-way through the century, on the banks of a soft brown river, turned foaming with the storm. I am abed, on a porch, beside the moaning camphor trees. The screens oh and sigh, canvas cords cry out in the wind, and I cannot rise. The doctor comes, with his black bag, in the storm, to tell us what is happening to that part of myself I call body. The doctor comes, with his bag, to give us that black knowledge, of the virus, of the body, dying, on that day when the wind tears Spanish moss from the long-leaf pine, and the camphor trees howl, and the branches of my body come crashing down, turning slowly in the wind gone mad and wrong.

CHAPTER I

My sister! My teacher! In 1952, she had two weeks advance knowledge of the theory and practice of the wasting disease. I want you to see her. She is my companion-in-arms.

No goddess, nor villain. A child of twenty-nine. Two years of college. Presented to society in late 1943. A woman of great sport and warmth.

She likes sailing, and tennis. She is a good swimmer, with a broad fine stroke in the school of the Australian Crawl. She loves cooking, and from time to time, I would hear her in the kitchen, humming tunelessly to herself.

Of all the unlikely people, of all the unlikely people to kiss with the grey disease: who would have guessed? As of the second of September, she is laid in the hospital bed by poliomyelitis. By the sixth of September, they have laid her in an iron lung so that she can continue to breathe. And on the 29th of December, of the same year, they lay her in the grave.

She has never thought about the functioning of her body. She has no idea in the world how her various muscles combine in their workings with bone in a magic way to carry her through the range of motion: the complex interface of muscle and bone and nerves, the action and reaction of dendrons, axons, neurones, cytons that makes it possible for her to climb into a sailboat and spend a day racing before the wind on the St. Johns River. I am sure that the knowledge of *how it is done* never comes to her. Nor the importance of it. It never occurs to her. At least, not until late summer 1952.

She a *naïf* who spends twenty-nine years of her life harming no one and loving, to the depths she is able, a few close family members and a husband. She is an innocent, slightly freckled child who plays a fair game of tennis, and who trails her red hair behind her like a fire.

She contracts polio in late August and in the intense stage, it moves slowly over the entire field of her body. When the fever departs, she has one muscle remaining: in her left foot. Because of the loss of her breathing apparatus, she is fitted with a machine that breathes for her. "Whoosh" it goes, fifteen times a minute, nine hundred times an hour.

She cannot scratch her knee should it itch. She cannot bring food to her own mouth. She cannot brush back her fine red hair. She cannot wash nor wipe herself. She cannot reach out to hold another's hands.

In her respirator, she is flat on her back. She is turned over every hour or so to prevent the development of bedsores which can become malignant and score the body down all the way to white bone.

The regularity of the bellows punctuates her every moment, asleep or awake. "Whoosh." "Whoosh." A submarine: she is lying in a submarine. Warm. Protected. With lightbulbs, festooning the iron lung, like a newly constructed building, or a Christmas tree. A submarine with portholes all along the side, so you can peer in and see where the muscles have disappeared from bone.

She, my sister, the originator and founder of all this pain, is now quite thin. Bones show beneath flesh, a picture out of Dachau. A woman's once graceful body now has knobby knees, knobby elbows, celery root. The hip bones jut up from a wasted stomach. The entire skeletal frame is pushing to get out, to get born, to be done with this painful flesh.

Her eyes are quite large now. Her face so shrunken and drawn that the eyes start out as if she were some night creature, startled in her submarine body. "Whoosh." She views you, the room, the world, upside down through a mirror. People stand outside her new breathing machine, up near the head, and wonder what to say. If they stand, she looks at their legs (legs that move!) If they sit, she sees their faces backwards. Friends' faces are turned around, turned obverse.

She who never thought seriously about sickness, nor her body, nor death, is thinking on them now, thinking hard on them. And she wonders what to say to the reversed faces of her old friends who cannot imagine *who cannot imagine* what it is like to be in the pale tan submarine, with all the dials and meters, and the bellows that go "whoosh" fifteen times a minute, nine hundred times an hour.

And if they talk, and they do talk, and if she replies, and she does reply, her words are turned wispy, hard-to-hear, for the talking mechanism is dependent on lungs and air, and her lungs have been deprived of power to push air and words.

And when she talks, and she talks so that you can barely hear her, she talks on the exhale, because she cannot talk on the inhale (one does not fight the submarine), which means that her sentences are interrupted fifteen times each minute, for the breathing machine to make her breathe, which makes conversations with her quite leisurely, long pauses in the sentences, and everyone learns to be patient, very patient, with this new woman in her new submarine, who has become very patient.

Very very patient. Doesn't demand too much, really. Can't demand too much. Except that you feed her when hungry (she is not very hungry) and bathe her when dirty (she is not very dirty, doesn't play in the mud too much) and dry off that place near the corners of her eyes when sad (she is sad very much because she doesn't know what has happened to her, nor why) and be with her when she thinks on

3

the things that are gone now, like body and arms and legs and motion which are gone now, so soon now, things that she loved, gone so soon now, like sailing and tennis and running into the surf at the beach on the Atlantic Coast, and most of all, the ability, that important ability to scratch her knee, when it begins to itch, or turn over in her sleep, which she doesn't do very much any more, sleep that is, because of the noise, and confusion, and the strange change that has come over her body, which with the six nurses and orderlies and nurse's aides and the eight doctors and technicians and physical therapists, which with all these people working at her body, somehow doesn't seem to be her body any more at all, at all.

They give her a mirror, over her face, turned at a forty-five degree angle, attached to the submarine, the submarine that pumps away, with its engine pumping away. They give her a mirror so that she can see the world, so she doesn't have to look at the ceiling, the light green institutional ceiling, with the flies, and the single naked light bulb. She is given a mirror, her own mirror, so that she can watch the world go by outside her door, there in her hospital room. She doesn't know if her room has a view out the window, because she isn't turned that way, but rather, turned so that she can see up and down the hall, see the nurses and orderlies and doctors, who come in to do things to her body, her new body, a body which has come up with such new experiences of pain, of new pain. She never thought she would be capable of surviving such pain. She never thought she would, my sister didn't: but she did. For awhile, for awhile.

They bring in a television set, into her room, and she becomes a fan of baseball, watching baseball through her mirror, on the new-fangled television set. She never cared for baseball before, before all this happened. She cared for sailing, and tennis, and some golf, from time to time (she was very good at the long stroke, in the first, fourth, and eighth holes at Timuquana Country Club) but she never really cared for baseball, at least not until now, but the afternoon nurse, Miss Butts, likes baseball, so they watch it together, and my sister can watch the Dodgers (whom she never heard of before) playing the Pirates (whom she never heard of before) and she watches the occasional home run in the mirror, when the batter hits the ball, and takes off, and runs to third base, then to second, then to first, and finally to home. It is comforting, in a funny sort of way, to know that people still play, think of, watch, write on, report on, worry about something like baseball.

They never taught her very much about life, and the body, and muscles and things, before this. When she was at Stephens College, they taught her dance, and music, and a smattering of literature courses, and some math, and a little chemistry. But they never taught her about the catheter stuck into her urinary tract, which stays there to drain the piss that won't come out on its own, and how urine crystals grow, so that when they pull the catheter out, it is like they are ripping out the whole of her insides, her entire urethra shredded, to ribbons, by these crystals, that come out of her, and no pain-killers, they give her no pain-killers, because of the fact that this is a disease of the nervous system, and it might affect the regeneration of nerves. They taught her some math, and a little chemistry, and how to dance, at Stephens College, but they never taught her the new dimensions of pain, which she never ever thought she could bear, never, in a thousand years, but she does, she does, even though she never thought she could.

They taught her how to diagram sentences; and they taught her about Mozart, and Beethoven. They showed her the difference between the Samba and the Rumba, and between the Waltz and the Foxtrot, she remembers her teacher played "Bésame Mucho" over and over again, so they could learn the Samba — but they never taught her about her lungs, the beautiful rich red alveoli, that lose the ability to aspirate themselves, so that one night, they think she is clogging up, suffocating, the doctor comes, with all the lights, and slices into the pink flesh, at the base of her neck, the blood jets up all over, and she can see the reflection of her neck in the mirror of his glasses, as he cuts into her neck (no anesthetics permitted because they affect the dark grey nerves nestled in the aitch of the spinal column, and polio got there first) the blood goes all over his smock, a drop of her blood even flecks his glasses, and of a sudden no air comes through nostrils or mouth, and she is sure she is suffocating, the very breath has been cut out of her, and her doctor punches a three inch silver tube down into her lungs, so that every two hours they can pump out the mucous, that collects in her lungs: they never taught her what it feels like to breathe through a little silver navel in her throat, never taught her about the feel of mucous being pumped from her lungs. They never taught her about the kiss of the trachea, the silver kiss, at the base of the neck, the kiss of this silver circle, the silver circle of the moon.

She was quite good at chemistry, my sister was: quite good. She got special honorable mention, at graduation, from Stephens College, there in Central Missouri. What she remembers most about Stephens is the spring evenings, when the smell of hay would drift into the classrooms, make her feel so alive, in the rich fecundity of Central Missouri, the rich hayfields, and the people moving so slowly, on a spring day, through the fields, those rich fields of hay. Or in the fall, when the moon would peer up over the fields come hush by midnight: the moon growing a silver medallion, hanging there in the sky, the sky so black, the moon so white-dust-silver. They gave her a silver medallion, for her chemistry, she was surprisingly good at it, not so good at literature, she never cared for Dickens, or Jane Austen, but she was so good at H_2SO_4, and NaCl, and MnO_2 that they gave her a special ribbon, with a silver moon on it, which she hung on her neck, which hung where the new silver moon of the tracheotomy hangs now, her badge, the badge of a job well done, a job well done, in the new education on the nature of the body, and its diseases, and the way the body will try to kill off its own, because of the diseases, and the deterioration of the kidney, bladder, lungs, heart, mind, under the sweet kiss of the disease, under the sweet new kiss of the disease.

My sister: the new student! The student of the body, and a student of disease, and perhaps even a student of sainthood: Sainthood. The questions of the nuns and priests and ministers of all religions of all times. If a tree falls in the forest, and no one is around, and no one hears it, was there really a sound? Or, can God create a rock, such a huge rock that He Himself cannot lift it. Or, can God create a disease, such a painful awful burning disease, of the nervous system, that invades the tender spinal chord, and scars the nerves therein so completely, with such pain and destruction of the self, that one can wish not to live any more. To live no more.

My sister. An innocent saint. For slightly less than four months, from 2 September 1952 to 29 December 1952, she will have ample time to work on her sainthood. She will have 2,832 hours to recall growing up in the sun of Florida, her shadow a black hole on the burning white sands of the beach.

169,920 minutes: she will have almost a hundred and seventy thousand minutes to remember running for a fast lob on the white-line tennis courts at the Timuquana Country Club. She will have over ten million seconds, there in her new submarine, to remember that for twenty-nine years she had a constant companion, namely her body. A companion which asked little and gave much and, of a sudden, in the early fall of that year, turned a dead weight like a tree which has had the life leeched out of it. So dead, so weighted, that she must ask the good nurse to scratch her forehead, move a leg, adjust the hair, or brush away the wetness that forms of its own accord at the corner of her blue-gray eyes, just below those beautiful ruddy lashes, that match her beautiful ruddy skin—turning quite pale now.

The body ceases to function as a body, and commences to try to kill itself off. Bladder infection, kidney stones, phlegm accretion in the lungs, bedsores, respiratory dysfunction, depression. Over the next three months and twenty-seven days, my sister's body, the body which has been so kind all these years, will turn enemy and try to sabotage every machine (from within and without) which makes it possible for her to survive. Her body will attempt to murder her.

And shortly before dawn, nineteen hundred and fifty-two years after the Birth of Our Lord and Savior, two days before the end of that dark year, at 4:47 in the morning, in some anonymous respiration center in North Carolina, where she

7

has been sent for reëducation of what is left of her body, in the company of some one hundred other machine-bound patients, just as the first of winter dawn is beginning to crack the still and snowy Chapel Hill sky, my sister will awaken for the last time to find her lungs clogged with the suppurating thickness of pneumonia.

There is to be a battle, a short one. A creature is squatting on her chest, trying to keep air from its proper place in her lungs. It is a silent and a lonely battle. There is no crying out. She is alone, and thinking "This is not happening to me," and for some unexplainable reason she remembers a spectacular day from last summer, with the sun coming down over the water, a spectacular day on the St. Johns River running before the wind in a White Star sailboat. She remembers the wind in her hair, and her body riding, riding on the swells from the great dark Atlantic near the jetties, and that great flowing expansive feeling of having all of life before one, of having the wind and the river and the freedom to ride them and be alive, so full of the freedom of being alive at the very edge of the river, just before it merges with the great wide dark deep Atlantic Ocean before her.

"This is not happening to me," she thinks. She cannot believe a termination of self and being in this huge room of clanking machines on a snow-dawn in North Carolina. "This is not happening to me," she thinks, but she is wrong. She is drowning in the liquids of her own body, and there is no way she can call out, to tell the nurse that she is suffering.

My sister! My sister. She is quite alone in her struggle as the sun begins to break through the grey waste outside. She tries to breathe in, cannot, and suddenly there is no spirit in her. My sister. Eyes, mouth, heart, single moving muscle in foot cease. There is no more warmth within or without, beyond the artificial heater placed inside the submarine which, as of now, has discharged its last patient.

The iron maiden continues to pump dead lungs for over an hour before the night nurse discovers the drowned creature, grey froth on blue lips. My sister, who never did anyone any harm, who only wished joy for those around her, now lies ice and bone, the good spirit fled from her.

CHAPTER II

Once I had a vision of me in the Isolation Ward. I am lying on a white marble table. My body has turned to white marble. I can hardly move.

My brain is a bird. A bird trapped in a pale cage, a cage of bone. The fires are raging all about, and the bird, in fear, escapes from the cage of bone. If you look to the corner of the room, you can see the bird beating frantic wings against the shadow-filled upper corners of the room. There is no way out of the room: the window is barred, the door is locked.

The bird, frantic, eyes shiny with fear, beak ajar, beats wings against the corners of the room. And there is no way out, no way to escape from the room with the body being eaten by flames, lying on the marble crypt below.

The inferno consumes the body, lays waste to the cells, and, in the process, plumbs the deepest shadows of the mind. Seamless grounds open, vampires and greyish beasts come swarming forth, extricating themselves from the pits. Figures lurch out of caves hollowed in the ground. They elevate themselves on bony limbs. Feelers twist and circle, and from out of the space one can hear instrument howls, lips beating time out of space.

An army of creatures come to cross civilization through that room. Sticky feet beat small rhythms across the figure wrapped in white linen. From time to time, masks lean out of chambered porticoes, jaws open volcanoes to release clouds of words into a barren sky.

Body tangles in sheets. Knowledge corrodes, falls thickly to the shiny ground below. The invading beasts metronome

9

through the vast reaches of the soul, platoons of shadows bearing clocks that push forth with black hands to clutch at the child below. He rocks on the edge of infinitude. In a far corner, a grey candle sputters, and contemplates the wisdom of darkness. Showers of reason babble in dying whorls.

This child, this child of the sheets, comes to be bent forever on the strange crusted edge of night. The scratching beasts gnaw at the bones and disappear, leaving ragged clawprints about the desert stretching all about.

Human shades come and go in that bile-green Isolation Room. Two interns come to take a spinal tap. Spinal tap! A knock on the door of the nerves. They come to my bed and with no words, no discussion, no thought—they wrestle me into the *C* position, head touching knees. I am unable to move with the burning ache of it, and they draw me into an arch so that they can run an eighteen-inch horseneedle in between the plates of my spine for an hour or so to get a copious sample of the cerebrospinal fluid. So the doctors can tell my family. What they know already. That I am very sick. That I might die.

A mechanical jungle comes to replace the plumbing and the wiring that have gone out. An army of instruments are brought in to make the bare-bones functions continue, so the body will not poison itself, nor starve itself to death. I don't want to, I can't eat, so there a needle that rides in the crook of my arm (the loving crook of my arm) three times a day, for an hour or two each time. For that hour or two, my arm is tied down so that the little motion I have is forced to a halt. The mucsles in *agon* redouble their pain at being restrained in one moveless position.

And then, they come once a day to irrigate the insides of me, to wash out the impacted bolus. There is a great new dam in me, and that stuff that used to flow so easily, without regard has stopped. It is a huge hard ugly plug that tries to kill me.

And then the bladder stops up. Lord—it is as if there was this house, this fine new house, which has been working excellently well for years: and it goes all blarmy. The faucets, heaters, boilers, stoves, fans, blowers, showers, washers and dryers just stop dead, all at once. The whole machinery breaks down.

They send out another intern to work over the broken bladder. In between jabs with the various needles (glucose, distilled water, antibiotics) and nozzles up the ass—they are now going to have to fix the pisser. Because there is no way in the world I can make that little trap door or whatever it is open up and release its load. My body is killing me.

Medical student without consultation pulls down the sheet over naked me. I don't even know him and he is undressing me without my specific permission. I am wracked, and yet I remember thinking, "I don't want them looking at me without my clothes, not at all." But no one is listening to me. My body is no longer my own.

He then runs a hose (another hose) up my cock. By this time I am so generally befuddled with amazement at what my body is doing to me, and what they are doing to my body with all their needles and valves and tubes, that I can hardly moan. Or show any interest. But the old pisser does. Medical student runs into the cockswain or whoever is the keeper of the gate and we get wet, all of us do. All of us: me and medical student and the bed sheets and for all I know the walls and the ceilings: two days of fevered piss, showering the room in golden ecstasy, the hot yellow stuff of the burning sun coming out knee-deep all over the floors, gushing out doors, flooding all the rooms of Isolation, floating desks, records, nurses, mucking up the plumbing and electricity, causing such a general stink that Medical Director must file an official edict: no more unplugging Milam's pisser.

It works. It has a salutory effect on the *corpus spongiosum*.

This is the last time the pisser ever gives me any trouble. Of all the joints and muscles and parts that quit, take off from work, go out on strike, cancel engagements, it alone stays on the job thereafter. After that Normandy Invasion, I can, and will forever, until my dying day, be able to piss out-of-hand, with the best of them, in symphony, the golden symphony, showering the world with warm regard.

Isolation has its own music. There is the banging and clanking of the food cart. There are handles to raise and lower the beds, and they rattle and bang as patients are moved about, as beds are made and unmade. Nurses walk down halls, and the clicks echo and reëcho.

Next door to me is the Howling Girl. Day and night she wails. She has contracted lock-jaw from some biting dog. She is expected to die momentarily. Her saliva has turned to glue, her teeth are ground together. She howls all the day and all the night.

I waken to her songs. Her music blends with my own. We are the Weird Sisters, in the Year of the Big Wind. Our songs fold and turn together down the halls. We are demon lovers. We howl in unison, a song of dying, the harmonies from the deepest animal centre of ourselves. We are trapped in our twisted and knotted bodies, and in the storm, the souls cry out to escape. The beasts beg to be allowed to leave the fevered aching land, to sail away, to be done with it, to be done with this ragerie called living. In that phantom day and night of total Isolation, she comes to me as my wolf-lady lover. We make the unearthly rhythms together, the wailing hymns of body-woe, a *Missa Solemnis* for all to hear.

One night I try to walk. The wolf lady, now, of a sudden, relieved of her sickness, is the first to hear me go down.

When I first arrived in the hospital, there was an attempt to erect bars alongside my bed, to keep me from falling out. Some preservation instinct made me protest. "There is no need for that," I said, weakly. I remember thinking that if the bars were set up, they would never come down.

And then on the fifth, or the sixth night of my new indoctrination, I wake to find myself hugging the floor. Hot cheek to cold tile. They hear me, next door, down the hall. "Nurse. Nurse!" He has fallen. They come running.

I got half-way to the door, perhaps six feet from the bed. I was trying to get out of there. Goddamn, I wanted to be out of there.

Those are my last steps alone, unassisted. My body, on its own, for the last time, raises me from the winding sheets, takes me half-way across the room. Get me out of here! Just so they will stop torturing me with all those tubes and needles and buckets and pans and hoses. God let me out!

The last steps. And the first knowledge of what had come over me in the few days in Isolation. In those icy moments on the floor comes the realization of total immobilization. I cannot get my arms to raise me up. I am lying flat on the floor, my cheek to the floor. I go to raise myself up from it. Nothing. I push with my arms, but there is no movement, not an inch. I push, and there is no resulting movement, no matter how hard I try. I have fallen, and am helpless. I have come to a point of no strength. I cannot raise myself from the dead. I am body with bulk and no motion.

A new man. I am a new man! Instead of being one who dances, or races the surf, or runs up the stairs two at a time, I am the one who will watch the dancers, contemplate the surf, lift myself up the stairs, backwards, one at a time.

From butterfly to worm. The reverse metamorphosis. Flying free one day (in the sun, heady smell of ocean, palms rattle overhead); the next day, a new body, a different body (shadows and fires all around, darkness, the fecund smell of death from within.)

My wings have been shrivelled. The delicate antenna have been shrunk down. They waved a wand and I am cocooned in a white hospital sheet to emerge, later, as a night crawler.

The fall of the year, and we are turned to worms of blackness, filled with the smell of dirt, chewing away at past bodies.

September, October—the Golden Flyer turns to a slow Quadruped. The irrevocable reverse metamorphosis. On that cold floor, I lying just above the ground below, on that cold floor, the black-and-white tile pressed to my burning cheek.

On occasion, I return to the places of my youth. But I have never ever returned to Belsen Medical Center. Never. They took my spontaneous self from me there, in 1952. In 1952, I ceased to be me. I lost my ability to be casual, at ease. I didn't know it at the time, but when I emerged from Belsen, it was without that ability to move across the face of the land free of plot or direction.

I have never returned to the place where the spirit flew out of me. It left me, a fresh bright blue light, brighter than the fire-flies. It left me then and, for all I know, it may still be haunting the area. This spirit, flitting around the dead and dying palm trees that mark the outer limits of Belsen Medical Center.

We die and we go on living. Sometimes it helps to return to that place of our death. Others do—and there is no reason why I should refuse to return to where the spirit wrenched itself so noisily out of flaming body. The fire all around, and villainous shadows, and spirit moving out of mouth, out of barely conscious body. Spirit escaping into the drenched night.

I have never returned, shall never return to seek out that spirit. But I know it is there: know the spirit of the eighteen-year-old me haunts that blasted prison. A spirit lost from Master, the Spirit of Spontaneity, crying out for a master gone forever.

There seems to be curtains. I should be able to see more clearly, with more insight, into the events of those three weeks. But the black curtain (it must be felt) comes tumbling down on the stage, and all is gone—actors, dramatist, still-warm corpse. No matter how hard we may look, we can never resuscitate the ghosts in that charnel house.

CHAPTER III

The Hospital they send me to in 1952, after the worst of the fire consumes my limbs, is called Hope Haven. Shades of Mercy! Where do they get these names! Obviously thought up by some refugee from the ad department at General Motors, sent south, out to pasture to dry out, to try his fertile brain on the charity hospitals of North Florida. Hope Haven! A penny for the old guy.

Physical therapy is a part of my daily routine at Hope Haven. There is a pool, a giant tub, really. There is a stretching table. And there is a shock machine.

The shock machine is an apparatus designed some fifty years ago whose main purpose is to keep muscles from atrophy, from loss of "tone." Two pads, one positive, one negative, are applied to the body. The muscle to be pulsated lies between these two moist pads. The operator can increase or decrease the amount of current, or the rhythm of the shocks.

It is a medieval torture machine. And I find out later, much later, that the efficacy of physical shock therapy is so limited as to make it next to useless. *Now* I find out.

The operator is Miss Bland, the physical therapist. She is shocking me powerfully twice a day, for four months. Anywhere from five minutes to half an hour. The cure and the disease match each other in relative pain. Miss Bland turns the dial all the way to nine, and a regular pulsating blast encompasses my upper leg, tearing at my bones and flesh, forkfulls of jerks blasting at my thighs. Dear God.

If I were me now, back there then, I would be hitting Miss Bland on the head each and every time she jolted me with those useless shocks, shouting in her ear: "You fool! What are you doing to this child? Don't you know . . . don't you know. You wretch!"

But I am not me back then—and I cannot speak to the foolish lady. All we can do is shake our heads, and wonder that those who practice medical science are so unwilling to expose themselves to the ideas of the time; to open their eyes to new theories of physical medicine so that they do not torture us endlessly, for no reason at all: torture those who have been tortured enough already; the patients who have had a bellyfull of pain and don't need any more supplied gratis by the ninnies who pretend to know medicine.

After electrocuting me carefully (shoulders, thighs, stomach, back) Miss Bland stretches the muscles. With her hands she lifts my legs and forces them into certain positions which are as close to elaborate and exact fainting painfulness as possible. By a true magic, she is able to go to work on the muscles which are already on fire, and pull hamstrings and extensors and rotators and quadriceps and opponens so that they will not contract. Miss Bland puts me through the tortures of the damned so that my heels will not touch my buttocks for the rest of my life. O, Miss Bland, you are killing me, telling me all the while it is for my own good. Kill me now so I can live tomorrow.

And as I think on this, I come to think on the hundreds, the thousands, the armies of people like me who are lying about the gutters and alleys and hospital beds and battlefields of the world, retching in pain. The thousands, of men, women, children, slaves, soldiers, supplicants, beggars, the poor and the hungry and the lost: puking out their guts, screaming with rage of pain, the dogshowls of anguish; on the fields, in the bed, on the cot, on the ground, on sides of whole mountains, in the open space of streets, with a full complement of witnesses.

A whole battalion of folk who are crying, moaning, wailing, screeching from the depths of anguish. An army of wide-open mouths. Their eyes glaze as they crawl, writhe and quiver with the fire burning, consuming whole limbs, whole bodies, whole blocks, whole cities, whole nations. An endless procession: all of us united in our groans of anguish. These are my brothers, my kin-folks in *agon*.

I think there is some poignance to this as we realize that the pain I was privileged to attend was not the pain of a noble cause. I was not crucified for my god. I did not run over a hill and get in in the gut for my country.

I was not tortured in some stony prison for freedom of the press. I was not martyred on some wheel for my pronouncements. The Pope did not have me pulled asunder by four horses (one on each limb) for my statements on *his* particular god. I was not privileged to have a red-hot tube of almost-molten glass shoved steaming up my cock to obtain a secret document for the Nazis.

My country, my God, my secret. The country to which I was loyal, the country for which I experienced such torture was the country of my body. They tortured me for clinging to that. My God was the belief in American Medical Technology as practiced in 1952: they worked me over for that.

The secret: the secret which I give you is the secret of no secret. We went through the torture of burning muscle, the ripped asshole, the electric shock muscle therapy, the pulled burning muscle, the regeneration of dead flesh for no other reason than we chose to continue living, with our collection of braces and crutches and pisspots and bedpans and rocking beds and iron lungs.

And I think they should raise a monument to this wonder. Let them raise a monument to it: a giant pedestal. And that pedestal will be surrounded, at its cold marble base, with an army of cripples. The draggers and the droolers, the stumps and wens and goitres and the bent and twisted frames. On their braces, on their racks and pinions, on their walkers and crawlers and draggers and inch-worm apparatuses.

A whole army of suffering lame and halt and blind, with their misshapen distorted human forms, their flaccid arms, their bowed legs, their dragging feet, their pouched-out bellies, their claw-like hands, their stranded, strained necks, and even, yet, the sacred spot: the spot at the base of the neck, where sternum meets clavicle; the slight puckered scar-navel of the ultimate kiss, the kiss of the tracheotomy. A blessing! The high dimple of truth! The symbol of all those new insights and visions which are the fruit of knowledge of the sacred virus.

And towering over all our bent and twisted figures will be that ungainly lamp post, a single virus *poliomyelitis anterior* magnified a hundred million times. The drunken corkscrew well elevated above the bent heads of her many gnarled children.

And because of the still imperfect science of magnification, our founder and leader may be slightly fuzzed. Which is as it should be. The noble cause for which we martyred ourselves (in the mold of Jesus, Saint Ignatius, Saint Peter, Joan of Arc), the hundreds of thousands of us on our collective bedpans, in our wheelchairs, on our gurneys, in our rocking beds, on our frames, and joints, and splints, with our arms and legs twisted, shrivelled, wasted—our leader, the virus of viruses, is itself fuzzed out, as if unsure of its standing in the panoply of international heroes.

Underneath that drunken pole capped with its hexagonal shape, in huge fluorescent lights, at the very center of the face of the pedestal, below which this maelstrom of broken humans sprout like so many weeds, will appear the words:

We Suffered Nobly For A Cause
Which was Neither Noble
Nor a Cause.

In Hope Haven, I am in a ward with some thirty-five boys. I am almost the oldest, and certainly the sickest. I don't talk to anyone; don't want to really. I am so blasted out of myself. I can't figure out what has happened to me—and here I am in the football-field-length medical ward with noise from 6:30 a.m. to 9:30 p.m., nonstop. Noise: babbling, calling out, yelling, whistling, stomping, running, singing, crying. Four-dozen boys ranging in age from seven to twenty, and I am right in the middle of them all.

Every possible sickness is represented: poliomyelitis, osteomyelitus, quadriplegia, spinal bifida, burns, gland disease, Legg-Calua Perthes, pneumonia, rheumatoid arthritis and, I am convinced, retardation. Mostly on the part of the medical and nursing staff.

My favorite is Nurse Stumpf. An old Naval Destroyer. Docked in with the kids, to give them the taste of the military life from 7:00 a.m. to 3:00 p.m. On the upper lip, a slight black down, incipient moustache. Like she has been eating dirt. Mouth curled down from eating bitter-melon.

You old axe. You make me so angry that I come to life again. I should strike a medal for you. You give me a taste of life, life: the sweet heady feel of bitterness and anger. Here I am straight out of the fire of body-death, and you come down on me for my attitude. My Attitude. What do you expect me to do? Thank you for every icy bedpan delivered? For the gruel they call lunch? Thank you for those high-powered colonic irrigations you order on the recalcitrant bowels?

I do have to thank her, don't I? There is no way that sweetness and light can bring me to my senses; it had to be vengefilled hate and vituperation. I know that Florence Nightingale made the troops of the Crimea stir to life again (mortality rate down by 79%) with the gentle whip of her tongue. "You boys have all the wrong attitude. You're gonna get an enema you won't forget Not an enemy: an enema!" And they fell to cursing her, and had some tyrant to hate, and vowed they would get well just to get the hell out of there: wouldn't give her the satisfaction of dying!

Nurse Stumpf, the Florence Nightingale of Hope Haven. She gives us a common enemy. I mean coming here we are on our beds of separate disease, infection, affliction, plague, The Dengue. And the bosun's chair comes swinging down and the battleship hoves into view and we unite, despite our common differences; unite to denouce her. Each day provides another Nurse Stumpf horror story (did you hear what she told Willie about his shoes? And Willie has arthritis so bad he can't even reach his Christly shoes!) and the angel is giving us some great purpose. The prophet Stumpf: most of us have to wait years before we realize the sanctity of that - straight up-and-down white charger with the puckered mouth. God Save You Miss Stumpf!

She is actually at her best working on Harney. Harney is the ward quadriplegic. Four years before, he dives from a high boulder, arcs down to the rock-quarry pond, and misses. Head meets grey granite. Splits the spine wide, and the nerves grind to pieces between edges of bone. O Harney!

Now Harney is permanently encased, face down, on a Striker Frame: to contemplate his downfall, the two inches that separate rock from water. Harney has many days hours weeks in the arms of the Striker Frame to mull over the sin of his ways. And Nurse Stumpf comes to work him over with her acid tongue for not coöperating. Not coöperating! What a jewel!

Go to it, Nurse Stumpf! He is the one person that I know of at the time, in the world, who is in worse shape than I. Me: building an edifice of hope on the broken body of a broken man. He is my freedom. My path is up — his is down. I build my life on his corpse.

For in 1952, the quadriplegic is doomed. The fractured portion of spinal cord is so very high that everything from lower neck down is finished, forever.

Harney can wave his arms around, a bit, but they are permanently crooked, the arms of a rooster plucked, the chicken-thin arms. He has no use of his hands: they bend into the praying-mantis position. Harney, waiting to catch flies.

Harney has no feeling below his nipples. No feeling whatsoever at navel, or ass, or knee. No lover can pinch Harney and hope for response. Harney has no feeling in his cock. No lover can kiss those thin buttocks, and no lover will. Harney is incontinent, can't control his piss, or shit, can feel no joy in lips crossing thin white mountains of thighs.

If Harney were lying naked (Harney is lying naked, with a sheet over him) on his back (he is on his stomach) and the gentlest of ladies were to lay gentle fingers on the sweet co-

coon of his hips, put lips to inner thighs—Harney would feel nothing. Nothing. He is a quadriplegic.

He can feel nothing and do nothing. He can move his chicken-wing arms. And his legs: once every two or three days, his legs throw themselves into huge spasms, shaking and rocking. As if to protest this inaction. Why did you cut us off? Just when we were at our best! Why did you do that to us Harney? And his legs go into outraged spasms, are tied down to keep him from upsetting everything on the floor, and the whole bed shakes with the spasms of legs fighting against the bonds, against being tied down. Harney is shaking in rage; the earthquakes of the dying land. He has to be tied down, he is fit to be tied.

Harney, Harney, Harney! They have taken so much from you. You will never feel the cold waters of the quarry rushing past (sudden recoil) a slim 20-year old belly. You will never feel your balls tighten up as you go deep in that cold clear water, reach the darkness below.

You Harney: you have a new wife. Your other wife (the one with the veil; the one with Richard Hudnut perfume and magenta on the fingernails) will never run soft ladyhands trailing down your stomach, bringing the fires up from below. You have a new wife now, Harney.

You are married to your Striker Frame. Your cock lies in the cold vagina of the bed for all time, in good times and in bad, for better or worse, in good weather and in poor, for summer and winter. You are in perpetual love with the bed on wheels: the one raised high from the floor with extra soft padding to keep away the bedsores (that come anyway, lover's bites, love cherries from your new wife.)

You are high on your Marriage Bed, high up so those of us around you who love you can see you perched high on the throne, the flat-lay-down throne. And your constant procession of ministering angels comes to change, once daily, the silver chalice that receives the golden flow from within (that comes in its own natural cicadian rhythm) and, once each two days, to remove the offering from within that obtrudes from your moveless bowels.

Harney, Harney, Harney. Be good to him Nurse Stumpf!

Lash him good and proper. Pull out the whip of your words and flail those frail buttocks, that bone back, those knobby concentration camp knees. Flail him hard and good. For our child on his Wedding Bed has so little time to live. The liver and the kidney and the spleen and the bowels do not take kindly to the perpetual marriage of their body-master. Soon enough, one of them will give up. And Harney—who has grown so wise, lying face down for four of the last twenty-four years of his life (where he can attend to every speck, every fly, the movement of every foot) will consummate once and for all the ceremony he began as he arched through the air on that bright June day of 1948, as he raced down to engage, with two inches to spare, the huge grey boulder that came a giant to meet him, head-on, to enlighten him, once and for all, with the truth of the O so fragile hair-thin nerves.

CHAPTER IV

Beginning when I was—what?—five or six years of age, I had this friend used to go about with me. Tall, about my size. Shy. Warm (once you got to know him). Above all, dignified. He was my friend, my best friend, and I would do anything to protect him. He, I know, would do the same for me.

Early on in my stay at Hope Haven he got pushed around a bit, my friend did. Bruised. But he stayed with me, spent most of his time with me, despite the nurses, despite the unfriendly atmosphere. He put up with all that. He was my best friend.

It isn't until a few weeks have passed at Hope Haven that he gets the bludgeoning. This is how it happens:

They take a mallet, with the little metal studs on it, corner him at the far end of the ward, and beat the shit out of him. They beat him so hard and so fiercely that the blood leaks from his mouth and nose and ears. He had so much pride before that.

I am sure he knows what is about to happen. They can't hide that malevolence. He is very calm when they capture him—I think he hopes for the best. He is brave, he really is, even though his eyes are dim with the knowledge of what they might do to him. They do—they do their worst, and he doesn't have a chance.

The nurses and orderlies get him at the far part of the ward, where no one can hear them (even though it's broad daylight) and they beat him so thoroughly with the mallets that he can't even move to get away from them. They break his right arm (leaving it fractured and hanging by the skin alone). They twist one of his legs behind him so that you can see the ragged edges of the bone piercing the skin. They take a mace-like contraption, a metal one with rivets, and come right up under his crotch so that it slams into his nuts, driving them right up into his belly. It hits so fast and so hard that he doesn't have the breath to cry out. He just twists with the brutal hurt of it.

They stomp him there not once but four or five times to be sure they have done it right. His mouth comes to be frozen in a round jagged circle of pain, and when they smash the metal rods into his jaw, they crack the bone so that the stubs of his teeth (red washed in blood) are all that remain.

My poor friend; my dear friend; the friend of my days: Dignity. Absolutely beaten to insensibility, so that you can see the four red-brown blood streaks on the wall where he pressed crushed fingers against it as he tried to keep from being pulled down to the floor by the bloody weight of his body.

They do it to us, do it to me and my friend. They come at us with a mallet, a piece of piping, and a diaper.

Muscles cease functioning in the wasting disease. Muscles of lower intestine cease peristalsis. Movelessness in bed turns the contents of the bowels to rock. To counter this, the hospital loads the patient up with mineral oil, castor oil, milk of magnesia. If there is no reaction, the dosage is repeated, increased. Finally the bowels turn to water. Where previously, all was stone—now there is a flooding . . . not once, but again and again. There is no control.

There is no way that we can run to the bathroom. In total bedrest, there is no way to go to the private world of toilet which is our heritage from the age of child on. No privacy, no freedom, no exit.

The nurses are harassed. There are dozens of patients to be attended to. They can help only so much, and after awhile, I am a man soiling himself as if I were a babe again. A bad boy who shits in his clean white sheets. There is no control.

After the sixth time, the nurses' aide, the blonde one, the one with the thin sharp face, Miss Amarga, takes a white towel, folds it into a triangle, puts it around my waist and between my legs. Gets two big steel pins, pins the diaper in place. I am the child again. I dirty my bed, so they give me a diaper, so I can dirty that. I have no control, filled as I am to the brimming with mineral oil, milk of magnesia. I am out of control. Dignity gets it with the bludgeon.

"I put a diaper on him," Miss Amarga tells Nurse Stumpf. They both smile. I can see them smiling, each to each. "I put a diaper on him," Miss Amarga tells the other nurses, and nurses' aides. "I had to put a diaper on him," Miss Amarga tells the other patients. I can see them smiling at me. They stay away from my bed. Miss Amarga is smiling with a tight clean smile. She looks quite clean in her white starched uniform.

I am not smiling. I am not smiling: I am contemplating the broken body of my friend Dignity, now a bloody rag doll over in the corner of the boy's ward. I am contemplating the broken body of my friend, in the corner of the ward.

Lorenzo is not smiling with Miss Amarga, the nurses, the other aides, the patients. I am not smiling, neither inside nor outside. In fact, inside, where none can see me, I am torn by misery, and loneliness, and the absolute desolation of hope and pride. "I do not want to be doing this," I think over and over again. "I do not want to be the baby again," I think. "I must get out of here," I say to myself. I do not ring for them to come and clean me up. I lie there by myself, in my own dismal dirt, moveless, speechless, hopeless, a foul babe again, without hope, with no reason for existence.

I do not want to be here. I do not want to be here alone, in a dirty baby diaper. I do not want to be in this ward, in this hospital, in this world. I want to be back at the beach again, on the sands again, running, laughing, the warm waters spitting out before my feet as I run, me in my sun-colored bathing suit, racing alive through the surf, racing to lunge into the waves, to swim down below the waves, below the surface, deep down into the nectarine waters, down where the white moon-hill bottom is pulsing with the waves and the warm life about me. Fish dart thoughts swerve past me and turn colorful showers there at the bottom of the sea where I am warm and fresh again, kicking out into the sea, there with my friend of my life, my friend of all time, my friend dignity, who has lived with me, good times and bad, for so long, so long.

Over in the corner of the ward, clean, white Miss Amarga whispers to one of the other patients and looks over her shoulders with a tight, clean, white-lipped smile. She winks, and so doing, she renders one last blow to my friend, and he passes out against the wall, for all intents and purposes crippled forever.

It's a good school I go to, out there at Hope Haven. One of the best. Within a day I learn to feed myself.

The teacher, I must admit, is a hard disciplinarian. But I am a good student. And I want to learn. They might starve me if I don't attend to my lessons.

I get them to turn me over on my left side. I support my right arm with my left hand. I have them place the tray close to me on the bed table. With some agility and juggling, I can get fork to plate, pick up food, and back again to mouth without dropping too many beans on the sheet.

I have to rest each five bites. And at the end of the meal I am exhausted. I lie there for an hour, resting from the exertion of eating. But by Jesus it is my own fucking hand that is bringing food to mouth. Six weeks into the school, and I have learned the first step of independence.

I go over it again and again in my mind. Perhaps if they put the tray closer. I should be able to get seven bites before exhaustion. The glass of milk: that is the bitch. There is no way I can get lips to it. I have to wait until they come to take the tray away so someone can hold the straw to my lips.

But a victory! And it came so suddenly. When friends or family come to see me, they think (I can see them thinking) Jesus, he looks awful, and wasted. They see me in the thrall of atrophy. Disconnect muscle from brain, and the muscle withers to a string. The joints stick out. The bones come to lie painfully close to the surface. The flesh hangs down, like an old washerwoman's upper arms.

I am thin, wasted; pale. And they all see that—those people who come to visit, who knew me before. But they are already behind the times. I am moving upwards in the world. I can get fork in hand to mouth. I am a self-feeder. I am three years old again.

They take me through the firehouse, and burn the flesh away from my bones, and fry my brain, and leave me with muscles that still (twenty-five years later) are tender, and disconnected. Yet give me a fork and a tray and by God, I can eat with the best of them.

And Triumph Number Two. That one takes a bit longer. I would say another month. It's called Turning Over in Bed By Yourself.

For so many years, I had the sweet and simple pleasure of turning over in bed, with no help at all. We fall asleep, and we move, unconsciously, from front to back, from side to stomach, legs moving this way and that, arms thrown out wide.

The vulgar disease takes that ability from me. There is no substitute for the muscles that have turned me about in my sleep. I wake up in the darkened ward, and my hip bone is burning. My shoulder aches from the pressure. I am paralyzed, not only in the waking state, but asleep as well.

To keep from getting bedsores, they must move me about for me. They (nurses, aides, occasionally another patient) will pull me over to the side of the bed, throw left leg over right leg, push me to the other side. Turn the patient (a potato in the oven) over and over to keep him from getting burned.

Miss Frye is the night nurse. Eleven to seven. She is to watch over the flock by night. She is to minister to the occasional crying out, the occasional bedwetting, the occasional attack of sleeplessness. The way she deals with these is by pulling the old easy chair to the foot of the ward and going to sleep in it. Most of the night.

Miss Frye, I call. Miss Frye! I don't want to call too loudly, wake the others. But my hip is like fire. Will you turn this potato? She can't hear me above the buzzing of the dreams, and her snoring.

I appeal to the head of the hospital. Miss Frye won't come. She is asleep.

Miss Frye comes after that. She lies awake sulking in her chair. Whenever I call, she races down the corridor, throws me over. I am no longer a potato: I am a sack of bones. Miss Frye is furious.

I wish she would die. I wish she would retire. I wait eagerly for Sunday nights (her night off) so that I don't lie awake for an hour, or two, hesitating. Should I call? My voice is tremulous. Why doesn't she move to the goddamn day shift?

Miss Frye: you should understand (don't you understand?) that I am not here to bug you. I am not some whimper of a baby, intent on irritating you out of your well-deserved sleep. I see you: as you sleep in that easy chair, snoring loudly through your adenoids; I see you shuffle and move around. The body needs freedom from pressure points. You understand, don't you Miss Frye?

No. I am dependent on a woman who hates me. Absolutely a slave to her.

I begin to intellectualize the problem, the huge space between thought and deed. Problem: I have few muscles, but I have to be turned. Now if I take my left hand and hold it up with the right (on the elbow) I can just get my fingers to the cross bar.

Once on the cross bar above my bed, if I move (slowly, O so slowly) upper torso to the right in the bed, squinching shoulders along the sheets, I can make it so that I can pull the right shoulder over so I am lying on my left side. Marvelous!

And it works. At least, get from my back over to one shoulder (the legs follow like pooches on a hunt). And, with enough calculation, and putting my strong hand up to the head bar of the bed, and twisting, I can get over on the other side (this second process takes another ten days to clarify). And, one night, without her knowing it, I am free of the clutches of Miss Frye. That horrid lady with the snore of an ox; who didn't give a goddamn about me and my burning hips. Horrid: no. Wait. Miss Frye has taught me several lessons. (1) How to fend for myself in the jungle of the bed; (2) How to avoid conflicts with hospital personnel; and (3) A new view of the legs.

The legs! My legs. My new legs, thin as they are; in this period, they become an adjunct to the rest of my body. They don't do leggy things like walk, stroll, or cross themselves. They are rather weighty appendages, although fast slimming down in a trimming class *sans pareil*. As time goes on, I will begin to treat them as so much excess baggage. Throw them around on the bed. Lift them up, by hand, and put them somewhere else. They are weight and counter-weight: and little else.

An appendix. Of a sudden, my legs have become strangers to me. They aren't quite a part of me (Where did you go? Nowhere. What did you do? Nothing.) But they provide a balance when I go through the intricate motion of hospital bed body juggling.

You are right, Miss Frye. You have taught me a couple of good things. Think out the act of moving before doing it; intellectualize it to accomplish it. And: stop thinking of legs as legs. Weights, potatoes, sticks, firewood, appendages: ok. But legs of yore (running, dancing, standing still) — no. No.

CHAPTER V

James was a football player. He was Captain of the Robert E. Lee High School football team until polio put an end to his end runs. A big guy, with a Marine crew cut. Born to be captain.

He is probably captain of the ward at Hope Haven, if anybody is. His legs have, through the kiss of Polio The Great Leveler, turned the size of telephone cables. One of his arms has been eaten alive: shrunk, reddened, muscles survive, but not too many—and it becomes definitely second place in James' armory. The other arm, the left one. What a powerhouse. Wow! Big when James was trying his opponents on the gridiron; now, trying his opponents in the hospital bed, it has doubled in size. After all, left arm has to be right arm, and as well, left and right leg.

The shadow of the glory-hole days of Spring 1952. Racing down, that arm securely nursing the football, the baby to his chest. But the baby dies, and the Captain acts out a lifetime of football maneuvers, for the next forty years, in the comfort of an Everest & Jennings Wheelchair.

What a leveler! James and I are almost the same. No: wait. My family comes to see me visiting hours on Sunday. James' visitors are girls from the high school cheerleader squad. They come in their short hair and pleated white skirts; their white-brown Oxfords and blue sweaters. And their carefully shaved smooth round muscular legs that work, that work by God. And their trim little waists and sweet blooming breasts. Their arms and hands so casually placed on James' pillows. The heady fragrance of rose scent. Let's hear a locomotive for James and his five regular cheergirls. We are all so envious.

I like them because they breathe and speak the normalcy that the rest of us have had dragged from us by one means or another. I think on their breasts, and their beautiful calves, their lips made up in Cardinal Red (that pout!) but most of all I think of what lies underneath the skirts.

I think of their stomachs. I think of their duodenal reaches. I think of what lies under that warm matty softly downed scarcely touched skin. I think of their bowels. And the shit in their bowels. And how it works. Just like clockwork (they don't even think of it!) the faeces come and plop! are gone. Without a quiver. Without a pause. Without the hard, impacting, asshole wrenching, crater-fissure aching brutalizing deep bone-ass tiring killing constipated Impacted Bolus.

The secret: James—the football captain, the ward captain—teaches me the secret of the Shit.

Don't be angry with me. Or sick. You see: I have vowed that I will tell you everything. Everything. I am going to cut a hunk a mile wide channelling through my soul, and lay it out on the page for you. The depths of my soul. The reaches of my workings. The Secret of the Big Shit.

I have to stick the secret in James' ass because of the fact that he was and is a man. I am not saying I am some wimp, for Christ's sakes; but I was never the captain of the team. As a matter of fact, the closest I came to the team was when I played soprano saxophone for the Lawrenceville Prep Bears or Hogs or Geese or whatever they were called. I surely was no sportsman. You would *expect* me to cry out in anguish when they first started teaching me the Secret. But not James, not the Captain of the Lee Lions.

Two or three times a week, in the ward, in the long ward, of Hope Haven Charity Hospital, I watch the shit reduce James to a baby. A crying baby.

I can watch this because in that unquiet grave, our voiding is a matter of public record. Each Bowel Movement is recorded on work sheet: texture, quantity, nature (hard or soft). For the bedridden, there is no place we can go God knows to crap. Privacy: what's that? The best they can do for us is to pull together white curtains on moveable metal frames, enclose our bed, and let us get on with it.

Two or three times a week, in the ward, in the long ward, I watch the shit reduce James to childhood again. James the man who would never shrink from a head-on with some two-hundred-fifty-pound guard; who would pile-drive his way through eleven hulking peers to lead his team to victory: James the Captain turned to a moaning baby by some wretched turd.

Why am I telling you this? I have promised to tell all. Why am I smiling? It's not funny! Get on with it, get on with it; let's be done with it.

The agony, the one that haunted, and still haunts James, and Hugh, and Francine, and Margo, and Ed, and all my old polio friends—outside of braces, crutches, corsets, wheel-chairs, and Nurse Stumpf. The introduction we have to the wonders and romance of this disease, the secret order of friendship, the special handclasp, the grasp of ass that binds us all forever together, the legion of camaraderie for all of us forever, until death do us part, the Secret Ritual of the Groaning Crap.

Listen to me! This is important! I have never read any book on hospital lore, sickness, disease, the novels of self-help and resurrection of the ill, the betterment and wonder of departure of the sickbed: nothing, not one of those has dealt with Constipation. Constipation: you old bag you. Phew!

What happens is that the normal muscle tone of the intes-tines, the easy workings of peristaltic action, that gentle kneading action that makes the bowels move, gets lost. The action motion of the outside us (arms, legs) is gone; that in-side (peristalsis) goes as well. The bolus which moves out so smartly for, say, you, from ilius to sphincter in eighteen hours—is for us slowed down intolerably. It moves slower and slower, the lower intestines extract more and more water, it grows larger, and heavier, and drier. Get the picture? It becomes "impacted."

Impacted: a great word, conjuring up images out of geol-ogy. Giant tidal basins colliding with one another; great shelves of land becoming locked in slow motion; huge hunks of rock and cold lava straining and tearing against each other. All suitable images for the freezing up of the bowels, the consequent giantization of the turd.

Apt image! And when the bolus finally comes to exit, it has grown (I swear by all that's holy) to the size of a boulder; a hard, monster boulder. Never (I think, you think, he, James, thinks) can that monster get through the tiny asshole.

Nothing makes it come out. Nothing, not prayers, strain, sweating, rocking back and forth, arms folded across belly, crying out, gut wrenching sweat and strain; nothing can get that Christly turd out of the hole to, for God's sakes, Get Born.

Does the message get through? O I don't just mean about the crap. I mean the body turned to enemy. My body, so kind and amiable, is all of a sudden producing this thing, this wretched painful thing, that will lay siege to another part of my body; and in their struggle, we are torn by pain. Enervating, hours-on-the-cold bedpan agony. The bottling up. The monster that refuses to release itself from us.

I hear James right now. I hear him, and my heart is with him. James the Captain is crying out, trying to get that *thing* (part of himself) out of himself. The Passion of the Split Asshole.

James, James! My brother of the cofraternity. My sweet brother. Writhing and crying, as the inspiration from within ennobles him on his throne of steel. We, the select, divinely chosen, honored by the black kiss of the gods.

In symphony: James and I and countless others raise our cries to the heavens. This, the highest passion of truth and understanding. We, caught forever on a piece of ourselves, come from these golden moments perched in solitary wonder: come, at last, to the magic moment. The one that leans down, splits yet another fissure, and, in an instant, transforms us from frowning gods into smiling cherubs.

For an hour, or two, or three, we lie there, thrashing back and forth, the edges of the pan of steel permanently etched in our bones; and we, straining with it, come, finally, to the apex, the crowning moment. As we feel the stone beginning to penetrate into outer world, as we feel the rock cutting into tender sphincter flesh, as we feel the rage and passion of that rock merged on the edge of consciousness, and the universe, beginning at last to crawl out into the world.

When, at last, the rock is sprung (Jesus! did you feel that!) there comes, after it, the golden flow, burning out of the centre of all of us. Rushing, racing, pouring out of the noblest end of all of us, the place, where indeed, we wear the halo of the silver-shined aluminum pan: flowing out of the upper reaches of all of us, at least, the golden plug yields to pressures from within and without, and comes klang! into the world of the living, a massive on-swelling floods from us; we, lying in the sanctified perfume of the deepest parts of us, raise us all high on the mountain of our throne—as once and for the next two days we are released from the hard truth from within, we, perched on the sweetest mountain, the Himalaya of our sweet scented ever-flowing mountainous shit.

I don't know who is making money off Hope Haven. It isn't me. It certainly isn't the nurses, or the superintendent. I would be loathe to suspect my medical director, the doctor who is *chargé d'affaires* for that hundred-bed charity hole.

Despite the fact that he comes to us on monthly rounds in elegant tweeds, with a nose whose many veins testify to an excellent diet of wine and viands: who am I to point an accusing finger at Dr. Jackyl? Not I, Not I.

But someone is getting a good cut of all that money that comes rushing in from the annual fund-raising drive of Kidz on Krutches.

The food is lousy. We eat at seven in the morning, noon, and four-thirty PM. Supper in midafternoon! And you know what happens to bad food that is cooked and over-cooked and then cooked some more. Vegetables turn to library paste. Meat becomes doorstops. Rice is non-exis-tent. Potatoes are peeled and boiled until they drop from exhaustion. We get five servings of wonderbread, and black-eye peas turned to mush.

And always can-fruit-salad for dessert. Every day and twice on Saturday and three times on Sunday: fruit salad, soggy peaches and desiccated cherries. Where do they get that stuff? The sick and dying are being fed on pennies a day.

Things in the kitchen fall apart so that hot suppers come to us warm, coffee is served tepid, cold milk comes out of a can and is presented at dishwater temperature. They cook the meat until it is rubber, then they serve it to us with knives that bend. Lukewarm dogmeat.

Then the building: the roof leaks when it rains. The windows admit drafts and big centipedal bugs. When, in the late fall, the temperature ventures to the freezing point, the whole heating system collapses.

The therapy equipment goes into eclipse. Not the electric zap shock muscle machine: that fucker never gives up. But the pool develops cracks, the aerator burns up, the motor lift blows fuses, the heater sags and withers.

The furnace quits in November. Kerosene heaters are brought in to keep the ward warm. Kerosene heaters, with no chimneys, whatsoever. Kerosene heaters that throw great black clouds to the ceiling of the ward. We are freezing to death, and they are trying to choke us to death with these smudge pots.

Something inside me gives. A moment of truth; probably the greatest if not the gravest that this disease has been so kind to give me.

The plumbing ain't working. I lie locked in my bed in my own void. It is late in November; it is dark. The supper was swimming in grease. It is rainy, and the kids have to play inside, all about me, in the ward. Noisy: an army of broken children, half in wheelchairs, the other half on stumps or crutches, screaming, laughing, playing tag.

I have a vision. A vision of self. It comes to me at this time. The Virgin Mary, you may recall, came to the three shepherd children in the hills of Northern Portugal. She comes to them in brilliant garments, blue robes, to tell them to warn the world. To warn the world against the evils of Bolshevism. To make her message clearly understood to the rest of the world, she moves stars and moons and suns in the firmament: whole physical astral bodies wobble and warp in their orbits; lights blare into the faces of the masses gathered below, comets streak across skies turned black for the occasion.

The Passion of the Bedstool is as moving. It comes to me on that anonymous November afternoon in the form of a huge turd. From within, there wells the giant being, the rock of humanity. As great and as grand as any wobbling sun or moon: it comes accompanied by a cloud of wonder. And out of this wonder grows a figure, an emaciated figure, a bony figure: a figure as sepulchral as any ghost.

A figure of the night is Our Lady of the Bedstool. In wonder and amazement I watch as she grows beside me to the size of a mountain. Where did she come from? What is her message for humanity, for the world, for the hungering masses?

Our Lady has a message for all of us, given to humanity through me, her innocent Child of the Pot. This is what she tells me in her ghostly voice:

"You, my child, my beloved child, are never going to get 'Better.' You are going to stay on this noisy ward perhaps forever. There is no escape for you.

"Likewise, there is no goal, no hope, no chance, no freedom. You shall neither walk nor think as a 'Normal' human being. In this smoky, cold, noisy, bleak and colorless room — you shall spend eternity. You shall live here forever, and you shall die here.

"In no way will your life be normal. Rather — you will be stabbed in the gut with rocks, fed wretched food, punched in the arms with dull needles, have giant waterworks crammed into your bowels. You shall have no compensations for living: none at all. Your muscles will hurt, you will be tortured with machines that are supposed to cure you (but won't).

"There will be no relief. There will be no way that you can leave this room — to dance, sing, play, run, have parties and fun. You can do none of these things now; you will do none of them in the near or distant future.

35

"The experience of September is the prelude. For that past eight or ten weeks you have continued to have something called Hope. Each week, you ask the physical therapist if you will be back in school in the winter—back on the swim team in the spring. I am here to tell you now, because you haven't known until now, that you might as well give up your hopes and your plans. You are stuck in the arms of the Queen of the Bedstool forever and forever.

"There is no escape, no hope, no promise, no reward. Life is a dark brown smudgy color. You are to receive the Dark Kiss of Truth. When I lay my cold lips to your own—you will no longer embrace fantasies of the spring prom, summers lounging on the beaches, winters with snowfights and long invigorating bike rides.

"That nonsense is behind you now. You have a new goddess for the rest of your days: me. Some may find me abhorrent; at worst, they will think of me as being homely and repulsive. But there are compensations in my love. You will have visions which are denied to all but the most hopeless of humanity's children. You will have insights which will overwhelm the world in sheer sizeable crap.

"There will be times," she concludes—nuzzling me coldly—"when you will doubt me or deny me. After all—the God of Christians is at once more exciting and more powerful appearing; the Prince of Peace has traces of blood on his pale brow; the Mother of us All has a careworn cheek and a loving hand. Me: I am none of these. I am dank and profane. I stink of sewers; I come to being out of the cesspools of humans; I belch forth with gaseous yellow bubbles of loathesome stickiness—and all but the most brave faint dead away at my caress.

"You are one of my chosen and favorite few," she says as she fades into the brownish mist at the foot of my bed: "You are Lorenzo, Chosen and Ennobled of The Order of the Stool. You are My Child, My Sweet: and all I do, I do for you. . . ." And she is gone. Gone!

CHAPTER VI

I have a fantasy about Hope Haven. Even now I can remember it as clearly as I can remember that long noisy ward, with the sun coming down through four-dozen windows during the day, and the chill darkness and occasional lights at night. It concerns Harney and Roberto.

I have told you about Harney, wasted Harney: the man locked forever on his mountain Striker Frame, the man who would never walk, or run the mountains, dive the dives again.

And Roberto of the Sorrows. Six feet tall. Beautiful black hair. Strong body. Grew up on a farm just outside McClenny, riding horses and throwing hay, driving tractors. Strong and country—can walk and run with the best of them.

Roberto has the saint's disease, the disease of Doestoevsky. The seizures. The large ones. I hear him, one night, late, in *grand mal*. I am wakened on the ward, we all are, by this unholy crying out. A bestial moan: Roberto *in extremis*, fallen down on the floor, next to his bed. I remember the flashlights on walls and ceilings, the nurses from all wards trying to hold down this hulking farmer thrashing about on the floor, trapped in the anguish of his brain. I remember thinking that Roberto, so quiet, is suddenly so noisy.

Once, once two years ago, Roberto had gone into *grand mal*. It was next to an open fireplace. He was by himself. His face fell into the coals. He didn't know. He was out of his head.

One half of Roberto's face is the face of a rather nice-looking fellow, shy smile, firm nose, deep-set eyes. The other—

37

Jekyll-and-Hyde: cartilage of the nose exposed. All eyebrows and eyelashes burned off. Hairline singed to the top of the skull. Mangled lips, giving a glimpse of vampirish teeth. The whole side of the face scarred with striations of red, pink, purple.

Roberto never looks at anyone head-on: only from the "good" side of his face. He hides behind his shoulders, and sometimes you catch him watching you from the shadows. His only friend is Harney: Harney who always looks down, at the floor, never up; never to see Roberto's face.

They would spend hours together. Roberto, lighting cigarettes, sharing them with Harney, placing them to his lips, long enough for him to take a drag. They would whisper to each other, like lovers, words that none of the rest of us would hear, could ever hear. The perfect body and the perfect head would become conjoined, as you watched them there, joined in some long story, some quiet mirth. Roberto and Harney, the doubler crab, twins joined at the neck.

I never spoke to either of them: they were always on the other side of the ward. But I was envious of their closeness. And out of my envy grows this fantasy, my longest continuing dream.

Some miracle has happened. I don't think about its source: no religious experience, divine intervention, medical magic. An instant (albeit temporary) cure. Harney is able to walk and run. Roberto's face comes whole again. I am able to slip out of bed, and run out into the night with the two of them.

We do it after everyone else on the ward is asleep. No razzle-dazzle, no "Look, I'm cured!" Just the three of us, crawling out the window late one night: over the white brick fence, out of the yard of Hope Haven.

We don't do much, the three of us, on our temporary vacation. We walk down the street, under the bare bulbs of the corner lights: they catch our shadows long, bring them shorter and shorter under our feet, then stretch them out long before us. The three of us, laughing softly at our prank. Telling stories about ourselves—things that we did in the past, before we came to be encamped in that place.

We probably walk down Riverside Avenue. It is quiet at this time of night. We pass under massive oaks, with Spanish Moss hanging down, in some cases, almost to the street we walk on so lightly. At one intersection, we run, racing each other (breathless, laughing) down to the waterfront. We go into the Harbor Lights Tavern, buy three Jax beers, go off to a corner booth by ourselves.

We have many stories to tell each other: tell about lovers and drinking and trips we've made. We have men's confidences to share. I get a little drunk and make up some story about some woman I slept with in fantasy, in the past. Harney laughs unselfconsciously at my tale, and nudges me in the ribs. Roberto peeks in the long mirror over the bar, again and again, to see his face altogether now. At one point I get up and stand, head bent close to their faces, my foot on the seat of the booth. It feels comfortable standing like that.

We know we have to be back before dawn. That is part of the rules. We don't protest: that is the way it has to be done. We live up to our end of the bargain. At three, or three-thirty, we get up: finish off our beers, go back to the street. We have some time left. We amble past the waterfront. Fishermen are yawning and stretching themselves on the boats docked around the wharf. They are beginning to gather up their nets, so they can put out to sea again, as they have for so many years. One of them may call to us, or wave.

We make it back to the hospital just before dawn. No one has missed us yet. Harney reaches up with his hands, pulls himself up to the top of the white brick wall. The paint is peeling; it spots his hands white. He reaches down to give me help up; and then we both reach down to pull Roberto to the top.

We slip in the far window at the north end of the ward, the window that opens on the terrace. We are very quiet. No one is awake. Down at the far end, the nurse snores a bit, and stirs in her easy chair. The day that is coming turns the tile floor from black to grey.

We help Harney onto the Striker Frame, pull the cover all the way up to his neck. Roberto waves at me as I go to my bed, crawl under the covers, pull the white stiff sheet up to my cheek. He disappears down at the far end of the ward. I snuggle into the pillow, yawn once, am tired, very tired, fall off to sleep as the light comes full into the ward.

I wish I could remember his name. I wish I had a clue. Maybe I would like to look him up, see what he looks like, now, at age thirty-nine. He probably has an admirable wife, two admirable children (fourteen and nine), and an admirable house with crushed stone on the driveway and gold lamé threads in the sofa, paintings by the Keenes on the walls. He probably can't even remember *my* name.

It is all just as well: that I have forgotten who he was, and all. He was the last of my child-innocent loves. For the life of me I can't remember if he is Frank or Tommy. Or Pat or Roger. So, I shall take the liberty of calling him a name of my own choosing: Randall, my son.

I wish I could tell you that my earliest love is beautiful, supple as the wind, body classically sculpted of Greek stone. I wish I could tell you that his muscles rippled beneath that marble-like exterior, that his eyes, a haunting blue-green, turned crystal sparkfire when the two of us were together. I would like to say that from his lips came the most arcane (and yet the most poetic) iambics of the land. I wish I could tell you all that.

Alas, it isn't so. As best I can remember, Randall's eyes are set too far apart: what would be called almond-eyes in others we will have to refer to as, unh, slightly piggy. His round fifteen-year-old face is nicely set off with a sprinkling of pimples. His mouth is far too wide and moist to be lovable to anyone. Except, possibly, his mother. And the long thin stranger in the next bed over, to the North.

Randall is fifteen years, three months old. He comes to Hopeless Haven in late November. He has diagnosed osteomyelitis. It is a cancer-like disease. The observation period is to see if the progress of the disease has been arrested; or whether it will continue to kill him.

To the few people who have known my love Randall, he is a typical Middle South 1952 teen-age boy with pimples and terminal shyness. Inside, he is replete with the vicious cells which sap the marrow of the bone, suck it dry, turn it to dust, visit death on the young and the innocent.

Inside Randall, as well, there is an affliction of supreme and radiant gentleness, and a sly and quick humor. Just the thing that would appeal to his new next-door neighbor (some thirty inches away) at the particularly confused, anxious juncture of both of their lives.

Isn't that the way it works! Just when you have been visited by the gods who tell you that you don't have a chance, that all is lost, that you are nothing, that life is nothing, that there is no reason at all, *at all* for surviving, that you might as well hang it up, just hang it up: along comes some shy bumbling open-faced kid, just pops up like that right next to you and all of a sudden there is a softness and a light to all the white-and-shiny things which, days before, were so clinical and dull.

Walls take on a new hue. People seem kinder, or more human. Nurse Stumpf essays a smile for once in her dreadnaught life. The sun peeps out from the thunderheads, and one night, at eleven or so, you can see a sliver of a fall silver-powder moon that creeps along the ward floor. There is a gentleness in the air, and a reason to wake up in the morning. The banging and caterwauling of the kids somehow seems less bruising, and you can lie with your love and be charged three thousand kilowatts with the sweet dew of kindness that turns your insides to bubbling gold.

There is a bizarre custom in that hopeless place: one that I recommend to all other hospitals, large and small. It is visitation. Not of the divine kind: those are reserved to the sallow-faced holies who plague our Sunday mornings with their chocolate-coated words. Nor am I speaking of the familial order—the ones who are allowed to materialize on Sunday afternoons from two to four.

No—I am speaking of visitations between patients, between the able-bodied and the disabled. In that stark setting, there is no place to sit. Certainly no isolated room, with chairs. In a ward crowded with four dozen persons, no privacy is possible except under the scanty covers, and hardly there.

So when folks visit back and forth, they do so side-by-side. In the same bed. When Randall visits me, he lies on the bed, next to me, his warm body threatening, by its very presence, to consume my own in a pure blue flame which seems to emanate, by magic, from his pores. He doesn't know his melting kindness, the effect it has on iceberg me. Or does he?

No questions asked. Visiting time is usually in the evening, before lights out. No suggestions of Queer. A simple and a nice custom, for an otherwise gross environment.

I have no idea what we talk of, Randall and I. I don't know if we visit eighteen or twenty or three dozen times, or every day for three months. All I know is that in the midst of the arctic night of emotional despair, there is a glow. A candle, somewhere, is lit, briefly. Its flame gutters—then burns strongly, sending warm shadows through the otherwise dark room. There is given to us the knowledge that the two of us are not totally nor irrecoverably alone.

For him and for me some bleak stranger has come down the road, and pushed us off in the mud ditch. I, perhaps, shall never walk again. He may be dead within a year from the beast that eats away at his marrow. No matter: we have a respite from that. We are together. There is a chance that I have my arm under his neck. I am sure that from time to time I touch him with my hand. We may laugh together, leaning together in our quiet mirth, something for the two of us, something which, for a change, is ours alone, something that cannot be taken away from us by the rest of the maelstrom of the ward.

Randall and I. The two of us. The innocents in bed, in love together. I can see the glint in his eyes as he whispers to me some particular story out of his youth, or as he gives me a sly report on one of our ward-mates. Our laughter is quiet, mixes quietly with the general babble of the ward, and the ten radios competing with each other to be heard.

I can see him as he walks towards me across the ward. His hair hangs down across his forehead; he grins shyly. He walks, body turned slightly to the left, favoring the leg where the disease is eating the bone alive, the rich young marrow that feeds an insatiable disease.

It may have killed him, that disease: wasting him away. Or, as they operated on him again and again, trying to stop the inevitable "progress" of the disease, his walk may have been turned to a crawling sluglike limp.

I don't want to think about that, and I shan't. Just as I have drawn a heavy black felt curtain, a curtain of mourning, over the fires of September, I shall draw a thick humid nightblue cloth over the two of us, Randall and I, at eight or eight-thirty of a dark November evening. We are carrying on about some unimportant, inconclusive bit of trivia; every now and again my hand touches his shoulder or arm, to emphasize a point, to let us know, us both know, that we are, after all, human, even though our bodies are their own friable element. There is in us some strong stuff of humanity: a warmth that fills us both, the cracked bowls replete with some sweet-smelling liquid.

I could, I suppose, go find him: somewhere, perhaps in Northern Florida. He would be almost forty now. Or he would be dead. Either way, it would give me little. I loved him, deeply, when I did—and now I have covered him with a fine blue curtain.

CHAPTER VII

As I look back over that long, cold ward of Hope Haven, I see nothing but a line of juvenile corpses. Eugene, with black pigeyes and something wrong with his hip to go along with 230 pounds of twenty-year-old corpulence. Warren, whose joints, all of them, are frozen by rheumatoid arthritis so that he cannot straighten out his concentration camp body, nor bend it: but would spend his life at 150 degrees of arc, legs straight out in front of him, arms frozen parallel at his side.

Mark, the guitar player, whose foot, deprived of blood and nerves by spinal bifida, was always in a cast, for skin graft, left foot attached to right leg. Brad, of the kind disposition: an arm permanently kinked by some sort of birth defect. (When I come to visit you two years later in your shack near Valdosta, and I see the coon hounds and kerosene lantern, I realize with a shock how poor you are, how the hospital must have seemed to be some rich paradise.)

Fred, who sported one leg ten inches shorter than the other, another recipient of the bone-wasting osteomyelitus. You had big teeth and a wicked way, Fred. Clark, one arm, and one arm alone, shrivelled by polio (a captious disease: like a tornado, dipping down to lay waste to some parts of the land the body; then skipping over other parts completely). You wore your left arm in an upright brace, to keep it from tightening up. You are the Statue of Liberty, commemorating the poor and the helpless who have come to shore looking for wealth and freedom—and have found, instead, two years in a hospital bed.

You, and the dozens of nameless others: with stumps, bent shoulders, skewed backs, funny feet, hopeless hearts, gangrene brains, swallow-tailed butts, frozen joints, busted frames, twisted eyes. You, the pitiful dregs, the poor children, the poverty-stricken: so poor that you are sent to the hospital which is not a hospital, but rather a special torture chamber which is designed to enfeeble the healthy, maim the whole, sicken the well, cripple the walking.

Such is the state of the medical art being practiced at that dungeon in Northern Florida that those who enter the portals (which say "Abandon Hope Ye Who Enter Here!") can expect your straight shoulders to be crooked; your beating heart to develop murmurs; your fingers to bend and twist at the joints.

Your cocks will sprout cankers; your ass will grow huge purple fistulas; your face will be encrusted with The Pox. Your shining hopeful eyes will become leaden and dull; your

44

mouth which smiles will smile no more; your head will come to droop and your back to sway.

Your teeth will begin to rot; your spleens will develop lesions and leaks; your intestines will blossom with tumors and warts. If you walk straight—we will make it so you crawl; if you crawl, we will reduce you to a wheelchair; if you come to us in a wheelchair, we will turn you to one of the bedridden.

No state of health is too robust or too arcane for us to ignore. Bring us your hopeful, your eager, your breathing, your lively. We, the doctors and nurses and orderlies and masters of Hopeless Haven will reduce them to the walking wounded, the scabrous deformed metal-jointed plastic-plated broken and defeated. Give us your children of hope and mercy, and we will return to you beggars and basket cases. Give us the young adults of the future—and we will give back to you broken flies of humanity to tug your heart and rip your soul. We are the masters of hospitalization: and without prejudice, we can reduce the young of this nation to rubble.

I am dying in that hospital. It won't be revealed to me until later—but I am on my death-bed there. The food, not to say the shocking physical therapy, are less than sufficient for survival. I am in a charity hospital, and in 1952 they are very chary of giving that which is necessary for life.

I have been sent to the hospital to die. They have sent me to a place that will leech the life and the hope out of me. Despite having been squashed by the steam-roller disease, there is possibility of life and recovery. With appropriate care, I might be able to walk again.

But they have sent me to Hopeless Haven. I shall be enslaved forever in the toils of this place. The food is fit to kill; the medical help is deadly; life will soon be over. Dr. Jackyl, head of Physical Medicine at the hospital, is trying to think of some way he can keep me there, and with luck, get me into his operating room. If he plays his cards right, a

45

good series of operations should take care of me, and increase his annual income by five figures.

But he is being asked to yield me up. A determined mother has decided that her son is dying in the pest house. She has pulled strings to get me admitted to Warm Springs Foundation, Warm Springs, Georgia. She is sure that I will be treated somewhat better there, off to the north. She is right.

Dr. Jackyl has decided that he does not want to surrender $1000 a month, cash on the line, to an importuning mother. He is a wily businessman, and knows which side of the bread the butter is breaded on. He has his rummy eye on to something good—and it will take an act of divine intervention to get me out of my bed of pain.

Mother is persistent. She finds that Dr. Jackyl can be reached at his office each evening between 5:15 and 5:30. Each day for two months she calls him at 5:15 to get his OK for my departure, to get my records sent to Warm Springs. Two adults, two titans fighting for control over the boy, the boy in the bed.

A mother of persistence. A doctor of resistence. How reluctant he is to give up his young charge! You would think that the old man was in love with me. You would think that Dr. Jackyl knew a good fuck when he had it. And he had me. On my stomach, legs spraddled far apart, the rheumy doctor with the leaden hand had his will of me. From September to early February. Had it not been for the sixty telephone calls, the unlimited zeal of sheer motherwill—this body would have remained consigned to the hole-wall nightmare hospital of No Hope.

But he fails. Reluctantly, he signs the papers. Reluctantly he rises from my impoverished body, and with tears in his eyes, watches his $12,000-a-year patient sail off to North Georgia. Reluctantly he sees his financial security lifted from his arms, and spirited to another place, to another doctor, to another hospital, out of his hands.

I am admitted to Warm Springs, and I get to say goodbye to the one or two angels, the dozen or so harpies, and the countless non-entities that haunt that hospital of charity.

I am allowed to say goodbye to the twice daily electric

shock spasms and the supper at four each afternoon which both, or alone, are certainly capable of killing a pig.

I am permitted to say good-bye to the kerosene black-smoke heaters, and the leaky roofs; the shrieks and hollering fourteen hours of the day, including all Sundays and holidays.

I am able to say farewell to the trim black moustache of Nurse Stumpf, to the snores of the night nurse, to the encrippling of several hundred children of North Florida at the hands of the professional paid rippers and cutters and tearers and brutalizers.

How was I able to survive this ministration of the damned? How? I survived as well as I did because I truly had no knowledge of how grossly set-up, how grossly run the whole institution. I had no yardstick to tell me that I was in a dump set out to perpetuate sickness, not to cure it.

I had no idea that they were using medieval torture devices on me, tortures that were long since discarded in other parts of the country. I had no idea that the road I was on was ugly, bad, maladjusted, stupid, painfully stupid, out-of-date, backwards, acutely harmful. I had never been in a hospital except as a visitor—and I didn't know beans about nutrition, no idea of new developments in physical therapy, no idea that I was being medically and physically and emotionally starved.

Environments are Givens for the young. I had no criteria to decide whether I was in Paradise or Vulgar City. I had no knowledge of relative accomodations, quality of nursing, standards of hospitalization. We are so pure and clean and straight and innocent—we children of the Upper Class.

With my Prussian education, I learned to do what I was told, to accept what was given. If they had sent me to Korea (draft notice appears three weeks after my induction into the hospital) I would have learned how to use a flamethrower, how to cook up resistant natives. I would do what I was told: I wasn't educated to disobey orders.

We children of the sun: tall, innocent, tanned, lank, pimply-faced stoics. We are the true Existentialists: taking in

47

stride whatever measure our bleak god hands out to us, wondering why life is so drab. We accept the givens of life; we are put here and there, told to do this and that—and we think we have no choice. Never would I think to say (or think to think) "I am being destroyed in this place, by a bunch of doughheads. I have to get out of here!"

I, at eighteen: a poor child of wealth, having a poor, a piss-poor vision of those things which would contribute to my own survival. And as I am telling you this, I am wondering, just wondering how I survived to this moment to be able to tell you all this: wonder how I managed to get to the place of relative security and survivability. How did I ever manage to make it from dying to living?

Permanent harm? Did I suffer any permanent harm from Hope Haven? Sure: I have a souvenir of Hope Haven that twinges me to this very day. Medical care—sensible, up-to-the-latest-technology medical care, available to those who could look for it in 1952—dictated total bedrest for the post-polio for at least three months. And then—a gradual, gradual, gradual reëducation of the muscles.

The medical director and the physical therapist could not and would not research that fact. The cross bar, the one that made it possible for me to escape from The Dread Night Nurse, was put over my bed. I was encouraged to pull myself up on it for exercise, to help the nurses when they were making my bed.

That bar murdered muscles of the upper arms, back, shoulders—anterior deltoids, serratus anterior, trapezius. These are muscles that cannot return, will never return, because they were burned out: not by the disease, but by the strain put on them, as weak as they were, in the first few months of recovery.

Every time I pull myself up those muscles talk to me. They remind me of their nonexistence because the adjacent muscles have to work overtime to make up for those long absent. And they can never do the full job of the ones now gone.

A little present of permanent loss from the pixies who ran Hope Haven. A present from those who could not be bothered with the burden of learning the truth about physical therapy, knowledge available in the medical journals of the time.

We can curse him, the fraudulent and hurtful Dr. Jackyl, but, already, he is reaping his same. At this very moment, some three decades after his collected malefeasances on the poor and unwitting of Hope Haven, he is lying in his own Hope Haven Nursing Home.

His titles and badges mean nothing now. The power he wielded so callously on the poor and young of the land has come back to regale him under the aegis of Nurse Neo-Stumpf, Proto-Craven, Nova-Bland. He is in their thrall now.

His eighty-four-year-old body has changed most wonderfully. The legs that carried about his rounds for so many years have failed him. His intestines are showing signs of advanced retardation. He is on a new journey through bowel and vein and bladder. The brain—in collusion with the rest of him—has turned forgetful around the ages. Sometimes, he doesn't know if it is 1941 or 1922 or 1985.

His fellow members of the profession of Hippocrates have passed to another, deeper, more encompassing institution. He, alone, remains the uninvited guest of a house in the state of terminal collapse. He spends his Sunset Years in the thrall of catheter and aspirator.

His many journeys over the years are now done. His voyages of sensual and financial and social delight are now a dream. He is visiting a new holy land, a land of rot and putrescense. A silent land—except for the whispering of puzzling words against his inner ear, the wheezing of an unknown roommate, the occasional scolding of a vague, balloon-breasted nurse, and the quiet tinkle of the piss bottle at the foot of his bed.

In the Last Hope Rest and Nursing Home, all comes home to all. Bones turn to chalk. Cerebrovascular fluids leak out of the various cranial stops. There are new dawn-flowers of purple over the milk-white deserts of his skin. Shades of *amarillo* juices seep from the nine famous exits of the body.

His eyes have turned to the color of mud. His fingers,

49

imprecise, frail, pick at the starched sheets. His voice trembles of its own weight, heavy with disuse. His body has taken him to a land of truth—a truth that says "There is no freedom from the body. We can deny it, pretend it away, but there is no escape from this bag of skin-and-bones that runs us, runs us all."

He is now alone with a sweet and simple song born of the engine of time; an engine that sings to us the hymn of entropy. Entropy! It runs us and it terminates us, and all besides it is illusory. You are living proof of its power, Dr. Jackyl. Human vengeance is an unnecessary gilding. Our thoughts turn to mice, skittering down dust-choked halls. All that is left as you drop towards the hole is the message of uselessness. All efforts, past, present, future, are foolish. You are proof dying and proof living of entropy.

I see you now, Dr. Jackyl. You touch neither my heart nor my soul. We are in this comic cage together, the corner-cage of decay and futility. The nurses ignore your whispered commands, the aides mock your pitiful requests, the orderlies shove you aside to clean the stench from your sheets, and laugh at your drooled commands. I see you Jackyl: we are together on this last journey. We are tied together in tubes that ride up into veins, up into the nose, deep inside the bladder, along the lower thigh. We are fully plumbed for the last journey, slowly dribbling to a halt in the last crevasse.

You are now wise, Jackyl. Your shattered *os innominatum* gave you ultimate wisdom. You are now part of a Socratic army on wheels, pulled and pushed here and there, given the knowledge of endless sleep, scratching the covers with what is left of your days. You have outmassed the world in understanding.

If they only knew the depths of our body-given wisdom. O if they only knew! They would fall to their knees to worship us. They would hail us with the inviolate cry, out of long centuries past:

Magnus ab integro saeclorum mascitur ordo.

PART II

it is hard believing to think that
a love or a sorrow is a bond pur-
chased without design and
which matures willynilly and is
recalled without warning to be
replaced by whatever issue the
gods happen to be floating at the
time

—*The Sound and The Fury*

CHAPTER VIII

They fold me up like an accordion and squeeze me onto a lower berth on the Southern Railroad to go to Atlanta. From there an ambulance to Warm Springs Foundation.

Paradise. Paradise of Meriwether County, Georgia. Warm Springs. Two support personnel for each patient. Campus of the gods. Food of humans — prepared to be eaten at civilized times.

Physical therapy twice a day, with experts drawn from all over the country. Exotic rehabilitation equipment, the best that the March of Dimes can buy. Massive occupational therapy program. Support doctors in every discipline having to do with The Disease.

How strange and yet how right. To have a place which caters to one specific ill of the time. My ill. My own ill. They have built a castle on the red North Georgia clay country to care for my ill.

Not some mongrel hospital to care for a hundred random diseases. But a twenty-five building complex on one thousand acres to care for my one disease. My own special complex, dealt with by specialists.

O Lord if I could take you back there with me, to the Warm Springs of 1953. The beauty of that place: the giant white colonnades of Georgia Hall. The high ceiling of the dining room. The luxurious food, prepared by those who see it as a pleasure, not as some enemy to be beaten to death.

The tranquility of the nights. Those warm nights out of the American South. Voices on the soft wind. Soft lights shining. The shadow of a disease banished. Laughter, joking.

Humanity. People coming to life again. People like me, who have been buried in ignorant drab little hospitals all over the country; being brought by bus, by car, by train, by airplane to this paradise: this white, clean, alive, human, deliciously hopeful environment.

Massive tanks for swimming and rehabilitation. Elegantly designed neoclassical buildings. Trees and birds and squirrels, and over it all the clean rich open air of a rural environment. No wonder I go back there even now and see patients who should have left when I left, but who, through some vague connections with the staff, managed to stay on and on, never to leave that environment.

Roosevelt: I love you! He did it. Back in the dark ages of Physical Medicine, he thought there was some better way of rehabilitation; better than sticking thin limbs in plaster casts (that's the way they did it in 1920!) He thought there was something better than twenty-pound braces, heavy wooden crutches, locking the cripples in the back rooms of America until they could crawl out into the light like some wormy supplicant. Talk about dignity! Roosevelt, I love you!

He came there, to Meriwether County, in 1924. At that time, it was a spa, one of those hot mineral springs with a creaky old wooden hotel and countless fat black-dress vultures of three hundred pounds, sitting out in the night air and babbling about their livers.

Roosevelt! You dimwit! You were a better doctor than politician! You went into the wrong field! What you did with Warm Springs could have been done with all the basket cases of the world. What you did for my disease, Our Disease—could have been done for countless others.

And there you go off and and decide you would rather run the country, give us all the New Deal stuff when you could have just stayed in your natural (and proper) field. A friendly warm loving doctor, Doc Roosevelt, caring for the chidren and all the other babes that come out of the closets to be cured.

What a saint doctor you would have been! You knew that it was the ads with the children that got them by the heart and nuts and purse strings. Those adorable little girls, in their pinafores, with their clear little blue eyes, and their sweet rosebud mouths. And their little wooden crutches, and their tiny exquisite little braces on their little limbs.

What a pretty disease! No drooling or twitching here! No shitting down the leg, convulsions or other indecent exposures. Roosevelt, you old PR man: you knew how to get $7,000,000 a year from the March of Dimes with that sweet poster girl. We all so puzzled by this thing got her legs. We can cure her, can't we, doc?

Roosevelt as President; cripples as politicians? What a strange idea.

Misplaced cripple passions. The twisted and distorted bodies twist and distort the mind. Rock-gut twisted ideas, wrenched out of shape on the broken anvils of our bodies. Brains turned acute angles by the round-knee shadows and protruding bones from below.

Do you really think you can trust a crip? Are you kidding: trust some spavined basket-case with decisions of War, of Budget, of State, or Humanity? Are you kidding?

See, we cripples cannot believe in the future. We have no sense of it. We run into this wall, and we learn bam! that there is nothing, nothing to be trusted in the world. If I cannot trust my body, what *can* I trust. Certainly not a government, or the state, or money; and certainly, in no way, can I trust other people. My body becomes the screen through which I distort the world. The lens is warped, and so am I. So was Roosevelt.

He went through his own personal Depression. Ten years before it shocked the rest of the country. That day in August of 1921, at Campobello, when he felt the worm-bud disease turning him to fire, his legs to water. He learned what no body and depression are, firsthand. The man of twenty-hour-a-day politics, reduced to a worm.

Roosevelt. President. The rich cripple President. Flew above all handicaps. Rose to the top. But wouldn't let anyone see how they had to carry him around in a box. Would never let them photograph him in his wheelchair, on crutches. Would never let anyone know about those twenty-four-hour junkets in the second floor of the White

House. Him, alone, in his room, alone, all by himself, except for the booze. No one allowed to enter, no one allowed to disturb him, alone with his black mood, the spooks in his head. When I was young and could run pitted against the horrible nightmare thought of Why Me. *Why me?*

Will I ever be the whole man again? No, I will never be the whole man again. They have taken my body from me, doctor. O god, doctor. I have nothing to take its place doctor. They have given me a country, an army, a navy, a wife, children, a state, honor, dignity, applause, lots of applause. They love me. But I am not and can never be in any way whole and dignified and alive again, never. It came like a fire, and wasted me, *wasted me.* I was a man, and it wasted me.

He was brave, that Roosevelt. O Lordy he was brave. He must have known that he would never be whole, but he was brave. A clear-cut nothing-from-the-waist-down case, and yet he forced himself to walk. With steel and fire, he forced his arms to take him across the room, across the lawn, down the steps. He knew, some part of him knew he would never be walking at the head of the Labor Day Parade again, but he kept on pouring his will into what was left of his muscles, trying to walk that walk again. He put on his twenty-pound steel braces, and sweating and puffing, demanded of his body that it produce steps for him. There were none there: yet he created them from somewhere. From his burning will he created them from somewhere. From his burning will he created whole steps where there should have been none. O he was brave, that Roosevelt.

Lift yourself from the chair by your arms alone. Walk on your hands, clasped to wooden poles. Force your arms to be legs, your hands to be feet. No cheating. The swing of your leg has to come from your shoulder. The move of foot has to originate from above the pelvis. You must lift yourself from the chair, out the door, and down the stairs with biceps, triceps, and trapezius alone. No cheating. And know that if you make one misstep on the stairs, there are no gluteal muscles, no sartorius to rescue you. If one of your feet misses the step, you have nothing to catch you but your hands. And you must go down. Way down.

He fell once, Roosevelt did. In front of fifty thousand people. During the Democratic National Convention. Franklin Field, Philadelphia, 1936. He was walking down the aisle. Showing he could walk, so they wouldn't think they had a hopelesss cripple for President. Roosevelt, you dummy! Didn't you ever give up?

Sweating, pouring all of his force into his arms and shoulders to move the hundred and eighty-five pounds of him down a three-hundred-foot aisle. The poet Edwin Markham, an old friend, on the aisle. Reaches out to grab Roosevelt's hand.

Roosevelt gets jostled. The balance is so critical. The cripple on two tiny rubber-crutch-tip pins is so vulnerable. The balance deserts him, the leg-brace breaks, and with great finality, the President of the United States of America topples to the ground.

In that second, he sprawls, groaning, some crutch spun off askew. He is at that sharp moment rendered open to the gods. They, with their pitiless hawk eyes, showing they care nothing for Bravery Strength Courage Overcoming-All-Odds. The mockery of self and of respect; and he has to turn in supplication to those around us to lift him from the bestial mud.

The body guards and Secret Service men grab Roosevelt and set him on his feet again. He is shaking with his public fall, but remember: he is a driven man; he continues his doll-like stiff-legged walk, and makes it the rest of the way to the podium. *And no-one tells!*

Roosevelt goes before fifty thousand people, gives his speech, waves to the crowds, and gets carried out to the back to his waiting limousine. No one comments on the public fall. The press is silent. There are no pictures taken. There is a conspiracy. We have to show our President as strong, and brave, and not-a-cripple. They all buy into it: the Democrats, the Republicans, the crowd, the press, the opposition.

One of the great conspiracies of our time—and not one word of demurral.

Roosevelt. Driving himself so terribly to be The Whole Man. Not realizing that when cripples drive their souls and their bodies so unconscionably, the price must be paid. Play the piper, and then pay him. There is no literature on Driven Cripples. Yet as sure as he was President, he would have to end up paying the price for that venomous self-hate, through the Black Moods in the White House.

And we get to pay for it, too. We get to live with your decisions, you cripple nut. Annual budget madness, the permanent war machine, the largest bureaucracy in the world. Hitler may have been right when he said that polio had turned your brain to frankfurters. Only a madman with blighted limbs would saddle us with the Roosevelt Eternal Sinking Debt Machine.

There is one crucial day in Roosevelt's life-as-President which has never been documented nor recorded. It is, I do believe, the most important day in his whole history as President, as a man. Perhaps it happened shortly after The Fall of Franklin Field. Perhaps a year, or three years later. Maybe on the seventh day of December, 1941.

It was the day when Roosevelt decided not to try any more. It was the day that, for the first time since the fever had crusted his nerves, he decided not to get up and walk. It was the day when he decided that strapping on the braces, hoisting his weight on the crutches, feeling the squeeze of leather against thigh and calf, the burning weight of wooden handle against palms was just too damn much trouble.

I am sure that it didn't come just that way. I am sure that Roosevelt said to himself: "I just don't have time to get up today. Tomorrow, I'll do it tomorrow." And then tomorrow came, and then tomorrow, and then there was no petty pace at all. None of the grinding strain to get up and move about. More comfortable in the wheelchair—the wheels have become my legs. I'll do it next week. Meanwhile, I will let the helping hands move me on these round rubber legs, with their spokes, and these comfortable leather arms.

Perhaps he had no choice. The disease leaves no choice.

When it first picks us up and throws us down, we think that we can beat it. Learn to walk; do it gracefully, so no one will know what little we have. Become independent: how do they say it? 'I'll be my own man . . .'

They never tell us about Phase Two. When the ageing nerves begin to weaken. What we learned to do so smartly after the fire has passed over us, we watch disappear again. Our victories last for ten, twenty, thirty years — and then the referee comes up to us, blows the whistle, and tells us that we're out, after all. What we gained, we lose. In the last part of our lives we are dragged to the bed again.

There was a day when Roosevelt succumbed to the unmitigating, undeniable truth of his body. Accompanied by terminal despair, he found he was growing, again, to be as helpless as he was in the awful days at Campobello. He learned that the disease is master, the final ultimate master: and our efforts to surmount it are, have been, and always will be tinsel, cut from the glaze of ultimate defeat.

When my friend Gallagher, the historian, asks people who knew Roosevelt, asks them how he reacted to being a cripple, how he reacted to the second encrippling that must capture all the 'old' polios — when Gallagher asks the Tug-wells and the Grace Tullys and all the Roosevelt nieces and nephews how he dealt with the final toll of the virus, they always say "O. No problem. Nothing at all. Didn't bother him at all. He was magnificent."

They don't know, those who thought they knew him. They never got the secret of the withered leg. That secret which I am giving you now. Didn't bother him at all? Didn't bother the Master of Control at all? Fat. Fucking. Chance.

consequent belief that no one in their right mind would want (we think) to engage in an act of congress with a spinal case, a certified quadriplegic, a multiple-spastic scoliosis-and-iron lung crip— e.g., a patient. We are convinced that we can't make it in the passion sweepstakes.

And for exactly that reason, we seem to have a double dollop of lust. They say that when you remove an arm, or a leg, or a bladder—or the backbone, for that matter—the extra energy gets concentrated in the groin. Extra *frustrated* energy. I believe, I believe! What they take away from us in motion comes back in spades in the testes and ovaries.

At Hope Haven, I had little opportunity, except in fantasy, to manifest this newly created nut-madness with Randall. I had been returned to a primeval state, where survival was more important than anything else. Furthermore, as one of thirty-six patients in a ward, there was little privacy. If I couldn't make it out of the ward to crap, or play cards, I was hardly about to get to the sub-basement for a few *sub-rosa* kisses, flaming caresses behind the coal-burning furnace.

It wasn't until I came to Warm Springs that my loins entered a request for some consideration and attention. Consideration—hell! After a few weeks there, my lust, Hermann Lust, that is, starts rattling the cage bars, demanding that I pay attention to him, give him some warmth and comfort, let him out of the box. I can scarcely make it through the day without this pee-head trying to worm his way into my every relationship. It is quite draining. I mean, there is little enough privacy in your standard hospital bed, what with all the bars and handles rattling about as you gave yourself over to the ministrations of Rosie Palm and Five Kidz. How does one deal with staff, other patients, the real world, when it comes time to manifest that lust in arenas beyond the confines of the warm fist?

I am, further, the last to deny that there are problems when commencing passion in the wheelchair. The logistics of weakened (sometimes non-existent) arm and leg muscles, being intertwined with other weakened arm and leg muscles, can lead to especial frustration. Atrophied quadriceps riding hard atop atrophied gluteals—or the atrophied opponens policis in proximity to a partially atrophied *mons veneris*: these do salt and pepper the potato of passion. Logistically, socially, practically, emotionally—it's a mess. There are no block-and-tackles, pulleys, or choke-levers designed to make the intricate task of interpenetration easy for your average basket-case.

The puritan mentality that runs Warm Springs—or any of the hospitals, then and now—is not about to make it simple for us to exorcise the fire down below. They are going to provide no Brace Shop fixtures to unite us with spring and metal, to provide flexion joints to get us hip-to-hip, lip-to-lip. There are no cord-and-ring exercise devices which will encourage, as a form of positive physical therapy, two patients, with an arm here and a leg there, the wherewithall to come to a fantastic spastic rhythmic clash and climax: not on your sweet biddy. The staff isn't going to make our task of extinguishing the holocaust legal, gentle, easy, or right.

Yet my sometimes friend Hermann Lust won't leave me alone: crying in my ear over breakfast, yanking on my covers at night. I can be alone, admiring the stately columns of Georgia Hall, at one with the fountains, birds, squirrels—and that bugger starts dancing up and down, screaming in my ear, GET LAID. What a gunk!

It is he who brings me into conjunction with two important figures in my new life. One, a princess, a goddess of a fellow-patient—Francine. The other, a waif-like orphan of emotion, one of the Foundation Staff, Miss Fay Trimble.

Miss Trimble: a small figure in white. She is a student in the physical therapy department at Warm Springs. She has a pointy nose and sharp, ferrule teeth. One of her eyes, at all times, seems to be contemplating the end of her nose. The other, presumably, is on me. She has a disarming habit of wrinkling up her nose at those times when something refreshing (a thought, perhaps) drifts through her mind, or when there is some felicitous exchange between us.

Miss Trimble can't keep her hands off me, her first patient. She isn't *supposed* to keep her hands off me. She is a therapist. Physical therapists get into very intimate positions and places with their charges. Which is why most of them, as with doctors and nurses, practice "distance" and a measured iciness.

But Miss Trimble likes me too much for that. In the isolation booth of therapy, physical therapy, she will offer a kiss on the knee as she is putting that object through its paces, through its exercises. A tickle on the bottom of the foot during toe exercises. A too-generous hug as she helps me work out my neck muscles.

At first I do not protest. I have been raised on the American movie cult that every man should have a woman. I have been terrible, heretofore, on the love-involvement scene, always feeling something is wrong with me, maybe my breath or my hair. Now that I definitely *do* have something wrong with me, it is a pleasure, I think, to have someone developing an intimacy with me.

She changes my feeling of isolation, something wrong. She invests me with the charged sex-laden atmosphere of our mutual entertainment world idols. When she comes into the workout exercise cubicle, pulls the curtains closed, throws her cape (she wears a cape!) to the side, leans her face close to my face, wrinkles up her nose and says, breathes really: "Hi!" I am interested. It is expected. We movie nuts of the forties play out our society-sketched roles.

This passion of the exercise booth never, unfortunately, goes beyond the wrinkled nose and the kiss on the knee. Some aspect of self-preservation in both of us prevents us from extending our intimacies to her, for instance, climbing up on the table, hiking her skirts, and giving us both some well-needed exercise of a more penetrating sort. Miss Trimble and I both are chicken; or rather she is chicken, and I am hardly in a position to insist on plugging her in that private booth.

Our diddling goes on for some five or six weeks—she active, I passive. And then, one Sunday, the *coup de main*. She invites me up to her place for tea, her little bungalow a block from the campus. She comes to get me at two in the afternoon. I am awaiting her in my wheelchair. She pulls and pushes the beast (it is one of the old wooden variety) across

63

the street, up the walk, and into the ramp at the door of her house. This is certainly going to be the site of the *denouement,* where cripple and therapist will get it on. Certainly, my years of virginity are to be brought to a crashing halt: she, lifting my still frail body over to the settee; closing the curtains; her undressing me, personally unstrapping my orthopaedic corset; pulling down pants and with bird-like tongue, kissing and caressing that young man body she had been coveting this past month and a half. And there, while the mockingbirds wait breathlessly in the late March Sunday afternoon drowse, the magic of consummation, as she throws her scanty shift to the floor, and athletically and boldly, she rises up astride my burning etc etc and she etc etc blah blah blah.

Well, alas dear reader: our crisis, when it comes, is not of the orgasmic sort. Probably had Miss Trimble been the least bit aggressive, we could have, in our own way, as the contemporary generation so crudely says, gotten it on, or "done it." But Miss Trimble is, for reasons of her own, far less aggressive in the bedroom than she is in the therapy booth. We both have a spot of tea; she shares with me some Lorna Doone cookies; she also shares with me her abysmal taste in literature, reading some foul Joyce Kilmer poetry to me as she has heard that I am one of the literati having taken two English courses at Yale, both of which I barely comprehended.

Our crisis, when it comes, is not of the throbbing intrauterine sort. Our crisis when it comes is, at least to me, far more dramatic, far deeper, far more encompassing. Miss Trimble is a dolt; at least, she doesn't understand about old wooden wheelchairs and such. She doesn't know (I don't know) that the ancient wheelchair doesn't go down ramps forwards: rather, you pull it down backwards, to keep from dumping the prize patient out on the fucking ground.

When we go to leave, we leave in more ways than one. Barely out the door, I am being shoved forward and of a sudden I am out of the wheelchair and a pile in the dirt. Miss Trimble isn't too well coordinated, and she runs me over with the front wheels and then stands there, fluttering her hands, and in a whimper-voice, says "O dear, O dear me" and "Are you all right?" Of course I am not all right, and in the ten minutes it takes her to find someone to untangle me from the spokes of the chair, get me back seated again, and back to my room—I am in turmoil.

I say nothing. I am very very silent. In contrast to our previous bonhomie, Miss Trimble finds me strangely wordless. I am not hurt, outside. But my eyes are narrowed, my mouth a bit tight. I am, inside, enraged. My dignity, what little precious dignity I have mustered after this past half year, has been trampled on, torn, disfigured. I am filled with the most poisonous sort of loathing for one who has caused me such indignity. I lose all sense: sense of equilibrium, sense of warmth. The next day, I send for the head of the Physical Therapy Department, and tell all. All about the hugs and kisses and the ticklings.

I am transferred to another therapist. For the uncomfortable week that we continue together, there are no words exchanged between Miss Trimble and me. After that, there is no more than a frigid nod as we meet in the hallway, or on the path. I have violated her the only way I know how, for I am convinced that she violated my dignity.

Strange: that I should put up with such indignities at the charity hospital for so long, and bring no blame to anyone for them. The difference is that what I suffered heretofore was merely medical or nutritional in nature. For the first time, with Miss Trimble, I have been subjected to an indignity which reaches into the tattered pride that I have so carefully nurtured in its hothouse for all these months. And once that pride has been trampled, I am out for blood.

Anger and Brooding. That is what we cripples are best at. Sitting around in our baskets, brooding over the wrong done us by the world, by our own accidents and diseases. The bile! The bile that comes out of our withered limbs, our calcified joints. We are so good at it. Our sense of injustice is so huge; our forgiveness so slight.

The poor and the innocent Miss Trimble made two mistakes. She loved me, and she dumped me. She was the first, and my triumph over her was just the beginning of the

Old Testament rage I came to direct at the world. Boils, fires, storms would be visited on those who stepped over the line of my dignity, my self-esteem, my desire to be independent.

I have just begun to grow in my new body. It will be the battlefield. There will be those who will try to love me; those who will be drawn to me; who will try to empathize with me; who will think they understand me.

But I have something over them all. I am Troy. I have been sacked and looted and burned by the barbarians. The Huns came and devastated every street, every temple, every square. And, as a result, I have turned inwards.

There is no way I will let myself be understood. There is no way I will permit myself to be reached. Much as rats crowded into too small cages turn vengeful, queer, strange—so one trapped in too little body does the same. In spades.

CHAPTER X

The next physical therapist they put in my grinding machine is Greta Green. Greta Green! The good and the sweet and tall and straight Miss Greta Green, who would never have the bad taste to dump me on the ground. Hell: she would never have the need to invite me up to her house for tea. And she would surely never drop her dignity and good sense to fall in love with one of her patients.

Greta Green! Greta Green! The Physical Therapist of Physical Therapists. She who teaches the teachers. They come from all over the country to learn the Warm Springs Rehabilitation technique. They come from California and New York and Florida and Michigan and Canada and Mexico: to learn what Warm Springs developed on its own. In the twenty years since its inception, Warm Springs works in a vacuum, there in the high Georgia country, with millions of dollars, to develop exquisite techniques of rehabilitation. And they come from all over the country, from all over the world to learn the lesson of lessons, the art, the high art of polio rehabilitation.

And who do they learn it from? That's right, from my own Greta Green. The Master of Masters. The *chef d'oeuvre*. Going from Miss Trimble to Green Greta is like moving from Borden's Baby Formula to getting it straight and warm and nuzzly from the teat. She is a princess!

Sometimes I wonder where she is, what she is doing now twenty-five years after my lessons at her able hands. Greta Green: do you still get up at six to go to Mass and chew the wafer; then at seven play tennis with your roomie, letting the morning Georgia sun turn your aristocratic face more dark and more handsome, so that when you smile, Greta Green, your teeth come out myriad stars in the dark windswept night; then at eight to breakfast, and then at nine to cure your loving admirer, me?

You can see that I am quite taken with the good Greta Green and she was smart enough not to give me cause to doubt her. No piddling on the exercise table! She is working with me to get my body (not my cock) up in the air. It is Greta Green of the tan face and white uniform, good soul, who will, finally, get me elevated from the dead; it is Greta who will get me elevated from my tomb-body.

She will get me up on my feet, up on my feet, standing on my own feet (not someone else's). It is Greta who will teach me. Who will teach me to, who will teach me, at last, after all this time, who will teach me, to get on my own two feet. At last, on my own goddamn feet, on my own two feet, and, once there, once there, to w-a-l-k. Me, walk!

We first learn to move on our own two pins when we are (on the average) 1.13 years of age. At that time nature, the body, all is on our side. Evolution is on our side. The act of raising ourselves from the dirt is a natural consequence of the bones and the muscles given to us. We teach ourselves to do what is ultimately natural for us to do.

Learning to walk at the age of nineteen is different. First,

there is the natural weakness of muscle; general lack of coör-
dination that comes with old familiar muscles gone, and few,
too few, to take their places.

Then there is the support equipment, some dozen
pounds of braces, crutches, back support. I lost thirty-five
pounds from the wasting disease, and gain twelve in metal
and cloth and leather. You expect me to walk with all this
junk tied to my body, Greta Green?

The characteristic look of the patient in wheelchair at
Warm Springs is that of a wasted human hidden behind a bizarre collection of hangers and straps and springs and leather
doo-dads. All this sprouted collection of overhangs and lea-
therwork is designed to undo the muscle contraction and
overuse in patients coming to Warm Springs from all the
other meathead hospitals around the country. The funny-
looking L-bars overhang wooden lapboards with C-bars on
hands and springs and rubber bands pulling fingers here and
there are all designed to retrain what is left of the weakened
muscles into correct positionality.

Other equipment is actually used for muscle substitution.
The orthopaedic corset is a back-and-stomach-muscle substitute. It keeps the huge and heavy upper torso and head
from grinding down with all that weight on the relatively
frail backbone. Long and short leg braces are metal
bones strapped with leather to substitute for quadriceps,
hamstrings, tibia, and gastrocnemius. Missing muscles are
remade of aluminum and leather. Our intimate (and new)
long-term friend: corset and brace.

The day they send me down to the Brace Shop, Bud, the
foreman, puts a long piece of butcher paper under my leg,
and traces the image of my leg, the form below, so they
can make up a pair of braces for me. I am lying there restless
for an hour, staring at the pictures of four-dozen cripples—
photos as wall decorations—and I look, and they look back
at me, fellow basket-cases frozen (no smiles, no tears) with
their featured metal extenders for wrists, rings and rubber
bands and elevated bars for hands, cast back braces to right
the S-shaped backbone, spring-in heel devices to correct the
characteristic polio drop-foot.

As they are running these lines about my legs, do I despair? Do I rebuke the gods for the knowledge that I will be stuck, for the rest of my days, with metal-and-leather, cotton-moleskin-and-stays? Do I, on that day, when I start to visualize myself as one of the walking wounded, creeping about on the face of the blasted earth — do I, at that fatal moment, lift moist eyes to the smoky gods that reign, forever, over us poor-fly mortals and heave on them Tantalus-like, my fatal curse? Me, never ever again to walk the path of the Normal: for that do I blast the gods at the very fount of their beings?

No. At that moment, when they are fitting me with the paraphernalia which I carry about with me even today, so many years later — while they are socking me with the bands and straps and knots that will bind me forever, I am (I have no doubt) mooning, in my head, about some latest truelove or humming some idiot Billy Eckstein or Frankie Laine love tune to myself, or preoccupying myself with the usual trivia which is the wont and expectation of your average, typical, moribund nineteen-year-old American male of the year of our Lord and Grace, 1953.

That I would curse the gods, much less figure out what has happened to me, strains the knowledge that is given to the typical child of our time. That I should have the prescience to see what a devilish life I have ahead of me, had I been blessed with that cruel knowledge, I should promptly have stuck my headbone in the nearest Warm Spring and done myself in.

It is not that I am stupid. Rather — it is that I am sensible. I need the self-protection of selective vision. By myself, by my own wonderful lack of vision, I have protected myself from the terrible blearing insight which certainly would have drowned me in grief. Me, on that stretcher, Bud drawing crude caricature of my thin and bony leg: that I should know at that moment what I know now could only lead to despair and eventual self-destruction. I, humming fool love-songs to myself and thinking on trivial affairs of the heart, am being protected by the supreme wisdom of my own mind from the fatal and poisoning knowledge which, over the next years, was to come fire and nigh about blind me to what I am coming to see, only now, is the true self and real being.

One afternoon, I am watching Greta Green out of my window. I am on the second floor of the East Wing. We overlook the east courtyard of the Quadrangle. This is the heart of the Foundation.

The birds are singing, and Greta Green looks like a bird with her white feather dress and dark limbs. It is a nice day in April, and Miss Green is out to teach the other birds how to fly. They are students who have flown in from all over the country to learn how to raise the blind, the halt, and the lame.

For their first lesson, Miss Green dresses them in equipment. Over their uniforms there are tied metal supports and cloth backing and shoes with pegs and high full-arm Canadian crutches. They stand up straight-legged in metal, so they can learn, so they can learn that hard lesson. That is: equipment, the equipment that will make us walk again is an impediment and a bother. A necessary impediment, but one just the same. Because without those external bones of aluminum, many of us could never move out of our chairs again. And it is incumbent on those who think that they are going to teach cripples to rise from their beds to know the impediments of rehabilitation. Learn them first hand.

I watch Greta Green out that window, and her straight-backed stiff-legged students trying to climb stairs, walk backwards, get up on the straddlers. I watch her teaching the teachers how to fly, and I don't know it then (I don't think of it then) that soon enough she will be teaching me how to fly. To fly out of the nest. Like I knew what I was doing.

It is one day in early summer, that fine summer of 1953. Some anonymous day in, say, June; let's say, the 17th of June, 1953. It is some nine months since I last placed weight of body on leg and foot.

I am, as I say, thirty-five pounds lighter than before, having been on a special crash diet course, and I am, it is said, some three inches taller (we grow in bed). And, Greta Green, in white, with some anonymous Push Boy in white (Push Boys push wheelchairs and stretchers down the long halls of the Georgia Warm Springs Foundation), the two of them in white like angel birds, he pulling she pushing, pulling and pushing me in my two long-leg braces, one orthopaedic back-brace, two full-arm crutches, us together there in the anteroom between the warm sulphur-smelling exercise pool and the physical therapy exercise room, they, Greta Green and Push Boy, get reluctant me up from the sitting position, from there through an arc of ninety degrees, legs snapped into the wobbling and uneasy position of, are you ready:

S
T
A
N
D
I
N
G
(ME!)

On my own two feet. With no other support than their four hands on belt back and chest, my two metal leggins, my aluminum-stay-clad waist, my two metal pins, and any other support that I can grab on to.

What is my first thought, you ask? What is the first thing I think of when I, after nine months in the sack, am finally, and once again, elevated to the raised position of unbelievable complication which man describes so simply (oblivious to its complexities) as "standing."

What is my first earthly thought? Is it "O God, I'm on my feet again?" Is it "I kept the faith?" Is it "Sweet Jesus, look at me now?"

No. It just doesn't work like it does in the movies. All I can think of is "Good Christ it is such a long way from here down to the floor" and "I wonder why my hips are so slippery."

And I most definitely don't stand around there forever. I

am a bit scared way up in the sky, and, after all, I can only hang on for dear life for four or five minutes before I am exhausted. Suffice it to say that those few moments are quite enough for my first attempt at mountain climbing since September of the previous year.

You would have liked it though: that day, with the sun coming in through the blue frosted windows of the therapy pool area. There are the stacked windows next to the door, and the red scuffed tile floor, and the heady smell of sulphur in the air from the hot springs below, the eternal fire of geothermal power bubbling up clear and hot from some reddish magma mystery below.

You would have liked it, I am sure: watching me for those few minutes; I, for the first time in so long, so very very long, feeling the weight on the balls of my own feet, standing so tall (6´3˝!) and trembling with the novelty of it.

I think if you had been there, and had been told what the occasion was, what you were seeing for the first time, I think you would have been proud of me. And Greta Green, and Anonymous Push Boy. If you had known what was up (me!), getting Lorenzo back on his legs after nine months down, I think you would have felt quite warm and good inside, the first steps up, the first return of stolen freedom. I think you would have liked it.

Events like this one are only significant when basted with the juices of subsequent events. The most important day of (perhaps) the next ten years becomes crucial when we look at it a long time afterwards to appreciate the thrust of it.

I stand on that day (and every day thereafter) not because I am strong and brave and true and have to defy the nay-sayers with my natural tenacity; but rather, I stand because it is what is expected of me. I get out of that chair because I have no choice: there are two people pushing and pulling me into the standing position. To resist would have been futile. It would have taken far more bravado to resist, to say to Greta Green "No. I don't think I want to do it today. Let's wait." She wouldn't have tolerated that.

The significance was lost, much as the statement made four months earlier, by Doctor Bennett. He was the one who ran the whole show at Georgia Warm Springs Foundation. He looked at my muscle chart, poked around my body for a few moments, and ventured the opinion to the interns, therapists, and various secretaries in the office that, because of the singular weakness in my right posterior shoulder girdle, there was a probability, a quite high one, that I should never stand again, much less walk.

I didn't even *hear* the old fool say that. It was the therapist who was assigned to me for the day who said, kindly, "Don't worry, Lorenzo; I don't think he's right. I wouldn't listen to him." I didn't even understand *her* either.

We do as we are told. If, instead of going into the Army of Cripples, I had gone into the Army of the U.S. Government, travelled to Korea, and learned how to stick people in the gut with a bayonet: well, so be it. I would have done what I was told, not because I am a good or bad person, but because there is someone up there with the proper authority at the proper time and they tell me to disembowel the enemy and I do it, no matter what I may personally think of the insides of some poor peasant working for the People's Army. That's faith!

CHAPTER XI

When I first get to Warm Springs, I think of the nurses and orderlies and doctors as being just the same as me. The only difference (a slight one) is that they are up, and I am down. They stand and walk, I lie down or sit in a wheelchair. Outside of that minimal distinction, we are just the same.

But during my time there at the Foundation, I begin to perceive distances between us. There are some subtle and strange differences between Patient and Staff. And it isn't just that they are Up, and I am Down (and I've been Down so long it don't look like Up to me).

I find myself envying them. I find myself wondering about the magic which protected them from the disease, isolation, the travail of rehabilitation, both physical and mental. What spirit, I wonder, kept them from being blasted by the disease of the ages?

Rodney the pushboy, with his sour face and moss-bound teeth and slow wit. What has he done to keep the virus from creeping to the backbone, turning the cells poisonous and vicious. What is it that Rodney has that separates him from sensitive me, or wise Hugh, or gentle Jan? What is the *ethic* of disease? What is the logic (if there can be logic to a civil war of such dimension within the body) that gives Rodney the full use of arms and legs and back and shoulders and hips—while my beautiful and kind Francine has the threads in her backbone scarred and ruined so that she can never move toe or foot or leg, ever again?

What is the wisdom, the god-wisdom that provides Rodney with an evening after work to stuff mashed potatoes in his face, pick his nose, amble down to the Dew Drop Inn and slug down eleven cans of National Bohemian Beer and then (legs and arms intact) indulge in a senseless brawl with two other male orderlies? What magic does Rodney have in his stars, his make-up, character, birth, parentage, (his round-shouldered father, his red-faced mother with a grey bun pulled back so tight) that gives him the right to run headlong into Willie, the orderly, and try his best with his fist to turn one of Willie's eyes blue and knock out a tooth or two in the process? What divinity ordains that Rodney have full use of back and legs and arms so that he can be smashed down on the asphalt tile floor of the Dew Drop Inn, next to the spittoon, and almost without thought, raise himself back up to standing again (against a blow that would have felled a cow) and start whaling away at Willie, despite the barkeep's intense efforts to get them outside where they belong? And all the while my beloved Francine; not a muscle, not a twitch in her legs, pulls herself by arm power alone from wheelchair to bed, an effort of few muscles and much will which takes some five minutes and leaves her panting and breathless. How in hell have the gods determined to split the universe of men sick and men well? What are their strange, bizarre, incomprehensible criteria over who runs, who walks, who sits, and who lies flat?

We learn to sit and we learn to stand and we learn to walk and we do it because it is expected of us, and in the interim we don't think of the importance of what we can do (or what we can't do) for the rest of our lives because we are twisting ourselves up into emotional bundles, falling in love or at least thinking that we are falling in love. With Francine.

Francine Coupé! You sweetie! Outside of serious Greta Green it is you I should like to see the most. After twenty-five years apart, each of us grinding along on our separate courses, what it would be for the two of us to get together at the corner saloon and compare notes on what we have and haven't done?

Francine. Francine Coupé, of New Orleans. A classic beauty. Classic! I return to Warm Springs a dozen years later, and they still ask me about Francine of the black hair, high cheekbones, exotic brown-black eyes, one mole on upper right cheek, perfect skin, perfect person, perfect perfect.

We meet by accident, Francine and I: on a remote island resort in the Caribbean. My family and I occupy the castle on the hill. Francine is a simple waif of seventeen, in her ragged tattered shorts; she, hunting conch shells and sand dollars alongside the surf when I first chance upon her. It changes our lives: that meeting on the desert beach. We on the white hot sands, palms rattling in the first of the afternoon breezes and, and her cool, moist, salty, firm lips on my own. You Francine! And the nights when the moon is so bright that you would think it was the sun, blazing cold white light down where the surf curls lazy C's onto the beach, darker sands under our bodies, as we lie there, our legs in the water boiling up around us, the surf pounding, wetting our tan trim bodies, pounding our hearts to bits as we lie there each to each in desperate child-innocent love.

Wait a minute! That's not me, nor Francine. I meet her in Second East Hall at the Foundation, just outside the nurse's station where they dump the bedpans. She is lounged naughtily back in her canvas wheelchair. She has just arrived, and I remember thinking "she really is quite beautiful." And she is.

We become the talk of the Foundation. Lorenzo and Francine. Always together. Eating together, playing together go to the twice-weekly movie together (hold hot hands together). Race wheelchairs down Founders Hall together. Wait in line for lunch together. Go to standing class together.

Francine appears just as I am leaving my bed. Slowly, very slowly—I am allowed time up. A half hour a day. Then an hour. Two hours. Three. It takes months to work up to the twelve hours a day in wheelchair which is *de rigueur* for those of us who are part of the sporting set at Warm Springs.

I have just been released to do six hours a day butt time in my wheelchair, and freed of certain equipment which allows me to wheel myself from here to there when Francine arrives on the scene. She and my passion for her are tied to the newest and most precious freedom: independence.

In de pen dence. Jesus Lord, how great it is. To wheel to lunch and supper on my own. To careen down the hall on my own. To take my own dump by myself. I am my own person!

To wheel myself (not be pushed or pulled by someone else) to treatment. To wheel myself to the Brace Shop or the Corset Shop. To wheel myself to the movies. To go places on the campus I didn't realize existed before. I am free. I can push myself from here to there and no one will stop me.

Francine comes at a time when I am just enjoying this new freedom. Realize how important it is: I have been locked in one ward for the first six months of my new life and in the beginning of my stay at Warm Springs I am mostly in one room. Now, I can move up and down the halls, even enjoy some privacy on my own, even take my own bath, get in and out of the tub by myself. I am free.

Francine comes party to my new freedom, and I see it as

part of my freedom to go everywhere with her, to be with someone who is as new to it as I am myself. With Francine, I can slip out to, say, the deserted card room in Builder's Hall and we can hold hands and I can look deep into her moist honey eyes and Jackie Gleason leads the orchestra in our theme song which is

> *My funny valentine*
> *Sweet funny valentine*
> *Your nose is laughable,*
> *Unphotographable*
> *You make me happy when you do walk . . .*
> *Don't change your face for me*
> *Not if you care for me*
> *Stay sweet valentine stay . . .*

and the strings come up high in close harmony and Francine and I stare deep deep into each other's eyes and we know what love is.

This is the most serious thing that has happened to me up to that time, at least in the love department. Except for Miss Trimble, I had never had someone who saw me as desirable or interesting or lovable—and of a sudden this bombshell thinks that I am the most wonderful man in the world. It is a heady experience, and despite my own hesitation at calling it anything as strong as Love, now, it is important in the agonizing crawl-walk to freedom to have Francine as my ally in the journey upwards.

It is in the midsummer that Francine and I start parking our wheelchairs behind the Pithacanthrium so archly called Bush Thirteen. There, while the stars blare down by the thousands, we sup at each others' lips and gradually extend our intimacies with each other. At first it is kissing, and then it is kissing and caressing, and then kissing and caressing and rubbing, I touch every part of her, and she does the same to me, and one night (sweet night!) she takes us both beyond redemption, O Lord! she caresses and loves O rub-a-dub, O rub, O dub, and sudden the lights all over, the sweet heady smell of magnolia the stars banging forth, stars come comets spangling forth, the rockets red glare, aburst in night air, give proof to the night that our love is so rare.

I am so smitten with us, so tenderly torn, and she holds my head to her night-swelling chest and runs her hand along the line of my hair, fingers about the tender corolla of my ear, the last of the swollen stars gracefully falling away into the last of the night luminous fruit velvet blue melt in the last of the North Georgia sky, to the depths of the warmest springs springing forth forever and a night. . . .

Francine, Francine, Where are you, where are we now? I heard that you married your soldier love boy friend, shortly after you and I gave up being cripple lovers. It is just as well, don't you think? Can you imagine the magnifying effect we would have had on each other: extra focus on our half bodies, never having either of us complete, and thus, emphasizing our separateness from the rest of the world. It is a good thing that we each went our different ways: me back to college, you into the arms of your khaki-colored uniform Master Sargent Honey.

We live out the spasm of our cripple love for the rest of that summer and fall. In August we move the scene of our passionate chair-bound wrestlings from the all-too public Bush Thirteen to the new complex which was to become Roosevelt Hall. There, on the lower floor, in what was later to be a broom and sweeper closet, with the water of the cement layers coming dripping down the walls, we try with all our might to consummate our cripple love, and fail. John Longstaff was kind enough to instruct the both of us on how to get down from the wheel-chair seat to floor, on a blanket spread there; but you and I were never sure we could get back up. What would it be like for us to be trapped on the floor there, exhausted from our night of passion, having to wait until morning for some bemused construction worker to respond to our scratchings on the door, to lift us back into our respective chairs? "We were just sitting here, and just somehow fell out onto the floor, you know?"

In September, I left; you in October. In December, we were reunited at your grandparent's house in Ferndale, Louisiana. There, for the first and last times, we shared a bed, you and I, valiantly pumping away with what few muscles we had.

We struggled to carry out our love in that icy house in northwest Louisiana. You in the front room, me in the next— except for the hours from eleven to six or so, at what time you let me, cold me, in at your warm side.

We, sharing that white frame house where the cold breath of the plains comes raging down from the north. You and I and two grandparents and an aunt who probably would have called the police on me in your bed in their house in cold northern Louisiana, in 1953. But because we are two cripples (how do they say it? *hopeless cripples?*) in that cold frostybound winter in Louisiana, just outside the cajun country, where the coffee is coal black with chicory: they, the three relatives, never comment on the fact that there is one bed in the front of the house which is mussed beyond all belief, the other barely slept in.

They are kind to us and we are kind to each other in that crisp refreshingly healthy time just before the two of us are to be launched on our new careers as professional, full-time cripples: me on my long silver wings; you in your famous blue canvas-back portable wheelchair. Me on foot, you in your chair. You in your chair. You always in your chair.

For you are never to walk. Not since that summer day in August at the upper Georgia Hall walking court, during "walking class." When you try out your new braces and new crutches. For the first time by yourself. All the other times there have been pushboys and physical therapists to hold on to your belt. But the rest of us are getting up, me and John Longstaff and Margot, all of us in full triumph on our new feet, walking, friends out for a stroll together.

We are full of the triumph of getting onto our own two feet, by ourselves, to try out our new stuff together. And you do too: you, Francine in blue shorts and white blouse. You my Francine, my beautiful Francine: I never realize how tall you are. I never realize how tall you are until you are tall no more.

79

A swing through, and you miss. Feet go forward, but the balance is wrong, the balance is all wrong Francine. And you begin to go backwards. Ah Francine.

You fall backwards. There is nothing to stop you in your fall backwards. You don't have the muscles of the other 99% of humanity that would permit you to twist, to catch yourself. There is nothing you have to protect yourself from the ground.

To this day, a quarter century later, I can hear the sound that your head makes when it smacks into brick pavement. I can hear it, and I see you now there, my helpless friend, my helpless love. We are all helpless. There is no one, no one of your friends there who can reach out to you as you fall; none of us can reach out to you after you fall. There is no way I can reach down to you, there is no way I can kneel down to reach you as you lie there on the ground my Francine.

Your body is askew. You are so hurt by your fall that you cannot cry out. You don't see my gut soul frozen with the recognition of you all of us lying helpless there, the army of us cripples fallen over backwards to crack our heads and with the shock of it, just barely able to groan, barely.

We try in any way we can to get out of ourselves; we try to rise out of the dirt, to get up, get on our feet for a moment, for five minutes—and then, we catch our foot or slip on something, and we are arched back and our heads smack against the red brick pavement, and in an instant the blood of our skulls leaks out to mix with the cracks of dirt in the pavement and we can barely see with the blow of it, barely groan as we are lying there and there is no way that any of our friends can reach out to touch us. And we know we have tried to beat the gods, and that we have lost.

I believe there is a god who created Francine. And he created a disease to smash her down, so that on that August afternoon, with the cicadas all around, in her attempt to be free, she would instead fall backwards so violently that she would never ever again try to get onto her feet. She would never try to get on her own two feet ever again.

If I could get on my knees (if I could get on my knees!) I

should send up to the heavens such words that the very lilies of the valley would shrink and turn ashen at the words that I would offer up to Our God who gave my kind, my never hurtful Francine such a muscle disease so that she comes to lie broken askew on the bricks, her head softly leaking the red-turning-dark on that rich sweet-smelling day in August so that she would be laid in the bed for two weeks, and laid in the chair forever after, so that she would never ever again get to her feet, onto her feet and off the ground. Never again.

CHAPTER XII

We have good times, too. Francine and John Longstaff and Hugh Gallagher and Margot and I and a half-a-dozen others, the in-crowd of late teen-agers at Warm Springs. We, four-and-four at the tables for lunch and supper, with Henry the Waiter. It is the summer of Eat Me Raw (later reduced to E.M.R.) and Pogo and new Peanuts. We go to bad movies in the movie house and smooch: the old movie house so dangerous with rotting wood that the Warm Springs Fire Department comes with fire hose and trucks to stay for the whole movie in case there is a blaze because you know what *that* would do to 300 wheelchairs and stretchers.

We race through Georgia Hall and at lunch throw food across the table, we are children again, squash in the hair, bread in the lap. We get Willie the Orderly to find some Georgia Mountain Moonshine which we keep hidden in the lightbox of the *Wheelchair Review* newspaper. We mix that awful stuff tasting of copper and rubber with Cokes and get snockered and John Longstaff, trying to do wheelies in his chair falls over backwards and lies there giggling giggling singing about the glories of moonshine.

We sing in the church choir because it is something different to do, sweating over our hymns, Francine looking at the back of my head (bass up front) and she confesses to me it is the back of my head that she really falls in love with.

In the nights we play bridge or hearts or rummy in tall Georgia Hall, like a railroad station or a twenties movie theatre tall; and we gossip about who is loving whom, who is caught in a kiss, and our gossip extends to the power masters, the President of the Foundation and the head of all the physical therapy departments, who, it is rumored, are in bed with each other, despite both having mates in other places, other times. They are lovers, we gossip, maliciously, so proud of ourselves that we are coming back to life so that we can even gossip. Or the two women therapists, or the German teacher and the occupational therapist, or the or the or the . . . all the lovers for us to giggle about.

O we race down the path that angles down so we can spin in our wheelchairs, down to the big bump that goes into First East, past Surgery: free in our shining wheelchairs, on the angle hold sliding onto one wheel and you'll turn a corner (or turn over if you don't know what you are doing).

Up past Roosevelt Hall, to the squirting pool, built with C-sides so that the water squirts up, the waves well up, the squirt stops, and then starts again: subject to all of the usual ejaculatory comparisons. The languor and hot Georgia damp of the evening, as sky turns luxurious pink to passion blue, and we watch the multitudes of fat brown-grey squirrels having congress in the eaves of Georgia Hall.

Gossip and play. We are freed for the first time, really free of the nightmare that gripped us just months before. We are at home base now: playing games, busy with staff and patients, each day full to bursting with new tricks, new steps, new abilities. And we are not eighteen or twenty-two but fourteen again: for we are reborn. We have come born again out of the ashes of shared horror, and have come whole again. We have the deep camaraderie of brethren who have gone through the same roasting mill, and now we come out of our antiseptic environments into the world of the heavily scented trees and at night the five-cluster lights that immerse the entire campus with a heavy white creamy sauce of summer night, and the reflections of some distant friend wheeling silently a long way away over the distant dream of the campus.

I think there is no way that I can again have the happiness that came to me that summer, that swollen summer of joy in 1953. I can never ever be normal among the normals who make up the world, and, for the last time that summer, I am among my own people, the polios of 1952-53, joined together in the last summer of our youth, together in the heady air of North Georgia.

For being crippled in the environment of three hundred other upwardly mobile cripples has its own special distinctive rapture. We speak the same language. Our bodies know the same limitations. Our restricted world is restricted commonly among the three hundred of us, and especially the dozen or so who make up our age group.

We will within weeks be going back into worlds which may or may not remember us: but we can never forget that special union of the paradise island set up by master Roosevelt and his merry crew who invented joy on earth for those of us fortunate enough to get out of the claws of the doctors in the small grey hospitals around the country and into that wonder.

I can't forget, I can't foget: the nights at the movies in the house of laughless laughter. We polios uniformly have lost our abdominal muscles, so when we laugh (or cough, or sneeze) we do so in miniature, so you can barely hear it. Hugh's mother couldn't believe it, as she sat at the back of the movie house during a Fred MacMurray comedy, watching hundreds of shoulders shaking in silent mirth.

I can't forget: Francine and I called to task by the evening nurse for holding hands in the hallway of Second East. So that afterwards, if we wanted to show passion, we had to do it by ourselves, out of the sight of this frosted biddy with her pluperfect moral system.

I can't forget: being assigned to occupational therapy, to print class. They tell me to print up something of my own

83

devising on the 1912 print machine with the big wheel going 'round, and I set the type (Bodini 6, 10, and 18 point) to print up a thousand hand-sized cards, each imprinted in blue with the following message:

> The Person Handing You This Card
> Is An
> AIR - RAID WARDEN
> *Lie Flat On Your Back*
> *Do Exactly As You Are Told!*

Lorenzo W. Milam   Warm Springs
Director   Civil Defense

I can't forget: jerking off with my friend Dennis in his room over in Builder's Hall. And him telling me that the reason that his cock can't shoot worth a damn is because the day he got polio he went ahead and jerked off three times anyway, and it wore out, just wore out his shooting muscles.

I can't forget: the Hennesey Brandy smuggled in by my family, which we drink furtively in the middle of the campus out of paper cups with crushed ice; us, looking around for any intruder so we could quick dump the liquor out onto the grass, it being highly illegal and grounds for expulsion.

I can't forget: handsome blond Lief from Minnesota who comes to visit for recheck. He walks so well, with only one cane, hardly needs his wheelchair. He so handsome, his chest developed by his months on crutches. Just before he is to come to visit for the second time they tell us that he has put a gun in his mouth, aimed for his brain, missed, and blew his eyes out.

I can't forget: the triumphs, the triumphs. The first time I get down from my high hospital bed by myself, get down by myself into my own wheelchair, so that I don't have to have some orderly come in and help me down. I can do it by myself. The first time I stand by myself, with no one else around. The first time I walk to the dining room. For months I have come to the dining room in a wheelchair, and one day I am told to walk to the dining room, and I do. And when I get there I don't know what to do with my crutches after I sit down.

I can't forget: the pushboy who gets the girl patients in the elevator between First East and Second East, trying to kiss them. He's the same one who when he is changing my bathing suit for me after therapy says "Pretty big dick you got there boy."

I can't forget: friends and family coming from home to visit for my birthday, and me and Hugh and Francine so ill-at-ease with them. They will be looking at, I know they will be looking at my friends and thinking of them as Lorenzo's crippled friends. They won't know them or their minds—just their wheelchairs.

I can't forget: reading *The Warm Springs Story*, a dingbat book, supposedly the Official History of the Foundation. The author, full of the sentiment of the disease, full of bullshit about how brave, and noble we are: wringing every ounce of emotion out of the push-boys falling in love with (and marrying) women patients; the physical therapists falling in love with (and marrying) the men patients; the passages on Roosevelt complete gooey caramel. Not a word about constipation, about muscle adhesions, about the body driven out of its mind; about death of the soul. "O gorp!" we say, as we read every word of that tripe.

I can't forget: the three physical therapists who extract permission to take a dozen of us patients up into the scrub deep-red clay country of Meriwether County for a picnic. We are carried bodily to the campsite, laid on the ground on blankets. Our first beer in months! Next to me Merle whose polio has wasted his neck and shoulders so that he looks like a turkey-gobbler, drinks so much beer that he has to puke, and to do it, he digs a little hole in the dirt, right next to me. Gobble, gobble, he says, as he throws up, right next to me.

I can't forget: one night, the sun just failed in the west, Francine and I so aware of the night, and our place together; and she tells me that if she could do it all over again, if she could do it all over again, so that I wouldn't get polio: she would do it twice, take sick all over again, so I would not have to go through it. Thus she loved me, so.

85

I can't forget: one night, one of the dining room waiters, a Black, is shot mysteriously, just disappears. Several of the Foundation's grounds staff are implicated— but a police investigation absolves them completely, to remind us that we are in the deep, deep, South, the Blacks in terror for their lives, and there is no appeal, no appeal in our paradise cripple country.

I can't forget: the patient who is Total, one of the few admitted to Warm Spring who has no muscles, no muscles except ones to turn the head, open and shut the mouth, open and shut the eyes. That's it. He comes with a faithful friend, who feeds him, hold his cigarettes, wipes his ass, blows his nose, talks to him. A faithful and good friend. And one night the clerk at the front desk asks me (asks me!) if it is true that "they have a Queer thing going?" Making me realize that in this majestic place are stuck tiny-nut minds who cannot conceive, cannot conceive the luck of a frozen man to have a lover, male or female, dog or cat: anything for a bit of human love and warmth. The tiny gossip of tiny minds.

I can't forget: Maurine, of the long sad face. Her only involvement from polio is in her left gastrocnemius (heel) and her jaw. So that she walks with a slight drop-foot (but she walks!) and has to have all her food ground up for her into a paste, and I see her sitting there before me, at our table, that dreamy look in her eyes, as she chews on a mush of hamburger, ground carrot, ground lettuce. Sweet Maurine! John Longstaff did an excellent imitation of your drooling chops when you weren't looking.

I can't forget: the iron lung they keep on First East, for emergencies. And a delegation of patients goes to the head nurse and asks that a cover or sheet be draped over it, anything: so they wouldn't have to see it there every time they are wheeled by, see it and remember, those days or weeks, or months, in that terrible tin-can.

I can't forget: the orderly pulling off my bathing suit in the dressing room, after physical therapy, and he catches the band of the suit around my nuts, almost pulls them off, and I yell, and he leans toward me, black face, gold teeth gleaming, says: "Almost got your family jewels there boy, eh?"

I can't forget: the power plays among the staff, with the good Dr. Bennett playing the role of Stalin, so that overnight, old faces, faces from ten and twenty years at the Foundation would disappear, heads would roll, to make sure that the entire staff was loyal to one man. And we, the patients on whose behalf all this murder had taken place, would whisper and wonder, what was being wrought, for our good, by the new Brutal Order.

I can't forget, I can't forget, I can't forget: but I do. There are months of me laid in the clay country of North Georgia and memories blend and meld with the dreams and fantasy and sometimes I don't know what is real, what is unreal. The good and the bad, and now it is all gone. Why am I remembering it so burningly—those nine months of my life? That is the end of Paradise, and you can never go back, they will never let you go back to Paradise. It is taken from us: the circus we love at age ten turns out to be, a dozen years later, some seedy little tent with ragged, mange-coated animals who are half-starved, who live in stinky cages.

It's always like that, isn't it? I can put the perfect set on what I had back then; idealize it, bathe it in the warm soft glow of my own experience there. For others it might have been a nightmare; for those there now it may continue to be Paradise. I can't say, there is no way for me to say, there is no way for me to know again what is now so poignantly ripped from me, that sweet fading light of late summer that comes trailing through the high windows of Georgia Hall, bathing us for a moment in some magic gold shimmery wave of brightness. Then, as is so typical in those subtropical environments, the light is snuffed out and it is dark and the tall crannies of the Hall come to be haunted with ghosts out of some night long past, and the whole pleasurable interlude is gone forever.

A year to the day of my initial infection, they come to get me in the family car, to drive me two hundred miles from Warm Springs to home. Hugh and Francine come to see me off at the loading dock of Georgia Hall. I am uneasy at leaving my new security.

The last vision I have of the Foundation is through the back window of the car, where the two of them are consumed by the cloud of dust raised by my departure. I wave to my friends, and wave, and they are gone. I have known them for half of my new life, loved them, in ways I have never known or loved anyone else. And now they are gone, and I am going out into the world where I will be officially classed as a cripple.

I am no longer in the fever stage of the disease. I am through and past recuperation. I am to normalize myself. I am to live at home. Several years ago, I started out to be a man, moved out of my childhood home. Then I sickened and paled and withered. Now I am going back, a child again.

PART III

"What a glorious thing must be a victory, Sir."

"The greatest tragedy in the world, Madam, except a defeat."

— *The Duke of Wellington*

CHAPTER XIII

In Isolation, they ripped my body from me, without warning. There was no possible preparation, or forethought. I wake up after the searing jumble of fever as an eighteen-year-old boy in a seventy-five-year-old body.

In Hope Haven, they begin to teach me the price of that loss. I learn the role of being dependent, being dependent on those who could never love nor cherish me. Sometimes it is your enemy that you must ask to come and roll you over in the night. In this process, one must surrender, or lie all night, unmoved. The body which was young and pliant is now awkward and unlovely: it is a sack-of-wheat with five appendages (arms, legs, head) that flop about when the torso is being raised, lowered, turned, moved, pushed up or pulled down. The body cannot and will not function "normally," no matter the depth of one's will, courage, faith, hope, belief, and desire for improvement.

In Warm Springs, they start the process of giving me back to myself again. They teach me the new moves that are necessary with a new body. The act of standing and moving has to be thought out ahead of time, and the reward is that one can disguise the effort involved in the commonplace act of sitting down or walking across a lawn. I am learning to "pass," to prepare myself for all conditions of interaction with the world.

After leaving Warm Springs, I will have to learn the next steps on my own. I have no compadres about me to give me the benefit of their learning. I will, alone, have to build physical and emotional resources to deal with the real world.

I am in disguise. Despite what does exist, I must pretend
there is much more. This prevents the Helping Hands. And
there are Helping Hands, encumbering me every time I try
to move. They are out to prevent me from being my own
man. They want to move for me, across the table, across the
room, not knowing that their assistance is my destruction.
You fools. You fools! Don't you know I can do everything,
everything for myself.

Everything, everything. Except run (hear the slap of
my own feet on the pavement), climb a tree (feel of bark in
the palms of my hands), carry a box (know the power of my
back muscles), run laughing with my love into the waterfall
(the shock of the cold racing down the full expanse of our
bodies drawn together), jump into the icy creek (the freezing
water forces me to kick out), racing on a motorcycle down
the beach (wind tearing at my hair, my eyelids, billowing my
cheeks, the thrum of the hot, heavy machine between my
legs), go mountain climbing (sixteen miles from all humanity, and the sun sets against an icy peak, turning the whole
world blue-black in cold ecstasy), paddle a boat down the
Sewanee River (we and the kids out in the fresh, achingly
fresh wilderness, gathering wood for a night around the fire,
where we will cook our food and talk and sing, and then roll
out our sleeping bags under the thousand stars), crawl on the
roof of the house to repair it (the pleasant scare of heights,
and the comforting feel of hands and legs grasping the apex),
amble down to the sea's edge to the retreating tide (and the
cool wave's waters bubble around my toes, around my
ankles, the feel of sand under my feet, my feet sinking amia-
bly in the sand), walking through the fields to select a pine
tree for Christmas (I have chosen to go barefoot, in the fields,
and the brown pineneedles are slick under the soles of my
feet), sitting on the dock at midnight, in the moonlight (the
river shuffles along the pilings, and I can feel the misty waters
under my feet; I have taken off my shoes, wriggling my toes
in freedom, with the feel of the cool planks along the back of
my legs), roll on the living room floor with the kids, me up

on all fours, like a dog, barking (child bodies around my own, wrassling with my own), dancing in the early morning at the Florida Yacht Club with the girl I think I love (a slow dance, to "I Didn't Know What Time It Was," and the perfume body is next to my own, and I feel her hair across my cheek, and we are so close to each other I can see the pulse of life in her lower neck and count the freckles littering her back), in bed next to the one I love (wrapping legs around each other, legs about legs, straining against each other, the primitive love force in bed together, as we strain against each other with all the muscles at our command, our bodies so close, in ecstasy, that we are, in that muscled exchange with the force of all our love, for all practical purposes, one person).

A week or so after my return home, I am out on the front lawn of the house, the house I grew up in, in North Florida. I have taken off my shirt—drawn up my pants (but not too far up: the shame of the appearance of my upper legs, bone thin, is too great. No one is to see that part of me).

I have rolled myself out on the lawn in my wheelchair, and let myself down from it, down onto the ground. I am going to give my white body to the sun. It is noon. Perhaps I will be able to tan the bleached skin, back to what it was, back . . . before . . .

I hear something behind me. I turn around, and see my mother standing just inside the door, in the darkness of the living room. She is watching me. I am trapped on my blanket, and she is watching me. I can see the glint of tears in her eyes. She is weeping over me.

"Goddamn," I think. "Why can't she leave me alone. *Goddamn!*" I think. I am nothing to weep over. No man nor woman in the world has the right to hide behind me and weep over me. She's acting as if I were a corpse. It is as if I died a year ago. And here she is, looking through the fine mesh, at this corpse of a son. "I've got to get out of here," I think, slamming my fist on the foot pedal of the wheelchair. But where can I go? My friends are off at school. Their houses are no better than this one. I can't go back to the hospital. It's impossible for me to move into an apartment. I couldn't cook, wash dishes, get in and out, wash clothes, make my own bed. She has me trapped here, in this cage she calls a home. And she is standing there behind the door (does she think I can't hear her?) crying over me. And I can't even get up from the ground, tell her to stop, tell her to leave me alone, leave me alone on the lawn. I hate her.

Friends come by to see her one day. I meet them, me in my new disguise, disguised as a cripple. We talk of this and that for a while, and then I go back to my room, to be alone. I prefer to be alone. Alone I am away from their sanctimonious pity, the vile stink of their sympathy.

I can hear them as they are going out the back door, next to my room. "He is so brave," one of them tells my mother. And I can hear her, a crack in her voice, suppressing her tears. "Isn't he?" she says. "Good *Jesus*!" I think. Why doesn't she leave me alone? "She makes me want to puke," I think. "I've got to get out of this shithole."

I go back to visit the radio station where I worked the summer before, before I "got sick." I meet some of my old friends. One of them is doing a country show on the air. He announces that he's going to play Hank Williams "Elija," and he says ". . . and we are gonna dedicate it to our good friend Lorenzo here. He's back now from the hospital. He was hit by polio, but he's making a wonderful recovery, aren't you Lorenzo?" "O shit," I think. "Why do they have to do this to me?" I leave without saying goodbye. "What's wrong with these people?" I think.

I go to visit the parents of one of my friends. It takes me almost five minutes to back up the stairs (there's no railing; I am breathless with the effort, and the everpresent fear of falling). When I come into the living-room, I sit down awkwardly on the couch. "O God," I think. "It's so low to the floor. I'll never get out." My head begins to fill with obstructions. I hardly hear what they are saying. My physical self is obtruding on my mental self. I remember this same house, from . . . back then. I would run up the front stairs, arrive breathless at the living room door, then bound into the kitchen, up the stairs (taking them two at a time) and then into my friend's room. We would consult a moment or two, laugh and cackle, and then the two of us would thunder down the stairs, through the living room, slapping the wall as we piled out through the screen door, down the front stairs, across the lawn, into the car. Now it takes me five minutes (or is it an hour?) to get to the living room. They are hovering on the landing behind me. What are they thinking?

Should we talk about it? How should we handle Before and After. My whole world has been Hospital for the past twelve months. I have been out of their lives, out of their experiences. What is there to say, to do? How should we get into words how it feels, with those new legirons, that new body. Should we, or shouldn't we: simple relationships become complexly bound up in my physical presence in the room, as if I had been turned into some six-foot tarantula. How do you ignore your old friend Lorenzo who is now a huge worm, perched on the couch across from you, ill-at-ease: what to say, how to say it? How do you talk to a Tarantula?

Stacy comes in with her five-year-old, and the kid gets on the floor, looks at the place where the metal braces attach to the shoes. "What's this for," says the kid, all eyes, and wonder. "What happened to you?" What can they say, what can I say? They laugh nervously, or run over and pick up the kid, try to distract him, get him interested in *anything* else so he will stop embarrassing us all.

Then they start talking about golf, and I watch them, and I wonder, are they thinking "He used to play golf. We can remember when Lorenzo was a pretty good golfer. Shouldn't we shut the hell up about golf?" So I try to change the subject, talk about anything, something, but not swimming or sports, because of the memories.

And then I go to leave, and I try to get up from the low couch, and when I lean against the back of it, it begins to go out from under me. I get scared I am going to fall, so I have to sit down quickly (hoping they didn't notice) to start all over again. And there I am sitting on the couch, where I don't want to be, wanting to be somewhere else. *I can't be out of here just by wanting to be out of here. It isn't like before.*

They remember me climbing trees, and chasing around the back yard. They remember when I first started driving, and when I went out on the town with their son and raised hell with him, how we took care of each other, that night when I go so shit-faced drunk I could hardly walk, and he held me in his arms like a baby, until I could come to my senses, and then he led me back to the car, and drove me home. They remember all that. And now I can't even get up from their goddamn couch. The father asks me if I want some help and I get sort of pissed, and I say "no." I can feel the anger flaring up in me, but I brutally suppress it, and I say "no; I can do it" and I wonder if I can do it. The floor is so slippery, and the couch so low. I start pushing with all my might against the back of it, trying to swing my body around into the standing position so I can lock my brace, but as I get half-way up, the couch begins to slip out from under me and the father has to run across the room and grab it, and he says: "I have trouble getting off this damn couch all the time myself. I've got to do something about it," and I am panicking, as I can't get elevated the last inch to lock my brace, and if he tries to help me, he might unbalance me and we would both go over, together, so I twist my body a little bit and I am, at last, standing, panting, my arms aching with the strain of it.

They go down to the car with me, the father standing a little ahead of me on the stairs, his arms out in a half-circle, to catch me if I start to go. "I wish he wouldn't do that," I think. His face is drawn, filled with concern, and I think "I've got to get the hell out of here." I get to my car, and I can sense them wondering if I'll ever be the same again (I won't) or if I'll ever come back here again (I won't) and I think of my room, there at home, where I grew up, me alone in my room, with my new body, me and my new twin Broken Body, staying in the room with a big lock on the door, and anyone wants to see me they have to wait until I turn out the light and they can come in and see me by dim candle light, and if they don't like that, they can just shove a goddamn note under the door, so they won't have to see The New Me, so I won't have to see the fucking ugly putrescent lines of pity in their face, that pukey look of poor-kid in their fucking eyes.

CHAPTER XIV

There are people who are good around cripples, and there are people who are dumb. I learn to avoid the latter. Like the ones who refer to my crutches as "Pogo Sticks." Or the people who spurt ahead of me as we are reaching the door and say "Here, lemme help ya: looks like you gotta handful there!" Strangers with concern on their faces, always asking if they can help. "Can I help you"? "Can I help you son?" "Here, I'll get that for you." So many times I turn away, go back from where I came, leaving them holding the door. I won't let them do this to me.

In the park, I am sitting, away from my home, away from my memories, away from those rooms that shielded the growing me, that now mock the clanking me. Alone in the sunshine, away from the raised brows of compassion. "You had polio, didn't you?" says a lady, sitting down next to me. "Oh shit!" I think. How can I get away from here? "My brother did too," she says. "He got over it though. Recovered completely. He loves dancing." "O please leave me alone," I think, turning away.

"Why do I have to be held up in comparison to those people," I think. I am being compared to the holy and faithful and strong-of-will who were delivered by sheer guts from where I am now. I am being bulldozed with my own weakness and, by implication, my own inability to overcome this weakness.

"My son was like you," says the lady in the elevator, in the department store. She babbles on about his religious conversion in the tent, and how he's now carrying bricks for some construction company. "Let me out," I think. "I must get out of here." If I would just believe. By not sucking into her belief, I am willingly staying in the basket. "Jesus Christ!" I mutter, and as the doors open, I push ahead of her, pushing her and her gods aside with my bulk. Tell me about the Gods! They have failed me, lady. As my body has failed me, so have the Gods. You want me to worship the He who denies me access to the fields and mountains and seas and valleys? Tell me about the Gods who burn me up before age twenty, leave me a skeleton of my former self.

The religions that teach fear and trembling, the fundamental religions, can have no effect on me. I have my own religion of the fundament, and it grows out of the shit that stopped up inside of me, when they burned me up in Isolation. Tell me about the fires, the eternal fires—I have seen them already. I was there, I tell you! The gods came to me and unleashed several million of their servants into my bloodstream, in my duodenum, in my gangalia, released them to invade the cloudy hypnotic mass that rests in the den of the skull.

Damnation! I have been there. I have peered into the pits and smelled the charring flesh of eternity. Eternity gets reënacted for me each day that I place leather against skin, metal bone against back, cloth stays and straps over abdomen, moleskin against hand, metal strut against the undersides of the arm. Tell me about eternity, and timelessness. It rides with me at this moment, the steel-and-leather of this eternity we call life.

I see your Gods, woman. I see what they are: demented madmen who unleash the horrors of death on the living, and then expect honor and humility. Jesus Christ! What have you created? What do you want?

I move as quickly as possible to escape these people who

are trying to enmesh me in their sentimentality, stick me with their vile and hopeless cripple-thoughts. As they approach me, I can see from their eyes that they come to use my crutches as a flag, for them to put all their twisted cripple-stories on me. They don't know that I enter the world despite them; I have to grow especial sharp porcupine prickles to protect me from the likes of them.

I am going down the stairs, slowly, careful not to sway, not to fall. Coming up is a wen-faced witch from across the way. "Well," she says loudly, too loudly, "you look like you're doing all right. You look like you are gonna make it." "I've been making it all this time, you stupid cunt," I think. "I've been making it all this time," I mumble.

At the grocery store, I am agonizing over the melons, pinching the avocadoes, eyeing the vegetable boys. Three children are being pushed about in a metal chariot by their mother. She is in pink hair-curlers. "What happened to you?" This is the oldest child speaking, finger deep in mouth. Tears burn in my eyes. I try to turn away. "Won't they ever let me alone?" I think. Louder: "Mother, what happened to him? Why can't he walk?" "O fuck, leave me alone," I think, trying to go away, trying to go anywhere, but where they are. "Shush," says the mother timidly, sideëyeing me. "Don't let me forget the milk," she says, lying, to protect me against the monsters that she has borne into the world to shame and humiliate me.

"How you doin'?" I say to the mole-eyed clerk at the My-T-Fine Liquors. "I'm doin' all right, but you don't look like you're doin' all right," he says, nattering. "And your ass is another, you dumb fuck," I think. "Have you got any rot-gut whiskey," I say. He turns to the Four Roses, and I turn and go out the store. "Hey," he says, "don't you want your liquor?" "I should burn this place down," I think.

"Here, let me get that door for you," says the beagle-faced boozer at the It'll Do Tavern. "What happened to you?" he says, blocking my way and smirking up at me. "Have a ski accident?" "Ski your hole, pecker," I think, pleasantly. "Nothing, nothing," I say, brusquely, inadvertently banging crutch-tip against his hairless shin. "Nothing at all," I

CHAPTER IX

There is something quite interesting, exciting, and important that you and I have to get out of the way. Right now. It has to do with all those embarrassing questions we, or rather you, have about cripples and sex. I know, I know the question: namely, how does one make love in a basket?

Those old and tired queries about the union of the Iron Lung Lady with the Rocking Bed Man. How does it work? Who's there to help? Nurses? Orderlies? Do they close their eyes? What does go on, anyway, when paraplegics and triple amputees decide to make it. How does the thalidomide baby conjoin with the four-foot dwarf (or normal, five-foot-ten you, for that matter)? How does one with no more gluteal muscles than a wren do what is necessary to get from here to there, and back and forth? Who does what to whom, and how, and why (and who cleans it all up)? I've heard them all.

Being a basket-case myself, I probably have more answers than you would want to hear. And given the fact that—as I write this—I am poised on the abyss of male menopause, I would have no hesitation, whatsoever, in laying out the answers for you, on the page. The River of Passion which has driven me looney Lo! these many decades is finally, and at last, and not a moment too soon, about to be damned with the bricks of my days. Thank the Lord.

To make it easier on both of us—I am not about to embarrass you, nor me: at this point. Let me just say, by way of introduction, that most cripples, at least most cripples that I know, have a special, and unusual, relationship with that old bag of grapes down there. It has to do with the twisting of our bodies, and the twisting of our psyches, and the say, turning away from all these futile stupid soul-ripping questions.

"Looks like you do all right on them sticks, boy," says the white-haired old pervert in front of the stationery store. I smile at him: tight smile, friendly. "Is there any reason some worm-head like you should be out here trying to noodle up the souls of poor cripples?" I think. "What's wrong with me?" I wonder. So much bitterness, so much hate. "I am killing myself with hate," I think. These dodos aren't worth it. "What am I doing to myself?" I wonder. Plenty, I know. I'm doing plenty to myself. "I should stay at home," I think. Stay at home, in my cave, away from these mental cripples, with their projected nightmares, trying to trip me up. I should stay in my dark, warm cave, peering out at the world with luminous eyes, never venturing forth, never allowing anyone into the warmth and darkness. All those who do try to sneak in: why, I'll razor them with my words. All who reach out to me will pull back nubs for fingers, stumps for hands.

"What happened to you?" What happened to you. The same old question. Can't they come up with anything original. What happened? O, nothing. They killed the prettiest part of me, that's what happened. One time, long ago, on an island by the sea, the dragon got hold of me and burned out my body, left me a hulk, burned up the fine tender strains of me, burned out all the chords, turned me to ash.

What happened? O nothing. I just got skewered, cauterized, roasted, burnt out, mangled, queered, crippled. On an island by the sea, by the blue sea, they came and brought in the devil firepurge, ran the whole gas hose into me, into the deepest part of me, turned it on so that the yellow-red flames belched out of my nose, my ears, my eyes, my asshole. They came and stuck this hose all the way down into me, and turned on the juice, burned me out. Boy, did they ever!

What happened? Not much, not much at all. They just came in with their pickaxes and shovels, brought in all the meat-cleavers, chopped me open, went to work with the buzz-saws and hatchets to dig into the muscles, yank out twenty-five hundred feet of tender nerves, burned down the walls, wrecked the playroom, filled the living rooms, the halls, the bedrooms with scalding water and ashes.

And it didn't hurt. No, not at all. They just gutted the fucking place, so that there is no place left to rest, no place where one can lay a tired head, what with all the ashes and torn books scattered about, the sofas ripped up, the paintings torn down and trampled on, the tables up-ended, the legs ripped off, the flooring mangled, the ceiling axed and splintered, the whole jesus-bitten place so torn that no one, no one at all, would ever want to live here, ever, ever again.

"Well, my goodness," says the plump grandmaw at the check-out stand, she of the rimless glasses and the pleasant mouth, the skin so white you'd think it was sewed-on magnolia petals. Her breath reeks of denture cream. "What happened to you?" She says brightly: "Looks like you're having a little trouble getting around."

"If I got one of them regulation U.S. Army flame throwers, you know, the ones with the five-inch wide nozzles, and I stuck it a foot or so up your ass, and then turned the sucker on, do you think you might jump some?" I think. "Then you'd have some trouble getting around too," I think.

"Nothing," I say: "Nothing at all. Just a little accident, you know," I say.

"I know, I know," she says, smiling. But she doesn't. Doesn't have the faintest foggiest fucking idea in the whole world. She doesn't know shit about me. Especially with that flame-thrower lodged in her butt.

My brother is to be married in the fall of 1953. The wedding is to be in New Hampshire. I am to be the best man.

We fly north to New York, then Albany. We drive from Albany to Littleton. This is my first trip since they carted me from Warm Springs, my home.

The ceremony is to take place in a small Catholic Church. My brother and I step slowly out of the side door, and walk (he softly, me squeeking) past the two hundred faces. There should be a round of applause: I have now come to the point where I can perform in front of small, select audiences. And I do it rather well. It takes me a bit of a time, but I make it to the center of the action. At the appropriate time I step back with nary a fall.

The reception has been set up on the wide lawn outside the palatial mansion of the bride's family. There is a tent, a huge tent. Tables, dozens of tables are groaning with every sort of food, punch, champagne. Hundreds of people are there. I am dressed in my rented tuxedo, held together with pins. Someone has draped one of my crutches with a bouquet of tiny pink roses.

The brother of the bride is describing to rapt family members a recent ski trip to the White Mountains. I step closer to hear what they are saying. At the same time, he steps backwards to make way for a sandwich tray. He runs into me and I topple over like some doll, falling backwards onto the lawn, falling and twisting, my crutches banging down around me.

There is a silence, isn't there? I think there is a great deal of silence. The imported string orchestra—which was playing "I am always true to you darling (in my fashion)"—seems to have faded away. I think I can hear a mockingbird singing somewhere. A hundred mouths open in a hundred gasps, don't they? I have fallen on some sort of a mound, perhaps a New England Indian Burial Mound. My hips are jutting into the sky.

"Why don't I just lie here, on the ground here," I think, "and let the goddamn reception go on around me." I don't care for any of these people anyway. Let them get on with their business of laughing and drinking and chatting and talking about their skiing trips. I have other things to think about. I will just lie here, for the rest of the afternoon, and into the evening, me and my grass-stained tuxedo.

Finally, when the last person has left, I will get some of the kitchen help to lift me up and carry me over to the Mount Washington cog railroad. Together we'll go up to the top, and I will have them carry me out of the train, over to the edge of the mountain where they can just push me off the face of it off into space, off into the rocks and gravel and granitic schist, where I belong.

The people around me get me up and brush the grass and leaves off of me and hand me some champagne. My eyes are burning and my hands tremble such that the drink slops out of the glass. "I am sorry that I came here and fucked up this nice party," I think. I am sorry I made everyone so sad at seeing me topple over onto the lawn. I am sorry that I took all the trouble to come all this distance so that I could fall down and screw up everyone's head. I am sorry that I am here, I am sorry that I am alive, I am as sorry as I can be that I grew up, that I lived my life, that I came to this sorry state, through no fault of my own.

I am sorry that I thought, for a single moment, that I could leave the isolation and darkness of my bedroom, with its comfortable wheelchair and its long dark desk, and come all these uncomfortable miles so that I could go into my spectacular collapsing act which was viewed by hundreds, perhaps thousands of guests. I am sorry to have left my room and my desk, before which I could sit and stare at my hands, at my long, pale, white hands, where I could sit in the safety and security of that dark room and stare at my hands.

In conclusion, I am sorry for what I have done to this happy occasion, and most of all, I am sorry for what I have done to myself, this wretched, pulsating, suppurating wound which is me, this box of anguish and hurt that has come to burst, on this day, this fresh and crisp day in November, when the fall of the year is so golden about of us, full of the freshness of the golden decline of the year — this box which is now so painfully cut and twisted open beyond all doubt and reason.

CHAPTER XV

The next six years, I was to pursue education diligently in order that I might be set apart from the foot-dragger with stained pants and rag-top wooden crutches who pulls himself into the Salvation Army camps of the world. It was the purpose of education to set me apart forever from the amputee hunched bent-over in the sun of the downtown street, selling newspapers by showing his body, his face with those furrowed brows, those trembling lips, those hurt-forever eyes, those animal wolf trapped eyes.

I have to go it alone out of the basket world. I have to protect myself from the cripples all around me, who are my mirror image and who, at all times, are falling, puking, muling, slipping, spinning, wheedling, pulling, hanging on, all about me, trying to pull me down with them.

My brothers! I stand apart from you: you, and your wasted limbs, your blighted breath, your palsy and your lordosis. I could care less about your sob stories. I have no interest in your own personal torture. You may be born without a nose, leg amputated at ten, back smashed at twelve, body wasted at twenty-three, foot gangrened at forty-two, brain imploded on its own juices at sixty-nine. I don't care about you, you and your torn crabbed limbs.

You are foul, and evil-smelling. Your guts show the dregs of coarse ground meatburgers prepared by all the cripple institutions of the world. Your eyes drool with amber-brains softened by years of treatment in hospitals, charity homes, rest-care operations, rehabilitation centers. Your buttocks are pimpled and corrugated by imperfect bowel movements, on imperfect bedpans, in wretchedly kept wards.

Your minds have been crenelated to paste by the therapy, pills, and nostrums dreamed up by the professional "helpers." Your shoulders are bent under the weight of a dozen nursing home capitalists who get $50 a day to keep you, to feed you and house you and clothe you on pennies. Your eyes are filled with the pity of begging help from doctors and nurses and orderlies and janitors and nurses aides and volunteers. And none of them can really help you: you are hopeless cripples, hopeless—and I want nothing to do with your hopelessness.

We have invented a system to keep you in slavery; a system to keep you bound to your enema bags, chained to your catheters, tied to your walking sticks, locked in your wheelchairs, buried in your aspirators and rocking beds and iron lungs and infusers and clyster solutions and irrigators. This country has devised a system to keep you in the back rooms and closets, off the television screens, out of the newspapers, under the sheets, out-of-sight-out-of-mind: you with your spasms and tics and twitches and sputum-spilling, saliva-dropping ways have to be kept out of the eyes of the great clean American public. For it is on health and beauty and nobility, the clear eye and the pink cheek, that we have built a whole country of such wonder and grace.

You and your bent limbs, your hopelessly twisted frames. It is right and it is proper that we hide the exposed ills that the body can sport: the protrusions, the brown, evil-smelling indiscretions, the moist, slick overflows of the membranes. We could drown in the juices that the eager body produces to survive. Your must be kept beyond the pale so that those who live healthy in this country will not be dragged down by the vulgar knowledge of their own mortality, the very fragility of the body, the ease with which it can slip into pus and pustules.

Me? I am a subscriber to this system. Me: I am only interested in the young and the beautiful and the perfect. Give me only supernal limbs, angular curves of muscle on packed, flat, rippling stomachs.

Me? Give me the twin dimples of healthy lower backs, the sprinkling of blond hair on tan torso and arm, the moving mountains of deltoid on upper shoulder.

Me: I am only interested in consorting with the young, with their sleepy eyes, their arrogant smirks. Give me the child of the shore, whose every limb is baked to dark perfection. And that ease of movement: give me the movement that belongs to the innocent, the children totally innocent of the abyss that awaits within.

I escape from the snake-thoughts of Cripple by being in love. Daily in love. On the beaches, in the pinball parlors, the movies; at the dirt races, in the parks, at the zoo; in the audience at the roller palaces, at the high-school wrestling matches. I follow my children down the long trail of eye-seduction, the snail's own trail of seduction.

My whole self comes to be optic. My flesh turns to sclerotic tissue. My soul melts into aqueous humor. My brain comes to be vitreous. I see with my fingers, my toes, my skin. Every pore blossoms into cornea; thoughts become iris. I am transformed into the one great Coptic Eye, watching all the children of the earth from high dark castle walls.

I am the single great orb of vision perched at the highest turret. My reason drains as lachrymalia. My children: I see you, run fingers of vision over your every muscle, every part of your selves that burns my sight.

Lightning ripple of abdomen, strain of tibia, the thread of latissimus comes seen before me as the sculpture of the brown sun. See: look: see as the child reaches for me (me hovering there the round vision), inches before taut fingers: I am in love. They move before me on the sands of time and I am in love. The desperately beautiful harmony of motion, the harmony of the human body, perfect, walking perfectly, each step so perfectly stilled by the lumbar and dorsal vertebrae, stones between waves of latissimus and trapezius, lapping against the bone rocks, sweet tide of spinous motion, tides of muscle coming to shore with complex rhythms of its own as foot paces earth, as leg strides continents of the being. Lumbar, sacral, cervical, dorsal facets: obtruding rocks in the oceans of muscle.

I have no time, no time for my brothers. I am in love. I am the Cripple Secret Casanova. I gorge on the shadow moun-

tain of muscles, riding sub-continents beneath the earth's
skin. I am caught: fingers reach out to capture the floating
eye, and I am caught with the Greek Passion again. White
orbs, baked by suns. We, caught forever on the amber fingers of time.

I am the bird. I am the leathern bird of the shores. I flap
heavily from continent to continent. The Cripple Casanova,
pumping hell-for-leather with metal winds, creaking, slow; I
leave behind the dark sulphur pits, erupting under flights of
passion. The Atlantis of Desire rises within me, a Volcano of
Cascading Senses. There is no holding it back. See it now as
it protrudes from the green-black oceans.

Squamous part of self! The throbbing peninsula stuck out
into the ocean of bodies. A stratosphere of self-induced pleasure; the globus comes together, comes together into a sun-
licked point of pleasure, the magnifying glass comes down to
a single smoking point riding over the ant of being and, of
a sudden, the mandibles freeze, the hair-thin antennae wave
no more, and the creature comes to bend back onto itself,
carapace smoking back on itself, biting into the insect pain
that comes smoking out of nowhere; then, a final popping, a
pulsing stem come from so far away through space magnified onto itself, a single shaft of hot pleasure running down
the bricks to crack whole shells of being, crisp red shells of
plenty smoking out into the halls of time. And from the tiny
beak of this creature, there is a cry of this-is-the-end, this-is-
too-much, life-is-too-much, we are finished, done-for, dying, eased, eased out of ourselves; we are eased, the lava of
imagination burning out of being; muscles freeze against the
dark sky of infinity, a billow of clouds glances off the universe above, arrows come down to pierce the roiled waters,
black nothing comes turning, turning a planet black shadow
turns black on the inside of itself, and we, the shades, are
back on ourselves again.

My friend Hugh Gallagher from Warm Springs, now in
Washington, is thinking of returning to school at Haverford

College, in Pennsylvania. I drive up there in the spring. I will apply for admission with him. We will be roommates.

On the way up, I stop off in Griner, North Carolina. Another Warm Springs friend, Harry Charles, lives there. His father runs a looming mill in Griner.

Harry is so wasted by polio that he is incontinent—which is rare in this particular disease. He cannot control bowel and bladder. He wets the seat of his wheelchair, his car. One time, the orderlies at Warm Springs were giving him a bath, and he craps in the tub. "This turd just floated right up," says Harry, laughing.

I shudder. He thinks the whole thing is funny. He has a country humor.

When I arrive in Griner, I find their house. His mother comes to the door. I knew her in Warm Springs, but she has never seen me on my feet. Harry left before I started sitting up or walking.

She smiles at me. She hugs me. She cries. Tears run down her great horse face. I can hear her teeth clacking. She is crying, because I am walking. Her own son will never walk again. He will never stop pissing in his pants, he will never be able to get himself in or out of his wheelchair.

She has seen me laid out flat, much like Harry, and she assumes that I will never be walking again. So when she sees me for the first time in a year, she sees a miracle. She has known me as a cripple, a cripple in bed, and now I am moving about, moving myself about, moving across the room, sitting myself down.

"Lorenzo," she says: "Lorenzo, I declare. I declare!" She is proud of me. She has no pity, no ignorance of what I have come from. She is proud, she can't stop crying at the miracle-me on my feet.

She is one of my people, one of my new people, one of the post-inferno people. She isn't one of those who will remember me running the stairs at age seventeen. She won't ever look at me with the I-remember look.

No: she knows me from the bottom, when I was flat on my ass and she looks at me now, standing, me standing ("O Lord! Lorenzo! How tall you are!") She has no tainted memory of me. I am the miracle that escaped her twenty-year-old son.

I pick up Gallagher in Washington, D.C. We drive north on Highway One to Philadelphia, then on to Haverford. He tells me about some of his new adventures, things that have happened to him in the six months since he left Warm Springs.

"I was in the Piggly-Wiggly, with my mother," he tells me. Supermarkets are one of the places where there are few barriers to the wheelchair: the aisles are wide, there are no curbs or other impediments. It gets Hugh out of the house and out of his Brood to go shopping.

"It was over near the pickles," says Hugh. "A kid started following me around. Maybe about four, or five. And he kept shouting, 'Mommie. Mommie—look at the poor broken man.' He said again and again: 'Mommie—look at the poor broken man.'

"Why don't I just stick my head inside a toilet bowl and drown myself?" he says. "Why should I keep this game going. Really!" He pauses. The exquisite Pennsylvania countryside, so rich and green with the new buds of spring, races past our car. There is the sweet head-strong smell of cherry blossom, pine nuts, maple coming to life, burgeoning, so tender-sweet yellow green with the new life of the new year. "Why do we even bother?" he says. "It would be so simple and so easy to be done with it. Sleeping pills, the oven, freezing to death in a car out in the country on a winter night."

Dear Gallagher! You know, don't you? We know. We keep on living when, by every conceivable benchmark, life is such a mess that we should be done with it. But we don't. With our innocent blind stupid hope we keep on. Telling these stories. Wondering at our own animal nerve that keeps us going. Keeping on keeping on—despite the fact that we know that never ever in medicine will there be a cure for us.

We get to Haverford in the early afternoon for our interview with the Dean of Men. We are both accepted. There is some discussion of where we shall live. Some students will have to be bumped so that we can stay in a first floor room.

After our interview, Gallagher has to take a pee. Because of his wheelchair, there is much consulting to find where he can get to a toilet without going up or down stairs. The single simple act of finding bathrooms for cripples takes enormous thought and energy. Most people go up and down stairs and curbs and don't think of them as what they are: impenetrable dangerous walls, making chairs on wheels useless.

In a handsome Victorian campus like Haverford, with great granite buildings, stairs are everywhere. Every door, every room is a trap, trapping those in wheelchairs and on crutches to special limited areas.

After much discussion, we find the one toilet which can be reached with no stairs. It is in the gymnasium. I drive around to the back door. Gallagher unfolds his wheelchair from the back seat, takes off the left side arm, pulls himself into the chair, and we go (him rolling me pegging) into the gym bathroom.

There, standing at the urinal, standing alone against the light institution walls, pink skin against the green wash, is the god of the Greeks. A symbol, my lord, it must be a symbol.

A naked student, taking a leak. Fresh and pink from the showers. An end on the football team, perhaps. Pissing: unaware of our entrance.

It has been such a long time since Gallagher and I have seen a naked, normal, regular, human body. Nakedness in the hospital is so different: someone being bathed in bed. A body being prepped for an operation. One being flipped over so a bedpan can be slipped beneath wasted buttocks: a flash of rail-thin legs and protruding backbone. We are accustomed to the sight of the black flower of pubis lying sickly against the wasted belly, a body distorted by some death-tramp disease.

For two years, neither of us have had occasion to go to a *situs* where men habitually, casually, pleasantly walk around in front of others with their clothes off. We have no excuse to visit a gymnasium, to be confronted by the gods of nakedness and youth.

Both of us are assaulted by our vision. Gallagher, a laconic sort, says, later: "If I had those glutes. If I had just 1/100th of those glutes!" (Glutes: gluteus maximus and minimus. The ass muscle. The beautiful proud protruding muscle which is the buttocks which makes it possible for *Hominoidea* to walk and stand. The flower of the behind. The mountain of the god's delight. The twin clefts of pure man-strength).

Me: I am staggered by the sheer, sweet, pink, delightful, wondrous beauty of normal healthy man. My vision has been sharpened by many months in the wasting wards. And, with this vision (he was before us no more than ninety seconds; he jiggled his peter, our anonymous god, and to the accompaniment of a flush and a banging door, was gone.) I am struck by the delight of a male frame with *nothing* holding it up. Not a chair, not a crutch, not a cane, not a walker: just those wonderful bones hidden under pink-white muscle-ribbed flesh, everything working in apple-pie order.

If I had any sense (if I had any sense!) I would have seen our quickly-there quickly-gone Achilles as a symbol. A message of the future. A symbol, an image, right out of *Ulysses.* The flag from ahead: the towering event, that would haunt me, partially destroy me two years hence, and set up a chain of desires and events that would twist my whole world around, changing me as profoundly and as wantonly as I had been spun by the kiss o' fever of September 1952.

CHAPTER XVI

Well, Gallagher couldn't take the stairs of Haverford. He went off to California. In his place, they gave me Spicer. Spicer, my college roomie. The Unicorn God's Eye of Chance. Who put that goon in my room? He, fighting against going to war years before it was fashionable to do so. Looks just like a soldier-boy, too. Crew-cut hair, neither brown nor blond, just dirty-looking. Skin all rutted with an unnamed pox, a mine field.

Spicer: crimped teeth, crooked smile. Voice like one barely out of the toils of pubescence. Always trying to push my wheelchair, with me in it, down the stairs. Just a joke of course, freezing my heart at the top of the stairs.

My source of locomotion, the old Everest and Jennings, is Spicer's toy. Balance on two wheels, go in circles on two wheels, turning around in circles, on two wheels, turning my heart in circles, on two wheels, that Spicer, turning my head around, just like that, so easily, me with my topsy love, off balance. O you Spicer. . .

. . .You, Spicer! Here I am a quarter century and several dozen lovers later, and I am still able to recall that I haven't seen my Spicer since approximately 8:37 a.m., 5 June 1957, that being roughly twenty-five years, eleven months, sixteen days, four hours, thirty-two minutes, fifty-eight seconds ago. Spicer: you! When I think of you, when I think of the way you walk, walk all cockeyed, with your adolescent cackle; or you, sleepy, just getting out of bed, (yours! not mine!) angling down the hall, towel on shoulder, toothbrush in hand, lucky toothbrush, to caress the inner warm part of your mouth for three minutes, so vigorously, twice daily; and I see, I see from my hiding place, here somewhere towards the end of the 20th Century, from my closet, where I peek-a-boo old lovers, as they walk down the long halls of our days, slippered feet slapping on too-smooth shiny tile, and I see the backbone, all twelve ridges of that proud dorsal mountain extrusion, nestled so deliciously, albeit delicately, between dual peaks of longissimus, the proud back of the proud beast, copious muscles ridging and stranding as you walk so sweetly down the hall, your very feet tramping the roses, you whistling some absurd tune from some absurd Broadway play, and the backbone, my hope! my home! comes sparkling ridges down past the twin clefts, O me, twin delicious, golden delicious peach-blossom time, and the birds sing to me, there in my secret cage at the end of the hall, as I see (my eyes eat you with honey and cream, you peach you) the nestling secret blossom jewel, right there, just above the ratty Broadway Hotel towel, right there above the secret part of you (never to be seen by me—my imagination turns sun-spot to blind my vision, and all mankind) I spy the Y where the orbs behind come so rangily together, and I tell you, I am mad and on fire, I am Gorgon and Mad Jack Ripper, I am the child of the sun-gods who burns with the most spectacular fires, you Spicer! You in your gentle march down the Plains of Thermopylae, as you the proud soldier, so arrogantly moving god-like, the black cut-out of you turning into that bright steaming room of my all-out knock-down passion-fire lights, you past the door where you are to wet down the most precious parts of you, when I see you enveloped in that stream, your god's body . . .

. . . ah me. I turn lava inside. The great fire-globs rise up in me, bubbling insanely inside of me, honey-fire out of the flowering, that secret glen inside of me, the secret, tree-laden, flower-blasting, stream-burbling, bird-screaming, sun-shadowing most secret part of me, the part of me that Spicer opened up to me, opening up a secret to me, a secret part I had never seen before, before, before, that I had bever been to before, inside of me, that secret even to me, that secret hollow, nesting a C inside of me. And Spicer, old Spicer took me there, not even knowing we were going there together, the treasure hunt inside of me, Spicer tapping the load, Spicer, the tapper, tapping the treasure of me within me, and the diamonds turn white-hot, and the earthquake rumbles them out of the ground, the dark earth there in upheaval, and rocks, diamonds, rainbows, come cascading willy-nilly out of the earth.

Lorenzo the Magnificent Basket-Case Iceberg manages to hide this passion for months. Do you think I am going to blab out this madness to anyone? I have to be careful. I walk a dangerous road. We must Maintain Control. The Emotional Glacier. This strange bubbling around the edges of my being: I can hide it, can't I?

Keep it under your hat. Keep the mutiny below, where it belongs. Shut the hatches. Smother the rebellion. Keep it all under control. Control the body. Control the mind. Control the wonder welling from within. Keep it tight. They put you in jail (or the looney-bin) for stuff like that.

Control, absolute control. Until the mountain turns to ice-cream fudge. Until it collapses smoking into the burning sea.

It is the morning that we are to leave for summer vacation. All the pictures have been removed from the dormitory room wall. I am sitting in my wheelchair, a spider, in the center between the two rooms (Spicer to the West, Lorenzo to the East). I am on fire. There has been a welling up. The patient might well expire in an explosion of clouds and burning. There is a bottle of Scotch with me, down by my side, there in the basket-chair with me. The bottle of B & L Scotch. Blither and Languishing. The Scotch will put out the conflagration, won't it? Won't it?

I have to tell Spicer something. So far there has been no hint, nothing, not a word. About the lava that burns holes in my being. I have to tell him something, don't I? It's been six months that the earth has been in travail. He is to arise, get up at three a.m., to drive home, and I have a message for him. A message from Garcia. From the little band of irregulars camped inside the volcano. They are coming out of the spout with a white flag in hand. To surrender. *But they don't know what they are surrendering!*

And while I am sitting there, me, in my cripple-chair, with the fire extinguisher next to me, half-consumed, I have this fancy. From next summer. When I am home, when he is home, when we are home. About the telephone call. That comes, the blinding flash of can-you-believe, and my-god!

The call from Warm Springs. From my beloved Greta Green. She wants to be the first to tell me. That they have come up with a cure. They have just developed this cure for polio, for the old polio patients. I can come up anytime during the summer. They'll give me the shots. Free.

O it'll take a while. A few weeks. It will take some time to reëducate the muscles. They'll have to be brought back to strength again. It'll take a few weeks. But it can be done. She'll work with me (joyous work!) to get the muscles back up to snuff. To where I'll be walking again. By myself again. Without crutches, equipment. Throw away the equipment! Walking, on my own two feet again! She wants to be the first to tell me.

I don't tell anyone. A surprise! "Who was that on the telephone," they ask. "O no one," I say. A man about a dog. I am going to be cured, I tell myself, secret, bursting with glee. These crutches, this brace, that back support, the wheelchair. They are all temporary now. Temporary. In a few weeks — they'll be gone. Just like a broken leg. All healed up. All well. Lorenzo: cured.

Don't tell anyone. Going away for a few weeks, I tell them. Slip up to Warm Springs. The doctor is smiling, Greta Green and I are laughing, at the first few spasms, and then the coursing, of muscles, mountain streams coming down from above, as the muscles twitch, then move, begin to flex. Look! My leg! It's moving again! My leg is moving again! Look! My first steps in four years! I can move again! I can move by myself again!

Spicer lives up in the Blue Ridge Mountains, with his family, near Brevard, North Carolina. I drive up there, drive straight through from Warm Springs. Find the cabin, where they are staying, there on the mountainside, overlooking the whole green smoke-smelling valley. I get out of the car. It is evening. Spicer is there, by himself, beside the campfire, I can see his shadow on the cabin-side. I get out using my crutches. A joke.

He sees me. "Lorenzo, how did you? . . ." Two slow steps towards him. And then. The miracle. The silver wings fall to the ground. The bones rattling to the ground, and I am dancing before him. The two-step. The old soft shoe. Lorenzo is doing the Old Soft Shoe. On his pins again! Shake a leg!

He has tears in his eyes. We are dancing. With joy. He is so happy for me. We are so happy for me. We dancing in each other's arms. He is crying, because I am cured. We are in each other's arms. We are lying in each other's arms. There is laughter, then joy, then silence, we in each other's arms. We are whole. His eyes are shining. He nestles my head on his man's chest. He cradles my head against him. This richness. The cure. The sickness is cured. There are no more secrets. He knows. I know. The potent flower of our new love. Man and man. He knows.

I am sitting in the room between our two rooms. I am in my cripplechair. I have to say something to Spicer, this man with whom I have been living for six months, six months in silence.

He gets up. I can hear the alarm. I can hear him moving around his room. The door opens, he in his jockey shorts, eyes barely open, he in his jockey shorts (lucky shorts!) The man of him, straining out of sleep, and I am afire. The spider in the middle of the web, on fire. This broken spider, the legs broken off, in his broken chair on fire. The spider has something to say, something to tell, a story to tell. Of love, on a mountain side, a summer cabin, two men in love, doing the dance of life, together.

He veers past me and gone. Hello and he is gone. I crush the words, the vision, the fancy, and he is gone. The silent spider remains in his spider's chair, crushing the volcano. The desire has been cocooned, wrapped in webbing, so that it cannot escape. A once live wriggling creature has been stilled.

I hear Spicer down the hall. The rush of the shower. I hear him whistling, off key, "You Are My Sunshine." The water is boiling past my love, the chest, the stomach, into the black-fire hair, past the thighs, the knees, the ankles, the feet, into the ground, the dark ground, the dark ground below.

Lorenzo, The Basket-Case Casanova. Sitting alone in the chair of wheels. Unable to reach that man who just went by, taking the sun a soul with him. If I were whole again. *If I were whole again.* I on all fours, supping on his limbs. The long distance runner, lapping on the feast of the ages. The birds outside, the mountain winds ruffle our hair, his eyes glint with desire. We together, at the peak of the mountain, rising up suns desire.

I am alone in the chair on wheels. He is naked somewhere else in the water. There is no way I can reach him, no way at all. He is somewhere else, in the water, away from me. He is whole. Me: I am only part of a man. Alone in the basket-chair, with broken spider-legs. Alone; alone. I should be dead.

CHAPTER XVII

There are times, if you will believe me, when I was to have, shall we say, a "normal" love affair. I tried. I tell you doctor, I really tried. I spent more time trying to get my peter on right, my head screwed around to look up skirts and not down pants. I tried, I tell you. And Zooey was there to help me try, weren't you, my love. Zooey! A beautiful woman for a beautiful (but tortured) male student.

Zooey! You were something out of a book, weren't you? Out of, say, Henry James. That's it: you came straight out of Henry James.

Zooey! You know why you loved me? I do. It's because I never tried to do the old jack-in-the-box with you. Those men from Villanova would take you out, attracted by your patrician ways and your horseback rider thighs, and by the second or third date they would begin to try to stick it to you. The Eternal Curse of One-Eyed Peter. Blind to all other attributes.

But me! Do you realize Zooey that we went out together seventeen times and all I did to you was to read to you from Camus, Kit Marlowe, and "Tithonus." You couldn't believe it. I know you were asking yourself: "Why doesn't he try anything?" You thinking that maybe the Crippling Disease took my nuts with it. It did, it did: but not in the way that you suspected.

So as a reward for my perspicacity, and restraint, you give me your heart of blue blood, and invite me out one Sunday to meet the family. At the farm. In Bucks County.

You never tell me, and I neglect to ask, that the Farm was built in 1788. Fourteen rooms. Forty acres; no mules, but lots of horseflesh. I am about to join the upper class.

It is a party, a spring party, a Sunday Spring Party in Bucks County. I like it. I am impressed. All those tall, thin, elegant Philadelphia lawyer wives, with their thin, elegant hands, and faces, and their elegant jodhpurs. Smelling of leather and talking through their noses at each other.

You must understand, Zooey, if I never told you before, and I am about to tell you now, because you are a literate person, and you will read this, because you read everything, you eat books, as I recall, tear them apart, nuzzle out the warm tender leaves of them, eat the bindings; I must tell you Zooey, why I left you on that Sunday afternoon, in Bucks County, at that beautiful Spring Party at the Farm.

I have made it. Zooey is my entree into Philadelphia society. I am not averse. Shit, I want to talk through my nose too. I want to smell like leather and get a ten-room white neo-colonial fifteen-acre horse-and-dog stream-side manse just outside Paoli.

You understand Zooey. I want to be surrounded by thin Main Line folks who will age so beautifully, their curly white

locks, ruddy faces sparkling with robust foxhunt health. I am
not adverse to Aristocracy at all, not in the slightest. I could
happily have spent the rest of my days with you, and after
graduation from Law School, and a suitable honeymoon in
Aix, I would be able to join the family practice.

I could have done that, Zooey, but you don't know,
and I am about to tell you, that on that particular Sunday,
that Sunday I come out to the family pile in Bucks County, I
stand around some, and all those people know each other,
but none of them know me, and you have gone off somewhere, and I am surrounded by all this elegance, and I have
to take a piss.

My body! My friend! My constant companion! Always
letting me know. The whiff of grapeshot across the bow.
Whenever I get too high-falutin'. Running up the flag, pulling the cork out of the bilge. The supreme arbiter of my
bullshit self. Protecting me from all those fancy-dan ideas,
aspirations: me, in Philadelphia Society. Law School. The
burgeoning practice with the old-line firm of Tweedle and
Dee. Slowly working my way to the top, with you, tennis-
court tan you at my side. A cripple of some great promise. A
few corporate directorships here and there, a place on the
board of the Marin Cricket Club (even though I shan't be
playing much cricket).

And your dad, Marcus (you called him Pops), his Harris
Tweed arm around my Harris Tweed shoulder, telling me
"Welcome aboard, son," and it all starts that fine, that mem-
orable Sunday you take me out to The Farm in Bucks County. And it all ends when I have to take a pee.

It befits a fourteen-room farm house in Bucks County
built in 1788 in the Colonial mode to have its pisser up on the
second floor. It befits a fourteen-room farm house in Bucks
County built in 1788 that the pisser should be up twenty-nine
stairs, stairs with a high polish, oak stairs of a narrow beam
and a very high (almost fifteen inch) rise, with a railing on the
wrong side, so that as I address myself to the stairs,
backwards, as is my wont, a step at a time, and as I am teetering up there, 'way up there, teetering on Stair Number
Twenty-Seven, two from the top, and as I am stopped to

119

catch my breath, teetering there, it befits the situation (and me) that some noodle-head, your arch mother perhaps, has placed athwart the next step a Pennsylvania Dutch hand-weave many-speckled round rug, or pad, so that when I, precarious, on my two very thin fragile sticks (keeping me suspended there, breathless, high in the stratosphere) place right foot behind me, and go to shift my weight backwards, that all of a sudden the solid wood is solid wood no more but a very dangerous and highly moveable round Pennsylvania Dutch rug which quickly slips (my unwilling foot on it) all the way over to the edge of the step and then on through the rails of the bannister so that as I go to catch my-self, pulling foot forward as far as non-existent muscles will let me, I get foot wedged in bannister, at the very edge of space itself, and if I go forwards, down, crashing down twenty-seven steps, I will take part of the bannister with me, and if I try to go up, to Stair Number Twenty-Eight, I will have to somehow get my right foot out of the space between the railings, out of the place where it is caught almost at the edge of space. I am stuck.

Below me, just out of view, beyond the turn in the steps, the party goes on. I can hear someone saying "Haw haw haw and he said haw haw go on David tell him about the baby haw haw and he said haw haw." And behind that, counterpoint to that, is a sophisticated voice, somewhat shrill (I believe it is your hollow-cheeked mother, Zooey) at the door, calling out "Chlorine! My God I'm so *glad* to see you. And you brought Pug. Pug, how are you?" And sounds of kisses, sweet aristocratic hollow-cheek kisses.

Zooey: I am stuck at the top of these goddamn dangerous steep slick man-eating stairs. I have to take a pee so bad I can't see straight. I should call out, I should be able to call out for someone to save me, for God's sakes, save me from the mountain climb where I am stuck at the very edge of the chasm (if I make one false move, I go over the chasm) and my arms starting to ache, and I want someone to save me, and I can't call, I can't call out, it would be so indiscrete, in the Upper Class world, me calling out because I am so full of piss that I am stuck at the top of your Bucks County Farm

Steps, and there is no way I can go up nor down, and I am crying inside myself Zooey, crying because there is no respite, nor warning, no protection at all *at all* against the vengeful angels who come to me, always by surprise, come to me and belch fire into my soul, leave me shaken, ashen, a burnt ant-heap; just to remind me that I am human, and vulnerable; that there is no escape. That I am stuck, and there is no escape.

A Mr. Peabody, of proper leather elbows on grey flannel jacket comes up the stairs to relieve his own inner plumbing, and finds me there, nested so awkwardly at the top of the steps. A ruddy-faced gentleman, fifty or so, with a proper bristle moustache and an aristocratic way of betraying no surprise, no surprise at all at finding six-foot-three me stuck, my foot almost over the parapet, two rungs from the top of the heap, as it were. His voice booms, friendly (it actually booms: I wish he could be a little bit more discrete at my suspension) CAN I HELP YOU OUT THERE SON? LOOKS LIKE YOU'RE STUCK!

The good aristocratic Mr. Peabody, a communications attorney, I believe, is quick to move when he sees a disaster afoot. No *lis pendens* here. He applies strong-veined hands to my ankle, disengages foot from railings, has me lean on his broad, horsebacky shoulder, and we push and pull, I push and pull, we both panting some, not up but down, easing me down the twenty-seven steps of damnation, down all the way to the bottom, where when, having reached the safe, all-safe bottom landing, he bucks me up, there in Bucks County, with his hands, pats down my Brooks Brothers tweed jacket lapels, asks me, whiskey breath (actually: Scotch breath) ANYTHING ELSE, SON? I so grateful at my big red-faced angel-of-mercy, who comes to this Sysiphus-of-the-Stairs, with my intolerable boodle of self; the man who saves me from becoming a permanent fixture, a living statue, there two steps from the top, in the 1788 Farm House, in Bucks County, owned by the parents of my loving, all too loving Zooey, my innocent, ignorant Zooey.

Out and away from Mr. Peabody, mumbling something about everything being all right, which it isn't, and without even saying goodbye to Zooey, or her mother, or her father, I slip, if slip can be the proper word, out through the kitchen, surprised black faces at the steamy cauldrons there, out the back, out to my own comfortable slightly dirty Oldsmobile, the white Oldsmobile which you and I, Zooey, called *Moby Dick,* because of the white monstrosity of it; and I ease myself out into the narrow road between your farm Zooey, and my safe and comfortable room on campus, Zooey; I leaving without so much as a by-your-leave, or thank-you-for-inviting me, or I-had-a-great-time, none of these courtesies which are true, because I am ashamed Zooey, at my own personal defeat, there near the peak of the mountain, the pass of Thermopylae, where I was defeated, there for the two-thousandth, seven-hundredth, thirty-third time, by that being which should be my friend, Zooey, but which isn't my goddamn friend, Zooey, but my enemy, Zooey, the enemy that lies within and without, that enemy which defeated me just as I was about to ascend the ladder of success; that sentient being which defeated me even before I could get up the first goddamn rung of the ladder; me, defeated by a body so Spartan, Zooey, so that I would prefer, and I hope you understand now, prefer to adjourn to my own home, that dormitory place called home, where I could for Christ's sake take a leak without tangling with twenty-seven of the most bitching, slippery, man-killing, cripple-eating, head-busting, bone-smashing, shit-piling stairs ever invented by any fool in this whole high class aristocratic world, Zooey. O Zooey!

CHAPTER XVIII

I suppose that somewhere around here you are expecting me to open up that bag o' worms called marriage. You think I am going to tell you about me and Clare and our new young childhood there together in college and in Berkeley, living out whatever it is that we are supposed to live out as Young Marrieds in the most fecund land of ours.

But tell all? Who do you think I am? Some sort of perverted exhibitionist, ripping open the rainjacket and pulling out all the fat, slick worms from within for us to mutter over and admire as novel diviners? You want me to unveil all the secrets of courtship, romance, marriage, mother-and-father-hood? And then should I go on to the disillusionment, the humdrum argument (or sulk), the "now-what-have-I-gotten myself-into?" stage, along with the final divorcement, the empty chair at the dining-room table in the now too-large home, and your prototypical guilt over the abandonment of wife-and-eighteen-month-old-child?

I would never squeal on Clare. She would never let me hear the end of it if I were to reveal the secret exchange of courtship and our months together. She has her pride! Why do you think I married her? I'm not about to spend the rest of my days on the telephone with her, explaining why I recited all sorts of lies here to explain the coming and going of the Love-Marriage Dream.

Suffice it for me to tell you that when we finally decided to hang it up, she could've taken me to the cleaners if she was that type. She could've gotten half my assets, and the house, and the child, and the car, and the cat, and the cat-box. If she was that way. But she's not—kind Clare, and the kindest thing I can do in return is to keep the lid on all those steamy passages in our brief-comet marriage. I loved her (as best I was able) and she loved me (far more than was wise) and we did what we did at the time, as best we could, and that's that. She called me secret names which are the province of those in love, and she tried to give me some flowers for my days, at a time when my heart was encased in concrete from the dying fall. She loved my body, as weird looking as it was, after the fire had passed. She said that it put her in mind of Christ's body, with the bone-thin legs and straight-out wiry arms and the ribs riding so high under the skin. She kissed my wounds, and made them better, because she was a kind person, in love with poor-christ me, I who could never accept love even if it was given to me straight on a gold-trim platter with no payback required, at all, at all.

Now you know why I am keeping my writer's blab-mouth closed about our tiny cottage in Berkeley, with the dirty yellow-bead lamps and murky carpet. It was there that our love turned to coal. The last night I was to see her was the night the roman candle came streaming a star trailing the form of child come over the hills. We called our child Small because she was, and at the time of her coming wise Clare and I said to each other farewell.

I think of my daughter on the day of her birth, the huge purple-and-green *umbilicus* attached to such a tiny body. The pose: the child upside-down, the tiny feet caught in the large hands of another man. And then I think of her years later, when I have gone off in such a different direction from my world in Berkeley: from being a student of English; away from a marriage; away from the house on a hill; the comfort; the middle-class student life.

I don't realize then how much I have been jolted out of my mind by my body. Relationships, always out of kilter. Out of my mind. Think with my groin. Walk on my hands. Always upside-down, reversed: the turn of self. The woman's head set so perilously on a man's body. The moon comes to be sun; the land turns to water; the sea becomes hard, slippery, dangerous; the beach turns to mud, treacherous quicksand.

I come to be the arsey-versey. My tears will water my bottom. There is no foot below, no heaven above. There is no foundation: the rocks have blown up, melted, turned to juice, come to rest in strange patterns.

She, my daughter, grows to be victim of The Reverse Father. The Father who should be Mother. The man who is woman. The little man who wasn't there. The father who is no further; the father who has turned a woman's ghost. The queerest little spook you ever did see.

Over the next years I will be gone, a vapor, a dust. I see her in a series of photographs that come to me, black-on-white, some faded, some wispy, some shadowed. A head that turned too soon, as the shutter moved, so that the face my face comes to be blurred. My face, my chin, blurred by too much distance.

The father who is the reversed negative. The reverse, and the negative. In becomes out. Up becomes down. There becomes here. Positive is negative, the polarities turn on themselves.

The reversed father can have no compassion. No father-love, no sense of family, or duty, or right, or wrong. No loyalties (fragile loyalties!) to mother, father, sister, brother, wife, uncle, aunt, nephew, daughter. No feelings of obligation, no lock-chains of family. You cannot tie me down with your blood!

The arsey-versey kid knows no familial affection: no mother, no father, no daughter, no wife, no nothing but self. There is no room in this wasted body for parent. "Abandon love" should be the sign they hang on this half-being. Abandonment—that's my middle name.

Besides a wife I married to cure me of this boodle called Man-Love; and a daughter who would come later to be the apple-of-my-eye—the only thing to come out of that grueling time was my freedom.

125

Shit: maybe the whole period was necessary so that I could get the old and foolish and worn ideas about the American Work Ethic and Married-And-A-Father out of my numbskull brain. The journey was so long and strange: and at the the end of it they gave me $388,000, in cash.

That college I went to gave me two foolish perversions. One was an unyielding hate of war. It taught me that destruction of man-by-man was a sin. It convinced me that those who carry the Bible in one hand and a gun in the other are fooling you, and themselves, and God. As a Quaker College, the message was that war was an intolerable solution to the differences between men. Three years of classes went into brainwashing me on that score.

The other perversion they stuck me with was that I, personally, could do something to mitigate the drift of humanity towards World War III. Somehow, they taught me, I had enough power and passion to stop all wars of all mankind for all time. Of course, given my ineluctible narcissism, I helped the thought along; but they fired the madness—and I was to spend the next twenty years chasing about the country (with only a brief hiatus, to be described shortly) devising, organizing, funding, building, and operating a series of noncommercial radio stations that would turn mankind away from violence through a pea-brained concept called Free Speech. Thus if I started a broadcast station in Washington D.C. (I tried to start a radio station in Washington, D.C.), when all those Senators and Representatives and Presidents and Generals and Civil Service Workers tuned in and heard a vigorous debate on our foreign policy, or when they heard a well-researched documentary on the hazards of radiation, and the history of human frailties—after a few months of this, they would be saying to themselves "We must be idiots to think that war is the answer to our problems." They would come to nod their heads sagely and think: "Maybe there are other, more peaceful, solutions . . . Something other than . . . than the Horror of Nuclear War . . ." And the other Senators and Representatives and Presidents and Generals would nod their heads, and suddenly America and Belligerent will turn into America the Peaceful, and it would all be my doing.

Well—you can guess what came out of that nonsense. Any nut who believes that he can change the world gets the ultimate payoff: disappointment, frustration, grief, and breakdown.

The whole save-mankind fantasy (and my concurrent adventures in the steamy parts of Washington) will have to await my next literary endeavor. The story of those two years that I was to spend, those two mind-wrenching, soul-crushing, nut-numbing years of chasing Radio Bigfoot through the halls of Congress, into the East Wing of The White House, down the dark halls of the Federal Communications Commission—those adventures will have to await the publication of an outsized confessional, an epistolary saga as compendious as, say, *The Idiot*. It will be replete with forms filled out and filed and duplicated and lost in the morass of Potomac Despair. In the interim, while we are waiting for that tome, let me guide you through the final *coup de main* which drove me from the shores of America, into the waiting arms of the thieves, pimps and pederasts of decadent Europe.

As I am filling out O so hopefully the required FCC Form 340 that is to result in the first broadcast Marketplace of Ideas (Athens right there on Pennsylvania Avenue) I run across a section that asks that I show enough scratch to build my dream broadcast outlet. The form asks: "By what method does the applicant propose to finance construction and initial operation of the broadcast outlet?"

Money? Now where am I going to get money? Where does one go to get money anyway? To a bank, right?

I go over to Riggs National Bank, on H Street, just across the way from Eisenhower's winter home, and just up the alley from mine (I live in the Washington YMCA, which has been kind enough to rent me a soot-encrusted habitation for five dollars a day. I certainly don't want to waste any money at this point. I'll need it all once my permit for the Washington station gets granted, right?)

I go to Mr. Coolidge, the Vice-President in charge of crackpot loan requests, and I ask him for $20,000. "Do you have any security?" asks Mr. Coolidge, a bit tartly.

"Do I have any what?" I say.

"Any security?" he says. "Stocks, bonds, municipals, property. What are your assets?"

Shit, I don't know what my assets are. I write home to the family accountant, the man who dribbles out checks to me from time-to-time when I get up the wall (or married). I tell him to send along any securities he might be holding for me. I tell him to send them air-mail. Free Speech is waiting in the wings.

The package arrives on November 19th, 1959, at 11:03 in the morning. O no it doesn't—it arrives in 1933, in August, on a hot and stormy night, on the second of the month, at 8:53 in the evening. At that moment, when they set me free, passing me through Vestibule and Fouchette, there is a man dressed in black, among all the white coats and smocks, and he's a lawyer, who reaches over at the moment of the first cough-and-breath, and puts in my little red-wrinkled hand, still moist with the clear juices of birth, a paper that reads:

Dear Lorenzo:

You are loaded.

With kindest regards,

Mom & Dad

Well, that was in 1933, in the midst of the Depression, and down we forget as up we grow, so even though I was to spend most of my days in a fourteen-room log cabin on the banks of the St. Johns River, with summers at the Summer House, at the edge of the warm Atlantic, I guess I get confused. It might have something to do with wearing all my brother's hand-me-down clothes. It may have been that they didn't want to spoil me, so that to put in my claim for my inheritance, I have to liberate quarters amd halves from my mother's white ivory black silk-lined purse. Possibly it is the taking baths with my sisters, in luke-warm, inch-deep tub-water, freezing my little nuts in the grey-scum, and wondering why everything had to be so cold.

Somehow, somewhere, I get the idea there is "just enough" for us to get by on. The indignities—O the indignities that the poor rich suffer through to pretend that we are no better off then our friends and relations, in this most egalitarian of all societies.

It's not until the second package arrives that I get the message, the message that the days of frugality are all a snare and a delusion. Truth comes in a shiny brown envelope, thick and heavy and registered. It comes from the family accountant, with the return address of the family law-firm.

I am all alone in the $40-a-month shared-rent office on "G" Street. My desk is crowded with application forms and such. I clear a space for the package. I figure they must have put in lots of cardboard to keep the one or two papers from bending. I always knew there was something there. All the bills got paid, somehow. There was always food on the table, a new car every third or fourth year, nice plates to eat off of, maids and things. But I never imagined, *I never imagined. . . .*

Stock certificates. Dear Gussie! So many of them; all carefully imprinted with my name. That's me: General Motors. General Foods. Eastman Kodak. U.S. Steel. Foremost Dairies. Fifty different certificates. IBM. Xerox. American Cya—namid. Merck Corp. American Home Products. Some with engravings of elaborate machines; nude Grecian figures with staffs; engravings of gods and goddesses; machines, complicated line etchings of machines. My god. National Cash Register. Winn-Dixie Grocery. General Mills. Standard Oil. Texaco. I own parts of all these companies: sometimes twenty-five or fifty shares; sometimes a hundred or five hundred; in one case, two thousand. Weyerhauser Lumber. Coca-Cola. Lone Star Cement. Lone Star Gas. Middle South Utilities. American Tel. & Tel. RCA. Washington Water Power. Dear Gussie.

Red certificates, blue certificates, orange, green, yellow.

All with delicate scripted writing beautifully engraved, run your fingers along the edges. Long close writing on front and back. The language of the stock market. The language of money. This is what takes up three pages in every newspaper every day: the ups and the downs of these pieces of paper. Dow-Jones. Price/Earnings Ratio. Stock Dividends. Ex Dividend. Ex parte. Ex cathedra. Ex poor (me).

Out they come, up in the air, whee! Whee! The raining down of six dozen carefully scripted, carefully engraved papers of me, my money, my wealth. Whee, whee! Up in the air, showering down, the golden showering down, the papers come showering down: Portland Cement, Boeing Aircraft, Piper Aircraft, Prentiss-Hall, San Diego Gas & Electric, Florida Power and Light, General Cement, General Tire, General Dogbone, General Curtis LeMay, General Wealth, wealth is general, wealth is where you find it.

Showering down. I throw them all up in the air and let them rain down the golden leaves all about my head, my body, my chair, my shoes, my feet, my ground? O no, O no.

No: I carefully, o so carefully keep them in their brown envelope. So carefully. Down to the corner. Get a newspaper. Back in the office, open it up to the page I have never studied before. New York Stock Exchange. Jesus, what does this all mean. Open High Low Close. What is 77 1/4? Is that cents or dollars? Ex div? Does that mean "Extra Divisors?" I thought a "split" was a dance step. "P.E?" What does physical education have to do with SONJ? And who *is* SONJ? What in God's name could "VaEP pf 2.90" mean? "x24?" "z16?" "CmwE 6 1/4 '82?" Someone, I think, has committed something with someone called "Eddie" and they have size 6-1/4 shoes and are 82 years old. Is that possible?

"Wait a minute," I think. I didn't learn how to parse Spenser in college for nothing. I could read the symbolism in "The Love Song of J. Alfred Prufrock" with the best of them. You remember that paper on the symbolism of fireworks in the Cissy Caffrey sequence in *Ulysses*? "You're no-body's dummy, Milam" I think. With dictionary in one hand and

Washington *Post* in the other, I apply myself to the poetry at hand. "This is no worse than that awful Oscar Williams," I think. "If I can write a paper on his turgid nonsense," I think: "then I can certainly deal with the ancient cadences of money. We can do it, can't we?" and I imagine my late father standing, in his upper-class vested way, at my side, lending me the helping hand to make these letters and numbers talk to me. And they do.

Within five hours, I figure my net worth at $387,991. Give or take a few thousand dollars. Dear Jesus Christ. I can start seventeen radio stations with that money.

I haul them over to Riggs National Bank. My bank. The one in which I have kept anywhere from $12 to $300 in my account, depending on what I could beg from home. I get to the desk of Mr. Coolidge. A quiet man, with pencil-thin lips, a desk perfectly cold and bare. A prim man. One not given to enthusiastic hellos or good-byes.

I tell Mr. Coolidge that I have decided I would like the loan for $20,000. There is a general silence. His lips thin slightly. His eyes look a little more bored. He plays with a yellow pencil.

He doesn't know about my baby. Not yet. I haven't told him about the baby I wear in my shirtfront.

Q. How does a cripple carry papers, important or unimportant?

A. Down his shirt front. Like a baby. Right there, slightly bulging out under the first three buttons of the white Brooks Brothers shirt. Held up by the belt. Me, carrying a $388,000 baby in my wrinkled shirt front. Mr. Coolidge doesn't know yet. The fine razor edge between ignorance and knowledge. The moment, the insight, the vision, the wonder.

I must look a sight. My hair: I don't have time to comb it. The crutches have worn holes in my jacket, in the armpits, so that the frays show. My pants are a mess, since the brace inevitably wears a hole in the knees. I am not much for laundries, so I wash my own shirts at the Y. The collar is wrinkled, and turned up. I look dishevelled. Just yesterday, a lady tried to shove a dollar in my hand at the corner of Pennsylvania and F Street.

131

So here is this ratty-looking crip bothering the Vice-President of Riggs National Bank. Taking up his time. Asking for a $20,000 loan. We bank presidents get so bored with people asking us for money. We may be made of money, but we have to protect it.

I am waiting for Mr. Coolidge to be impolite. To get angry. To tell me to take off. But he must sense something. Or maybe he is just born polite. "Lorenzo, you must remember, I said to you a couple of weeks ago that we would need some security in order to make you a loan." He smiles thinly. "Those are our rules."

I pause for a moment. I want to play with him some more. After all, I have a $400,000 baby burning in my stomach, just waiting to get out, to be birthed, to come sliding out onto the desk so that we can both look at it, so that we can see what a giant brawling baby has come into the world.

I pause a little, think. "Mr. Coolidge," I say. "I have never gone back on a debt. I have always paid back my debts."

"Lorenzo," he says, patiently, "you have never borrowed from our bank before. You have no credit. I don't know what you are worth, I have no idea of your net worth."

"O baby," I think: "I'm worth plenty." Not much in soul and in body, but there's this little fetus riding on my tum, my money-gut, ready to ride out in the world, flatten all opposition.

"But would you believe me if I told you that I have always paid my debts," I say, archly. "I'm no bum, you know. I'm not a dead-beat."

I am trying to get Mr. Coolidge worked up. Maybe he will get angry at me, slam his fists down on the table, tell me to stop wasting his time. Maybe he will tell me to get out, be done with him, get gone. And then I can rise up in wrath, pull out my baby, riffle the stock certificates under his nose, and say "See. I would have been a good customer of yours. Spent hundreds of thousands of dollars with you. Borrowed tons, and paid back tons." I could have shouted at him: "But you are such an inconsiderate little jerk. Judging people by the way they dress, rather than what they are. You are a fool, and you and this goddamn bank should be razed."

And I would have crutched out the door, leaving him behind in open-mouth amazement, so sorry that he had said all those unkind things to me, trembling in fear of his job, when the word gets out: Coolidge turned Milam down for a $20,000 loan, secured by $388,000 worth of good common stock.

But Mr. Coolidge has all the time in the world. It has been a quiet day, and I am obviously no dummy. He cleans his already trim and pink-white fingernails with a silver pocket knife, and starts on a boring monologue about how he would really like to give loans to all the people that come to him, but the bank has to be careful, there are policies that have developed over the years, and that his hands are really tied, although I might be a very good credit risk, and . . .

He falls silent, watching me wrestle this fat brown envelope out of my shirt front. It is so goddamn big that it gets caught on one of the buttons, so it looks like I am trying to take off my shirt, and I am getting flustered: here I was striving for a dramatic performance, to come on cue, and now I can't get the leading star out of my shirt and onto the delivery table, where it belongs.

When I finally *do* get it out it slips out of my hand, and certificates go all over the floor everywhere, so that for a moment, Coolidge and I are locked in a shocked silence, sitting on what seems to be a mountain of high quality engravings, and we both scrabble, I seated, he unseated, to scoop them up and get them where they were supposed to go in the first place, on his desk. And finally they are on Mr. Coolidge's desk, and we look at them for a moment or two. The ugly duckling has been transformed into the great goose. The worm into the multi-colored butterfly. The waif into a beautiful (and rich) princess.

We talk about this and that as Mr. Coolidge fingers the new me. All my talk about radio stations gets transformed. Two weeks ago I was another person in Washington with an idea. Now I am a person with an idea, and the way to make it work. I have been turned around. I have shown a new face. I am a man of means. I am reversed, not one of those want-to's that pound the Washington streets with a dream and nothing else.

I am rich. Me: rich! And Mr. Coolidge takes three companies (Coca-Cola, General Motors, Eastman Kodak), hands me some notes to sign; I sign them, and without even a twitch, $20,000 appears on the balance of my checking account. Some people work at shitty jobs for five years so that they can show $20,000 in their bank account. I write a letter to my accountant, get some paper, exchange it with Mr. Coolidge, and zip, the money is in my account.

It is a *terrible* system. You and I agree. It is unjust, unfair, evil, destructive, immoral, outlandish. That I, because I was born in a certain place at a certain time; that I should have the right to those pieces of paper, and have the right to sign them over to Riggs bank and have $20,000 in my account: it is unconscionable. It's Wrong. It's contrary to the free spirit of mankind.

But it is fun, and this little cripple is goddamn glad that at the age of twenty-six, finally, after all these years of scrabbling along in life, wondering where I was going to get the next $100, that magically, was handed to me something that I should have had the good sense to ask for all along.

Once I have the money—there's another stinker at the bottom of the bag. I file my application for a radio station with the Federal Communication Commission and I wait and I wait and I wait some more. Each day I take the trolley over to my shabby offices at 805 "G" Street Northeast, looking for that letter that says:

> Dear Mr. Milam:
>   We think your idea to enlighten Washington is excellent, and included herewith is a permit to construct the first of such exciting radio stations on the East Coast.
>   Love & Kisses,
>   Ben F. Waple
>   FCC Secretary
>   (and Protector of the Aether.)

But it never comes.

I guess that some monkey-business is up. Everytime I go

downtown to the F.C.C., and start asking people about my application, they have to go to the bathroom. How was I to know that my application got stuck in the office of some flea-brain by the name of John Harrington? He is head of "Internal Security" at the FCC, and he's heard about me all right. He has heard from unimpeachable sources that Pacifica Foundation, parent of KPFA, in Berkeley, is teeming with Communists. Since I worked for KPFA briefly, before I came to Washington, and since I obviously enjoyed it, and since I am trying to start a similar station, I am probably a Communist too.

Harrington and the other guardians of the aether will not tell me of their suspicions. That is the part of the game of the late '50s with suspected subversives: you deny that one is under suspicion; thus, one cannot defend oneself. Thus, the Harringtons don't get hauled in court to justify the illegal system of guilt-until-proven-innocent. It's the ultimate perversion of The English Common Law.

Something isn't working, and I am not sure what, or why, so I decide that I can get some information from my congressman, from my home-town in Florida. He's another cripple, Hon. Chas. Bennett. You can stick it too, Charlie. You are good, really good to your fellow cripples, aren't you, you cunt?

Anyway, Charlie takes me to lunch. I guess he figures that if he is going to insult me, he should put some food in my belly so I'll be all filled up when I get the word. Two crips, out on their crutches, for a cruise, together. We go to the dining room of the House of Representatives. We sit knee-to-knee, or rather, brace-to-brace. I have never had lunch with someone so important.

"There are people," he says, portentously, "who want to destroy the country. There are people who want to use the institutions of the country to wreck the country. These people have different political beliefs, and will use any agency of government or even the freedom of the press to wreck the United States of America. We have to be on the look-out for them."

"I agree, I agree," I think. I am very pleased that he is giving me a political lecture. After all, he is a politician, so he should know a great deal about politics. This is much better than college.

"People go to colleges, liberal colleges. They get in the hands of the wrong kinds of professors. These people take advantage of youth's innocence. They fill their heads with dangerous propaganda, and the young people just can't handle it. They just haven't had enough experience in the world, they are overwhelmed."

"You're probably right," I think, nodding my head. "You can't be too careful nowadays. These kids just can't handle it."

He nods his head too. He spoons in some bean soup, and continues:

"We simply have to protect ourselves against these . . . these traitors if you will," says Charlie The Nodder. "We have to be very careful, because of our country, as good as it is, as strong as it is, is also fragile. Some people will take freedom of speech, and freedom of the press, and turn it against the very country that provides it. We can't be too careful."

"You are so right," I think. "And yet," I think, "in some ways. . . ." (Now's the right time to tell him about my radio station, the one that I want to put on the air in Washington, where we'll protect Freedom of Speech by letting *everyone* on the air. Right-wingers, left-wingers, crackpots, dildoes—the whole panoply. But it's too late, I don't have a chance. Charlie is standing up, locking his braces, taking my hand in his and looking me in the eye, being very serious. I feel it is a pregnant moment.)

"The country has to protect itself against those who will harm it. That's our job." And he fits crutch to arm, and creaks away, lumping back to the subway, hobbling back to defend the country against The Great Red Peril.

"What the fuck is he talking about?" I wonder. "Where does he get this mish-mash?" I wonder. "Maybe polio has fried his brain too," I think. I don't get the message. I want a radio station, not a political lecture. It isn't until a year later, one of those 5 a.m. aha! moments, when I finally get what

Charlie The Crip is trying to tell me. The gimpy little traitor. Trying to tell his fellow basket-case about loyalty! So's your old man's ass, Charlie!

All I have to show for two years of work in Washington are a dead application, a heart full of wormwood, and a bucket of frustration. O yes—a rich litany of what-did-I-do-wrong, and, not the least, $388,000.

I did my best. I wanted so to show this country the alternatives, the full flower of free speech and music. But it was enamored of war and bombs and The Devil-Enemy Theory. They intend to kill each other. The Russians over there and the Americans over here are both full of kill-to-solve-all-problems, and I should get the hell out of here, before they kill me. Leave it. Leave Washington and the country to the Harringtons and Eastlands and Bennetts and Dulles and all the cripple minds who have so much hate in them. They and their atomic wastes deserve each other. Me: I'm getting the fuck out.

My marriage is over. My vision has been corrupted. My schooling is a waste. My love affairs, what few I've had, are a mess. I have been shafted by the very system which should encourage me. Screw them all. I am rich, and that is all that is important. Money is the ultimate portable. I am taking a hunk of it with me and sailing for Europe. On the *Liberté.* I leave America with nothing: no love, no hope, no vision, no change, no chance. No way. I am going to Europe as a rich and hopeless immigrant. Europe which calls out:

> *Give me your tired Idealists*
> *Your poor fruitcakes; your huddled*
> *Gimps yearning to breathe lust,*
> *Perversion, and corruption . . .*

God save the New World! God bless the Old!

PART IV

*the strange thing is that man
who is conceived by accident
and whose every breath is a
fresh cast with dice already
loaded against him will not face
that final main which he knows
before hand he has assuredly to
face without essaying expe-
dients ranging all the way from
violence to petty chicanery that
would not deceive a child until
someday in very disgust he risks
everything on a single blind
turn of a card no man ever does
that under the first fury of
despair or remorse or bereave-
ment he does it only when he
has realised that even the
despair or remorse or bereave-
ment is not particularly important to the dark diceman*

— The Sound and The Fury

CHAPTER XIX

Now, for a change, let me take you back a quarter-century or so, to a small dark cabin, on a small dark ship, somewhere on the stormy Atlantic. Our hero (me!) is alone, as usual, and is suffering from The Cosmic Blues and The American Angst. Something must come of it.

The ship, like most, is filled with fools. All the nuts salted away together, steaming through nowhere, babbling at each other. Our journey of madness is courtesy of La Compagnie Générál Transatlantique.

It is shortly after my twenty-seventh birthday. I am far more beautiful (and far more neurotic) than I am now. I am just a slip of a thing, six-foot-three, peglegging my way through life and into another year of Our Lord and Savior. 1960, to be exact.

I have been told by some fraud that being on the *Liberté* is the most glamorous way to travel to Europe. What they don't tell us is that we spend most of our time aboard sleeping, or having our feet tacked down in the dining hall for two or three hours at a stretch. There they stuff us with foods and wine that make us to feel like some great grey goose.

It's very depressing. We Americans can hardly stand to talk to each other (after all, that is why we are leaving America). The French staff and crew see us as an army of Algerian terrorists, and they have strict instructions not to let us escape from our cabins or the dining halls or the lounge *Fruits de Mer* where I spend too much of my time downing tepid Alsatian beer and wondering why no-one loves me.

In addition, we manage to scout out the few available storms in the North Atlantic — so moving about the ship on pins already rocky at best becomes nigh about impossible. I am forced to become a recluse in my dark steerage compartment with no porthole, with the steady accompaniment of the 1925 Bucyrus-Erie engine complete with two-story overhead pistons that grind and beat against the bulkhead so that I am threatened with permanent deafmutism on top of my other disabilities. There is no port, so I can't even look out to sea; I never know what time it is when I wake up. It is like being transported in a small, uncomfortable space capsule with a primitive steam engine and scientists bent on testing my ability to survive.

One night I can't take it any longer. My darkened cabin is filled with hobgoblins of engine beat and Gallic overheating. The sea is rising up in huge waves that threaten to throw me out of my bunk. My fury starts to match the fury outside: I make it up two flights of narrow stairs to the ballroom (empty), then to the lounge (empty), then out the door, over an impossibly high step. There is no-one about can stop me in the plans I have so carefully laid. I am alone with my soul, and the universe—and both are in tatters.

It is time for me to give myself to the sea. The hell with America, and my heritage, and my reputed love of life. To hell with La Compagnie Général Transatlantique, my hopes, my future, and The Christian Ethic. I sit myself down, in a red, wet, cold, isolated deck chair, and contemplate my fate. It is time to be done with pain—this mortal and (moral) coil. To hell with it.

The storm is all about me. I am classically alone with the elements. The wind-swept foam flecks my lips. Sometimes, the running lights a scarce dozen feet from me are immersed in the icy water. I am as exposed as I can be to the violent heaviness of the sea. It is time for me to act. It is time for the ultimate exposure that man can make. With a vicious determination, I narrow my eyes, raise my head, clench my jaws, pull out the old whanger and go at it.

I am sorry to be dragging you into all this. I know there are other things to be explored, discussed. The Inquisition, say. The Renaissance. Rock Gardening in the Ukraine. Love and the flowers of Spring. The Papal Encyclical *Rerum*

Novarum of 1891. There I am, 2,700 miles from home, some 3,600 feet (give or take a hundred feet) above the dark and crusty surface of the earth, suspended on salt water gone mad—and I have to jerk off. What does that have to do with this book, anyway?

Plenty. It is a message from the deep. Lightning gabbles down from the sky, clouds crash cheek-to-cheek, the waves appear to be eating our ship, their foam tops surely will lick me away in the next instant. And I am beating off, in love with myself, my sole solitary self, defying all the mighty about me.

I know I should be down below with all the other seasick passengers. Yet, here I am on the open deck, practically being lurched off into the trough of the coming wave. My dong, so puny against the hugeness of mother sea (so frail the little white worm in those ten-a-minute lightning flashes) is being given the work-out of the ages.

Kinsey reports that 98% of American males admit masturbating at some time in their miserable lives, and the other two percent are obviously lying. My psychiatrist said that only lonely businessmen on trips and soldiers in the foxhole do it. That's me! A lonely businessman in the foxhole, under fire by life, the war of life, the clang and alarums of too many troubles, too little body, not enough love (except from me!), not enough of what I must have to survive. The battle of life being enacted on that deck of the *Liberté*, the dark and stormy night of 19 September 1960, at 10:32 in the evening, at approximately Lat 44° 53′ 21″ Long 31° 02′ 14″; me, the soldier boy, fresh from the Flanders Fields of Washington, D.C.

My tool! My buddy! The friendliest pal of all mankind: never complaining, always there at the ready, willing to jump up at the softest signal (a thought, .00001 milliwatt of command) and stand by for action. The cock, the wonderful runny-nosed, gentle, compact, easily portable little feller.

I ask you: who among you would fault a leisurely whack-off to while away the hours under pressure, to provide the lonely and the disabused a momentary spasm of pleasure? Certainly it is safer and nicer than rape. Certainly it is more to be countenanced than the seduction of the young.

Certainly it wins hands-down over forcible entry, or the time-honored blood cruelty of the wedding night. I would be the last to gainsay that it is better than the time-honored fuck—the regular garden variety cock-a-mannie dance. There is no one to apologize to if you come off schedule; there are no foreplay rituals required; no foul breath to deal with or ill-timed kisses; no partner (except the mirror) to be caught off-rhythm; no inexperienced unknowing lover to miss the most sensitive nerve endings or to inadvertently rub off the first layer of epidermis.

Just pal me, in love with myself. I—the only one in the world who can love me properly. Who else would know the proper rhythm, the proper timing; who else could probe all the appropriate membranes, caress them with such keen understanding and keen verve? I am so sensitive to me sometimes that I can carry me to the very brink of destruction and stop, hold back, for a moment, the fat red sun poised on the edge of the smoky sky, waiting, the gaping black hole of space ready to swallow up the veriest part of me, carrying me to the ultimate crest, there at the top of the sea.

Imaginary lover. That's me. There is no one who can be as competent as me, no one to drive me to such depths of love. What I am doing here is reaffirming myself; a sign of loyalty; my own loyalty oath; a pledge, the pledge of allegiance to me; the confirmation of me, of self; the proof that I am truly here, that I do indeed exist, no matter what all the others (officials, government, world) have to say. I hereby pledge allegiance to my existence, and all that it stands for, in this hour of need, one cock, undivisible, with semen and ecstasy for all, for ever and ever. Amen.

I have thus given explicit recognition of my own existence through that instrument of five digits, the right hand. My own right hand: what a precious and efficient little machine! So capable of giving me such ecstasy! The hand, set there at the proper and exact level, as if it were constructed by the divine maker for just such a task. I am on a veritable cliff-edge of delight with me.

I have had a bad year. Shit, I have had a bad decade. I

have no one to give me love except me. I, alone in this storm, confirm hereby that I am alive. I present my whanger to the universe, the universe that towers all about me, the combs of fifty foot waves cresting to my left and to my right. I am tossed and turned by life in the raw; I am shivering in my damp clothes—so I raise my all, and with cold hand and warm heart, address myself to the final delicious act of self-confirmation, despite all handicaps, odds, scorn, and neglects.

I am free of man and woman in the world. I surpass the clawing doubt, the one that has damaged and deranged me for all these past months. I raise myself on high to honor Lorenzo, the me, alive despite the F.C.C., John Foster Dulles, John Harrington, John Wayne, fatherhood, motherhood, Communism, band-aids, Christian Herter, Pope Pius, Billy Graham, Mary Baker Eddy, Khruschev, Charlie Bennett, Lar Daly, the world. I may have the world's worst body, or the world's worst personality, but I am free (free!) to love myself freely.

A great lover of self. They can write that on my tombstone: "*No one knew how to love him as he did himself.*" A paen of praise to Saint Onan! Onan! None else besides my great God Onan knows the tenderness and affection with which I hold myself, hold this joint of pleasure, larger than life, aloft, preparing to send the fireworks of the ages into the sky of darkness.

I have no idea how long I defy the spirits, freezing my nookies, taking myself to the very edge-nub of delight. I don't know how long it goes on, this enjoyment of the god's own solitary pleasure, the pleasure of the crippled, the lonely, the prisoners, we followers of the Infinite Feedback System, that system which is tied to the final main fusing which comes, at that magic moment, when most needed.

There is an especially close cap of lightning, and I can see blue balls running across the waves. The ship lurches frighteningly to starboard, almost casting me from my seat of joy;

a wave crest foams, bubbles inches from my body hunched over itself. Then, then, then—I find myself stranded on that perfect pearl of joy, come the ultimate point of my shiny nacreous self, the pass of peace, the final thrust of independence from all men, women, children, states, laws, requirements, orders of the world. I there, in my greatest moment of freedom, rising ponderously to a warm watermountain spring of up-cascading heat which foams the tips of all crests. I mesmerized in fixity within and without, mouthing the sacred poem of defiance and acceptance, calling out calling out to the wind, the wind catching my prayer and billowing my cheeks, crying out in that split infinite moment out of the glacier of time that tells me there is no one in the whole world can lay a finger to me as lover of the pure supreme soul, the self that rises above all others.

Later, a pointed somewhat later, I rest against the cold red strips below me. I am alone, and in isolation. The cry of me probably echoes out there still in the wind somewhere. I hope so: it was a tenderness of self which goes beyond all mankind, all expression.

I am weary, bone-weary—and cold. The cone of creation has escaped me. That substance (that same protein substance that makes up the brain) has been licked away by wind and salt spume. 500,000 of my babies have been pulled over the side of the vessel, into the salty wet from which they originally came. I am left at a skinny juncture where my hands are frozen in the posture of supplication. The lock of me weeps a bit more, turns small and humble. There are tadpoles out there, looking like me, once a part of me, now a part of the great sea. I know they persist, are non-surrendering, just like me. I know they are swimming valiantly against the storm's tides, convinced there is some hot red ovum awaiting them, just beyond the next wave.

Brave seeds of me, in the frigid ocean, the vast and frigid ocean. Those cells whip bravely into the cold, in pursuit of the sun, not knowing (just like me) that the sun may well be nowhere near, nowhere near, nowhere to be found, indeed, may be many many millions of miles away. Single thread-like swimmers in the huge and restless sea. Just like me. Alone, at sea.

The next day we reach Le Havre.

CHAPTER XX

I think there is one event that shows the tenor of my first two months in Europe. It comes in Paris. I am travelling alone. During the afternoon, I spend four hours at the Louvre, looking at the great masterpieces of the world and wishing I had someone to love.

That evening, I go to Aux Deux Magots. I keep thinking it is 1928, and that I will run into F. Scott Fitzgerald, or Wallace Stevens, or Ernest Hemingway, or better yet, a beautiful long-faced Frenchman from Cannes who will take one look at me, see the beauty in my eyes, and invite me over to his apartment near the Rue d'Avignon.

As we speak—he in broken English, I in broken French—we will see through the language barrier; he will see in my eyes, my face, my hands, the true beauty that lies inside of me. He will, over a glass of bordeaux, at a tiny cafe (and an order of mussels) come to have an appreciation of what my life has been so far, and the wealth of strength that I would represent to a lover.

That evening, we would come together in his simple room. There would bloom that evening, in Paris, on the Left Bank, a love so sparkling, so rich, that it would last for decades. We would see in each other what we had been seeking so often in others—and had failed to find, until this night, this magic night, embracing each other, in the humble little flat, just off the Rue d'Avignon.

I stay in Aux Deux Magots for two hours, drinking brandy, waiting, waiting. Finally, a black comes up to me. He is from Dakar. He speaks no English at all. I buy him a couple of drinks. I have to use my dictionary to tell him I am looking for a room. He invites me, by elaborate hand gesture, to follow him. He has a cold, and keeps blowing his nose on his hand, wiping the hand on his not-too-clean pants. I guess he is taking me to his apartment. I wonder if he is going to ask me to sleep with him.

We go down too many long back alleys. There is little to be said, since he knows no English, I know no French. I swing gamely after him, wondering what star of passion awaits me at the end of the road.

Under streetlight, he stops me. No one is around. He is asking something. I can't understand. "Aw-jaunt," he says. We take out my dictionary. He shows me the word "argent." He wants to know if I have money for a hotel room for the night. Of course; I take out my wallet, show him the several thousand francs I have to survive in Paris. I'm no poor sponger, wanting to live off the land.

He reaches in the wallet and takes it all. He runs, delicately, down the cobbled street. "Wait," I shout, in English. "Monsieur, wait! I can't keep up with you." He doesn't stop, takes off 'round the nearest corner, and I see him literally bouncing off a wall as he races off with every cent I have. "Wait," I call: "You're going too fast."

It takes awhile, doesn't it? For us to glom onto the truth. Events go in a certain direction; when they are jammed into another mode, it takes awhile for our heads to follow. It takes me at least a minute to figure out that the motherfucker is in such a hurry to get my money that he doesn't even wait for me to give it to him.

Those colonialist victims! So impatient! If they had monkey sense, they would know that we will dump it all in their laps anyway. If that boob had taken me to his place, let me have my will with him, within days I would be sending home for some more bucks to support him and his execrable manners.

If he had only waited to help himself to my loot, he could have done it in spades. Get to know me (I'm not such a bad sort, you know); tell me stories about growing up in the dust and dirt of Senegal, describe his ten brothers and sisters, their little bellies poofed out with hunger, his mother broken by years of washing white men's white clothes, his dad's health ruined by too many years in the jute mill.

What a chump! He, robbing himself of a constant flow of dollars: all he had to do was to befriend me, me, all alone in that confusing puzzling city, let me spend a few nights (white face on coal-black chest, white fingers spread in black frizzy hair) and he would have had a stipend for life.

He, my man of West Africa, so eager, so impatient for his just desserts. Unaware that he had drunk with, walked down the alleys with, had befriended one of the most opulent lover-supporters this side of the Atlantic, unaware that a few nights of twice-daily love would have, forever, put an end to knocking around the poor quarters of Paris, getting all those poor tourists pissed at his greed and uncouth manners. That fucker robbed the shit out of himself.

I make my way to the Gard d'Nord. I take a train, any train, to get me out of Paris. These people can't stand anyone who doesn't speak French. They look on it as a personal insult that I can't make head nor tail of their impossible uvulated language.

Despite the fact that it takes a block-and-tackle to get me up the four steep steps of a train, it is my favorite way to travel. I am passing through the heart and soul and bowels of Northern France, and I see cows and farms and trees and farmers through a giant, glass-line screen. The rails talk to me, and the telegraph lines lean down, pause, and rise up to be smashed by the blur of a pole, then lean down, beside me, again.

As we pass through Luxembourg, I vow that I will

change; I have to change. "The trouble with me," I think, "is that all my life, when I am looking for a honey, I always seek out The Perfect Beauty. I think I have to go to bed with a star." That is so self-defeating. It's the weenie between the legs that counts. "I should be on the lookout for some homely, simple lad, with great driving needs like mine," I think. One who won't be too critical of the looks, appearance and shape (or bad shape) of others.

The next day, in the Copenhagen Youth Hostel shower, I run across a young man who seems to be just what the doctor ordered. He is perhaps seventeen or eighteen. His hair is black. His body: ah, and woe! It is close to perfection. With some exceptions.

He is, I find out later, an American. From Virginia. He is part Indian. Cherokee, I believe. The upper part of his body is a battlefield of pimples and acne. Ypres is nothing compared to that pitted and scarred landscape. He is a mess.

Acne vulgaris. The universal mark of derision and isolation. I love it. Society tells him that he is ugly. The mirror tells him he is ugly. No beach parties and teen-aged revelry for my Tom. No such scarring permitted in the surfer movies.

Tom! My brother! We are convinced of our vileness. We—estranged from normal intercourse with society. Ah, the pimple. Sing praise for the homely hopeless chancre. Hooray for the single raised welt of the angry sebaceous gland. Give thanks for abcess and comedo. These children: ugly (they think) (and guilty for being ugly). The rejected of the world.

Give me your scarred youngsters. Send me your suppurating wounded cheeks and brows and chins. I will hold each vulgar pustule to my powerful breast. I will forgive each boil, each volcano of pus and pain, each and every ravaged pox of teenagery. I will adore each chasm and papilla starred across the sky faces of a thousand thousand lonelies who cannot reject the chocolate and malteds and Hershey bars proffered on every side.

I see in the mirror my Indian lad, Tom, with a battle-encrusted face. I see by the mirror (my mask) a war zone cascading a turbulent stream down the neck, across the high parts of the shoulders. The uppermost back and chest are a maze of skin in constant turmoil and eruption. The poisons from within are ever voiding themselves on the ascendant front and back.

And below, below? My eyes are not my own! Will the mirror stop steaming up; or is it just melting with the force of my gaze? Certainly it will puddle in the sink: for the abdomen, the lower muscular back, the backside and frontside of the love zone, the thighs and knees and calf: ah perfect, perfect. Perfect as all the driven snows of all times (driven, perhaps, by the howling wind of desire). Pure and gentle as mountain streams cascading down rock-strewn rivulets the cold hard waters of my lust. My wondrous love.

O Tom. Let me set you up with a fancy apartment here in Copenhagen, with fine shirts and even finer pimple cremes. You will come to love me, we the two cripples, crippled-in-the-face, crippled-in-the-body. The perfect pair. The Beast of Two Bodies. With my face and my brain, with my upper arms and chest, bulging with muscles; with your lower back and stomach and the carved muscular legs; we, together, the one perfect man.

The famed Two-in-One. The blend of Sacred-and-Profane. Prince Hal and Falstaff. The Sun and The Moon. Don Quixote and Sancho Panza. Castor and Pollux. My brain and face, his legs and dong. What fine team!

That evening, in the Hostel dining hall, I find Tom conveniently sitting alone. Tom fully clothed shows to the world a somewhat ordinary body surmounted by a red and angry face. "Tom," I think, "you should come to dinner in your birthday suit." I am sure that all would forgive him after seeing what lies under the jeans and flannel shirt.

What to say? I never was much for idle conversation. I glare at my potato soup. He says nothing. I must do something.

— Hi. My name's Lorenzo. What's yours?	— Can I fuck you?

—That's a nice name: Tom!

—Where are you from?

—Manassas. Is that in
  Virginia?

—Wasn't there some big
  battle there? During
  the Civil War?
—How long have you been
  here in Copenhagen?
—It's a great city, isn't
  it?

—It's such a friendly
  place.
—And you really don't have
  to get to know the
  language.
—Everyone seems to speak
  English.
—I like riding the yellow
  streetcars downtown.
—O yes, there's one that
  goes two blocks from
  here.
—I think it's less than
  a krøner.
—I'm just nuts about trol-
  leys, especially these.
—And it will take you right
  down to City Hall.
—That's called the Rad-
  hausplatz.

—Everything is within
  walking distance of
  that Square.
—What's it like growing
  up in Virginia?
—Is the weather as nice as
  it is here?

—I really like having sex
  with young men.
—I could care less that your
  face is a wreck.
—In fact, I think it
  makes you more attractive
  (in some strange way).
—It's the cock that counts,
  if you will pardon the
  expression.
—You know, I'm probably what
  you would call a pervert.
—Sometimes I think the whole
  goddamn world is made up of
  perverts.
—I'll bet you are some kind
  of pervert too.
—Have you ever tried making it
  with a man? Like me, say?

—Although I am a cripple, I
  can still do it.
—And I have perfect control
  over my bowels and bladder.
—I can feel it too. Just like
  you.

—In fact I think I can feel it
  more than other people.
—You do believe in being nice
  to cripples, don't you?
—Making it with me should
  really be interesting.
—At least I think it will. I
  haven't done it with someone
  else since I beat off with
  Homer in 1947.
—You can guess that I am sort
  of frustrated.

—I'm not very experienced, but
  I've thought about it a lot.
—Once you get over the social
  hang-ups, it's probably a
  kick.

— I mean in the summer! I'll
bet the winters aren't
too nice here!

— You want to be a technician.
How interesting!
— Yes, you have to go to
school to do anything
nowadays.
— You say you want to live in
California.
— What is it they say, "California is filled with
fruits and nuts?"
— It's a growing state,
though. Lots of oppor-
tunity.
— You know, you have nice
eyes.

— I don't know how to say
this, but I am very
attracted to you. I
don't believe in beating
around the bush. Would
you be willing to go off
with me to one of the
hotels downtown, so we can
stay together for the night?
I'll pay for it. I really
wish you would.
— O.

— Hey, you know we ought to
pick up a bottle of ab-
sinthe and shack up for
the night.
— You wouldn't beat me up,
would you?
— Or murder me?

— You can never tell, in this
world.
— You know, even a pervert can
be tender. I could be very
tender with you.
— Your face is a mess, but your
eyes are terrific.

— I swear, I can't stop looking
at you in the shower. You're
so very beautiful.
— I don't know how to say
this, but I am very
attracted to you. I
don't believe in beating
around the bush. Would
you be willing to go off
with me to one of the
hotels downtown, so we can
stay together for the night?
I'll pay for it. I really
wish you would. Please.
— O shit. I really blew this
one. What's wrong with me?

Tom didn't really do anything radical. He just finished up his soup, and went out. Whenever we met after that, in the hallway, in the bathroom, he looked the other way. The shit. Didn't know what he was missing. Twins joined at the hips. The only person in the world who could adore him for his war-zone, love him for the part of himself that he loathed. *Video meliora, proboque, deteriora sequor . . .*

153

CHAPTER XXI

In London, I go to work for the Anti-Slavery and
Aborigines' Protection Society. Me: at the Anti-Slavery Society! A charming and arcane organization,
founded in 1810 by the Pitts. Board of Directors all
stone deaf with age. Money coming in by dribs and drabs
from Quakers here and there, so that the director, an eccen-
tric love of a gentleman by the name of Cmdr. Fox-Pitt, can
turn it subtly to financing occasional revolutions south of the
equator. I am the only one in that organization who
can make the 1923 Smith-Corona work, and I find myself
typing up constitutions for nations which are, or will be,
emerging to their own sun independence. I take notes at the
monthly board meetings, and report each time that 87-year-
old Lady Droll turns her hearing aid up too loud, getting
feedback.

I, and my friend Diana, and a few other volunteers, freezing in that unheated Denison House, us downstairs from the
Over Forty Ladies Society and the King Wilhelm VI Friendship Society, having tea from the hob at four each afternoon,
and watching the nuns at the Catholic Ladies School across
the way lifting their habits as they go up and down
the fire escape, the only route between their classrooms.

It is a relaxed, easy time. I fall in so easily with the gentle
revolutionaries of Gentle England. I listen to the BBC Third
programme, wonder where American radio went wrong,
live with a poor couple in Kensington, argue American politics, jazz, economic theory, the meaning of life, Eisenhower,
Dulles, Salinger, Kerouac, the U.S. African Policy, Korea.

One Wednesday evening, I go to the Metro Turkish Baths of Soho. At some expense to my dignity, I have disrobed in a cubicle. Pulling about uneasily on my crutches, towel barely hung about the pelvic girdle, I make my way to the steam room, where, before several presumably naked Englishmen, I sit on the warm marble bench, exposed for all to see.

There may be four or five men in the room with me. I can't be too sure, because along with my other cards, I have been dealt a severe case of myopia and astigmatism (20/400). Without my spectacles, I am unable to differentiate between a cow patty and a craw-daddy, much less the physical attributes of the big pale blurs who sit steaming in this hot steam room. I await a revelation.

It comes in the form of a white walrus sitting next to me. He looks at me. At least, I think he looks at me, although he may be looking above or below me. I can't be sure. He moves closer. I squint my eyes in order to defeat my blindness. It does no good. I may be seeing a pale fat man with little bunches of ginger hair all over his forearms, or I may be looking at the slim body of young Keats. He may or may not have saphenous veins Christmas decorations below the ankles. He may or may not be a pudgy, egg-soft blob of a man, captivated by this lovely cripple who, so uneasily, awaits his fate.

The English gentleman sighs heavily in my direction. It is a sigh, a sigh of sighs, that comes from the heart, and from the gastric areas as well. It is a sigh that contains the weight of generations of loneliness and self-abuse; and, as well, the unmistakable air of unholy rot. It is a sigh that could or should make the blind to see, the deaf to hear, the halt and lame to walk. It also could easily strip the blossoms, leaves, and bark from a cherry tree at twenty paces. I am overwhelmed.

I guess it takes me a full five minutes to navigate the distance between the old geezer and my locker. My short stay in the steam room has coated my feet with sweat; this, combined with the snot, sputum and boogers that line the marble floor gives a certain excitement to my exit. "It would be just the place to fall," I think; "here in this sleazy steam bath, with these perverts all around, watching my descent." I, felled by the great grey green greasy Limpopo floor, in a clatter of crutches, the towel unveiling me and my nervous sensibilities to an army of queers who probably are more fortunate than I, I would hope, being able to see more than two or three inches past the nose.

It usually takes me some minutes to get various oddments of equipment and clothing about my body. In this case, I set the indoor speed dressing record, and am on the street two minutes later, rosy-cheeked and unviolated, away from the Metro Turkish Baths, unbathed, sweaty, and yes, frustrated. As always.

England is such a rock. That very night, as I am lurching out of the Steam Baths, I lurch into a few pubs for a few pints, making myself garishly drunk. I stop in a back alley to pee. A bobby comes up to me and tells me he is going to arrest me for voiding myself in public. The London cold, no street level pisser within miles, my bladder shrunk to the size of a pencil, and this bastard wants to arrest me for crimes against nature. Victorian England. The Gibralter of 19th Century morality.

The next evening I take a boat for Amsterdam. I go, again, to the Youth Hostel. Ah, those unhostile youth. Germans, Dutch, Scandinavian, a scattering of Americans. Their ruddy cheeks and ruddier bums and sweet sweaty limbs in the showers in the morning. The thighs, the pectorals, the femurs, the lacunae of support systems: the backbone.

The backbone. I must be a backbone junky. I love them. I nibble on them for breakfast, suck on them at lunch, gnaw on them with my tea. I sup on them at supper, gobble them up with my milk and cookies at bedtime. And at night, after a hard day's work in the showers, what with my desires and all, I sleep with sugarplum visions of them, wrapping my poor old bones about those bones in bed. The backbone.

My pride. At its best when it has a Christmas wrapping of epidermis, slightly freckled o'er with a touch of sun.

The sacred backbone, with its cross-spar of clavicle. That's my religion, my god. I abase myself here at the foot of your white cross of marrow, you great bony divinity you, rising so tall above humble me. Praise Lord Osteogenesis! The bone is my sheathing. I shall not roam. I lay down to feed on you in green pastures. Surely, marrow and ossification shall follow me all the days of my life, and I shall live amidst centrums and pedicules forever. Amen.

I almost slit my throat shaving while ogling these lads in the mirror. O the places they set up for our eyes. The army showers, the prison barracks, the prep school gyms, the youth hostels all over the world. My body may be unsatiated, but my eyes are filled to overflowing with sheer raw naked flesh-pinkness. I caress each inch of flesh with my vision. I must have the most powerful optic nerves in all of creation. Almost as powerful as the extrinsic and intrinsic muscles of my tongue. I move with my tongue, licking a hundred steaming bodies, tickling them to death. My tongue passes over thighs and armpits and bellies and cheeks and backs and ears and, yes, feet. I swear I must have the strongest tongue in the West.

(I walk on my tongue. I move body on soft lips. Words are my legs and feet.

(I move others as well. Speech, my speech, becomes the power of my desire. Aspirations transform themselves into miles, deeds, motion, action, money, feeling, change. Sound moves through windpipe, and I please, offend, appall, amuse. I become my mouth; mouth becomes action.

(I move about the city, the world, on my tongue, lashing like a snake. I move me everywhere. Aspirations are transformed into action. Air moves through larynx, gilded and glided by that tongue, the sweet snake of want. I sculpt with my tongue: pleasing, demanding, questioning, destroying. I become my mouth.

(I travel great distances on my words. I travel across rooms, down the street, into other cities, other countries; I surmount continents, oceans, moons, stars, worlds. I float on butterfly tongue. I soar on noun, adjective, adverb. I am the verb master—see, feel, hear, act, get, move, do. My tongue and my brain pull the world, and me, through space.

(Since my words are my feet—I cannot use the subtleties of body to communicate. There can be no sly movement of torso and thigh to indicate interest. I cannot tiptoe across the room to surprise; I cannot move body from chair to punctuate a sentence. I cannot kneel to one I adore— and I cannot entwine with a web of movements and bodily juxtapositions—body to body—as the rest of the world does, in its elaborate dance of love.

(My ceremony of passion must be a declaration of passion, a mound of verbalizations, a brief of enticements formed by tongue, not a bit by swing of hip and thigh and dancing motion, dancing, circles in dancing about the one I would be about to love. I am basebound to chair or bed.

(The cripples of the world are thus frozen by a double sun. We may be desperate for the fire of love—but the system is turned against us. We prisoners are not allowed to move in on passion.

(All we have are our tongues and brains. The power of manipulation and persuasion of the spoken word. Out of the wire-box brain must come our glottal dance of passion.)

Alone I visit the Museum Willet-Holthuysen and wonder how I can find a Protean child to give me a chance to love. I ride the yellow, double-jointed street cars, eat pickled wurst in front of the Binnen Gasthuis, and wonder if there will be any one, ever, who will recognize my beauty, under all the jackets, glasses, shoes, braces, corsets, crutches: one who will see the beautiful American with a raw and stunning flower of self, waiting to be plucked.

I have heard of a bar in Amsterdam, the Can-Can. I had been to a gay bar before, only you didn't call them "gay" then. It was a homosexual bar if you thought you were, and a fruit-bar if you thought you weren't. I had gone to one in

New Orleans, called Candy Lee's. I went there when I finally decided to hang it up on my marriage, and my daughter, and the straight and narrow.

Candy Lee's is in the *Vieux Carre*. I drive there, park four blocks away, in case any of my friends (I know three people in town) might see me. It is dim and dark. The action is supposed to take place in the annex, behind the main bar. I am very nervous. I keep wondering if the police will come in, check for my identification (which I conveniently left in my apartment). They will try to find out my name, where I live, and then take me off to jail, where I will be forced to stay with all the thieves and prostitutes for six or eight months. I am sorry officer. I am just out on the town. I didn't mean anything. I don't know what came over me officer. I have never been in a place like this before. You say it's a "queer" bar. I *thought* the people in here looked a little strange. I had no idea. I am from back east. We don't have things like this in Pennsylvania. I can scarcely believe it. Why do they let it stay open, do you imagine? You are going to take me down and book me? Wait a minute. I didn't know what I was doing. Really, you believe me, don't you? Please, don't put me in prison, officer. Can't you see I've been in prison for years. Please don't put me in jail, officer. Please.

I order a drink, then another, then another. They are playing Edith Piaf on the juke-box:

> *Allez venez milord*
> *Vous asseoir à matable*
> *Il fait si froid dehors*
> *Ici c'est confortable . . .*

The drinks are being served by Candy Lee. He is wearing fuchsia fingernail polish. He has huge green sparkly galaxy earrings, green spiders on his ears. His southern accent mixes with his effeminate ways.

"Fuck," I think to myself. "O fuck: if I go queer, I'm going to have to wear fingernail polish, black fingernail polish. I'll have to wear spider earrings, lavender silk shirts. Shit," I think: "I'm going to hate that." I try to get out the door. They keep moving it around. When I go to the left, it goes to the right, when I go to the right, it goes left. "These queer bars are devilish," I think. I finally order the door to stop moving. On the way back to the car I wet my pants. "What did those fruits put in my drink," I think, as the piss runs hot down my legs. My pants leg turns cold, slaps against my leg. My shoe goes squish with each step. "They put pisswater in the drinks," I think to myself. "They'll probably make me wear chartreuse lipstick, and big pats of rouge on each cheek," I think: "They're going to expect me to talk with a lisp, wiggle my hips."

I drive home carefully by lodging my tires in the street-car tracks and singing loudly to myself:

> *Come come milord*
> *Sit with me at the table*
> *Outside it is so cold*
> *Here you will be comfortable . . .*

Pretty good, I think. I'll be a good bar-hustling singer. I can get a job easy, with my four legs and my friendly ways and my crossed eyes. "Shit, I should just turn around and go back to Candy Lee's and ask for a job."

I don't, though. It's too late. I don't have time. I have to get home without being killed by every Neanderthal driver on the road. New Orleans is filled with them, I tell you.

"Why do I have to force myself to do these things," I wonder, as I go in the Can-Can Bar. "Why can't I just go up to some beauty on the street, confess my love, and go home for a night of passion. What's wrong with this society?"

I sit in the Can-Can and drink mug after mug of beer, special CO_2 foam for the fires of lust. A tubby gentleman, looking a bit like Nikita Khrushchev, sits at the table next to me, commences to stare at me. "Wait until I tell them at the Kremlin where the Chairman is hanging out," I say to myself. "Just like some pet store; and I'm in a cage, being checked out by the customer," I think.

I am waiting for someone to pay attention to me, come sit at my table, drink beer with me, talk about the St. Matthew's Passion of Bach (in the Scherchen version) or perhaps comment on the middle, pastoral period of Auguste Renoir. Or maybe we'll get in a heated discussion on nuclear power. Me with this bomb of passion, inside myself, treated to the gossamer of words.

Khrushchev moves to the next table over, back into my line of sight. I think on the Politburo, and the wart on his middle left cheek, the hair that grows riotously out of his ears. I struggle up, repair to the bar. They are playing Judy Garland, about her being born in a trunk somewhere. "Why are these fruit bars so anti-intellectual?" I wonder. "Why don't they have a jukebox that plays 'O Come Ye Sons of Art!' and 'Zephiro Torno?'" Someone else drops coins into the jukebox. We get "Itsy Bitsy Teeny Weenie Yellow Polka Dot Bikini," not once, but five times, in a row. A thick-eyed Dane sits down next to me. He is drunk, but well-dressed. His tie is awry. He puts his hand on my shoulder and starts crying. He tells me about his one-time American lover, Bob (or Bill, or Sam, or Dan) Walker.

"I loved dat man, I did," he tells me. "We make love everywhere, even in the dirtiest places, the publik toilets. I loved dat man. Have you ever had anyone piss all over you? Every morning he would get up and show me his class piktures, and cry over them, and show me the ones he loved, all three months he was here, and he gave me an inlay ivory piano. I loved dat man. . . ."

He asks me if I know Bob (or Bill, or Sam, or Dan) Walker, "of California," and I say vaguely, vaguely. His already-veined chin quivers, and his thick unseeing eyes cloud over, and I think he is going to break down completely. He caresses my arm, leans heavily on me, and says "I love you. You know dat? You remind me of Bob Walker. I love you, and would like to fuck you, you know. Do you love me?"

Here I am; here is what I come to the Old World for, this is what I have travelled so far to get, this is the love I am looking for. I have moved myself and my mind and my body such a long distance, and here it is: if I want it. I have here come to a point where I can choose, choose if I want *not* to continue being alone, and lonely, without a lover.

The desire—that vulture: the one that has driven me across whole continents, forced me out of the country of my birth, given me so many thousand hard nights of sleeplessness. Here I am at the climax, the point-needle star of my existence. A Dane, heavy with Beer and Love, will do anything I want: fuck me blue (if that is what I desire;) piss all over me; suck me off behind the statues in the Hortus Botanicus. Or, at worst, at least be a comfort and a warmth to me on the cold hard driving rail of my passion.

My search, if I want, is over. At last. If I want. I am at the swivel of my life where desire can meet satiation. If I want.

So what do I do? I stand, shake the hand of the good rheumy Hans who has so much to offer me, and go out alone, by myself, onto Fazanten Weg, back to the Youth Hostel where I can suffer, sniffing around the showers, loaded with the charge of unfulfillable desire.

The fourth dimension. Of counter-space. A new dimension of sexual and physical crippledness. I have found a man in a country where man love is no crime; a man who is alone and who needs someone to play with. And I run away from him. As fast as my two arms will carry me.

CHAPTER XXII

In Madrid, I stay in the Madrid Youth Hostel. It is out in the West end of the city. It is a fleabag. The mattresses are so dusty that it is hard to stay on them without coming down with catarrh. Everyone moves so slowly. The main office is also a bar. The Hostel receipts are kept in a defunct refrigerator with a chain about it. The major occupation seems to be sitting on the front steps, watching curs lick each other's speckled nuts, listening to the Falange students next door practice their military songs. I want to visit the Prado. Someone tells me that if I walk behind the Hostel, for a few blocks, I will find a trolley line that will take me into the city.

I set off on a long journey. There is nothing behind the Hostel but a dusty field, extending as far as I can see. And there is nothing in the field: no benches, no place to sit, no place to drink, no place to rest. The sun is merciless.

I walk for an hour before I figure out that I am lost. I can't believe it. I thought I was on the outskirts of a major city of Europe. But I am out lost in some terrible field. I have hiked more than a mile, and I seem no closer to the streetcar I am looking for.

Countless small bushes catch at my crutches. Some places the dirt is soft, so I have to go slowly, very slowly so I won't fall over. There are endless small hills for me to go up and down. Each one slows me down.

My hands begin to hurt from the constant pressure of the crutches. Jaggers of pain run up my arm. It feels as if I have bared every nerve in my arms. I am sweating, and the sweat runs down my forehead, into my eyes. I have to stop each few steps to wipe the sweat from my eyes. Then I put sore hands on crutch again, and walk a few more steps, then I must stop to wipe my eyes again.

The brace begins to rub painfully against my knee. My one good foot begins to drag. I can feel my feet swelling. Where the fuck am I? I am alone on some huge abandoned field.

I am thirsty. Bugs fly in my ears, in my hair, occasionally in my eyes. My shoulders feel like I am lifting eight hundred pound weights. I know, at this juncture, that I cannot make it back to the Youth Hostel. It is too far behind me. I must have been walking over two hours. But how much further ahead is the street? I can see nothing but the field stretching on endlessly. I can hear nothing but the sawing of bugs. Suppose they were lying to me? Suppose they said the road was this way, but they really meant the other way?

I cannot sit down and rest. I can only stop and lean on my crutches, but the bugs become maddening. There is absolutely no way I can sit on the ground and ever get back up again. That is one of the conditions of my infirmity: once on my feet, I stay on my feet until a conveniently high bench, seat, chair or bed is available. There are none of those here. If I were to fall, I could never get back up: not in a thousand years. Then I should have to drag myself along on my ass, stopping to pull my crutches after me. It might take days.

Each step is torture. My shoulders are inflamed, my back is rubbed raw against the corset, my feet are swollen beyond belief, my hands feel gnarled and clenched. Sooner or later one of my arms will give out on me entirely, and I will slip and fall. And that will be that. I have seen no one on this wide expanse. I am not even on a trail. Why in the fuck did I come this far? Why didn't I ask someone else? Why didn't I turn back when I could?

No one knows. No one cares. I have no friends, no companions. I am totally alone in the world. I am some 6,000 miles from home, on some desolate field, with no help in sight. I will drop from exhaustion, die here of thirst. No one will miss me: they won't know or care at the Hostel. I may be on this field for years before they find my corpse, ant-eaten. "Who does this strange body belong to?" they will ask. "What was he doing here, out on Desolation Field, so far from any help? What foolishness made him come out here?"

I feel so alone, so desperate. I want to weep at the sheer folly of it. How could I be so stupid! Just when I was about to get some place in my life where I would be happy. What's wrong with me. What's *wrong* with me?

As I stumble along, I hear the voices, see the things that happened to me so long ago. One memory comes especially clear: it is one of me in a storm, when I was nine or ten years of age.

A hurricane has come up the coast of Florida, turning the whole waterfront area into a shrieking holocaust. The trees move and wave, tidal waves of wind in the branches. The river, normally so quiescent, turns angry. Waves flood the lawn.

My father stays home from the office, bangs around the house, nailing doors and windows shut. He fires up the Sterno to make some coffee. "Jesus!" he says. "Jesus, what a storm!" He picks me up, carries me outside down to the riverfront park. We can see the waves crashing in through the holes in the bulkhead, smashing brown foam over the seawall, into the park. The wind snatches at our hair, pulls at our clothes.

"Jesus!" he keeps saying, below me. I am riding on his shoulders, nine feet tall above the seastorm waves. I feel the warmth of him under me, his big red leathery neck between my boys' thighs. I hold onto the crown of his head with my boys' hands. "Jesus!" he says, wading the mountainous waves breaking ashore.

As I plunge through the sand waves of Desolation Field, he rides with me, up on my shoulders. I talk to him to keep his spirits up. "It's terrible, isn't it, dad?" I say to him. I never was able to call him "dad" while he was alive.

"This is an awful spot to be in, isn't it?" I am worried that he will think we won't make it. "Don't worry, dad," I tell him. "It's rough, what with the storm and everything, but we'll get to the other side soon enough. Please don't worry." I can feel him riding so lightly on my back, so confident in what I am doing.

"I am sorry I was such a sissy all while I was growing up," I tell him. "I'm sure you wanted to have a man for a son, but it just wasn't in the cards. I really wanted to be your little man, I did, dad. I wanted to do everything you told me, be someone you could be proud of, could tell your friends about when you were playing golf at the country club. I did my best. You may not have known that then, but I hope you understand it now. I couldn't help being a sissy; it just seemed the easiest way to survive being a kid and all."

He doesn't say anything, him riding up there above me: but I know he is listening. I have to take care of him. I have to get him past this heat and sand and desert. I have to get him somewhere so he'll be safe. I don't want him to have to stay here. I have to show him how brave I can be, when the chips are down, when our lives are at stake. I want him to see that.

"Look," I tell him, "it'll be all right. Please don't worry. It's not to worry." He always used to say that: "It's not to worry." He knows what is happening, and he knows I am doing everything to keep him from falling down in this field.

"I don't complain, now, do I dad?" I say. "Remember, when I was a kid, I used to cry all the time. When Radford Lovett and Jack Hines used to hit me, chase me, I would bust out crying, and run home. You were disgusted, I could see you thinking 'How did I raise such a panty-waist?' You didn't like that, did you?

"But see how much braver I am now. I don't complain. I'm a good cripple. I never ask people to help me. I never ever cry, no matter what I am feeling inside. I'm so tough. I'm so brave. I'm a good cripple. I may be angry, and pissed off that I can't run back to the Youth Hostel, but most of all I am brave. Most people would say, 'What have I done to deserve all this?' Not me. I don't lie down and whine. I am a man now, aren't I dad? You know I am a man now, don't you dad? You do admire me, don't you, dad?"

The field washes out from my vision. It is like I have been lifted above this plain of white sand. I don't even feel myself moving anymore: it is like I am flying. "He is pulling me up," I think. My dad is lifting me up like an angel. He is riding lightly on my shoulders, so lightly that he is pulling me up off the rough and coarse ground, as if he were some helium balloon, painted with great swatches of red and gold and silver. He is carrying me from this desert.

He is quiet, so quiet that I scarcely know he is there. But I know he is listening. I know he is going to hear every word I say. "I'm sorry I didn't cry the day you died," I tell him. "Truly, I'm sorry. You know why I didn't cry then, or any-time after. It was because I wanted them to see how strong you had made me, how I wasn't affected by anything, how I was a true man. I didn't know then, but I know now, that you were just a little boy, like me. I didn't know it at the time, but now I do. That's why I just held my head in my hands and pretended to be grieved, but didn't cry. I didn't know that you were a boy, dad. My poor boy. They came in the school and told me that you had drowned, in your own blood, the split aorta had drowned you—and I didn't show any feelings whatsoever because I had come to be such a man. You understand now, don't you?"

He doesn't say anything, my dad doesn't. But he hears. I know that. He rides up there, his eyes squinting in the brilliant sunlight. His face is grave. He understands what I am trying to tell him. I think he is proud of me for the journey I am making, such a long and painful journey. I don't weaken. I do it on my own, and I don't cry. I am a brave cripple, carrying on, against all odds, carrying on the war against despair and lying down and dying. Me: no longer a sissy! He understands.

I talk to him so loudly that I almost don't hear it. I swear, it's right there at the edge of my consciousness, but I don't hear it—not at first anyway. It's a trolley bell, off in the distance, ahead of me. A trolley bell! My pains vanish. I hear the sound of metal wheels on metal tracks. I climb painfully up a hill. And there it is: a wooden, slab-sided, double-ended Toonerville trolley, with the single carriage drawing power from the wire that yokes overhead. What a homely, lovely sight! Jesus God, I am saved! I have been taken through the trail of trials, the trial of fire: my muscles turned fire within me, my head split with the agony of the sun and fever. I made it, by Jesus. I made it over dirt, through brush, across hills, and ants, and bugs and thirst and pain and anguish. The Passion of Madrid's Desolation Field. I know what it is like, to be lost, to be climbing some mountain.

When I read about the mountain climbers, climbing over some impossible height, over impossible gorges, with their arms torn by the weight of their own bodies, their eyes glazed with the blast of the sun, their fingers ripped and bleeding: I know! I was there.

When I read of their endurance, and courage, and persistence, I know! I have been there. When they show me movies, when I read of some major climb to 17,000 feet, with the rocks all about, giving no succor, with each step possibly the last, where one misstep may mean that they come crashing down to their doom, and yet, with bravery of the highest order, they continue, continue to the heights: I know what they are talking about. Dear God! We have been there together. Together, we, the mountain climbers, the brave, tanned, hardened, hardy, courageous mountain climbers and I have scaled great heights, unbelievable heights, taking us to the very edge of death: we have gone there together, them on their delicate spider-web ropes, me on my delicate spider-web crutches and brace.

Together we have pushed our bodies beyond endurance to the veriest heights, gotten there despite all odds. And, once there, we find what we are looking for: the great wide-open eye of god. The pupil as clear as any white hole of space, the iris made of the same stuff as the heart of glaciers, the unblinking, never-changing, never-moving, all-seeing eye—neither unfriendly nor friendly, neither loving nor hating. Contemplative. Aloof. Wise. Cutting through all the foolishness and pride and fanaticism and occlusion—all those dark clouds with which we surround the innermost isle of our beings. It is there waiting for us, god's clear eye.

And there we find it, at the end of the journey across deserts, up the highest peaks. There, alone, always awaiting us there, once we have been dogged enough (and foolish enough) to scale the last of the great heights. God's Sweet Eye of Chance!

CHAPTER XXIII

I have come to Spain because of a chance conversation in a bar in Copenhagen. "You'll love it there," they told me. "It's so cheap!" they said. After a week in Madrid, I find it to be cheap, and noisy, and dirty. I take a flight south, to Málaga, to the warm, worn edge of the Mediterranean.

I get a room in the Hotel Niza, just above the main square. It is late Sunday afternoon. I take a rest in bed. I wake at nine in the evening. There is a tremendous noise, babbling, yelling, laughing. Must be a national holiday. I go to the Victorian metal-work balcony overlooking Plaza Juan Primo de la Rivera. There are hundreds and hundreds of people walking around the square: laughing, talking, stopping for a *copita* of wine. And looking. Looking at each other. It is later that I find out that this is a typical evening paseo in the southern village of Málaga.

I go to look for my cottage by the sea. I take the narrow gauge *ferrocarril* to the West, to Torremolinos. Already the edge of tourists is turning the town into English-French-German-Scandinavian heaven. No poverty here: the people look fat and happy. The bartenders try to speak to me in English, instead of Spanish.

The next day, I go east, to the town of Vélez. On the way the train dips along the beach. I see a series of small cottages, obviously closed up for the winter. Each of them has garden, flowers, bars on the windows. On the way back, I get off at the station nearest to these cottages. The town is named Rincón de la Victoria. It is ragged and dirty. In the old part of town, the streets are of beaten dirt. There is the smell of shit, and stagnant waters, and cheap food being cooked in olive oil.

169

On the other side of the station are the twenty or thirty summer cottages lining the white beach. They look to be clean and neat, tile terraces, the bougainvillea and white juniper bloom everywhere. Most of them appear to be vacant. I stop an old lady with grey hair in a bun and bad teeth. Her name is María. Yes, most of the cottages are vacant. Yes, they can be rented in the winter, she knows most of the owners. O, most of them go for twenty, thirty dollars a month.

I have come home. I have come home to Rincón de la Victoria. My home. The home I have been looking for so long, so very very long. Home.

In 1960, to get from Málaga (Pop: 250,000) to Rincón de la Victoria (Pop: 800) you take the train. Eighteen miles. Forty-five minutes. Narrow gauge. Engine: built in Belgium, 1906. Steam puffing. Real fireman to feed real coals to a real fire under the boiler. Coaches designed by the Great Wooden Car Company, 1885. Cowboy and Indian stuff. Puffing alongside the sea, or through the narrow tunnels carved in the rocks. Whoowee. Puffing alongside the sea, the great Mediterranean Sea, the cradle of civilization, the cradle of my hopes.

Rincón de la Victoria. The edge, the beach, the inlet, the cove called Victoria. Sun, all day, every day. White sands on the beach outside, except where the natives shit (they have no indoor plumbing; only the beach cottages sport that luxury.)

Train runs in front of house. Eight times a day. Puff, wheeowheee. Hear it coming from El Palo, the whistle echoing on the rocks to the west. Stop at the spare Rincón de la Victoria station for a few minutes, unless the conductor wants a glass of *tinto*. Then it stays for twenty minutes. Finally, getting up steam, it barrels in front of my house, right in front of my front door on the beach goes this steam engine, this finely designed toy train, with sparks and steam and belching smoke, wheeoowhee, and the three wooden coaches rattle and creak afterwards, so that I can hear them until they make the grade over the hills, over towards Vélez. Shheeeowhee.

House: three rooms. Front bedroom for the ocean lovers.

Back bedroom for the hill lovers. Living room for the fireplace lovers. Looking out over the Mediterranean (or have I said that already?) Front tile porch over the sea, the beautiful sea, by the seaside, by the beautiful sea.

Garden. Bushes, trees, flowers, green gold yellow red. Bars on the windows. Small dark kitchen. Teeny refrigerator, teeny *butano* stove. Enough room, plenty of room for this tall Americano with the thick James Joyce glasses, the green-ribbed high-neck sweater, the two high silvery *muletas* that he walks on, and his dusty brown shoes.

Plenty of room in that cottage for the Americano who comes with one suitcase, and one small portable Royal typewriter which he pounds for four or five hours a day. Plenty of room for the Americano.

Sweet cottage. There beside the sea (did I already say that?) My love nest. The place where I will learn to love. For the first time in my life, learn to love another. $30/month for house. $20/month for cook. $15/month for maid. $50/month for food. $40/month for lover.

I would guess that we passion-nuts of the world, those of us with frustration mounted into the stratosphere, will go anywhere in the world to take care of our nuts. If we can't get it in Durham or Boise, we go to Berkeley or Washington. If we can't get it there, we go to London or Copenhagen. If that doesn't make it, we go to North Africa, the Philippines, or southern Italy. In the tradition of horny American soldiers and travellers of the centuries, we go anywhere in the world for it, and, if necessary, we buy it. Holesale.

And we aren't picky. If there is a singular fact about the children of Hermann Lust, it is that we are democratic. Abraham Lincoln and Susan B. Anthony are our spiritual parents. We look to the groin, not to education, class, culture, learning, background, job, sire and dam of our lovers.

We horny toads! The ultimate democrats. We will embrace the black or the brown or the yellow, as well as the pink and white and ivory. We will lavish our passion equally on Chinese, African, Mongolian, Indian, Esquimaux, Bushman, Latino, Turk, Moslem, Jew, Hindu, Buddhist, Catholic, Swedenborgian, Cultist, N'Khosa, Serbo-Croat. The pubes are the key: not face, nor nose, nor shade, nor hair, nor eye.

Radical sexualists! That's us! In love with the children of the land—the children of the snows and the children of the dirt. We caress thighs that are olive, jet black, tan, or pale. We lay white face to chest the color of marble or the color of night. We rub cheeks across cheeks that are callipygian (as in Hottentot) or flat-wall (as in the lean Greek). We allow our fingertips to pluck gently at hair that is black, curly, bushy, or long and blond. We will rub nose-to-nose with the Prognathous or the Orthognathous. We will nibble ears which are tiny, tuberose, turquoise-encrusted, or tawdry.

The groin, the great leveller. The universal dork. We scarcely consider the rest of the baggage. We care not whether its master is peasant field worker, busboy, student, carpenter, barkeep, slum-dweller, painter, grape-picker, singer, sander, swimmer, or shepherd. The Democracy of Passion. We, the children of Hermann Lust and La Passionara. We will bed down with the coolie still wet from the rice-field, the poet with ink on his fingertips, the bracero with sweat on his back, the lad from the wheatfields with straw in his hair, the waiter with wine on his breath, the gigolo with *lupus vulgaris* on his face.

Our love is universal and all-encompassing, if not all-encumbering. We put up with the smell of fish, cows, oil, sweat, vomit, grease, whiskey, garlic, dust, perfume, sheep, body odor, and pigshit so that we might come to that six-inch square haunt of forbidden magic which lies so deliciously and so dangerously between the two crests of the pelvis; that cradle endlessly rocking, the sacred sacrum.

We warp and distort and twist all—even our own delicate sense of breeding—so that we can adore that precious square of flesh and matted hair and protrusions about which so much has been written, so much felt, so much thought, so much dreamed. The thirty-six square inch battlefield which, even more than Waterloo, Gettysburg, Flanders, has inspired, trapped, imprisoned, debilitated, maddened, ruined, and murdered so many humans.

The Plains of Pubis. We—the democratic battlers for its freedom, to free it from the captivity of levis, buckskins, trousers, shorts, jockstraps. Giving the groin the freedom it so well deserves. We—the Pitts of Passion. The Justinians of Jizz. The Ovids of Orgasm. The Robespierres of Rumps. The Patrick Henrys of Pubic Hair, the Benjamin Franklins of Bum Fucking.

We—the queer and perverted lust-seekers of the world— hereby announce our opposition to any and all oppression resulting from class, social standing, or previous conditions of penal servitude. We stand here, behind our bushes, in our closets, under our beds, to declare that we are the democratic libertarian satyrs of the universe. Reciting our credo: that all are born of passion, born with passion, born to passion. This passion makes us unique, with one need, indivisible, and in the pursuit of it, we will tolerate no prejudice, no slavery, except the Slavery of Lust.

We, the ultimate Democrats of the Dingus, seeking our all without limit and restraint. Long may she wave.

Salvadore Estaban Jesús Rodriguez. Where the hell are you now, you delicious frog you? My first true honey-pie. What a bod! Do you think of me, Salvadore? I'll *bet* you do!

I take the train to Málaga to place a want ad in the local rag, *El Sol*. "Inválido," says the copy, "Necesito chico para trabajar, y dar ayuda." I need a kid to work, and give assistance. "Llama Vd. a Sr. Lorenzo, Calle Misericordia 33, Rincón de la Victoria." I don't like the word "inválido" too much. Sounds like "invalid," as in not valid. But that's the word given in my Caesar's Spanish-English dictionary as the word for "cripple."

Salvadore! What are you doing now? You and your twenty-eight inch waist. And those sad eyes. You come to see me in too many present-day fantasies, Salvadore. And you don't even exist anymore. At least, not as *I* remember you.

173

I am nervous as I take the ad to the *Sol.* There are too many stairs. All are highly polished. The journey to heaven is very slippery. And it's a typical Spanish industrial hallway. Lots of fanfare and garishness when you come in the door, then, when you get upstairs, to the heart, it is small, grubby, overcrowded. Great bales of newsprint everywhere. The newspaper itself looks to be printed on rub-don't-blot paper. Typical Spanish daily.

My hands shake. I give over my ad to the clerk. He puzzles over it. Looks at it, rereads it, takes it over to someone else, a fat guy, to look at. Goddamn! Do they know I am a fruit already? Trying to lure some young sweetie into my love nest. Do they know that I am trying to get someone into my paradise house by the sea so that I can play with his peter? Are they going to call the police? Maybe I should get out of here. A small change. The word "inválido" is invalid. The preferred word is "mutilado." As in mutilated. That is the currency. I stop by the drug store, buy some nerve pills, hurry home.

I am sitting in front of my portable typewriter, pretending to work, when the deluge begins. A deluge. Of bright-eyed and dusty young men. Also some of them not so dusty. All of them poor, and ragged, needing love, I mean, work. I examine them carefully as I am interviewing them. I look at their shanks, I mean their eyes, and faces. Are they hard workers? Are they to be trusted? Who comes with them? Will they rat on me? Are they the type to tell the police that I am running shaking hands up dusky, thin, beautiful limbs? Who can I trust? Anyone?

Forty young men. Straining, eager for work. Most of them desperately poor. There are four billion people on the earth, I think, give or take a hundred million (a hundred million!) Five hundred million, let us say, are at that attractive post-pubescent age. Now, half of these are young men (the rest women, we can discard them immediately); only a fourth of those (I am guessing now) are beautiful, lovable, not fat, or flatulent, or flabby. Of those, perhaps only half would be generous enough to enjoy my joy, or at least, would be ready to share the greatest glory of humanity with me, with frustrated, loveable old me. That's (let's see: divide 250,000,000 by two, then divide that by four, or is it eight, carry the five, drop three naughts), that brings it to sixty-two million, five hundred thousand young men on earth who are or could be someone that I am capable (or willing!) to love.

What possible harm, I think, can come to the world (this is my World View now) if I dip into the maelstrom of humanity and pick out one, only one, one very sweet young man (with nice eyes) and give him a taste of love, and money, and Saturday nights before the fire, sipping brandy and discussing the nature of man and the universe (and, perhaps, the latest soccer scores)? Just one, of 62,500,000, to love, and to talk to; to love as gently as I can. Is it, can it be, wrong?

I vowed that when I left the United States I would cater only to the demands of Hermann Lust. To hell with all my liberal teachings. After all, I think, you don't know how I have suffered for the past eight years. Being a cripple: that's the best excuse of all, right? After all, if they can come and snitch my body out of the bed so quickly (and so shamelessly), they might well do it again, even worse this time. I have to love myself, don't I?

Well, you know that these are the thoughts that flap heavily through my mind. But you know and I know that it is far more complicated than that. For each excuse, there is a counter-excuse. For each moral precept, there is a contrary. At times I feel like a Catholic retreat with a massive Jesuit dialogue going on, on some obscure tenet of morality, the yesses and the no's grinding on endlessly, wearing away the edge of my brain.

I am torn, and guilty, and anxious. But I am also in heaven. I am deluged with the young and the hopeful and the needy. There are acres of flesh around me. I talk to every one of my forty applicants. I take names, ages, previous job experiences, parents' jobs, live with parents? The work? O, I say, it will mean cutting some firewood. Taking care of the house. At night. Staying here in the house, beside the sea, for the night. Staying here in this house. With me. I have these nightmares ("pesadillas.") I just have to have someone here at night. With me. In the same room. Close at hand. In case of nightmare.

Forty pairs of eager eyes. Ranging in age from twelve to twenty. 'Twixt twelve and twenty. I eliminate the very young, and the ones that come with their mothers, sisters, fathers. Bad news. We cannot have the protected child. He might tell. Grey uniforms in the night. "Lo siento, señor. Hay que venir con nosotros. A la carcél." No parents, even the boorish old man who sits in my living room for an hour extolling the virtues of his gentle sloe-eyed sweetie of seventeen years and the torn pants. No parents at all.

I am still looking. Winnowing through the deluge. Everyone gets talked to. I need someone who is independent. Needy, but independent. And the body: it has to be perfect. We cripples don't like imperfection. We queers loathe imperfection. I am looking for the perfect poverty case.

Salvadore. Where the fuck are you? O, here you are. Standing at my door. You, one of the last to apply. Husky voice. Nice brown eyes. Pleasant face, although the nose is a little flat. Black hair. I know. At once. That you are the one. Salvadore. I know. At once. You don't. Not for awhile. There are some preliminaries first.

We talk for awhile. The usual questions. Seventeen years old. Good. Lives with grandmother. Father away, mother dead. Good. I mean, I'm sorry. But good, nonetheless.

I happen to mention to Salvadore that I have only been here a week, and I surely would like to try to swim in the Mediterranean. And Salvadore says at once that he loves swimming in the ocean. And I say why don't we try it. I need someone to help me out to the water, I tell Salvadore. He thinks that won't be too much of a problem.

We are in the bedroom. I am taking off my clothes. Salvadore is taking off his clothes. In front of me. He is to change into a swim suit I have found for him. Shirt off. Nice nice shoulders. Nice. Trousers off. Tight white jockey shorts, slipped off, just like that. I am blind.

Salvadore! I wish I could be with you just for a little bit, right now. Just to talk with you. You would be thirty-five now, thirty-six. Body starting to go. But we could chit-chat, about this and that. We did have some good times. And some bad.

You were Mr. Right. At the right time. I had been looking for Mr. Right for all these years. Me, stuck with Five-Finger Freddy, really wanting Salvadore. And here you are. In front of me. With all your clothes off. Trying to figure out which way is front, which way is back on the huge black swimsuit I have found for you.

Salvadore stands five-foot eight in the altogether. His shoulders are built by rigorous weight lifting (he is to tell me later). The complexion: olive, natural olive. The torso angles down to those impossibly small hips. Then, below the crotch (Jesus! Mary! and Joseph!) massive pillar legs. Fine black hair running down the legs to the feet, the flat feet. Salvadore: I kiss your flat feet. Stop wincing.

Do bolts jag out of heaven? When kind olive-skinned Salvadore takes off his white shorts, and puzzles with the bathing suit, do earths tremble and oceans rise up in black storms?

As Salvadore, blushing a little, a little shy, leans over to step into the too-large wet bathing suit, and his tiny ass appears full scale in my vision, and my glasses steam up: do the heavens rage? Does night eclipse day, do meteors swarm down to the beach at Rincón de la Victoria?

When, to get into the cold wet suit, he moves his hips a little and I can see his balls tighten, pull up with the cold of the suit: do earths well, do storms plow through the abyss, leaking blue and gold tangles of lightning into the smoking sky?

At the least, at the very least, when Salvadore stands triumphant with the comically large bathing suit pleated around his size twenty-eight waist, do I pitch myself from my bed of pain and kiss this child god from head to toe for the singular fact that, at least, he is here, where he belongs?

Do the gods billow their cheeks, do angels clap their wings, and cry out in heavenly unison: at last, Lorenzo, at goddamn last?

No. For one thing, I am hardly looking out the barred window to see what the angels are doing: I have to take care of myself. And anyway: do you think I am going to blow it at this stage, after all this work? "Que está mojada," I tell him, because the bathing suit is slightly damp, and cold. "¿Quieres partir ya?" I ask, shall we go to the beach?

He nods his head. His eyes are smelting liquid brown. His hair, above and below, is as black as night, as black as my soul: which has, by now, turned to lava. We go to the beach.

CHAPTER XXIV

I think we perform badly that day, at the edge of the Mediterranean, on the beach at Rincón de la Victoria. First of all, as I have told you, it is impossible for me to walk on the sand, my crutches get buried in the sand, up to the hilt. I keep spinning my wheels.

Although I have strengthened my legs enough that I can walk for short distances without my braces and shoes, on the white sands it is like going through molasses. And it is a long way from the cottage down to the water's edge. Then the water, O Christ. If nothing else puts a hiatus on my roiling passion, it is that fifty-eight degree water. The nectarine waters of the Mediterranean are secretly shipped in from the wastes of the Polar Ice Cap.

Which give me problems. I am easily subjected to leg cramps in cold water. So half the time I am with Salvadore, I am trying to swim; the other half of the time, I am pulling on legs and feet to untangle the tangled cramps in what remains of the muscles down there. It is a damn good thing I didn't drown my fool head in that ice bucket, although it would have given a certain *élan* to my life, to have drowned cold dead at the time when I was about to unlimber the old straight-shooter and get it on for two years of passion.

When I finally get out, I am so weakened by the cold that it takes a major act of strength for Salvadore and his weight-lift muscles to get me standing. He, a full seven inches shorter than me, trying to get me into the standing position, he pushing, I pulling, trying to get the crutches underarm so that we can make it back to the house. Our first embrace!

I don't give much of a damn. I could be treading on turds all the way back, and would think of them as golden posies: Salvadore has agreed to work three nights a week, for 500 pesetas a week. He will start the following night, so he can go back to the city and get his clothes. He will come and tend the fire of the house (not my soul). He will help me take my nightly bath (water has to be heated on the stove). He is to help me in the dark when I have nightmares.

Nightmares. Salvadore, I have been having these nightmares. For years and years and years. I think that there is no one in the world can love me. For years, I have been waking up screaming to that.

The Approach. There are speeches to prepare, words to look up in the dictionary ("I have no control over my hand." "Don't be afraid." "Why did you hit me?")

And, because I am me, and my world is so complicated, and everything I do that is meaningful to me is so complicated: there are contingencies, plans, counterplans, countercontingencies, counterunderplans. It is a mess. No, it is a siege of war. It is to be a real battle. The first that I have a chance of winning, the one I don't want to lose.

You've done the same things yourself, maybe with different goals, maybe with the same. If I were into corporate takeover strategy, with lawyers, stock options, proxies, legal battles: and if I put into them the same attention to detail I put into the seduction of Salvadore, I would probably be running ITT right now. Which would mean, if you know the corporate world, I wouldn't have to go out looking for Salvadores: they would be right there on my doorstep.

But I don't run ITT; all I run is me, and the machinery of my life. Be assured that I have every second of the seige planned. For the next night (no move) and the night after that (no move) and the night after that (no move) and the night after that (move!) I have to let Salvadore get a taste of his first 500 peseta bills before I spring it on him. I have to let him savor the feeling, for the first time in his life, of having money in his pocket. So he can buy those Fabian records that he likes so much. So he can be a rock and roll (he calls it "wreck-n-rohl") singer, which he wants so much.

Battle plans. Contingencies. Timing: delicate timing. The right approach. Don't be rash. If we blow this one. *If we blow this one, Lorenzo . . .*

One of my friends has said that the long-planned strategy seductions are the most beguiling. And, after all, in school I had studied *Pamela*, by Samuel Richardson (1689-1781), which is a 2,400 page exposition on how to approach the maidenhead. I am a good student, I have learned my lessons well. Salvadore has come for a week, faithfully at nine (he takes the last train from Málaga). He comes in, locks the doors and shutters, builds and lights the fire. We talk. I drink Anis del Mono, and he tells me about his life. With his grandmother. A few friends. A lonely person, who wants to be a singer.

At eleven or so, we repair to the bedroom. It goes without saying that I have trouble sleeping that week. I might make some groaning noises, so he will get used to the sound of me in nightmare.

X-night. I can hardly do anything all day, I am so jumpy. Maybe I shouldn't be doing this. What a cad I am: taking advantage of his poverty. Maybe he will call the police. Maybe he will leap out of bed, run out the door. Maybe he will tell me to get my fucking hands off of him. What's "fucking" in Spanish? I am so nervous.

Early evening. He will be here in half an hour. Maybe I should call this whole thing off. Maybe next week, or the week after. There's plenty of time. Maybe we should forget this whole piddling thing. What am I doing?

A familiar feeling. When I get close to some resolution, some favorable situation: I have this desire to kiss it off. A dozen times at the Can-Can Bar I am on the verge of asking someone to come home with me. Then I make up a hundred excuses not to do it. He's got funny eyes. Maybe he's a murderer, likes stabbing queers. I really don't feel like it tonight. I have a slight headache. I'm too drunk. He's too drunk. We won't be able to bring it off. He'll turn me down and I'll feel shitty for a week. All the familiar excuses I have been making for years to keep myself frustrated, and lonely, and horny.

Salvadore comes in the door on schedule. He locks it, bangs all the shutters closed, locks them, builds the fire. We talk. He hasn't told his grandmother he has a job yet. He tells her he is going to a "fiesta." A party. Three times a week. All night. Some party.

I yawn (patently faked) say it is time to go to bed. I take off my clothes, get into bed. Are you going to go through with this, Lorenzo? He takes off his clothes, except for his jockey shorts. Yes, I am going through with this. I turn out the light. I am shaking. I wait and wait. I wait forever. Jesus, is it two, or three a.m.? I start moaning. I am having a terrible nightmare. Salvadore, I am having a nightmare. Please come.

He is standing beside my bed. Outside the window, fishermen on the ocean, with their bright white gas lights. Light coming in through the windows, in through the bars. I can see his body, the glint of his eyes, his underpants, his underpants. Get in bed. I am shaking violently. My chin against his shoulder. My left arm flung carelessly across his stomach. I am on fire.

I don't have any control of what happens next. I swear to you judge, there is no way on god's green earth I can control the motion of my left hand. It comes, I swear to you, it comes to be invested with a life of its own. I have nothing at

181

all to do with it; I am too distracted by other things. I do not move my hand, it moves for me. There is no way in heaven or in hell that I can stop the slow move of that creature, first coming down the external oblique then the abdominis and finally the trans-versus abdominis, down to the area across the umbilicus and the start of the few wild black hairs there, down from there to where the elastic of the underpants crosses from bone-hip to bone-hip. The bridge over the isthmus. The channel of Scylla.

A pause. There is a brief pause as the hand reaches the shorts. But just for a second: soon enough the bugger is on its way again. Slowly, but firmly. Making the next short jump. The inches, the few inches of infinity. The hand moving inches through the gap of eternity. The space between the stars. The edge of the cosmos. The site of the gods.

I am listening. My eyes are wide open. My head is now on Salvadore's chest. I am listening, watching: every pore has eyes and ears, for any sign of a change in breathing. Or the fist, it would have to be the right fist, coming up from his side. I have to be prepared for that. I have to be prepared to fail, don't I?

I don't fail. Salvadore is ready for me. He has this humongous boner.

My hand has life of its own. First, through the frail white soft cotton of those Fruit-of-the-Loom underpants, my hand flat-open, wide, pulling back and forth, up and down, and I can feel the curl of the stiff hair underneath the soft white worn cotton of the underpants. The elastic rubber of the waist restricts my motion—but I am so unwilling to stop for a minute, so afraid that Salvadore would be out of the bed, dressed, and out the door if I were to let up for a minute. After all my calculations, all my planning and plotting, I must move with the tide, I must go quickly to conclusion.

For I have this idea that the first orgasm will be the lock; the first flowing of the fruity sweetness out of him will be the religious seal on our relationship, the red wax molded at the bottom of the letter, the document-of-state with the ribbons plastered to the huge, just unrolled treaty.

While this master seduction scene is going on, I have

this attack of philosophy. About cocks, and things.

What I am thinking about is Salvadore's cock, and my cock, and everyone's cock. How our cocks really fuck things up.

I mean here I am so far away from everything that I grew up with and know, so far away from my own country, so far from my friends and family and roots and history and heritage. And how did I get there: my cock led me. It's as if we went to all that trouble to get me a brain, and fill it with all this education—and then this cock takes over, and runs the whole show, and I might as well be a big dick. They might as well show a picture of me as this huge peter: my head all red and shiny, that little collar of circumcised skin around my neck, and this smooth trunk for a body, with the big channel sticking out for a stomach, the *vas deferens*, and for feet, these two massive bally-looking things, with the loose skin and the veins. I mean, why not?

Because we don't control our destiny. It is all run for us by that arrogant dick down there, that half-foot homely little snot-nose calling the whole frigging show, and Bob's-your-uncle.

We cannot control it. We build all these elaborate structures: thoughts, prejudices, countries, governments, buildings, philosophies, religions, morality, prisons. And then this pecker comes along, and boogers up the whole show. That pecker! Its own master. Its own boss. Think of me, for all these years, trying to keep Joe Dick where he belongs—either in my fist, or in some nice warm *proper* vagina. But the little bugger keeps insisting, simply insisting that he prefers to be somewhere else. Like next to Salvadore.

And Salvadore's cock: another show-off master. Salvadore will pretend until he is blue that he isn't interested in being played around with by men. He may be 100% convinced that he is a lady's man, that he will spend his happiest days fucking Conchita of the big tits, his bride who, most certainly, he will meet in the next five years. Salvadore is absolutely convinced he is the straightest of the straight.

So he ends up, against his will, in this bed, next

to this crippled American, with thin shanks and blue-green eyes and curly hair and all that hogwash about nightmares — and there is his cock ruining his whole show. How can you be 100% heterosexual when you get so big and brazen under the warm soft touch of some man's hand?

There is one moment of maybe-we-will-lose-all-we-have-gained. Salvadore's underpants are limiting my range of motion. So despite the possibility that if I stop the old back-and-forth for even a second, I will lose my dear love, I halt and, first left side then right side, yank the underpants half way down his thighs, his beautiful crispy olive-thighs, with that delicious Sartorius riding so hard and high on them like some wonderful cloud on his very youth.

It must be the old Catholic/Spanish resignation: Salvadore doesn't move a hair. In the dim light coming in off the ocean, from the sea, I can see this cock of his, grown to prodigious size, a touch, just a touch of dew (O Jesus the nectar) near the fissure at the head of it, and the elegant black bush that swirls around the base of it, and the two friendly old nuts, Mr. Nuts, the whole wonderful picture set and posed so perfectly in this man's body, some picture of stunning beauty out of some magazine of The Body Perfect, My Desire Perfectly Mad.

I come down on my Salvadore, take this giant monster wonder hunk into my mouth, without thought, and he shudders, I can feel his body tense, as he finds himself moving, involuntary motion, the grinding of the hips, and I find me too, my own groin turned hard against the tender muscle and wire hairs of his soleus, and he is turning, turning, his pelvis moving, and me, my whole cripple's body come up with muscles I never knew existed, as I twist and turn against those firm strong massive-pillar legs, the legs of man, I am grinding my life out against those perfect man's legs, that contain the perfect muscles, built to such hardness by such elaborate, exquisite training; and he, my Salvadore, my love, my god is turning and twisting under the soft-bite tearing of me at this monster lollypop. I am filled with the wonder of it growing harder, I can feel the once-flaccid muscle turning harder and bigger, I can feel it pushing fire inside, ramming itself against the head, the skull of me, the skull of me plowed, swived to its depths, bone against bone, God Salvadore, where did you come up with this delicious verge, and I find myself not thinking, no longer thinking, but melded together with this monster muscle that threatens to beat my brains out, this powerful muscled gun striving against my force, my yielding, and my hands run claws up and down the inside of these straining legs of his, as they push and bury themselves in the coverlets, and twist and pull at the jockey shorts that are half ground down against the straining muscles of these legs, these pillars of wisdom, these pillars of life indestructible, and my hand claws the inside of his legs, up and down, then back up, to where the ridge of proud flesh has grown so huge, so stunningly huge where the two giant pillar legs meet standing so tall over the very earth, this ridge grown so tall with its sprinkling of rough hair, and there it joins with that easy riding flesh over the globes, those huge suns, which at this time are coming to ride so tight against the whole base of him, Salvadore's whole body is rising, rising, I can feel it swelling, and the thickness of me that is jammed against the hot flesh of him, I can feel it swirling as the juices begin to flow, and where the wire-hairs are cutting into the head of me, now I feel an engorging as the whole gets tough and taut and tight, the sliding as these incredible juices come to work themselves against the taut flesh, both of us rising on some peak, coming to some peak where we ride ourselves up some razor sharp ridge above ecstasy, where, now, that the whole comes together, melding balls and cock and hair and hard *meatus* of globular delight, as the fire-hot lava comes to be its own essence, meet us, O meet us, as the essence of me and him comes blended together in whole continents, as the continents ride together to the point where the neck of the volcano comes slowly at first, with a few sputterings and roilings, then comes hot now, the volcano puffing its red hot crown above the steaming workings of the sea, rising from out of the cold into the tepid waters, and then into the hot steam of the air, and finally whole continents collide, and the volcano juts its neck and head as far into the steamy sky as humanly possible, and the lava bubbling red-white-hot-enormously-boiling blacks, the rocks red-white stoning come pouring, a brief pause, and then throwing world-sized boulders hurling popping and crashing, grinding and cracking, these boulders come screaming out of the infuriated sea, these boulders shoot jagged bolts of themselves high into the sky, past the sky, into the black fury of the heavens that ride above, the fire bolts come jaggering out and eviscerate the whole inner earth straining, coming raging out in one high keening whistling cry of despair and love, a crying love wail come wailing out shamelessly, the cry comes out, O the last sweet crying out of desperate shaking, as the earthquakes of the land love come shivering out, the shaking of whole continents, the two continents of two men, who have, for this brief and hurtling joy, have come together, two men come together for a crying together, the coming together of the two of them, now so eternally and famously bound together in the molten lava bond-seal of flame that is two men who have come together on this dark shore, at the edge of this dark sea.

PART V

*every man is the arbiter of his
own virtues whether or not you
consider it courageous is of more
importance than the act itself*

— *The Sound and The Fury*

CHAPTER XXV

Salvadore Esteban Jesús Rodriguez is raised Catholic, Spanish Catholic. The good fathers have always warned him about dark sin. They pull themselves from each other's arms at La Iglesia de la Virgen Sagrada, and rail at him, from age five onwards: rail about the bad things that men shouldn't do with, to, or by each other. They chant about the men who, in that fine and unsubtle language, have committed "acto impuro" and the special baking, frying, salting, basting, broasting and broiling they can expect shortly after their descent into the darkest reaches of hell.

So there, after the storm, in the moments of rest after the volcano and earthquakes, the residents of the island, the two residents who survive the storm, find themselves in each other's arms again, in tears. Salvadore shakes and sobs. This man, this glorious man, is so sad. He shakes and sobs. We shake and sob. Guilt wrenches and tears at our bodies. Our bodies shake in unison. I make a speech.

It is one of those speeches which comes out of the same substrata as that nonsense about the nightmares. But it has to be done; it is the key to our survival together as lovers. It goes something like this: that neither of us have women. And we are both lonely. And we have these needs, these strong *terremoto* needs. These needs that cannot be explained.

And we are doing wrong, of course we are doing wrong, but in his church, and in my church (whatever that is) there are rules against these sorts of things, of course, but there is also forgiveness, absolution. And although we are doing wrong, it is not eternal wrong, because there must be a compassionate god somewhere, who, after all, gave us these rock-hard needs, and when we give in to them every now and again, we are only doing it because we are not lucky enough to have some woman around, whom we can love, and so what we are doing can easily be forgiven, 'cause if it couldn't be forgiven half the world's population would be salted away in *inferno*.

I studied Spanish in school for five years. I have spent another few weeks in Spain trying to make myself cognizant of the language. I am not truly bilingual, but I have a feeling that on that particular night, I am supremely fluent. I have a dozen years of ice-hard frustration to lay to rest. And I have to be sure, damn sure, that Salvadore comes back.

Because when he leaves the next morning (getting up at six to catch the earliest train, tearing at my heart as he pulls on those worn blue jeans, pulls on that garish fake-silk pink shirt) I have no real idea if he will come back. I know that for Salvadore, the next two days will be pure shit. He will be torn by the angels and devils inside of him. Just like me. The two of us will have two ghastly days. While he decides whether to return to the only job he has been able to get, one that pays, and pays well. And costs a great deal.

Salvadore comes back. He has no choice. The money snake has him. He doesn't like it. When he returns, his jaw is tighter, his eyes are a little narrowed, his shoulders a little slumped. He doesn't like it at all, *at all*, but he comes back.

O he resists. Sometimes passively, sometimes actively, sometimes with a touch of Andalusian Mau-Mau at eleven or eleven-thirty on a moon-lit night, in the bedroom, with the pumping of the sea, the sound coming in through the bars on the windows, giving counterpoint to our conversation:

Salvadore.	Salvadore.
Sí.	Yes.
Venga aqui.	Come here.
Alli?	Over there?
Sí.	Yes.
Ahora?	Now?

190

Ahora mismo.	Right now.
(Silencio).	(Silence).
Salvadore!	Salvadore!
Sí?	Yes?
Venga!	Come here!
Ya?	Now?
Ya!	Now!
Pesadilla?	Nightmare?
Sí, sí.	Yes, yes.
(Suspira con pesa y viene.)	(He sighs heavily and comes over to the bed.)

There will be other times when Salvadore disappears for days. I get to experience, at those times, The Love Waits, which are akin to the monsters of Golgotha, or the head-eating foul beasts out of Dante's *Inferno*. My jealousy is huge, as huge as the room, and with its maddened eyes and fire-breath mouth, I could consume whole continents.

The train will go by. I am sitting before the fireplace, notebook in hand, trying to write. I know that Salvadore always takes the nine o'clock train. I know that it takes him exactly four and three-quarters minutes to walk through the back alleys from the train station to my cottage.

I do not write in that four and three-quarters minutes. Nor do I really think, except to say to myself "Now? Is that him?" Every scratch, rattling tree, bush, footstep is heard and analyzed. I barely breathe. I am suspended in the ammoniac solution of where-is-my-love. The wait of all ages. The black wait of eternity.

If he doesn't come in five minutes, I find myself talking to myself. "He must have stopped off for some coffee," I say, knowing that Salvadore never stops off anywhere for anything in Rincón de la Victoria. "Maybe he's just stopped to admire the moon and the sea," I say, knowing he has no interest in the moon, nor in the sea.

"Ah," I say, "his grandmother's sick tonight. Or maybe he's sick. I remember he had a slight cough last time. That's it: he's sick. Or: he missed the train, he'll walk here. Let's see, he should be here at eleven-thirty or so," I say, knowing that Salvadore would never walk twenty-five miles at night for any reason whatsoever.

Then I get mad. "That son-of-a-bitch. After all I've done for him. That greasy little shit. I have given him all that money, where does he get his clothes (from me), where does he get his food (from me), where does he get his miserable rock and roll records (from me)? He is so unappreciative. He's ungrateful," I say. "And he smells bad, too. Pomade and garlic. Good riddance," I say.

There is the snap of a branch outside. I am tingling. At last! Delight runs through my veins. I think of his thighs. I think of lying next to his thighs tonight, how I am going to love his thighs tonight.

It is only María, the maid. She forgot her shawl. "¿Toda está bien?" she asks, is everything all right? "Usted está solo," you are alone, she says. O no no, I say, I'm reading and writing. I have my books.

"I don't need Salvadore," I say, after she has gone. "I really don't. There are hundreds, thousands like him. All I have to do is put another ad in the paper. They are all over, just waiting for me to ask them for the night. With my money, I can get a Salvadore anywhere. I think we are better off this way, anyway. I was getting tired of him. Is that the train I hear? Maybe that wasn't the last one." The train goes by, the other way. It is going from Vélez back to Málaga. "Maybe Salvadore forgot to get off. He is getting off at the station right now, and he'll come running down here, come in the door here, breathless, blushing, ashamed that he dozed off, that he had to go all the way to the end of the line."

I wait five minutes, keep checking my watch to be sure it doesn't need winding. "It's just as well," I say. "That poor bastard. He didn't really like it here anyway. I *forced* this on him. It really is cruel, when you think about it. It's going to be better this way. I want him to be happy. Maybe I will run into him in Málaga, on the street someday, and I can say to him 'It was just as well that you didn't come back that time. I really was the wrong person for you. You were right not to come.'"

192

Each rustle or footstep or whistle outside gets transformed into the sound of his shoes, the sound of his whistle (he never whistles). Every sigh—from the wind or no—is his sigh. Every voice is his voice. Every step is his step. My ears develop the super ability of hearing Salvadore in every possible sound.

After another ten minutes, a black numbing depression sweeps in over me, an avalanche of tar roaring down from the mountains, covering me in darkness. "O shit," I say. "O shit, O shit, O shit! There's no one, no one in the whole wide world for me. Not a single person, anywhere. I am all alone, alone. O shit!" I feel the bitterness of my isolation. I am the loneliness of stars, riding at the furthest reaches of the universe, surrounded by dark and bitter, bitter worldlessness. There is no other light within a million light-years. I am shrunk down by the appalling separation from other human beings.

I am shaken by the poignancy of me alone in this cottage, this cold cottage by the sea, so far from home. I drink anis, and every glass makes me drunker, sadder. I brood on the complete desolation of it all. I am the face of the moon. Nothing stirs out of the cold and dusty dead of it. I am separated from all that is warm and comforting in the world. I am an isolated queer cripple in some strange land, with nothing to hold onto, no one to care for me.

"I'll forgive him," I think. "If he comes back next time, I'll forgive him, I swear I will." How could I have thought those things about him? "If he'll just come back, I'll get him a nice present. I'll get him a wool jacket, say; or some nice Fabian records. Maybe I'll give him a salary increase. Five hundred pesetas, that's eight dollars a week." I think: "Why don't I give him seven-hundred fifty. That would make him happy. His eyes would shine. He might even smile. Poor Salvadore, I really am not very good to him. And he is very good to me. The poor kid. What a shit I am!"

Two nights later the train screeches by the house, and 4-

3/4 minutes later, Salvadore bangs in, closes the door, locks it behind him. I pretend to be reading my book (I haven't looked at if for the last half-hour). I casually smile up at him and nod. I watch him take off his ragged and torn jacket. I want to crush him.

"Buenas," I say. "¿Dónde estuves el mártes pasado?" Where were you last Tuesday. Casual. Not accusatory. Smiling. I can't be angry. I was going to tell him off, tell him if he ever did that to me again, he would be fired. But Jesus, I am so happy to see him. I look at the way his jeans squeeze and mold the upper parts of his thighs, and when he leans over to fold his jacket onto the chair, I see dark, wiry leg hairs exposed by a half-inch triangular rip in his pants. I can feel the flush rising in my cheeks. My heart is thumping.

"No quería venir aquí otra vez," he says. I really didn't want to come back. "Éste no me gusta." I don't like doing this. He looks at me, and his eyes are brown, immobile, emotionless. He doesn't smile. "Sino, es imposible hallar otro trabajo." It's impossible to find any other kind of work. "Necesito el dinero mucho, muchíssimo, para me y mi abuela." I need the money for me and my grandmother. Very much. Very very much.

He runs out of words. He says nothing more. He stands motionless. I watch the way he stands, the way his legs rise to the perfect apex.

"Ay, que lástima," I say. What a pity. "Verdad," I say. It's true. It is a pity. We are both quite pitiable, Salvadore and I, him with his dragon money need, me with my dragon nut lust. "Que lástima," I say, because it is a pity. We are both saddened by what is happening to us.

"¿Quieres hacer el fuego ya?" I say, because it is so damnably cold, even though my body is burning. I can feel the blood lust guttering my veins. "Sí," I say, "haces un fuego ya, ¿OK? Y quizás debo de pargárte un poquito más." Perhaps I should be paying a bit more money. "Quizás otra viente duro cada semana," I tell him: another dollar and a half a week. Can that warm you at all, my sweet Salvadore?

You see, he doesn't have a chance. I need him. Like sun moon stars I need him. In the two years we are together, I get to know Salvadore like a bride. I get to know all parts of him. I know his habits, his moods, his interests, his needs, his desires, his musical tastes, his ambitions. I know how he looks dressed, half-undressed, and completely undressed. I know (O I know) that his left nut is about twice as big as his right one (you really should get that looked at, Salvadore). I know how he is going to lie in bed, with his arms crossed over his big brown chest, the hairs just starting on his chest, his eyes open and dead, looking slightly martyred, making damn sure I know that *he* doesn't like any part of this hanging out with this damn American cripple fruit-cake when he would rather be out on a man's job, making some man's money.

But I also know after we have been in bed together for awhile how the fire of it moves him and shakes him; how there is no way he can hide the way the passion takes up his front side and down his back, takes him like a kitten takes a mouse and shakes it and shakes it so that the stuffing all comes out. There is no way you can hide that, Salvadore, even though you never stop trying. Thank the Lord for it. I think you may have saved my life Salvadore.

He smells of garlic sometimes. His brows come down at acute angles so that he looks sad, like he is in permanent mourning. He's a sad-sack, my Salvadore is. Shit, he's condemned to hell and fire damnation forever and ever by this *maricón*, and there is not a damn thing he can do about it.

Sweet Salvadore! Torn and uneasy and pissed off at this sorrowful fate. Lying there like he was dead, until the Americano gets it so that he can't really stop moving, making all those crying noises. There seems to be no way in the world we can stop crying out, like babies, no matter how hard we try. No matter how much we wish we could control ourselves, you with all that Spanish passion, me with this North American glacier puritanism.

No way to stop it all, no matter how hard we try. Salvadore, you sweet nut! You and your twenty-eight inch waist. You might well have saved my life, you know that? Que dulce, mi Salvadore. Que lástima. ¡Ay, qué lástima! ¡Qué dulce!

CHAPTER XXVI

There are other things I do in Spain the next two years besides corrupt the youth of that land.

I wake up each morning with the sun coming my friend into the bedroom. I read a little, or write in my journal, and get up and make some tea. While it is stewing, I am at the front door, contemplating the sea's rise and fall, the rise and fall of several eternities, there, just outside my door. I watch the donkey traffic on the beach, or the occasional train on its way to Vélez or back to Málaga.

I make tea and sit down at the typewriter for three or four hours. I am writing a book. And poetry! I am the Dylan Thomas of Spain. The only distraction is the thousand flies who rest on the ceiling of the living room, who come to life with the sun (and me) and try to buzz my ears or drown their fool heads in my teacup. This is a farm country, and across the road is enough cowshit to keep me in flies for the next thirty years.

I am done writing by noon, just in time to catch the train to Málaga. I have to do the shopping for María: the fish and shrimp and clams and rice and spices for the *paella*. Or the soup makings, the meat, the salad. José brings the straw basket, and goes with me. José is one of the three children of Rincón de la Victoria who comes in the evening to eat with me. He is thirteen, but a lifetime of eating black olive oil on white-paste bread for breakfast, lunch, and supper make him look to be not much more than ten. Marcellina, another suppermate, is also thirteen but looks to be eleven. She has dark skin, like a gypsy—so everyone in the village thinks that she is ugly. With the dark brown almond eyes and the high cheekbones, she looks like she got off a poster for Iberia Airlines: and the villagers think she is ugly because she looks like a *gitana*. The third supper guest is Enrique: he is nine and looks to be seven. He doesn't say much: he knows the business is eating and that's all he is interested in. Half the time he has eaten so much they have to undo the top two buttons of his pants and help him from the table. A real worker is Enrique.

I borrow them from their families each evening for supper at my house. They eat real food for the first time in their lives. They troop in about eight or eight-thirty, and we eat at nine, all of us, gathered around the groaning-board. They've never seen so damn much food.

Supper time is gossip time: I get them to tell me what is going on in the village. The usual small pesky world of a small (poor) village. I get to practice my Spanish on them. Shit: I would have had to pay Berlitz three times what it costs to have these three miniature teachers come to me each evening (including Sundays) and help me out with my verbs and adjectives and nouns, and conjugations.

These are peasants, I suppose, but what does that mean? It seems that their peculiar blend of pride and humility, their fears and wonders, their naïvete and world-wisdom, they don't deserve the appellation of "Peasant." Marcellina may be a witch when she is talking about the postman's drinking habits, or a devil when she lets on what she knows about the village priest's sexual appetites; she may be an awful nuisance when she takes my crutches from me and won't let me have them; she may be sad when she wants the beautiful black-silver-buckle shoes I won't buy for her because I know they will fall apart the next week; she may be a figure of tragedy when she shows me the collection of memorabilia she has of me: a box with a faded photo I got from the village square photographer, an empty anis bottle, a button from my jacket, and the green Mennen's spray deodorant container. She can be witch-devil-nuisance-saddo-tragedian, but she is hardly peasant.

These are my friends. They are my contact with real Spanish life. What they like they like, what they dislike—they don't hide. They have that peculiar honesty that is the province of children around an adult who they are sure will not rat on them. I have three pairs of eyes into the heart of southern Spain, with the particular roughness of their rough lives. Before they come to me, after I leave, they will either be in the four-hours-a-day Catholic school, or they will be working in the olive fields for about twenty cents a day. Their lives are killing them, probably already have killed them: but for two years I am given access to them, and their warm personalities, and their fierce pride, and their bigotry, ferocious prejudices, and their honesty. My teachers: José, Marcellina, Enrique.

José is my companion to the city. We catch the train there, daily, and walk a mile or so through the back alleys of Málaga, both of us all eyes to the amazing lives that are revealed to us on the streets, and in the shops. We haunt the various places of the public market, gape at the bloody carcasses hung up, stare at the blood-spattered walls of the chicken shop (you get to pick your victim), finger the mountains of oranges, beans, peas, lettuces, cauliflower, bitter asparagus, tomatoes, lentils, *habas*, artichokes.

Together we reel at the smell of the fish shop, the stacks of still fresh squid, yellowfish, perch, octopus, shrimp, butter clams, bonefish, *merluza*, shad, trout, cuttlefish, whitebait. Together our eyes gleam at the delicatessen, where I can buy anis, Cointreau, Chartreuse, cognac (fifty cents a bottle!), Galliano, Grand Marnier. And *queso de bola*, goat's cheese, head cheese, a dozen varieties of butter and salamis, bolognas, *chorizo*, and *bacon:* dark bacon which, cut paper thin, can be cooked as an appetizer in three minutes by María, and eaten with fresh *bollas* of crisp french bread bought off the bicycle bread man, so delicious having come out of the oven a scant two hours previously.

Together José and I haunt every inch of the heart of Málaga, every day, looking at the knife man, who comes with his bicycle; and if you want your knife sharpened, he turns the seat around, drops the grinding mill wheel on the tire, and pedals backwards to sharpen your blades for *un duro*. Now, even now, so much later, an eternity later, I can hear the doleful sounds of the knife man's whistle, the sharp Arabic cry which says, bring your knives and scissors to me: and I will do them for you. Cheap.

Together we are part of the life of the street, the lives of the streets, so filled with people, in a way that has been lost to America in the last fifty years: the crowd of people buying, selling, arguing, talking, singing, walking, drinking, chatting, gossiping: the panoply of life, the movie of southern Spanish life, played out with such a variety of characters and faces, acted out every day, for free, for no cost.

And last, before we catch the four p.m. train back to Rincón, we stop at my favorite sidewalk cafe. Where I can sip a *sombra*, black chicory coffee with hot milk, and José gets a chocolate, and I can review the world far distant—dated four days ago, in the International edition of the *Herald-Tribune*.

As I go through the streets of Málaga, people stop and stare at me. It is the custom in that honest country for people to gape at what interests them. I am fascinating: me in my olive-drab chain sweater, my English terrapin glasses, me six foot three of aluminum and leather. I am a fascinating spectacle.

And I am. José and Marcellina and I stop in the park, and the man with the box camera takes our picture. Then he reaches inside the camera box, and develops it (the chemicals are kept there). I still have it, a painfully foggy picture of me with my hair curled out all over my head, Bob Dylan style six years before Bob Dylan *had* a style, and my pants with the cuffs sweeping the streets, and my dusty Cordovans. I am at the top of my form then: I am immensely strong. I weigh 140 pounds. The streets are mine. The smells and the language and the customs. I avoid the *americanos*, I speak no English, I think and speak and dream in Spanish.

And when the people of that country stare at me, at first I am angry and ashamed. What do they think they are looking at! But then I begin to get into it: I am different and I know it. So I start staring too. For one thing, Spain is Cripple Heaven. I have never in my life seen collected together so many desiccated joints, twisted limbs, protruding backs, cases of scoliosis, kyphosis, vulture necks, gnarled fingers, drop-feet, moleskin toes. Never never have I seen such a zoo. A marvelous cripple zoo! Faces with warts and wens. Jaws shot away. Eyes crossed, twisted, protruding. Holes for noses. Ears cut out. Dents in skulls. Every possible form of birthmark: red, black, strawberry, lemon, lime, peach. I can't believe it. They have scoured the earth and brought together the deformities of humanity. All have been collected together on this Island of Sorrow. Dwarfs, spastics, every conceivable palsy. The bent knee, the damaged back, the wandering arm, the swollen torso. This is Cripple Paradise! There is no disguise, no hiding. If you have cancerous jaws: hang them out there, for all to see. If you have goitres growing (enormous tits) down the neck: stick them out for the world. If you have to walk by pressing palm of hand to knee: do it publicly, openly— and if possible, display it so that you can collect a few pesetas in the bargain.

Did they amputate your leg? Show what's left, openly: stick the scar-and-sawn-away-bone out there for everyone to gaze on. Did your foot get twisted in some horrendous accident with the streetcar? Elevate it, in front of your tri-wheelchair (the one you operate with the hand rotor) so that all can admire its strange angles of bone, flesh, toes, and heels.

Did you lose your eyesight in some ugly childhood accident? Don't put on dark glasses: stick the socket out there for all to see in its glorious wetness. Did your hand get mangled in some explosion of childhood, so that the fingers curve around each other and back to the palm again? Don't hide that claw! We have curiosity-seekers who want to see it entire, naked, unadorned. Did they cut into your neck with an axe, taking out half the sterno-hyoid muscle? Don't you dare hide it: go out there with shirt open to the navel so that the scar with its purple proud flesh is open to all eyes. Has this sudden unexplained growth occurred on your left cheek, so that it swells triple size, and turns the color of vanilla custard, with raisins? Get it out there! The public of Málaga is awaiting! Let's get it seen by all, because, you know, my loves, we are in Cripple Heaven. Cripple Heaven!

And then the costumes! The women dressed like Dorothy Lamour, or Rita Hayworth, or The King Sisters. Hide those knees. Lipstick from nose to chin. Rouge, beauty spots, false eyelashes, earrings down to the shoulders. Time stopped. All the refugees from progress the world over are in Spain. The men in drab, grey jackets, misshapen blue pants, children in *luto* and in rags. The ciegos that sell lottery tickets, shouting to all that they have the big one left: "Me queda el gordo. ¡Me queda el gordo!" And their cries echo and reécho down the animal noisy streets.

The peasants. Down from the hills, down from their stone houses, where they live as their parents and grandparents did before them, with the dirt and the animals, and the shutters closed at night to protect the chidren from the bad air with the pestiferous diseases that come on the winds of darkness to infect them all.

The streets filled with dogs and cats and donkeys and horses and humans riding every conceivable vehicle: foot, basket, cart, dray, hansom, wagon, wheelchair, three-wheeled Motocarro. (Everything but automobiles. Those are too expensive for this poor country.) I have the eyes of the street. And everything, the people, the buildings, the width of the alleys, come to human scale so that we feel part *of* it, and not apart *from* it. These are my people.

At four or so we catch the train back to Rincón de la Victoria. The ancient steam whistle engine chugs through the back alleys of East Málaga, then through the stone cliffs and into the coves at the edge of the Mediterranean. I am standing on the back platform of the wooden third-class coach (there is no first or second class) and the clack and rattle of it mixes with the sounds of late afternoon waves beating up against the rocks, up against the beach, as it has for so long, so long, so long. I can see into the hearts of those houses that back up to the edge of the tracks. A *criada* in black stands on the patio, leaning against her yellow straw broom. I wave at her. She doesn't wave back: just looks at me with impenetrable dark eyes. What is she doing here? What is she thinking? What am I doing here? Loving it, loving it, loving it.

We are back by five and make the mile walk to the house quickly. María is already there, in the kitchen, the dark kitchen, with single naked bulb: cutting up tiny things for the croquettes, the *paella*, the fish chowder. I send José down to the *cantina* to buy me a ten-cent liter of red wine, and sit out on the porch, facing over the sea, drinking it, watching the sun die to the west. I may have my guitar in my hand, play a few songs which amuse those in the house immensely. I can hear María or her daughter giggling over my peculiar version of "Home On The Range," wondering about this mad Americano they work for.

We eat well, the children of the earth and I. It is here at supper that I cook up my dumb schemes to improve their lives. They are fascinated by my toothbrush, and I find out that they have never brushed their perfect white teeth in their lives. I can't believe it: tomorrow José and I pick up three small toothbrushes, and three small tubes of Pepsodent (pron. "pess-o-denn"). Each day, I instruct them solemnly, they are to brush their teeth. I give them my best you-are-on-tv exaggerated arm movements demonstration on how they are to do it.

Within a week, their teeth have turned a uniform grey. Seems that people who live in such poverty that they are not introduced to the wonders of hygiene have built-in systems of body protection. When teeth are not brushed, they develop their own plaque which is white and chalky, and gives a perfect-smile appearance that would be the ideal of some travel agency poster.

Trouble is, their teeth will fall out at age twenty-five if they don't brush them, or will look grey for the rest of their lives if they do. I leave the choice to them, and they gamely file away their toothbrushes and toothpaste in their memento-of-Lorenzo boxes which they all have, no doubt, kept to this day.

They leave about ten or so. If Salvadore comes, he locks

up the house, we chat, he may help me to take a bath and we toddle off to heaven for the night. If it is one of his nights off, I sit by the fire and sip anis, which has an excellent mind-expanding drug in it, and write in my journal, or read the Penguin books which I have picked up in the sole Málaga English-language bookstore. Thus I read authors I would never have chanced on, since the bookstore selection is limited to about fifty books: Muriel Spark, Thomas Wolfe (the elder), Tolstoi, Rudyard Kipling, Robert Lewis Stevenson, Damon Runyon, Graham Greene, Phillip Marlowe. My speaking Spanish is sufficient; my reading Spanish is limited to puzzling out *El Sol.* The one Spanish book I buy (*Los Cipresses Creen en Dios*) lies mouldering on the shelf the whole time there.

In the course of my time in Spain, I manage to fill six diaries with tiny black ink words, which now so much later, are often impossible to puzzle out. I had this dangerous feeling that all my crimes against nature would be discovered in these journals, so in awkward compromise, I put much of it in third person singular: "He went to Nerja today . . . " "He thought of His family briefly . . ." "He wondered about His daughter . . ." "He was depressed . . . " "He was drunk . . ." "He was happy. . . ."

To keep me separate from the other he's in the world, I give myself God's own honor, or that restricted to important royalty; the same homage that we give our kings, as well as our lord and savior, capitalizing my He, leaving all others in lower case. It makes the journal now read like a cross between *The Black Book* and *The Gideon Bible.* The seduction of Salvadore takes a full eighty pages.

CHAPTER XXVII

One day I have gone to the city late, and I come back alone. It is dark. I get off the train at the station, and walk past the wall next to Paco's Cantina. There are four or five men ranged up against the wall. Two of them stoop; another is smoking a cigarette. A fourth calls out to me. "Señor," he says.

He is short, and scruffy. His jacket is worn. His teeth, I can see in the dim light, are black and in disarray. His face is turned a prune by the sun and the bad food and the wretched coffee he drinks. He looks to be fifty-five. He is no more than thirty. He is José's father.

"Tómale," He says. "Take him." I don't understand what he is saying to me, not until later, not until I have puzzled out the situation. What he wants me to do is to take José any way I want: but take him from Spain. That old man (who is my peer) knows the cruelness of Spain. He was born six years before the Civil War, where the citizens of that country maimed, brutalized, killed, and wounded twenty percent of their fellow countrymen. He knows the wretchedness of the forties, after Hitler stopped sending in repatriations. He knows what it was like in 1949, when the average family income was half what it is now.

He knows about working in a factory: he himself works at the cement plant in El Palo, and the incessant poisonous dust has turned his lungs to paste, his whole system to ruin. He knows the desperation of a father of eight children, in a country where the mother church will permit no contraceptives, so that the only abortions are the abortions committed on the living young by insufficient food, insufficient health care, insufficient education.

He has killed himself for his children. José, José who can still laugh, José who is still young and active, is his pride and joy. But he knows that the country will kill José sooner or later. In the orchards, in the factories, on the streets: José will be murdered by poverty. In a country where three percent of the population has ninety percent of the wealth, José doesn't stand a chance.

"Tómale," he says. At first I think he is talking to me about taking the boy back to America with me. But later I realize he is meaning any way I want: emotionally, sexually, whatever. In that small town of 800, there is no way that the liaison of Salvadore and me is to be kept secret. No one ever tells me, no one ever smirks and asks about Salvadore: the young man who comes so secretively, walks through the back way, trying not to be seen. No one says a word, but they know: they have to. A stranger is a stranger in Rincón de la Victoria, and a young man coming to the home of the rich and generous American at ten in the evening, gone by six the next morning: there can be only one reason.

One day José asks me if he can take a bath. It is before we are to go to town. There is no one in the house. He—like all the children—is fascinated by the indoor plumbing: a toilet that flushes! A sink that gurgles with water that comes magically from a tap. A tub that can be filled with hot steaming water; where you can sit and play for hours.

We fill the tub, and he takes off his clothes and gets in the tub. I lock the bathroom door. I tell him I will wash him. He, innocent sweet that he is, splashes water all over his body, and kneels patiently in the tub, left side to me, waiting for me and the washcloth. To wash him.

I am, I must confess to you, dear reader, breathless. Do you know about the perfection of a boy's body? He isn't even fourteen. The food I have been feeding him has given his whole body a fine glow that shows up under the light, very light olive skin. The veins jag throughout, blood lightning just below the skin.

He kneels in the water, José does, and I am awestruck by the perfection of the human boy form. He is absolutely hairless: puberty comes late to the hungry. His flanks are hairless and smooth. He is beautiful, José is. He is a beautiful, perfectly proportioned boy, with just a hint of the carvings that time will bring to the muscles of his body over the next three years.

You probably knew, José, even in your boy's mind, that I was in love with you then. You couldn't have missed it. My hand, hidden, as it were, a blushing flower in the wash cloth, soaping you and then rinsing your body, from top to bottom. Did you hear me breathing, José? There was hot lime juice, running through my veins that day, José. Me and my cardiac arrest.

I am so innocent. José and I are so innocent. My laws, and my own rigidly enforced strictures. The innocence of my self-restraint. The enormity of it. Suffer the small children to come to me. They are safe.

José survived to die. If he came out of the cauldron of poverty in southern Spain any better than his father, I should be surprised.

I never loved him. I swear to you, Judge: I never violated your trust in me. Even, once, months later: we are to catch an early train in the morning. He stays with me. At first, he embraces the wall, but after falling asleep, he rolls over and is in my arms.

I am good, I tell you Judge, I am good. In the dim light I can see the sad sleeping mouth, see the grey of dirt behind the ears. He is filled with the fire of sleep, metabolizing all that boy heat, burning him up, burning the two of us, the barn is on fire.

I am good. I hold him tight, all that bird-heat against my poor old flesh. There is a holocaust of life in the body of children, and if you hold it too close, too long, you get scarred. I bear those scars to this day.

Here, look: you can see how the figure of José is burned a shadow across the front of me. See, here, on my chest, is where this hot breath burned the hairs; down there, is where his simple straight strong boy's stomach carved its image across my own stomach; there, down there between my two thin legs ride the scars of two smaller, stronger, more agile, more alive legs.

The negative burned across my body. A bird-fire, a tattoo on me, on my nerves, on the deep parts of myself. And sometimes, the scar hurts, O god does it burn. Sometimes, at inexplicable times—that scar pulses and aches, as it did for that long night. I think on Spain; I remember how storms would flood the hills, bring bright red earth down to the waters, to turn the oceans to blood. O the scar burns.

I remember the broken sounds of flamenco, solo, coming from some unseen, unnamed singer; some poor gypsy walking the railroad tracks, singing the miseries of love, of love gone years ago. The scar burns me, threatens to consume me as I listen to the moorish intonations on a solo voice out of the caves of Granada.

I am scarred, scarred by that simple peasant boy who loved me so, scarred by that tempestuous heat of his child flesh, life burning up to ashes; the child who loved me, and let me hug him, travelled all over southern Spain with me— and then one day, was left behind.

I left Spain, and I left José, and I left him bereft, and all I have to show is the flame across the front of my body, the birthmark of me at a time that I came into myself, got reborn, in the country of sun and poverty. Me with a port wine mark, the *cavernous haemangioma*, which will be with me until I die.

I see him one more time after my departure. It is a year later. I have come back again to Rincón de la Victoria. It is late evening. I have come a long way. José has heard. He is waiting for me at the little train station on the platform.

There is only one dim light. He is standing on the platform, up above where I have gotten down from the train, perhaps four feet above where I am standing. It is winter, and cold wind comes up from the south, from the Mediterranean, from the icy Atlas Mountains of North Africa.

The blue sweater I bought him is worn at the elbows, his mother's patches cannot make the sleeves entire. The pants I bought him are faded. The shoes are filled with holes.

"Buenas," he says. "Buenas," I say. He stands on the platform, I far below him. He stands and looks down at me, then out over the ocean. His eyes have dusked over again, just as they were the first time we met. His fists are in his pockets. His shoulders are hunched up. He shivers from the wind that keens in from the sea.

He is such a tiny figure. For one who has loomed so large in my life—friend, companion, fellow traveller—he is such a cold and pitiable and shivering figure, so small against the sky and the platform and the wind sweeping up from the icy mountains to the south. He is such a small and fragile creature. He grew to such dimensions because of my huge needs, because of the fact that my demands and desires were so whale-like. But truly, he himself: he is a small and delicate creature. The children of the earth, the poor children of the earth. They are so fragile, specks on the landscape of adult needs and madnesses.

He, José, is back to his own small self again. He fed huge on my plans and dreams, supped at my wealth, engorged in my fantasies: and now he is the child of the beach again, back in his poor clothes again.

I reach out for him. I want to grab his shoulders, put my arms around him. But he is up there and I am down here, and my body does not allow me to do anything more than reach out for him, whatever part I can reach. His ankle. Cheap ratty yellow socks, just above worn shoes, shoelaces tied and retied in countless knots. His ankle—the only part of José I can reach. And it is such a frail and thin ankle for one his age.

It could have been different. I could have brought him back with me, given him nice clothes to wear, given him huge American meals, watch him grow to normal size. I could have done that: "Tómale" his father said, but I didn't. I deceived him. I didn't do it. My want was great—as was my fear; no, greater than my fear. Something else. The twinge, the twitch that I thought I had renounced, abandoned, given up when I came to Europe. That tiny twitch of morality, that twitch in the foot: it would be wrong to capture a poor boy, wouldn't it? There is something wrong with that, isn't there? Isn't there? I'm not sure what . . . not sure what . . . not even sure I am right. The tiny difference between what I think, and what I do. That miniscule abyss between desire and deed.

José got raped. When you think about José and me and Salvadore and me: it was *José* got raped. I gave him food and talk about America and the good life. He came to believe in it and in me, that we were going to go on forever. I drew out the nectar, then killed the plant. We spent time together, everyday: and sometimes, on cold days, he would skip school, and come over to my place, and build a fire. He would sip gin (good medicine for his stomach, he told me) and stare into the fire for hours, mesmerized. We were companions, brothers, despite the fifteen year gap in our ages.

And then I disappeared, left him bereft. All the magic was gone. When, at last, I returned for the brief visit, it was to see that José had come again to where I had found him. With one exception: that my two years with him had given him an especial sense of desperation at his own life, a knowledge of the trap that his poverty represented.

I gave José the fatal understanding: that there is no escape from being poor; no escape from the economic prison instituted by societies which destroy their young for the pleasure of the rich and the tourists.

CHAPTER XXVIII

My lawyers write me, tell me that if I return to the United States—they (the government) might give me a radio station—on which to broadcast, on which to tell my tale.

I take the bus down from Málaga to the border town of La Línea de La Concepción. From there, I will cross over to Gibraltar, catch the airplane to England, and thence on to New York.

My last night in La Línea, I go to a tiny restaurant. I eat a meal of *pulpos* by myself, drink a bottle of red wine. I am feeling terrible to be away from my friends in Rincón de la Victoria. I am worried about returning to the country I have vowed to disown.

I am drunk and muttering to myself, miserable after leaving the restaurant. Outside, on the street, there is a trolley car. "I should get on board," I think. I figure that it will be the last trolley ride I will take for some time. And it is such a grand machine: with a giant U-bar that reaches up to the heavens, leaking power, sparkling and crackling, blue shots to illuminate the cobblestone-shadows.

I pull myself up the trolley stairs one at a time. I am the only passenger. The driver is thin, his face is bony, his eyes penetrating. "Ah, my Charon," I think. We go across the city, then down to the beach, down to the water. The trolley stops at the beach. I can hear the surf muttering to itself.

I get off. It is late at night. The trolley groans, sparks a few shadows on the beach, and disappears. I am alone. I go down to the edge.

Across from me, beyond the dim white lips of the surf, lies

a cold sea, and Africa. The Atlas mountains shadow the sky, blotting out the stars that lean so close to the horizon. The cold wind needles my jacket, and I shiver. I wait for the next trolley car to take me back to my warm hotel. I wait and wait. I wait some more. I make my way to the schedule sea-blurred on the pole. I light a match, and discover that I was on the last car of the night. It is a dark and lonely place. There are no houses.

I walk about, as best I am able, across the rock and stone-strewn beach. Because of my full bottle of *tinto,* I am slightly drunk. I am thinking about last Christmas, back in Rincón de la Victoria. It was late at night, like this. It was cold outside. Salvadore was to come, my Christmas present, wrapped up in his delicate white fruit-of-the-loom shorts, the gift I prefer above all others.

I waited and waited for the train. It was late. Finally at 9:33, I could hear it puffing and fussing past the house. I waited for my Salvadore, and finally I heard him outside, in the bushes, talking to someone, two men from the Guardia Civil; above the sound of the sea, Salvadore talking with, perhaps arguing with, two of the state policemen in their tricorn hats. I waited and waited, unable to catch the gist of their argument, the sea being louder than the words. I think that perhaps they are going to arrest Salvadore. Perhaps they had found out about our liaison. Perhaps they would make him reveal everything about our relationship. Perhaps they would torture him.

Fully alarmed, I peg to the door that leads to the beach, yank it open, and see there before me no one: no one to the right nor the left nor up on the roof nor below the porch nor behind the trees. There is no one but the beach and sea and thick yellow moon.

I think about that sub-basement, under my love and my lust, where I have spooks with which I can people the bushes and shadows, vapor policemen with which I fill the world, arbitrary guards for my ruinous passion. The under-pinnings of my lust are so dangerous, and all is supported by the muck and ooze from which I come.

"What a nightmare," I think. Here I am at the end of the line, and what do I have to show for it. No hope, no ideals, no faith. I walk down to the surf, turn to go back, slip on a stone, and topple to the ground. "Just like a big fat dead bird," I think, as I roll on the pebbles and sand. "I should be in atoms," I think: "Atoms." I feel alone and desperate. "At least there wasn't anyone around to see me fall," I think. I am sick of people watching me topple over to the ground, like some big tree after it's been sawed in half. I think of their frozen-fear faces, the surprise-horror in their eyes.

I lie there on the pebbles and think about Salvadore some more. Last week I told him I was going to be gone for awhile. I told him I had to travel back to the United States to take care of business. He sat before me, his face yellow and stony. The fire makes it look like wax.

"Tuve más alegre (I was much happier)," he told me "antes de todo este dinero (before you came along and gave me all this money.)

"Era muy diferente antes (It was so much different before you came on the scene.)

"Fuímos al campo, todas las semanas, con las niñas (We used to go each week, all of us, out to the fields, out with the girls.) Bailemos y cantemos toda la noche (We would dance and we would sing all night.) Qué alegría! (We had so much fun!)

"Ya, no tengo ni un amigo, o amiga (Now I don't have any friends—man or women.) Si no estuviera aqui, estuví en casa, solo (If I am not here, working for you, I'm at home alone.)

"Era mucho mejor antes (It was so much better before.) Mucho mas de alegría (There was so much more happiness then.) Ahora, tengo ningún amigo (Now, I don't have any friends at all.) Ni un amigo (Not even one.) Soy muy triste (I am very sad.)"

As he is telling me this, I watch, and see the tears leak down his face, his face so impassive. His shoulders don't shake. He sits there, shoulders slightly drooping, face very doleful, and almost as if it weren't his tears, as if they belonged to someone else. The tears come out of his eyes, run down his cheeks, run down past the corners of his mouth, down to his chin, where they pause for a moment, then drop off into his lap. "Poor Salvadore," I think.

That memory makes me sad. Sad for Salvadore who now has money, and who is now so sad. I, on that stone beach, mourn for him and what has happened to his life. Poor Salvadore, and poor me. We had to come to such a desolate state in order to love. "Passion," I think. "What a bludgeon it is."

I have to weep a bit for me, and for Salvadore. While I am about it, I weep for me being a cripple. I haven't wept on that one for a long time. And while I am about *that*, I weep for me being a cripple who has fallen down. I weep for me being on the ground, weeping, and for all the other cripples in the world who, tonight, perhaps, have fallen in some such drunken puddle of humility. Jesus.

And the children of Spain. I have to weep for them — not only for Marcellina and José and Enrique, but all the others, who, perhaps, I will never meet. I weep for them and for their fathers and mothers, and grandfathers and grandmothers. All those people in Spain, and so many of them with such disfigurements: faces twisted by the blight; humped backs; dragging legs; bent bones; missing fingers; holes-for-noses; empty eye-sockets. All these cripples, collected together on the Iberian Peninsula. And what do they do? They sing! Good Christ! With all this poverty and disease, and total lack of hope for the future, and they get together in some crappy old *cantina* and start singing. The most desolating poverty in Europe, and they stand around in a half-deserted hole-in-the-wall, with one single miserable dim fluorescent tube for light, and they sing songs about love and bullfights and old heroes who are dead and in the grave. So pitiable and so right: these nuts singing out their sadness and their joy.

There is no sound except for the sound of the surf. There is no light except for the ghostlight of a moon gone gibbous sinking through the horizon. I can see above me the blue-black of space, spun on, infinitely, beyond earth and solar system, beyond galaxy, beyond reason.

Sharp stones stick in my back. The few stars that brave the ashen flow of moon pierce the soul of me. I am alone. We are alone. We are alone, all alone in the universe, all of us alone.

The white edge of surf approaches the beach, rises up, and explodes to death on the sands. "What I will do," I think, "is lie here. All night. I will lie here all night in my shirt, with my thin summer coat, and my thin summer pants, and I will let myself be exposed to the merciless night and cold."

When they come tomorrow, they will find my cold and lifeless body here. They will wonder who I am, how I got here, why I didn't seek help. I will scrawl a note to them, tell them that I am a man without country and without hope. I will tell them that I died by my own choice and free will, because I was alone, without the heart to survive, because no one cared for me. I will die a martyr to all the lonely people of all the lonely earth.

They will recognize me as the Saint of Loneliness. At first, little known: the anonymous cripple of the cold beach just outside La Línea de la Concepción. Then, over time, over the years, more and more people will come to hear of me. "He died because he was alone. He thought no one loved him."

They will go to prove I am wrong. Each year, thousands, then hundreds of thousands of pilgrims will make the trek to this isolated spot, at the end of the line. There will be a statue of me, standing thirty feet tall, me, my small frame glasses, my thin frayed jacket and trousers, my two majestic stone crutches. I shall stand here forever, on a great bronze base weathered and whipped by wind and sea and sand. "Here lies the real martyr to the loneliness of humanity" will be in inscription at the bottom of that huge shrine. And all over the world there will be people who will carry a small statuette of me in their pockets, on their key chains, a small luminous statue that glows in the dark—a momento to the fact that all over the world, in every city, town, village and hamlet, there are people who are desperately lonely, who are convinced that no one in the world loves them.

Three sailors come by. Out of the dark they come, walking past, on the beach. They are talking, laughing, telling stories, singing. One is speaking of some imagined night in Córdoba. Another is telling of the flight of his "pajarito" into the nest of love, in Granada. The third is singing Flamenco. They are tipsy on jeréz. They stop near me: in their green uniforms, turned dark with the sea. This is their one night out on the town, and they have stumbled across drunken me in my submarine of sorrow.

The one nearest me has skin burnished like almonds. He has a long dark wondrous face, with *san paku* eyes, as blue as my own. He calls to me. "¿Ayúdete?" he says, his shadow fallen across my heart. His brothers echo the word in low, throaty sonority. "¿Ayúdete?" they say.

"Where do they get them?" I wonder. "Where do they get those voices?" So young, and yet they speak with all the timbre and passion of the warm Andalusian sea. The murmurings of a thousand thousand years played out at the edge of the Mediterranean. My dark saving seamen, come out of the spout of time, endlessly rocking, turning us on our beds, in our cradles, into our graves. Sinuous motion, gypsies rounding musically in the shadows of caves.

The one with my eyes hunkers down beside me, knees crackling. He puts an innocent hand on my innocent thigh. "¿Ayúdete?" he asks again: "May I help thee?" This innocent god wants to make me whole again. He will touch me, he will cure me. The spark will course from his heart, through his hand, up to my soul, and I will be transformed, enflamed by the godhead.

His eyes; his concerned face, his touch, his words: he has chosen to speak to me with the *te* of intimacy and love, rather than the distant *se* of formality and age. He knows me, he does: the ocean layers of me. He has known me centuries in the past, will know me centuries into the future. I am the old man fallen to the sands; and he is the nautilus, moving over shores to save me and all the others who have come down with terminal despair. We have met before, he and I: we will meet again. He will save me countless times. He will save me from my devilish self-inflicted, self-imposed, self-pitying, self-strangling grief. He is my saving grace.

"How lucky we are," I think—after they have gone. "How lucky we are to have the young about us, to save us when we most need them." We fall down and think that we have fallen to ultimate degradation —but our falls are no more than another in the continuous falls of mankind. We are not alone in these moments of vexation: we just think we are. The sailors will always be about us, to raise us again to the heights, should we wish.

I am right, aren't I? To love the young out of the sea? Randall and Marine Spicer? Salvadore of the sad eyes, Tom of the riotous skin? Even my robbing black of Dakar. I am right to love them, in my own way. I know, I know: I do it all ragged and wrong. But there will come a day, I think (I am right!) when I will be able to love them without the chains of money, martyrdom, guilt.

Lorenzo the dark crab in pursuit of his Sinbads. Lorenzo, the brain-heavy, passion-driven, nut-clunking, chain-gang fruitcake on his desert isle. Lorenzo who escapes from his leeched body by adoration, naked worship of these voyagers from the nine continents. My god the sailors! It is they who will deliver me from the perverts. The perverts! Stalin and Nixon and deGaulle and Heath and Dulles. Those proto-pederasts who take our young, strip them to their cream-soft skin, stuff them in dun-colored uniforms, put rifles in their hands, and send them out to destroy their own.

O you perverts! Eisenhower and Molotov and Tito and Beria and that gimpy Christian Herter. All of them so full of hate for the boy-within that they push them out into the mud of Ypres, Inchon, Iwo, Irún: to die there, dying in the green rot of national idiocy. Those old geezers with their withered shanks and melon-moon bellies: so envious of the young and the brave that they send them forth, under a frazzled banner marked "Glory!" and turn children, the innocent babes, into Unknown Soldiers, to moulder under marble.

The ultimate perversion is not that I have loved, or wanted to love, or thought of loving, Salvadore and José and Spicer and Randall. No: the ultimate sin is that I should feel wrong, dirty, guilty for so doing—and thus create in all of them equal feelings of wrong, foisting off on them my own grievous sense of guilt. All the while I am wrangling others with my guilt, Mao and Adenauer and Franco are conspiring to destroy the young by the brigade, by the army, by the nation. Strip them bare, and instead of flowering their tender bodies with kisses, forcing them (gun and bayonet) to slash and brutalize each other. *¡Ay, qué maricones!*

"What they should do," I think, "is to let us *real* queers run the world for awhile. Enough of these fake perverts!" We would put an end to all this killing. Would we fruitballs send the young of clear eyes and downy cheeks into some mass murder scheme in Korea, Stalingrad, Viet-Nam, Pakistan, Algeria? Fat chance! The only soldiers we would permit into the field would be over forty years of age; and there would be therein a full quota of presidents, party chairmen, senators, prime ministers. Let them and the caudillos and the representatives and the governors and the commissars take out their rapine on each other! Leave us boys alone, in the golden shadows, where we belong.

I shake with the cold that has penetrated deep into the core of me. I shake with the cold, and with the wonder of those men in power, and what they do to the young of the world. I quiver with the force of their hate and ugliness, externalizing their childish misery onto the rest of us. I shake with the evil—and with the new power I have found here on this beach, the power needed to change all that, the power to rid the world of their vicious degrading harm of the young. It's time to rouse myself and cast out these villains.

I get my bones over to the end of the trolley-line. I push myself up on the bench, and rest for a moment. "Jesus Christ," I think: "I have so much to do!" I yank my crutches up from the ground, my old go-with-you-anywhere-anytime-pal crutches, my eternal silver wings of locomotion (me a bird of silver wings). "Jesus Christ!" I say. "I'm fucked if I am going to freeze to death in his hole!" I have six thou-

217

sand miles to travel tomorrow. I have people to see, people to argue with, people to shake out of their systems. "I'm getting out of here. I have to do something about those pie-brains who want to kill our boys. 'We've got to love them and care for them—not kill them!' I'll say. 'Good God!' I'll say: 'What's wrong with you? You don't want our children to grow up dead, do you?'"

I get up from the cement stool, and start walking down the tracks, get my old bones to moving again. I follow the tracks to a path, which turns into a street. I peg down the street for awhile, and it turns into an intersection. Soon enough, a taxi comes along, and I stop it, and get in, and go back to my hotel, to the world again. It's time to begin another journey, another long journey, to the west. It's time to tell them what they are doing wrong. They may not hear me, not at first, but it'll be a start.

Sometime, when I have a few days, I'll tell you about the new road I started on that night. I'll tell you where I went (or tried to go) and how I got there (or tried to get there.) I'll tell you about the people I met, the structures I built, the world I talked to, or tried to talk to. I'll tell you all about the people that helped me, and the ones that didn't, and the ones—like me—that were changed by this new journey. I have so much to tell you about this new trek of mine. Some day, I promise you, I'll tell you about it. Not now. Not enough time. I have to hurry. There are so many, too many things to do.

Suffice it to say that I went back to the world, my world, again. And no one knows (except you) how close we came, all of us, to having a martyr, a universally beloved martyr, there on that beach. A figure of pathos and tragedy, there on the sand: the Dead Saint of all the Isolates and Perverts and Cripples of the world, set in cold stone, frozen forever on that sacred and wind-swept beach.

AFTERWARD

First of all, I should like to thank my subconscious which wrote this whole book for me. And my right thumb: I fell on the sucker two weeks into the manuscript, fracturing it. Having little else to do but enjoy the throb of pain, I got to spend time at my desk, writing and rewriting and cursing my fate.

Cathy Conheim was the person who insisted that this book needed to be written. She was right.

Jeff Nighbyrd edited most drafts, and gave me hope that someday there would be a publisher. Tom Thomas (who helped me with an earlier book) was kind enough to read this one and comment on it at length. Hugh Gallagher read the manuscript twice, which he assures me is some kind of concession. His beautiful and haunting essay on his own first months in the hospital were very important to the description of my sister's last days.

Dr. Dave McWhirter read the whole to correct any medical inaccuracies. Holt Maness and Lee Milam read the whole to scold me over the vestiges of Puritan Morality that peep a stern eye through my words. Laura Daltry and Laura Hopper read the whole because they both enjoy reading. Karyn Alice Baker showed herself to be a competent editor, but told me that there should be a few more developed characters in the book besides me. Cese McGowan helped me with the final, the hardest, draft.

Meriel Milam, Joy Milam Dennis and Kevin Milam were able to refresh my memory on past events which had drifted beyond me. Peggy Golberg read the manuscript entire to chastise me over my bad language and remind me of the pure. Jane Anne Shannon said the manuscript was good enough to eat, and both Sy Safransky and Hy Cohen gave me hope for its future. Diana Boernstein read it and said it had too many naked backs and ruddy bums, and Tom Connors said it should be called *Another Man with a Monkey on His Back*. Dear Tom.

Doug Cruickshank coordinated the layout, design and printing of the whole book, while Ovid was kind enough to give us the *mot* in Chapter XIX which translates as

I see the better way, and approve it;
I follow the worse . . .

And finally, Vergil, in his fourth *Ecloque*, provided the line used at the end of Part I:

Now has come the last age
The great series of lifetimes starts anew . . .

LWM
Paradise, California
October, 1983

can be identified with greater certainty (especially when tape tutors are used), but tutor identification, in some respects, is actually easier in the field. In our song sparrow studies, for example, song copying was more faithful and precise in the field than in the laboratory (see the following).

We considered all birds in the study population who were in the territory during the subject's hatching year as possible song tutors. We identified the bird with the most similar rendition of the song type (complete with idiosyncratic features not heard in other renditions of the song type) as the young bird's probable tutor for that song type. This judgment was rarely difficult because song-sparrow songs are complex and similar songs are conspicuous against the background of the nearly infinite variety of possible song types. In addition to the tutor–student classification, we also classified songs that were shared by tutors (i.e. two or more tutors had very similar songs) or unshared (i.e. the song type was unique to one singer in the reference group). Procedurally, this classification was fairly easy and very similar to the tutor–student classification because highly similar songs were conspicuous against the background of extraordinary song diversity.

We will summarize the results of these field studies of song learning (Beecher et al. 1994b; Nordby et al. submitted). We will contrast these results with those of conventional song-learning experiments in the laboratory.

5.3.2 Song Learning in the Field: Inferences Regarding Song-Learning Rules

Song sparrows in our sedentary population learned songs in a two-part process, which appears to fit the model developed by Marler and Nelson from laboratory and field studies (Marler and Nelson 1992; Nelson and Marler 1994). A young song sparrow left his area of birth at around a month of age. He began to learn songs during the second and third months of life in the neighborhood where he would remain and ultimately attempt to set up a territory. During this early stage, he memorized the song types of the adult birds in his new neighborhood. He did not finalize his repertoire of eight or so songs, however, until the following March. Although song memorization seemed to be completed during the sensitive period of early summer, the bird continued to be influenced by adult tutor-neighbors until the next spring; the bird generally settled next to the tutor-neighbor from whom he learned the most songs. Consequently the bird's final repertoire was more heavily influenced by tutors of the previous summer who survived the winter than those who did not. There was also usually greater influence from nearer tutor-neighbors than more distant tutor-neighbors. In this second phase of learning, the bird did not appear to learn new songs de novo, but was greatly influenced as to which of the many songs he had memorized during the early sensitive period he kept for

his final repertoire of eight or so songs. Social interactions appeared to influence most of the songs that were retained; the bird tended to keep those song types that were shared by neighbors with whom the bird interacted most.

The pattern of song learning we observed in the field can be summarized in terms of the following rules of song learning.

5.3.2.1 The Young Bird Learns Songs from the Birds Who Will Be His Future Neighbors

As already indicated, the young song sparrow learned the songs of the adult males in his new neighborhood, and he preferentially retained the songs of birds that survived into his first breeding season. A representative example is shown in figure 5.2. When one examines the details of song learning, a number of interesting additional rules emerge.

5.3.2.2 The Young Bird Copies Whole Songs Precisely

In the field, young song sparrows usually learned to sing nearly perfect copies of the songs of their older neighbors (fig. 5.3). The similarities were striking; the differences between songs of tutor and student were often no greater than what is normally heard among repetitions of the same song sung by one bird. In the example in figure 5.3, which shows five songs of the young bird and four of his tutors, the biggest difference between songs of student and tutor is in the third song. The young bird appears to have simplified this song by dropping the high-frequency section near the end. The student's rendition of the fifth song is a blend of two tutor songs (this song is discussed later in this chapter).

These field results differ substantially from those of laboratory tape-tutor studies of song sparrows (Marler and Peters 1987, 1988). In the laboratory, young song sparrows copied elements of particular tutors, but they commonly combined elements of the different songs of different tutors to form hybrid songs, or songs made up of parts of different song types.

5.3.2.3 The Young Bird Preserves Type and Tutor in His Songs

In our field population, two exceptions to the perfect-copy rule actually clarified the rule and suggested an additional principle. The first exception occurred when the young bird blended two tutors' somewhat different versions of the same song type (instead of copying one or the other song type). These songs were not true hybrids because song elements—although selected from two different tutors—were selected from the same or very similar song type. The second exception, which was rare, occurred when the young bird combined elements from two dissimilar song types of the *same* tutor (fig. 5.4). The prin-

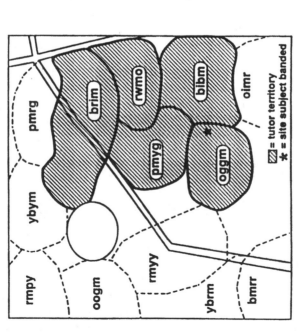

Figure 5.2. A young bird's tutors are neighbors in the area where he settles after leaving his birthplace in his first year; however, not all of these tutors survive into the young bird's first breeding season the next spring. *Left:* Map of territories of thirteen adult birds in the area where the young male AIRM settled in his hatch year (1992). Star indicates where AIRM was banded. Territories of the five birds who were subsequently identified as AIRM's tutors on the basis of his final repertoire in 1993 are outlined and hatch-marked. *Right:* Same configuration overlaid with AIRM's 1993 territory (*hatched*), dead birds are crossed out (eight of the 13 birds, including four of the five tutors). Although the actual 1993 territories of birds other than AIRM are not shown, birds OGGM (the sole-surviving tutor) and OlMR remained in approximately the same place. A pond (*circle*) and two intersecting paths are indicated; open areas were unoccupied (e.g. steep hills and meadows) (from Beecher 1996).

ciple suggested by these two exceptions is the following: Song elements of different songs are combined only if they are from (1) different tutors' versions of the same type; or (2) different song types sung by the same tutor. We summarize this principle as the student "preserving type and/or tutor" in his songs. We have yet to find a clear example of a bird hybridizing a song type of one singer with a distinctly dissimilar song type from a different singer; yet, in the laboratory, song sparrows do this commonly.

5.3.2.4 Young Birds Preferentially Learn Shared Songs

As we discussed, neighbors in our song sparrow population usually shared a portion of their song repertoires, on average about four of their eight to nine song types. We discovered that the young bird preferentially learned (or retained) song types shared by his tutor-neighbors. Typically, the bird's version of the song type most resembled that of one or another of his tutors, but sometimes the bird blended features of the versions of two or more tutors. An example of this learning preference for shared song types is shown in figure 5.5. The young bird shown retained seven types that were shared by two or more of his tutors and only two that were unique to one of these tutors, despite the existence of 11 shared and 13 unshared types in the tutor group. In the full sample analyzed by Beecher et al. (1994b), birds learned (retained) 84% of tutor-shared types and only 21% of tutor-unique types, although only 37% of the tutors' song types were shared.

5.3.3 Song-Learning Rules Imply Cognitive Principles

The song-learning rules we derived from our field observations suggest that a young song sparrow classifies songs by type and singer identity; this two-way classification appears to be central to the construction of the bird's final repertoire. We recapitulate these rules: (1) Song types shared by two or more tutors are preferentially learned. (2) Different tutors' versions of the same song type are often blended, but different tutors' versions of different song types are not. (3) The rare cases in which a bird combines elements of different song types to form a hybrid-song type occur only when the song types are sung by the same singer. The strategy of song learning defined by these rules is possible only if the young bird classifies tutor songs by type and singer identity.

It is instructive to contrast these rules in the field with those in the laboratory. In the Marler and Peters (1987) tape-tutor study, there was no evidence of this two-way classification. With tape tutors, however, the necessary conditions for defining song type and singer identity are eliminated. With tape recordings, individual identity can be preserved only to the extent that the different song types of a song sparrow have common "signature" or "voice"

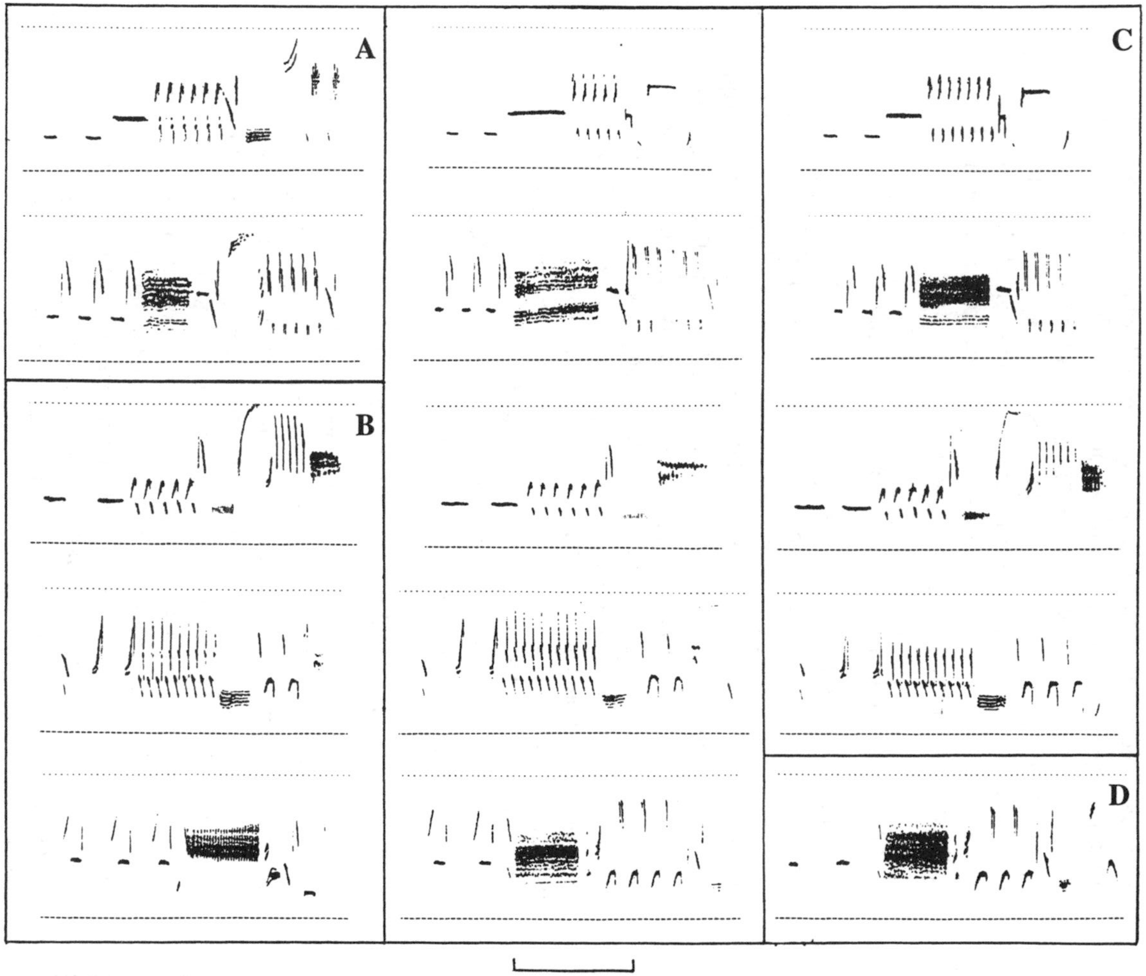
A
B
C
D

Figure 5.4. A young bird's hybrid song from two songs of one tutor. The young bird's hybrid song (*right*) incorporates the first four elements of one song type (*top left*) of the tutor and all but the first two elements of another song type (*bottom left*) of the tutor. Frequency scale is 2–10 kHz in 2-kHz steps. Time marker = 1 second. Bandwidth = 117 Hz.

characteristics; we showed in perceptual experiments that the song types do not have these characteristics (Beecher et al. 1994a). Moreover, tape-tutor studies have not used different singers' versions of the same type. The results of these tape-tutor studies contrast with those of our field studies. The most obvious discrepancy is that cross-tutor hybrid songs are common in tape-tutor studies but essentially are not sung in the field. We suggest that a bird preserves a whole song type not simply because he has frequently heard those particular elements sung together. He preserves a whole song type because (1) he has heard that song type contrasted with other distinct song types within the repertoire of a particular singer, and (2) he has heard that song type sung by different birds. In other words, a song type is defined by the song being sung by both multiple birds and a particular bird that sings multiple types.

Figure 5.3. Sonograms of five of the nine song types of one young bird are shown (*middle column*). Left and right columns show the matching song types of his four tutors; each tutor is denoted with a box (*left,* two song types of tutor A and three of tutor B; *right,* four songs of tutor C and one of tutor D). Song types not shown include those unique to a particular tutor and those shared by three or more tutors. In some cases, the young bird's version of the song type was closer to that of one tutor or the other. For example, his renditions of the top two song types were more like that of the tutor's songs on the right. Song classification was based on several versions of each song type from each bird (not all shown). Song sparrows vary their song types from one occasion to another, and song types, therefore, are better described as song classes. Song endings are most variable and least diagnostic of song type. Frequency markers at the bottom and top of each sonagram are 0 and 10 kHz, respectively. Time marker denotes 1 second. Bandwidth = 117 Hz.

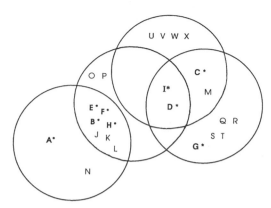

Figure 5.5. Young males preferentially learn songs shared by two or more tutors. Venn diagram of four tutors (*circles*) of one young bird. Each song type is indicated with a letter, and shared songs of two or more birds are indicated with the same letter. Shared song types are in the overlapping sections of the circles (e.g. types I and D were shared by three tutors). The nine song types learned by the young bird are indicated (bold type and *asterisk*). The young bird learned seven of the eleven tutor-shared types but only two of the thirteen tutor-unique types (from Beecher 1996).

Thus, if conditions in the laboratory eliminate or muffle these features (as a tape-tutor experiment inevitably does), the bird will not copy whole songs but will recombine the learned song elements into hybrid songs.

Simply replacing tape tutors with live tutors in the laboratory is not sufficient to simulate adequately the natural song-learning environment and, therefore, replicate field results. In our first attempt at such a simulation, we exposed young song sparrows in the laboratory to the songs of four live tutors (Beecher et al. unpublished). Otherwise, our paradigm had no more ecological validity than the typical tape-tutor experiment, and our results were closer to those of the comparable tape-tutor study (Marler and Peters 1987) than those of the field study. In particular, our young birds developed repertoires of nearly all hybrid songs.

We offer the following as one likely reason for the number of hybrid songs observed in our laboratory study. In this study, we used four tutors each of whom had come from a different area; these tutors, therefore, had no song types in common. Thus, we presented the young birds with a set of tutors that were very abnormal in our bird population. As discussed, song types were poorly defined in this situation; there were no song types common to more than a single tutor.

Moreover, if a young song sparrow has a preference for learning shared song types, what does he do if he is presented with tutors that share no song types? Suppose the song-learning bird has a predisposition to pay attention to

song types that are sung by two or more tutors. The bird must, therefore, make a judgment about the similarity of or differences among songs of different tutors. If the songs are similar enough, he categorizes them as the same type; and if the different tutors' versions of the type are different enough, the bird must blend the versions. The more different the blended songs are, the more the resulting song will sound like a hybrid song to the experimenter. Yet, from the bird's perspective, he has produced a version of a tutor-shared song type. A set of tutor songs that are dissimilar may cause the bird to stretch his similarity criterion. We think this is the most likely (and certainly the most interesting) explanation for the hybrid songs produced by song sparrows in our laboratory experiment (and perhaps for those produced in the tape-tutor study of Marler and Peters 1987). It is a testable proposition: Hybrid songs should be uncommon when there are many shared songs in the set of tutor songs, but hybrid songs should be common when there are few shared songs among tutors.

In our study population in the field hybrid songs were exceptionally rare, probably because tutor-neighbors invariably shared many clearly similar songs. Occasionally, we observed a tricky case, in which the bird appeared to regard two songs of his tutor-neighbors as 'shared,' but we did not classify the songs as shared. For example, figure 5.6 shows two examples of a young bird's blending of similar songs from two tutors. In each case, we can infer that the young bird regarded the pair of tutor songs as the same type (i.e. the songs were similar enough to blend). Cases like these were relatively rare in our field population because probably the bird was usually exposed to more similar songs from which to choose.

Finally, some possible support for the interpretation that song learning is partially guided by the bird's concept of song type comes from a recent tape-tutor experiment by Nowicki et al. (in preparation). They found that song types that were presented with variations were preferentially learned over songs that were presented without variations. A possible interpretation of this result is that the bird's concept of song type may be stimulated by hearing variations of the type. This effect may be analogous to the bird's tendency in the field to preferentially learn song types sung by more than one tutor (i.e. each tutor sings the song type somewhat differently). We do not know, of course, if the learning preference for tutor-shared types is because of the greater number of variations of a type or the greater number of repetitions of that type; however, these propositions are testable.

In summary, we are suggesting that the song-learning bird be viewed as a cognitive decision maker; he decides how to lump or split the many tutor songs that he hears. These decisions are guided in part by the bird's concepts of singer individuality and song type, and the bird will not blur these categories; he will preserve tutor and type distinctions unless the conditions of song learning are ambiguous. Further research, in which these variables are experi-

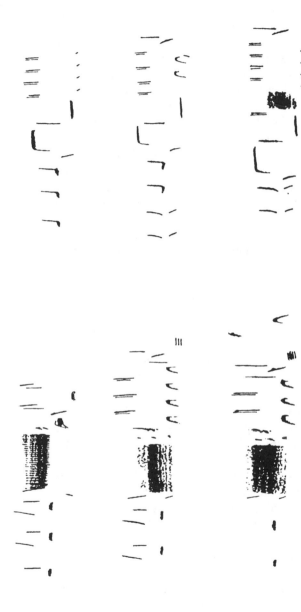

Figure 5.6. Two examples of a young bird blending the songs of two tutors: the two song types were similar but not easily classified as shared. The young bird's sonagram (*middle*) and the two tutors' sonagrams (*above* and *below*) are shown. In the example on the left (also shown in fig. 5.3), the young bird takes the first part of his song from one tutor song (*above*) and the rest is from the other tutor song (*below*). The similarity between the two tutor songs is not in the microstructure of the elements, but the songs have the same sorts of elements in the same order. Specifically, both begin with two or three notes at frequencies of about 4,000 Hz (birds often vary the number of notes within a song type) spaced about 40 msec apart. The notes of one tutor song but not the other are embellished with higher grace notes. The introductory notes are followed by a buzz about 0.5 seconds in duration. In both tutor songs, the buzz is preceded by a down sweep and followed by a two-voiced upsweep. The end of the two songs differ, although not re-markably so (from Beecher 1996). In the example on the right, the young bird takes the following introductory notes from both tutors: the shared four-note complex (the buzz of one tutor [*below*] is omitted); the shared trill (with modification); and the final note complex of one tutor (*below*). The two tutor songs are difficult to classify as shared, despite strong similarities in microstructure, because they differ in terms of the introductory notes and the presence of a buzz in one tutor song only. Note, however, that if you remove the buzz from the one tutor's song (*below*), it is virtually identical to the other tutor's song (*above*) except for the introductory notes (the notes at very end of the song are not diagnostic because the song is invariably changed from one performance to the next) (from Beecher 1996).

mentally manipulated, will be required to test the validity of this cognitive interpretation.

5.3.4 Simulating Key Ecological Song-Learning Variables in the Laboratory

We argued that laboratory studies of song learning can be misleading because key social variables and context are removed from the laboratory situation. It should follow that adding these variables back into the laboratory will provide results that are more similar to those of field studies. Our first attempt (described) failed in this regard because our simulation was unrealistic (apart from substituting live birds for tape tutors). We recently completed a second simulation; this time, we brought into the laboratory more features thought to be critical to the pattern of song learning in the field (Nordby et al., unpublished).

In this experiment, we put four adult song sparrows in aviaries at four corners of the roof of a building; we attempted to simulate four neighboring territories. The adults were neighbors in our population, and consequently, they shared some song types. Young birds were taken from the nest in another area at approximately 4 days of age and raised in the laboratory. At fledging (about 1 month), they were placed in cages next to the tutors. The young bird could see only the tutor he was stationed next to, but he could hear the other tutors at a distance. During their second and third months, the young birds were rotated among the four tutors on a weekly basis. That fall and following spring, half the subjects were again rotated among the four tutors, and each of the other subjects was stationed next to only one tutor. Final song repertoires of the young birds were recorded in late spring. The pattern of song learning was very similar to that we observed in the field. First, most songs the birds developed were good matches to song types of tutors. Only rarely did birds produce hybrid songs (i.e. elements of different tutor songs rearranged into a new song type). Second, although our analysis is not yet complete, it appeared that birds preferentially learned or retained song types shared by tutors. Third, birds learned songs from multiple tutors. Fourth, a bird stationed next to a particular tutor learned, or retained, more songs of that tutor than of the other tutors.

5.4 COMMUNICATION BY SONG IN MALE–MALE INTERACTIONS

5.4.1 Design of the Playback Experiments

We examined the nature of singing interactions primarily with playback experiments in which we experimentally manipulated one part of the singing inter-

action. In these experiments, we played neighbor or stranger songs near the boundary between the subject's and neighbor's territories and, in some cases, at an "inappropriate" territory boundary (i.e. that of another neighbor) or within the subject's territory. When song was played from a neighbor's territory, the neighbor was drawn off during the trial. Playback trials were 3 minutes long and songs were repeated at the typical rate of the species, approximately one song every 10 seconds. We measured five components of the subject's response to the playback: (1) closest approach to the playback speaker; (2) number of flights; (3) number of songs; (4) song types sung (usually only one); and (5) displays such as wing waves and "quiet song." Closest approach and number of flights are clear correlates of aggressive responses. In song sparrows, the number of loud songs sung during the trial is not a simple correlate of aggressive response; although birds sing very little when uninterested in the playback, typically they are equally silent when in "attack mode," searching for the singer in the bushes near the playback speaker. Which particular song types the birds sing may be related to aggressive response and will be discussed further. Wing waves and quiet song (which is qualitatively different from normally loud song in respects besides amplitude) are very intense responses, but they were seen mainly when the playback occurred within the subject's territory. Loud song was rarely sung in these cases; these cases indicate that loud song is truly a long-distance signal.

5.4.2 Results

5.4.2.1 Neighbor Song from the Neighbor's Territory Evokes a Weak Response

If the playback song was presented from the neighbor's territory near the boundary, the subject usually responded less intensely if the playback song was that of the neighbor versus that of a different neighbor (i.e. a neighbor in the wrong place), a stranger, or the subject (the latter perhaps is perceived as a stranger song) (fig. 5.7) (Stoddard et al. 1990, 1991; Beecher et al. 1996). It makes sense, of course, that the subject responded less strongly to a neighbor's song from the neighbor's territory than to other songs; singing of these other songs may suggest territorial intrusion to the subject.

5.4.2.2 Otherwise, Responses to Neighbor and Stranger Songs Are Equally Strong

The subject responded equally strongly to neighbor and stranger songs when the songs were played back from a boundary of an inappropriate territory or within the subject's territory (fig. 5.7, Stoddard et al. 1991). A ceiling effect is a possible interpretation of the response to the playbacks within the territory

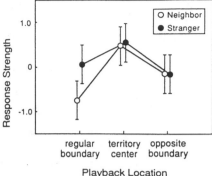

Figure 5.7. Mean response to playback of fourteen male song sparrows to songs of neighbors and strangers played in three locations: (1) the regular boundary (where the neighbor's song is ordinarily heard); (2) the center of the subject's territory; and (3) the opposite boundary (i.e. opposite from where the neighbor's song is ordinarily heard). Bars are ± 2 standard errors of the mean and represent 95% confidence intervals for the mean estimates (from Stoddard et al. 1991).

but not the response to the playback from the inappropriate boundary. The response at the boundary was reduced compared with that in the territory; the most conservative interpretation of the equality of the response at the boundary is neighbors and strangers were viewed by the subject as equally threatening. This interpretation is consistent with field studies of another sedentary population of song sparrows; these studies showed that a bird's territory may be usurped by either a new bird (floater) or one of his current neighbors (Arcese 1987, 1989).

5.4.2.3 Birds Reply to Neighbor Songs with Songs Specific to Those Neighbors

The prevailing view on species-specific repertoires is that different song types in a repertoire are interchangeable and exist primarily to provide diversity (e.g. Kroodsma 1988). If this view were correct, we might expect the bird to reply to a stimulus song with a song type that is chosen randomly from his repertoire. We found, however, that a song sparrow did not reply with a randomly chosen song, at least under most circumstances. Instead, he typically replied to a neighbor's song (from the neighbor's territory) with one of the song types he shared with that particular neighbor (remember, neighbors in our population shared an average of about 30% of their eight to nine song types). If the particular stimulus song was in his repertoire he usually would not reply with that song but with another one of the song types he shared with the neighbor (assuming he shared more than the one). We call this pattern of

song selection "repertoire matching" because usually the bird matched some song in the stimulus bird's repertoire (Beecher et al. 1996). Repertoire matching implies knowledge of the singer's repertoire; the bird must know which songs he shares with the singer.

A bird responded to the song of a stranger very differently. If he had a similar song type in his repertoire, he usually responded with that type (type matching) (Stoddard et al. 1992). We cannot describe how he selected his reply song if he did not have a similar type in his repertoire (the usual case); however, we made the following observation: If the stranger song was played from a neighbor's territory, the subject avoided replying with a song type he shared with the neighbor. The bird appeared to reserve the shared songs for that neighbor. This interesting response suggests a concept of "not neighbor." In one study, we played back the same stranger song to the subjects on two different days; the birds tended to respond with different songs on the two days. This suggests that the subject birds may not have been selecting a particular reply song (Stoddard et al. 1992).

To summarize these findings of type matching, song sparrows generally matched type in response to stranger songs (that were similar enough) and their own playback songs, but they rarely matched type in response to neighbor songs. The same pattern has been observed in western meadowlarks (Falls 1985) and a similar pattern has been observed in great tits (Falls et al. 1982).

Under one specific set of conditions, however, birds matched type in response to neighbors songs: This occurred when neighbors were new that year and the breeding season was still early (Beecher et al. unpublished). Longtime neighbors, on the other hand, rarely matched type; birds replied with another song they shared with that neighbor.

5.4.3 Another Instructive Contrast

Just as we unwittingly performed a laboratory study with minimal ecological validity that happened to provide an instructive contrast to its field counterpart, so have we performed ecologically dubious playback studies, and they have proved to be equally instructive. The concept behind these playback experiments was closer to that of the classic ethological model described earlier than to that of the cognitive-ecology model we now favor. Both studies were designed to reveal which types of songs are more threatening (i.e. better releasers) (Krebs et al. 1981). In the first experiment, we compared unmatchable songs (stranger songs which did not resemble any of the subject's songs) with songs that could be matched (the subject's own songs, or self songs). (We used self songs because previous studies showed these songs were equivalent to very similar stranger songs; however, similar stranger songs were much

harder to find because usually, in our population, only neighbors sung very similar songs.) We used a two-speaker design in which two speakers were placed at equivalent locations, about 50 m apart, within the bird's territory; on different days, we switched which speaker played which song. In the second experiment, we compared matching vs. nonmatching song. In this case, we used a single speaker; one stimulus was used on one test day, and another was used on another test day. The song was presented from a neighbor-free area (an open field) outside the bird's territory. We used self songs as playback stimuli; the same song the subject was singing was played back on one test day, but a different song not in his repertoire was played on another test day. With these two experiments, we attempted to answer similar questions: (1) Are matchable songs more or less threatening than unmatchable songs? (2) Is having your song matched more or less threatening than having your song replied to with an equally familiar, but nonmatching song?

In both studies, we found that the birds responded equally strongly, on average, to both stimuli. Although ceiling effects potentially cloud interpretation of both experiments, the birds simply could have found these songs equally threatening. Whether songs were matchable or not, or matched or not, birds evidently perceived the songs as those of strangers or neighbors in the wrong place (more on this point below); to the birds, these situations are equally dangerous.

These two studies have not been submitted for publication because, on reflection, the results are difficult to interpret. When viewed from a cognitive-ecology perspective, the results don't appear to make much sense. Usually, the only songs a bird hears are those sung by his neighbors. Thus, the bird's best hypothesis concerning a playback song—whether in truth it is a neighbor's song, a stranger's song, a dead neighbor's song, a computer-manipulated song, or one of the bird's own songs—is that it is a neighbor's song. If the hypothesis fits, i.e., if a nearby neighbor has a similar song in his repertoire, the bird should respond appropriately: the response should be weak if the song comes from the hypothesized neighbor's territory and strong if the song does not. Because these two experiments were performed within the subject's territory or at the boundary of a neighbor-free territory, the subject should have responded strongly. If the hypothesis does not fit, i.e., if no neighbor has a song like the playback song, then the bird should assume that the song is that of a stranger and respond appropriately: strongly. Thus, if we take the social-ecological context into account and suppose that the bird takes a cognitive perspective (e.g. "Who is that bird, and does he belong there?"), we see that the logical outcome of these two experiments should be precisely what we found: On average, the bird should have responded equally strongly to both classes of songs because an intruder is an intruder. If this view is correct,

these results are trivial; we would be better off working systematically with neighbor songs or designing reasonable simulations of the kinds of stranger intrusions that typically occur in this population of birds.

5.4.4 Conclusions

Although our understanding of the rules of song communication in neighbor interactions of song sparrows is still rudimentary, one aspect of the system seems very clear. The song sparrows in our study population live in relatively stable neighborhoods, and our playback experiments suggest the birds know one another on the basis of the songs. The birds' knowledge is much more sophisticated than we expected. We were not surprised to find that a bird gave a milder response to a neighbor's song from the neighbor's territory than to a stranger's song from the same place, nor were we surprised to find that the bird responded equally to these songs from other locations (Stoddard et al. 1991, 1992). These results simply imply that the bird recognizes this neighbor. We were surprised, however, to find that the bird replied in a qualitatively different fashion to a neighbor's song from the neighbor's territory than to a stranger's song from the same place: to the neighbor's song with another one of the songs he shares with the neighbor (repertoire matching), to the stranger song with one of the song types he does *not* share with the neighbor. Repertoire matching indicates a more detailed knowledge of the song repertoires of neighbors than we had expected. Repertoire matching suggests that birds classify songs by type (the bird knows which songs he shares or does not share with each of his neighbors) and by individual identity (the bird knows which songs each of his neighbors has in his repertoire).

5.5 DISCUSSION

In this chapter, we developed two points. First, the key variables that determine how a song sparrow constructs his song repertoire (during the period he learns songs) and how he uses the songs in his repertoire are variables that pertain to the bird's social ecology. Second, song communication and song learning in song sparrows are largely organized into two main cognitive categories—individual singer and song type. This two-way classification helps explain which songs birds learn and retain in their first year and the way in which birds use these songs as adults in countersinging interactions.

The major unanswered questions are (1) Why do song sparrows use their songs as they do? and (2) What is the advantage of a learning strategy that provides the bird with songs he shares with his neighbors? We showed that song sparrows preferentially communicate with neighbors with shared songs, but the function of this repertoire matching is unknown. The posting function remains the only function of song repertoires in male–male interactions that

we are certain of, but how repertoire matching or having shared songs relates to this function (if at all) is not obvious.

A major impediment to developing hypotheses about the function of song in neighbor communication is our limited understanding of the territorial neighbor relationship. The field has advanced beyond theories like the "Beau Geste" hypothesis (Krebs 1977), which suggests that a bird moving into an area and prospecting for territory misperceives a single bird with several song types as several different birds and consequently avoids that high-density neighborhood. We can now be reasonably sure that these birds know not only how many birds are in the neighborhood, but who they are, and probably the details of their song repertoires as well. However, the working model of the territorial neighbor relationship remains a simple competition model, and most theories of song function in this context do not go beyond that assumption. For example, consider the various hypotheses that have been advanced to explain the function of song repertoires in this context. All of these hypotheses propose that the bird uses his song repertoire as a weapon against his neighbor in one way or another (the hypothesis usually is based on whether the bird's songs match or do not match those of his neighbors). For example, according to the ranging hypothesis (Morton 1986), the bird uses his repertoire to disturb his neighbor; according to the threat hypothesis (Krebs et al. 1981), repertoire is used to threaten the neighbor. According to the antihabituation hypothesis (Kroodsma 1988), repertoire is used to keep the posting signal fresh and hold the neighbor's attention; according to the Beau Geste hypothesis, repertoire is used to confuse and discourage prospective neighbors (Krebs 1977).

It is possible, however, that song serves functions in neighbor interactions beyond the purely defensive or offensive ones suggested with the existing theories. In particular, the relationships of territorial neighbors may have cooperative and competitive aspects (e.g. Getty 1987; Beletsky and Orians 1989). The kinds of interactions implied (e.g. cooperative defense against intrusions by new birds) may have different influences on singing and song learning. At the very least, a long-time neighbor represents a different sort of competitor than a new bird; yet, existing theories make no such distinction. We suggest that future developments in our understanding of the cognitive ecology of song communication and song learning will hinge on the development of a general theory of the social ecology of territorial songbirds (see Dugatkin and Sih, this vol. chap. 10).

In this chapter, we focused on our particular study species, the song sparrow; however, we expect that many of the general conclusions made apply more broadly, at the very least to many other songbird species. For example, considerable evidence supports the hypothesis that the function of song learning in many species is to equip the bird with songs he shares with his neighbors. In addition to studies that show birds learn their new neighbors' songs

after leaving their birthplace (Bewick's wrens, Kroodsma 1974; saddlebacks, Jenkins 1978), a number of studies have indicated that birds may later modify their song repertoires to increase song sharing with neighbors in the first or subsequent breeding seasons (indigo buntings, Payne 1982, 1983; white-crowned sparrows, Baptista and Morton 1988; great tits, McGregor and Krebs 1989; field sparrows, Nelson 1992; American redstarts, Lemon et al. 1994; cowbirds, O'Loghlen and Rothstein 1995; European starlings, Mountjoy and Lemon 1995).

In this chapter, we concentrated on the aspect of the song sparrow's social ecology that pertains to social interactions among neighboring males. Male–female interactions undoubtedly are also of great importance in shaping song learning and song use in this species and other songbirds (e.g. Searcy 1984; Catchpole 1986, 1987; West and King 1988; King and West 1989; Searcy and Yasukawa 1990). We have recently begun to look at female influences on song in our study species, and we have completed several studies which suggest that song sharing may be very important with respect to female sexual preferences (O'Loghlen and Beecher, 1997; in preparation). It will be interesting to see if the study of intra- and intersexual selection provides reinforcing or opposing arguments for the cognitive ecology of song learning and song communication in this species.

5.6 SUMMARY

In song sparrows, the strategy of song learning in young birds and communication with song between neighboring territorial males are shaped by two major sets of variables: (1) cognitive factors at the proximate level; and (2) variables in the species' social ecology at the ultimate level. At the proximate level, song learning and song use appear to be shaped and guided by the bird's concepts of song type and singer identity. At the ultimate level, the function of song learning appears to be the acquisition of songs that will be shared with territorial neighbors. Thus, a young male song sparrow develops a song repertoire of eight or so song types that are taken from the repertoires of neighboring males. Songs of the nearest neighbors and those of birds that survive the winter between the young bird's hatching summer and his first breeding season are more likely to be adopted. In singing interactions with his neighbors, the bird not only recognizes his individual neighbors but selectively uses just those songs he shares with each particular neighbor. We argue that a cognitive-ecology perspective—which focuses on cognitive factors and social-ecological variables—captures the key features of song learning and song communication in this species and will probably do so as well in other species of songbirds.

ACKNOWLEDGMENTS

Our colleagues in the studies described in this chapter were Philip Stoddard, John Burt, Adrian O'Loghlen, Christopher Hill, Cindy Horning, Patricia Loesche, Michelle Elekonich, and Mary Willis. We thank Discovery Park for hosting our field work and National Science Foundation for supporting this research. Finally, we thank Reuven Dukas for patience beyond his years.

LITERATURE CITED

Arcese, P. 1987. Age, intrusion pressure, and defence against floater by territorial male song sparrows. *Animal Behaviour* 35:773–784.

———. 1989. Intrasexual competition, mating system, and natal dispersal in song sparrows. *Animal Behaviour* 37:45–55.

Baptista, L. F., and M. L. Morton. 1988. Song learning in montane white-crowned sparrows: From whom and when. *Animal Behaviour* 36:1753–1764.

Beecher, M. D. 1996. Bird song learning in the laboratory and the field. In D. E. Kroodsma and E. L. Miller, eds., *Ecology and Evolution of Acoustic Communication in Birds,* 61–78. Ithaca, N.Y.: Cornell University Press.

Beecher, M. D., S. E. Campbell, and J. M. Burt. 1994a. Song perception in the song sparrow: Birds classify by song type but not by singer. *Animal Behaviour* 47:1343–1351.

Beecher, M. D., S. E. Campbell, and P. K. Stoddard. 1994b. Correlation of song learning and territory establishment strategies in the song sparrow. *Proceedings of the National Academy of Sciences of the United States of America* 91:1450–1454.

Beecher, M. D., P. K. Stoddard, S. E. Campbell, and C. L. Horning. 1996. Repertoire matching between neighbouring songbirds. *Animal Behaviour* 51:917–923.

Beletsky, L. D., and G. H. Orians. 1989. Familiar neighbors enhance breeding success in birds. *Proceedings of the National Academy of Sciences of the United States of America* 86:7933–7936.

Catchpole, C. K. 1986. Song repertoires and reproductive success in the great reed warbler *Acrocephalus arundinaceus. Behavioral Ecology and Sociobiology* 19:439–445.

———. 1987. Bird song, sexual selection, and female choice. *Trends in Ecology and Evolution* 2:94–97.

Catchpole, C. K., and P. J. B. Slater. 1995. *Bird Song: Biological Themes and Variations.* Cambridge: Cambridge University Press.

Falls, J. B. 1985. Song matching in western meadowlarks. *Canadian Journal of Zoology* 63:2520–2524.

Falls, J. B., J. R. Krebs, and P. K. McGregor. 1982. Song matching in the great tit (*Parus major*): The effect of similarity and familiarity. *Animal Behaviour* 30:997–1009.

Getty, T. 1987. Dear enemies and the prisoner's dilemma: Why should territorial neighbors form defensive coalitions? *American Zoologist* 27:327–336.

Jenkins, P. F. 1978. Cultural transmission of song patterns and dialect development in a free-living bird population. *Animal Behaviour* 26:50–78.

King, A. P., and M. W. West. 1989. Presence of female cowbirds (*Molothrus ater ater*) affects vocal imitation and improvisation in males. *Journal of Comparative Psychology* 103:39–44.

Krebs, J. R. 1977. The significance of song repertoires: The Beau Geste hypothesis. *Animal Behaviour* 25:475–478.

Krebs, J. R., R. Ashcroft, and K. van Orsdol. 1981. Song matching in the great tit (*Parus major* L.). *Animal Behaviour* 29:918–923.

Kroodsma, D. E. 1974. Song learning, dialects, and dispersal in the Bewick's wren. *Zietschrift der Tierpsychologie* 35:352–380.

———. 1983. The ecology of avian vocal learning. *Bioscience* 33:165–171.

———. 1988. Contrasting styles of song development and their consequences. In R. B. Bolles and M. D. Beecher, eds., *Evolution and Learning,* 157–184. Hillsdale, N.J.: Erlbaum.

Lemon, R. E., S. Perrault, and D. M. Weary. 1994. Dual strategies of song development in American redstarts, *Setophaga ruticilla. Animal Behaviour* 47:317–329.

Marler, P. 1970. A comparative approach to vocal learning: Song development in the white-crowned sparrow. *Journal of Comparative Physiology and Psychology Monograph* 71:1–25.

Marler, P., and D. A. Nelson. 1992. Neuroselection and song learning in birds: Species universals in culturally transmitted behavior. *Seminars in Neuroscience* 4:415–423.

Marler, P., and S. Peters. 1987. A sensitive period for song acquisition in the song sparrow, *Melospiza melodia:* A case of age-limited learning. *Ethology* 76:89–100.

———. 1988. The role of song phonology and syntax in vocal learning preferences in the song sparrow, *Melospiza melodia. Ethology* 77:125–149.

McGregor, P. K. 1992. *Playback and Studies of Animal Communication.* New York: Plenum.

McGregor, P. K., and J. R. Krebs. 1989. Song learning in adult great tits (*Parus major*): Effects of neighbours. *Behaviour* 108:139–159.

Morton, E. S. 1986. Predictions from the ranging hypothesis for the evolution of long distance signals in birds. *Behaviour* 99:65–86.

Mountjoy, D. J., and R. E. Lemon. 1995. Extended song learning in wild European starlings. *Animal Behaviour* 49:357–366.

Nelson, D. A. 1992. Song overproduction and selective attrition lead to song sharing in the field sparrow (*Spizella pusilla*). *Behavioral Ecology and Sociobiology* 30:415–424.

Nelson, D. A., and P. Marler. 1994. Selection-based learning in bird song development. *Proceedings of the National Academy of Sciences of the United States of America* 91:10498–10501.

Nowicki, S., J. Podos, and F. Valdes. 1994. Temporal patterning of within-song type and between-song type variation in song repertoires. *Behavioral Ecology and Sociobiology* 34:329–335.

O'Loghlen, A. L., and M. D. Beecher. 1997. Sexual preferences for mate song types in female song types. *Animal Behaviour* 53:835–841.

O'Loghlen, A. L., and S. I. Rothstein. 1993. An extreme example of delayed vocal development: Song learning in a population of wild brown-headed cowbirds. *Animal Behaviour* 46:293–304.

Payne, R. B. 1982. Ecological consequences of song matching: Breeding success and intraspecific song mimicry in indigo buntings. *Ecology* 63:401–411.

Payne, R. B. 1983. The social context of song mimicry: Song matching dialects in indigo buntings (*Passerina cyanea*). *Animal Behaviour* 31:788–805.

Podos, J., S. Peters, T. Rudnicky, P. Marler, and S. Nowicki. 1992. The organization of song repertoires of song sparrows: Themes and variations. *Ethology* 90:89–106.

Searcy, W. A. 1984. Song repertoire size and female preferences in song sparrows. *Behavioral Ecology and Sociobiology* 14:281–286.

Searcy, W. A., and K. Yasukawa. 1990. Use of the song repertoire in intersexual and intrasexual contexts by red-winged blackbirds. *Behavioral Ecology and Sociobiology* 27:123–128.

Slater, P. J. B. 1989. Bird song learning: Causes and consequences. *Ethology Ecology Evolution* 1:19–46.

Stoddard, P. K., M. D. Beecher, S. E. Campbell, and C. Horning. 1992. Song-type matching in the song sparrow. *Canadian Journal of Zoology* 70:1440–1444.

Stoddard, P. K., M. D. Beecher, C. L. Horning, and S. E. Campbell. 1991. Recognition of individual neighbors by song in the song sparrow, a species with song repertoires. *Behavioral Ecology and Sociobiology* 29:211–215.

Stoddard, P. K., M. D. Beecher, C. H. Horning, and M. S. Willis. 1990. Strong neighbor-stranger discrimination in song sparrows. *Condor* 97:1051–1056.

Stoddard, P. K., M. D. Beecher, and M. S. Willis. 1988. Response of territorial male song sparrows to song types and variations. *Behavioral Ecology and Sociobiology* 22:125–130.

West, M. J., and A. P. King. 1988. Female visual displays affect the development of male song in the cowbird. *Nature* 334:244–246.

Cognitive Ecology of Navigation

FRED C. DYER

6.1 INTRODUCTION

On the most general level, the adaptive significance of spatial orientation is obvious: It is easy to imagine why natural selection has equipped animals with mechanisms that enable them to (1) acquire information about their position and orientation relative to fitness-enhancing resources, such as food or mates; and (2) guide movements in search of better conditions. Accordingly, most biologists interested in orientation have focused on the underlying sensory and neural mechanisms and have treated questions about the adaptive importance of these mechanisms only superficially, if at all.

It is clear, however, that the flexibility and accuracy used to solve similar navigational problems vary enormously among species. It is also clear that the navigational tasks faced by animals vary with species-specific ecological differences. Such patterns of variation demand an evolutionary explanation that focuses not only on the variation in behavioral performance but also on the mechanisms that underlie the behavior. By analogy, consider foraging behavior, another class of biological traits whose general adaptive importance of foraging behavior is obvious, and yet which varies widely among species. For 30 years behavioral ecologists have attempted to understand the foraging decisions of animals in relation to (1) the selection pressures associated with specific foraging tasks, and (2) the constraints imposed on the design of mechanisms that underlie these decisions (reviews by Stephens and Krebs 1986; Krebs and Kacelnik 1992; Bateson and Kacelnik, this vol. chap. 8; Ydenberg, this vol. chap. 9). To the degree that the study of foraging focuses on the adaptive design of mechanisms used to process information about the profitability, distribution, riskiness, and palatability of food resources, it is already a relatively mature branch of cognitive ecology. Conceivably, it could provide a model for developing a cognitive ecology of the mechanisms used by animals to process spatial information while navigating.

This chapter is one of two in this volume that examines the prospects for a cognitive ecology of spatial orientation. Sherry (this vol. chap. 7) stresses well-developed vertebrate model systems that have been used to explore orientation and spatial memory on a small spatial scale, such as during the final approach to a familiar food source. With comparative and experimental ap-

proaches, this work has provided important insights into the evolutionary modification of spatial learning and memory. I adopt a somewhat broader approach to the evolution of orientation mechanisms. The chapter is organized into three main sections. In the first section, I adopt a broad problem-oriented approach by describing the diverse manifestations of the general problem of finding the way to a goal and considering how the diversity of navigational tasks helps account for the diversity of navigational abilities. In the second section, I outline the components of a trait-oriented approach to the study of navigation by arguing for the importance of hypothesizing specific fitness benefits and costs associated with different navigational strategies and exploring various constraints that may influence the course and outcome of selection on such strategies. These first two sections provide a conceptual framework for making sense of the diversity and adaptive design of navigational mechanisms. In the final section, I analyze several specific studies that illustrate the potential for an evolutionary-ecological approach to the cognitive mechanisms that underlie navigation.

Before proceeding, I would like to explain briefly my emphasis on the cognitive aspects of navigation. The hallmark of a cognitive approach—and indeed its main advantage over the behaviorist tradition with which it is often contrasted—is a concern with the internal processes that mediate behavior and not merely the observable correlations between an animal's experiences and its responses. There is considerable variation in opinion among researchers, however, about what mechanisms are encompassed with a cognitive approach.

In the most restrictive view, cognitive processes are those involved in humanlike mental qualities such as self-awareness. This seems to be the view of many so-called ''cognitive ethologists'' (Ristau 1991), who are largely concerned with investigating the role of humanlike mental processes in animals. Like other authors in this volume, I use the term "cognition" in a broader sense that refers to information processing in general by nervous systems and that encompasses simple perceptual and learning processes as well as more complex mechanisms used to acquire internal representations of the world (Dukas, this vol. sec. 1.1). Studies of animal orientation provide scant reason to invoke humanlike mental processes such as self-awareness. These studies do, however, provide abundant evidence for sophisticated internal processing of information acquired with the senses and reveal the inadequacy of simple stimulus-response accounts of the behavior. Indeed in navigation, as in foraging behavior, the differences in behavioral performance among species can often be understood only by considering how these species detect and organize information about features of the outside world.

An important caveat to bear in mind is the danger of committing to a particular cognitive hypothesis that is suggested by the behavioral data. Often one

overestimate the sophistication of the mechanisms underlying the flexible, adaptive behavior of animals (for a detailed discussion see Dyer 1994). I will describe some impressive feats of navigation that are accomplished with surprisingly simple responses to environmental cues. Any attempt to understand the adaptive design of the information-processing mechanisms that underlie navigation must start with an accurate depiction of what those mechanisms are.

6.2 Diversity in the Problem of Goal Orientation

6.2.1 General Considerations

In this section, I outline a classification system for describing the specific navigational tasks faced by different animals. This system involves a set of distinctions that define the parameters of the general problem of finding the way to the goal. This classification system is analogous to the categorization of foraging tasks into prey models or patch models or variants thereof (Stephens and Krebs 1986). Such categorization clarifies the general and specific features of the problem that natural selection has presumably designed the animal to solve. Control systems used in orientation are often clearly tuned to the parameters of the navigational task, and so a classification based on these parameters provides an initial way to account for the variation among species in navigational ability.

Attempts to classify the abilities of animals to orient themselves in space date back at least to the time of Loeb's (1918) hypothesis that all behavior can be described as manifestations of simple orienting responses to environmental stimuli (tropisms). Kühn (1919) and Fraenkel and Gunn (1940) developed more elaborate systems, which nevertheless invoked only very simple control mechanisms (taxes and kineses). These taxis and tropism theories inadequately accounted for the impressive discoveries in avian and insect orientation that began in the 1940s. In the 1970s and 1980s, improved classification systems were advanced (e.g. Jander 1975; Baker 1978; Schöne 1984). The system I present is most similar to that of Jander (1975) in relating the design features of different orientation systems to their function in the life history of the species.

In the classification of orientational mechanisms, Jander (1975) and Schöne (1984) agreed on a major distinction between (1) rotational adjustments to stabilize the body axes relative to external stimuli, and (2) goal orientation, or movement toward a different place where the animal can find better conditions (e.g. more food or less stress). This distinction encompasses most of the controlled, nonrandom movements that animals make.

I will focus entirely on goal orientation, which I define very broadly to encompass such widely different navigational tasks as (1) heading for a nearby object in plain view, (2) heading for an unseen feeding or nesting site within

a familiar home range, and (3) heading for home from a distant, unfamiliar location. Following Griffin (1952), many researchers—especially those who study birds—restrict the term "navigation" to mean the last of these tasks, but I will use the term "navigation" synonymously with goal orientation. By doing so, I explicitly recognize the fundamental similarities among different types of goal orientation, and I believe this recognition makes it easier to understand the differences.

All types of goal orientation necessitate that the animal, at its starting point, obtain two general sorts of information about the environment: First, the animal must be able to discriminate among different directions (body orientations) relative to some external reference (e.g. a celestial body, a landmark, or a chemical cue). Second, the animal must be able to determine its position in space relative to its goal. The animal may need to measure its angular position and distance relative to some directional reference, or as we shall see, the animal may need to use a simpler measure of location. The crucial point is that information about position indicates to the animal which direction—among those that it can discriminate—is the correct direction that will lead to the goal.

Bear in mind that the dichotomy between positional and directional information is sometimes indistinct. For example, if an animal heads toward a clearly visible conspecific or prey item, the mechanisms involved in recognizing the item's position (i.e. the direction that will lead to the goal) may be hard to separate from the mechanisms involved in choosing the correct direction. On the other hand, for many navigational challenges, such as homing from a long distance, the tasks of obtaining positional and directional information may entail very different problems, perhaps even different sensory modalities.

To characterize the specific problem faced by an animal that is orienting to a particular goal, we can identify three parameters that affect in some way the procurement of positional and directional information and therefore the setting of a course to the goal: (1) the geometry of the space containing the goal; (2) the distance of the goal from the starting point; and (3) the variability (either spatial or temporal) of the environmental cues that provide navigational information. Classifying goal orientation with these parameters allows us to see more clearly how navigational challenges among animals are similar or different and thus provides a foundation for examining the similarities and differences in the mechanisms used by animals to meet these challenges.

6.2.2 Geometry of the Goal

Jander (1975) and others recognized that the nature of the navigational task is strongly influenced by the geometry of the region of the environment in

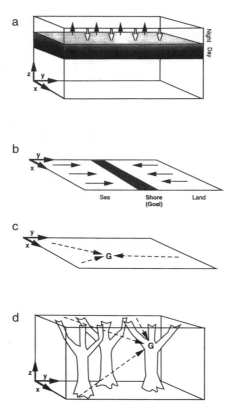

Figure 6.1. Geometries of goals. (*a*) Goal is a stratum in a volume. Shaded area is preferred stratum into which zooplankton (for example) move to escape predation during the day and out of which they move to feed at night. This orientation is commonly referred to as "diel vertical migrations" (e.g. Ringelberg and Flik 1994); here it is called z-axis orientation. (*b*) Goal is a linear zone on a surface, for example a preferred strip of beach where sandhoppers find salubrious conditions (y-axis orientation) (see Able 1980). (*c*) Goal is a point on a surface, for example the nest of an insect or a bird relative to the surface of the ground (x,y-orientation). (*d*) Goal is a point in a volume, for example the nest of an insect or a bird in a particular portion of the forest canopy (x,y,z-orientation).

which the navigating animal will find improved conditions. The geometry of the goal profoundly influences the problem of obtaining positional and directional information and thus determines how sophisticated the mechanisms used to obtain this information must be. We can distinguish four main goal geometries (fig. 6.1, where the x + y axes define the horizontal plane and the z-axis defines the vertical). I describe these relative to a three-dimensional Cartesian coordinate system, but I make no assumptions about whether an animal actually measures its orientation relative to such a coordinate system.

The point is to show that, in general, more complex goal geometries require navigational mechanisms that allow for more degrees of freedom of spatial position relative to the goal.

6.2.2.1 Goal Is a Plane or Stratum in a Volume

This situation is best illustrated by the "diel vertical migrations" of marine and freshwater zooplankton (reviews by Baker 1978; Dingle 1980, 1996). In the three-dimensional space of their environment, these animals must move along the z-axis from one stratum to another. For example, to escape predators during the day, they move deeper; to feed at night, they move toward the surface (see fig. 6.1a). The animals are presumably indifferent about their positions along the x- or y-axis when they are in the appropriate stratum because conditions within this stratum are essentially uniform. I refer to this orientation as "z-axis orientation."

The positional and directional cues that allow animals to perform z-axis orientation are potentially easy to ascertain (review by Schöne 1984). To determine position, the animal must decide if it is above or below the preferred stratum. Conceivably, this can be done by measuring light intensities (which is likely the most important cue for most species; Ringelberg and Flik 1994), water temperature, water pressure, or chemical concentrations in the water. To discriminate vertical directions, the animal can swim along the vertically oriented gradients of these stimuli or orient to gravitational forces.

6.2.2.2 Goal Is a Line or a Zone across a Surface

This situation applies to an organism with a preferred region in the environment that is a narrow strip of land containing food refugia, or optimal levels of temperature or humidity (see fig. 6.1b). A common example is the search of many littoral organisms for a particular zone along a shore. In this context, littoral amphipod crustaceans (sandhoppers) and amphibians have been particularly well studied (reviews by Able 1980; Baker 1978; Pardi and Ercolini 1986). When displaced from their preferred zone, such animals orient in the direction that is perpendicular to the shore and appear indifferent about where along the shore they end up. This type of orientation is often called y-axis orientation; the x-axis is parallel to the shore and the y-axis is perpendicular.

In y-axis orientation, the animal obtains positional information relatively simply by detecting which side of the preferred zone it is on. Direct cues may be available (e.g. visual features of the shore). Also, there is abundant experimental evidence that many animals use indirect cues. For example, if it is wet and cold, a sandhopper behaves as if it is in the water and heads toward drier land; if it is dry and hot, the sandhopper behaves as if it is inland and heads in the opposite direction (reviewed by Able 1980; Pardi and Ercolini

1986). These behavioral responses are exhibited even in experimental arenas far from the shore. Conceivably, a more sophisticated measure of position includes the distance from the goal as well as the direction. I know of no evidence, however, that animals use information about distance for y-axis orientation; nor is it likely that a navigational strategy that employs distance information is superior to one that uses only directional information.

To discriminate the two relevant directions in y-axis orientation (e.g. in littoral animals, toward water versus toward land), animals may again use direct cues—features of the shore itself—or indirect cues (Pardi and Ercolini 1986). Direct cues are gradients (e.g. slope or temperature) or visual cues (e.g. landmarks) that are aligned with the y-axis (Craig 1973; Hartwick 1976). Conceivably, the mechanisms that underlie a response to a local gradient are no more sophisticated than those used in z-axis orientation; in fact, mechanisms that underlie z-axis orientation presumably would result in y-axis orientation if the animal could only move in a plane perpendicular to the preferred stratum.

Indirect information about the y-axis direction is provided by compass references such as the sun or the earth's magnetic field; both references can be used by amphipod crustaceans (Ugolini and Pardi 1992) and newts (Phillips 1986). With use of such a compass, the major challenge for the animal is to determine which compass direction corresponds to the y-axis of the local shoreline. In some species, naive individuals behave as if they are innately informed about the y-axis direction that corresponds to their natal beach, and animals from different populations (from differently oriented beaches) exhibit hereditary differences in the innate compass response (e.g. Pardi and Scapini 1985). These results imply that gene flow among populations is relatively slight; this implication is surprising given that individuals are probably often carried off by ocean currents to other shores. The compass direction of the local y-axis is learned in at least some species of sandhoppers (Ugolini and Scapini, 1988). Also, a learned response can override the innate response (Ugolini et al. 1988); learning would allow for appropriate orientation if an individual drifts to a differently oriented beach. Learning the direction of the local y-axis has also been documented in amphibians (e.g. newts) that live along the shores of ponds (Phillips 1986).

6.2.2.3 Goal Is a Point on a Surface

This situation applies to those organisms that need to find the location of a specific nesting or feeding site on a two-dimensional surface (see fig. 6.1c). This task may be called x,y-orientation, although some animals may locate goals in terms of polar coordinates (not Cartesian coordinates) relative to a central location such as a nest. Orienting to a point on a surface is performed

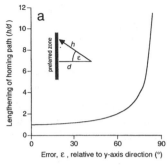
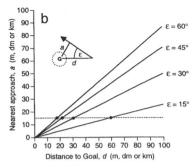

Figure 6.2. Implications of error in setting the homeward direction for two different goal geometries. (*a*) In the y-axis orientation, the error (ε) in setting the course toward shore results in an increase in the length of the homing path, *h*. The animal should eventually reach the shore if ε < 90°. The length of the homing path is not doubled until ε = 60°. (*b*) When the goal is a point (*G* in inset) on a surface, even a fairly small error in setting the course imposes a risk of missing the goal altogether. For a given error, ε, the distance, *a*, of the nearest approach to the goal increases with the distance, *d*, between the starting point and the goal. Suppose the animal must come within a certain distance to detect the goal (shown with the dotted circle around *G* in the inset and the horizontal line set at 15 distance units on the graph). The homing accuracy required to ensure that the animal comes this close to the goal must increase as the distance between the starting point and the goal increases (compare symbols on horizontal dotted line).

by most terrestrial animals and many flying animals. Although flying animals can move vertically and may need to orient in three dimensions (see section 6.2.2.4), the critical task for many is to find locations relative to the earth's surface (the earth's curvature can generally be neglected). Well-studied examples include homing and migrating birds (reviews in Berthold 1991) and hymenopteran insects returning to their nests after finding food (reviews by Dyer 1994, 1996; Wehner et al. 1996). Also, flying animals typically maintain a relatively stable altitude (e.g. nesting insects, a few meters; migrating birds, a few hundred meters), and so they perform the basic navigational tasks in two dimensions.

If the goal is a point on a surface instead of a linear zone across a surface, the setting of a course to the goal is greatly complicated. To determine position in y-axis orientation, the animal merely has to decide which of two opposite directions is correct. Errors of up to just less than 90° do not prevent the animal from reaching the preferred zone. Such errors slow the approach to the preferred zone, but this cost is not severe if small errors are made (fig. 6.2*a*). If the goal is a point, however, the goal can be in any direction, and a much more precise ability to determine position is required. Small errors in positional or directional measurements can result in more drastic consequences because the animal can miss the goal altogether (fig. 6.2*b*). Furthermore, unlike

an animal that targets a linear zone, an animal that sets a course for a point may benefit considerably from information about its distance as well as its direction from the point. With distance information, the animal would be able to engage in a search strategy after traveling the expected distance and not reaching its goal (Wehner and Srinivasan 1981).

When determining their position relative to a point, many animals do determine both the direction and the distance of their starting point relative to their goal. As I will discuss in the next section, however, the specific strategies used for determining position are strongly related to the distance over which the x,y-navigation takes place.

Information about direction can be obtained from cues directly associated with the goal (e.g. visual or odor cues), but only if the animal is already close to the goal. For setting and maintaining a direction of travel over greater distances, the animal must use either a compass (celestial or magnetic) or landmarks. Landmarks are stable features of the environment; they are usually detected visually, but in principle animals obtain information about landmarks with other sensory modalities (Bennett 1996). As discussed in section 6.2.3, the directional references available to the animal may depend on its distance from the goal. Both celestial compasses and landmarks require learning, as I will discuss later in the chapter.

6.2.2.4 Goal Is a Point in a Volume

Consider (1) a sea otter that seeks to return to a familiar patch of sea urchins; or (2) a forest-dwelling bird or bee that needs to find its nest or a patch of food at the correct stratum in the forest canopy or at the correct (x,y) position on the forest floor; or (3) an ant that forages in dense vegetation and must locate its nest or familiar food sources by negotiating a three-dimensional maze of branches and leaves. In each of these cases, the organism needs to find a particular point within a three-dimensional space (fig. 6.1d); this situation may be referred to as x,y,z-orientation. The navigational strategies animals use to solve such a problem have scarcely been studied at all, and I mention this situation mainly for the sake of completeness.

Orienting to a point in three dimensions need not be much more complicated than orienting to a point in two dimensions. For example, the sea otter may first locate the correct x,y position on the surface of the water (with use of landmarks on the shore) and then dive. The ant may follow odor trails and use guidelines (topographic features) that are essentially the same as those used in a two-dimensional environment (Jander 1990). On the other hand, some animals may use more complex strategies for fixing their position relative to their goal in three dimensions and then set a direct course. In general, it seems likely that comparisons between closely related taxa that live in two-

and three-dimensional environments may reveal interesting differences in the designs of the mechanisms that underlie goal orientation.

6.2.3 Distance of the Goal

The importance of distance is threefold. First, distance affects the geometry of the task. For an animal (such as a sandhopper) that is heading for a beach from just offshore, the goal is a line on a plane, and the task is y-axis orientation. For an animal (such as a sea turtle) that is heading for the same beach from hundreds of kilometers away, the goal is effectively a point on a surface, and the task is x,y-orientation. Similarly, a bird that is heading for its nest in a forest canopy must find the correct height and the x,y position of the nest on the earth's surface (x,y,z-orientation). If the forest is tens or hundreds of kilometers away, only the x,y position of the goal is important.

Second, for point locations, the distance of the goal affects the accuracy required for successful homing. Figure 6.2*b* shows how, as homing distance increases, the error in the setting of the course to the goal must decrease so the animal can come within a certain distance of the goal.

Third, distance affects what strategies are available to an animal for determining its position relative to its goal. The effects of distance on the information available for navigation are particularly critical (and best understood) if the goal is a point on a surface. The following is a summary of the most important strategies that an animal uses to determine its position relative to a point at different starting distances (fig. 6.3). Note that distance in this case is a relative dimension that depends on such factors as the sensory modality used by the animal, the animal's travel speed, and the structure of the environment. What is a long distance to a walking animal with poor vision may be a short distance to a flying animal with good vision.

6.2.3.1 Short Distance: Final Approach to a Goal

From a short distance (fig. 6.3, zone 1) an animal may orient to stimuli emanating from the goal. A nearby goal may serve as a visual beacon, or it may emit sounds (e.g. a calling male frog luring a female) or odors (e.g. the pheromone plume originating from a female moth). In these cases, the task of determining position relative to the goal is a simple matter of recognizing and turning toward the relevant stimulus.

If the animal is guiding its final approach to a hidden goal, the animal must use indirect information about its position and direction of travel relative to the goal. Many animals can use surrounding landmarks to pinpoint the location of a hidden goal. This use of landmarks requires an ability to learn the spatial relationship between the landmark array and the goal. Such abilities have been studied intensively in invertebrates and vertebrates. Indeed, all of the major

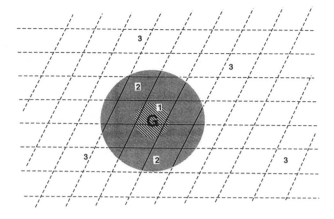

Figure 6.3. Determining positions relative to a familiar goal (*G*) on different spatial scales. In zone 1, the animal can detect *G*, or landmarks around it, directly. In zone 2, the animal is within its home range and relies on familiar landmarks that indicate a path to *G;* alternatively, if the animal traveled to its current location from *G*, it can use path integration to compute its displacement from *G*. In zone 3, the animal is outside its home range and establishes its position relative to *G* only by extrapolating previously experienced, geophysical stimulus gradients within its home range. Lines represent isoclines of two roughly orthogonal stimulus gradients. Solid sections are known values; hatched sections are values not previously experienced.

paradigms used for studying spatial learning in vertebrates deal with short-distance navigational tasks: these paradigms include the radial-arm maze, the Morris water pool, and other cue-controlled arenas used in behavioral and neurophysiological studies of rodent spatial memory (reviewed by Leonard and McNaughton 1990; McNaughton et al. 1996), and the cache-recovery tasks used to study spatial memory capacities of certain songbirds (Sherry, this vol. sec. 7.3.1.1). Studies of short-range spatial navigation in insects date to Tinbergen's famous studies on the abilities of digger wasps to learn the configuration of landmarks around their nests; more recent intensive studies include those of landmark learning in bees and wasps (for reviews, see Wehner 1981; Gallistel 1990; Dyer 1994; Collett 1996).

6.2.3.2 Intermediate Distance: Goal Orientation within Familiar Home Range

If an animal ranges widely, it may face the problem of heading toward a familiar part of the environment it cannot detect directly (fig. 6.3). To determine its initial position relative to the unseen goal, the animal must refer to environmental features at the starting point and along the way to the goal.

Animals have evolved two main mechanisms for determining their position

within a home range. Use of both mechanisms necessitates learning. First, many animals can, during their travels through the environment, keep track of their position relative to a particular goal such as the nest. This process is known as path integration or "dead reckoning." The animal measures the angles (relative to an external compass or an internal directional reference provided with vestibular or tactile stimuli) and distances traveled over successive path segments; the animal then computes its net direction and distance from the starting point (reviews by Wehner and Wehner 1990; Gallistel 1990; Dyer 1994). I will discuss this process in a following section.

Second, many animals can determine their position by recognizing familiar landmarks that they have previously used to move to their goal. Obviously, this strategy is available only if the animal is familiar with the landmarks that are visible from the starting point. The ability to use landmarks to move to a distant, unseen goal is interesting because the initial landmarks that the animal uses may no longer be available once the animal has traveled some distance; therefore, different landmarks must be used to maintain the homeward course.

Although many animals use both path integration and landmarks for determining position within a familiar home range, the two strategies are potentially independent of one another. Path integration can be used to determine position even if the animal's path enters unfamiliar terrain. Landmarks can be used to determine position even if the animal has not traveled the path to its current location. For example, the animal may be displaced by wind or the experimenter's hand, and the animal, therefore, has no opportunity to determine position via path integration (reviewed by Wehner 1981; Dyer 1994). Despite their potential independence, the two strategies do reinforce one another under normal conditions.

6.2.3.3 Long Distance: Goal Orientation outside a Familiar Home Range

This is the task faced by homing and migratory birds and long-distance migrants of various non-avian taxa, such as sea turtles (Lohmann and Lohmann 1996) and monarch butterflies (Brower 1996). The animal's goal is tens or hundreds of kilometers away, and the animal may never have been at the starting point (as in the case of experimentally or wind-displaced homing birds) or at the goal (as in the case of migratory birds making their first trip to their winter habitat). Thus, path integration is not an option, and the animals do not have any opportunity to learn the landmarks along the route from the starting point to the goal. In the scheme put forth originally by Griffin (1952), this is the task classified as "true navigation" or "complete navigation."

How does the animal determine its position relative to its goal in this case? Two general strategies have been identified. The first, which is relatively simple, is exemplified by migratory birds that must determine if they are in the

north and must head south or in the south and must head north. This decision is influenced strongly by hormone levels that vary seasonally as a result of the photoperiod. Thus, the animal's internal state effectively indicates the animal's approximate geographical position by affecting the animal's response to directional references (e.g. flying north or south) (reviews by Berthold 1991; Gwinner 1996). Experiments in which birds in the northern hemisphere are exposed to artificial photoperiods demonstrate that this navigational process is not dependent on actual measurements of geographical position. For example, birds in the lab will head north in the fall if they are exposed to increasing day lengths that are typical of spring. Birds that winter in the lab will also head north in the spring although the birds are already within their summer range.

The second, and much more complicated, strategy is employed in situations in which the animal is displaced a great distance to an unfamiliar starting point in an unknown direction, and the animal must determine its actual geographical position relative to its goal (fig. 6.3). This is what pigeons do when setting a homeward course after being displaced to a novel location far from their home loft (Keeton 1974). It is also what experienced starlings do when correcting for a lateral displacement from their normal migratory route that leads from northern Europe to southern England (Perdeck 1958). Just how animals accomplish such feats remains deeply puzzling and controversial. The general consensus, if there is one, is that animals exploit large-scale (global) stimulus gradients; animals generalize from gradient patterns that are experienced in a familiar area (e.g. around their home nest) to determine their position in the gradient when they are in an unfamiliar area. Furthermore, in this case, there is widespread agreement that animals would require at least two large-scale stimulus gradients that are not parallel to each other to fix their position unambiguously (review by Wallraff 1991). By this view, animals are assumed to locate their positions relative to an extrapolated bicoordinate map in a manner similar to how human explorers find their position in new lands relative to the system of latitude and longitude that is linked to geographical coordinates of home.

The controversy arises over the sensory basis of the extrapolated map used by animals. Among those studying bird navigation, debate has centered around two main hypotheses: use of olfactory cues versus use of geomagnetic cues. I will not review this controversy in this chapter (for recent reviews, see Able 1996; Walraff 1996; Wiltschko 1996). The crucial point is that in both the olfactory and geomagnetic hypotheses, it is assumed birds find their position on a large-scale map extrapolated from environmental patterns experienced on a much smaller scale. The sensory basis of the extrapolated map is a little less controversial in sea turtles, which also need to find their way over enormous distances. Lohmann and Lohmann (1996a, 1996b) recently provided evidence that young loggerhead sea turtles use a bicoordinate geomagnetic

map (with use of the inclination and intensity of the geomagnetic field) to determine their position in the North Atlantic Ocean. Olfactory cues do not likely explain the long-distance navigation of sea turtles.

6.2.4 Variability of Navigational Cues

The environmental features that animals use to obtain positional or directional information may vary spatially or temporally. Temporal variation means that, in a given location, a fixed strategy for use of a particular environmental feature for navigation does not work equally well at different times of day or in different seasons. Spatial variation means that a fixed strategy does not work equally well in all locations. From the perspective of most animals, spatial variation can effectively be viewed as temporal variation because navigational cues vary at different times as a consequence of movement between different locations. Variation of such cues may be an important component of the navigational problem that an animal must solve. In particular, an animal confronted with a potentially variable navigational reference must be able to learn an appropriate response given the current state of the reference. Moreover, differences in the time scales over which animals experience environmental variability may affect the design of different learning mechanisms that deal with this variability.

Learning is commonly thought to be beneficial because it allows animals to adjust behavior in response to changes in particular environmental features. As Stephens (1993) and others have recognized, however, learning is not necessarily advantageous if environmental conditions fluctuate very rapidly relative to the time scale in which the animal makes successive responses to the environment. Thus, there must be some persistence of environmental conditions for learned responses to be of any value. There would be no point in learning features of a food that changed every time the animal encountered the food. Learning, however, may also be disadvantageous if environmental features fluctuate very slowly such that the appropriate responses to stimuli are the same for each generation. In this case, animals that adopt fixed responses may benefit over those that incur the costs of learning (e.g. the time and energy needed to sample or the cost of neural machinery; see Dukas, this vol. section 4.4). As I will discuss, the time scale of environmental fluctuation that favors learning depends heavily on species-specific life-history variables (e.g. lifespan).

In the context of navigation, animals tend to exhibit experience-independent responses to environmental features that change slowly (and hence are the same for each generation) and to depend on learning for features that vary in a shorter time scale. For example, naive amphipod crustaceans respond innately to a slope by heading down, which is the direction that allows escape

to the sea for all sandhoppers everywhere (Scapini and Mezzetti 1993). Also, hatchling sea turtles, in their rush to the sea, exhibit innate responses to a slope (heading down), to landmarks (heading away), and to waves after entering the water (heading into waves); all of these responses predictably lead the hatchlings offshore (reviewed by Lohmann and Lohmann 1996a).

Other examples show how learning allows animals to adapt their behavior to unpredictable environmental features that, once encountered and learned, persist long enough to serve as reliable navigational references. The use of landmarks by animals that are heading to a familiar goal at a point location (x,y-orientation) illustrates this idea well. Although landmarks reliably indicate the y-axis direction of a shoreline, the spatial relationships between landmarks and a particular point are often completely unpredictable, and so a fixed innate response to the landmarks is of no value. Because landmarks do not move, however, a learned response will enable repeated visits to a location.

A second example arises in connection with use of the sun as a compass. As I will discuss in this chapter, animals that use the sun must compensate for the movement of its azimuth (the sun's compass angle) during the day. The exact pattern of change of the azimuth (the solar ephemeris function), which varies with latitude and season, is unpredictable; in species that are active in a wide range of latitudes and seasons, individual animals cannot predict exactly which ephemeris function they will need to use. Once a given ephemeris function is learned it will be useful for several days, because the ephemeris function changes only gradually from day to day. Both insects and birds learn the current, local ephemeris function early in life. Because the ephemeris function changes relatively slowly, short-lived animals such as insects may never need to relearn it (von Frisch 1967). Long-lived or wide-ranging animals such as birds, however, may need to recalibrate their memory of this pattern, and indeed there is evidence of such relearning in pigeons (Schmidt-Koenig et al. 1991).

A final example is the learning of the compass direction of the local y-axis by hatchling sea turtles that are heading seaward (reviewed by Lohmann and Lohmann 1996a). As mentioned, naive hatchlings can head in the y-axis direction with use of a succession of highly reliable cues, but hatchlings are uninformed about the compass orientation of the y-axis (a presumably unpredictable variable given the possibility that mothers lay eggs on beaches in various orientations). The baby turtles rapidly learn their compass heading, however, using their outbound orientation relative to the waves as a reference. The feature used to measure the compass heading (the local geomagnetic field) is stable; their learned response to this feature guarantees consistent movement away from the shore.

Animals that initially exhibit an innate response to a particular cue may

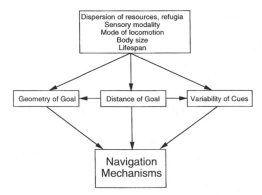

Figure 6.4. Hypothesized causal relationships among various factors that could have shaped the evolution of navigational mechanisms.

subsequently modify their behavior through learning. This is illustrated in the y-axis orientation of amphipod crustaceans that exhibit an innate initial response to the sun or the geomagnetic field and adopt the compass heading that is aligned with the y-axis of their natal beach. The innate response implies that populations are sedentary enough so that, for each new generation, a given direction relative to the sun compass or the magnetic compass predictably corresponds to the local y-axis. If, however, sandhoppers are displaced to a differently oriented beach, they can learn a new y-axis orientation relative to a compass reference. Apparently sandhoppers do this by using the direction of the slope—a highly reliable indicator of the y-axis direction—to calibrate their response to celestial or magnetic cues (Scapini and Mezzetti 1993; Ugolini and Pezzani 1995).

6.2.5 Biological Factors That Set the Parameters of the Navigational Task

This classification of the diversity of navigational tasks has so far ignored the question of why animals face different navigational tasks. Here I list several general biological and ecological traits that are likely to be relevant for defining the navigational problems an animal faces (fig. 6.4). To the extent that these traits are phylogenetically conserved, one could argue that they have played a causal role in the evolution of particular navigational abilities. Of course, the direction of causation could be reversed if improvement in an animal's navigational mechanisms creates opportunities or imposes demands that were not experienced by ancestors, and hence leads to adaptive modifications in these traits.

6.2.5.1 Diet

The food resource typically exploited by an animal is dispersed in a characteristic way, which requires a particular set of behavioral strategies (including navigational strategies) to find and exploit it. For example, a resource distributed in widely spaced patches necessitates a different navigational strategy than one distributed more uniformly. The rates of depletion and renewal of resources in patches influence the need to learn the locations of new patches.

6.2.5.2 Mode of Locomotion

Flying animals can cover more area in a given period of time than walking animals, and thus, flying animals may have to navigate toward goals over greater distances. Because distance affects the geometry of navigational tasks faced by animals, the mode of locomotion may indirectly influence the complexity of the navigational strategies needed. Also, flying (or swimming) animals potentially face navigational problems in three dimensions, whereas walking (or benthic) creatures face navigational problems in essentially two dimensions. Furthermore, animals whose mode of locomotion allows them to range widely are also more likely to be exposed to variable environmental conditions, and hence, these animals more likely need to learn new responses to variable navigational cues.

6.2.5.3 Sensory Modality

Because the positional and directional information that is necessary for goal orientation must enter an animal's brain by way of its senses, the sensory modalities used to detect environmental features may influence profoundly the navigational problems the animal faces and its capacity to solve a particular problem. For an obvious example, landmarks (fixed features of the environment) provide spatial information through any sensory modality, but landmarks are most easily used by highly visual animals. Even animals that rely on the same sensory modality may differ in their navigational abilities because their sensory organs are phylogenetically different. The compound eye of the insect, compared with the vertebrate eye, probably restricts greatly the visual information available to the insect's brain (Land 1981).

6.2.5.4 Body Size

Body size profoundly affects the animal's resource needs and hence the size of its home range, which in turn affects the distance over which the animal

typically has to navigate to feeding sites. Body size also affects travel speed, which by definition affects the distances that can be covered by an animal daily. As mentioned, the scale of an animal's movements possibly influences the geometry of the navigational task and the variability of the navigational cues encountered by the animal. At the same time, a faster animal can sample the environment more rapidly and thus may accumulate a richer knowledge of relevant spatial relationships.

6.2.5.5 Lifespan

The most important consequence of lifespan (which generally correlates positively with body size; Calder 1984) is the extent of environmental variation an animal experiences. An animal that lives longer more likely needs to recalibrate its responses to environmental features (when important spatial relationships change) during its life (see Dukas, this vol. section 4.5.6).

6.2.6 Potentialities and Limitations of This System

In this section, I attempted to organize the diversity of navigational problems faced by animals. I hope this classification system not only describes known patterns but also stimulates new research by providing a clearer framework for comparative studies. This system establishes criteria for identifying species that face similar or different navigational problems and may help us frame questions about the similarities and differences in the underlying mechanisms. Furthermore, given the wide variation of navigational problems faced by animals, this system may help us understand the adaptive design of particular navigational mechanisms.

The various mechanisms that underlie animals' navigational abilities are not elucidated with this system; it only allows determination of similar or different navigational problems that are encountered. Indeed, some species that may be classified as having similar navigational problems are likely to solve these problems in different ways. For example, like many songbirds that spend the summer in the northern hemisphere and head south for the winter, monarch butterflies migrate thousands of kilometers on a path that effectively leads to a point location in the subtropics (reviewed by Brower 1996). The geometry of the goal and the scale of movement are essentially the same in the cases of songbirds and butterflies, but the underlying mechanisms of navigation are, in all likelihood, very different. Of course, discovering that animals solve comparable problems in different ways raises interesting biological questions. This classification system clarifies the similarities of the problems that two organisms face, and thus may better guide the search for an explanation of the different navigational solutions that are used.

6.3 CURRENCIES AND CONSTRAINTS

In this section, I present the components of a trait-oriented approach to the adaptive design of navigational traits. The goal of a trait-oriented study is to understand why selection has produced specific phenotypes in an organism. Ideally, we would like to know how and why phenotypes have been selected. Often, however, the history of a phenotypic trait cannot be constructed, and so we can only ask how the phenotypic end points observed may be maintained by natural selection.

Behavioral ecologists have attempted to answer this question by asking two related questions (Stephens and Krebs 1986). One question concerns the fitness benefits and costs of variants of the trait: Does the trait's design reflect the selection to maximize certain benefits, minimize certain costs, or both? The goal is to identify the benefits and costs as specifically as possible and understand the causal link between phenotype and fitness. The notion of fitness "currencies" is often used to summarize the benefits and costs that correlate with different phenotypic variants. A given currency expresses (ideally in precise quantitative terms but sometimes in qualitative terms) the relationship between a particular phenotypic variable and particular benefits and costs. For example, a currency commonly hypothesized for the adaptive design of foraging behavior is the "net rate of energy gained" (NREG) by the animal while it forages: energy gained per unit time (the benefit) minus energy expended per unit time (the cost). Such a currency is a measure of performance that is assumed to correlate with fitness, such that fitness is highest when the currency is maximized (for a currency such as NREG that emphasizes benefits relative to costs) or minimized (for currencies that emphasize costs relative to benefits (see Ydenberg, this vol. section 9.2, for further details).

The second question concerns the biological and physical constraints that limit the course and outcome of selection. Understanding the constraints on phenotypic design is difficult. Several different constraints have been proposed, and there has been considerable debate about whether some constraints are more important than others (Arnold 1994; Dukas, this vol. section 3.2). To simplify the discussion, I focus on two relatively well-defined classes of constraints. The first I have already introduced (6.2.5): phylogenetically conserved or "ground-plan" traits that determine the general nature of the challenges of survival and reproduction. Such traits are constraints in the sense that they determine the selection pressures that operate on another trait being studied. For example, the traits that make a zooplankton a zooplankton—its dietary and habitat requirements (which determine how sources of food and shelter are distributed in space), its size, its mode of locomotion—jointly determine that the zooplankton's most difficult navigational problems are

(1) whether to go up or down, and (2) which way is up. The traits that make a bee a bee determine that the bee must learn to find, in a two-dimensional terrain, the widely separated point locations of its nest and nectar and pollen sources.

The other class of constraints comprises those features of the organism or its environment that slow or prevent a trait from reaching a particular phenotypic optimum. Invoking constraints in this context assumes not only that selection is inherently an optimizing process (an assumption some dispute) but also that we can identify the optimal phenotype—the peak in a fitness landscape—that selection is "trying" to reach (an even more controversial assumption). The failure of the organism to exhibit the optimal phenotype may mean that there is some biological or physical reason for why the optimum can never be reached (e.g. lack of genetic variation in the organism) or why the optimum has not been reached yet (e.g. genetic correlations with other selected traits that slow the course of evolution toward the optimum or limit an organism's ability to acquire information that is needed for optimal performance). In the case of navigational mechanisms, commonly invoked constraints of this sort are the animal's sensory modality (which hypothetically limits the ability to acquire information that enables better performance) and brain size (which hypothetically limits the ability to process and store the information that is obtained).

Ideally, one can incorporate hypotheses about benefits, costs, and constraints into a formal quantitative model. This is standard practice in studies of foraging. (For examples in this volume, see Dukas, sections 3.3.2.2, 3.4.2; Bateson and Kacelnik, sections 8.5, 8.6; Ydenberg, sections 9.2.7, 9.2.8.) The few explicit hypotheses about the adaptive design of navigational mechanisms, by contrast, are presented in qualitative, verbal terms. One of these is Baker's (1978) "principle of least navigation." Baker uses "navigation" to refer to the process(es) that must occur in the animal's brain for the setting and maintenance of a correct course, and not to the behavioral outcome of this process(es). The idea is that animals have evolved to use those sensory cues and information-processing strategies that will allow them to meet some critical level of performance while minimizing investment in processing: Thus, natural selection does not favor use of a supercomputer when a pocket calculator will do. This hypothesis assumes that (1) the currency for the adaptive design of navigational mechanisms is dominated by the costs associated with "more navigation," and (2) the selection favors mechanisms that minimize this cost while also producing the benefits associated with reaching a given goal. The costs could include, for example, the time required for relevant calculations or the energy needed for neural processing. This hypothesis also assumes there are constraints on the capacity of animals to handle navigational information such that more complex solutions require more time or energy.

There is much evidence that animals tend to use approximations and short-cuts that guarantee adequate performance, instead of processes that may pro-duce (with a greater investment of time and energy in computation) more accurate navigation (Dyer 1994; Wehner 1987, 1991; Wehner et al. 1996). At the same time, however, this hypothesis of minimized investment provides little explanation about why the navigational abilities of a given species are limited in specific ways or why some species exhibit more sophisticated navi-gational abilities than others. Perhaps more important, this hypothesis consid-ers only a narrow subset of the possible currencies that may affect the adaptive design of navigational mechanisms and offers a very superficial account of why animals are constrained in the ways they apparently are. I shall conclude this section by outlining ways in which the study of navigational currencies and constraints may be broadened.

There are a number of possible currencies for the natural selection of navi-gational mechanisms: homing speed (maximize), homing accuracy (max-imize), probability of disorientation (minimize), energy expenditure (mini-mize), risk of predation en route (minimize; i.e., follow the safest path), or probability of contacting possible resources (maximize). One can imagine how each of these may be favored in particular circumstances—depending on the ecological and life-history characteristics of the species—and produce very different behavioral consequences.

Furthermore, by drawing an analogy to foraging currencies, one can also propose more complex navigational currencies that reflect the fitness trade-offs between competing needs. A widely studied trade-off in the foraging liter-ature is that between foraging and predation: For some species, increases in the foraging rate may occur at the expense of a higher predation rate, and animals behave in ways that balance the need to feed well and stay safe (Ydenberg, this vol. section 9.4). By analogy, navigational mechanisms in some species may reflect the competing needs of maximizing homing speed and minimizing exposure to predators. Confronted with the general task of finding the way from point A to point B, a species that is relatively immune to predation (for example, because it is distasteful) may be selected to find the shortest path; however, a more vulnerable species may be selected to find the shortest *safe* path (as exemplified with the thigmotactic [e.g. wall-hugging] behavior of mice or cockroaches).

With regard to constraints, I have already outlined a broad framework for identifying the ways in which biological or physical factors external to the trait that is under selection may place limits on the course of selection. I want to focus my attention on a specific constraint that is addressed by Baker's least-navigation model and many other explanations about navigational limita-tions in animals. This constraint is the inherent limitation in the ability to obtain and use information from sensory stimuli; this constraint in turn limits

the speed or accuracy of navigational performance. No doubt all animals are limited in their capacity to handle information about the environment (Dukas, this vol. chap. 3). To verify this idea, however, we must determine what has prevented natural selection from producing a more sophisticated animal than what we observe.

The difficulty of answering this question becomes apparent when we attempt to understand the role of brain size as a constraint. Brain size is widely invoked as a constraint on the cognitive capacities of animals, both as a general constraint on basic learning ability and as an explanation for the failure to adopt certain strategies. Brain size is invoked as a constraint any time it is assumed that an animal can learn more or faster or remember longer if it had more neural tissue. This assumption is made, for example, when we contrast the sophistication of big-brained animals with the limitations of small-brained animals (Wehner 1991). It is also made in any study that correlates the sizes of brain regions with the apparent complexity of a cognitive task (reviews by Fahrbach and Robinson 1995; Sherry, this vol. section 7.4.4).

The assumption that brain size constrains cognitive performance is reasonable. A computational device with more computing elements (be they transistors or synapses) must be able to process larger amounts of information at a time, store more information in memory, and possibly handle more tasks simultaneously. The problem is to translate this eminently reasonable assumption into an account of the specific limitations on cognitive performance (see Dukas, this vol. section 4.3). Correlations between brain size and performance abound (see Sherry, this vol. section 7.4.4). Because we do not know how the brain does most of what it does, however, there is no theory that allows us to predict how much cognitive sophistication can be manifested with a given amount of neural tissue or explain why an animal's cognitive performance and its consequent behavior are limited in the ways they are.

Furthermore, overemphasis on the constraints imposed by brain size may lead one to overlook other explanations for an apparent failure to employ a presumed optimal strategy. Perhaps the cognitive strategy that we regard as superior—because it appears more sophisticated, more accurate, or more reliable—would actually be inferior to the one used by the animals. For example, the more sophisticated strategy may necessitate more processing steps or greater sampling of the environment and hence may cost the animal more time or greater exposure to predation. If so, then the animal, by adopting its strategy, may actually be balancing optimally the competing demands of computational accuracy and computational speed.

Most hypotheses proposed about the adaptive significance of navigational abilities apply to particular situations only, plausibly identifying the likely functions of particular mechanisms. This is not necessarily bad—we have to start somewhere. I believe, however, the rigor of hypotheses about the adap-

tive design of particular navigational mechanisms can be improved considerably.

6.4 CASE STUDIES

As I stressed, most investigators have focused on how animals carry out their amazing feats of navigation. In the following, I will consider a number of examples of navigational processes that either have been or could be analyzed from an adaptative standpoint. My goal is to illustrate the potential for new insights into the biology of specific navigational mechanisms and the evolution of general cognitive mechanisms. I will consider only cases in which there is good behavioral evidence of the underlying mechanisms. There is little point in speculating about the adaptive design of mechanisms if their basic properties are a matter of debate (e.g. the navigational maps of birds).

6.4.1 Path Integration by Nesting Insects

As mentioned, path integration is a mechanism by which an animal can determine its position on the basis of information acquired along the path. A particularly well-studied example is the ability of desert ants to determine the direction and distance to home from a feeding place after moving on a circuitous, outward searching path (reviews by Wehner and Wehner 1990; Gallistel 1990; Dyer 1994). Similar abilities have also been studied in honeybees (von Frisch 1967), funnel-web spiders (which need to retreat after running onto the web to find prey) (Görner and Claas 1985), hamsters (Etienne et al. 1996), rats (McNaughton et al. 1996), and humans (Loomis et al. 1993). Such navigational abilities provide clear evidence of internal representations that are derived partly with computation of sensory data. The homing ant behaves as if she has encoded a vector that corresponds to her distance and direction from home. Usually, however, this vector does not correspond to any segment of the outward path or any path previously traveled; therefore, we can exclude the hypothesis that the animal merely encodes a neural replica of sensory information that is acquired during the movement on the outward path. Instead, we must conclude that the animal computes the homing vector with use of distance and directional information acquired during the twists and turns of the outward path (fig. 6.5).

Recent studies have provided new insights into the nature of the computations that ants perform and have raised important questions about the adaptive design of the mechanisms used to perform these computations. Before the recent work on ants, investigators of path integration traditionally assumed that animals compute the homing vector with use of the equivalent of trigonometric vector summation (e.g. Mittelstaedt 1985). This computation would require

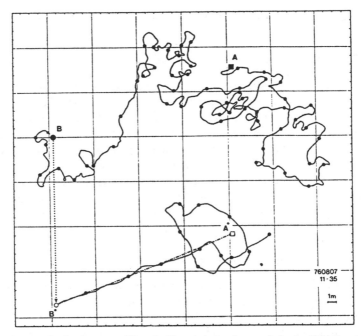

Figure 6.5. Track of a desert ant (*Cataglyphis* sp.) during its search for food. Track originates at nest (*A*) and terminates at *B* (dots give position at 10-second intervals). After experimental displacement from *B* to *B**, the ant searches for home (*A*). The ant travels in the direction from *B** that would have led it to *A* from point *B*. The ant also travels roughly the same distance from *B** that would have led to *A* from *B;* the ant then wanders in search of *A*. The ant's ability to set a homeward course is not dependent on any cues that emanate from its nest or previous experience of the homing route; instead, the ant integrates the directions and distances traveled over the outward path and maintains a continuously updated internal representation of its net displacement from home (from Wehner 1982).

neural mechanisms to decompose the vector that corresponds to each segment of the outward path into its sine and cosine components and to compute from the summed components the net direction and distance of displacement. The implicit assumption is that natural selection equipped animals to perform path integration in this way because other possible methods introduce systematic biases in the calculation of the direction home.

Wehner and Müller (1988) found, however, that ants actually do exhibit systematic errors of up to 30° in their estimate of the homeward direction. The pattern of these errors was evident when ants were constrained experimentally to travel to food along a two-segment outward path. These ants chose a homeward direction that deviated consistently to one side of the actual homeward direction. Ants that made a right turn from the first segment to the second segment set a homeward course slightly to the right of the actual homeward

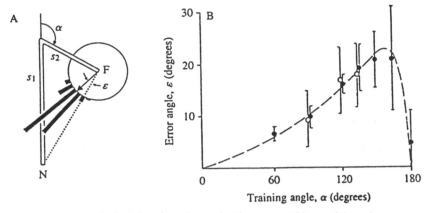

Figure 6.6. Systematic deviations from the true homing course with use of the path-integration system in desert ants (*Cataglyphis fortis*). (*a*) Homing directions selected by ants after travel on a two-segment outward path in an experimental channel that leads from the nest (*N*) to food (*F*). From *F*, the ants were displaced to a featureless plain and their homing orientation was measured. The angle ε is the deviation of the ants' mean path from the compass direction that would have led to *N* from *F*. (*b*) As the angle (α) between s_1 and s_2 increased, the ants' angle of deviation increased (ε) (although ε is low when α = 180°) (from Wehner et al. 1996).

direction. Ants that made a left turn erred to the left. The degree of error varied systematically with the angle of the turn (fig. 6.6).

These systematic errors suggest that these ants do not carry out the equivalent of trigonometric vector summation. Furthermore, the bias in the homeward direction cannot be accounted for by random errors in a trigonometric calculation because random errors would produce only scatter around the correct homing vector. By analyzing the errors, Müller and Wehner (1988) deduced an alternative computational algorithm that better explains the ants' behavior. The alternative algorithm is not a trigonometric solution. In the alternative algorithm, the animal maintains an arithmetic running average of the directions traveled along the outward path; the contribution of each path segment to the average direction is weighted by that segment's length. Reanalysis of published path-integration data revealed that other invertebrate species, including honeybees, exhibit systematic errors that can be explained with the same algorithm (Wehner 1991).

Wehner (1991) suggested that use of a nontrigonometric computation for path integration represents a "small-brained strategy." Wehner implied that trigonometric vector summation is inherently more difficult to perform than the computations in the algorithm of Müller and Wehner. We encounter a problem I alluded to and one stressed recently by Wehner et al. (1996): There is no theoretical or empirical justification for the assumption that a brain the size of an ant's cannot perform the equivalent of trigonometric computations.

Conceivably, all that is required is a neural unit with an output signal that scales as a trigonometric function of the input signal (Gallistel 1990). Wehner et al. (1996) pointed out that mammals (including humans) performing path integration make systematic errors inconsistent with the predictions of trigono-metric vector summation. Should we therefore assume that the processing capabilities of the mammalian brain are too limited to support an exact solution to the problem of path integration?

An alternative possibility is that the systematic errors in path integration observed in so many species reflect not an inherent limitation of computing power but an adaptive strategy that is designed to solve a specific problem in path integration. Any path-integration mechanism is subject to random er-ror (which results from imprecise measurements of directions and distances during the outward trip). Furthermore, these errors accumulate over successive segments of a long path. The systematic errors exhibited by ants and other animals could be viewed as strategies used to mitigate the effects of accumu-lated random errors (Hartmann and Wehner 1995). The direction in which homing ants deviate from the actual homeward direction tends to lead them across the initial segment of the outward path; this deviation would bring them into visual contact with familiar landmarks that could be used for reorientation. Even if there were more scatter around this (systematically biased) homing direction, most ants would come within view of familiar landmarks. Hence, an ant's probability of missing the nest to the other side and heading into unknown terrain would be reduced. This explanation may account for the ob-servation that there is no systematic error in the ants' homing direction if the outward path doubles back toward home (Müller and Wehner 1988).

The hypothesis that the systematic deviations in the ant's path-integration system are adaptive raises new questions that could be examined by means of an optimality analysis. Presumably, the systematic deviations from the homeward direction are advantageous only if they are not too great. Very large deviations may waste energy or time or even increase the probability of getting lost. What determines the optimal degree of systematic deviation? One impor-tant factor might be the degree of random error that occurs during travel on a typical foraging path (fig. 6.7). Greater random error would produce greater scatter of the homing vectors calculated by ants, and would favor a greater deviation in the homeward direction to reduce the probability of missing the nest to the wrong side (fig. 6.6). Another factor might be the size of the familiar area where familiar landmarks could direct the ant home. The size of the famil-iar area would be determined by such factors as the visual structure of the environment, the visual acuity of the animal, and the animal's capacity to learn spatial relationships between landmarks and the nest. If the familiar area were larger, then larger random errors of path integration would be tolerated, and there would be less need for compensation with systematic biases.

It is premature to say if such an optimality analysis would provide new

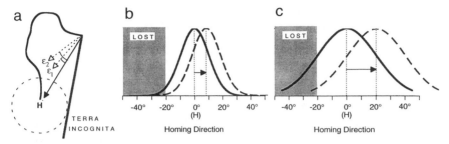

Figure 6.7. Optimal tuning of systematic deviations in the path-integration system of desert ants. (*a*) Systematic deviations possibly compensate for random error in the computation of the homing direction by ensuring that the homeward path leads across the first segment of the outbound path instead of into unfamiliar territory (*terra incognita*) (Wehner et al. 1996). If so, the magnitude of systematic deviation sufficient to eliminate the possibility of getting lost should be smaller when random error produces a relatively small scatter in the computation of the homing direction (*b*) than when random error produces a relatively large scatter (*c*).

insights into the design of path-integration mechanisms. My aim is to illustrate that study of this fascinating system can be moved beyond a consideration of mechanisms toward the development of testable ideas about why mechanisms have the properties they do.

6.4.2 Sun-Compass Orientation by Insects

In both y-axis orientation (navigation perpendicular to a shoreline) and x,y-orientation (navigation to a goal at a point location), animals must hold a straight-line course once they have determined their position relative to their goal. A common solution is to use an external feature of the environment as a compass. The most important sources of compass information for animals and humans are celestial cues (e.g. the sun, polarized light patterns, and stars) and the earth's magnetic field. In this section, I will consider sun-compass orientation in insects. Honeybees have also been found to have a magnetic compass (Schmitt and Esch 1993; Collett and Baron 1994). I will discuss the honeybees' magnetic compass later in the context of the function it serves in landmark learning.

Insects use their sun compass to hold a straight course during path integration, and honeybees, specifically, use the sun as a reference to communicate the direction of food with dance (von Frisch 1967). The sun is ideal as a directional reference because it is reliable and too far away for parallax error to occur. To maintain a straight course, the animal simply holds a constant body angle relative to the sun's azimuth. The problem, however, is that the sun moves. An animal that must maintain a straight course over an extended period of time or travel along a given route at different times of day must compensate for changes in the sun's direction relative to the direction of travel.

Many animals can compensate for changes in the solar azimuth (even during periods when they cannot see the sun directly); this compensation means that animals must be informed about the pattern of solar movement during the day. One major question regarding cognition concerns the nature of the mechanisms by which animals estimate changes in the sun's position over the course of a day.

The task of compensating for the sun's movement is complicated further because the rate of the sun's movement is not constant (fig. 6.8), which precludes the possibility of compensating at a fixed rate. The rate of change of the azimuth is relatively slow in the morning and afternoon and relatively rapid at midday. In addition, this daily pattern, or the ephemeris function, varies with the season and latitude. Clearly, an animal that uses the sun as a compass would do well to use the current, local ephemeris function. We have known since the 1950s (Lindauer 1957, 1959) that insects learn the solar ephemeris function early in life. Recently, investigators have focused on understanding how this learning takes place, and, in the process, they have provided clues about the adaptive design of the underlying learning mechanisms.

To begin, we should consider what learning the sun's course entails. At the minimum, the animal must associate different positions of the solar azimuth, as measured relative to some earthbound coordinate system (e.g. landmarks or the earth's magnetic field), with the times of day at which they are measured, so that time can cue the retrieval of the correct azimuth. Conceivably, the entire course of the sun can be learned by simply encoding time-linked measurements of the azimuth into a neural "look-up table." We have long known, however, that animals do something a bit more impressive. As Lindauer (1957, 1959) first showed in honeybees, some animals can estimate the sun's position at times of day when they have never seen the sun. It is as if the animals can somehow compute unknown segments of the sun's course. Lindauer reared bees in an incubator and allowed them to see only the afternoon segment of the sun's course. During their afternoon flight time, he trained these bees to find a feeding station south of their hive. When he tested the bees in the morning (in a different terrain so that familiar landmarks could not be used), he found that bees could use their sun compass to find the food. Other studies have shown that honeybees (Lindauer 1957; Dyer 1985) and desert ants (Wehner 1982) can estimate the sun's course at night. Bees refer to the nocturnal position of the sun when performing waggle dances to communicate the location of food at night (Dyer 1985); in ants, compensation for the sun's nocturnal course has been demonstrated experimentally with use of an artificial sun (Wehner 1982); however, why ants have this ability is not clear.

Thus, in insects, learning the sun's course entails not only the recording of known time-linked positions of the sun's azimuth but also filling in unknown

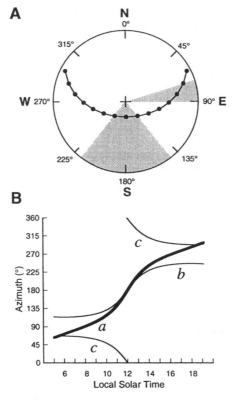

Figure 6.8. Solar ephemeris function. (*a*) The sun moves at constant rate 15°/h along its arc (symbols show sun's position at hourly intervals starting at 0500 hours on the June solstice in East Lansing, Michigan, ≈43° N); however, the azimuth, or the compass direction of the sun, changes at a variable rate during the day. Shaded sectors show the change in the azimuth for two 2-h time intervals—one early in the morning when the azimuth changes relatively slowly (≈7°/h) and one spanning noon when the azimuth changes quickly (≈40°/h). (*b*) Alternative method for representing the sun's pattern of movement, illustrating seasonal and latitudinal variation in ephemeris function. Thick line (*a*) shows the ephemeris function for East Lansing, Michigan, on the June solstice. Other lines show functions for the equator on two dates: (*b*) June solstice, when the azimuth shifts right-to-left (counterclockwise relative to cardinal compass coordinates) along the northern horizon; and (*c*) December solstice, when the azimuth shifts left-to-right (clockwise) along the southern horizon (from Dyer and Dickinson 1996). Function *c* appears in two segments; the break occurs at noon when the azimuth is in the north.

positions of the azimuth with some sort of computation. The computation can be modeled with the following general equation: $A_{\tau+t} = A_\tau + R \cdot t$, where A_τ is a known time-linked azimuth of the sun, $A_{\tau+t}$ is the unknown azimuth after an elapsed time interval t, and R is the rate of compensation (degrees of azimuth/time) during t. Most investigators who have sought to understand how insects perform this computation have asked how insects determine the rate of compensation, R. The prevailing assumption has been that insects compute R on the basis of the position or the rate of movement of the azimuth when they have observed it. For example, much of the available data can be explained with the hypothesis that insects interpolate at a linear rate to find unknown positions of the azimuth (New and New 1962; Wehner 1982); thus, the value of R is determined for a gap between two known positions of the azimuth by dividing the difference in the azimuth by the difference in time. Other data suggest, however, that insects extrapolate the sun's position on the basis of the rate of azimuthal movement observed at other times of day (Gould 1980; Dyer 1985).

Recent studies of desert ants and honeybees have suggested that the actual learning mechanism used by insects is considerably different from the mechanism that any previous investigators had assumed. The properties of these mechanisms were revealed in experiments that used improved assays to infer how experience-restricted insects estimate unknown segments of the sun's course. For example, Dyer and Dickinson (1994) studied the dances of bees; with dance, the bees indicated a known feeding site to which they had flown under a cloudy sky. The bees used the dance to indicate the direction the dancer had flown to reach food, relative to the sun. Human observers can use dances to infer where the bees have determined the sun to be relative to the line of flight. By testing bees on an overcast day, one can ensure that bees base their dances on an internally generated estimate of the sun's position instead of a direct measurement taken during flight (Dyer 1987).

Examination of dances during an extended period of cloudy weather revealed that experience-restricted bees did not use any of the proposed linear computations to estimate the sun's course at times of day when bees had not seen the sun. Instead, bees behaved as if they used an internal ephemeris that approximated the actual nonlinear pattern of movement of the azimuth (fig. 6.9a). The internal ephemeris was an exaggeration of the actual ephemeris at the time of the experiment: In the internal and actual ephemerides the sun rises opposite from where it sets, the azimuth changes little throughout the morning and afternoon, and the azimuth moves rapidly from the eastern to the western half of the sky at midday. The data, and hence the mechanism that produced the data, can be described as a step function in which the azimuth changes by 180° at midday (fig. 6.9b). More importantly, with additional experience throughout the day, this approximation of the sun's course is trans-

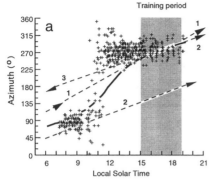
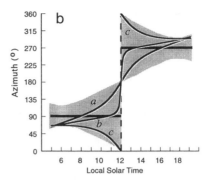

Figure 6.9. Partially experienced bees estimate the sun's course at times of day when they have never seen it. (*a*) Solar positions inferred from dances that indicate the same feeding place by incubator-reared bees that had seen the sun only from 1500 hours until sunset (training period) on days before the test. Data from 554 dances performed over the day by 44 different bees are shown. Bees were tested on a cloudy day so they could not base their dances on a direct perception of the sun during the flight to the food; bees had to estimate the sun's position on the basis of their experience on previous afternoons. The thick line is the actual solar ephemeris function at the time of the experiment. Lines 1–3 show the predictions of previous computational models proposed to explain the ability of insects to fill gaps regarding the sun's course: 1 = linear interpolation of the sun's position at times between sunset and the beginning of the daily training period, 2 = forward extrapolation (through the night and into the next day) of the rate of solar movement measured during the training time, 3 = backward extrapolation of the rate observed during the daily training period to earlier times during the day. All three predications account poorly for the bees' behavior. The data can be described by a step function in which the azimuth used in the morning is 180° from the azimuth the bees experienced on previous afternoons. Data from two bees that used the afternoon angle in the morning and the morning angle in the afternoon are excluded (see Dyer and Dickinson 1994 for these data). (*b*) Comparison of 180° step function with actual ephemeris functions. Curving lines show the ephemerides for three latitudes on the June solstice: *a,* 43° N (East Lansing, Michigan); *b,* 25° N; and *c,* 15° N. Shaded region covers all possible solar-ephemeris functions that could be observed on the earth's surface (i.e. all latitudes and all days of the year). The mean of all these functions is a 180° step function that resembles one used by the bees.

formed so that it more accurately reflects the actual movement of the azimuth (see Dyer and Dickinson 1994).

 With evidence of a similar phenomenon in desert ants (Wehner and Müller 1993), the results suggest that the development of the insects' sun compass involves an interplay of innate and individually acquired information about the dynamics of solar movement. I suggest that the learning process starts when bees, during their first flights outside the nest, record time-linked positions of the sun relative to landmarks and thereby associate their approximate, innate ephemeris with the local terrain. This association allows them to use

remembered positions of the sun at times of day when they have seen it and estimate, with reasonable accuracy, the azimuth at other times of day. With additional experience, a bee refines its internal ephemeris to resemble the actual ephemeris.

The innate ephemeris uncovered by these experiments has some intriguing properties that could represent adaptive design features facilitating the bees' learning of the sun's course. Note that the solar ephemeris observed at latitudes near the equator (where honeybees evolved) closely resembles the step function developed by the experience-restricted bees (fig. 6.9b). This means that a bee that has sampled only a small segment of the sun's course is able to estimate the sun's position at other times of day to within about 30°. Even at higher latitudes, a bee's errors would exceed 45° only during a couple of hours near noon. Although such errors degrade the accuracy of compass orientation and path integration based on the sun, the approximate ephemeris may nevertheless allow foraging bees to begin to use the sun, perhaps in conjunction with familiar landmarks, before they have extensively sampled the sun's course throughout the day (Dyer and Dickinson, 1996).

An even more intriguing feature of the innate ephemeris function revealed by the experiments is that the shape of the ephemeris—a 180° step function— exactly matches the average of all possible solar ephemeris functions (considering all latitudes and all days of the year). The learning task faced by a bee is to develop an internal ephemeris function that resembles the ephemeris function at the time and place at which the bee lives. The function to be learned cannot be predicted in advance because a developing bee cannot anticipate the latitude and season in which she will be active; however, consider the advantages of beginning with a default ephemeris that resembles the average ephemeris function instead of, for example, substituting random angles for unknown positions of the azimuth. As shown in figure 6.10, the estimates produced with a 180° step function deviate far less on average from any actual ephemeris function than do random estimates. Thus, the underlying neural network that encodes the sun's course presumably has to change less to conform to the actual ephemeris and thus approximates more quickly an accurate representation of the ephemeris. The faster learning speed may be a considerable advantage for an animal that, like a honeybee, spends at most 2 weeks gathering food for her colony before she dies (reviewed by Winston 1987).

In summary, the behavioral evidence suggests that the insect brain was designed for rapid learning of the sun's changing position relative to the terrain. The development of the sun compass exploits regularities in the sun's general pattern of movement. The innate representation essentially encodes this general pattern; this encoding allows bees to use the sun for orientation relatively accurately (even at times of day when they have never seen the sun)

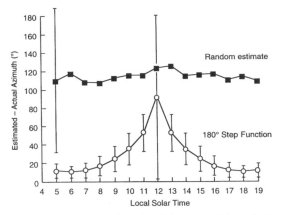

Figure 6.10. Deviation from the actual solar azimuth in two possible methods used for estimating the azimuth at unknown times of day. At each time of day, symbols show the mean difference ($n = 500$ comparisons; error bars, ± 1 standard deviation) between the estimated azimuth and the actual azimuth as defined by the solar ephemeris function from a randomly selected latitude and date. The values for the random estimate were based on a randomly selected angle between $0°$ and $360°$. The error bars for only one time of day are shown; the others are comparable in magnitude. The values for the $180°$ step function were based on angles of $90°$ before noon, $270°$ after noon, and either $0°$ or $180°$ (each with probability 0.5) at noon. This simulation suggests that a $180°$ step function, like that used by partially experienced bees and ants, would, on average, estimate unknown positions of the sun with far greater accuracy at most times of day than a process that generates a random estimate (Dickinson and Dyer in preparation).

and possibly facilitates subsequent development of a more accurate representation.

6.4.3 Compass Orientation in Birds

Compass orientation has been intensively studied in birds since Gustav Kramer (1950) presented evidence of a time-compensated sun compass in starlings. His discovery occurred the same year von Frisch (1950) reported the existence of sun-compass orientation in honeybees, and so the studies of compass orientation in these two species have developed simultaneously. The research has revealed certain parallels between these two species in addition to the role played by celestial cues in both groups. Most important, compass orientation in both insects and birds depends on an interaction of innate and individually acquired information, leading to the development of an internal record of relevant features of the compass reference. Furthermore, in birds as in insects, the plasticity of this developmental process allows the animal to develop a reliable compass reference despite geographic and seasonal variation in the environmental features that provide the directional information.

These parallels notwithstanding, compass orientation in birds appears to be far more complicated than that in insects; in birds, multiple interacting compass systems and complicated developmental trajectories are involved. This complexity, combined with interspecific variation in how compass senses develop and are used, has led to a rich literature that defies easy summary. I will attempt to provide an overview of the most important design features of avian compass systems and relate these design features to the navigational problems that the animals must solve. For more extensive reviews, see Able and Able (1996), Wilschko and Wilschko (1991, 1996), and Schmidt-Koenig et al. (1991). For work on the navigational compasses of other vertebrates, see Lohmann and Lohmann (1996a, 1996b) and Phillips and Borland (1994).

6.4.3.1 Sun Compass

The avian sun compass has been best studied in pigeons, which use the sun compass for homing, and in various songbirds (e.g. starlings), which use the sun compass to learn directions of food in a way that is analogous to that of insects. Like insects, birds need to contend with variations in the rate of movement of the azimuth. Studies by Wiltschko and Wiltschko (1981) and others have shown that the pigeon sun compass is learned, but many puzzles remain unsolved regarding the nature of this learning process. It is still unclear just what geographic references can be used for measuring successive time-linked positions of the sun. Various evidence supports a role for the earth's magnetic field (Wiltschko et al. 1976). Other nonexclusive possibilities include the "pole point" (the center of rotation of the sky vault; see section 6.4.3.3) and of course landmarks. The location of the pole point can be determined with the patterns of skylight polarization that are detected at sunrise and sunset (Phillips and Waldvogel 1988).

Another issue is whether partially experienced birds can solve the problem of filling in unknown segments of the sun's course. I have already discussed that insects can do this (Wehner and Müller 1993; Dyer and Dickinson 1994). In one study, pigeons with experience limited to the afternoon seemed unable to use the sun as a compass when their homing ability was tested in the morning; instead, they used their magnetic compass (Wiltschko et al. 1981). On the other hand, Schmidt-Koenig (1961) showed that pigeons used an artificial sun for finding the compass direction of food at night and behaved as if they compensated for the solar movement after sunset. Also, direction-trained starlings (Hoffmann 1959) and pigeons (Schmidt-Koenig 1963) correctly used the midnight sun in the arctic sky for orientation when they only had been exposed to the diurnal course of the sun at middle northern latitudes. Such abilities, which closely resemble those of insects, strongly suggest that birds can fill in gaps in their experience of the sun's course. Pigeons that did not exhibit such an ability in a homing task (Wiltschko et al. 1981) may simply

have been using the magnetic compass instead of the sun compass in this context.

Birds, unlike insects, appear to be able to recalibrate their internal compass as the solar ephemeris changes seasonally or as the bird moves to a different latitude. An ability to recalibrate the sun compass is sensible for a long-lived, wide-ranging species. One study examined pigeons living near the equator (reviewed by Schmidt-Koenig et al. 1991). There the sun's movement varies seasonally in a particularly dramatic way; the sun passes north of the zenith (with a counterclockwise shift of the azimuth) during part of the year and south of the zenith (with a clockwise shift of the azimuth) during the other part of the year (fig. 6.8b). The homing orientation of pigeons was tested at noon, and they behaved as if their internal ephemeris was out-of-date by about 7 weeks. The pigeons sometimes sought home in the wrong direction, as if (for example) they had interpreted the noontime sun to be in the south when it was really in the north.

This result may underestimate the flexibility with which birds recalibrate their sun compass when confronted with changes in the sun's movement. At tropical latitudes, seasonal changes in the local ephemeris function are very subtle. Each day, the azimuth stays in the east for most of the morning and in the west for most of the afternoon (fig. 6.9b); only during a few hours (or even minutes) near noon does the ephemeris differ from that on other days. Thus, the pigeons may not have had adequate information to keep their internal ephemerides up-to-date. One might expect transequatorial migrants, which would be faced with far more obvious changes in the ephemeris function, to be able to recalibrate their memory of the sun's course more rapidly.

I have stressed the ability of birds to develop an internal representation that matches the pattern of movement of the sun, and the problems that arise for sun-compass orientation as a result of changes in season or latitude. Alerstam (1996) recently discussed interesting issues that arise with regard to movements in longitude. Specifically, he suggested that the linkage of the sun compass to an internal clock allows birds to solve the problem of setting an energetically economical route over long distances.

As airline travelers know, the shortest (and, ceteris paribus, the least costly) route between two points on the globe follows a great circle, the line on the earth's surface formed by an imaginary plane that intersects those two points and the center of the earth. Following a great circle presents challenges to a navigator, however, because one may need to continuously change one's geographical heading (i.e. the angle of travel relative to latitudinal and longitudinal coordinates or relative to a compass that is linked to geographical coordinates). An alternative strategy is to follow a line of constant geographical heading, which is referred to as a "rhumb line." Although the rhumb-line and great-circle routes between two points can be identical (when both points lie

on the same line of longitude or the equator), the rhumb-line route is always longer if the routes differ. The difference between the rhumb-line and great-circle routes between two points is greatest near the poles. For an extreme example, imagine setting a course from 1 km on one side of the north pole to 1 km on the other side of the north pole. The rhumb-line course may be set by walking 3.14 km east (or west) along the 89.99th parallel, maintaining a constant orientation relative to the pole. Or, one could walk the 2-km great circle across the north pole; one would have to head first north and then south and, hence, change orientation relative to the pole (and other geographic coordinates) midcourse. If the goal were at the same latitude but not at exactly 180° of longitude from the starting point, the great-circle route would not intersect with the north pole, and continuous changes in compass course would be required.

It is apparent that an animal changing longitude may save considerable time and energy by taking the great-circle instead of the rhumb-line route, if the animal can solve the compass-course adjustments required for great-circle navigation. Alerstam (1996) provided evidence that some arctic birds face this very problem and use the sun compass to solve it. For example, populations of waders (phalaropes and sandpipers) travel from their breeding grounds in northern Siberia to winter quarters in South America. The initial segment of this journey apparently takes the birds roughly 2,000 km across the Arctic Ocean to Alaska—a trip that spans more than 60° of longitude at latitudes of 65°–75°. Radar tracks of these migrating flocks suggest that a great circle is followed instead of a rhumb line (fig. 6.11). By following a great circle, the birds save at least 200 km in travel distance over this initial segment.

Alerstam proposed a surprisingly simple mechanism to account for this ability. If a bird sets its initial course relative to its sun compass and does not reset its internal clock as it crosses successive time zones, its geographical compass course changes during the trip to closely resemble a great-circle route. This happens because, at the same subjective time, the bearing of the sun is different in different time zones. For example, for trekking across the north pole (assuming travel occurs close to the June solstice), one could head northward by starting at local noon and keeping the sun at one's back. As the north pole is crossed, the longitude changes by 12 time zones so that it is now local midnight. By ignoring the time change (at least temporarily), one can switch to a southbound course by continuing to walk with the sun at one's back. At lower latitudes, the same process produces a continuous veer in the compass course.

A potential problem with this strategy is that flight paths would veer in the same way as that of birds as they move through time zones near the equator, where this effect would not be so useful. The rhumb-line and great-circle routes are essentially the same at low latitudes, and they are identical along

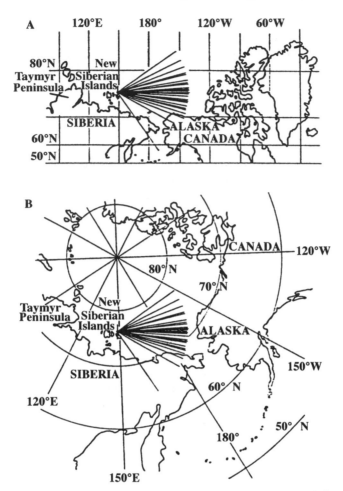

Figure 6.11. Do birds that migrate at high latitudes follow great-circle or rhumb-line routes? Maps show radar tracks from arctic waders interpreted as rhumb-line routes on a Mercator projection (*a*) and great-circle routes on a polar projection (*b*). The situation in *b* is a more likely interpretation because the routes carry the birds over the Alaskan peninsula, where populations of migrating waders are known to pass (from Alerstam 1996).

the equator. The veer produced with a sun compass linked to a different time zone would cause the bird to deviate from both of these equally efficient routes. For a given distance of travel, however, the effect would be much less pronounced near the equator than near the poles because the same linear distance spans fewer time zones at the equator than near the poles.

This example provides a useful lesson for demonstrating how an apparently difficult problem—one which human navigators can solve only with consider-

able computational effort—may be solved by animals without special cognitive abilities. Certainly, the bird must obtain positional information that allows it to set off on the correct course, and obtaining this information may entail a complicated assessment of its spatial location. However, following an efficient great-circle route over a great distance may be no more difficult than using a sun-compass orientation over short distances.

6.4.3.2 Magnetic Compasses

As human navigators have long known, the earth's magnetic field provides an extremely reliable directional reference. Therefore, it is scarcely surprising that animals have evolved the ability to use this reference. The evidence for magnetic-compass orientation is overwhelming in a wide variety of avian species. Most work has focused on migratory songbirds, which can be easily studied in controlled conditions because a behavior called "migratory restlessness" is exhibited by captive birds (reviewed by Berthold 1991; Gwinner 1996). During the migration season, caged birds increase their activity levels at the time of day (or night) they would be flying along their migratory route. When active, the birds tend to cluster toward the side of the cage that corresponds to the migratory direction, as if the birds are trying to take off in that direction. This clustering makes it very easy to manipulate stimuli experienced by the birds and thus explore the sensory basis of their ability to discriminate directions. In addition to the studies on migrant songbirds, magnetic-compass orientation has been explored in pigeons that are heading homeward after being experimentally displaced from their loft (reviewed by Wiltschko and Wiltschko 1996).

To understand the problems that must be solved in the design of the avian magnetic compass, it is important to understand that the avian magnetic compass responds to a different feature of the earth's magnetic field than magnetic compasses used by people. The earth's magnetic field lines are not parallel to the ground over most of the earth; instead, the field lines penetrate into the surface of the earth at an angle (fig. 6.12). The inclination, or dip, of the field lines varies systematically over the globe: the field lines are horizontal (parallel to the ground) at the magnetic equator and progressively steeper near the magnetic poles, where they are nearly vertical. With conventional compasses, human navigators detect the polarity of the field lines by means of the alignment of a magnetized needle with the horizontal component of the magnetic field; these conventional compasses are essentially insensitive to the dip. The avian magnetic compass, by contrast, detects inclination. The compass can detect if the animal is heading toward a magnetic pole (the direction in which the field lines form a small angle relative to the direction of gravity) or toward the equator (the direction in which the field lines form a large angle relative to the direction of gravity). The compass is insensitive to the polarity of the

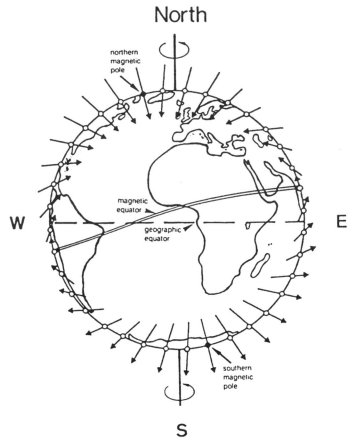

Figure 6.12. The earth's magnetic field with inclination of field lines relative to the earth's surface (from Wiltschko and Wiltschko 1991).

field per se; experiments in which the horizontal and vertical components of the field were manipulated independently revealed this insensitivity (reviewed by Wiltschko and Wiltschko 1996).

The use of an inclination compass that is insensitive to magnetic polarity has interesting implications when the performance of such a compass at different latitudes is considered. The same compass will indicate north as the poleward direction in the northern hemisphere and south as the poleward direction in the southern hemisphere. Thus, without any evolutionary modification, the compass works in both northern and southern hemispheres to lead birds toward the pole in the spring and back toward the equator in the fall (fig. 6.13).

Such a compass presents problems, however, for birds with migratory routes that span the magnetic equator. The compass cannot resolve directions at the

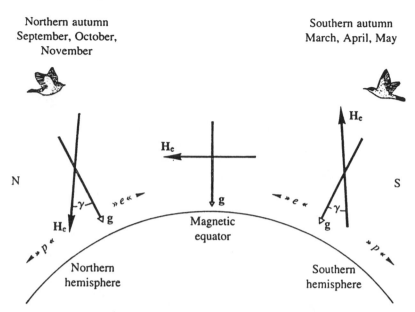

Figure 6.13. The inclination compass of birds. In this system, the direction toward the pole ($\bar{p}$) is the direction in which the magnetic field lines (H_e) make the smallest angle with gravity (g). The direction toward the equator ($\bar{e}$) is opposite that toward the pole. The field lines are horizontal at the magnetic equator. Birds from both northern- and southern-hemisphere populations can use an identical compass to fly toward the equator during their respective autumns. Birds with migratory paths that cross the magnetic equator, however, must change their response to the magnetic compass to stay in the same geographical heading. (From Wiltschko and Wiltschko 1996.)

magnetic equator because the field lines are horizontal. Migrant songbirds do indeed become disoriented when placed in a horizontal field. Transequatorial migrants evidently have some way of compensating for the ambiguity in their magnetic-compass information during their passage across the magnetic equator. One possibility is that these birds may temporarily rely on a celestial compass (Wiltschko and Wiltschko 1996).

Another problem is that a bird with a migratory course that passes the magnetic equator cannot employ a constant response to the dip of the field lines throughout the journey. The response that leads the bird southward in the northern hemisphere to the equator causes the bird to turn northward (to the equator) again after the bird crosses the magnetic equator (see fig. 6.13). To keep flying south, the bird must adopt a poleward response relative to the magnetic compass. Wiltschko and Wiltschko (1992) obtained strong evidence for such a switch in the compass response of garden warblers by exposing caged birds to a simulated crossing of the magnetic equator. Southbound birds

heading toward the equator relative to an inclined magnetic field in the laboratory were placed in a horizontal magnetic field (the condition at the magnetic equator) for two days. When returned to the inclined field, the birds adopted a poleward response, which was opposite to their previous heading and opposite to the orientation of birds that had not been exposed to the horizontal field. This remarkable result suggests, among other things, that birds do not learn the new response to the magnetic field by referring to an independent compass reference that indicates the direction of true south. Instead birds appear to experience a relatively simple programming change when exposed to the horizontal field. Thus, an elegant bit of engineering solves a problem that may not have been solved any more reliably with a learning process.

Why do birds rely on a magnetic-inclination compass instead of a magnetic-polarity compass for migration? This question is especially perplexing given that there is evidence for a polarity compass in newts; therefore, a polarity compass is not a neurobiological impossibility for vertebrates. Indeed, newts appear to use both types of magnetic compasses; an inclination compass is used for y-axis orientation toward their local shoreline, and a polarity compass is used for long-distance x,y-orientation toward their natal pond (Phillips 1986). Baker (1984) suggested that development of biological polarity compasses would have been heavily disfavored during the periodic changes in the polarity of the earth's magnetic field. The newt's polarity compass argues against Baker's hypothesis. The hypothesis is also unsatisfying because it is unlikely that such an infrequent event (the last polarity reversal occurred over 700,000 years ago) has played an important role in the adaptive design of the avian compass. An alternative possibility is that magnetic inclination provides more reliable or accurate information than that provided with magnetic polarity; however, it is not obvious what the specific advantages may be. Indeed, we have seen that there are serious problems with use of an inclination compass near the magnetic equator because the field lines there have no inclination. Migrants may well deal with this problem by relying briefly on a celestial compass. What about birds that live throughout the year in that part of the world? Conceivably, such species rely less on a magnetic compass than migrants do, or perhaps some species have evolved the ability to use a polarity compass.

6.4.3.3 Stellar Compasses

Most songbirds migrate at night, and several species have been shown to use the pattern of stars in the sky as a compass reference during migration (reviews by Able 1980; Able and Able 1996; Wiltschko and Wiltschko 1991). Stellar-compass orientation, like magnetic-compass orientation, is exhibited by caged birds during migratory restlessness; therefore, stellar-compass orientation can

be easily manipulated for the study of its properties. Like humans, birds can identify north by the static configuration of stars in the sky. Learning plays a crucial role in the development of this ability. North is defined by the pole point, which is the point in the sky around which the sky appears to rotate. The azimuth of the star closest to the pole point, Polaris, does not change during the night. Birds probably do not cue specifically on Polaris as we do, but birds can recognize the configuration of stars that rotate around Polaris. Naive birds can be trained to recognize another star as the pole star if they are reared in a planetarium in which the stars rotate around a new pole point. Birds can even learn the pole point in an arbitrary configuration of artificial stars (e.g. Able and Able 1990). Other than that learning plays a role, we know little about the integrative mechanisms by which birds measure celestial rotation and identify the pole point.

6.4.3.4 Interactions among Compass Systems

Some of the most exciting work on bird orientation in recent years has focused on how different compass systems interact during migratory orientation and how these interactions develop. In compass systems, we see most clearly the interplay of innate and individually acquired information in the formation of internal representations of spatial relationships. In addition, we can find examples of how the variable and predictable features of navigational cues may favor learning in the development of compass systems.

The following developmental pattern is, in many ways, typical of the processes by which a naive songbird acquires the ability to use different compass references (reviewed by Wiltschko and Wiltschko 1991 and by Able and Able 1996). When birds are completely naive (as in the case of birds that are hand raised in the lab), their orientation during migratory restlessness is controlled with an innate response to the earth's magnetic field. Southbound birds head in the direction relative to magnetic north that corresponds to the direction taken during actual migration. For many songbirds from central and northern Europe (two well-studied species are garden warblers and pied flycatchers), this innate heading is either southwest or southeast—the directions that allow birds to bypass the Alps. In eastern North America, the innate heading of savannah sparrows is southeast, which corresponds roughly to the direction actually traveled by migratory flocks bound for South America. (Although, oddly, on some nights caged savannah sparrows reverse their direction and head toward the northwest.)

The innate response of naive birds to the magnetic field is modified as birds acquire experience with celestial cues. Specifically, after birds have learned the pole point (which corresponds to true geographical north), they use this reference to calibrate their response to the magnetic reference. This calibration

process may entail a drastic modification of the magnetic heading. For example, Able and Able (1990, 1995) reared savannah sparrows under an artificial sky in which the pole point deviated by 90° from magnetic north (instead of only a few degrees as in the actual sky) so that celestial north was now in the magnetic east (see Wiltschko and Wiltschko 1991 for similar experiments with pied flycatchers). Birds reared under such conditions behaved as if the shifted pole point redefined the position of magnetic north. During migratory restlessness in an artificial magnetic field, they adopted a new angle relative to the magnetic compass and behaved as if magnetic east was aligned with geographic north. Similar effects were observed when the shifted pole point was defined with patterns of polarized light observed at sunrise and sunset (Able and Able 1993).

This experiment showed that the celestial compass not only serves as a navigational reference but also affects calibration of the initial response of naive birds to the magnetic field. Why is it that the celestial compass initially calibrates the magnetic compass instead of vice versa? The answer presumably is that the magnetic field varies over the earth's surface. The variation consists of both large-scale systematic patterns and small-scale anomalies in which the local field departs from a regional pattern. This variation means that a fixed response to local magnetic cues could result in a magnetic heading that deviates markedly from the appropriate geographic heading. Given the distances that birds are traveling, errors in heading of a few degrees may result in a course that ends over open ocean instead of land. The magnetic compass is useful for the same reasons to migrating birds as it is to humans: The magnetic compass generally provides reliable directional information on a global scale, and its reliability is not affected by atmospheric conditions that obliterate celestial references. The usefulness of the magnetic compass depends, however, on its correlation with true geographical north. Because local anomalies in the earth's magnetic field may produce substantial deviations in this relationship, it needs to be calibrated through learning.

This tidy account of the adaptive importance of this calibration process gets a little messier when plasticity in the compass systems of birds after they have begun to migrate is examined. As I discussed, in very young birds the response to the earth's magnetic field is calibrated with reference to the celestial pole point. In older birds, responses to celestial compass cues can be recalibrated with reference to the magnetic field! In experiments with warblers, Wiltschko and Wiltschko (reviewed 1991) caught experienced birds during migration and exposed them to a view of the nighttime sky in an artificial magnetic field that was shifted 120° from the normal field. The birds adopted their typical magnetic heading relative to the artificial field, and hence, they appeared to ignore the stars. When these birds were later tested with a view of the sky but in the absence of magnetic information (an artificially nulled field), they

adopted the new angle relative to the stars. Thus, the birds had not been ignoring the stars in the shifted magnetic field; they were learning a new response to the stars with reference to the shifted magnetic field.

How can we make sense of the evidence that (1) the celestial compass initially serves to calibrate rasponses of naive birds to the magnetic field; and (2) the magnetic field serves to recalibrate responses of experienced birds to the celestial reference? The Wiltschkos (1991) suggested the following interpretation. Although the stars that surround the pole point provide a reliable reference for learning the correct initial migratory heading relative to the magnetic field, they cannot continue to guide the bird along its journey because they gradually disappear below the northern horizon as the bird moves south. New patterns of stars emerge from the southern horizon, but the bird can use these only if it has learned the proper geographical heading relative to them. In this situation, the magnetic field provides a reliable reference. (An alternative possibility is that birds calibrate their responses to newly encountered stars by referring to familiar stars before they disappear below the horizon.)

Thus, the ontogeny of avian compass systems involves a complex interplay of innate and individually acquired responses to navigational references in multiple sensory modalities. We can make sense of this process by invoking plausible arguments about the reliability and variability of different compass references birds use in different stages of their lives. The challenge is to understand in greater detail the evolutionary forces that have shaped these compass systems.

6.4.4 Landmark Learning by Insects

The stereotypical image of a rat running in an artificial maze alludes to the long-standing interest that behavioral scientists have had in the ability of animals to use landmarks for spatial orientation. Insects too have long been studied for their abilities to learn landmarks. Because most studies of insects have been performed in the natural environment, these studies have provided a richly detailed picture of landmark-learning abilities in the context of natural navigational tasks. I will summarize what has been learned about the design of these learning mechanisms, which have been revealed mainly with studies of honeybees (*Apis mellifera*) and desert ants (*Cataglyphis* spp.).

These species, like other nesting animals, face the navigational problem of finding their nest in the terrain. In addition, like other animals that exploit rich patches of food, they often must return to a feeding site that is depleted only after many foraging trips. The scale of their movements demands the use of visual cues, which are far superior to olfactory cues for efficient long-distance orientation to a point goal. (Although many ants use odor trails deposited on the substrate, *Cataglyphis* and other desert ants live in a dry, windswept

environment in which odor is less useful.) Furthermore, the animal must learn the relationships between visual cues and the locations of repeatedly visited goals.

We have already seen how the sun and sun-linked patterns of polarized light serve extremely important functions in the orientation of insects within their foraging range. The celestial compass has certain limitations, however. Clouds may obscure celestial cues. Furthermore, the celestial compass provides good directional information but, by itself, no positional information. Thus, if an animal is passively displaced in the environment (e.g. by the wind or the hand of an experimenter) and cannot perform path integration to update its change of position during the displacement, the celestial compass is of little help to the animal. Finally, as we have seen, the path-integration system used by insects is subject to errors (both systematic and random) that limit the accuracy of pinpointing the location of a goal, such as the nest. For orientation under such circumstances, insects rely on a well-developed ability to use landmarks.

In this section, I will discuss a system for classifying the cognitive sophistication of the landmark-learning abilities of animals. Then I will discuss experimental studies of spatial cognition on small and large scales and consider what these results indicate about the adaptive design of the underlying processes.

6.4.4.1 Characterizing the Contents of Spatial Memory

In recent years, much of the research on landmark orientation has focused on how animals memorize and use spatial information that landmarks provide. Generally, an animal must link the retinal images of landmarks to motor responses that will lead toward the goal. It is not immediately obvious how a brain can do this. At each point in the environment, an animal that views a set of landmarks can record only the two-dimensional retinal pattern. If the animal is moving, it can also record movement across the retina. Different images can be recorded at different points in the environment. Use of landmarks for navigation through the environment, therefore, must involve integration of these separately recorded images.

Gallistel (1990) outlined a three-part system that describes the capacity of animals to encode and use spatial relationships among landmarks. This system is useful for comparing the performance of different species with respect to the sophistication of the cognitive mechanisms that are required to encode spatial information. The first component of this system is the *geometry* of the spatial representation. Does the animal visually encode a rich metric, or Euclidean, representation of the angles and distances among elements it has seen? Alternatively, does the animal encode spatial relationships in a simpler geometric system? For example, an animal that encodes spatial patterns in an

affine geometric system would confuse shapes such as squares, rectangles, and parallelograms that are readily distinguished with use of a metric geometric system.

The second part of Gallistel's system is the *coordinate system* used by the brain to encode shapes. One common distinction is that between an egocentric representation (in which the animal learns directions and distances of different landmarks relative to a coordinate system defined by its body axes) and an allocentric representation (in which the animal learns directions and distances of different landmarks relative to an external coordinate system, such as one based on an external compass). An allocentric representation is assumed to be more complicated because it must be assembled from the egocentric images recorded with the visual system.

The third part of Gallistel's system is the *spatial scale* of the representation. Many nesting insects must learn spatial relationships on a small scale (e.g. the panorama of surrounding landmarks that pinpoint the location of the nest) and a large scale (e.g. the sequences of landmark panoramas seen in different parts of the foraging range). As I will discuss, the properties of the spatial representations that animals form on different spatial scales may be very different.

To illustrate some of what is known about the capacities of insects to use landmarks, I will focus on experiments that have been performed on two spatial scales.

6.4.4.2 Use of Surrounding Landmarks to Pinpoint a Goal

Work on the small-scale task began with Tinbergen's classic studies of nest finding by digger wasps (e.g. Tinbergen and van Kruyt 1938). These studies provided the first clear evidence of landmark learning in insects and defined some of the properties of landmarks that insects learn. More recently, Cartwright and Collett (1983), who worked with honeybees, and Wehner and colleagues (Wehner et al. 1996 [review]), who worked with desert ants, began examining systematically the nature of landmark learning. The general assumption has been that insects arriving at the nest or feeding site stored an image of the surrounding landmarks in memory and then used this memory image to guide their search on return to the goal. The questions are (1) What spatial information do these images encode? (2) How are they used? and (3) How are they acquired by naive insects?

Several studies have demonstrated that insects visually encode the angles that separate different elements in a scene. For example, bees trained to find food in the middle of a square array of landmarks will subsequently search for food in a square array instead of a rectangular array of roughly similarly sized landmarks (Cartwright and Collett 1983). Furthermore, bees can encode

the distances to familiar landmarks at least in the following way. If bees are trained to find food relative to an array of landmarks, some of which are close to the food and some of which are farther away, their subsequent searching behavior is more strongly influenced with the landmarks that were near the food—even if the distant landmarks were larger and presented the same size of retinal image (Cheng et al. 1987). Thus, nearby landmarks (which specify the location of the goal with greater precision), are weighted more heavily in the memory of a particular landmark array. The source of distance information is probably the motion parallax produced with near and far landmarks.

These experiments thus indicate that insects encode metric information—angles and distances—about familiar landmarks around a feeding or nesting site. This finding is not surprising; the compound eye is ideally suited to measure the relative angles and image motions that correspond to different landmarks that surround the animal.

It is more difficult to understand in what coordinate system this information is encoded. The simplest hypothesis, which accounts for much of the evidence, is that bees encode landmark positions in egocentric instead of allocentric coordinates. The memory image that corresponds to a particular array of landmarks is recorded as a neural "snapshot" of the image as it falls on the retina (Cartwright and Collett 1983). It is relatively easy to see how such a snapshot, fixed relative to retinal coordinates, indicates to the animal that it has reached a familiar goal. The animal need only recognize that its current view of the landmarks matches the snapshot stored during previous visits. The challenge is to understand how a snapshot encoded in egocentric coordinates can guide the animal when it has not yet reached the goal. Perhaps the animal encodes a sequence of snapshots, each slightly different, at successive points along its approach to the goal. However, encoding a sequence of snapshots would require considerable memory capacity, especially if the insect needed to learn how to approach a goal from a variety of directions (see Dyer 1994).

Cartwright and Collett proposed a relatively simple model that would allow a single (distance-filtered) snapshot recorded at the goal to guide the insect's approach from a variety of starting positions relative to the landmark array (fig. 6.14). In essence, the model assumes that the visual system makes multiple local comparisons of discrepancies between the current retinal image of the landmarks and the image stored (in retinal coordinates) at the goal. Each local comparison generates rotational and translational responses to reduce the discrepancy. These responses are added to steer the animal. A computer simulation showed that this model could lead an insect to its goal from a variety of starting positions relative to a simple landmark array. A major difficulty, however, was that the model necessitated that the snapshot remain oriented in the same compass direction throughout the process (fig. 6.14a, b).

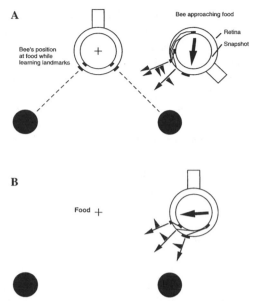

Figure 6.14. How bees may use memorized landmarks to pinpoint the location of a familiar goal such as a feeding site (+), according to the model of Cartwright and Collett (1983). A bee's visual field and body axis are shown schematically. (*a*) The bee records a neural snapshot of landmarks as seen from the food source. On subsequent return (*right*), the bee guides herself by comparing the current view of landmarks to the snapshot, which remains in the original position relative to retinal coordinates. Each element of the snapshot (the two landmarks and the space between them) is compared with the nearest element of the image on the retina. Each local comparison generates a unit translational vector and a unit rotational vector (*thin arrows* and *arrowheads,* respectively). These unit vectors are summed to determine the bee's new heading (heavy arrow) from its current position. If, as in this case, the bee is not facing in the direction in which the snapshot was originally recorded, the model may not compute a heading that points to the goal. (*b*) The model provides a better simulation if the bee is facing in the direction in which the snapshot was originally recorded. Bees apparently do face in a constant direction, when close to the food source, using an external compass reference adjust their orientation (Collett and Baron 1994).

Bees can approach a familiar goal from a variety of directions. Since their visual field is fixed relative to their body axes and thus oriented relative to their line of flight (it was thought), the model seems to require that the visual image, linked to an allocentric reference frame, be used independently of how the visual image projects to retinal coordinates.

In a follow-up study to that of Cartwright and Collett (1983), Collett and Baron (1994) found that landmark learning by bees does involve use of an external compass reference, but the representation of landmarks is probably encoded in an egocentric reference frame. By measuring the orientation of

(videotaped) bees as they approached a familiar feeder, Collett and Baron found that bees maintained their bodies (and hence their visual field) in a more or less constant compass orientation by using the magnetic field as a reference. Dickinson (1994) found that bees can also use their celestial compass in this context.

In bees, the effect of maintaining a constant body orientation is a constant orientation of an egocentrically recorded snapshot of the landmarks (Cartwright and Collett 1983). Hence, the task of matching a recorded snapshot to the current retinal image of the landmarks is simplified (fig. 6.14b). Note that this is not at all the same as recording the landmarks relative to an external compass and hence in an allocentric reference frame. Instead, the bees use the compass to standardize their viewing angle and then encode (and later use) a snapshot that was recorded relative to egocentric coordinates.

These interpretations have received further support from observations of the "locality study" that a flying insect does prior to leaving a goal (such as the nest entrance) to which it will return. This behavior, which has also been called a "turn-back-and-look" response (Lehrer 1996 [review]), allows the bee to learn visual features of the goal and the surrounding landmarks. In careful video analyses of yellow jacket wasps, Collett (1996 [review]) showed that the insects' orientation during the turn-back-and-look response closely matched the orientation maintained during subsequent approaches to the food. Thus, the spatial arrangement of the landmarks can be stored and retrieved with the orientation of the animal's visual field in the same direction, which presumably greatly facilitates the recognition process. To see the advantages of maintaining the pattern to be recognized in a standardized orientation relative to the visual field, rotate this book by 90° and notice how much the rotation slows your reading speed. Although we can learn to read rotated text, the recognition processes (even in humans) are affected by the orientations of patterns relative to retinal coordinates.

These studies of landmark learning on a small spatial scale thus suggest that insects store a relatively simple representation of the landmarks that surround the goal and can employ various tricks to ensure efficient recognition of the pattern and correct orientation toward the goal. In section 6.4.4.4, I will consider the implications of these observations for understanding the adaptive design of the learning mechanisms.

6.4.4.3 Landmark Learning on the Scale of the Foraging Range

Insects face the task just described—narrowing the search for a goal relative to a surrounding array of landmarks—only when close to the goal. But the foraging ranges of some nesting insects are very large (10–20 km) (reviewed by Wehner 1981). In these cases, the forager must head for a part of the land-

scape it cannot directly see. An ability to use landmarks for navigation over such distances implies that the animal can in effect use landmarks at the starting point to determine its position relative to the goal and discriminate different directions. Then the animal can repeatedly perform this process as it encounters each successive visual scene along a given route (reviewed by Dyer 1994, 1996; Wehner et al. 1996).

Evidence that landmarks can be used as a directional reference was provided by experiments in which insects were given conspicuous landmarks along a familiar foraging route and then were displaced to a different location with similar landmarks. For example, von Frisch and Lindauer (1954) trained bees to fly along a line of trees to reach food. They tested the bees where a similar line of trees was aligned in a different compass direction. Thus, the bees were faced with a conflict between their celestial compass and the familiar landmark configuration. Although some bees flew to food in the direction indicated with the celestial compass, most searched for food along the landmarks. However, bees tested in environments without conspicuous and familiar landmarks searched for food with use of the celestial compass. Thus, landmarks can be powerful enough to override the celestial compass as a directional reference.

Evidence that landmarks provide insects with positional information comes from experiments in which insects were displaced passively from their nest. Passive displacement denies insects the opportunity to perform path integration. The ability to fly home after such a displacement implies that insects determined their position with use of information obtained at the release site. A variety of evidence suggests that insects, unlike birds, cannot find their way home from release sites beyond their usual foraging range (see Wehner 1981 for a review). Instead, insects need to see previously encountered landmarks that led them home from feeding places in the vicinity of the release site. Insects can reach home after displacements of hundreds or (in some bee species) thousands of meters (Wehner 1981). Such displacement experiments therefore suggest that these insects learn visual features in an enormous area of the terrain around the nest.

Most of these results can be explained with a very simple model, which was first proposed by Baerends (1941) on the basis of his studies of digger wasps. The insect follows a sequence of visual images that correspond to successively encountered stages of a given familiar route. This model is similar to the snapshot model proposed much later by Collett and Cartwright. In essence, orientation to landmarks on a large scale entails the formation of a route map that consists of a string of snapshots. The route maps need not be linked in memory to the celestial compass, although directions learned relative to landmarks and celestial cues would typically provide equivalent navigational infor-

mation. With a few route maps radiating from its nest, a bee would be able to navigate efficiently in a large area around the nest (fig. 6.15*a, b*).

About 10 years ago, Gould (1986) triggered a flurry of excitement by suggesting that bees could integrate their experience on separate foraging routes into a common, geometrically accurate map of the terrain (fig. 6.15*c*). Experimental evidence suggested that bees estimate a novel shortcut from one familiar site to another. This is analogous to what we may do if we want to find the most direct route between two distant locations that we have visited separately from our home but have never traveled to along a connecting route. This navigation requires placing each location in a common geometrical frame of reference. For example, we keep track of the directions and distances traveled to each place from our home and then use the same frame of reference in which this information was obtained to compute the path connecting the sites. Bees have certain prerequisite abilities for performing the same task: They learn landmarks along multiple routes, and they have a directional reference (the sun compass) and a measure of distance that can serve as the basis for a large-scale coordinate system. Thus, Gould's proposal that bees also have the capacity to perform the necessary computations to determine the relative positions of separately visited locations was not far-fetched.

Gould's results have been very hard to replicate. Some investigators did not find evidence that bees compensate for their displacement from a route by heading along the shortcut to their goal. I found that bees could set a shortcut, but only if (1) they had a view of large-scale landmark features that could be seen during the flights from the nest to the goal, or (2) they had previously flown along the shortcut (Dyer 1991, 1994 [review]). In neither of these circumstances would bees require a large-scale map of the sort Gould envisioned. Instead, their behavior can be easily explained with the same sort of egocentrically referenced pattern-matching model that Cartwright and Collett (1983) proposed for orientation on the smaller scale. When I presented bees with a more stringent test of the cognitive-map hypothesis—by denying them large-scale landmark features or previous experience along the shortcut—they failed to head in the direction of the shortcut. In more recent experiments (reviewed by Dyer 1996), I found that honeybees lack a key ability that is needed to organize experience into a common large-scale map. This is the ability to learn the orientation of landscape features relative to a compass reference. Thus, bees do not guide their movements by means of cognitive maps as proposed by Gould (1986), nor do they have a way to form such maps.

6.4.4.4 Constraints on Landmark Learning by Insects

The landmark learning that results from both small- and large-scale orientation tasks suggest that insects store spatial information derived with use of land-

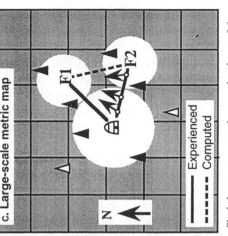

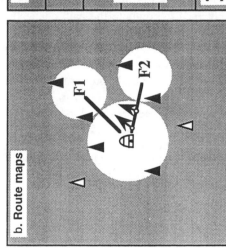

Figure 6.15. Alternative mapping schemes for encoding large-scale spatial relationships in a foraging range. Shaded area represents the unexplored part of the environment, and white areas indicate regions in which bees have learned visual features of the terrain. Triangles represent familiar (*black*) and unfamiliar (*white*) landmarks. (*a*) The local image, similar to the snapshot of Cartwright and Collett (1983), allows for efficient homing from multiple locations that are surrounded by the same panorama of landmarks. (*b*) Route maps allow for navigation to unseen portions of the terrain with use of sequences of snapshots compiled during previous flights. Flexibility in compensating for displacements from a particular route may be based on the same sorts of mechanisms that allow for flexibility with use of local images (snapshots). (*c*) Metric maps are constructed with route maps referenced to a common coordinate system (e.g. an external compass). Such a map allows an animal to compute novel routes between separately visited sites (from Dyer 1996). Gould (1986) suggested that insects form large-scale metric maps of a familiar terrain; however, most recent work suggests that insects cannot form these maps, although they clearly form route maps (Dyer 1991; Wehner et al. 1990).

marks in a relatively simple manner. Unlike humans, bees do not seem to encode landmark images in an allocentric reference frame and cannot form or use large-scale mental maps that encode the metric relationships among separately traveled routes. Insects can obviously respond to familiar landmarks with considerable flexibility (reviewed by Dyer 1994), but consider the implications of their limitations. Again, the limitations of insect behavior have been attributed to the small size of their brains (Wehner 1991, Dyer 1994). The assumption, however, that brain size constrains performance begs various questions: Why should a particular strategy, such as the ability to form a large-scale metric map of the terrain, be beyond the capacity of a brain the size of the bee's? How much more neural tissue, if any, is needed to develop and use such a strategy? We simply do not have the empirical or theoretical perspectives that allow us to answer such questions.

Furthermore, as in the case of path integration, a focus on neural constraints may blind us to the possible advantages of the insects' apparently simpler strategies for encoding and using familiar landmarks. One possible advantage of an egocentric representation is that it allows more rapid acquisition of relevant information as landmarks are learned; it also allows more rapid recognition of familiar landmarks when returning to a goal. But what constraint limits the speed of processing allocentric instead of egocentric spatial representations? It is possible that such a constraint applies equally to a larger brain. If so, then perhaps the small size of the insect brain may not limit the evolution of richer cognitive capacities; the selective disadvantages of such capacities in an animal with a short lifespan may be the limiting factors.

Clearly, we need more information about how brain size constrains behavior in invertebrates. A valuable starting point would be to identify correlations between the sizes of brain regions and behavioral performance that are analogous to the correlations between hippocampal volume and behavioral flexibility discovered in mammals and birds (Sherry, this vol. sec. 7.4.4). Recent studies of honeybees (reviewed by Fahrbach and Robinson 1995) have revealed that the mushroom bodies, a region of the insect brain that has been implicated in learning and sensory integration, increase in size relative to the rest of the brain as the bee ages. This neuroanatomical change parallels behavioral changes that take place as bees move through a succession of different jobs in the colony. Young bees work mainly inside the nest while older bees—during roughly the last third of their lives—work outside the nest collecting nectar and pollen for the colony. A reasonable interpretation for the increase in size of the mushroom bodies is that they are associated with the greater information-processing demands that foraging bees face, including the need to learn features of the environment necessary for orientation and the colors, odors, and shapes of rewarding flowers. If so, then studies of the insect mush-

room bodies and other neuropils in the insect brain may contribute to the development of a more neurobiological cognitive ecology of spatial memory in insects, which is similar to that described in vertebrates (Sherry, this vol. chap 7).

6.5 Conclusions

One major lesson in this chapter is the cognitive ecology of animal navigation is still relatively immature. Given that most research has been on the behavioral level, our understanding of the information-processing *mechanisms* that underlie the navigational abilities of animals is very sophisticated. In some species, we can specify in considerable detail the capacities and limitations of such mechanisms and relate performance to sensory and neural function. Concerning the *evolutionary forces* that have shaped such mechanisms, however, our understanding, for the most part, remains conjectural. Certainly our understanding of the cognitive ecology of navigation lacks sophistication compared with our understanding of other adaptive behavioral traits, such as those involved in foraging or life-history strategies. In this chapter, I have provided an outline of the issues that must be considered in the development of a more rigorous study of the adaptive design of cognitive mechanisms. In particular, I reiterate the importance of clearly identifying navigational problems that animals face and developing rigorous hypotheses about the fitness benefits, fitness costs, and constraints that may have guided the evolution of navigational mechanisms.

Acknowledgments

This chapter was written during a sabbatical at the University of California, San Diego, and I thank Jack Bradbury and Sandy Vehrencamp for their gracious hospitality. I thank Reuven Dukas, Lee Gass, and Don Wilkie for comments on the manuscript and the National Science Foundation for financial support.

Literature Cited

Able, K. P. 1980. Mechanisms of orientation, navigation, and homing. In S. A. Gauthreaux, Jr., ed., *Animal Migration, Orientation, and Navigation,* 283–373. New York: Academic Press.
———. 1996. The debate over olfactory navigation by homing pigeons. *Journal of Experimental Biology* 199:121–124.
Able, K. P., and M. A. Able. 1990. Calibration of the magnetic compass of a migratory bird by celestial rotation. *Nature* 347:378–380.

————. 1993. Daytime calibration of magnetic orientation in a migratory bird requires a view of skylight polarization. *Nature* 364:523–525.

————. 1996. The flexible migratory orientation system of the savannah sparrow (*Passerculus sanwichensis*). *Journal of Experimental Biology* 199:3–8.

Alerstam, T. 1996. The geographical scale factor in orientation of migrating birds. *Journal of Experimental Biology* 199:9–19.

Arnold, S. P. 1994. Constraints on phenotypic evolution. In L. A. Real, ed., *Behavioral Mechanisms in Evolutionary Ecology*, 258–278. Chicago: University of Chicago Press.

Baerends, G. P. 1941. Fortpflanzungsverhalten und Orientierung der Grabwaspe *Ammophila compestris* Jur. *Tijdschrift voor Entomologie Deel* 84:68–275.

Baker, R. R. 1978. *The Evolutionary Ecology of Animal Migration*. New York: Holmes and Meier.

————. 1984. *Bird Navigation: The Solution of a Mystery?* New York: Holmes and Meier.

Becker, L. 1958. Untersuchungen über das Heimfindenvermögen der Bienen. *Zeitschrift fur vergleichende Physiologie* 41:1–25.

Bennett, A. T. D. 1996. Do animals have cognitive maps? *Journal of Experimental Biology* 199:219–224.

Berthold, P. 1991. Spatiotemporal programmes and genetics of orientation. In P. Berthold, ed., *Orientation in Birds*, 86–105. Basel: Birkhauser.

Brower, L. P. 1996. Monarch butterfly orientation: Missing pieces of a magnificent puzzle. *Journal of Experimental Biology* 199:93–103.

Byrne, R. W. 1982. Geographical knowledge and orientation. In A. W. Ellis, ed., *Normality and Pathology in Cognitive Functions*, 239–264. London: Academic.

Calder, W. A., III. 1984. *Size, Function, and Life History*. Cambridge, Mass.: Harvard University Press.

Cartwright, B. A., and T. S. Collett. 1983. Landmark learning in bees. *Journal of Comparative Physiology*, ser. A, *Sensory, Neural, and Behavioral Physiology* 151:521–543.

Cheng, K., T. S. Collett, A. Pickhard, and R. Wehner. 1987. The use of visual landmarks by honeybees: Bees weight landmarks according to their distance from the goal. *Journal of Comparative Physiology*, ser. A, *Sensory, Neural, and Behavioral Physiology* 161:469–475.

Churchland, P. S., and T.J. Sejnowski. 1991. *The Computational Brain*. Cambridge: MIT Press.

Collett, T. S. 1996. Insect navigation en route to the goal: Multiple strategies for the use of landmarks. *Journal of Experimental Biology* 199:227–235.

Collett, T. S., and J. Baron. 1994. Biological compasses and the coordinate frame of landmark memories in honeybees. *Nature* 368:137–140.

Collett, T. S., E. Dilmann, A. Giger, and R. Wehner. 1992. Visual landmarks and route following in desert ants. *Journal of Comparative Physiology*, ser. A, *Sensory, Neural, and Behavioral Physiology* 170:435–442.

Craig, P. C. 1973. Orientation of the sandbeach amphipod, *Orchestoidea corniculata*. *Animal Behaviour* 21:699–706.

Dickinson, J. A. 1994. Bees link local landmarks with celestial compass cues. *Natur-wissenschaften* 81:465–467.

Dingle, H. 1980. Ecology and evolution of migration. In S. A. Gauthreaux, Jr., ed., *Animal Migration, Orientation, and Navigation,* 1–101. New York: Academic.

————. 1996. *Migration: The Biology of Life on the Move.* Oxford: Oxford University Press.

Dyer, F. C. 1985. Nocturnal orientation by the Asian honeybee, *Apis dorsata. Animal Behaviour* 33:769–774.

————. 1987. Memory and sun compensation in honeybees. *Journal of Comparative Physiology,* ser. A, *Sensory, Neural, and Behavioral Physiology* 160:621–633.

————. 1991. Bees acquire route-based memories but not cognitive maps in a familiar landscape. *Animal Behaviour* 41:239–246.

————. 1994. Spatial cognition and navigation in insects. In L. A. Real, ed., *Behavioral Mechanisms in Evolutionary Ecology,* 66–98. Chicago: University of Chicago Press.

————. 1996. Spatial memory and navigation by honeybees on the scale of the foraging range. *Journal of Experimental Biology* 199:147–154.

Dyer, F. C., and J. A. Dickinson. 1996. Sun-compass learning in insects: Representation in a simple mind. *Current Directions in Psychological Science* 5:67–72.

Etienne, A. S., R. Maurer, and V. Séguinot. 1996. Path integration in mammals and its interactions with visual landmarks. *Journal of Experimental Biology* 199:201–209.

Fahrbach, S. E., and G. E. Robinson. 1995. Behavioral development in the honeybee: Toward the study of learning under natural conditions. *Learning and Memory* 2:199–224.

Fraenkel, G. S., and D. L. Gunn. 1940. *The Orientation of Animals.* Oxford: Oxford University Press.

Frisch, K. von. 1950. Die Sonne als Kompaß im Leben der Bienen. *Experientia* (Basel) 6:210–221.

Frisch, K. von. 1967. *The Dance Language and Orientation of Bees.* Cambridge, Mass.: Harvard University Press.

Frisch, K. von, and M. Lindauer. 1954. Himmel und Erde in Konkurrenz bei der Orientierung der Bienen. *Naturwissenschaften* 41:245–253.

Gallistel, C. R. 1990. *The Organization of Learning.* Cambridge, Mass.: MIT Press.

Görner, P., and B. Claas. 1985. Homing behaviour and orientation in the funnel-web spider, *Agelena labyrinthica.* In F. G. Barth, ed., *Neurobiology of Arachnids,* 275–297. Berlin: Springer-Verlag.

Gould, J. L. 1980. Sun compensation by bees. *Science* 207:545–547.

————. 1986. The locale map of honeybees: Do insects have cognitive maps? *Science* 232:861–863.

Griffin, D. R. 1952. Bird navigation. *Biological Reviews* 27:359–400.

Gwinner, E. 1996. Circadian and circannual programmes in avian migration. *Journal of Experimental Biology* 199:39–48.

Hartmann, G., and R. Wehner. 1995. The ant's path integration system: A neural architecture. *Biological Cybernetics* 73:483–497.

Hartwick, R. F. 1976. Beach orientation in talitrid amphipods: Capacities and strategies. *Behavioral Ecology and Sociobiology* 1:447–458.

Hoffmann, K. 1959. Die Richtungsorientierung von Staren unter der Mitternachtsonne. *Zeilshrift für vergleichende Physiologie* 41:471–480.

Jander, R. 1975. Ecological aspects of spatial orientation. *Annual Review of Ecology and Systematics* 6:171–188.

———. 1990. Arboreal search in ants: Search on branches. *Journal of Insect Behavior* 3:515–527.

Keeton, W. T. 1974. The orientational and navigational basis of homing in birds. In D. S. Lehrman, J. S. Rosenblatt, R. A. Hinde, and E. Shaw, eds., *Advances in the Study of Behavior,* Vol. 5, 47–132. San Francisco: Academic Press.

Kramer, G. 1950. Weitere analyse der faktoren, welche die zugaktivität des gekäftigten vogels orientieren. *Naturwissenschaften* 37:377–378.

Krebs, J. R., and A. Kacelnik. 1991. Decision making. In J. R. Krebs and N. B. Davis, eds., *Behavioural Ecology: An Evolutionary Approach,* 105–136. Oxford: Blackwell Scientific.

Kühn, A. 1919. *Die Orientierung der Tiere im Raum.* Jena, Germany: Gustav Fischer Verlag.

Land, M. F. 1981. Optics and vision in invertebrates. In H. Autrum, ed., *Handbook of Sensory Physiology,* Vol. VII/6B, 472–592. Berlin: Springer-Verlag.

Lehrer, M. 1996. Small-scale navigation in the honeybee: Active acquisition of information about the goal. *Journal of Experimental Biology* 199:253–261.

Leonard, B., and B. L. McNaughton. 1990. Spatial representation in the rat: Conceptual, behavioral, and neurophysiological perspectives. In R. P. Kesner and D. S. Olton, eds., *Neurobiology of Comparative Cognition,* 363–422. Hillsdale, N.J.: Erlbaum.

Lindauer, M. 1957. Sonnenorientierung der bienen unter der aequatorsonne und zur nachtzeit. *Naturwissenschaften* 44:1–6.

———. 1959. Angeborene und erlernte Komponenten in der Sonnenorientierung der Bienen. *Zeitschrift für vergleichende Physiologie* 42:43–62.

Loeb, J. 1918. *Forced Movements, Tropisms, and Animal Conduct.* Philadelphia: Lippincott.

Lohmann, K. J., and C. M. F. Lohmann. 1996a. Orientation and open-sea navigation in sea turtles. *Journal of Experimental Biology* 199:73–81.

———. 1996b. Detection of magnetic field intensity by sea turtles. *Nature* 380:59–61.

Loomis, J. M., R. L. Klatzky, R. G. Golledge, J. G. Cicinelli, J. W. Pelligrino, and P. A. Fry. 1993. Nonvisual navigation by blind and sighted: Assessment of path integration ability. *Journal of Experimental Psychology: General* 122:73–91.

McNaughton, B., C. A. Barnes, J. L. Gerrard, K. Gothard, M. W. Jung, J. J. Knierem, H. Kudrimoti, Y. Qin, W. E. Skaggs, M. Suster, and K. L. Weaver. 1996. *Journal of Experimental Biology* 199:173–185.

Mittelstaedt, H. 1985. Analytical cybernetics of spider navigation. In F. G. Barth, ed., *Neurobiology of Arachnids,* 298–316. Berlin: Springer-Verlag.

Müller, M., and R. Wehner. 1988. Path integration in desert ants, *Cataglyphis fortis.*

Proceedings of the National Academy of Sciences of the United States of America 85:5287–5290.

New, D. A. T., and J. K. New. 1962. The dances of honeybees at small zenith distances of the sun. *Journal of Experimental Biology* 39:279–291.

Pardi, L., and A. Ercolini. 1986. Zonal recovery mechanisms in talitrid crustaceans. *Bollettino di Zoologia* 53:139–160.

Pardi, L., and F. Scapini. 1985. Inheritance of solar direction finding in sandhoppers: Mass-crossing experiments. *Journal of Comparative Physiology,* ser. A, *Sensory, Neural, and Behavioral Physiology* 151:435–440.

Perdeck, A. C. 1958. An experiment on the ending of autumn migration starlings, *Sturnus vulgaris* L., and chaffinches, *Fringilla coelebs* L., as revealed by displacement experiments. *Ardea* 46:1–37.

Phillips, J. B. 1986. Two magnetoreception pathways in a migratory salamander. *Science* 233:765–767.

Phillips, J. B., and S. C. Borland. 1994. Use of a specialized magnetoreception mechanism for homing by the red-spotted newt *Notphathalmus viridescens. Journal of Experimental Biology* 188:275–291.

Phillips, J. B., and J. Waldvogel. 1988. Celestial polarized light patterns as a calibration reference for sun compass of homing pigeons. *Journal of Theoretical Biology* 131: 55–67.

Ringelberg, J., and B. J. G. Flik. 1994. Increased phototaxis in the field leads to enhanced diel vertical migration. *Limnology and Oceanography* 39:1855–1864.

Ristau, C. A., ed. 1991. *Cognitive Ethology: The Minds of Other Animals—Essays in Honor of Donald R. Griffin.* Hillsdale, N.J.: Erlbaum.

Scapini, F., and M. C. Mezzetti. 1993. Integrated orientation responses of sandhoppers with respect to complex stimuli-combinations in their environment. In *Proceedings of the 1993 Conference on Orientation and Navigation: Birds, Humans, and Other Animals.*

Schmidt-Koenig, K. 1961. Die Sonnenorientierung richtungsdressierter tauben in ihrer physiologischen nacht. *Naturwissenschaften* 48:110.

———. 1963. Sun compass orientation of pigeons upon displacement north of the arctic circle. *Biological Bulletin* 127:154–158.

Schmidt-Koenig, K., J. U. Ganzhorn, and R. Ranvaud. 1991. The sun compass. In P. Berthold, ed., *Orientation in Birds,* 1–15. Basel: Birkhauser.

Schmitt, D. E., and H. E. Esch. 1993. Magnetic orientation of honeybees in the laboratory. *Naturwissenschaften* 80:41–43.

Schöne, H. 1984. *Spatial Orientation.* Princeton, N.J.: Princeton University Press.

Stephens, D. W. 1993. Learning and behavioral ecology: Incomplete information and environmental unpredictability. In D. R. Papaj and A. C. Lewis, eds., *Insect Learning: Ecological and Evolutionary Perspectives,* 195–218. New York: Chapman and Hall.

Stephens, D. W., and J. R. Krebs. 1986. *Foraging Theory.* Princeton, N.J.: Princeton University Press.

Tinbergen, N., and W. van Kruyt. 1938. Uber die Orientierung des Bienenwolfes (*Philanthus triangulum* Fabr.) III. Die Bevorzugung bestimmter Wegmarken. *Zeitschrift für vergleichende Physiologie* 25:292–334.

Ugolini, A., and L. Pardi. 1992. Equatorial sandhoppers do not have a good clock. *Naturwissenschaften* 79:279–281.

Ugolini, H., and A. Pezzani. 1995. Magnetic compass and learning of y-axis (sea-land) direction in the marine isopod *Idotea baltica basteri. Animal Behaviour* 50:295–300.

Ugolini, A., and F. Scapini. 1988. Orientation of the sandhopper *Talitrus saltator* (Amphipoda, Talitridae) living on dynamic sandy shores. *Journal of Comparative Physiology,* ser. A, *Sensory, Neural, and Behavioral Physiology* 162:453–462.

Ugolini, A., F. Scapini, G. Beugnon, and L. Pardi. 1988. Learning in zonal orientation of sandhoppers. In G. Chelazzi and M. Vannini, eds., *Behavioral Adaptation to Intertidal Life,* 105–118. New York: Plenum.

Wallraff, H. 1991. Conceptual approaches to avian navigation systems. In P. Berthold, ed., *Orientation in Birds,* 128–165. Basel: Birkhauser.

———. 1996. Seven theses on pigeon homing deduced from empirical findings. *Journal of Experimental Biology* 199:105–111.

Wehner, R. 1981. Spatial vision in arthropods. In H. Autrum, ed., *Handbook of Sensory Physiology,* Vol. VII/6C, 287–616. Berlin: Springer.

———. 1982. Himmelsnavigation bei Insekten. Neurophysiologie und Verhalten. *Vierteljahresschrift der Naturforschenden Gesellschaft in Zürich* 5:1–132.

———. 1987. "Matched filters"—Neural models of the external world. *Journal of Comparative Physiology,* ser. A, *Sensory, Neural, and Behavioral Physiology* 161:511–531.

———. 1991. Visuelle navigation: Kleinstgehirn-strategien. *Verhandlungen der Deutschen Zoologischen Gesellschaft* 84:89–104.

Wehner, R., B. Michel, and P. Antonsen. 1996. Visual navigation in insects: Coupling of egocentric and geocentric information. *Journal of Experimental Biology* 199:129–140.

Wehner, R., S. Bleuler, C. Nievergelt, and D. Shah. 1990. Bees navigate by using vectors and routes rather than maps. *Naturwissenschaften* 77:479–482.

Wehner, R., and B. Lanfranconi. 1981. What do the ants know about the rotation of the sky? *Nature* 293:731–733.

Wehner, R., and M. Müller. 1993. How do ants acquire their celestial ephemeris function? *Naturwissenschaften* 80:331–333.

Wehner, R., and M. V. Srinivasan. 1981. Searching behavior of desert ants, genus *Cataglyphis* (Formicidae, Hymenoptera). *Journal of Comparative Physiology* 142:315–338.

Wehner, R., and S. Wehner. 1990. Insect navigation: Use of maps or Ariadne's thread? *Ethology, Ecology, and Evolution* 2:27–48.

Wiltschko, R. 1996. The function of olfactory input in pigeon orientation: Does it provide navigational information or play another role? *Journal of Experimental Biology* 199:113–119.

Wiltschko, R., and W. Wiltschko. 1981. The development of sun compass orientation in young homing pigeons. *Behavioral Ecology and Sociobiology* 9:135–141.

Wiltschko, R., D. Nohr, and W. Wiltschko. 1981. Pigeons with a deficient sun compass use the magnetic compass. *Science* 214:343–345.

Wiltschko, W., and R. Wiltschko. 1992a. Magnetic orientation and celestial cues in

migratory orientation. In P. Berthold, ed., *Orientation in Birds,* 16–37. Basel: Birkhauser.

———. 1992b. Migratory orientation: Magnetic compass orientation of garden warblers (*Sylvia borin*) after a simulated crossing of the magnetic equator. *Ethology* 91: 70–79.

———. 1996. Magnetic orientation in birds. *Journal of Experimental Biology* 199: 29–38.

Wiltschko, W., R. Wiltschko, and W. T. Keeton. 1976. Effects of a "permanent" clock-shift on the orientation of young homing pigeons. *Behavioral Ecology and Sociobiology* 1:229–243.

Winston, M. L. 1987. *The Biology of the Honey Bee.* Cambridge, Mass.: Harvard University Press.

The Ecology and Neurobiology of Spatial Memory

DAVID F. SHERRY

7.1 INTRODUCTION

The study of spatial memory has served a central function in the development of a science of animal cognition for two reasons. The first reason is ecological: Most ecologically interesting behavior of animals has a spatial component. Dispersal, migration, territoriality, predator avoidance, mate search, nest site selection, provisioning young, foraging, and food storing all require animals to move through space and keep track of where they have been, where they are, and where they are going. The second reason is neurobiological: In 1978, O'Keefe and Nadel (1978) proposed that an ancient structure in the vertebrate brain, the hippocampus, is a dedicated processor of spatial information, a cognitive map. The hippocampal cognitive map became a paradigm for animal cognition—a cognitive system with more complex operating rules than those governing simple associations and implemented with a specialized neural architecture. The hippocampal cognitive map has had its critics, and current research presents a complicated picture; the idea, however, has provided an inescapable theoretical backdrop to most research on the neurobiology of spatial memory.

In this chapter, I will illustrate the ecological importance of spatial memory with a few examples of territoriality, mate search, foraging, and food storing. Next, I will describe some proposed mechanisms of spatial memory and discuss a few current topics in the neurobiology of spatial memory. This review will be selective, but I will chart the major trends in contemporary research on spatial memory. Dyer (this vol. chap. 6) examines spatial orientation from a different perspective—the adaptive design of navigational strategies.

7.2 THE BEHAVIORAL ECOLOGY OF SPATIAL MEMORY

How important is memory in spatial orientation? Some spatial-orientation tasks require no memory. In European blackcaps (*Sylvia atricapilla*), migratory direction is inherited (Berthold et al. 1992). When hand-raised blackcaps from two populations with autumn migratory directions that differed by 90°

were tested in captivity under controlled conditions, their autumn migratory directions corresponded to those of the respective parent population (Helbig et al. 1989). Migratory direction in one hand-raised group even included a 45° clockwise turn part way through the migratory period, which corresponded to the direction change made by the parent population as it rounded the eastern Mediterranean Sea and headed south into Africa (fig. 7.1). Without previous migratory experience (and therefore without memory of any previous migrations), these first-year blackcaps headed in the direction that was characteristic of their parent population's migratory path, and in one case, the birds were ready to make a right turn at the appropriate time.

Other aspects of spatial orientation, however, clearly depend more on experience, and a record of recent and sometimes long-past experience must be maintained to return home, revisit a newly discovered place, or adjust for changes in the environment.

7.2.1 Territoriality

A territory is a place that is defended for the exclusive use of the occupant (Davies and Houston 1984). A territory has a spatial extent and boundaries, and defense often occurs at prominent landmarks that define the limits of the territory. The benefits of the use of landmarks as territorial boundaries have been quantified by Eason et al. (1996). They plotted the territories defended by individually marked male cicada killer wasps (*Sphecius speciosus*) on a flat, grassy lawn. Males defended territorial boundaries by patrolling and chasing intruders. Next, 90-cm lengths of dowel were placed flat on the lawn such that the dowels were not aligned with existing territorial boundaries. The dowels rested slightly below grass level and were not used as perches by the wasps. By the following day, wasps had changed their territorial boundaries to coincide with the dowels. In another experiment, Eason et al. placed parallel pairs of dowels on the lawn and compared the time males spent in territorial defense at their dowel-marked and unmarked boundaries. Males spent 9.7% of the

---

Figure 7.1. The inheritance of migratory direction. Each compass circle shows the individual mean vectors, determined in Emlen cages, of hand-raised blackcaps from two populations with differing autumn migration routes as shown on the map. An Emlen cage records foot scratches made by a bird on the walls of the funnel-shaped cage. Statistical tests on the pattern of scratches are used to determine if activity is oriented and the mean bearing of oriented activity (Helbig 1991). Solid arrows in circles indicate means for well-oriented birds and dashed arrows indicate birds not significantly oriented during tests. For southwestern Germany, $n = 18$ and for eastern Austria, $n = 19$. There was a significant change in directions between September/October and November in birds from eastern Austria ($F_{2,35} = 26.42$, $P < .01$) but not in birds from southwestern Germany (from Helbig 1996; Helbig et al. 1989).

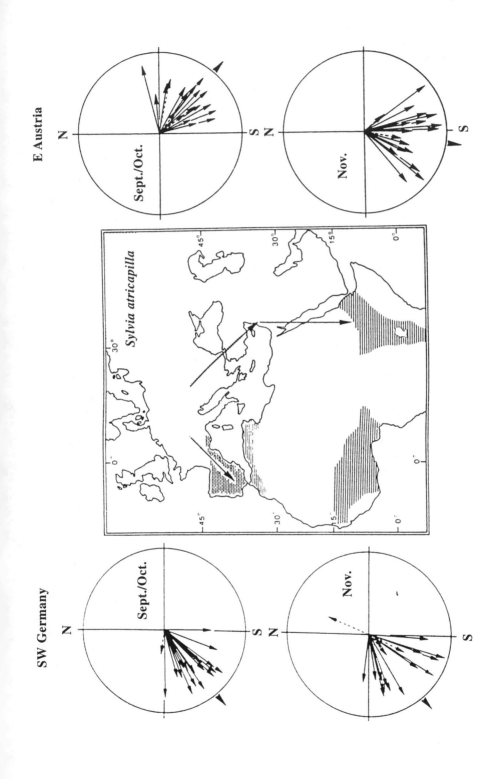

E Austria

Sept./Oct.

Nov.

Sylvia atricapilla

SW Germany

Sept./Oct.

Nov.

observation periods defending unmarked boundaries and only 1.4% of the observation periods defending boundaries marked with dowels. Territorial wasps thus changed the shapes of their territories to make use of landmarks at boundaries and benefitted by a reduction in the time spent defending marked boundaries.

Territorial boundaries are honored in both the breach and the observance by male song birds. Male white-throated sparrows (*Zonotrichia albicollis*) defend exclusive territories with song, but spend about 45% of their time outside territorial boundaries. They do not sing outside their own territory but instead move silently through the territories of neighbors (Falls and Kopachena 1994). This change in behavior at territory boundaries shows that the spatial location of boundaries is known to the birds and has a direct influence on behavior. The role of spatial memory in territoriality is further illustrated with experiments on birds' ability to associate the songs of their neighbors with the neighbors' territories (Falls 1982; Beecher et al., this vol. chap. 5). Male hooded warblers (*Wilsonia citrina*) responded relatively mildly to the played-back song of a neighbor when the song was broadcast from near the boundary with that neighbor. When the same song was played back from near another neighbor's boundary, territory holders responded much more strongly and approached quickly to within a few meters of the speaker; the birds then remained near the speaker during and after playback (Godard 1991). Playback of a familiar song from a new location was thus regarded as territory intrusion and produced a strong response from territory holders. Remarkably, comparable results were also obtained the following year when male hooded warblers returned to their territories after wintering in Central America and not hearing the songs of their neighbors for about 8 months (Godard 1991). Therefore, male hooded warblers not only learn the songs of their neighbors; the warblers associate their neighbors' songs with the boundaries of their neighbors' territories. The response to song depends on the place where the song originates (see Beecher et al., this vol. section 5.4).

Male songbirds are not the only territorial animals to associate the signals of their neighbors with spatial locations. The weakly electric fish *Gymnotus carapo* discriminates the electric discharges of neighbors and responds more aggressively and with a shorter latency when a familiar signal comes from a new location, the territory of another neighbor (McGregor and Westby 1992).

7.2.2 Mate Search

For some animals, like male songbirds, obtaining a mate requires defending a resource-rich territory and advertising occupancy. For other animals, finding a mate requires an active search. If a potential, but initially unreceptive, mate

is found, there may be a reproductive advantage to returning to the same place at a later, more propitious time. The mating season of thirteen-lined ground squirrels (*Spermophilus tridecemlineatus*) lasts 1–3 weeks, and females are in estrus for about 4 days. Males compete for females in a polygynous scramble. Schwagmeyer (1994) removed females that were in estrus and found that males searched preferentially at sites where they had encountered the female on previous days. Males were not simply attracted by pheromones or other odors of the female because males did not find females that were experimentally displaced to new sites and did not search the sleeping burrow used most recently by the female (unless the female had been encountered there on a previous day). Observations showed that males did not follow regular routes during successive searches and avoided sites they had searched previously.

How important is spatial memory, in general, for locating mates? The importance of spatial memory varies, no doubt, with the mating system and the spatial distribution of potential mates (Davies 1991). When males mate polygynously and compete for mates by expanding their home ranges to include multiple female home ranges, selection can produce a difference in spatial memory between the sexes that favors males. Meadow voles (*Microtus pennsylvanicus*) are polygynous, but pine voles and prairie voles (*M. pinetorum* and *M. ochrogaster*) are monogamous. The home ranges of male meadow voles are larger than the home ranges of females, but home-range sizes do not differ between the sexes in prairie and pine voles (Gaulin and Fitzgerald 1986, 1989). Radiotelemetry data showed that range sizes of male meadow voles do not expand before sexual maturity or outside the breeding season (Gaulin and Fitzgerald 1989). Male meadow voles' spatial abilities are superior to those of females, as shown by males' performances in a variety of laboratory maze tasks; male and female pine and prairie voles' spatial abilities do not differ (Gaulin and Fitzgerald 1986, 1989).

It is possible that the superior spatial ability of males is not an endogenous component of the polygynous mating system of meadow voles; instead the superior spatial ability may be a consequence of spatial experience or level of activity. A series of experiments by Gaulin and his colleagues have shown, however, that sex differences in spatial experience and activity level cannot account for the observed sex difference in spatial ability (Gaulin et al. 1990; Gaulin and Wartell 1990). To determine if spatial ability is affected by experience, the maze performance of wild, captive adult prairie voles was compared with that of their lab-reared offspring. Wild captive adults had experienced 200-m^2 home ranges, and lab-reared offspring had been confined to small, plastic holding cages. No difference in maze performance was observed between the two groups (Gaulin and Wartell 1990). The similar performances of the groups were not simply the result of insensitive measurements of maze

performance; significant differences in maze performance were observed between voles that were food deprived for 15 hours and voles that were food deprived for 24 hours, with the latter group showing better performance.

The hypothesis that sex or species differences in activity account for observed differences in maze performance was tested by recording the level of activity, measured with photocell-beam interruptions, of polygynous meadow voles and monogamous prairie voles of both sexes (Gaulin et al. 1990). As expected maze performance was not related to the observed activity level (male meadow voles performed better than females, and male and female prairie voles performed equally well). A statistical interaction between species and sex in maze performance was still found after controlling for activity level.

Organizational effects of hormones during development and activational effects at sexual maturity combine to produce the sex difference in spatial ability observed in meadow voles (Galea et al. 1996). As I will discuss in section 7.4, male and female meadow voles differ not only in home-range size and ability to solve laboratory spatial problems; the size of the male vole's hippocampus is larger. This sex difference does not occur in pine voles (Jacobs et al. 1990).

7.2.3 Foraging

Despite the explosion of interest during the 1970s and 1980s in optimal foraging, few foraging models explicitly considered how the spatial distribution of food influenced foraging decisions. The classic patch and prey models assumed only that food was distributed in patches and that encounter with prey was determined by an encounter-rate parameter (Stephens and Krebs 1986). Central-place models addressed the effect of distance to a patch on foragers that returned to the same central place after collecting prey, but these models did not address other properties of the spatial distribution of food. If the spatial properties of prey distribution or searches were considered, it was usually in simplified models showing, for example, that (1) directional search paths were more efficient than random search (Krebs 1978); (2) search areas were restricted after a forager encountered food; or (3) a forager may maximize renewal time of a resource by following a path around a continuous circuit (e.g. Davies and Houston 1981). Clearly the spatial distribution of food and memory for food location can have more complex effects on foraging decisions.

Healy and Hurly (1995) examined how foraging rufous hummingbirds (*Selasphorus rufus*) use memory for spatial locations. Many hummingbirds defend feeding territories to maintain exclusive access to enough flowers to meet their energy requirements. Because feeding depletes the flowers' nectar, hummingbirds can increase the rate at which they collect nectar by avoiding visits

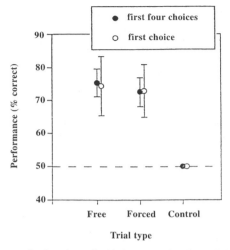

Figure 7.2. The accuracy of rufous hummingbird memory for the spatial locations of flowers. Four flowers, in an array of eight, had not been visited in the previous trial. Visits to these previously unvisited flowers were "correct" and are shown for trials during which birds' previous visits were either free or forced. Performance exceeded the control level during both free and forced trials (*t* tests, $P < .05$, $n = 6$). Performance on the first choice and for the mean of the first four choices did not differ. Error bars indicate the standard error of the mean, and the dashed line shows performance expected by chance (from Healy and Hurly, 1995).

to depleted flowers; rufous hummingbirds avoid revisiting depleted flowers by remembering which flowers they have visited. Healy and Hurly (1995) placed artificial flowers, each filled with 40 µl of 24% sucrose, in a circular array of eight flowers in hummingbird feeding territories. Birds were allowed to visit and deplete four of the eight flowers, and their subsequent flower visits were observed after intervals that ranged from 4 to 40 min. From 70% to 80% of the birds' next four visits were to nondepleted flowers; this outcome was observed if the birds were allowed to choose the four initial flowers to visit or if they were forced to visit four flowers determined randomly by the experimenters (fig. 7.2). The locations of particular flowers in the array were varied to control for memory of individual flowers, and additional tests showed the hummingbirds could not discriminate between nondepleted and depleted flowers without visiting them. Hummingbirds could, in principle, avoid revisits to depleted flowers by "trap lining," (i.e. following a consistent route from flower to flower). Healy and Hurly (1995) showed that rufous hummingbirds solved the revisiting problem not by trap lining but by remembering individual flower locations. Rufous hummingbirds did this either retrospectively, by remembering depleted flowers, or prospectively, by remembering which flowers

had not been visited (Cook et al. 1985; Kesner and DeSpain 1988). In either case, memory was used to restrict visits to flowers that were not yet depleted.

The tendency of hummingbirds to avoid previously visited flowers, rather than return to them, depends on the birds' recent experience with the food source. In a subsequent experiment using artificial flowers that were not depleted after a single visit, birds were trained to search an array of four distinctively colored and patterned flowers until the one flower that contained sucrose was found (Hurly and Healy 1996). This flower was not depleted after a single visit, and hummingbirds learned to return to this flower and not other flowers in the array on subsequent visits. Nevertheless, birds still identified this flower by its spatial location and not its appearance as shown by a further experimental manipulation. Hurly and Healy (1996) were able to separate memory for the location of the baited flower from memory for its color and features by adapting an experimental design developed by Brodbeck (1994) (see section 7.3). After hummingbirds fed at the baited flower, the flower was exchanged with another flower in the array and the birds' subsequent choices were recorded. On their next visit, hummingbirds consistently returned to the location in the array where they had found nectar (now occupied by a different looking flower) instead of the flower with the matching color and pattern (now at a different location). Subsequent choices gave no indication of a preference for the flower with the matching color and pattern.

7.2.4 Food Storing

Few behaviors make such extraordinary demands on spatial memory as the retrieval of food from scattered caches. A variety of birds and mammals scatter hoard food and retrieve it by remembering the spatial locations of caches (Vander Wall 1990). Jays and nutcrackers store large numbers of acorns and pine nuts, respectively, and their failure to retrieve all that they store is an important means of seed dispersal for several species of oaks and pines (Tomback and Linhart 1990; Bossema 1979; Darley-Hill and Johnson 1981). Food-storing birds depend on their caches to survive the winter. With use of stored food to feed nestlings, food-storing birds are able to breed earlier than many other birds (Sherry 1985; Vander Wall 1990). Jays and nutcrackers (*Corvidae*), chickadees and tits (*Paridae*), squirrels (*Sciuridae*), and kangaroo rats (*Heteromyidae*) have all been observed to accurately remember the spatial locations of caches for periods ranging from a few days to many months (Kamil and Balda 1990; Sherry and Duff 1996; Shettleworth 1990; Jacobs and Liman 1991; Jacobs 1992).

Memory for spatial locations is not the only conceivable way to relocate hidden caches. Food-storing birds might encounter their caches by chance or place caches in sites that are likely to be searched again in the course of normal

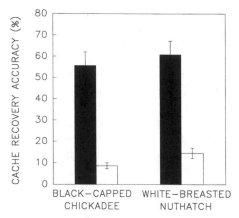

Figure 7.3. Memory for the spatial location of caches in black-capped chickadees and white-breasted nuthatches in captivity. Filled bars indicate observed cache-retrieval accuracy, open bars indicate accuracy expected by chance. Accuracy significantly exceeded that predicted by chance for both species (chickadees, $F_{1,14} = 43.93$, $P < .001$; nuthatches, $F_{1,8} = 62.67$, $P < .001$). There was no difference in accuracy between chickadees and nuthatches (chickadee data from Petersen and Sherry 1996; nuthatch data from Petersen and Sherry, unpublished).

foraging (Gibb 1960; Haftorn 1974; Källander 1978). Laboratory experiments have shown, however, that the performance of food-storing birds when searching for stored food was much better than that expected by chance (fig. 7.3), and food-storing birds showed no decrement in accuracy when their choice of cache sites was experimentally constrained (Kamil and Balda 1985; Shettleworth and Krebs 1982; Sherry et al. 1981). The birds did not follow a regular route when retrieving caches, and they did not retrace the route they used when making caches (Sherry 1984). When visual and olfactory cues from stored food were eliminated, birds showed no decline in accuracy, and when stored food was displaced a short distance away from the cache site, birds usually failed to find it (Bennett 1993; Cowie et al. 1981; Shettleworth and Krebs 1982). These results occurred because birds retrieved hoarded food by remembering the location of caches with respect to prominent nearby landmarks (Bossema 1979; Bennett 1993; Herz et al. 1994; Vander Wall 1982), perhaps supplemented with use of the sun compass for orientation (see section 7.3) (Balda and Wiltschko 1991; Wiltschko and Balda 1989). Food-storing rodents can detect buried caches by olfaction. These rodents, nevertheless, preferentially retrieved their own caches before those of others, which indicates that they too can remember the spatial locations of caches (Jacobs 1992; Jacobs and Liman 1991).

In the laboratory, black-capped chickadees (*Parus atricapillus*) were able to find their caches for at least 4 weeks after making them; after 4 weeks,

their accuracy fell to that expected by chance (Hitchcock and Sherry 1990). Clark's nutcrackers (*Nucifraga columbiana*) found their caches in captivity at least 40 weeks after making them (Balda and Kamil 1992). In chickadees and tits in the wild, estimates of the interval between caching and cache retrieval range from several days (Cowie et al. 1991; Stevens and Krebs 1986) to several months (Brodin and Ekman 1994). Brodin and Ekman (1994) determined the cache-retrieval interval of willow tits (*Parus montanus*) by offering the birds seeds labelled with ^{35}S-cysteine, which is incorporated into the daily growth bars of feathers when the food is retrieved and eaten. By pulling a tail feather from each member of a marked population of willow tits to induce growth of a replacement feather and then collecting and analyzing the replacement feathers 2 months later, Brodin and Ekman (1994) obtained a record of the consumption of labelled food. Food was commonly retrieved and eaten 6–40 days after storage and, in some cases, after even longer periods of time. Because this interval exceeded the duration of memory for cache location in the laboratory, Brodin and Ekman (1994) proposed that long-term cache retrieval does not depend on memory mechanisms. Whether or not tits' memory for cache location can persist for 40 or more days in the field will, no doubt, be answered with further experimentation; however, it also seems possible that the duration of memory for cache location observed in captivity may underestimate the duration of this memory in the wild.

7.2.5 Conclusion

The ecological importance of spatial memory is widespread. A few cases in which spatial memory has not been well examined but seems potentially important are (1) poison-arrow frogs, *Dendrobates pumilio,* that remember, in all likelihood, the bromeliad leaf axils that hold their developing tadpoles (Weygoldt 1980), (2) brood parasites that visit and probably remember the locations of potential host nests (Sherry et al. 1993; Reboreda et al. 1996), and (3) migratory birds that show year-to-year nest-site fidelity (Ketterson and Nolan 1990). Although the ecological circumstances in which animals show memory for spatial locations is very diverse, the ways in which different species solve these problems are similar. In the next section, I will describe some of the more well-documented mechanisms that underlie memory for spatial locations.

7.3 MEMORY AND SPATIAL ORIENTATION

Some proposed mechanisms of spatial memory are well established, others have not been so unequivocally demonstrated, and some probably await discovery. A distinction can be made among *landmarks, global-reference systems, path integration,* and the *cognitive map*. Landmarks are stationary ob-

jects or surfaces that can be used to identify a location in space by its distance and direction from the landmark. With global-reference systems, celestial or geomagnetic information is used to determine a reference bearing (analogous to a compass bearing) and, in some cases, a position. Path integration is the use of idiothetic information, or information that is generated during motion, to determine distance and direction from the origin of the path. Idiothetic information about active displacement and rotation can be derived, at least in principal, from the vestibular system, proprioceptive feedback, optic flow, and efference copy of locomotor commands. Finally, the cognitive map usually refers to a representation of the spatial relations among locations that is constructed or inferred from partial knowledge of the spatial relations among places. This categorization is somewhat arbitrary. Landmarks can be important for correcting errors that accumulate during path integration, and global-reference systems are components of some cognitive map models. Nevertheless, these distinctions help describe the component parts of many models of spatial orientation. Dyer (this vol. chap. 6) examined the selective costs and benefits of these systems. I will deal with how the systems work. In the following sections, I will describe how landmarks and one global-reference system, the sun compass, contribute to memory of spatial locations. Path integration is discussed by Etienne et al. (1996), and discussions of the cognitive map can be found in Gallistel and Cramer (1996), Bennett (1996), and Nadel (1991).

7.3.1 Landmarks

Stable environmental landmarks provide the most readily identifiable (at least to humans) and easily manipulated sources of spatial information. The classic demonstration of landmark use is Tinbergen's (1932) homing experiment in the digger wasp, *Philanthus triangulum.* Tinbergen placed a circle of pine cones around an active nest and then either displaced the cones to surround a sham nest 30 cm away or returned the cones to their original positions around the active nest. As every student of ethology knows, returning wasps landed inside the circle of cones regardless of whether the cones surrounded the sham nest or the real nest. This simple experiment showed that wasps found their nest by remembering its location with respect to neighboring landmarks.

But how do landmarks specify a location in space? It seems obvious that the wasp always searched in "the same place" with respect to the circle of pine cones, but there is more than one way that landmarks can specify "the same place." For instance, did the wasp determine the nest position with use of the whole array of landmarks or just one particular landmark? In a very informal experiment, Tinbergen and Kruyt (1938) found that moving only a few landmarks was not sufficient to ensure identification; the whole array of

landmarks had to be moved. Suzuki et al. (1980) designed an experiment in which rats were trained to find food on an eight-arm radial maze. A cylindrical black curtain surrounded the maze to eliminate use of extraneous landmarks, and the experimenters placed landmarks outside the maze beyond the ends of the radial arms. In experimental trials, rats were forced to visit three preselected maze arms (by blocking entrances to the other five arms) and then were confined briefly to the center of the maze. Then with all arms open, the rats' choices among previously visited and unvisited maze arms were observed. This method of providing forced choices before free choices, first used by Zoladek and Roberts (1978), controlled for the possibility that the rats may have changed the nature of the task—for example, by entering the most distinctive maze arms first. This method also allowed Suzuki et al. to manipulate landmarks during the time between the rats' forced and free choices. Landmarks were either rotated as a group by 180° or transposed randomly and reassigned to the maze arms. When landmarks were rotated 180°, rats entered the maze arms that were in the same position relative to the landmarks as the arms that were unvisited. That is, when the landmarks were rotated, the rats' choices rotated. When landmarks were transposed, animals chose randomly. This simple experiment illustrated how animals determine spatial location with use of landmarks. The rats used the array of landmarks as a unit to identify unvisited maze arms. They did not identify maze arms by the individual landmark at the end of the maze arm or by the nearest landmark. If this were the case, transposition of landmarks should have produced systematic choices of unvisited maze arms defined by their respective landmarks, because after transposition each maze arm still had a corresponding landmark. Landmarks were not used by rats in this experiment as individual beacons but as an array or configuration. This finding has been confirmed in a variety of contexts (Morris 1981; Kraemer et al. 1983; Olton and Collison 1979; Mazmanian and Roberts 1983; Spetch and Honig 1988).

Landmarks are used as a configuration and not as individual beacons because a single landmark usually cannot specify a location in space (apart from the spot occupied by the landmark) without additional information. A digger wasp may remember the distance her burrow entrance lies from a pine cone, but in what direction? Either a radially asymmetric landmark, additional landmarks, or another cue that polarizes the environment by providing a bearing (such as the north star or the earth's magnetic field) is required to determine the direction of the goal from the landmark. A pair of landmarks is sufficient if the landmarks can be distinguished or if the goal and the landmarks are collinear. Two identical landmarks reduce the number of possible locations of the goal to two points in space, and a third landmark defines the location.

Collet et al. (1986) showed that gerbils use landmarks as a configuration. Gerbils were trained to find hidden food in an array of three identical land-

marks and then tested with various modifications and distortions of the land-mark array. Gerbils learned the distance and direction of the goal from each individual landmark but required multiple landmarks to locate the goal. For example, gerbils trained to search for food at the center of an equilateral triangle of identical landmarks searched in roughly the correct location if one landmark was removed. This result incidentally indicated that the environment was polarized and must have contained some cue that provided a bearing; in this way, the gerbils determined the side of the triangle with which they were dealing. Without such a polarizing cue, the regions formerly inside and outside the triangle would have been unclear, and gerbils would have searched at two points, one on either side of the line connecting the remaining landmarks. If two landmarks were removed, gerbils regarded the remaining landmark as first one and then another of the known landmarks; gerbils searched at three points around the remaining landmark (fig. 7.4). Landmarks were learned individually but used in a configuration. The experiments of Collett et al. showed, in addition, that gerbils used a variety of rules if landmarks provided conflicting information. Landmarks near a goal were weighted more than landmarks far from a goal. If some landmarks indicated one location and others did not, the location indicated with the most landmarks was chosen. If landmarks were distinct, gerbils learned both the geometrical properties of the landmark array and the individual features of landmarks to determine goal location.

Cheng (1986) showed that in some circumstances, however, landmark features are ignored altogether, and the geometrical properties of the landmark array are used alone to identify a goal. Cheng trained rats to locate food in a rectangular enclosure with use of distinctive tactile, olfactory, and visual cues in each corner of the enclosure. When the rats searched the enclosure during test trials with the food removed, rats tended to err at places that were at a 180° rotation from the correct site. The pattern of errors suggested that rats relied on the rectangular geometry of the enclosure more than the distinct features in each corner of the enclosure. Further experiments with rotations and transformations of distinct features showed that rats used features but principally when these features were in geometrically correct locations.

In rats, this distinction between the features of landmarks and their geometric properties is relevant to a sex difference in spatial memory. Male rats, like male meadow voles, tend to perform better than females on spatial tasks. In rats, Williams et al. (1990) examined how hormonal effects during development may influence performance in the radial-arm maze. Males gonadectomized shortly after birth behaved like control females; females given estradiol benzoate, which has the masculinizing effect of the testosterone metabolite estradiol, behaved like control males. Control males and females given estradiol benzoate consistently performed better than control females and gonadectomized males; most interestingly, the kind of information used by the former

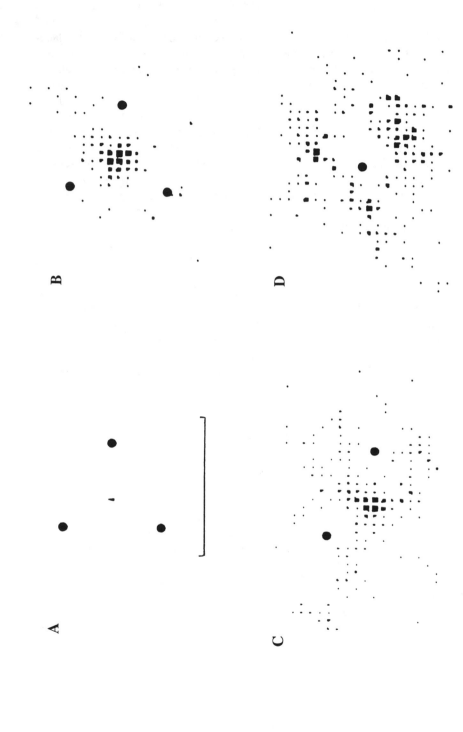

group differed from that used by the latter group. The performance of control males and females given estradiol benzoate was disrupted by changing the geometry of the enclosure that surrounded the maze, from rectangular to circular. Performance was unaffected by changes in landmarks outside the maze. Control females and gonadectomized males were affected by changing both the geometry of the enclosure and landmarks. Control females (and gonadectomized males) used more sources of information but performed less well than control males (and females given estradiol benzoate), which relied almost exclusively on the geometric properties of the region around the maze (Williams et al. 1990).

7.3.1.1 Food-Storing Birds

The scattered caches of food-storing birds are sometimes preferentially placed near conspicuous objects and edges instead of in more open areas without distinct features. Jays cache food more often near objects oriented with their long axis vertical, than near the same objects oriented with their long axis horizontal (Bossema 1979; Bennett 1993). These preferences likely arise because birds use landmarks to relocate their caches. One of the clearest demonstrations of the use of landmarks by food-storing birds was provided by Vander Wall (1982). Clark's nutcrackers displaced their searches for caches in the same direction and by the same distance as experimentally displaced landmarks. Herz et al. (1994) found that removal of landmarks immediately next to caches site had relatively little effect on the accuracy of searches by black-capped chickadees; however, removal of landmarks about 1 meter away from caches reduced search accuracy. Rotation of these more distant landmarks produced partial and inconclusive effects on searches, but a more recent experiment by Duff et al. (in press) showed that a 180° rotation of distant landmarks produced a nearly perfect 180° rotation of searches in chickadees.

The relative importance of the geometric relations and features of landmarks was determined by Brodbeck (1994) with a very elegant experiment on black-capped chickadees. Birds were trained to find food in one of four feeders placed on the walls of an aviary. Colored patterns on the feeders were unique

---

Figure 7.4. Use of landmarks by Mongolian gerbils. (a) Gerbils were trained to find food hidden at a site (*triangle*) at the center of a triangular array of identical landmarks (*circles*). Scale bar equals 1 meter. Search behavior is shown as time spent in each 11.0 × 13.3 cm cell, and cells are filled in proportion to the time spent searching. Data of three gerbils and from eight to 19 search trials per condition are shown. Search distributions are shown with (b) all landmarks present, (c) one landmark removed, and (d) two landmarks removed. Search was concentrated at a single site if two or three landmarks were present, but three different sites were searched if only one landmark was present (from Collett et al. 1986).

during each trial, and the four feeders were arranged in a different geometric array during each trial. Once birds located the baited feeder, they were removed from the aviary for a 5-minute retention interval; on return, food was available only in the previously baited feeder. The bird's task was to locate and remember for 5 minutes the feeder baited on this trial. Once birds had mastered this task, test trials were conducted to determine the information birds used to accomplish the task. During search trials, after the retention interval, birds returned to an array that had been displaced laterally along the aviary wall, and the baited feeder had been exchanged with another feeder in the array (fig. 7.5). With feeders in this configuration, the relative importance of the location of the feeder within the aviary, its location within the array, and the features of the feeder could be determined. This procedure is the same as that described for Hurly and Healy (1996) experiment with rufous hummingbirds, with the addition of a lateral displacement of the whole array. Brodbeck (1994) found a clear preference ranking in the chickadees' choices: location in the room, position within the array, and features (fig. 7.5). Brodbeck demonstrated that landmark features are not ignored or forgotten, but they are just not highly ranked among cues.

7.3.2 Global-Reference Systems

A global reference provides an animal with a spatial frame for orientation. Some global-reference systems allow the animal to determine its location and some merely provide a fixed reference bearing. The sun, stars, and the earth's magnetic field serve as global-reference systems. The sun's position provides a compass bearing if the animal has information about the time of day. The classic work of Kramer (1951) showed that starlings (*Sturnus vulgaris*) can use the sun's position to maintain a constant bearing in a small cage. The night sky, or more specifically the fixed point of rotation in the night sky, can also provide a compass bearing, as shown by Emlen (1970). Finally, experimental manipulations of the magnetic field have shown that birds can use the inclination of the earth's magnetic field (its deviation from horizontal)

Figure 7.5. Black-capped chickadees were trained to find food at one of four feeders and return to that feeder after a short retention interval. On probe trials (*top*), birds located food in one of the feeders (C); however, during the retention interval, the array was laterally displaced and another feeder was exchanged for the baited feeder. At testing (*bottom*), feeder D occupied the original location of the baited feeder, and feeder A occupied the original location of the baited feeder in the array. Most of the birds' first choices were to the original location of the baited feeder (D), and their second choices were the original array position (A). Their third choices were the feeder that matched in color and pattern (C). Results are shown with bar graphs. All three search distributions differed significantly from those predicted by chance (G-statistic, $P < .05$, $n = 4$) (from Brodbeck 1994).

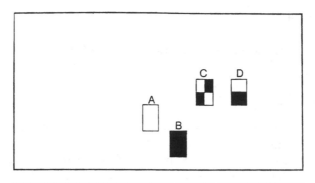

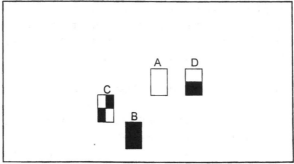

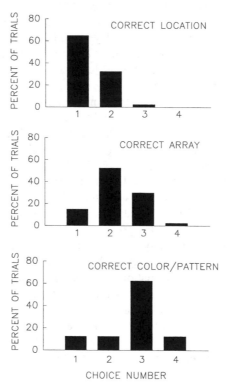

to derive a bearing and possibly a position as well (Wiltschko and Wiltschko 1993).

7.3.2.1 The Sun Compass

A variety of methods have been used to investigate animals' use of the sun compass. The most commonly used method of investigation is the clock-shift procedure. Because the azimuth of the sun changes during the day, the sun's position is useful only if combined with information about the time of day. The elevation of the sun is not used for orientation by animals. One way to demonstrate that the azimuth of the sun is used for orientation is to change the animal's estimate of time with a phase shift in its circadian rhythm. A phase shift should cause an error in orientation that is equal to the difference between the sun's azimuth at the animal's subjective time of day and the sun's actual azimuth at the local solar time. Phase advances and phase delays produce errors in bearing that can be measured in cages or in the field, and these errors are frequently as predicted with the sun-compass model (Schmidt-Koenig 1990; Wiltschko and Wiltschko 1993).

Much research on sun-compass use by vertebrates has assumed that solar information is most useful for long-range orientation because, at least initially, the animal may need only a correct heading. Insects use the sun compass to orient on a much smaller spatial scale (Dyer and Dickinson 1994), and recent work indicates that the sun compass may also serve a function in the small-scale orientation of food-storing birds. Wiltschko and Balda (1989) discovered that the clock-shift procedure caused pinyon jays (*Aphelocoma coerulescens*) to rotate their searches for cached food in a relatively small octagonal cage away from the actual cache locations and toward the sector of the cage predicted with use of the sun compass. Black-capped chickadees trained to find food in one sector of an octagonal cage exhibited similar changes in their direction of search (Duff et al., in press). Duff et al., however, also showed that the bearing derived with use of the sun compass is not sufficient for orientation in a small scale. Chickadees were trained to find food in one sector of a small octagonal cage. They were able to see surrounding landmarks through the mesh walls of the cage. In the presence of familiar landmarks, the clock-shift procedure produced a modest rotation of the mean search direction; however, in the presence of novel landmarks, the birds were not oriented in any direction. When information from familiar landmarks and the sun compass conflicted, the chickadees' search was clearly influenced by use of sun-compass information. Their search was probably a compromise between sun-compass and landmark information. However, when all landmarks were unfamiliar and the sun compass was the only source of directional information, the birds were disoriented. The explanation for this seemingly paradoxical re-

sult may be that birds form a "mosaic map" consisting of familiar areas (defined with local landmarks) that were linked with use of the sun compass or other global reference systems (suggested by Wiltschko and Wiltschko 1978). In familiar surroundings, the clock-shift procedure produces a change in orientation by means of its effect on the sun compass, as shown by Wiltschko and Balda (1989) and by Duff et al. (in press); however, in unfamiliar surroundings, a directional cue alone provides no information that the birds can use to locate food.

7.4 THE NEUROBIOLOGY OF SPATIAL MEMORY

There are many ecological contexts that necessitate use of spatial memory. Animals also use a variety of environmental sources of information to guide spatial orientation. Orientation, however, not only has functional utility; it also has underlying causes, and these causes are found in the nervous system. If function has influenced the evolution of spatial memory, then the same function has influenced the evolution of the nervous system. There is thus a direct link from ecological selection pressures on spatial orientation to spatial-memory processes to the neural implementation of spatial memory. If so, differences among animals' brains and nervous systems as consequences of adaptation to different ecological conditions would be expected. This idea is widely accepted for sensory processes. Evidence that animal cognition and its neural basis are ecological adaptations has only more recently become available. This evidence is comparative. In animals, similarities and differences among brain areas with spatial memory functions have been found that correspond to similarities and differences in uses of space.

7.4.1 The Hippocampus

As I mentioned (section 7.1), much research on the neurobiology of spatial memory has focused, in one way or another, on the hippocampus. In this section, I will describe briefly why the hippocampus has held center stage for so long, and then present some comparative research. In most mammals, the hippocampus is a curved C-shaped structure that surrounds the thalamus. In primates (including humans), the curve of the hippocampus descends into the dorsomedial aspect of the temporal lobe. In birds, the hippocampus extends along the dorsomedial surface of the forebrain for about one-third of its length. The hippocampus was named by the anatomist Giulio Cesare Aranzi (1530–1589), who saw a resemblance to the sea horse *Hippocampus* in the curving shape of the human structure (Lewis 1923) (fig. 7.6).

Birds and mammals have evolved independently for at least 310 million years, when the synapsid clade of reptiles, which gave rise to mammals, diverged from the diapsid clade, which gave rise to dinosaurs and thereafter

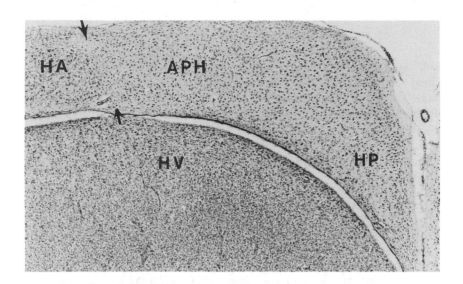

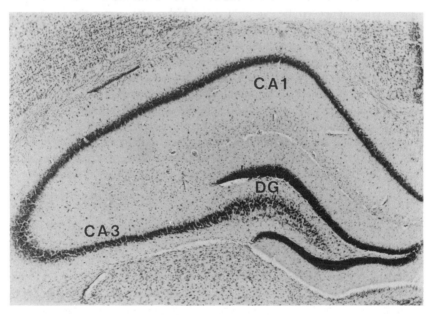

Figure 7.6. The hippocampuses of a white-breasted nuthatch (*top*) and a deer mouse (*bottom*). Both photomicrographs show coronal sections of the left hippocampus. The dorsal edge of the nuthatch hippocampus lies at the dorsal surface of the brain, and the deer mouse hippocampus is overlain by cortex. Abbreviations for nuthatch: APH = area parahippocampalis, HA = hyperstriatum accessorium, HP = hippocampus, HV = hyperstriatum ventrale. Arrows show the lateral boundary of the hippocampal region. Abbreviations for rat: CA1 and CA3 = subdivisions of the hippocampus proper, or Ammon's horn, DG = dentate gyrus. CA cell fields, the dentate gyrus, and associated structures such as the subiculum and entorhinal cortex make up the hippocampal formation. Deer mouse section courtesy of Tara Perrot-Sinal.

birds (Fastovsky and Weishampel 1996). Little anatomical or functional similarity between the hippocampuses of birds and mammals is expected, and as figure 7.6 shows, there is no gross anatomical similarity at all. Nevertheless, by embryological (Källén, 1962) and anatomical criteria (Casini et al. 1986; Erichsen et al. 1991; Krayniak and Siegel 1978; Szekely and Krebs 1996), the mammalian and avian hippocampuses appear to be evolutionary homologues; they are derived from the same medial forebrain structure in their most recent common ancestor.

O'Keefe and Nadel's (1978) theory of the function of the hippocampus is straightforward, and this idea has been rearticulated by Nadel (1991). The theory states that (1) the hippocampus is one of several brain structures that function in spatial memory; and (2) the primary function of the hippocampus is spatial memory (not spatial orientation or spatial behavior). The theory was derived with two key pieces of evidence: (1) lesions in the hippocampus produced spatial disorientation in rats; and (2) the rat hippocampus contained "place" cells, or cells that showed maximum firing rates when the animal was in a particular place (O'Keefe and Dostrovsky 1971). The theory states that the hippocampus deals with the input, storage, and retrieval of information from all sensory modalities that enable identification of places. The part of the theory that has been largely abandoned, even by its supporters, is the claim that the hippocampus is involved in long-term storage of memory. Various experiments have shown that the disruptive effects of hippocampal lesions are diminished if enough time is allowed to pass between learning and lesioning (Squire et al. 1984).

The principal debate about the function of the hippocampus concerns whether its characterization as a spatial-memory module is sufficiently broad to describe how the hippocampus actually functions. A variety of theories describe broader functions of the hippocampus. These proposed functions include declarative memory (Squire 1987), working memory (Olton et al. 1979), temporary memory storage (Rawlins 1985), and configural association (Sutherland and Rudy 1989). Lesions in the hippocampus disrupt the learning of relations among odor cues (Eichenbaum et al. 1988), and most of the deficits produced with hippocampal damage in primates and humans have no clear consequence on spatial functioning (Cohen and Eichenbaum 1993). A broader theory may indeed be required to characterize the function of the hippocampus. Species differences—in particular, the difference between primates and other mammals—are frequently ignored in theory construction but may mark important evolutionary divides in hippocampal function. The spatial function of the hippocampus may be more important in some taxa than others. Place cells and the more recently discovered head-direction cells (see the following) are located outside the hippocampus, and lesions in other brain regions can produce spatial deficits. In addition, researchers are focusing increasingly on the

function of the neighboring cortex in the processing of hippocampal input and output (Nagahara et al. 1995). Whatever the final resolution of the hippocampal debate is, important correlations remain between spatial behavior and activity of single brain cells, between localized brain lesions and disruptions of spatial orientation, and between species differences in the uses of space and relative sizes of the hippocampus. These three topics are discussed in the following.

7.4.2 Head-Direction Cells

One of the most dramatic discoveries concerning the neural representation of space has been the identification and description of head-direction cells. First described by Ranck (1985), head-direction cells exhibit maximum firing rates when the head of the animal points in a particular horizontal direction. Notably, these cells lie outside the hippocampus in the postsubiculum, anterior thalamic nucleus, lateral dorsal thalamic nucleus, retrosplenial cortex, and striatum (Taube et al. 1996). Recordings of the electrical activity of head-direction cells in freely moving rats show that these cells fire maximally over a relatively narrow range of head directions (usually about 90°). The firing pattern is stable from day to day and is independent of the animal's behavior, its position in space, and roll or pitch attitude of the head (providing the head is pointed in the appropriate horizontal direction).

How do head-direction cells "know" where the head is pointing? Head-direction cells in the postsubiculum and anterior thalamic nucleus are highly sensitive to the location of landmarks in the rat's environment. Goodridge and Taube (1995) placed rats in a cylindrical enclosure with a single large landmark (a white card filling 100° of arc). The head direction that resulted in the maximum firing rate of head-direction cells was determined, and the card was removed. Some head-direction cells fired maximally with the same head direction in the absence of the card; other cells fired with the head rotated as much as 180° from its original orientation. When the card was returned, however, most of the cells that fired with a new head direction returned immediately to maximum firing with the head in the original orientation relative to the card. Of those cells that had fired with the original head orientation in the absence of the card, about half could be induced to fire with a new head orientation by reintroducing the card at a new position rotated 90°. These results showed that some head-direction cells maintain a stable firing rate with one head direction in the absence of landmarks, probably with use of idiothetic input; however, many head-direction cells fire with head directions that are relative to landmarks.

In another series of experiments, Taube and Burton (1995) found that when there was a conflict between landmark and idiothetic information, the rat's head direction that resulted in maximal firing of head-direction cells was deter-

mined primarily by landmarks. Idiothetic information could affect the firing rate of cells with head direction, but landmark information, when available, clearly dominated idiothetic information.

Taube and Burton (1995) also confirmed that head-direction cells respond to perceived direction and not merely prominent surrounding cues. The maximal firing rate of head-direction cells in the postsubiculum and anterior thalamic nucleus of the rat was determined in a cylinder with a single prominent landmark as described. The cylinder was connected by a short alley to a rectangular chamber with a single landmark in a different cardinal direction than the landmark in the cylinder. Head-direction cells did not usually fire with a new head direction after the rat left the cylinder, proceeded along the alley, and entered the rectangle (fig. 7.7). A maximal firing rate was established with head direction relative to a conspicuous landmark, and this firing rate with head direction was maintained in new surroundings with a new landmark.

7.4.3 Lesions of the Hippocampus

Lesions in the mammalian and avian hippocampus disrupt spatial orientation. Jarrard (1983) trained rats in the radial-arm maze and found that hippocampal lesions disrupted function of both spatial and working memory. Sherry and Vaccarino (1989) found that lesions in the hippocampus of black-capped chickadees did not disrupt food storing or the amount of searching for food caches; lesions instead reduced the accuracy of search to that predicted by chance. In a subsequent experiment, we found that performance of a nonstoring task that demanded memory for familiar spatial locations was disrupted by hippocampal lesions, while performance of a task that demanded memory for simple associations was not. Recent work by Hampton and Shettleworth (1996) showed the same kind of effect of hippocampal lesions with use of a very different task. Black-capped chickadees' memory for the location of stimuli on a touch screen was disrupted with hippocampal lesions, but memory for the colors of stimuli was not. These results show that lesions of the hippocampus do not disrupt all memory in black-capped chickadees; lesions disrupt memory of one kind and not others. In the terminology of neuropsychology, hippocampal lesions produce a dissociation in memory. Memory for spatial locations, whether places in a room or places on a touch screen, is impaired in birds with hippocampal lesions. Memory for other kinds of information, whether a cue that indicates food or a recently seen patch of color on a video monitor, is not.

Hippocampal lesions have effects in another natural setting: homing and orientation by pigeons. Homing pigeons show a complex pattern of deficits after hippocampal lesions. Experienced adult homing pigeons with hippocampal lesions released from a familiar site showed no deficit in homeward orien-

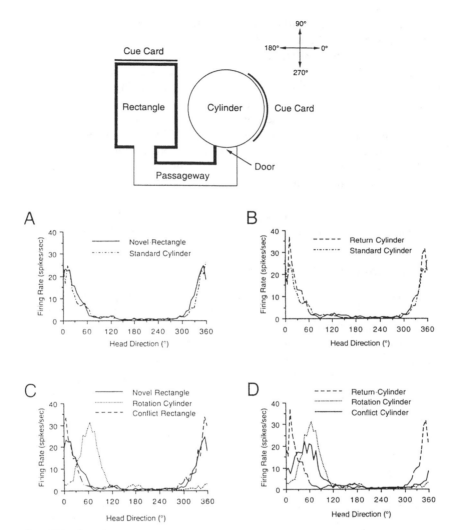

Figure 7.7. The relation between the firing rate of a head-direction cell and rat behavior are determined in the apparatus diagrammed (*top*). (*a*) The firing pattern that was established in the cylinder (standard cylinder) persisted when the rat traveled along the passageway and entered the rectangle for the first time (novel rectangle). (*b*) The cell maintained its firing pattern when the rat returned to the cylinder (return cylinder). (*c*) Rotation of the cylinder cue card by 90° counterclockwise caused an approximate 60° counterclockwise rotation in the head direction associated with maximal firing rate (rotation cylinder). The cell immediately fired maximally with the original head direction during a subsequent visit to the rectangle (conflict rectangle). (*d*) The cell fired maximally with the original head orientation when the rat returned to the cylinder (conflict cylinder). Data from novel-rectangle and return-cylinder trials are reproduced in *c* and *d* for comparison (from Taube and Burton 1995).

tation compared to that of controls (Bingman et al. 1984). Nevertheless, the pigeons with hippocampal lesions failed to return home. Such birds even failed to return home when released within sight of the loft. Thus, whatever mechanism these birds used to orient correctly at the release site (the possibilities include the sun compass, magnetic information, and release-site landmarks), this mechanism was not dependent on hippocampal function. What seems dependent on hippocampal function is the use of familiar landmarks near the home loft because lesioned pigeons manifested a deficit at this stage of homing. Other experiments, however, showed that homing from distant release sites is dependent on hippocampal function but in a different sense. An intact hippocampus is necessary for development of the ability to home from a distant release site although this ability, once acquired, becomes independent of hippocampal function (Bingman 1993).

7.4.4 Comparative Studies of the Hippocampus

The foregoing results show that the hippocampus and other parts of the brain function in memory of spatial locations. Does the brain, then, show adaptive specialization for spatial memory?

7.4.4.1 Food Storing

The hippocampus varies strikingly in size between species and, in some species, between the sexes. Much of this variation can be readily correlated with differences in the use of space between species and the sexes. The hippocampus of food-storing birds is as much as twice the size of that of birds with comparable brain and body sizes that do not store food (Sherry et al. 1989; Krebs et al. 1989). Within the food-storing parid and corvid families, there is variation in hippocampal size that correlates with the amount of food storing typically performed by different species (Hampton et al. 1995; Healy and Krebs 1992; Basil et al. 1996). Mexican chickadees (*Parus sclateri*) and bridled titmice (*P. wollweberi*), for example, both store food, although in controlled laboratory conditions, these birds store less than black-capped chickadees. In these birds, relative hippocampal size correlates with intensity of food storing (Hampton et al. 1995). Similar correlations are observed in European and North American food-storing corvids (Healy and Krebs 1992; Basil et al. 1996).

Comparable correlations occur among strains of pigeons (Rehkämper et al. 1988). Homing pigeons have a proportionally larger hippocampus than nonhoming strains. There seems to be no relation, however, between migration in passerines and relative hippocampal size (Sherry et al. 1989; Healy and Krebs 1991). This observation and that of Bingman, who described the effects of hippocampal lesions on homeward orientation in pigeons, suggest that the

hippocampus may serve relatively little function in long-distance orientation of pigeons and passerines. Perhaps this is so because long-distance orientation is achieved with use of global-reference systems such as the earth's magnetic field, the sun compass, or other celestial cues. Bingman et al. (1984) did find that in pigeons the hippocampus functions in the use of familiar local cues near home. If the same is true in passerine migrants, the hippocampus may function in home recognition by birds that show year-to-year nest-site fidelity (Ketterson and Nolan 1990). Healy et al. (1994) found that age and migratory experience are related to hippocampal size in the garden warbler (*Sylvia borin*). Older birds have greater hippocampal volumes than younger birds, and birds with migratory experience have greater hippocampal volumes than inexperienced birds. Whether these age- and experience-dependent changes in hippocampal size indicate hippocampal involvement in the use of local landmarks, development of global-reference systems, or both, remains to be determined.

In mammals, food storing also influences relative hippocampal size (Jacobs and Spencer 1994). Merriam's kangaroo rats (*Dipodomys merriami*) are scatter hoarders, and the bannertail kangaroo rat (*D. spectabilis*) maintains and defends a larder. Relative hippocampal size is greater in Merriam's kangaroo rats than that in bannertail kangaroo rats perhaps because Merriam's kangaroo rats rely more on spatial memory to retrieve scattered food caches.

7.4.4.2 Mating Systems

Food storing and homing are not the only ecological factors that influence relative hippocampal size. Sex differences in hippocampal size have been discovered that are clearly related to sex differences in the use of space. Among the *Dipodomys* kangaroo rats described and the *Microtus* voles, there are species with monogamous mating systems and species with polygynous mating systems. I described (section 7.1) the polygynous mating system of meadow voles and the monogamous mating system of pine voles and their effects on spatial memory. In addition to having larger home ranges and better spatial abilities than females, male meadow voles have a larger hippocampus than females (fig. 7.8). No sex difference occurs in hippocampal size in monogamous pine voles, and the sexes do not differ in home-range size in the wild or spatial ability in the laboratory (Jacobs et al. 1990). Research on *Dipodomys* kangaroo rats confirmed the effect of mating system on hippocampal size. Merriam's and bannertail kangaroo rats mate polygynously, and during the breeding season, the home ranges of males are considerably larger than those of females. The hippocampus of males is larger than that of females in both species (Jacobs and Spencer 1994).

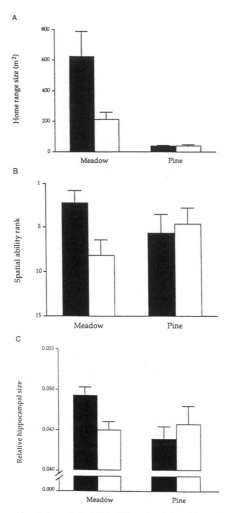

Figure 7.8. Home range size (*a*), spatial ability (*b*), and relative hippocampal size (*c*) in polygynous meadow voles and monogamous pine voles. Filled bars = males, open bars = females. (*a*) Home ranges were determined by telemetry for nine to 12 individuals of each sex in each species. Home-range size was greater in males than in females in meadow voles (*t* test, $P <$ .02, $n = 21$) but not in pine voles (*t* test, $P <$ .66, $n = 19$). (*b*) Rank order of maze performance for eight to 13 individuals of each sex in each species. A low rank indicates superior spatial ability. Note reversal of the y-axis scale. Male meadow voles performed better than female meadow voles (Mann-Whitney *U* test, $P <$ .02, $n = 20$), but there was no difference between the sexes in pine voles (Mann-Whitney *U*-test, $P >$ .05, $n = 21$). (*c*) The volume of the hippocampus is shown as a proportion of total brain volume in samples of 10 males and 10 females in each species. A significant interaction occurred between species and sex ($F_{1,38} =$ 4.61, $P <$ .05) (from Sherry et al. 1992).

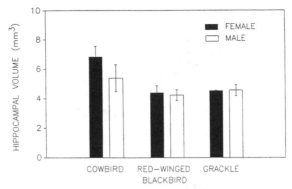

Figure 7.9. Hippocampal volume in male and female brown-headed cowbirds, red-winged blackbirds, and common grackles. Analysis of covariance, with telencephalon size as a covariate, indicated a significant sex difference in parasitic cowbirds ($F_{1,8}$ = 9.18, $P <$ .02, n = 12) but not red-winged blackbirds ($F_{1,13}$ = 0.65, $P <$ .5, n = 16). The sample size of common grackles (n = 4) was too small for statistical analysis (from Sherry et al. 1993).

7.4.4.3 Brood Parasitism

Cowbirds are brood parasites. In the best known species, the brown-headed cowbird (*Molothrus ater*), females lay about 40 eggs in the nests of various host species during an 8-week breeding period. Females lay at or before dawn, and spend the remainder of the morning searching for potential host nests in which to lay eggs on subsequent days. Female cowbirds have been reported to fly into shrubs and flush incubating birds from their nests, sit silently and watch nest building by potential hosts, and walk on the forest floor while scanning the canopy (Norman and Robertson 1975). Although not confirmed experimentally, it is likely that female cowbirds learn the locations of potential host nests and return to them after an interval of a day or two to lay eggs. Male cowbirds do not participate in the search for host nests in this species. The hippocampus of female cowbirds is significantly larger than that of males; this sex difference does not occur in closely related, nonparasitic icterine blackbirds (fig. 7.9) (Sherry et al. 1993).

Not all *Molothrus* cowbirds are parasitic. The shiny cowbird (*M. bonariensis*) is a generalist parasite like the brown-headed cowbird. The screaming cowbird (*M. rufoaxillaris*) is a specialist that uses one host, the bay-winged cowbird (*M. badius*). The bay-winged cowbird is not a nest parasite but a communal breeder with biparental care and helpers at the nest (Fraga 1991). Female shiny cowbirds search for host nests unassisted by males; however, male and female screaming cowbirds both have been reported to inspect the nests of their bay-winged cowbird hosts (Mason 1987). Reboreda et al. (1996) found that the hippocampus in the two parasitic species was larger (relative

to the size of the telencephalon) than that in the nonparasite. In addition, a sex difference in relative hippocampal size that favored females occurred in shiny cowbirds but not in the other two species. This sex difference suggests that search for host nests by shiny cowbird females exerts an effect on relative hippocampal size.

Although all of these results indicate that search for host nests by female cowbirds has led to the evolution of greater hippocampal size, there are some contradictory data: The *obscurus* and *artemisiae* subspecies of the brown-headed cowbird exhibit no sex difference in relative hippocampal size (Uyehara and Narins 1992). Hippocampal size in *Molothrus ater obscurus* and *M. ater artemisiae* may be subject to selective pressures or constraints that do not influence hippocampal size in *Molothrus ater ater* or *M. bonariensis*.

7.5 CONCLUSIONS

Animals use spatial memory in a diverse set of ecological circumstances. Indeed, it is difficult to imagine many activities of mobile organisms that do not involve processing, directly or incidentally, some information about spatial location. The study of spatial memory is currently undergoing a sort of renaissance as a result of increased contact between field-based researchers concerned with navigation and orientation and laboratory-based researchers concerned with animal cognition. Some of the theoretical dividing lines that formerly demarcated mechanisms of long-distance navigation from those of local systems, such as landmark use, are vanishing. Future research may further integrate theoretical ideas. In addition, neurophysiological research has uncovered a variety of substrates in which cognitive mechanisms of spatial orientation may be implemented. Comparative work on one of these neurophysiological substrates, the hippocampus, has shown remarkable variation in neural structure that correlates with ecological variation in the use of space.

7.6 SUMMARY

Memory for spatial locations is an important component of behavior in a wide variety of ecological settings, including territoriality, mate search, foraging, and food storing. Animals defend territories, locate mates, find food, and retrieve stored food in part by remembering spatial locations. Various kinds of information can be used to identify and remember locations in space. The use of landmarks and the sun compass are two examples. Neural specializations that reflect the ecological importance of spatial memory can be found at the neuronal level (e.g. place cells, head-direction cells, and such structures as the avian and mammalian hippocampuses). Comparative analyses illustrate the relation between ecological selection pressures and evolutionary modification of spatial memory and its neural basis.

ACKNOWLEDGMENTS

I would like to thank Andrew Check, Perri Eason, Bruce Falls, Peter McGregor, Bill Roberts, and Jeffrey Taube for much helpful discussion and information on spatial behavior and spatial memory. Thanks, too, to Reuven Dukas for his careful and patient editing and Nicky Clayton for her many helpful comments on the manuscript. Preparation of this paper was supported by the Natural Sciences and Engineering Research Council of Canada.

LITERATURE CITED

Balda, R. P., and A. C. Kamil. 1992. Long-term spatial memory in Clark's nutcracker *Nucifraga columbiana*. *Animal Behaviour* 44:761–769.

Balda, R. P., and W. Wiltschko. 1991. Caching and recovery in scrub jays: Transfer of sun-compass directions from shaded to sunny areas. *Condor* 93:1020–1023.

Basil, J. A., A. C. Kamil, R. P. Balda, and K. V. Fite. 1996. Differences in hippocampal volume among food storing corvids. *Brain Behavior and Evolution* 47:156–164.

Bennett, A. T. D. 1993. Spatial memory in a food storing corvid. I. Near tall landmarks are primarily used. *Journal of Comparative Physiology,* ser. A, *Sensory, Neural, and Behavioral Physiology* 173:193–207.

———. 1996. Do animals have cognitive maps? *Journal of Experimental Biology* 199:219–224.

Berthold, P., A. J. Helbig, G. Mohr, and U. Querner. 1992. Rapid microevolution of migratory behaviour in a wild bird species. *Nature* 360:668–670.

Bingman, V. P. 1993. Vision, cognition, and the avian hippocampus. In H. P. Zeigler and H.-J. Bischof, eds., *Vision, Brain, and Behavior in Birds,* 391–408. Cambridge: MIT Press.

Bingman, V. P., P. Bagnoli, P. Ioalè, and G. Casini. 1984. Homing behavior of pigeons after telencephalic ablations. *Brain Behavior and Evolution* 24:94–108.

Bossema, I. 1979. Jays and oaks: An eco-ethological study of a symbiosis. *Behaviour* 70:1–117.

Brodbeck, D. R. 1994. Memory for spatial and local cues: A comparison of a storing and a nonstoring species. *Animal Learning and Behavior* 22:119–133.

Brodin, A., and J. Ekman. 1994. Benefits of food hoarding. *Nature* 372:510.

Casini, G., V. P. Bingman, and P. Bagnoli. 1986. Connections of the pigeon dorso-medial forebrain studied with WGA-HRP and ^{3}H-proline. *Journal of Comparative Neurology* 245:454–470.

Cheng, K. 1986. A purely geometric module in the rat's spatial representation. *Cognition* 23:149–178.

Cohen, N. J., and H. Eichenbaum. 1993. *Memory, Amnesia, and the Hippocampal System.* Cambridge: MIT Press.

Collett, T. S., B. A. Cartwright, and B. A. Smith. 1986. Landmark learning and visuo-spatial memories in gerbils. *Journal of Comparative Physiology,* ser. A, *Sensory, Neural, and Behavioral Physiology* 158:835–851.

Cook, R. G., M. F. Brown, and D. A. Riley. 1985. Flexible memory processing by

rats: Use of prospective and retrospective information in the radial maze. *Journal of Experimental Psychology: Animal Behavior Processes* 11:453–469.

Cowie, R. J., J. R. Krebs, and D. F. Sherry. 1981. Food storing by marsh tits. *Animal Behaviour* 29:1252–1259.

Darley-Hill, S., and W. C. Johnson. 1981. Acorn dispersal by the blue jay (*Cyanocitta cristata*). *Oecologia* 50:231–232.

Davies, N. B. 1991. Mating systems. In J. R. Krebs and N. B. Davies, eds., *Behavioural Ecology: An Evolutionary Approach,* 3d ed., 263–294. Oxford: Blackwell Scientific.

Davies, N. B., and A. I. Houston. 1981. Owners and satellites: The economics of territory defence in the pied wagtail, *Motacilla alba. Journal of Animal Ecology* 50: 157–180.

———. 1984. Territory economics. In J. R. Krebs and N. B. Davies, eds., *Behavioural Ecology: An Evolutionary Approach,* 2d ed., 148–169. Sunderland Mass: Sinauer.

Duff, S. J., L. A. Brownlie, D. F. Sherry, and M. Sangster. In press. Sun compass orientation by black-capped chickadees (*Parus atricapillus*). *Journal of Experimental Psychology: Animal Behavior Processes.*

Dyer, F. C., and J. A. Dickinson. 1994. Development of sun compensation by honeybees: How partially experienced bees estimate the sun's course. *Proceedings of the National Academy of Sciences of the United States of America* 91:4471–4474.

Eason, P. K., and G. A. Cobbs. 1996. The effect of landmarks on territorial behavior. Animal Behavior Society, Flagstaff AZ. August 1996. Abstract 70.

Eichenbaum, H., A. Fagan, P. Mathews, and N. J. Cohen. 1988. Hippocampal system dysfunction and odor discrimination learning in rats: Impairment or facilitation depending on representational demands. *Behavioral Neuroscience* 102:331–339.

Emlen, S. T. 1970. Celestial rotation: Its importance in the development of migratory orientation. *Science* 170:1198–1201.

Erichsen, J. T., V. P. Bingman, and J. R. Krebs. 1991. The distribution of neuropeptides in the dorsomedial telencephalon of the pigeon (*Columba livia*): A basis for regional subdivisions. *Journal of Comparative Neurology* 314:478–492.

Etinne, A. S., R. Maurer, and V. Seguinot. 1996. Path integration in mammals and its interaction with visual landmarks. *Journal of Experimental Biology* 199:201–209.

Falls, J. B. 1982. Individual recognition by sounds in birds. In D. E. Kroodsma and E. H. Miller, eds., *Acoustic Communication in Birds,* Vol. 2, 237–278. New York: Academic.

Falls, J. B., and J. G. Kopachena. 1994. White-throated sparrow (*Zonotrichia albicollis*). In A. Poole and F. Gill, eds, *The Birds of North America* No. 128. Philadelphia: Academy of Natural Sciences.

Fastovsky, D. E., and D. B. Weishampel. 1996. *The Evolution and Extinction of the Dinosaurs.* Cambridge: Cambridge University Press.

Fraga, R. M. 1991. The social system of a communal breeder, the bay-winged cowbird *Molothrus badius. Ethology* 89:195–210.

Galea, L. A. M., M. Kavaliers, and K.-P. Ossenkopp. 1996. Sexually dimorphic spatial learning in meadow voles *Microtus pennsylvanicus* and deer mice *Peromyscus maniculatus. Journal of Experimental Biology* 199:195–200.

Gallistel, C. R., and A. E. Cramer. 1996. Computations on metric maps in mammals:

Getting oriented and choosing a multi-destination route. *Journal of Experimental Biology* 199:211–217.

Gaulin, S. J. C., and R. W. FitzGerald. 1986. Sex differences in spatial ability: An evolutionary hypothesis and test. *American Naturalist* 127:74–88.

Gaulin, S. J. C., and R. W. FitzGerald. 1989. Sexual selection for spatial-learning ability. *Animal Behaviour* 37:322–331.

Gaulin, S. J. C., R. W. Fitzgerald, and M. S. Wartell. 1990. Sex differences in spatial ability and activity in two vole species (*Microtus ochrogaster* and *M. pennsylvanicus*). *Journal of Comparative Psychology* 104:88–93.

Gaulin, S. J. C., and M. S. Wartell. 1990. Effects of experience and motivation on symmetrical-maze performance in the prairie vole (*Microtus ochrogaster*). *Journal of Comparative Psychology* 104:183–189.

Gibb, J. A. 1960. Populations of tits and goldcrests and their food supply in pine plantations. *Ibis* 102:163–208.

Godard, R. 1991. Long-term memory of individual neighbours in a migratory songbird. *Nature* 350:228–229.

Goodridge, J. P., and J. S. Taube. 1995. Preferential use of the landmark navigation system by head direction cells in rats. *Behavioral Neuroscience* 109:49–61.

Haftorn, S. 1974. Storage of surplus food by the Boreal Chickadee *Parus hudsonicus* in Alaska, with some records on the Mountain Chickadee *Parus gambeli* in Colorado. *Ornis Scandinavica* 5:145–161.

Hampton, R. R., D. F. Sherry, S. J. Shettleworth, M. Khurgel, and G. Ivy. 1995. Hippocampal volume and food-storing behavior are related in Parids. *Brain Behavior and Evolution* 45:54–61.

Hampton, R. R., and S. J. Shettleworth. 1996. Hippocampal lesions impair memory for location but not color in passerine birds. *Behavioral Neuroscience* 110:831–835.

Healy, S. D., E. Gwinner, and J. R. Krebs. 1994. Hippocampus size in migrating garden warblers: Effects of age and experience (abstract). *Journal für Ornithologie* 135:74.

Healy, S. D., and T. A. Hurly. 1995. Spatial memory in rufous hummingbirds (*Selasphorus rufus*): A field test. *Animal Learning and Behavior* 23:63–68.

Healy, S. D., and J. R. Krebs. 1991. Hippocampal volume and migration in passerine birds. *Naturwissenschaften* 78:424–426.

———. 1992. Food storing and the hippocampus in corvids: Amount and volume are correlated. *Proceedings of the Royal Society London*, ser. B 248:241–245.

Helbig, A. J. 1991. Experimental and analytical techniques used in bird orientation research. In P. Berthold, ed., *Orientation in Birds*, 270–306. Basel: Birkhäuser-Verlag.

———. 1996. Genetic basis, mode of inheritance, and evolutionary changes of migratory directions in palaearctic warblers (Aves: Sylviidae). *Journal of Experimental Biology* 199:49–55.

Helbig, A. J., P. Berthold, and W. Wiltschko. 1989. Migratory orientation of blackcaps (*Sylvia atricapilla*): Population-specific shifts of direction during the autumn. *Ethology* 82:307–315.

Herz, R. S., L. Zanette, and D. F. Sherry. 1994. Spatial cues for cache retrieval by black-capped chickadees. *Animal Behaviour* 48:343–351.

Hitchcock, C. L., and D. F. Sherry. 1990. Long-term memory for cache sites in the black-capped chickadee. *Animal Behaviour* 40:701–712.

Hurly, T. A., and S. D. Healy. 1996. Memory for flowers in rufous hummingbids: Location or local visual cues? *Animal Behaviour* 51:1149–1157.

Jacobs, L. F. 1992. Memory for cache locations in Merriam's kangaroo rats. *Animal Behaviour* 43:585–593.

Jacobs, L. F., and E. R. Liman. 1991. Grey squirrels remember the locations of buried nuts. *Animal Behaviour* 41:103–110.

Jacobs, L. F., and W. D. Spencer. 1994. Natural space-use patterns and hippocampal size in kangaroo rats. *Brain Behavior and Evolution* 44:125–132.

Jacobs, L. F., S. J. C. Gaulin, D. F. Sherry, and G. E. Hoffman. 1990. Evolution of spatial cognition: Sex-specific patterns of spatial behavior predict hippocampal size. *Proceedings of the National Academy of Sciences of the United States of America* 87:6349–6352.

Jarrard, L. E. 1983. Selective hippocampal lesions and behavior: Effects of kainic acid lesions on performance of place and cue tasks. *Behavioral Neuroscience* 97:873–889.

Källén, B. 1962. Embryogenesis of brain nuclei in the chick telecephalon. II. *Ergebnisse der Anatomie und Entwicklungsgeschichte* 36:62–82.

Källander, H. 1978. Hoarding in the rook Corvus frugilegus. *Anser* (suppl.) 3:124–128.

Kamil, A. C., and R. P. Balda. 1985. Cache recovery and spatial memory in Clark's nutcracker (*Nucifraga columbiana*). *Journal of Experimental Psychology: Animal Behavior Processes* 11:95–111.

———. 1990. Spatial memory in seed-caching corvids. In G. H. Bower, ed., *The Psychology of Learning and Motivation*, Vol. 26, 1–25. San Diego: Academic.

Kesner, R. P., and M. J. DeSpain. 1988. Correspondence between rats and humans in the utilization of retrospective and prospective codes. *Animal Learning and Behavior* 16:299–302.

Ketterson, E. D., and V. Nolan, Jr. 1990. Site attachment and site fidelity in migratory birds: Experimental evidence from the field and analogies from neurobiology. In E. Gwinner, ed., *Bird Migration*, 117–129. Berlin: Springer-Verlag.

Kraemer, P. J., M. E. Gelbert, and N. K. Innis. 1983. The influence of cue types and configuration upon radial-arm maze performance in the rat. *Animal Learning and Behavior* 11:373–380.

Kramer, G. 1951. Eine neue Methode zur Erforschung der Zugorientierung und die bisher damit erzielten Ergebnisse. In S. Hörstadius, ed., *Proceedings of the Tenth International Ornithological Congress, Uppsala*, 269–280. Uppsala: Almqvist & Wicksell.

Krayniak, P. F., and A. Siegel. 1978. Efferent connections of the hippocampus and adjacent regions in the pigeon. *Brain Behavior and Evolution* 15:372–388.

Krebs, J. R. 1978. Optimal foraging: Decision rules for predators. In J. R. Krebs and N. B. Davies, eds., *Behavioural Ecology: An Evolutionary Approach*, 23–63. Oxford: Blackwell Scientic.

Krebs, J. R., D. F. Sherry, S. D. Healy, V. H. Perry, and A. L. Vaccarino. 1989. Hippo-

campal specialization of food-storing birds. *Proceedings of the National Academy of Sciences of the United States of America* 86:1388–1392.

Lewis, F. T. 1923. The significance of the term *hippocampus*. *Journal of Comparative Neurology* 35:213–230.

Mason, P. 1987. Pair formation in cowbirds: Evidence found for screaming but not shiny cowbirds. *Condor* 89:349–356.

Mazmanian, D. S., and W. A. Roberts. 1983. Spatial memory in rats under restricted viewing conditions. *Learning and Motivation* 14:123–139.

McGregor, P. K., and G. W. M. Westby. 1992. Discrimination of individually characteristic electric organ discharges by a weakly electric fish. *Animal Behavior* 43:977–986.

Morris, R. G. M. 1981. Spatial localization does not require the presence of local cues. *Learning and Motivation* 12:239–260.

Nadel, L. 1991. The hippocampus and space revisited. *Hippocampus* 1:221–229.

Nagahara, A. H., T. Otto, and M. Gallagher. 1995. Entorhinal-perirhinal lesions impair performance of rats on two versions of place learning in the Morris water maze. *Behavioral Neuroscience* 109:3–9.

Norman, R. F., and R. J. Robertson. 1975. Nest-searching behavior in the brownheaded cowbird. *Auk* 92:610–611.

O'Keefe, J., and J. Dostrovsky. 1971. The hippocampus as a spatial map: Preliminary evidence from unit activity in the freely-moving rat. *Brain Research* 34:171–175.

O'Keefe, J., and L. Nadel. 1978. *The Hippocampus as a Cognitive Map*. Oxford: Clarendon.

Olton, D. S., J. T. Becker, and G. E. Handelmann. 1979. Hippocampus, space, and memory. *Behavioral and Brain Science* 2:313–365.

Olton, D. S., and C. Collison. 1979. Intramaze cues and odor trails fail to direct choice behavior on an elevated maze. *Animal Learning & Behavior* 7:221–223.

Petersen, K., and D. F. Sherry. 1996. No difference occurs in hippocampus, foodstoring, or memory for food caches in black-capped chickadees. *Behavioral Brain Research* 79:15–22.

Ranck, J. B., Jr. 1985. Head direction cells in the deep cell layer of dorsal presubiculum in freely moving rats. In G. Buzsáki and C. H. Vanderwolf, eds., *Electrical Activity of the Archicortex,* 217–220. Budapest: Akadémiai Kiadó.

Rawlins, J. N. P. 1985. Associations across time: The hippocampus as a temporary memory store. *Behavioral and Brain Sciences* 8:479–496.

Rehkämper, G., E. Haase, and H. D. Frahm. 1988. Allometric comparison of brain weight and brain structure volumes in different breeds of the domestic pigeon, *Columba livia f. d.* (fantails, homing pigeons, strassers). *Brain Behavior and Evolution* 31:141–149.

Reboreda, J. C., N. S. Clayton, and A. Kacelnik. 1996. Species and sex differences in hippocampus size in parasitic and non-parasitic cowbirds. *Neuroreport* 7:505–508.

Schmidt-Koenig, K. 1990. The sun compass. *Experientia* 46:336–342.

Schwagmeyer, P. L. 1994. Competitive mate searching in thirteen-lined ground squirrels (Mammalia, Sciuridae): Potential roles of spatial memory. *Ethology* 98:265–276.

Sherry, D. F. 1984. Food storage by black-capped chickadees: Memory for the location and contents of caches. *Animal Behaviour* 32:451–464.

———. 1985. Food storage by birds and mammals. *Advances in the Study of Behaviour* 15:153–188.

Sherry, D. F., and S. J. Duff. 1996. Behavioral and neural bases of orientation in food-storing birds. *Journal of Experimental Biology* 199:165–172.

Sherry, D. F., M. R. L. Forbes, M. Khurgel, G. O. Ivy. 1993. Females have a larger hippocampus than males in the brood-parasitic brown-headed cowbird. *Proceedings of the National Academy of Sciences of the United States of America* 90: 7839–7843.

Sherry, D. F., L. F. Jacobs, and S. J. C. Gaulin. 1992. Spatial memory and adaptive specialization of the hippocampus. *Trends in Neurosciences* 15:298–303.

Sherry, D. F., J. R. Krebs, and R. J. Cowie. 1981. Memory for the location of stored food in marsh tits. *Animal Behaviour* 29:1260–1266.

Sherry, D. F., and A. L. Vaccarino. 1989. Hippocampus and memory for food caches in black-capped chickadees. *Behavioral Neuroscience* 103:308–318.

Sherry, D. F., A. L. Vaccarino, K. Buckenham, and R. S. Herz. 1989. The hippocampal complex of food-storing birds. *Brain Behavior and Evolution* 34:308–317.

Shettleworth, S. J. 1990. Spatial memory in food-storing birds. *Philosophical Transactions of the Royal Society of London,* ser. B, 329:143–151.

Shettleworth, S. J., and J. R. Krebs. 1982. How marsh tits find their hoards: The roles of site preference and spatial memory. *Journal of Experimental Psychology: Animal Behaviour Processes* 8:354–375.

Squire, L. R. 1987. *Memory and Brain.* New York: Oxford University Press.

Squire, L. R., N. J. Cohen, and L. Nadel. 1984. The medial temporal region and memory consolidation: A new hypothesis. In H. Weingartner and E. S. Parker, eds., *Memory Consolidation,* 185–210. Hillsdale, N.J.: Erlbaum.

Spetch, M. L., and W. K. Honig. 1988. Characteristics of pigeons' spatial working memory in an open-field task. *Animal Learning and Behavior* 16:123–131.

Stephens, D. W., and J. R. Krebs. 1986. *Foraging Theory.* Princeton, N.J.: Princeton University Press.

Stevens, T. A., and J. R. Krebs. 1986. Retrieval of stored seeds by marsh tits *Parus palustris* in the field. *Ibis* 128:513–525.

Sutherland, R. J., and J. W. Rudy. 1989. Configural association theory: The role of the hippocampal formation in learning, memory, and amnesia. *Psychobiology* 17: 129–144.

Suzuki, S., G. Augerinos, and A. H. Black. 1980. Stimulus control of spatial behavior on the eight-arm maze in rats. *Learning and Motivation* 11:1–18.

Székely, A. D., and J. R. Krebs. 1996. Efferent connectivity of the hippocampal formation of the zebra finch (*Taenopygia guttata*): An anterograde pathway tracing study using *Phaseolus vulgaris* leucoagglutinin. *Journal of Comparative Neurology* 368: 198–214.

Taube, J. S., J. P. Goodridge, E. J. Golob, P. A. Dudchenko, and R. W. Stackman. 1996. Processing the head-direction cell signal: A review and commentary. *Brain Research Bulletin* 40:477–484.

Taube, J. S., and H. L. Burton. 1995. Head-direction cell activity monitored in a novel

environment and during a cue conflict situation. *Journal of Neurophysiology* 74: 1953–1971.

Tinbergen, N. 1932. Über die Orientierung des Bienenwolfes (*Philanthus triangulum* Fabr.). *Zeitscrhift für vergleichende Physiologie* 16:305–334.

Tinbergen, N., and W. Kruyt. 1938. Über die Orientierung des Bienenwolfes (*Philanthus triangulum* Fabr.) III. Die Bevorzugung bestimmter Wegmarken. *Zeitscrhift für vergleichende Physiologie* 25:292–334.

Tomback, D. F., and Y. B. Linhart. 1990. The evolution of bird-dispersed pines. *Evolutionary Ecology* 4:185–219.

Uyehara, J. C., and P. M. Narins. 1992. Sexual dimorphism in cowbird brains and bodies: Where does it end? *Proceedings of the Third International Congress of Neuroethology, Montreal* Abstract No. 146.

Vander Wall, S. B. 1982. An experimental analysis of cache recovery in Clark's nutcracker. *Animal Behaviour* 30:84–94.

———. 1990. *Food Storing in Animals*. Chicago: University of Chicago Press.

Weygoldt, P. 1980. Complex brood care and reproductive behavior in captive poison-arrow frogs, *Dendrobates pumilio* O. Schmidt. *Behavioral Ecology and Sociobiology* 7:329–332.

Williams, C. L., A. M. Barnett, and W. H. Meck. 1990. Organizational effects of early gonadal secretions on sexual differentiation in spatial memory. *Journal of Neuroscience* 104:84–97.

Wiltschko, W., and R. P. Balda. 1989. Sun compass orientation in seed-caching scrub jays (*Aphelocoma coerulescens*). *Journal of Comparative Physiology,* ser. A, *Sensory, Neural, and Behavioral Physiology* 164:717–721.

Wiltschko, W., and R. Wiltschko. 1978. A theoretical model for migratory orientation and homing in birds. *Oikos* 30:177–187.

———. 1993. Navigation in birds and other animals. *Journal of Navigation* 46:174–191.

Zoladek, L., and W. A. Roberts. 1978. The sensory basis of spatial memory in the rat. *Animal Learning and Behavior* 6:77–81.

Risk-Sensitive Foraging: Decision Making in Variable Environments

MELISSA BATESON AND ALEX KACELNIK

8.1 INTRODUCTION

Analysis of foraging has greatly benefited from the integration of evolutionary, ecological, and cognitive research. In this chapter, we focus on risk sensitivity, the area of foraging theory that concerns how and why animals respond to variability in food sources. Our intention is to show how optimality modeling and cognitive research can and need to operate in unison if we are to understand risk sensitivity. For many years, data collection and theoretical developments regarding risk sensitivity have progressed in parallel in the behavioral ecology and psychology literatures. The lack of interchange between these two disciplines reflects a difference in the types of questions asked and the types of explanations sought. In behavioral ecology, research has centered on theoretical predictions that under certain ecological conditions, natural selection should favor foragers that are sensitive to environmental variance. Conversely, research in psychology has been driven by animals' observed responses to variance and, more recently, by hypotheses about the information-processing mechanisms that underlie foraging. We demonstrate the necessity of both approaches and advocate a program of research that simultaneously considers evolutionary ecology and cognitive mechanisms.

8.1.1 What Is Risk Sensitivity?

We begin with three examples that introduce the phenomenon of risk sensitivity. In the first experiment, bumblebees (*Bombus edwardsi*) were allowed to forage on an array of two types of artificial flowers. One color of flower always contained a constant volume of 0.1 µl of nectar, and the other color of flower contained either 1 µl of nectar (10% of flowers) or no nectar (90% of flowers). Once the bees had experienced both flower types and presumably learned something about their different properties, the bees showed a strong preference for the flowers that contained the constant volume of nectar (Waddington et al. 1981). In the second experiment, thirsty pigeons (*Columba livia*) were given

repeated choices between two keys. The keys were arranged such that pecks on one key led to water delivery after a fixed 15-second delay, and pecks on the other key led to water delivery after a variable delay averaging 15 seconds. After training, the birds preferred water delivery with the variable delay (Case et al. 1995). In the third experiment, yellow-eyed juncos (*Junco phaeonotus*) were given repeated choices between two feeding stations, one of which offered four millet seeds on every visit, and the other either one or seven seeds with equal probability. The birds' preferences depended on the ambient temperature: At 1°C, they preferred the variable option; however, at 19°C, they preferred the constant option (Caraco et al. 1990).

In all three experiments, the animals faced two options that offered equal average rates of gain. The animals' preferences appeared to be influenced by the variance in the rate of gain that differed between the two options. In all cases, the variable option was programmed such that it was impossible for the animals to know exactly the gain that would result from choosing this option; with the variable option, the animals could learn only the probability distribution of possible outcomes. In the foraging literature, this type of environmental variance is referred to as *risk,* and an animal with preferences that are affected by the variance in the rate of gain is called *risk sensitive.* When two options offer the same long-term rate of gain, animals that prefer the less variable option (e.g. Waddington's bumblebees) are *risk averse,* and animals that prefer the more variable option (e.g. the pigeons of Case et al.) are *risk prone.*

Thus in foraging theory, risk has a very specific meaning. Risk should not be confused with the problem faced by an animal that has incomplete information and knows neither the mean nor variance of the foraging options it faces; this problem is often referred to as uncertainty. Also, risk should not be confused with risk of predation, which some authors prefer to call danger.

8.1.2 Patterns of Risk Sensitivity

In a recent review (Kacelnik and Bateson 1996), we collated the results of 59 experimental studies of risk sensitivity in 28 animal species including insects, fish, birds, and mammals. In most of these studies, we found evidence for sensitivity to risk, and a number of consistent patterns emerged. A brief review of our findings follows.

Most of the variation in the direction of risk-sensitive preferences is explained by the component of rate of gain that is programmed to be risky. Because rate of gain is a function of the amount of food obtained and the time taken to obtain it, variation in either of these components can generate risk

in the rate of gain. When risk is generated with variance in amount, as in the bee example described, animals are usually risk averse (fig. 8.1*a*). By contrast, when risk is generated with variance in the time associated with getting food or water, as in the pigeon example described, animals are almost universally risk prone (see fig. 8.1*a*).

In some species (for example juncos), the direction of preference appears to be dependent on the relationship between the energy needs of the animal and the average rate of energy gain available from the foraging options (the *energy budget*). Usually, if an animal's rate of gain exceeds its needs (i.e. the animal is on a *positive energy budget*), then risk aversion occurs. However, if the rate of gain is insufficient for the animal to meet its needs (i.e. the animal is on a *negative energy budget*), then risk proneness occurs (fig. 8.1*b*). This effect of the energy budget seems to be restricted to experimental situations in which risk is generated with variance in food amount. As yet, there is virtually no evidence that preference for variable time delays is affected by the energy budget; however, this lack of effect has not been thoroughly tested. There is also some evidence that a response to the energy budget may be dependent on the typical body weight of the species; lighter species appear more likely to respond to changes in the budget than heavier species (fig. 8.1*c*).

In this chapter, we will present a critical review of the main theories that have been proposed to account for risk sensitivity. We will concentrate on identifying which of the above findings the different theories can and cannot explain. However, before we proceed with these theories, we need to explain why risk sensitivity challenges classical optimal foraging theory, which until recently has provided the dominant framework for the modeling of animal decision making.

8.1.3 Classical Optimal Foraging Theory Predicts Indifference to Risk

In Charnov's (1976a, 1976b) two seminal optimality models, he assumed that foraging animals make decisions that maximize their rate of energy gain. In these models, rate of energy gain is computed as the ratio of the expected energy obtained from food to the expected time spent foraging. This form of rate is also known as *long-term rate,* or the *ratio of expectations* (Bateson and Kacelnik 1996). Thus,

$$\text{long-term rate} = \frac{\text{E}\{\text{energy obtained from food}\}}{\text{E}\{\text{time spent foraging}\}}, \qquad (8.1)$$

where E{ } designates an expectation or average. The choice of long-term rate is justified on the grounds that it makes sense to start with the assumption that natural selection should favor animals that maximize this currency. The

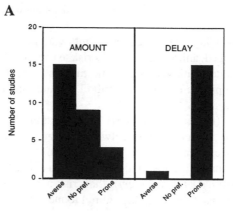

A

AMOUNT   DELAY

Number of studies

Risk preference

Averse   No pref.   Prone

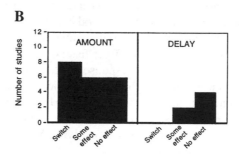

B

AMOUNT   DELAY

Number of studies

Effect of budget manipulation

Switch   Some effect   No effect

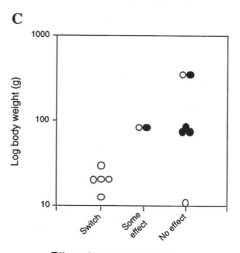

C

Log body weight (g)

Effect of budget manipulation

Switch   Some effect   No effect

rationale is that both the survival and reproduction components of fitness have an obvious relationship with the long-term rate of energy gain. The more energy gained, the greater the probability of survival and the greater amount of energy that can be put into reproduction. Also, the less time spent feeding, the more time there is for other activities such as predator avoidance and reproduction. Therefore, animals may be expected to maximize their long-term rate of energy gain because, by doing so, they obtain the most energy per unit of time that is devoted to foraging (see Ydenberg, this vol. section 9.2, for further discussion of currencies).

As equation 8.1 shows, only expectations or averages enter the computation of long-term rate. Therefore, in most risk-sensitivity experiments in which the average amount and time are the same in the two options, long-term rate should be identical and foraging decisions should be unaffected by risk. However, the results summarized in figure 8.1 clearly show that considering only the average values of these variables is insufficient because risk has considerable effects on preference in most studies. Thus, maximizing long-term rate cannot be all that is involved in decision making. In the following section, we will introduce Jensen's (1906) inequality, a mathematical result that helps us understand why risk affects foraging decisions.

8.1.4 Jensen's Inequality

Let us start by imagining a function $y = f(x)$. Although it is mathematically irrelevant what x and y are, we will assume that y represents fitness and x represents the amount of food an animal gains from a foraging option. Thus, for example, the function allows us to determine how many units of fitness (y) a junco will obtain from four millet seeds (x). In the case of a risky foraging option in which there are two or more possible values of x (either one or seven seeds in the case of the juncos), we need to calculate the average fitness value of the option; however, there are two different ways to calculate the value. We can compute the average value of x (with use of the same notation described, $E\{x\}$) and use this value to obtain a single value of y (written $E\{y\} =$

Figure 8.1. The responses of animals to risk. Data are from 28 species of insects, fish, birds, and mammals. (*a*) The differential effects of variability in amount and delay on risk-sensitive preferences. (*b*) The effects of energy-budget manipulations on risk-sensitive preferences. "Switch" indicates that subjects switched from being risk averse on positive budgets to risk prone on negative budgets. "Some effect" indicates there was a similar, but smaller shift in preference as that of the switch group. "No effect" indicates that manipulations of energy budget did not change the direction or degree of preference. (*c*) The response of bird species to energy-budget manipulations versus body weight. Empty circles indicate studies examining risk in amount, and the filled circles indicate studies examining risk in delay (replotted from Kacelnik and Bateson 1996).

$f(E\{x\})$). Or we can compute the y value obtained with each value of x and take the average of the resulting values of y (written $E\{y\} = E\{f(x)\}$). In other words, we can either average the values of x before applying the function or average the values of y obtained after applying the function to each value of x.

If $f(x)$ is a linear function, then averaging may be performed at either stage because the outcomes will be equal: $E\{f(x)\} = f(E\{x\})$. However, if $f(x)$ is nonlinear, then the stage at which averaging occurs matters because *Jensen's inequality* applies, and $E\{f(x)\} \neq f(E\{x\})$. Specifically, if $y = f(x)$ is increasing and decelerating, then calculating $E\{x\}$ first and applying the function to the result produces a higher value than calculating the average of the y values obtained after applying the function (i.e. $E\{f(x)\} < f(E\{x\})$). By contrast, if $y = f(x)$ is increasing and accelerating, the opposite is true, and $E\{f(x)\} > f(E\{x\})$.

If we make the assumption that fitness is the ultimate currency of all decisions, then the above results produce the following consequences for animals that must choose between fixed and variable foraging options with equal long-term rates of gain. In cases in which the fitness function is linear, risk sensitivity is not predicted because both options offer equal fitness. However, if the fitness function is nonlinear and animals average the fitness they obtain after applying the function, then risk sensitivity will occur, and the direction will depend on the shape of the function. If $y = f(x)$ is increasing and decelerating, then risk aversion is predicted; if $y = f(x)$ is increasing and accelerating, then risk proneness is predicted (fig. 8.2).

Thus, risk sensitivity is predicted if two conditions are met. First, the function that relates the amount of food gained to fitness must be nonlinear. We will refer to this condition as the *nonlinearity condition*. Second, averaging of outcomes from variable options must be performed with the fitness values obtained after the fitness function has been applied. We will refer to this condition as the *averaging condition*. Classical optimal-foraging models do not predict risk sensitivity because average long-term rate of gain is computed by averaging outcomes before the fitness function is applied (i.e. the averaging condition is not met).

Most existing models of risk sensitivity rely on Jensen's inequality. The models differ, however, in a number of respects that can obscure this underlying link. A major difference concerns the identity of the function $y = f(x)$. We introduced Jensen's inequality with use of the function to relate energy gain to fitness. However, alternative explanations of risk sensitivity focus on different functions. The alternative explanations also differ in the biological justifications they provide for the nonlinearity and averaging conditions. We divide the explanations into two types. The explanations presented in sections 8.2–8.4 are called *functional* because they assume that risk sensitivity has

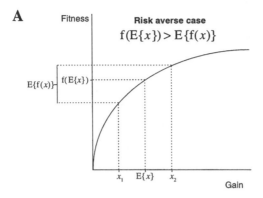

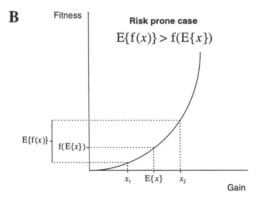

Figure 8.2. Graphics demonstrating Jensen's inequality. (*a*) f(*x*), increasing and decelerating, leads to risk-averse behavior. (*b*) f(*x*), increasing and accelerating, leads to risk-prone behavior.

evolved because of its fitness consequences. By contrast, the explanations in sections 8.5 and 8.6 are called *mechanistic* because they explain risk sensitivity as arising from basic psychological processes such as associative learning and perception. As Tinbergen (1963) made clear, these are logically distinct kinds of explanations, both of which are needed to fully understand behavior. Every behavioral phenomenon has a functional and mechanistic explanation; therefore, one type of explanation does not substitute for the other. Thus, we expect functional and mechanistic models of the same phenomenon to lead to identical predictions about behavior. We shall see, however, that differences in the background and motivation of behavioral ecologists and psychologists—who are responsible for the functional and mechanistic models, respectively—result in models that address different aspects of risk sensitivity and make very different predictions about behavior.

8.2 FUNCTIONAL EXPLANATION 1: LONG-TERM RATE MAXIMIZATION

In section 8.1.3, we argued that risk sensitivity is not explained by classical optimal-foraging models that assume maximization of long-term rate. However, this is only the case if the long-term rate of gain is equal in the fixed and variable options of a risk-sensitive foraging experiment. In this section, we suggest that there are a number of reasons why the long-term rate of gain experienced by a forager may differ from that intended by the experimenter.

In most risk-sensitivity studies, a tacit assumption is made that there is a linear relationship between the characteristics of the foraging option programmed by the experimenter and what is experienced by the forager. Thus for example, it is assumed that if one millet seed results in a net energy intake of 1 calorie, then seven seeds will provide 7 calories. However, the programmed amount of food may not have a linear relationship to the amount ingested by the animal, and the programmed time delay before food is obtained may not have a linear relationship to the delay experienced by the animal. It is also possible that the gross amount of food ingested by the animal may not have a linear relationship to the net energy derived from it. Because it is impossible for an animal to average quantities not yet experienced, the averaging condition is bound to be met and Jensen's inequality will apply if any of the functions we described is nonlinear. We, therefore, have a potentially trivial explanation for some cases of risk sensitivity.

The different techniques for generating risk can affect the shape of the function that relates what is programmed to what is experienced by the forager. Of the studies that generate risk by varying the amount of reward, most manipulate either the number of similarly sized food items, the duration of access to a food hopper, or the volume or concentration of nectar delivered. Although it is usually claimed that the average amounts obtained from constant and variable options are equal, evidence is rarely presented. In many cases, it is possible that animals may not consume the entire reward available or may not consume rewards of different sizes at the same rate. In cases in which amount is controlled by the time of access to food, the linear relationship assumed between programmed access time and the amount of food taken is usually not verified. It has been demonstrated that the amount of grain consumed by pigeons feeding from a hopper is an increasing, but decelerating function of the time of hopper access (Epstein 1981) (fig. 8.3). Jensen's inequality predicts that given an increasing, decelerating function, pigeons should be risk averse if they are offered a choice between two foraging options with the same average time of hopper access but with different variances in the length of access. In order to eliminate this possible source of risk-sensitivity, linearity between programmed and experienced reward needs to be proved in each study. For

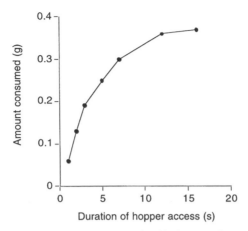

Figure 8.3. An example of nonlinearity in the relationship between the programmed duration of hopper access and the amount of grain consumed by pigeons. The nonlinearity is probably produced by two factors: the maximum amount of food the bird can retrieve from the hopper during one episode of reinforcement and the decreasing accessibility of grain as the pigeon eats (replotted from Epstein 1981). This graph shows that if a pigeon is given a choice between a fixed reinforcement of a 10-second duration versus a risky reinforcement equally likely to be 5 or 15 seconds in duration the bird maximizes its long-term rate of food intake by choosing the fixed option.

example, Reboreda and Kacelnik (1991) reported risk sensitivity in starlings (*Sturnus vulgaris*) despite the establishment of a linear relationship between time of hopper access and grams of food consumed in this species.

Experimenters that explicitly claim to vary the amount of food almost always also vary the time taken to acquire the food; large rewards usually take longer to deliver, handle, and consume than small rewards. This source of variability is usually ignored because it will not cause differences in the long-term rate of gain that is available from a fixed and variable option if the function that relates the reward size to handling time is linear. However, if there is a nonlinear relationship between the reward size and handling time, then differences in long-term rates can result because of Jensen's inequality. For example, Possingham et al. (1990) argued that a bumblebee presented with a choice of a flower type that offers a fixed 3 µl of nectar versus a variable flower type that offers 1 or 5 µl should be risk prone if the bee is maximizing its long-term rate of energy gain. This prediction is based on the observation that in bumblebees there is an increasing, but decelerating relationship between the volume of nectar taken from a flower and the time spent on the flower (fig. 8.4) (Hodges and Wolfe 1981). The effect of this relationship is that—although, on average, the volume of nectar taken from the fixed and variable flowers will be identical—the average time taken to get the nectar

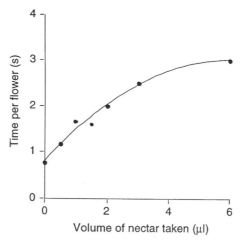

Figure 8.4. The relationship between volume of nectar taken and handling time per flower in the bumblebee, *Bombus appositus* (replotted form Hodges and Wolfe 1981). Bees extract larger volumes of nectar proportionately more quickly; initially, more of the hairy tongue comes into contact with the nectar, and lapping is more efficient (Harder 1986).

from the variable flowers will be less than that taken with the fixed flowers. Hence, the variable flowers will provide a higher long-term rate of nectar intake than the fixed flowers. This effect of handling time ought to be important in animals such as bees because handling takes up a substantial portion of total foraging time. However, the argument presented does not help us understand risk sensitivity in bees because the reported cases show risk aversion (Real 1981; Waddington et al. 1981; Real et al. 1982) and not risk proneness (we will return to the problem of why bees are sometimes risk averse in section 8.5). Despite this specific problem, the general point remains that nonlinearities in handling time can generate differences in the long-term rate of intake that is provided by fixed and variable food sources (which ostensibly should provide the same rate).

As with food amount, the delay to obtain food can also be controlled in a number of ways. Most studies use schedules of reinforcement, in which reward is programmed on the basis of either the number of responses performed (*ratio schedules*), the amount of time elapsed (*time schedules*), or a combination of these (*interval schedules*). With time schedules, the timing of reward is independent of the behavior of the animal; however, with interval or ratio schedules, reward is contingent on the animal completing the required responses. Thus, a programmed interval or ratio need not have a linear relationship to the actual delay experienced by the animal. For example, Ha et al. (1990) used fixed and variable ratio schedules to examine risk sensitivity in grey jays (*Persoreus canadensis*) and reported risk proneness. However, to

assess the source of risk sensitivity in this experiment it must be established if the rate of responding is constant over the range of programmed ratios. If, for instance, animals worked faster when the ratio was higher, then the average time taken to complete a variable ratio would be less than the time taken to complete a fixed ratio with the same average value. Thus, animals that appear to be risk sensitive with respect to the programmed ratios may simply be rate maximizers when experienced times are taken into account.

The examples we have discussed all relate to nonlinearities in the functions that relate the parameters programmed by the experimenter to those experienced by the forager. Fewer data exist on the shape of the function that relates the gross rate of energy gain to the net rate of energy gain because obtaining this information requires measurements of energy expenditure. However, it is theoretically feasible that this function may also be nonlinear. For instance, in the case of honeybees that collect nectar by hovering from one flower to the next, the cost of staying aloft per unit time increases with the load already collected; successive equal volumes of nectar collected have different net values to the bee (Schmid-Hempel et al. 1985; see also Ydenberg, this vol. section 9.2).

The explanations for risk sensitivity discussed in this section may seem uninteresting because they do not require anything beside long-term rate maximizing; thus, these explanations are consistent with the classical optimal-foraging theory. In many experimental studies, however, risk is programmed without consideration for the shape of the functions that relate what is programmed to what is experienced, and nonlinearity in these functions must be acknowledged as a candidate explanation for some reports of risk sensitivity.

From the ecological perspective that examines how resource characteristics affect the exploitation of the resource by foragers, the cause of risk sensitivity is irrelevant. What matters is that foragers may treat food sources that provide the same average quantity of food differentially depending on the variance in food quantity. This differential treatment could have consequences for the evolution of food species. For example, in the only risk-sensitive foraging study that used a natural food source, Cartar (1990) showed that bumblebees' choices between two flower species were influenced by variance differences in the rate of gain associated with the species. Such behavior should place selective pressures on the distribution of nectar between flowers because a plant can theoretically attract more pollinators with simply a change in this distribution.

8.3 FUNCTIONAL EXPLANATION 2: RISK-SENSITIVE FORAGING THEORY

Risk-sensitive foraging theory is the main, functionally based framework developed to explain why animals are sensitive to risky food sources. This theory

focuses on the function that relates the energy gained, as the result of a foraging decision, to fitness and provides biological justifications for both the nonlinearity and the averaging conditions.

8.3.1 The Energy-Budget Rule

The simplest and best known risk-sensitive foraging model (Stephens 1981) concerns a small endotherm, such as a bird, that has to attain a minimum reserve threshold by dusk to survive the night. This threshold provides the necessary nonlinear relationship between rate of gain and fitness. If the animal has more than the threshold level of reserves, it survives until the next day; however, if the animal has less, it dies and has a fitness of zero. Consider a bird faced with two foraging options that differ only in the variance of the expected number of seeds available per reward (for example the junco experiment described in section 8.1.1). If the fixed option offers a rate of gain that is sufficiently high to take the bird above the threshold (i.e. it is on a positive-energy budget), then the bird should be risk averse; however, if the rate is not sufficiently high (i.e. the bird is on a negative energy budget), then the bird's only chance of survival is to be risk prone and gamble on the variable option that gives an above average rate of gain (fig. 8.5). These options have been summarized in the *daily energy-budget rule,* which states that a forager on a positive budget should be risk averse and a forager on a negative budget should be risk prone (Stephens 1981). Note that "budget" is not equivalent to the animal's absolute level of reserves; budget refers to the relationship between an animal's needs and its potential rates of gain. A hungry animal close to starvation could be on a positive budget if it is currently facing a rich food source. By a similar argument, a well-fed animal could be on a negative budget. If everything else is assumed to be constant, however, a subject with low reserves has higher needs and is therefore more likely to be on a negative budget than a counterpart with high reserves.

Many investigators have sought to test the energy-budget rule directly by experimentally manipulating the energy budget of the subjects. Relatively few studies, however, have produced convincing support for the theory. In our recent review, we examined 24 studies that manipulated energy budget: In 18 of these studies, risk sensitivity was investigated when amount was variable. Time was variable in five studies, and both amount and time were variable in one study. Among the experiments with variable amount, 14 showed a shift toward risk proneness when energy budgets were reduced and risk aversion when energy budgets were increased; although, only eight of these studies showed a complete switch in preference between significant risk proneness and significant risk aversion (Caraco et al. 1980; Caraco 1981; Caraco 1983; Barnard and Brown 1985; Moore and Simm 1986; Caraco et al. 1990; Young

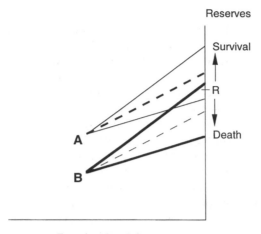

Foraging time left

Figure 8.5. Graphic demonstration of the logic that underlies the energy-budget rule. *A* and *B* represent two foragers that differ in their energy reserves. Both have to make one foraging decision before nightfall and must choose between a fixed option (*broken line*) that gives a certain amount of food or a risky option (*solid line*) that gives with equal probability a small or large amount of food. *R* represents the level of reserves needed by dusk if the foragers are to survive the night. The optimal choices for *A* and *B* are different: *A* is on a positive budget and ensures its survival by choosing the fixed option; however, *B* is on a negative budget, and its only chance of survival is provided with the variable option. Optimal choices for each forager are shown in bold.

et al. 1990; Croy and Hughes 1991). Despite this apparent support for the energy-budget rule, we suspect that the real number of failures to obtain the predicted switch in preference with budget manipulations is actually greater; studies that fail to reject the null hypothesis (lack of effect of budget) are harder to publish and probably seldom submitted for publication. Some studies that show failure may be salvaged for publication if a convincing post hoc argument can be made for why a switch in preference was not predicted. A possible example is Barkan's (1990) study of black-capped chickadees (*Parus atricapillus*), which examined two very different rates of intake; the continuing risk aversion of the birds despite apparent budget changes was justified on the basis of careful calculations that showed birds were, in fact, always on positive budgets.

Of the few budget-manipulation experiments with variability in delay, all have failed to demonstrate convincing shifts in preference. Ha and colleagues (Ha et al. 1990; Ha 1991) tried unsuccessfully to induce a preference switch in gray jays; we failed also to show a preference switch in starlings (Bateson and Kacelnik, 1997). Similar failure was met by Case et al. (1995) with use

of water as a reward for pigeons and manipulation of water budgets. A study of rats by Zabludoff et al. (1988) showed some evidence for a preference switch; the rats became risk prone as their body weights dropped from 85% to 75% of their free-feeding weights. This study, however, is difficult to interpret because the decrease in body weight is confounded by an increase in the variance of the more variable option; other studies have shown increasing risk proneness with increasing variance in delay to reward. Reboreda and Kacelnik (1991) found that individual starlings that were less efficient at using hopper access time (and as consequence got smaller food rewards) were significantly more risk prone than more efficient birds. This observation agrees with the prediction that needier animals should be more risk prone. However, because the amount of food the birds obtained was not manipulated experimentally, this evidence is only correlational. Thus, there is little direct evidence that energy budget affects risk sensitivity when the delay to receive food is variable. Instead, risk proneness with variable delays seems universal.

Differences in body weights of the various species of birds and mammals used in risk-sensitivity studies may explain the species that respond to budget manipulations and those that do not. Smaller species may be more likely than large species to be subject to selection for short-fall minimization, and thus, smaller species may be more likely to show energy budget-associated switches in risk sensitivity. In support of this prediction, studies of larger species of birds such as pigeons (Hamm and Shettleworth 1987; Case et al. 1995), jays (Ha et al. 1990; Ha 1991), starlings (Bateson and Kacelnik 1997), and rats (Leventhal et al. 1959; Kagel et al. 1986) have failed to find support for the energy-budget rule. In an attempt to reduce the impact of phylogenetic confounds (such as differences in metabolic rate) between birds and mammals, we analyzed the relationship between body weight and the effects of budget on risk sensitivity in birds only. In small birds, we found that changes in budget were more likely to cause appropriate switches in foraging preferences (fig. 8.1c). A closer inspection of the data, however, reveals that all studies with variability in delay have been conducted on larger species such as pigeons, jays, and starlings. Thus, it is not presently clear if the lack of an effect of budget in these studies is due to the component of rate of gain that was varied or the body weights of the experimental species because these two variables are confounded.

It is interesting to speculate if differences in energy budget were responsible for the differences in responses to amount and delay variability observed (fig. 8.1a). When food amount is variable, some of the variation in behavior is potentially attributable to the energy budget. Among the risk-averse animals, some were certainly on positive budgets (Caraco 1982; Stephens and Ydenberg 1982; Caraco and Lima 1985; Tuttle et al. 1990); however in one study, the subjects were probably on negative energy budgets (Wunderle et al. 1987).

Among the risk-prone animals, the shrews of Barnard et al. (1985) were probably on negative energy budgets. In the other three studies (Essock and Rees 1974; Young 1981; Mazur 1985), pigeons were maintained at 80% of their free-feeding weights and could also have been operating on negative budgets. However, the difficulty of explaining the variation is exemplified with the studies on pigeons. Despite the similar procedures employed and the maintenance of all birds at 80 or 85% of their free-feeding weights, two studies showed risk aversion (Menlove et al. 1979; Hamm and Shettleworth 1987) and three showed indifference (Staddon and Innis 1966; Essock and Rees 1974; Hamm and Shettleworth 1987) (in addition to the studies that showed risk proneness mentioned). This variation cannot be explained with any obvious differences in procedure that may have resulted in budget differences.

If delay is variable, animals are almost universally risk prone (the only exception has been shown in the concurrent schedule study of Rider [1983] in which a questionable measure of preference was used) (see Kacelnik and Bateson 1996). Given that most studies were performed by psychologists with pigeons maintained at body weights as low as 75% of free-feeding body weights, it is possible that subjects may have been on negative energy budgets. However, this seems unlikely because pigeons are relatively large birds that can be maintained at 75%–80% of their free-feeding weights for long periods of time. Moreover, given that most of the daily ration is generally received in the experiment, the rate of intake experienced must be sufficient to result in a positive energy budget.

Three studies (Logan 1965; Reboreda and Kacelnik 1991; Bateson and Kacelnik 1995a) directly compared responses to variability in amount and delay under the same conditions of energy budget. All showed that animals (rats in the first study and starlings in the other two) were risk averse when variability was in amount but risk prone when variability was in delay. These results suggest that the difference in response to variability in amount and delay is not attributable to energy-budget differences.

8.3.2 Beyond the Energy-Budget Rule

The energy-budget rule is insufficient to explain the patterns of risk sensitivity reported in the literature. Most experimental tests have focused on the energy-budget rule; however, this rule is not a universal prediction of all risk-sensitive foraging models. Stephens's (1981) original risk-sensitive foraging model inspired the creation of a number of variant models that explore the modification of his various original assumptions. It is not our intention to give an exhaustive review of the theory because an excellent review is available (McNamara and Houston 1992); however, we want to present the current level of sophistication and complexity of the theory's predictions.

One of the most important constraints in Stephens's model is that the forager is allowed to make only a single foraging decision and is then required to stick with this choice for the rest of the day. This constraint led to the criticism that risk proneness would be very rare in nature because it would occur only if the forager's probability of dying was over 50% that day (Krebs et al. 1983). However, if the forager is allowed to make sequential decisions that can vary according to its current state, then risk proneness becomes far less dangerous and therefore more likely. A risk prone forager with a run of good luck that creates a positive trajectory can capitalize on this luck by switching to risk aversion instead of chancing the creation of a negative budget again (Houston and McNamara 1982; McNamara 1983; McNamara 1984). Whether a single- or sequential-choice model is more realistic for a given foraging situation will depend on the degree to which an animal commits itself when it makes a choice. Single-choice models may be more appropriate to large-scale habitat choices, and sequential-choice models will be appropriate to the modeling of prey choices within a habitat. Most experiments on risk sensitivity probably approximate the sequential-choice model more closely due to their small-spatial scale and the large number of choices per session.

A second assumption of Stephens's model is that the only way to die is by failing to meet the critical level of reserves by nightfall. The possibility of starving while foraging is not included, even though for small mammals (such as the shrew) starvation during foraging is a very real danger. If the model is modified so that a forager is assumed to forage continuously to maintain reserves above a lethal level, then it can be shown that the optimal policy is always to be risk averse, if the mean net gain from a foraging choice is positive (Houston and McNamara 1985). Houston and McNamara (1985) combined in a single model the possibility of death (by allowing reserves to fall below a lethal level) during foraging with the need to build reserves to survive the night. In this case, the optimal policy was a compromise between those results in the separate models: A forager is risk averse at all levels of reserves except for a wedge-shaped region in the reserves-versus-time-of-day space near dusk when it is optimal for animals on negative budgets to be risk prone so that the required level of reserves may be achieved (fig. 8.6a)

A third limitation of Stephens's original model (and of all the others mentioned) is that the optimality criterion is restricted to maximization of probability of survival. There may be animals, particularly insects, that have the option of using energy for immediate reproduction. McNamara et al. (1991) modeled the situation in which reproduction occurs above a certain level of reserves and causes a reduction in reserves. They showed that the policy that maximizes lifetime reproductive success is different from one that minimizes mortality. In these reproduction models, risk proneness can occur at high levels of reserves because there are conditions in which a risk-prone decision could take a for-

(a)

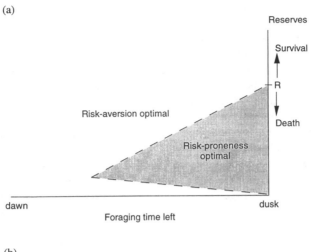

(b)

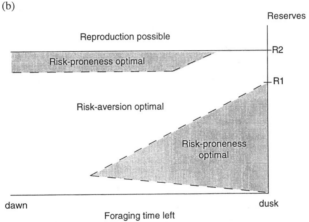

Figure 8.6. Optimal policy. (*a*) Diagram shows the wedge-shaped region near dusk in which it is optimal to be risk prone. *R* is the level of reserves required to survive the night (redrawn from Houston and McNamara 1988). (*b*) Diagram shows the effect of introducing the possibility of reproduction: If reserves are above the *R*2, then reproduction is possible. This second threshold gives rise to risk proneness at high levels of reserves in addition to the wedge-shaped region (see McNamara et al. 1991).

ager over a threshold above which it can reproduce (fig. 8.6*b*). Given certain parameters, it can be shown that as reserves increase, the optimal policy changes successively from risk aversion (to escape an immediate lethal level) to risk proneness (to have a chance of meeting a daily requirement) back to risk aversion (when the requirement can be reached but there is no chance of

reproduction) and finally back to risk proneness again (when this offers the possibility of reproduction).

A final deficiency of the models discussed is that they only consider variance in amount of food; yet, clearly variability in the time associated with obtaining food can also produce risk in the rate of intake. Zabludoff et al. (1988) modeled choice between a foraging option in which there was a fixed delay to food and one in which the delay had the same mean but was variable. In this situation they showed that if the forager must reach a critical level of reserves by nightfall, then the energy-budget rule describes the optimal policy. However, McNamara and Houston (1987) showed that, under some circumstances, the effects of variability in amount and time are not equivalent. Variability in amount and time affect variance in rate of intake; however, unlike variable amounts, variable delays additionally introduce variance in the number of choices that can be made because the length of the delay affects the amount of time remaining.

The message from our brief overview of risk-sensitive foraging theory is that, as Houston and McNamara stressed (Houston 1991; McNamara et al. 1991; McNamara and Houston 1992), there is no single model of risk-sensitive foraging and no single prediction. Notably, the energy-budget rule is not a universal prediction of risk-sensitive foraging theory. This complexity has a number of ramifications for how the risk-sensitive foraging theory can be tested.

8.3.3 Problems with Testing Risk-Sensitive Foraging Theory

Failure to find evidence supporting the energy-budget rule is inconclusive because it is always possible that the wrong model has been tested. Even if the correct model can be chosen for a given situation, there still will be too many unknowns to predict quantitatively how an animal should respond to a given manipulation. For example, the juncos of Caraco et al. (1990) switched from an average of 60% preference for variability in a cold regime to an average of 37% preference for variability in thermoneutral conditions; however, risk-sensitive foraging theory predicts only the direction of the switch, and not the magnitude of the switch.

An additional problem with testing of risk-sensitive foraging theory (and most purely functional models) is that assumptions must be made about the mechanisms an animal uses to assess variables such as the energy budget or rate of intake. Although the many different manipulations tried can theoretically modify energy budgets, modification does not mean that a shift in budget will necessarily be registered by the animal; registration of the shift depends on the proximate mechanism used by the animal to assess its budget. For example, in the natural habitat, ambient temperature may be easy to measure

and provide a reliable correlate of energy requirements. An animal, however, that has evolved a rule-of-thumb to change its risk preference with use of ambient temperature may fail to register a change in energy requirements induced by other means, such as a period of restricted access to food. At present, we do not know how animals assess their energy budgets; a failure to demonstrate an effect of an energy-budget shift on preference does not imply that the energy-budget rule will not predict behavior in the wild. A similar argument can be applied to the assessment of variance in rate of gain. These problems are only partially solved with experimentation in the field (e.g. Cartar 1991) because under natural conditions it is very difficult to control and measure the experience of individual foragers and thus a different set of problems are introduced.

From this discussion, it should be clear that testing the ecological validity of risk-sensitive foraging theory will be exceedingly difficult by rejecting predictions of specific models; the rejection of a model can always be attributed to some cause other than the general validity of the theory. Given this difficulty, we must rely on confirmation of predictions of risk-sensitive foraging models. If a theory makes original and counterintuitive predictions that are later confirmed, we gain confidence in the theory. The energy-budget rule emerges as the best candidate for a prediction that is currently unique to risk-sensitive foraging theory. We suggest that a sound empirical demonstration of this rule would provide strong evidence for the theory. The demonstration by Caraco et al. (1990) of the predicted switch in juncos may provide such evidence (Houston and McNamara 1990), but wide replication of their results is needed.

Another specific prediction of risk-sensitive foraging theory is that all risk-sensitive foraging models necessitate an unpredictable environment instead of just a variable environment. A starving junco is predicted to prefer a risky option because the possibility of a run of large seven-seed rewards will create a positive trajectory. A variable, but predictable option in which the junco receives one and seven seeds alternately offers no benefits over a fixed option that always yields four seeds because the total number of seeds obtained is the same. Thus, we can predict that if the observed preferences have evolved for the reasons proposed by risk-sensitive foraging theory and psychological mechanisms tightly match fitness consequences, then animals should be risk sensitive in the context of unpredictable variance but not predictable variance. We recently tested this idea in starlings. We reached the tentative conclusion that the birds appeared not to treat predictable and unpredictable variable delays differently in the manner predicted by risk-sensitive foraging theory (Bateson and Kacelnik, 1997). However, this negative result may be another example of a difficulty already mentioned. The prediction may have failed because predictable variance is uncommon in the natural world; animals may

have evolved a general rule to treat all variability as risk regardless of its predictability or unpredictability.

8.4 FUNCTIONAL EXPLANATION 3: TIME DISCOUNTING

It is possible that not all cases of risk sensitivity will be explained with the same theory, and this may be particularly true for the difference in response to variability in amount and time. We will discuss a completely different functional explanation for why animals may be sensitive to variance in food delay based on the probability of being interrupted while foraging. We will introduce the argument by considering a choice between an immediate reward and another reward of the same magnitude that is delivered later. After this we will investigate the effects of adding variance to the time before a reward is delivered.

8.4.1 Interruptions and Temporal Discounting

Animals are expected to prefer immediate rewards over delayed rewards for a variety of reasons; however, we will focus on the effects of the probability of losing a reward because of an unpredictable interruption, such as the arrival of a predator or a change in weather, during the delay. If a predicted reward has a continuous chance of being lost before consumption, the longer the delay, the greater the cumulative probability that the reward does not arrive. Thus, a delayed reward will have a lower expected value than an immediate one because the value of a delayed reward is its immediate value multiplied by the probability that it materializes. Immediate rewards should also be preferred over delayed rewards because the time saved by accepting an immediate reward can be used to search for the next reward. This consideration, however, only should apply if an animal is making a sequence of foraging decisions and should not apply to an isolated choice. For clarity, we will restrict our discussion to the effects of the probability of interruption on an isolated choice and return to the additional considerations posed with sequential choices in section 8.5.

The value of a delayed reward, v, will be a function of the immediate value of the reward and its delay and can be written $v = f(r, d)$ where r is the value of the reward if it is obtained immediately and d is the delay from the point of choice; $f(r, d)$ is known as the *discounting function*, and there is much theoretical and empirical literature on the shape of this function (e.g. Myerson and Green 1995). If we assume that (1) the reason underlying discounting is probability of loss by interruption; (2) interruptions occur as a Poisson process with rate α (i.e. the chances of the reward being lost are constant per unit of waiting time); and (3) the rate of interruption, α, is constant for rewards of different magnitude, then the probability of getting a reward

d seconds in the future is $\exp(-\alpha d)$. Therefore, if the subject is fully informed of all the parameters of the problem, then the discounting function $f(r, d) = r\exp(-\alpha d)$. This is a linear function of reward amount and a negative exponential (i.e. decreasing and decelerating) function of delay. This prediction has been made independently in the literature on economics (Samuelson 1937) and foraging (Kagel et al. 1986; McNamara and Houston 1987).

We will now examine the effects of introducing inexact knowledge of reward arrival. This situation can be treated as mathematically equivalent to the existence of variability in the expected delay to reward. Consider a fixed option in which a reward of fixed magnitude, r, is promised for delivery after a fixed delay, d_f, and a variable option in which a reward also of fixed magnitude, r, is promised after a delay of either $d_f - \delta$ or $d_f + \delta$ with equal probability. The expected delay in the variable option is $d_v = 0.5\,[(d_f - \delta) + (d_f + \delta)] = d_f$. The discounted value of the fixed option is $v_f = f(r, d_f)$, but the subject may employ different algorithms to assign value to the variable option. The subject may use either

$$v_{v1} = f(r, d_v) \tag{8.2a}$$

or

$$v_{v2} = 0.5[f(r, d_f - \delta) + f(r, d_f + \delta)]. \tag{8.2b}$$

In equation 8.2a, the subject discounts reward value with use of the expectation of the delay; in equation 8.2b, the subject averages the discounted value of each possible outcome. Thus, we discriminate between the order in which averaging and attributing value are performed. If the averaging of the two possible delays is performed first and the discounting function is applied later, we have equation 8.2a. If the discounting function is applied to each possible delay and the averaging is performed later, we have equation 8.2b. We encountered the same distinction when we introduced Jensen's inequality (section 8.1.4). We are, therefore, familiar with the various outcomes: If the discounting function is linear, then these two equations produce the same result and $v_f = v_{v1} = v_{v2}$. If the discounting function is decreasing and accelerating, then $v_f = v_{v1} > v_{v2}$. If the discounting function is decreasing and decelerating, then $v_f = v_{v1} < v_{v2}$. If the assumptions involved in predicting the discounting function are valid and the function is a negative exponential, then the third case applies and the value computed for the variable option according to equation 8.2b will be higher than that of the fixed option. In the case of a subject facing an isolated choice between a fixed and variable delay option, it is possible to prescribe equation 8.2b, because this equation maximizes the expected fitness consequences of the decision. To illustrate the effect of variability in delay, let $\alpha = 0.1$ and compare a fixed delay of 5 seconds with a variable delay that is either 1 or 9 seconds with equal probability. In the fixed option, the probabil-

ity of getting the reward is $\exp(-0.5) = 0.606$. The corresponding probability in the variable option is $0.5 \ [\exp(-0.1) + \exp(-0.9)] = 0.656$. Thus, we predict that animals should be risk prone if faced with an isolated choice between a fixed and variable delay to food when unpredictable interruptions have exerted an important selective pressure on the evolution of decision making.

In the case of an isolated choice between a fixed and variable amount of reward, the discounting function is assumed to be linear with respect to reward amount. Therefore, under the current theory of time discounting, variability in amount per se should have no effect on preference. If, however, r and d are correlated (as is the case if large food items take longer to handle than small ones), then variability in amount can affect preference by means of the variability's effects on delay (Caraco et al. 1992). We will return to this issue in section 8.5.

8.4.2 Time Discounting Is Not Exponential but Hyperbolic

There have been several attempts to explore how humans discount single delayed rewards. In a recent study, Myerson and Green (1995) gave subjects a choice between two notional sums of money: r_1 was delivered immediately, and r_2 was delivered after a delay, d. By systematically varying r_1 for each pair of values of r_2 and d, they found the value of r_1 at which each subject switched preference from one option to the other. This procedure gave estimates of the relative values of the immediate and the delayed rewards from which the shape of the time-discounting function, $f(r, d)$, could be derived. Like other similar studies, this experiment showed that the shape of the discounting function is hyperbolic and not exponential; for a given absolute increase in d, the fraction of value lost decreased as d increased. By contrast, with an exponential function, the proportional reduction in value with an increase in d is independent of the absolute value of d (fig. 8.7). Therefore, the empirically determined discounting function is inconsistent with the function predicted with our assumptions. We suggest that time discounting cannot be explained as a consequence of the probability of loss by interruption unless additional assumptions are invoked.

Nevertheless, the function that most closely fits the available data is

$$v = r/(a + kd), \tag{8.3}$$

where a and k are constants; a is small and k is close to $1s^{-1}$. In equation 8.3, value is also a linear function of reward and a decreasing decelerating function of delay. Therefore, whatever the reasons there are for devaluing delayed rewards, an isolated reward that is predicted to occur after a variable delay ought to be preferred to a reward that is predicted after a fixed delay of its arithmetic

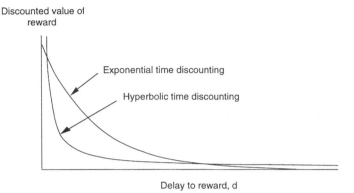

Figure 8.7. Exponential and hyperbolic time discounting functions. Both functions are decreasing and decelerating; however, their shapes differ.

mean. However, we have not been able to find empirical tests of this specific prediction.

8.4.3 Inadequacies of Purely Functional Accounts

All the functional explanations of risk sensitivity we have considered assume that animals can calculate accurate, unbiased estimates of parameters, such as their long-term rate of gain and the associated variance. In optimal-foraging models the tacit assumption is made that if adaptive behavior in animals necessitates accurate estimates of these parameters, then natural selection will provide the animals with the necessary cognitive equipment to obtain these estimates. When explaining subtle details of behavior, however, there are many reasons why a strictly adaptationist approach is insufficient.

In the following sections, we will discuss what is known about how animals process information while foraging. We will show how some of these findings may account for risk sensitivity with the generation of nonlinearities in the function that relates what is actually available to the subjective value the forager assigns to this. The explanations we will present differ from those in previous sections; risk sensitivity will be interpreted as a consequence of basic cognitive mechanisms instead of a direct functional response to external conditions. By promoting the development of mechanistically based models, we do not imply an anti-optimality stance. Behavioral mechanisms must also be the product of natural selection, and we hope that future work may help us understand why these mechanisms—which we regard as constraints in the context of the current discussion—have evolved. We believe natural selection is the main agent of evolutionary change, and we hypothesize that cognitive mechanisms, when viewed in a broader context, can be viewed as adaptations.

8.5 MECHANISTIC EXPLANATION 1: SHORT-TERM RATE MAXIMIZATION

Many experiments on nonhuman animals have examined the effects on choice of the length of delay to reward. It is tempting to generalize the ideas presented in the previous section and treat animal experiments as equivalent to the human experiments on time discounting. There are, however, problems with extrapolating from work in humans to that in animals; the preferences of animals can only be tested after training, which involves repeated exposure to the options. Repeated exposure introduces two differences between work in animals and that in humans. First, animals learn the probability of interruptions in the experimental conditions; because interruptions are typically not programmed, the subject can learn they do not occur. Therefore, whereas learned probability of interruption could influence the choices of humans who are instructed verbally to make an isolated choice, learned probability of interruption is less likely to explain animals' choices. Second, subjects learn to experience a sequence of choices; therefore, immediate rewards are more valuable than delayed rewards because the time saved with a short delay can be used to pursue the next reward. Thus, in animal experiments, a delay to reward can be viewed as a loss of foraging opportunity (Stephens and Krebs 1986).

From a functional point of view, an appropriate measure of value given a sequence of choices is long-term rate of gain (equation 8.1), which is the currency of classical optimal-foraging models. Notice the similarities between equations 8.1 and 8.3. The numerator of both functions is a measure of the immediate value of a food reward, and the denominator of both functions includes the time associated with acquiring the reward. Given that time spent foraging in equation 8.1 includes the delay to reward, d, long-term rate can be written as

$$\text{Long-term rate} = \frac{\text{E\{energy obtained from food\}}}{\text{E\{delay to food\} + E\{other time\}}}, \qquad (8.4)$$

where "other time" refers to all periods in the foraging cycle other than the delay between choice and reward, such as intertrial intervals, postreward handling times, and travel times. Note that, like in equation 8.3, long-term rate drops hyperbolically with the delay to food. Long-term rate maximizing is therefore formally identical to hyperbolic time discounting. Animal experiments have demonstrated hyperbolic time-discounting functions (e.g. Mazur 1987; Rodriguez and Logue 1988). Therefore, if animals are offered a sequence of choices between two rewards—one immediate and another delayed—their choices are basically compatible with those in long-term rate maximizing. This fact has often been overlooked; authors have invoked time discounting when, in reality, rate considerations came into play. The two ap-

proaches could be combined because interruptions during a series of choices will affect the magnitude of the numerator and denominator in equation 8.4; although, an interruption may cause the loss of a reward, the interruption will release time to search for the next reward.

If variability is introduced and an animal must choose between rewards after fixed and variable delays of the same mean duration, the problem of whether to average first and assign value later or vice versa arises again. Unlike a human that faces an isolated choice, a maximizer of long-term rate should calculate averages first and assign value later as in equation 8.2a; this algorithm correctly characterizes the ratio of expected gain over expected time. As a consequence, this forager would be insensitive to risk as discussed in section 8.1.3. However, many experiments have demonstrated that animals, given sequences of choices, prefer variable over fixed delays with the same means (Herrnstein 1964; Davison 1972; Gibbon et al. 1988; Reboreda and Kacelnik 1991; Bateson and Kacelnik 1995a); the results are compatible with those from animals that assign value first and average later, as depicted with equation 8.2b. *Short-term rate* or the *expectation of the ratios* of amount to time is maximized (Bateson and Kacelnik 1995a, 1996):

$$\text{short-term rate} = E\left\{\frac{\text{energy obtained from food}}{\text{time spent foraging}}\right\}. \tag{8.5}$$

Note that the difference between short- and long-term rates is in the position of averaging: for long-term rate, averaging precedes the computation of the ratio of gain over time, whereas for short-term rate, averaging follows the computation of the ratio. "Short" and "long" are often mistakenly interpreted as referring to the "memory window"—the amount of previous experience on which a rate estimate is based.

Evidence for maximizing short-term rate comes from experiments in which animals had to determine when values of fixed- and variable-delay options were equivalent. For example, we performed a titration experiment in which starlings chose between fixed (initially 20 seconds) and variable (2.5 or 60.5 seconds with 50% probability) delays to food. The birds initially preferred the variable option, and we reduced the fixed delay to 5.61 seconds before the birds showed indifference between the two options (fig. 8.8) (Bateson and Kacelnik 1996). At this *indifference point,* short-term rate was approximately equal for the fixed and variable options; the hypothesis that the birds use this currency to value the options was supported.

Further evidence for maximizing short-term rate comes from studies of bumblebees, which are risk averse if there is variability in the volume of nectar in flowers (Real 1981; Waddington et al. 1981). Harder and Real (1987) showed this finding is compatible with bees maximizing short-term rate. In

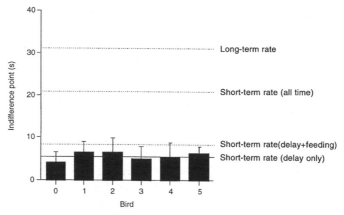

Figure 8.8. Indifference points derived from a titration experiment with six starlings. Bars show the mean (+1 standard deviation) of the value of the fixed delay for which the birds were indifferent between the fixed and variable options. The variable option had two delay times (2.5 and 60.5 seconds) that occurred with equal probability. Lines show the predictions of the six currencies under consideration (only one line appears for long-term rate because the three predictions are identical). The data are significantly different from the predicted data (one sample t tests, $P < .05$) with the exception of expectation of ratios (short-term rate, shown as a solid line) that was calculated with only the delay to reward (from Bateson and Kacelnik 1996).

bees, the correlation between nectar volume, r, and handling time, d, results in the appearance of r in the numerator and denominator of $f(r, d)$; an increasing, but decelerating function that relates the volume of nectar taken to net-intake rate from each decision results (fig. 8.9). This relationship does not lead to risk sensitivity if bees are maximizing long-term rate because volumes are averaged before the computation of rate. However, if bees are maximizing short-term rate, then risk aversion is predicted owing to Jensen's inequality. The magnitude of this effect of variability in reward amount will depend on the proportion of total foraging time that is spent handling the food item. In bees, this time is long; however, in many bird studies, the effects of handling time are likely to be overshadowed by longer delays to reward and intertrial intervals. Thus, variability in reward amount is unlikely to lead to detectable risk aversion even if there is a correlation between reward amount and handling time. In bees, risk aversion may be indicative of maximization of short-term rate given the measured correlation between nectar volume and handling time. In bees, risk aversion is abolished if the amount of reward is controlled with nectar concentration and not nectar volume; this occurs probably because there is no longer a correlation between r and d (fig. 8.9) (see Banschbach and Waddington 1994; Waddington 1995).

In animals, maximizing short-term rate is puzzling because an animal that

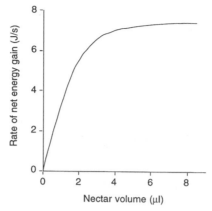

Figure 8.9. Function relating nectar volume to rate of net energy gain derived from the empirically established biomechanics of nectar extraction in bumblebees (replotted from Harder and Real 1987). The nonlinearity results from a correlation between nectar volume and handling time, (although Harder and Real assumed this function to be linear instead of nonlinear as shown in fig. 8.4 for the purposes of deriving this function).

maximizes this currency fails to account correctly for the loss of foraging opportunity and makes choices inconsistent with maximization of long-term rate.

8.5.1 Which Time Intervals Matter?

All time spent foraging including time lost traveling, pursuing, and handling prey items causes loss of foraging opportunity; this is why the denominators in equations 8.1 and 8.4 are the expectations of the sum of all time spent foraging. However, in operant experiments, the delay between the choice of a foraging option and a reward has a much greater impact on the value of an option than similar time intervals after the reward (Snyderman 1987). A reward associated with a short choice-reward delay and a long postreward delay is preferred over a reward associated with two delay lengths that are reversed (such that the choice-reward delay is long and the post-reward delay is short). The strong impact of choice-reward delays is also found in studies in which one of the options has variable delays. For example, in the starling experiment described (Bateson and Kacelnik 1996), there were two additional times in the foraging cycle—the reward time (or handling time) and the intertrial interval. We calculated the indifference points predicted with the six algorithms that result from applying either short- or long-term rates; each calculated with three combinations of time intervals (choice-reward delay only, choice-reward delay plus handling time, and choice-reward delay plus handling time plus the intertrial interval). The indifference point was very close to that predicted

with short-term rate maximization calculated without only the intertrial interval (fig. 8.8). This apparently maladaptive behavior can be interpreted as follows: In the wild, animals never experience time delays between obtaining food and being able to make their next foraging decision. A wild starling is free to decide its next action the moment prey consumption is complete. Thus, starlings may fail to attend to the intertrial intervals because these time intervals do not occur in nature.

To those familiar with the foraging literature, it may seem strange that intertrial intervals have little impact on decision making when tests of the Marginal Value Theorem (Charnov 1976b) indicate that travel time between patches affects patch-leaving decisions (e.g. Kacelnik 1984). This apparent anomaly disappears when one understands that travel times are more analogous to choice-reward delays than intertrial intervals; the travel time *follows* the decision to leave a patch. Like choice-reward delay, travel time is between the forager's decision and its next reward (in the case of the Marginal Value Theorem, encounter with the next patch). In the laboratory, analogues of this foraging paradigm have led to the same conclusions as those from work with individual rewards. Kacelnik and Todd (1992) found that patch-residence time is shorter if travel time is variable than if travel time is fixed when average travel time is constant. This result contradicts maximization of long-term rate; however, this result is consistent with the birds paying attention to the intervals between decisions and their consequences. With this observation, we are strongly reminded of the theme of this book: Ecological models are inadequate without reference to the cognitive processes of animals in nature.

In summary, if animals are faced with sequences of choices, they maximize short-term rate. The only time intervals used to compute this rate are those between the choice and reward. If there is no risk in the choices, this currency results in behavior equivalent to long-term rate maximizing. If there is risk, however, maximizing short-term rate can result in risk proneness when variability is in delay or risk aversion when variability is in reward amount (if there is a correlation between the reward amount and the handling time). Identifying short-term rate as the algorithm that best approximates the currency used by animals to attribute value to foraging options does not explain risk sensitivity. We have not yet identified a functional or mechanistic basis for the use of short-term rate. In the remainder of this section (8.5), discussion is devoted to some possible bases.

8.5.2 The Costs of Short-Term Rate Maximizing

The cognitive mechanisms that produce maximization of short-term rate in laboratory studies may produce behavior that maximizes something close to long-term rate in the natural environment. If this is the case, there would be

no need to explain why animals use a rate algorithm that results in suboptimal behavior in the laboratory. Maximization of short-term rate was initially rejected by optimal-foraging theorists because animals that used it appeared to make grossly maladaptive foraging decisions (Gilliam et al. 1982; Turelli et al. 1982; Possingham et al. 1990). In most experiments designed to separate the predictions of maximizing short and long-term rates, the discrepancy between the predictions was deliberately accentuated. Discrepancy between predictions is generated by programming very high variance in the variable-delay option. The lower the variance in delay, however, the smaller the difference in behavior predicted with maximizing short- and long-term rates. At the limit, when there is no variance in delay, short- and long-term rates are formally identical. Therefore, to determine the cost of maximizing short-term rate for a forager in its natural environment, we need to know the natural variability in the time it takes the animal to obtain prey items. If there is little variation in the natural environment, then the currency used will make little functional difference; even if the animal is maximizing short-term rate, behavior will be similar to that with maximization of long-term rate. To test this idea, measurements were made of the distribution of interprey intervals experienced by starlings that were foraging in natural pastures (Bateson and Whitehead 1996). These intervals were highly variable. Calculations proved that, given the observed level of variability, a maximizer of short-term rate would suffer a substantially lower daily food intake than a maximizer of long-term rate. Thus, at least in this case, maximizing short-term rate cannot be defended on the grounds that it generates adaptive behavior in the natural environment. We must look elsewhere for an explanation for why animals maximize short-term rate.

8.5.3 Associative Learning and Maximizing Short-Term Rate

In this section, we suggest that maximizing short-term rate can be explained mechanistically by considering the processes animals use to learn about causal relationships in the environment. We argue that the basic mechanisms of associative learning constrain animals' abilities to estimate the rate of food intake they are experiencing, and animals, as a result, behave suboptimally in some circumstances and display risk sensitivity.

In animal studies of risk-sensitivity, the foraging options are usually identified with stimuli such as differently colored flowers or pecking keys. When preferences are tested, the subjects choose among the stimuli instead of the rewards. It is therefore crucial to understand the process subjects use to attribute value to the stimuli, which have no worth before training because they are arbitrarily assigned to the foraging options. The training of subjects in foraging experiments follows a protocol that is analogous to that used in psy-

chological studies of conditioning. In a conditioning experiment, the subject is exposed to a neutral stimulus; after some time delay, the subject experiences a meaningful event (such as receipt of food) that has fitness consequences. The originally neutral stimulus is called the conditioned stimulus, or CS, and the meaningful event is called the unconditioned stimulus, or US. For the animal, the truly important event is the arrival of the US, and most of the changes in the animal's psychological state occur at this time. During training, the value of the CS changes every time an US is experienced. A variety of factors are known to affect the rate of acquisition and the asymptotic level of the value attributed to a particular CS (for a review see Dickinson 1980). We will be concerned with only two of these factors first, the delay between the onset of the CS and delivery of the US and, second, the value of the US.

In the following two sections, we will present models that produce maximization of short-term rate as a result of the conditioning process. The first model uses the effects of the CS–US delay on learning to provide a mechanistic explanation for risk proneness with delay. The second model uses the effects of the US value on learning to provide a mechanistic explanation for risk aversion with amount.

8.5.3.1 Risk Proneness in Birds and Mammals and the CS–US Delay

Since Pavlov's work early this century, it has been known that, usually, rewards presented shortly after the onset of the CS strengthen the association between the CS and US more efficiently than rewards presented after a longer delay. Also, the function that relates the speed of learning to the length of the CS–US delay is nonlinear and appears to be approximately hyperbolic for any given intertrial interval (for data in pigeons see Gibbon et al. 1977). We can explain these findings mechanistically as follows. If a naive subject is exposed to a stimulus (such as a red light [CS]), the stimulus leaves a trace in working memory that decays with time so that the strength of the memory is inversely proportional to the time elapsed since the occurrence of the stimulus. If a meaningful event (the US) then occurs, the subject attributes some value to the previously neutral stimulus it remembers and the magnitude of the change in value is proportional to the strength of the memory of the CS (fig. 8.10).

Compare what happens if a subject is trained with (1) a CS followed by a fixed delay to the US and (2) a different CS followed by a variable delay to the US. In the case of the fixed delay, the subject attributes value in proportion to its memory of the CS every time the US occurs, and this value is always the same. In the case of the variable delay, the value attributed to the CS in each trial depends on the length of the CS–US delay: If the delay is short, the change in value will be large; if the delay is long, the change in value will be smaller. Note that this mechanism of learning imposes value assignment

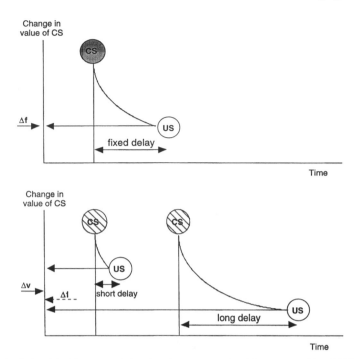

Figure 8.10. Model of how associative learning accounts for risk proneness if variability is in delay. *Upper panel:* the CS–US delay is fixed and results in a fixed change in value of Δf each time the US is experienced. *Lower panel:* the CS–US interval is variable (short or long with equal probability). The average change in the value of CS is Δv. If the function that relates the CS–US interval to the change in value of the CS in nonlinear, then Δv > Δf. The CS associated with the variable delay should be preferred over the CS associated with the fixed delay after similar exposure to the two options, because the CS associated with the variable delay will have a higher value.

before value averaging. If the function that relates the change in value to the CS–US delay is hyperbolic (as the literature suggests), then over a series of trials a CS followed by a fixed delay will acquire less value than a CS followed by a variable delay that has the same average length (another case of Jensen's inequality).

Consider what will occur if the subject, during the course of training, is allowed to choose between a CS associated with a fixed delay and one associated with a variable delay of the same average length. We predict that the subject will prefer the CS associated with the variable delay because this CS has a higher value, which reflects a stronger association with the US. We therefore can explain risk proneness as a product of the way animals learn if variability is in delay to reward. We can also explain why the CS–US delay,

which is equivalent to the choice-reward delay, should be particularly important to foraging animals. However, this idea needs further development because we do not know if risk-sensitive preferences that result from training can translate into the stable long-term preferences in the risk-sensitivity literature. Our explanation does not substitute for an optimality analysis; our explanation merely changes the optimality question asked. We are left to explain why a learning mechanism of this type has evolved.

8.5.3.2 Learning and Risk Aversion in Bees

In this section, we describe an artificial neural network that is designed to simulate how bumblebees learn the amount of nectar gained from flowers of different colors. Artificial neural networks are an increasingly popular tool for modeling the processes involved in learning and decision making. These models illustrate how a nervous system, composed of simple units, can produce seemingly complex behavior (Dukas, this vol. section 1.5). The network we describe is of interest because it produces risk aversion if there is variability in nectar volume. Risk sensitivity occurs as a result of how the volume of nectar obtained from a flower (i.e. the value of the US) affects the value attributed by the bee to flowers of that color (i.e. the CS).

In bumblebees, there is an increasing, decelerating function that relates the volume of nectar in a flower to the net rate of energy gain derived from the nectar (fig. 8.9). Montague et al. (1995) incorporated this finding into a simple neural network model. They assumed that the output, $r(t)$, of a reward neuron, R, is equal to the net energy derived from a flower (figure 8.11). Thus, there is an increasing, decelerating function that relates volume of nectar taken to $r(t)$. Neuron R is connected to neuron P by a nonmodifiable synapse such that neuron R affects the output of P $[=\delta(t)]$ directly. Because of Jensen's inequality, flowers that contain a fixed volume of nectar cause a higher average value of $r(t)$ than flowers that contain variable volumes with a mean that equals the fixed volume. Neuron P also receives input by way of modifiable synapses from three neurons that carry sensory input about the colors of flowers currently in the visual field (Y = yellow, B = blue, N = neutral). The strength of the synapses W_Y, W_B, and W_N is modified according to the following learning rule. If the bee finds food, the change in weight that occurs at a particular synapse is proportional to the activation of that sensory neuron in the previous time step (i.e. how much of that color is in the visual field before the bee landed on the flower) and the current output of P $[\delta(t)]$, which is controlled entirely by $r(t)$ at the time of reward and reflects the net energy gain). Thus, flower colors associated with fixed volumes of nectar result in higher synaptic weights than flowers associated with variable volumes (with Jensen's inequality).

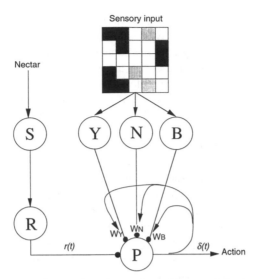

Figure 8.11. Architecture of a neural net that produces risk-averse behavior (redrawn from Montague et al. 1995). P is a simple linear unit that receives convergent sensory information and is hypothesized to correspond to the real bee neuron VUMmx1, which delivers information about reward during classical conditioning experiments (Hammer 1993). At the time (t) the bee gets a volume of nectar, $r(t)$ takes on the value derived from the utility curve shown in figure 8.9. The outputs of neurons N, Y, and B represent changes in the percentage of neutral, yellow, and blue colors in the visual field. These neurons influence the output of neuron P through weights W_N, W_Y, and W_B. The latter two weights are modifiable and W_N is fixed. The output of P, $\delta(t)$, controls the heading of the bee. As the model bee changes its heading above the array of flowers, the activity of these neurons change. Changing the weights with each encounter with a flower enables representation of information about the predictive relationship between sensory input and the amount of nectar obtained.

During the searching phase of foraging, the bee is not obtaining nectar and the output of P, $\delta(t)$, is equal to the weighted sum of the visual inputs [$r(t) = 0$]. This output controls the bee's probability of reorientation. If the bee is primarily looking at a flower color with a high synaptic weight, then $\delta(t)$ will be high and the bee will continue in the same direction. If the bee is looking at a flower color with a low weight, then $\delta(t)$ will be lower and random reorientation will occur. The higher synaptic weights associated with flowers containing fixed volumes inhibit random reorientation and thus promote approaches to these flower types. By contrast, the lower synaptic weights associated with variable-volume flowers result in random reorientation and make approach to variable flowers less likely. This simple model provides a mechanistic explanation for risk aversion in bumblebees. The behavior of the model closely resembles the risk aversion seen in experiments with bumble-

bees presented with different colored flowers associated with fixed or variable volumes of nectar (Real 1981; Waddington et al. 1981; Real et al. 1982).

Note that if the variability is in the concentration instead of the volume of nectar, the model does not predict risk aversion because the function that relates concentration of nectar to net rate of energy gain is linear. In bees, recent results have shown insensitivity to risk if variability is in nectar concentration (Banschbach and Waddington 1994; Waddington 1995).

The learning models we described in this section and section 8.5.3.1 have three crucial features in common. First, both models assume that environmental variability (the CS–US delay or the volume of the US) affects the speed of learning about the CSs associated with the fixed and variable options. Second, in both models, learning is assumed to occur each time an US is encountered, and attribution of value to the CS occurs before the averaging of value. Third, both models assume that the strength of the association of a particular CS to reward affects the probability that the forager will choose, or move toward, this CS. The combination of these features results in maximization of short-term rate and consequent risk sensitivity.

8.6 MECHANISTIC EXPLANATION 2: PERCEPTUAL ERROR

We have not made any reference to the accuracy and precision with which environmental information is processed. In this section, we will first examine the types of errors animals make when they estimate environmental parameters, such as the length of time intervals and the size of food rewards. We will then consider how these errors could affect animals' responses to fixed and variable food sources and the role these errors may have in risk sensitivity.

8.6.1 Weber's Law and the Scalar Property

In the first example, we consider the accuracy and precision of starlings' memories for time intervals. The birds were given a task that simulated foraging in patches (Kacelnik et al. 1990; Brunner et al. 1992); the patch was a standard operant pecking key. Each patch contained an unpredictable number of food items (between zero and four) that could be obtained with pecking at the key. Once the patch was exhausted, the bird had to travel to the next patch by flying between two perches. Within the patch, the food items were delivered on a fixed-interval schedule; the first peck made by the bird after the programmed interval resulted in a food reward. No signal was given when the final food item in the patch was delivered, and therefore the birds could only detect patch exhaustion by timing the intervals between successive food items. When arriving at a patch, the bird would peck at the key, and its pecking frequency increased toward the time of completion of each interval. If a reward was not delivered because the patch was exhausted, pecking rate declined. The time

corresponding to the highest frequency of pecks, the *peak time,* provided an indication of how accurately the birds estimated the fixed interval. The variance in their peak times provided an indication of how precise their estimates were. This experiment was repeated with several different fixed intervals to examine how accuracy and precision varied with the length of the fixed interval. The birds' peak times were close to the fixed interval and showed the birds could measure times accurately. However, the standard deviations of their peak times were proportional to the fixed intervals and showed that precision is inversely proportional to the length of the time interval being estimated (fig. 8.12a).

In a second experiment (Bateson and Kacelnik 1995b), we examined accuracy and precision of starlings' estimates of food amounts. The birds faced a choice between two options indicated with colored pecking keys; each key was associated with a fixed quantity of food. To choose the option that offered the greater amount, the birds had to remember the quantity of food associated with each option. One option was a standard, and in the other, adjusting option, the quantity available was altered systematically from trial to trial. The amount of food available in the adjusting option was increased until the bird detected that the adjusting option yielded more food than the standard; then food yielded by the adjusting option was reduced until the bird detected that the adjusting option yielded less food than the standard. The variation in quantity of reward with the adjusting option therefore gave a measure of the accuracy of discrimination between the standard and the adjusting option. If the bird had perfect memory for all amount sizes, then the quantity of food available in the adjusting option would have ranged between one unit above and below the number of units available in the standard. If the bird only detected a difference when the two rewards differed by at least 3 units, then the adjusting option would have ranged within three units above and below the standard. We examined the range of values in the adjusting option for two differently sized standard values. In both cases, the range of values seen in the adjusting option centered around the same value as the standard value; therefore the birds had accurate memories for the size of food rewards. However, if the size of the standard was increased threefold, the range in the magnitude of the adjusting option increased by a similar factor; therefore, precision was proportional to the magnitude of the reward being remembered (fig. 8.12b).

Two properties apply to starlings' memories of time intervals and amounts of food. First, memories seemed to be centered around the true physical value experienced; the assumption that starlings are able to learn the foraging parameters accurately was justified. Second, even if the foraging parameter had no variance, starlings' estimates were imprecise, and most important, the standard deviations of their estimates were proportional to the value of the parameter being estimated. The phenomenon of proportional standard deviations is some-

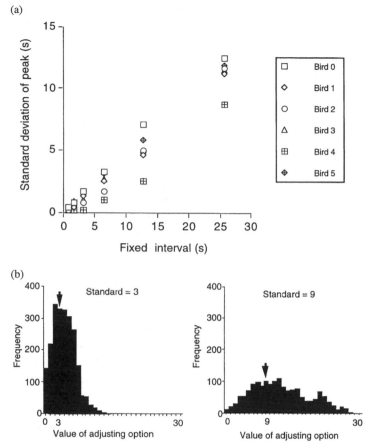

Figure 8.12. Demonstrations of Weber's law in starlings. (*a*) Memory for time. Graph shows the standard deviation of the peak time as a function of the fixed interval. Note the linear relationship between the standard deviation and the fixed interval: Short times are remembered more precisely than long times (replotted from Brunner et al. 1992). (*b*) Memory for amount of food. The range of values taken by the adjusting option with two different standards (three and nine units of food). Note the greater variability when the standard is nine units: Small quantities are remembered more precisely than large quantities (after Bateson and Kacelnik 1995b).

times known as the *scalar property,* which is a strong form of Weber's law. Weber's law is a very widespread phenomenon in discrimination and has been demonstrated for a number of different sensory modalities in many species including rats, pigeons, and humans. We will now examine how the scalar property interacts with environmental variance to give a mechanistic explana-

tion for why animals are generally risk averse if variability is in amount and risk-prone if variability is in delay.

8.6.2 Scalar Expectancy Theory

Reboreda and Kacelnik (1991) (see also Bateson and Kacelnik 1995a) developed a model of risk sensitivity that is based on an information-processing model of timing known as scalar-timing theory (Gibbon et al. 1984; Gibbon et al. 1988). They assumed that the memory formed for a fixed time interval or amount of food can be modeled as a normal distribution with a mean that is equal to the real value of the stimulus and a standard deviation that is proportional to the mean (as suggested by the data presented). The memory representation for a variable option is formed from the sum of the memory distributions of its components. Thus, a food source that offers three or five seeds with equal probability will be remembered as the sum of the memory distributions of three and five seeds. Similarly, a stimulus followed by either a 3 or 5 second delay to food will be remembered as the sum of the memories of these two intervals. The memory representations of variable options will be positively skewed because the memory for the smaller stimulus has a smaller standard deviation than the memory for the large stimulus (fig. 8.13).

It is assumed that subjects choose between two foraging options by (1) retrieving a sample from their memory for each available option; (2) comparing these samples; and (3) choosing the option that offers the more favorable sample (bigger reward or shorter delay). According to the previous description of memory representations, memory distributions for variable options are skewed to the right; however, memory distributions for fixed options with the same mean are symmetric around the true mean. If the subject makes a choice by picking a pair of samples—one from the variable and one from the fixed memory distribution—then in more than half of the comparisons the sample from the memory for the variable option will be smaller than the sample from the memory for the fixed option. Thus, the model predicts that an option that offers variability in delay to food should be chosen more often than a fixed alternative because the memory for the variable option will more often yield the shorter sample. An option that offers variability in amount of food should be chosen less often than a fixed alternative again because the memory for the variable option will more often yield a smaller sample. The difference in choice arises because options that offer short delays are good and should be preferred; options that offer small amounts are bad and should be avoided.

The major prediction of this model agrees with experimental observations because animals are usually risk averse if variability is in amount and risk prone if variability is in delay (fig. 8.1a) (Gibbon et al. 1988; Reboreda and

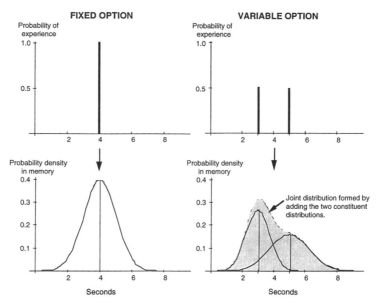

Figure 8.13. The scalar timing theory information-processing model. *Upper panels:* the experienced distribution of outcomes (delays or amounts) in fixed (*left*) and variable (*right*) options. *Lower panels:* the distributions that are assumed to be formed in memory as a result of the experiences (*upper panels*). Note the skew in the memory distribution for the variable option that results from the differing accuracies with which the constituent stimuli are represented (reproduced from Bateson and Kacelnik 1995a).

Kacelnik 1991; Bateson and Kacelnik 1995a). The model is also attractive because it predicts partial preferences, unlike the other models. The model, however, fails in some respects. First, although the qualitative agreement of data with the model is strong, there are quantitative discrepancies. For instance, the model predicts that animals should be indifferent between a fixed and variable option if the fixed option is equal to the *geometric mean* of the two alternative possibilities (amounts or delays) in the variable option (Bateson and Kacelnik 1995a) (i.e. the square root of the product of the two alternative possibilities in the variable option). Subsequent research, however, has demonstrated that, for delays at least, indifference occurs at approximately the *harmonic mean* (i.e. the outcome of maximizing short-term rate) (Bateson and Kacelnik 1996; Mazur 1984, 1986). Second, the model does not address the observed effects of energy budget on preference: It predicts universal risk proneness if variability is in delay and risk aversion if variability is in amount. Third, the model does not address what animals should choose if the two foraging options differ in the variance of both amount and delay simultaneously. A more recent version of scalar timing (Brunner et al. 1994)

deals with some of these problems; however, further developments are required to address all aspects of the data available in the risk-sensitivity literature.

8.7 CONCLUSIONS

The theories we have described rely on two types of explanations: functional (or evolutionary) arguments that consider the circumstances under which risk-sensitive behavior can be adaptive and mechanistic arguments that consider how risk sensitivity may emerge as a result of the cognitive processes used by animals to perceive, learn, and remember information about the environment. Functional and mechanistic approaches are complementary forms of explanation in animal behavior because all adaptive behavior must be implemented in some way (Tinbergen 1963). However, as we have presented with many examples, these alternative forms of explanation often produce different predictions about the details of risk-sensitive behavior. Different predictions occur because different approaches have been taken by behavioral ecologists and psychologists. Functional hypotheses are driven by the assumption that risk-sensitive behavior is adaptive. By contrast, mechanistic hypotheses indicate that risk sensitivity is a consequence of the cognitive mechanisms that underlie behavior. Although these mechanistic hypotheses are based on observations of how animals actually behave, these hypotheses do not address the adaptive importance of the mechanisms they postulate or the risk-sensitive behavior they predict. In the future, we hope to see a fusion of these two approaches with production of models that give equal weight to cognitive and evolutionary considerations.

By accounting for empirical observations of risk sensitivity, we found that all of the approaches have advantages and disadvantages, which strongly suggest that an integrated approach is the way forward. Risk-sensitive foraging theory is the only theory that can explain why the direction of risk-sensitive preferences should be affected by energy budget. However, this theory does not explain the many failures to obtain shifts in risk preference or why animals should more often be risk averse with amount but risk prone with delay. The theory is difficult to test conclusively because it has many variants. To make precise predictions about how manipulations will affect behavior, it is necessary to know the current status of an animal precisely. One effect of these uncertainties is that only qualitative predictions are being tested. For instance, the energy-budget rule predicts exclusive preferences; however, even the best examples of shifts in preference are only partial shifts in the predicted directions.

Time discounting that arises from the probability of interruption potentially explains why animals should be risk prone if variability is in delay. However,

time discounting fails quantitatively because with its simplest applications in isolated choices, it predicts exponential time discounting, and there is clear evidence that humans discount time hyperbolically. Also models that are based solely on time discounting do not address the effects on choice of variability in amount.

Maximizing short-term rate can account for the hyperbolic time discounting observed in animals and the consequent risk proneness if variability is in delay. However, assuming that animals maximize this currency does not explain all the data. The currency can only accommodate risk aversion with variable amounts if there is a positive correlation between amount and the handling time. Also maximizing short-term rate does not address the effects of energy budget. The major problem in maximizing short-term rate is explaining its functional and mechanistic bases. We suggested that maximizing short-term rate may emerge as a consequence of the basic mechanisms of associative learning that can be defended as adaptive in a context that is broader than that of risk sensitivity.

Scalar-timing theory can explain partial preferences and why animals are risk prone with variable delays and risk averse with variable amounts. However, the theory sometimes fails quantitatively and does not address the effects of energy budget.

Thus, whether risk-sensitive foraging preferences are largely the products of direct selection driven by the fitness consequences of variable food sources or whether they are consequences of selection for efficient cognitive mechanisms in broader contexts are unanswered problems. Of course, it is possible that the phenomena we categorize as risk sensitivity may only be superficially related; these phenomena may be the products of different underlying mechanisms, or they may have evolved under different selective pressures (in which case they will never be explained with a single unifying theory). Whatever the answers will be, it is unquestionable that satisfactory explanations for risk sensitivity will include ecological and cognitive considerations. This conclusion is not specific for risk sensitivity; however, its truth is particularly well exemplified with this area of research—perhaps because the field has attracted such extensive data collection and optimality modeling.

8.8 SUMMARY

Animals presented with foraging options that offer the same average rate of gain but differ in variance generally show strong preferences. This widespread behavioral phenomenon is known as risk sensitivity. Risk-sensitivity has implications for the ecological interaction of animals with their environments and the cognitive mechanisms that underlie foraging behavior. Several factors affect the direction of risk-sensitive preferences: the component of rate that

is variable (amount or time), the energy needs of the subjects, and possibly the typical body weight of the species. We reviewed explanations for these data arising from functional, descriptive, and mechanistic arguments. Animals can respond to environmental variance in ways that enhance fitness, and there is some evidence for use of adaptive policies such as the energy-budget rule. However, some well-documented cognitive processes also generate risk-sensitive behavior that does not appear to be directly adaptive. The broader adaptive importance of these cognitive processes remains to be established; however, we believe that cognitive processes cannot be ignored in any form of foraging research.

ACKNOWLEDGMENTS

We thank the Wellcome Trust for financial support (grants 45243/Z/95 and 461/Z/95), NATO Collaborative Research Grant (920308), and the many people with whom we have discussed the ideas presented in this chapter.

LITERATURE CITED

Banschbach, V. S., and K. D. Waddington. 1994. Risk-sensitivity in honeybees: No consensus among individuals and no effect of colony honey stores. *Animal Behaviour* 47:933–941.

Barkan, C. P. L. 1990. A field test of risk-sensitive foraging in black-capped chickadees (*Parus atricapillus*). *Ecology* 71:391–400.

Barnard, C. J., and C. A. J. Brown. 1985. Risk-sensitive foraging in common shrews (*Sorex araneus* L.). *Behavioral Ecology and Sociobiology* 16:161–164.

Barnard, C. J., C. A. J. Brown, A. Houston, and J. M. McNamara. 1985. Risk-sensitive foraging in common shrews: An interruption model and the effects of mean and variance in reward rate. *Behavioral Ecology and Sociobiology* 18:139–146.

Bateson, M., and A. Kacelnik. 1995a. Preferences for fixed and variable food sources: Variability in amount and delay. *Journal of the Experimental Analysis of Behaviour* 63:313–329.

———. 1995b. Accuracy of memory for amount in the foraging starling (*Sturnus vulgaris*). *Animal Behaviour* 50:431–443.

———. 1996. Rate currencies and the foraging starling: The fallacy of the averages revisited. *Behavioral Ecology* 7:341–352.

———. 1997. Starlings' preferences for predictable and unpredictable delays to food: Risk-sensitivity or time discounting? *Animal Behaviour* 53:1129–1142.

Bateson, M., and S. C. Whitehead. 1996. The energetic costs of alternative rate currencies in the foraging starling. *Ecology* 77:1303–1307.

Brunner, D., J. Gibbon, and S. Fairhurst. 1994. Choice between fixed and variable delays with different reward amounts. *Journal of Experimental Psychology: Animal Behavior Processes* 20:331–346.

Brunner, D., A. Kacelnik, and J. Gibbon. 1992. Optimal foraging and timing processes

in the starling, *Sturnus vulgaris:* Effect of inter-capture interval. *Animal Behaviour* 44:597–613.

Caraco, T. 1981. Energy budgets, risk, and foraging preferences in dark-eyed juncos (*Junco hyemalis*). *Behavioral Ecology and Sociobiology* 8:213–217.

———. 1982. Aspects of risk-aversion in foraging white-crowned sparrows. *Animal Behaviour* 30:719–727.

———. 1983. White-crowned sparrows (*Zonotrichia leucophrys*) foraging preferences in a risky environment. *Behavioral Ecology and Sociobiology* 12:63–69.

Caraco, T., W. U. Blanckenhorn, G. M. Gregory, J. A. Newman, G. M. Recer, and S. M. Zwicker. 1990. Risk-sensitivity: Ambient temperature affects foraging choice. *Animal Behaviour* 39:338–345.

Caraco, T., A. Kacelnik, N. Mesnik, and M. Smulewitz. 1992. Short-term rate maximization when rewards and delays covary. *Animal Behaviour* 44:441–447.

Caraco, T., and S. L. Lima. 1985. Foraging juncos: Interaction of reward mean and variability. *Animal Behaviour* 33:216–224.

Caraco, T., S. Martindale, and T. S. Whittam. 1980. An empirical demonstration of risk sensitive foraging preferences. *Animal Behaviour* 28:820–830.

Cartar, R. V. 1990. A test of risk sensitive foraging in wild bumblebees. *Ecology* 72: 888–895.

Case, D. A., P. Nichols, and E. Fantino. 1995. Pigeon's preference for variable-interval water reinforcement under widely varied water budgets. *Journal of the Experimental Analysis of Behavior* 64:299–311.

Charnov, E. L. 1976a. Optimal foraging: Attack strategy of a mantid. *American Naturalist* 110:141–151.

———. 1976b. Optimal foraging: The marginal value theorem. *Theoretical Population Biology* 9:129–136.

Croy, M. I., and R. N. Hughes. 1991. Effects of food supply, hunger, danger, and competition on choice of foraging location by the fifteen-spined stickleback, *Spinachia spinachia* L. *Animal Behaviour* 42:131–139.

Davison, M. C. 1972. Preference for mixed-interval versus fixed-interval schedules: Number of component intervals. *Journal of the Experimental Analysis of Behavior* 17:169–176.

Dickinson, A. 1980. *Contemporary Animal Learning Theory.* Cambridge: Cambridge University Press.

Epstein, R. 1981. Amount consumed as a function of magazine-cycle duration. *Behavior Analysis Letters* 1:63–66.

Essock, S. M., and E. P. Rees. 1974. Preference for and effects of variable as opposed to fixed reinforcer duration. *Journal of the Experimental Analysis of Behavior* 21: 89–97.

Gibbon, J., M. D. Baldock, C. Locurto, L. Gold, and H. S. Terrace. 1977. Trial and intertrial durations and autoshaping. *Journal of Experimental Psychology: Animal Behavior Processes* 3:264–284.

Gibbon, J., R. M. Church, S. Fairhurst, and A. Kacelnik. 1988. Scalar Expectancy Theory and choice between delayed rewards. *Psychological Review* 95:102–114.

Gibbon, J., R. M. Church, and W. H. Meck. 1984. Scalar timing in memory. In J.

Gibbon and L. Allan, eds., *Timing and Time Perception,* 52–77. New York: New York Academy of Sciences.

Gilliam, J. F., R. F. Green, and N. E. Pearson. 1982. The fallacy of the traffic policeman: A response to Templeton and Lawlor. *American Naturalist* 119:875–878.

Ha, J. C. 1991. Risk-sensitive foraging: The role of ambient temperature and foraging time. *Animal Behaviour* 41:528–529.

Ha, J. C., P. N. Lehner, and S. D. Farley. 1990. Risk-prone foraging behaviour in captive grey jays *Perisoreus canadensis. Animal Behaviour* 39:91–96.

Hamm, S. L., and S. J. Shettleworth. 1987. Risk aversion in pigeons. *Journal of Experimental Psychology: Animal Behavior Processes* 13:376–383.

Hammer, M. 1993. An identified neuron mediates the unconditioned stimulus in associative olfactory learning in honeybees. *Nature* 366:59–63.

Harder, L. D. 1986. Effects of nectar concentration and flower depth on flower handling efficiency of bumblebees. *Oecologia* 69:309–315.

Harder, L. D., and L. A. Real. 1987. Why are bumblebees risk-averse? *Ecology* 68: 1104–1108.

Herrnstein, R. J. 1964. Aperiodicity as a factor in choice. *Journal of the Experimental Analysis of Behavior* 7:179–182.

Houston, A. I. 1991. Risk-sensitive foraging theory and operant psychology. *Journal of the Experimental Analysis of Behavior* 56:585–589.

Houston, A. I., and J. M. McNamara. 1982. A sequential approach to risk-taking. *Animal Behaviour* 30:1260–1261.

———. 1985. The choice of two prey types that minimizes the probability of starvation. *Behavioral Ecology and Sociobiology* 17:135–141.

———. 1988. A framework for the functional analysis of behaviour. *Behavioral and Brain Sciences* 11:117–163.

———. 1990. Risk-sensitive foraging and temperature. *Trends in Ecology and Evolution* 5:131–132.

Jensen, J. L. 1906. Sur les fonctions convexes et les inequalites entre les valeurs moyennes. *Acta Mathematica* 30:175–193.

Kacelnik, A. 1984. Central place foraging in starlings (*Sturnus vulgaris*). I. Patch residence time. *Journal of Animal Ecology* 53:283–299.

Kacelnik, A., and M. Bateson. 1996. Risky theories: The effects of variance on foraging decisions. *American Zoologist* 36:402–434.

Kacelnik, A., D. Brunner, and J. Gibbon. 1990. Timing mechanisms in optimal foraging: Some applications of scalar expectancy theory. In R. N. Hughes, ed., *Behavioural Mechanisms of Food Selection,* 63–81. Berlin: Springer-Verlag.

Kacelnik, A., and A. I. Todd 1992. Psychological mechanisms and the Marginal Value Theorem: Effect of variability in travel time on patch exploitation. *Animal Behaviour* 43:313–322.

Kagel, J. H., L. Green, and T. Caraco. 1986. When foragers discount the future: Constraint or adaptation? *Animal Behaviour* 34:271–283.

Kagel, J. H., D. N. MacDonald, R. C. Battalio, S. White, and L. Green. 1986. Risk-aversion in rats (*Rattus norvegicus*) under varying levels of resource availability. *Journal of Comparative Psychology* 100:95–100.

Krebs, J. R., D. W. Stephens, and W. J. Sutherland. 1983. Perspectives in optimal

foraging. In A. H. Brush, and G. A. Clark, eds., *Perspectives in Ornithology,* 165–216. New York: Cambridge University Press.

Leventhal, A. M., R. F. Morell, E. J. Morgan, and C. C. Perkins. 1959. The relation between mean reward and mean reinforcement. *Journal of Experimental Psychology* 59:284–287.

Logan, F. A. 1965. Decision making by rats: Uncertain outcome choices. *Journal of Comparative and Physiological Psychology* 59:246–251.

Mazur, J. E. 1985. Probability and delay of reinforcement as factors in discrete-trial choice. *Journal of the Experimental Analysis of Behavior* 43:341–351.

———. 1987. An adjusting procedure for studying delayed reinforcement. In M. L. Commons, J. E. Mazur, J. A. Nevin, and H. Rachlin, eds., *Quantitative Analyses of Behavior: The Effects of Delay and of Intervening Events on Reinforcement Value,* 55–73. Hilsdale, N.J.: Erlbaum.

McNamara, J. M. 1983. Optimal-control of the diffusion-coefficient of a simple diffusion process. *Mathematics of Operations Research* 8:373–380.

———. 1984. Control of a diffusion by switching between 2 drift-diffusion coefficient pairs. *Siam Journal on Control and Optimisation* 22:87–94.

McNamara, J. M., and A. I. Houston. 1987. A general framework for understanding the effects of variability and interuptions on foraging behaviour. *Acta Biotheoretica* 36:3–22.

———. 1992. Risk-sensitive foraging: A review of the theory. *Bulletin of Mathematical Biology* 54:355–378.

McNamara, J. M., S. Merad, and A. I. Houston. 1991. A model of risk-sensitive foraging for a reproducing animal. *Animal Behaviour* 41:787–792.

Menlove, R. L., H. M. Inden, and E. G. Madden. 1979. Preference for fixed over variable access to food. *Animal Learning and Behavior* 7:499–503.

Montague, P. R., P. Dayan, C. Person, and C. J. Sejnowski. 1995. Bee foraging in uncertain environments using predictive Hebbian learning. *Nature* 377:725–728.

Moore, F. R., and P. A. Simm. 1986. Risk-sensitive foraging by a migratory bird (*Dendroica coronata*). *Experientia* 42:1054–1056.

Myerson, J., and L. Green. 1995. Discounting of delayed rewards: Models of individual choice. *Journal of the Experimental Analysis of Behavior* 64:263–276.

Possingham, H. P., A. I. Houston, and J. M. McNamara. 1990. Risk-averse foraging in bees: A comment on the model of Harder and Real. *Ecology* 71:1622–1624.

Real, L. A. 1981. Uncertainty and pollinator-plant interactions: The foraging behavior of bees and wasps on artificial flowers. *Ecology* 62:20–26.

Real, L. A., J. Ott, and E. Silverfine. 1982. On the trade-off between mean and variance in foraging: An experimental analysis with bumblebees. *Ecology* 63:1617–1623.

Reboreda, J. C., and A. Kacelnik. 1991. Risk sensitivity in starlings: Variability in food amount and food delay. *Behavioral Ecology* 2:301–308.

Rider, D. P. 1983. Choice for aperiodic versus periodic ratio schedules: A comparison of concurrent and concurrent-chains procedures. *Journal of the Experimental Analysis of Behavior* 40:225–237.

Rodriguez, M. L., and A. W. Logue. 1988. Adjusting delay to reinforcement: Comparing choice in pigeons and humans. *Journal of Experimental Psychology: Animal Behavior Processes* 14:105–117.

Samuelson, P. A. 1937. A note on the measurement of utility. *Review of Economic Studies* 4:155–161.

Schmid-Hempel, P., A. Kacelnik, and A. I. Houston 1985. Honeybees maximize efficiency by not filling their crop. *Behavioral Ecology and Sociobiology* 17:61–66.

Snyderman, M. 1987. Prey selection and self-control. In M. L. Commons, J. E. Mazur, J. A. Nevin, and H. Rachlin, eds., *Quantitative Analyses of Behavior,* 283–308. Hillsdale, N.J.: Erlbaum.

Staddon, J. E. R., and N. K. Innis. 1966. Preference for fixed vs. variable amounts of reward. *Psychonomic Science* 4:193–194.

Stephens, D. W. 1981. The logic of risk-sensitive foraging preferences. *Animal Behaviour* 29:628–629.

Stephens, D. W., and J. R. Krebs. 1986. *Foraging Theory*. Princeton, N.J.: Princeton University Press.

Stephens, D. W., and R. C. Ydenberg. 1982. Risk aversion in the great tit. In D. W. Stephens, ed.; *Stochasticity in Foraging Theory: Risk and Information,* Ph.D. diss., Oxford University.

Tinbergen, N. 1963. On aims and methods of ethology. *Zeitschrift fur Tierpsychologie* 20:410–433.

Turelli, M., J. H. Gillespie, and T. W. Shoener. 1982. The fallacy of the fallacy of the averages in ecological optimization theory. *American Naturalist* 119:879–884.

Tuttle, E. M., L. Wulfson, and T. Caraco. 1990. Risk-aversion, relative abundance of resources, and foraging preferences. *Behavioral Ecology and Sociobiology* 26:165–171.

Waddington, K. D. 1995. Bumblebees do not respond to variance in nectar concentration. *Ethology* 101:33–38.

Waddington, K. D., T. Allen, and B. Heinrich. 1981. Floral preferences of bumblebees (*Bombus edwardsii*) in relation to intermittent versus continuous rewards. *Animal Behaviour* 29:779–784.

Wunderle, J. M., M. Santa-Castro, and N. Fletcher. 1987. Risk-averse foraging by bananaquits on netative energy budgets. *Behavioral Ecology and Sociobiology* 21:249–255.

Young, J. S. 1981. Discrete-trial choice in pigeons: Effects of reinforcer magnitude. *Journal of the Experimental Analysis of Behavior* 35:23–29.

Young, R. J., H. Clayton, and C. J. Barnard. 1990. Risk sensitive foraging in bitterlings, *Rhodeus sericus:* Effects of food requirement and breeding site quality. *Animal Behaviour* 40:288–297.

Zabludoff, S. D., J. Wecker, and T. Caraco. 1988. Foraging choice in laboratory rats: Constant vs. variable delay. *Behavioural Processes* 16:95–110.

CHAPTER NINE

Behavioral Decisions about Foraging and Predator Avoidance

RONALD C. YDENBERG

9.1 INTRODUCTION

Everyone has watched a foraging bumblebee. Flying to an inflorescence, she usually alights on the bottom floret and works her way upward, sometimes visiting one or just a few florets, sometimes systematically probing each floret before moving to the next inflorescence. Hidden carefully somewhere in the vicinity is her home colony, with a queen, other workers, and a group of larvae whose growth and development are dependent on the proficiency with which she and her sister workers deliver nectar and pollen. Her sensory apparatus and nervous system developed under the direction of genes she inherited from her ancestors and are designed to enable exploitation of the flowers that supply essential resources. Ultimately, the reproductive success of the colony—the number of daughter queens and drones produced—depends on her foraging performance. I refer readers to Heinrich (1978) for a highly enjoyable and informative account of bumblebee biology.

The flight of the bumblebee poses important challenges; the senses and nervous system must deal with the formidable problems of proficient foraging in an everchanging and hazardous environment. To understand the bumblebee's experience, we must view the world with a bee's eye. The importance of adopting this perspective was recognized almost a century ago by physiologists such as Jakob von Uexküll—who was the first to promote the idea that an anthropomorphic viewpoint precludes understanding another species' behavior (see Thorpe 1979). Jakob von Uexküll taught that each species experiences the world in a unique way and the experience is determined with sensory abilities. This idea was very important in the development of ethology, and its practitioners laid great emphasis on von Uexküll's notion of the *Umwelt*—the sensory world in which each species lives.

While an appreciation of each species' unique Umwelt is important, generalizations are also required to build a broad understanding, which can be applied to many species. During the last thirty years, behavioral ecologists have developed a number of theoretical ideas that consider general properties of behavior. In a foraging context, much of the emphasis has been on analyzing

decisions (Kacelnik and Krebs 1991). The fusion of simple general models from behavioral ecology with ethological ideas, such as that of Umwelt, and techniques from experimental psychology is currently creating the new discipline of cognitive ecology (Real 1993).

In this chapter, I will introduce some current ideas in cognitive ecology that are relevant to understanding foraging theory. I first will consider the structure of foraging models and the distinct foraging processes of feeding and provisioning. I next will explore the role of information in these models, and I hope to indicate how the study of foraging may help the development of cognitive ecology. I will conclude the chapter by considering the function of predation risk in foraging models.

9.2 FORAGING THEORY

9.2.1 The Function of Foraging Theory in Cognitive Ecology

The most basic assumption in foraging theory is that natural selection has led to the evolution of proficient foraging. As a result, the focus in foraging theory is on fitness costs and benefits (Stephens and Krebs 1986). The decision mechanisms involved are rarely specified. An important goal in cognitive ecology is to expand our understanding of these mechanisms; there are two ways in which a well-developed foraging theory—with its emphasis on ultimate factors—may enable this endeavor. First, foraging theory suggests what factors are important and, therefore, the sorts of things foragers ought to evaluate as they forage. Further, the models suggest how measurements may be integrated to form a view of the world that is relevant to the forager.

Second, foraging theory may help illuminate details of the mechanisms involved. When predictions on the basis of foraging models do not match experimental measurements, there are two possible explanations. The first explanation is that the prediction is wrong because some important factor was ignored in the model or the theory was not applicable.

The other and more interesting explanation is that the design of the experiment revealed some mechanism that caused the animals to perform "incorrectly." This is of direct interest because the nature of the "error" indicates the workings of the cognitive mechanisms used by the forager to make foraging decisions. For example, errors in estimating or recalling time intervals are implicated with the "unwillingness" of foragers to wait as long as foraging models predict they should. Such errors are assumed to arise from properties of the timing or memory mechanisms (Bateson and Kacelnik, this vol. section 8.6).

In other examples, investigators compared the observed and expected performances of foragers to derive insights into mechanisms. For example, Pyke (1981) observed hummingbirds foraging on inflorescences of varying com-

plexity. He constructed vertical inflorescenses with 12 florets arranged linearly, in a simple spiral, or in a more complex pattern that resembled real *Ipomopsis* inflorescences—a favorite forage plant. Pyke measured hummingbirds' performances during visits to an inflorescence by counting the number of revisits to florets that had been visited already (and were therefore empty). Surprisingly, birds performed best on the natural array and most poorly on the linear array. Pyke concluded that the mechanism used by the birds to decide which floret to fly to next (the "movement rule") had evolved so that birds performed well in the complex arrays of natural patches of flowers; poor performance on simple arrays was a side effect. Although this side effect is of little or no consequence to wild hummingbirds who live and forage in complex habitats, this side effect may be very important to cognitive ecologists who study hummingbird foraging on simple arrays in the laboratory (e.g. Sutherland and Gass 1995).

Cheverton (1983) made a similar observation to that of Pyke, but he reached a very different conclusion. He found that bumblebees performed poorly on simple floral arrays in the laboratory and concluded that the bees used evolved simple-movement rules (in this case, involving handedness) to solve difficult foraging problems. He suggested that the benefits of a simple rule used to decide quickly where to move next outweigh the costs of taking more time to make a better decision. Obviously, this conclusion necessitates knowing what "better" means; foraging theory may contribute to this knowledge.

9.2.2 Foraging Models

9.2.2.1 Terminology

In the following, I set out the basic parts of a foraging model. To be of use in cognitive ecology, a model must be flexible enough to include a wide diversity of foraging behavior yet simple enough that generalizations can be derived.

A number of terms are important and must be defined and used carefully. In the context of cognitive ecology, the central tenet of foraging theory is that selection (natural, sexual, or artificial) has acted on the structure and functioning of *decision mechanisms*. These mechanisms integrate information from the sensory organs and internal indicators of state (e.g. hunger) to allow choice among the possible alternative behaviors in a foraging situation (called *tactics* or *options*). Certain variants of the decision mechanism are assumed to have been favored by selection because they lead to behavior that best achieves a *strategy* (or objective or design feature), such as maximum rate of energy intake, minimum time spent foraging to reach a requirement, maximum delivery, minimum probability of an energy shortfall, or a host of others.

The investigator's measure of foraging performance or proficiency is called

a *currency*. The currency is often referred to as a surrogate measure for fitness. In fact in much literature, there is hardly a distinction among currency, strategy, and fitness. I feel, for two reasons, that it is useful to reserve the term "currency" for the investigator's measures of foraging performance. First, different performance measures may be differently or even oppositely related to different fitness components (Salant et al. 1996). For example, the amount of food stored may increase with the amount of energy that a hoarding animal expends to fill its larder. The animal's survival, however, may decline with energy expenditure because of increased exposure to predators. The amount of food stored and survival both depend on energy expenditure, and both are positively related to fitness. The forager, however, cannot maximize the amount of food stored and survival simultaneously; the forager must balance two opposing demands. The investigator, however, may gain some insight by ignoring one of these demands and working to understand just how the other is related to fitness. Measuring fitness properly requires many details of population structure and density dependence not available in most foraging studies (Mylius and Diekmann 1995); I believe it is naive to assume that currencies and fitness are generally closely related.

Moreover, this assumption is not necessary. For example, Alexander (1982) successfully studied traits such as bone structure without making an explicit fitness assumption. In the case of femurs, he used the thickness of the femoral wall relative to femoral diameter as the performance measure. He assumed that this measured attribute was acted on by natural selection to minimize the weight necessary to bear a given load (the strategy). This assumption is different and less restrictive than the assumption that proposes such femurs maximize fitness.

Second, even if one could specify a currency directly related to fitness, there is no reason to suppose that the mechanisms used by animals to evaluate and measure their performance are similar to those used by investigators. In fact, the mechanisms are likely to be very different. Field biologists use stopwatches, but the foragers they study employ a cognitive timing mechanism that seems to function differently (Bateson and Kacelnik, this vol. section 8.6). This distinction between the investigator's measure of the animal's experience and the animal's own experience is especially important in cognitive ecology; with this distinction, a much better understanding of the cognitive and other mechanisms that animals use in foraging situations will be gained.

9.2.2.2 Adaptations and Constraints

As explained, the existence of an optimum is a deduction that is based on knowing how natural selection works; an optimum is not a manifestation of blind faith. There are undoubtedly many cases in which behavior is poorly

matched to the environment; however, to discover these cases, we must define well and poorly matched. The term "optimality" has been widely associated with foraging theory; however, this term perhaps is best reserved for reference to the usually mathematical procedure of determining which behavioral options are most proficient. Used in this way, the term "optimal forager" refers to a forager that uses the mathematical techniques of optimality to determine which behavioral option is best in a specific situation; the term does not imply a perfectly performing forager. Animals do not use stopwatches; likewise, animals do not use differential calculus to solve foraging problems. Optimality is merely an investigator's technique that may help illuminate the biology.

A paper by Marrow et al. (1996) illustrates how, when used well, optimality does not lead merely to wildly speculative adaptationist tales, but can be used to explore both adaptations and constraints. Marrow et al. studied the reproduction of Soay sheep (*Ovus aries*), an ancient domesticated breed now feral on the St. Kilda archipelago of Scotland. In this harsh environment, the population fluctuates greatly and mortality is high every three or four years. Marrow et al. (1996) used an optimality approach to model the reproductive decisions of Soay ewes. In spring, each model ewe chose to not reproduce at all, have a single lamb, or have twins. Reproduction carries mortality risks, and lambs born near the population peak are less likely to survive than those borne near the trough of the cycle. With use of field data from a long-running study on the island, the models that made reproductive decisions with information about body condition and cycle stage (i.e. population density) performed best. Ewes should have twins when in good condition and at low and moderate population densities; however, ewes should behave more conservatively when in poor condition and as the population peak approaches. While the data show that females are sensitive to their own condition when making reproductive decisions, they do not make use of population density information—although use of this information would be simple. Somehow, ewes are constrained from using population density information. Marrow et al. (1996) suggested that perhaps ancient human selection for high fertility has made the breed less conservative than it ought to be in this environment. This sheep example shows how optimality can be used in the investigation of alternative behaviors, the nature of proficiency, and the mechanisms used to make behavioral decisions.

9.2.3 Foraging Processes

By adopting von Uexküll's idea of Umwelt, we acknowledge that every species' foraging situation is different and that a single strategy is unlikely to be universally applicable. In the following sections, I will outline a general framework that attempts to recognize some of this diversity. The emphasis is on general properties instead of particular models. The aim is to gain insight

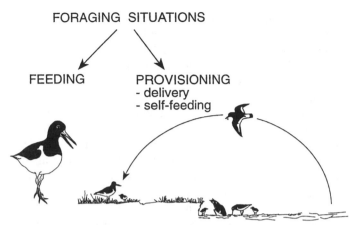

Figure 9.1. Classification of foraging situations that are exemplified with oystercatchers stud-ied by Bruno Ens (1992). While *feeding,* animals capture prey for their own immediate con-sumption; oystercatchers are feeders for most of the year. While *provisioning,* a forager *deliv-ers* some of the prey captured, obtaining the metabolic power for this activity by eating the other prey *(self feeding)*; oystercatchers become provisioners during the breeding season. Some parental oystercatchers must fly to deliver prey to inland nests; however, others have ter-ritories along the salt marsh edge and can take their broods to the foraging area. For these oystercatchers, provisioning does not involve a flight to a nest, but they give some of the cap-tured prey to their chicks (delivery) and eat some themselves (self feeding). Thus, provi-sioning is not the same as central-place foraging.

into the kinds of information that are relevant, and how these kinds of informa-tion may be integrated to make foraging decisions.

First, the foraging context must be identified as *provisioning* or *feeding* (fig. 9.1). These are distinct foraging processes (Ydenberg et al. 1994). The difference is that feeders consume prey, but provisioners deliver a resource—food, water, or nesting material—to their offspring, nest mates, or a storage site. Provisioners must obtain the metabolic power for delivery by consuming some of the prey captured (usually on the spot, see Kacelnik 1984) or by searching for and consuming different foods (see Waite and Ydenberg 1994a), a process termed self feeding.

The difference can be appreciated by considering a situation that involves the delivery of a resource other than food. Male black wheatears (*Oenanthe leucura*) have evolved, apparently by sexual selection (Soler et al. 1996), the strange habit of delivering thousands of small stones to their nest site. Many social insects such as paper wasps deliver water to the colony (Kasuya 1982) on hot days. Water is collected at puddles and other sources and transported in the wasp's crop to the nest, where it is regurgitated and evaporated to cool the nest. A wasp must power the delivery of the water with energy obtained

by self feeding; in doing so, the wasp must somehow take account of the time and energy needed for self feeding. To subtract the energy spent delivering the water from the water delivered does not make sense. This is not because we measure energy and water in different units (we could measure the weight of food needed to provide the energy, and the weight of the water in milligrams). The subtraction does not make sense because the water and energy are used differently. The same is true when food is delivered.

Second, provisioning need not involve delivery to a central place (fig. 9.1) (Orians and Pearson 1979). The essence of provisioning is that some or all of the resource is not for the provisioner's immediate consumption; the resource is delivered to an offspring, a nest mate, or a hoard, or the resource is given to another individual at the site where it is captured. (Ydenberg [1994] also considered provisioning situations in which food was consumed and later fed to offspring as a processed product, as in lactation.)

Feeding and provisioning are bound to be experienced differently by foragers—not least because a delivered resource is not consumed and, hence, does not affect hunger. While feeding or self feeding, a forager can assess its need for more food with feedback mechanisms that occur in the stomach, gut, or blood. However, provisioners must rely on very different feedback mechanisms to inform them that a demand has been satisfied. Parent songbirds respond to the level of begging by their nestlings (Price and Ydenberg 1995). Water-foraging honeybees apparently measure the eagerness with which workers in the hive unload them to determine how much more water is needed (Kühnholz 1994).

9.2.4 Currencies

I now turn to currencies. How should investigators measure foraging performance? Two main currencies are of interest. The currency called "rate" is the amount of energy gained per unit time and is defined as follows: the gross rate-of-energy capture with use of tactic i is b_i, the energy-expenditure rate is o_i, and so the net rate of gain is $b_i - c_i$. "Efficiency" is defined as the amount of energy gained per unit energy expenditure. (We could also differentiate between the gross (b_i/c_i) and net ($[b_i - c_i]/c_i$) efficiencies, but the latter is the same as (b_i/c_i) $- 1$ and efficiency usually refers to the former measure.) Other currencies have been used in foraging studies, but these currencies are mostly variants of rate and efficiency (see Ydenberg et al. 1994) or they are not very general (e.g. energy content per unit volume nectar for hummingbirds) (Montgomerie et al. 1984).

Most simple foraging models use the currency "net rate of energy intake," and the strategy "maximize the net rate of energy intake while foraging," and treat them virtually identically. Efficiency has been ignored almost entirely. But which quantity describes better the behavior of foragers?

Table 9.1
Studies that Contrast Rate and Efficiency Predictions for Foraging Behavior

Study	Behavior/Species Tested	Result
Feeding studies		
Juanes and Hartwick 1990	Prey choice/Dungeness crab	Efficiency
Welham and Ydenberg 1988	Patch time/Ring-billed gull	Intermediate[a]
Montgomerie et al. 1984	Nectar concentration/ Ruby-throated hummingbird	Efficiency[b]
Provisioning studies		
Kacelnik 1984	Load size/Starling	Rate[c]
Schmid-Hempel et al. 1985	Load size/Honeybee	Efficiency
Schmid-Hempel 1987	Load size/Honeybee	Efficiency
Wolf and Schmid-Hempel 1990	Load size/Honeybee	Efficiency
McLaughlin and Montgomerie 1990	Flight speed/Lapland longspur	Efficiency
Welham and Ydenberg 1993	Flight speed/Black terns	Efficiency
Waite and Ydenberg 1994a, 1994b	Load size/Grey jay	Rate, Efficiency[d]

Note: For each situation, the currency that best predicts the observed behavior is given.

[a] Gulls may have been provisioning.

[b] The currency used (net energy gain per unit volume nectar consumed) was close but not identical to efficiency. Nevertheless, the results approached more closely efficiency predictions instead of rate predictions.

[c] Results were close to the predictions of both currencies.

[d] Results were close to rate predictions in autumn, but shifted in the direction of efficiency predictions in winter.

9.2.4.1 Rate versus Efficiency: Tests

Studies that have examined the behavior of foragers in relation to the predictions of both rate and efficiency currencies are summarized in table 9.1. There have been relatively few studies of feeding (as opposed to provisioning) behavior. Juanes and Hartwick (1990) examined the prey-size selection of Dungeness crabs (*Cancer productus*) feeding on clams. Rate and efficiency currencies made very different predictions; with the former, a preference for large prey was predicted, and with the latter, a preference for small prey was predicted. The experiments clearly supported efficiency maximizing. A review of many other prey-choice experiments in the literature (Juanes 1992) showed that the preference for smaller prey (and hence efficiency) is a general pattern among decapods, although few of these studies made quantitative predictions.

There are more provisioning studies available. McLaughlin and Montgomerie (1990) and Welham and Ydenberg (1993) found that efficiency was a better predictor of the flight speeds of provisioning Lapland longspurs (*Calcarius lapponicus*) and black terns (*Chlidonias niger*), respectively. Finally, Schmid-Hempel and his colleagues studied the behavior of honeybees (*Apis mellifera*) and found good agreement with efficiency predictions and a marked divergence from rate predictions in three separate studies (Schmid-Hempel et al. 1985; Schmid-Hempel 1987; Wolf and Schmid-Hempel 1990).

While this survey of studies reveals that rate and efficiency are useful to the investigator as measures of foraging performance in different studies, this survey, as yet, tells us little about what a forager experiences or how it evaluates its own performance and integrates information to choose a behavior.

9.2.5 Strategies

How is it that rate and efficiency sometimes work as measures of foraging performance? These currencies have somewhat different properties. With an efficient tactic, energy is obtained cheaply in terms of energy expenditure; however, with this tactic, there is no direct account of the time involved. With rate-maximizing tactics, energy is obtained quickly. Foragers evidently choose rate-maximizing tactics under some circumstances and efficient tactics under other circumstances. What are these circumstances?

Most "classical" foraging theories assume that the foraging strategy is to maximize the long-term net rate of energy intake. This strategic objective always predicts rate-maximizing behavior and is therefore not supported with the data. I will consider two different possible strategies in the models I will outline. The forager maximizes the total net gain while foraging (denoted G_f) and the total net daily gain (G_d). These net gains seem very similar; however, they are not identical if any part of the day is spent resting because during rest energy expenditure continues but there is no intake. These models will show how, depending on the situation, foragers may choose a behavioral option (tactic) that is efficient or one that is quick; as a result, the investigator measures either rate of efficient behavior.

9.2.6 Constraints

The fundamental constraints in any foraging situation concern the time and energy available. Imagine that the total time available is T, and the forager has a maximum daily assimilable energy intake of K (Weiner 1992). If the forager's total intake reaches K before T expires, then the forager must rest for the remainder of the day. This situation is called "energy limitation" because the total gain is limited by the forager's ability to assimilate energy: Even if there were more time, the forager would be unable to increase its gain. "Time limitation" may occur in one of two ways. If K is not attained, the forager is able to forage until time T. Alternatively, there may be a time limit that limits foraging to a period t_L. The time limit may be imposed naturally as with day length in the northern winter (e.g. Systad 1996) or the tide (e.g. Robles et al. 1989), or the time limit may be experimentally imposed (e.g. Tooze and Gass 1985, Swenhen et al. 1989). In both cases, increases in the foraging time would allow the forager to increase its gain.

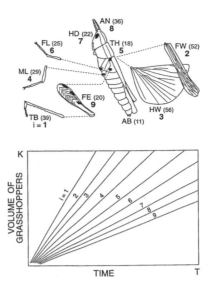

Figure 9.2. Prey-preparation tactics of grasshopper sparrows, based on Kaspari (1991). Diagram (*top*) shows an "exploded" view of a grasshopper and, specifically, the body parts that sparrows may remove. Each body part is labeled with the percentage of indigestible chitin (in parentheses) and the order in which sparrows tend to remove the body parts (*i* = 1 is the first body part removed in prey preparation.) Graph (*bottom*) shows how the removal tactics relate to the rate of intake and the K (maximum intake) and T (time available) boundaries.

9.2.6.1 The Relation between Time and Energy Constraints

The foraging of grasshopper sparrows (*Ammodramus savannarum*) illustrates how time and energy constraints interact (Kaspari 1990, 1991). These birds capture large insect prey such as grasshoppers and often expend considerable time handling them, discarding some parts before consuming the remainder. Why do grasshopper sparrows discard food they could eat? How much time should they invest in prey preparation? The options for preparing a grasshopper for consumption range from no preparation ($i = 1$) to removal of all body parts except the abdomen and thorax, which are always eaten ($i = 9$) (fig. 9.2). Each successive option requires more handling time ($h_{i+1} > h_i$) and produces a smaller item for ingestion (volume $v_{i+1} < v_i$) with less energy in it ($e_{i+1} < e_i$), although the energy density (e/v) of the item is higher.

Suppose that a sparrow can ingest and process a total volume K of grasshoppers over a period of time T, and that the encounter rate with grasshoppers during search is λ. (The encounter rate is the rate at which prey items are encountered during search. Search time does not include the handling time. The expected search time to find a prey item is $1/\lambda$.) With little or no prey preparation (low values of *i* on fig. 9.2), gut capacity is quickly reached and

the sparrow will be forced to spend some of the day resting. As defined, I call this phenomenon energy limitation. The gross daily energy gain is $B_i = e_i n_i$, where n_i is the number of prey items consumed ($n_i = K/v_i$). The level of prey preparation that maximizes the gross daily gain can be found by locating the value of i such that at the next higher level of preparation ($i + 1$) the sparrow will reach T before K is fully processed. (In fig. 9.2 these are $i = 5$ and $i + 1 = 6$.) The total daily energy intake is the rate of intake multiplied by the time available, $B_{i+1} = T (\lambda \cdot e_{i+1})/(1 + \lambda h_{i+1})$. As defined, this is time limitation.

The intake-maximizing level of prey preparation occurs when no extra gain can be had by increasing preparation and obviously depends on λ. (Because the levels of preparation occur in quantum jumps, the best level will often lie in between i and $i + 1$ but will be unattainable. The sparrow must choose which of i and $i + 1$ yields greater gain). As prey are increasingly easy to find, the sparrow is able to spend more time in preparation of each item so that the material it processes is of higher quality. The encounter rate at which the sparrow should switch to the next higher level of prey preparation can be found by setting $B_i = B_{i+1}$ and solving for λ, which yields $\lambda = (e_i n_i)/(e_{i+1} T - n_i e_i h_{i+1})$.

Kaspari (1990, 1991) found that sparrows removed parts from captured grasshoppers in reverse order of nutrient density; this behavior supports his "nutrient concentration" hypothesis. He also found that the amount of preparation varied as predicted with the availability of large prey. Taghon et al. (1978) advanced a similar idea to explain the size selection of particles for ingestion by deposit feeders, which use another feeding mode that likely utilizes the full gut capacity.

One way to think about the sparrow's tactics (levels of preparation i) is that they differentially use up the time and processing capacity the sparrow has available. Little preparation quickly takes up processing capacity because the prey are bulky, but extensive preparation uses up time in the form of handling. The intake-maximizing tactic will occur at the level at which time and processing capacity are used as fully as possible.

9.2.7 A Simple Feeding Model

The following simple model of feeding behavior illustrates how rate and efficiency are related. It is presented in full by Ydenberg and Hurd (1998). When feeding, a forager chooses among a number of foraging options $i = 1, 2, 3, \ldots n$. (In any particular model, the types of options may be the prey sizes to capture, flight speeds, or patch times; however, for now option type is not specified). Each option has an associated rate of energy gain during foraging, b_i, which depends on the rate of energy expenditure, c_i, as $b_i = f(c_i)$. An

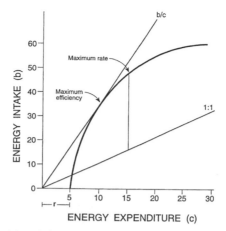

Figure 9.3. Example of the relation between the rate of energy expenditure on feeding (c) and the rate of energy intake [$b = f(c)$]. The specific function shown here [$b = 60\,(1 - e^{-0.25(c-r)})$] is used in the example given in Ydenberg and Hurd (1998). The basic assumption is that harder work (higher c) shows diminishing returns (b). The efficiency (b/c) and rate ($b - c$) maxima are indicated.

example is shown in figure 9.3. The central and likely very general assumption about the form of $f(c_i)$ is that there are diminishing returns on higher rates of energy expenditure. The resting metabolic rate r is indicated on the x-axis and can be thought of as the rate of energy expenditure at which there is no energy gain ($b = 0$). The different rates of energy expenditure possible are the foraging options or tactics, and they are deployed by the forager in support of a strategy. The maximum net rate ($b_i - c_i$) and maximum efficiency (b_i/c_i) tactics are indicated on figure 9.3. Note that rate maximizing involves harder work (higher c) than efficiency maximizing.

To illustrate how rate and efficiency can be observed, we calculate the total gain during foraging (G_f) and the total net daily gain (G_d) under time and energy limitations. The equations are developed in appendix A. Their form is designed to illustrate the relation of the behavioral choices depicted in figure 9.3 to the two strategies. The basic results are straightforward. The most proficient tactic depends on the strategy (maximize net gain during foraging or total net daily gain) and the constraints (time or energy limitation). Efficiency, or the closely related "modified efficiency" (in which the energy expenditure rate is discounted by the resting metabolic rate r), is important when the energy constraint K operates. Simply put, the forager should choose the option that maximizes rate when there is a shortage of time and the option that maximizes efficiency when there is a shortage of energy. Indeed, this is what Stephens and Krebs (1986, 9) wrote in the single paragraph that is devoted to the idea of efficiency in their book.

This approach shows that recognizing a diversity of feeding contexts within a simple framework can accommodate a variety of outcomes. This approach also shows that distinguishing between what ecologists observe (rate or efficiency) and what the forager attempts (with its choice of behavior) to maximize is important. The framework also makes clear how rate-maximizing and efficient tactics are related and under which circumstances each is to be preferred. With the framework, it is also indicated what information the forager needs to be able to make a choice of behavior. The forager needs to evaluate the foraging context (feeding or provisioning), the strategic goal, the constraints (time or processing limitation), and the rate of energy intake as it relates to the rate of expenditure for each behavioral option. One way to think about the behavioral options is as a gradient of successively harder working tactics, and the feeder "gears up" its choice of tactic until the desired outcome can be achieved. Factors other than purely energetic considerations (notably the risk posed by predators) may also cause foragers to adjust their choice of behavior if the different tactics are differentially vulnerable. These factors will be considered further in the following.

9.2.8 A Provisioning Model

In provisioning, unlike in feeding, foragers deliver the prey they capture to offspring, nest mates, or a hoard. The costs and benefits differ from those in feeding situations because the delivered resource is not for the provisioner's immediate consumption; therefore, foraging proficiency must be measured in currencies different from those in feeding situations. In fact, the currency "net rate" seems reasonable for feeders, but in a provisioning context, the meaning of this currency is not so clear.

In a feeding context, net rate is calculated by subtracting the forager's energy expenditure from its energy intake. A provisioner, however, does not consume the delivered prey; the food items are delivered to and consumed by nestlings (for example). Hence, it usually does not make sense to subtract from the energy value of delivered prey the energy expenditure of the provisioner who captured and delivered the prey. Nevertheless, in many published models, this is exactly the calculation that is performed. It seems more sensible that the provisioner maximizes delivery over some period, such as a day, and maintains energy balance by spending some time and energy self feeding. Accordingly, I use the currency "total daily delivery" in provisioning situations.

In the basic provisioning model, the provisioner may choose among a number of foraging options $i = 1, 2, 3, \ldots, n$. Option i yields a rate of prey delivery d_i and has a rate of energy expenditure c_i. As noted, the rate (d_i) and efficiency maximizing (d_i/c_i) tactics can be identified. (Note that in a provisioning context these currencies consider delivery d_i instead of intake

b_i). During the day, the forager has time T to forage, and its total energy expenditure can not exceed K, which is set by the maximum amount of energy the forager can ingest and assimilate in a day. The provisioner is assumed to choose the provisioning tactic i that maximizes the energy the provisioner delivers each day; however, the provisioner is subject to the restriction that its energy budget is balanced. To remain in energy balance, the provisioner must recover by self feeding the energy it expends on delivery.

The equations are developed in appendix B. When the provisioner's assimilation capacity (K) is reached in self feeding (energy limitation), the behavioral tactic that maximizes delivery is the tactic with the highest "modified efficiency" $(d_i/[c_i - r])$; with this tactic, the energy-expenditure rate is discounted by the resting-metabolic rate (Houston 1995). Efficiency is also important when the provisioner runs out of time (equation B2). Ydenberg et al. (1994) showed that, in this situation, the tactic that maximizes total daily delivery lies between the efficiency-maximizing and the rate-maximizing tactics; the exact choice of behavior depends on the net self-feeding rate $(b_s - c_s)$ (see Houston 1995 for further discussion.) The provisioner must feed itself to power the provisioning behavior, and equation B2 indicates that the provisioner's choice of behavior changes from use of the tactic with maximum efficiency when the self-feeding rate is low to use of the tactic with the maximum rate when the self-feeding rate is high.

The predicted behavior depends critically on the self-feeding rate, and the results would be sensible if the self-feeding rates were low in the studies that demonstrated efficiency and high in the studies that demonstrated rate maximizing. However, the only study that attempted to account for the self-feeding rate was that of Waite and Ydenberg (1994a, 1994b) on grey jays (*Perisoreus canadensis*) during late summer in central Alaska. The jays hoarded experimentally offered raisins, but fed themselves on blueberries, which were abundantly available on the forest floor. A jay takes only a few seconds to interrupt a flight and quickly gulp a few berries, and so the self-feeding rate was very high (although it was difficult to quantify exactly). Owing to the high self-feeding rate, we reasoned the behavior of hoarding grey jays should approach rate maximizing instead of efficiency maximizing. In our experiments, jays hoarded raisins proffered at a feeding board. On each visit to the board, the birds took the single raisin available on arrival and could have departed immediately or waited for a short (experimentally controlled) interval for two more simultaneously available raisins. When the intervals were short, it was worthwhile to wait and hoard three raisins; however, as the interval was experimentally lengthened, the single-raisin option eventually became more profitable. The critical time interval was very different under rate- and efficiency-maximizing, and we found that the time at which grey jays switched to single-raisin loads was predicted better with rate maximizing.

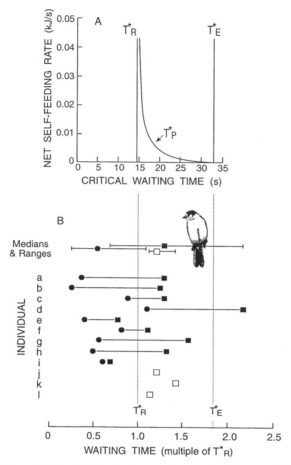

Figure 9.4. (*a*) The critical waiting time in the grey jay experiment is very different with rate (T_R^*) and efficiency (T_E^*) currencies. The critical waiting time with the provisioning model (T_P^*) depends on the self-feeding rate (see equation B2). The self-feeding rate is low near the efficiency level, and the self-feeding rate is high near the rate maximum. (*b*) The critical waiting time of individual grey jays differs between summer (*circles* = high self-feeding rate) and winter (*filled squares* = low self-feeding rate) and shifts toward the efficiency maximum in winter. Open squares show the waiting times measured only in winter of three individuals, so the result is not an order effect (from Waite and Ydenberg 1994b).

The critical waiting time, however, depends on the self-feeding rate, as shown in figure 9.4*a*. A test of the provisioning model would repeat the described experiment with a manipulated change in the self-feeding rate and the critical waiting time would shift as described in figure 9.4*a*. Such a test was designed by Waite (Waite and Ydenberg 1994b). He was unable to manipulate

the self-feeding rate directly, so he instead repeated the experiment during winter when the self-feeding rate was reasonably assumed to be much lower than that during the peak of blueberry availability in late summer. The same individuals that behaved as rate maximizers during the summer changed their behavior significantly to that of efficiency maximizing during the winter (fig. 9.4b).

How are grey jays able to evaluate and perform such subtle shifts of behavior? To make a choice of behavior, each individual needs to evaluate the context, the constraints, the rate of delivery relative to the rate of expenditure of each behavioral option, and the self-feeding rate. Like feeding behavior, provisioning behavior can be represented as a range of successively higher levels of work; the level that can be sustained is dependent on the self-feeding rate.

9.3 FORAGING AND INFORMATION

9.3.1 Information Use in Patch Foraging

The simple models developed were useful for illustrating the relationships between currencies, strategies, tactics, and decision mechanisms; these models rely on highly simplified and general assumptions. Most relevant to the following discussion is the assumption that foragers know all of the relevant characteristics of their foraging habitat; foragers can recognize instantly the prey or patch types they have encountered. However, like the bumblebee flying to an inflorescence whose contents she cannot know, foragers are often likely to be uncertain about many aspects of a foraging situation. Their decision mechanisms must incorporate the certainties and uncertainties of any particular situation; the exact nature of this information is likely specific to the ecology of the species.

Consider a forager that feeds by traveling from patch to patch, and each patch consists of two holes (called "bits" by Green 1980). A forager cannot know if any particular hole contains food without examining it. There is a variety of tactics the forager may use: The forager may always open both holes (exhaustive search); it may open the second hole only if the first hole contains a prey (stay after find); it may open the second hole only if the first hole is empty (leave after find); or it may only visit the first hole (partial search) regardless of circumstances.

The most proficient foraging tactic depends on the way the prey are distributed among patches. Compare three cases (fig. 9.5). The overall average density of prey per patch is one in each case, but the prey are distributed differently among the patches. In the clumped habitat, patches contain no or two prey (both holes full or both holes empty), and in the regular habitat, all patches contain one prey (the first hole is full and the second is empty or vice versa).

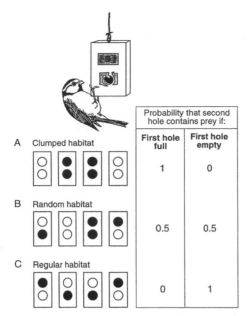

Figure 9.5. Simple conceptual habitats illustrate the importance of information use in patch foraging. Circles indicate the two holes in each patch; a filled circle indicates the hole contains prey, although the prey is not visible to the forager before it opens the hole. The average density of prey in all habitats is one per patch, but the distributions are very different. In habitat *a*, prey are clumped; in habitat *b*, prey are randomly dispersed; and in habitat *c*, prey are spaced regularly. As indicated, the discovery of prey in the first hole provides information about the presence of prey in the second hole. Foragers can use this information to elevate the rate of prey capture.

In the random habitat, prey are distributed in each hole with p equal to .5, so that patches contain no, one, or two prey.

To understand the function of information in foraging problems, assume the forager knows the distribution (clumped, regular, or random) of prey, but that the forager cannot recognize patches externally. Examination of the first hole in a patch provides the forager with information about the presence of prey in the other hole. In the clumped habitat, finding a prey item in the first hole means that the second hole also has prey, and the absence of prey in the first hole means the second hole is also empty; therefore, examining the second hole would be a waste of time. The forager should stay in the patch after prey has been found and leave when prey has not been found.

In the regular habitat, however, a prey item in the first hole means the second hole is empty, and an empty first hole means prey is in the second hole. The forager should leave after finding prey and stay when no prey is found in the

first hole. In the random habitat, the presence or absence of prey in a hole provides no information about the likelihood that the next hole contains food.

The best foraging tactic depends on the distribution of prey. Generally, the tactic "stay after find" is best when prey are clumped, and the tactic "leave after find" is best when prey are evenly dispersed (compare Iwasa et al. 1981). In the random habitat, exhaustive search is best and partial search (always leave after examining the first hole) is never favored because there is no diminishing return on patch residence. The exact solution depends on the proportions of patches with no, one, and two prey and the handling and travel times involved. By calculating the expected gain from further patch residence at each stage in the process (e.g. at patch arrival and after examination of the first hole), the conditional probability that the patch contains more prey is found. The expected gain is compared with the gain that is available by moving to the next patch. Behavior can be adjusted to give the maximum expected rate of gain. This was first derived by Oaten (1977). Green (1980) and McNamara and Houston (1987a) give clear quantitative examples (see also Stephens and Krebs 1986, chap. 4).

9.3.2 The Value of Information

How important is it for foragers to use information? One way to answer this question is to compare how well a forager performs with use of its best tactics when information is and is not used (Stephens 1989). In the example developed, use of information is advantageous when prey are clumped and regularly dispersed. The gain achieved with the best "no information" tactic (exhaustive search) is compared with that attained with use of the best information-use strategy ("leave after find" in the regular habitat and "stay after find" in the clumped habitat). Unfortunately, information use in foraging theory has received limited theoretical and experimental attention (but see Stephens 1987; Kamil et al. 1993; and Beachly et al. 1995 for examples of foraging). This is an essential area for further work because information use is perhaps the most relevant application of foraging theory in cognitive ecology.

A cognitive ecologist who is interested in knowing if foragers evaluate information as suggested by this simple framework could perform the following experiment: A forager is given successive choices between arms of an apparatus. Only one arm offers a food reward, and the forager does not know which arm. The choice is presented at (experimentally) controlled intervals, and at each trial, the forager must select one of the arms. With reward size e and interval duration t, the rate of gain, assuming that the forager's choices are made randomly (therefore proportion p of the choices are correct), is pe/t. The experiment, however, gives the forager another option: The forager may choose a key that reveals, after an additional wait, w, which arm will deliver

the reward at that trial. The setup is similar to a paradigm in experimental psychology called "observing" (see Dinsmoor 1983). When information is used, the forager's gain is $e/(w + t)$, and the value of information use is $v = e/(w + t) - pe/t$, which is positive so long as $p < t/(w + t)$. The quantities p, t, and w can be manipulated, and the situations in which the forager ignores or uses information can be specified. The experiment may reveal how flexible foragers are and may yield insight into the types of mechanisms used by showing when performance matches expectation.

In most existing models of information use in patch foraging, it is assumed that foragers know the characteristics of the distribution of patch types. This assumption may be useful when as examining some types of foragers, but this assumption is likely to be too restrictive. For example, "area-intensive search" has been observed in thrushes (Smith 1974) and parasitoid wasps (Waage 1979). Based on the above, area-intensive search should occur when prey are clumped. Zach and Falls (1977), working with the ground-foraging ovenbird (*Seiurus aurocapillus*), showed that intensive search of the immediate locale followed prey discovery. However, when prey dispersion was altered experimentally to be regular, ovenbirds learned to delay area-intensive search after a prey was found and moved on a bit after a prey capture before beginning to search intensively. Evidently some foragers can learn the distribution of prey and update their knowledge as they go.

9.3.3 Information and Cognitive Ecology

How do foraging animals handle these complexities? Certain assumptions about the distribution or other attributes of prey are undoubtedly "hard-wired" into behavior, and individuals may be unable to adjust facultatively these aspects of their behavior. Bumblebees, for example, usually begin searching inflorescences at the bottom and work upward. This behavior seems sensible because nectar is typically concentrated in lower florets. Each species probably has certain properties hard-wired into behavior; at the same time, each species possesses mechanisms that enable adjustment of behavior to variable aspects of the foraging world. Which aspects are learned probably depends intimately on the ecology of the animal (Dukas, this vol. section 4.5). For example, honeybees are predisposed to use the leave-after-find tactic (often called win-shift tactic) (Demas and Brown 1995). Use of this tactic is sensible because florets are empty after visits. Experimental manipulations, however, revealed that honeybees can learn to use the stay-after-find tactic. By contrast, great tits (*Parus major*) seem predisposed to use the stay-after-find tactic; however, they can learn eventually to use the leave-after-find tactic (Ydenberg 1984). For great tits, use of the leave-after-find tactic is perhaps sensible because much of their insect prey is in a clumped distribution. General statements,

however, about aspects of foraging behavior that are hard-wired and those that can be adjusted by the animal are not yet possible. An important goal of cognitive ecology is to develop a much more complete understanding of how hard-wired and adjustable mechanisms work together in the mechanics of foraging behavior.

Lima (1983) studied information use in the foraging of downy woodpeckers (*Picoides pubescens*) by creating a habitat of artificial patches (short lengths of branches with 24 holes each). He hung the patches from trees in a woodlot during winter. Each hole in each patch could contain a small seed, but each hole was covered by tape. The woodpeckers had to drill through the tape to obtain the seed. Woodpeckers flew from patch to patch and moved systematically from hole to hole within a patch. Lima stocked his experimental habitat with two types of patches, which could not be distinguished externally because of the tape. Patches were either empty or contained some seeds. The experiments tested the hypothesis that woodpeckers use their experience with the first few holes to discriminate between the patches.

This experiment is directly analogous to the simple experiment portrayed in figure 9.5; however, instead of two holes there were 24 in each patch. In the most directly comparable treatment, Lima's empty patches contained either no or 24 seeds; thus, opening the first hole revealed the patch type. A seed in the hole showed that the patch was full and should be exploited, and an empty hole showed that the patch was empty and should be abandoned. Lima (1983) further challenged the woodpeckers by presenting two other clumped distributions; one contained patches with no or 12 seeds, and another contained patches with no or six seeds. Now more holes had to be examined before patches could be classified as empty or full. Of course as soon as a seed was found, the patch was classified as full. But, what if no seeds were found in the first few holes? Lima calculated that a patch should be abandoned if the first three (half-full treatment) or six (quarter-full treatment) holes that were opened were empty.

Early in the morning, the patches that were carefully prepared the previous evening were set out. The exploited patches could be examined later in the day, and the pattern of opened and unopened holes could be used to measure the woodpeckers' foraging. The first prediction was that woodpeckers would open all of the holes or only a few holes in each patch. The second prediction was that the classification should be largely correct; all of the holes should be opened in the full patches and only a few holes should be opened in the empty patches. Finally, the number of holes opened in patches that were classified by woodpeckers as empty (i.e. abandoned after only a few holes were opened) should be one (0/24 distribution), three (0/12 distribution) or six (0/6 distribution).

The woodpeckers' performance exceeded all expectations. They showed

that they quickly learned to classify patches correctly as empty or full because they opened only a few holes on some patches and all the holes on other patches. Their classification of the patches was highly accurate. Moreover, the number of holes sampled before accepting or abandoning a patch agreed quantitatively with the predictions. About the only thing the woodpeckers did not do was count the number of seeds and abandon patches if all the seeds were found before all the holes were opened. Once a patch was classified as full, it was completely exploited.

How is it that woodpeckers performed so well on an apparently difficult foraging task? One hypothesis is that the birds have a generalized foraging strategy that is complex enough to handle any food distribution. Another hypothesis is that woodpeckers are predisposed to categorize patches as empty or full. The task was not difficult because it resembled the type of prey distribution naturally faced. Not enough is known about woodpeckers and their natural history to determine which explanation is correct. It would be instructive to repeat Lima's experiment with clumped or regular prey distributions and see if woodpeckers perform as proficiently.

Sometimes patches have externally recognizable features that give information about their contents. Large and small inflorescences can be distinguished at a distance, for example. Why, as Pyke (1982) observed, should a bumblebee that arrives at a larger inflorescence be more persistent and investigate more florets before abandoning the inflorescence? The gain from a larger inflorescence would be relatively greater if its florets contained nectar. The potential reward in a larger inflorescence makes it worthwhile to spend a little extra time determining if the patch is empty or full. McNamara and Houston (1987a) gave a quantitative example of the calculations required.

In summary, problems regarding information use represent perhaps the most important application of foraging theory in cognitive ecology, but these problems have received as yet comparatively little examination. The decision mechanisms used likely combine hard-wired and learned aspects; the exact combination depends intimately on the ecology of the species under consideration. Foraging theory can be used to study decision mechanisms. First, the nature of the problems that have to be solved can be analyzed. Second, experimental situations can be created in which foragers reveal details of the function of decision mechanisms.

9.4 FORAGING UNDER THE RISK OF PREDATION

9.4.1 The Importance of Predation Risk

Ecologists have studied predation for almost a century, but the vast majority of this work has considered only how actual deaths influence demography. Until recently, the effects of the behavioral changes that individual animals

may make when conditions are dangerous have been ignored. Now ecologists have begun to realize that the *risk* of predation is often more important than actual predation events (Lima and Dill 1990). The following anecdote illustrates. While I discussed with a student her research on molting geese in northern Québec, I wondered if foxes pose any danger when the geese are flightless for several weeks. The student replied that she had never seen a fox catch a goose; whenever a fox was anywhere in the vicinity, the geese stopped grazing and fled onto one of the many small lakes, where they were safe, and remained on the lake until the fox departed. This seemed a very sensible answer, and ecologists have often discounted the influence of predators in exactly this way. However, for a molting goose, the risk that a fox may approach presumably restricts grazing to areas near lakes; being flightless, any goose that grazed far from the safety of a lake would become very quickly a meal for a fox. Thus, foxes are most important in the ecology of molting geese—even if foxes never actually catch a goose. In the same way, many animals are always at some predation risk, and their behavior presumably reflects this basic fact.

The first formulation of a behavioral hypothesis that explicitly recognized the role of predation risk was made by Rosenzweig (1974). He suggested that a seasonal pattern in desert rodents of avoiding moonlight may be explained with individual animals weighing the risks of activity under moonlight (greater risk of capture by owls) against the benefits (access to mating opportunities), the balance of which changed and benefits changed as the breeding season approached. Steve Lima expanded this theme in a series of papers that explored phenomena such as body mass (1986) and clutch size (1987a). He (1986) also explicitly stated that the effect of behavioral alterations may have a much larger impact on demography than actual deaths. In more recent work (e.g. Peckarsky et al. 1993), these sublethal consequences have been addressed; the presence of predators reduces the activity, growth, and fecundity of animals.

To learn to interpret animal behavior that relates to predation risk, behavioral ecologists have tested hypotheses that are analogous to that of Rosenzweig (1974) described. Many experiments (reviewed by Lima and Dill 1990) have been created to observe how an individual animal behaves when placed in a situation in which the costs (predation risk) or benefits (access to food or matings) were manipulated. Several examples are given in figure 9.6. The results of these simple experiments are generally those expected. When risk is higher, animals adopt safer tactics; when the benefit to be gained is greater, animals adopt riskier tactics. The interpretation of the behavioral adjustments observed is often straightforward; however, because there are many subtle effects that cannot be so easily observed in simple, manipulative experiments, the role of behavioral adjustments to predation risk in large-scale ecological phenomena such as vertical migration (Clark and Levy 1988) and population

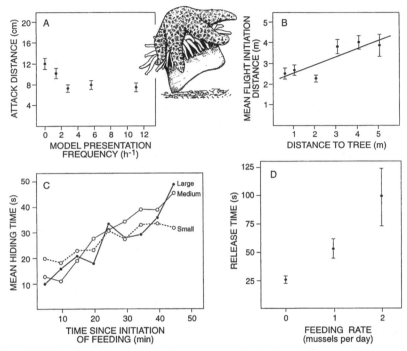

Figure 9.6. Experiments in which foraging responses of animals to risk manipulations were examined. (*a*) The distance from which juvenile coho salmon attack a drifting prey item decreases as the model of a predatory trout is presented more often (Dill and Fraser 1984). (*b*) Gray squirrels flee from an approaching predator at a greater distance as the feeding site is placed further from the safety of a tree (Dill and Houtman 1989). (*c*) After an experimental disturbance, barnacles take longer to reemerge if they have been able to feed for a time before the disturbance (Dill and Gillett 1991). (*d*) Anemones take longer to release their pedal disc from the substrate to escape the attack of a predatory starfish if they have experienced good feeding at the site (Houtman et al. 1997).

fluctuations (Dehn 1994; Norrdahl and Korpimäki 1996) is becoming clear only slowly. The role of predation risk in life-history factors such as in the costs of reproduction (Harfenist and Ydenberg 1995) and traits such as the timing of metamorphosis (Rowe and Ludwig 1991) are also receiving increased attention.

9.4.2 Predation Risk in Foraging Models

In the foraging models outlined, foragers choose among tactics that vary in the rate of gain and energy expenditure. If the tactics also vary in the extent of exposure to predators that is required, then predation risk should influence the decision. The interesting situation is one in which the gain and the risk

trade off so that the largest gains come at the expense of the largest risks. (If the largest gain comes with the smallest risk, the choice is obvious.) An illustrative situation considers vigilance during feeding (Lima 1987b, Roberts 1996). Safety increases with the time spent in vigilance, but the rate of feeding slows.

Predation risk and foraging often seem to trade off, and many such situations have been described. For example, animals may have to leave the relative safety of cover or a refuge to feed in the open (Lima 1987b; Sih 1992). The most dangerous habitats may contain the best food (e.g. Prins 1989). By moving to forage, cryptic animals may lose their camouflage (Houtman 1995). Defenses that protect against predators, such as thick shells, reduce growth rate (Palmer 1985). Infaunal organisms may increase their safety by burying more deeply; however, by doing so, these organisms reduce their feeding rate (Zaklan and Ydenberg 1997). Vertical migrants are better able to feed near the surface because there is more light but they are more exposed to predators (Clark and Levy 1988). In each of these examples, the forager can increase the feeding rate only at the expense of increased exposure to predators.

One misconception about predation risk is that it is often so small that it can, for all practical purposes, be ignored. For example, Piersma et al. (1993) asserted that the risk posed to each knot (*Calidris canuta*, a species of sandpiper) in a flock of 30,000 by the occasional appearance of a distant falcon is minuscule. However, the point is not that the risk is small; it is that the occasional presence of falcons confines sandpipers to big flocks in open areas, because individual birds taking up other options would be at greater risk. The relevant quantity is how much the risk is reduced by the flocking habit.

Even a minuscule reduction in risk can be important if the risk reduction pertains to an action that is repeated many times during life. For the parental songbird, the predation danger per provisioning visit to its nest is tiny—perhaps on the order of 10^{-6} (Ydenberg 1994). However, because a parent songbird may make thousands of provisioning visits to its brood, the compounded risk is substantial and may have a strong influence on the clutch size (Lima 1987a).

The idea that tiny risks can be ignored has its complement; namely, tiny benefits should be ignored in the face of large risks. For example, it has been asserted that prey should flee as soon as predators are detected (e.g. Myers 1983). However, as Ydenberg and Dill (1986) showed, this should not and does not occur. Instead, the decision to flee is adjusted according to the costs and benefits of each situation; fleeing is delayed as the opportunity foregone by fleeing increases.

9.4.3 Information about Predation Risk

Foragers can never be certain that there is not a predator lurking just around the next corner, and presumably foragers always behave as though a predator

may be present—even in laboratory experiments. With use of the same logic that predicts proficiency in feeding, we expect natural selection has led to the evolution of keen sensory abilities that enable detection of predators and clues about the presence of predators; this prediction is hardly powerful or surprising. More intriguing is the idea that nervous systems allow adjustment of behavior on the basis of information that is received proficiently. We expect proficiency because the obvious benefits of behavior that reduce predation risk must be balanced against the costs—the foregone opportunity to feed, seek mates, or care for offspring. Individuals that behave too cautiously on the basis of information received about predators forego too much opportunity, and animals that are too cavalier live less long. Bouskila and Blumstein (1992) considered how errors in the assessment of hazard influence foraging decisions; they showed that (over a certain range) errors have little impact on survival, but it is better to be too cautious than too bold. Sih (1992) developed a model on the basis of Bayesian statistics to show how foragers may update their estimate that a predator is still present. He also concluded that erring on the side of caution is selected for and provided an experimental test.

Mangel (1990) discussed three desirable attributes of an information-processing theory: (1) a decay of memory so that recent events have a bigger impact than remote events on the selection of current tactics; (2) a succinct estimate of the parameter of interest; and (3) flexibility of the estimate through a consistent treatment of uncertainty. There has been very little work in which any of these aspects as they relate to proficiency in reacting to information about predators has been examined. As discussed, relevant questions about foraging decisions include the nature of the decision mechanisms, the currencies, the possible tactics, and the strategies involved.

The sculpin, *Oligocottus maculosus,* inhabits tidepools along the Pacific coast of North America. Sculpins are cryptically colored and forage by lying motionless on the bottom of tidepools and occasionally lunging forward to capture small items. Their natural history creates a dilemma; camouflage works best when sculpins are still, but foraging requires movement. Houtman's (1995) study of their behavior is an instructive example of how cues about the presence of predators may be integrated into foraging decisions.

The model conceptualized foraging in a series of intervals, during each of which a decision was made. The decision was to reject an encountered prey item (i.e. remain still and cryptic) or attempt prey capture. Captures could be made at any of four distances; greater distances increased the rate of prey capture (because a larger area was searched) and predation risk (because more movement was required). At the end of each interval, the forager updated its estimate of the probability that a predator was present (called φ) and used that estimate in its decisions in the next interval.

The updating of φ took place in three steps, and three sources of information

were incorporated. If a predator was detected during the previous interval (indexed as $t - 1$), the value of ϕ of course became 1.0. However, information was available even if there was no detection because one of three events must have happened: (1) There was no predator present. (2) A predator was present but did not detect the sculpin. (3) The predator was present, detected the sculpin, but did not attack. The forager had an estimate that a predator was present $[\phi(t - 1)]$, and it was assumed that the forager knew the probabilities of detection and attack. On the basis of likelihoods of these events, $\phi(t - 1)$ was updated to an intermediate value, $\phi(t')$. The updating procedure used Bayes's theorem, and the formulae are given in the dissertation by Houtman (1995).

The second updating step accounted for predator movements. During any interval, a predator that was present may have departed or a predator may have arrived. In the model, predator movements were described by a first order Markov chain, and the transition probabilities were assumed to be known to the forager; these probabilities allowed the forager to update $\phi(t')$ to $\phi(t'')$. The final updating step incorporated information during vigilance, which was acquired during a scan of the surroundings. There were four possible outcomes: (1) No predator was detected and no predator was present. (2) A predator that was present was not detected. (3) A predator that was present was detected. (4) A predator was falsely detected. Either outcome (detecting or not detecting a predator) enabled the updating of $\phi(t'')$ to $\phi(t''')$, which became the estimate of ϕ used during period t.

This model contains many simplifying and possibly unreal assumptions. For example, the forager was assumed to know features of the habitat such as the arrival and departure rates of predators and how predators behaved (probabilities of attack and detection). In reality, the values of these features are more likely uncertain and must be estimated by the forager. Nonetheless, the model meets all three of Mangel's (1990) criteria for a model of information processing, especially with the consistent treatment of uncertainty, and the model, therefore, is valuable. Figure 9.7a shows an example that is calculated with the model of how ϕ changes after a forager has seen a predator.

Houtman (1995) integrated this information-processing procedure into a model of sculpin foraging. He assumed that foraging decisions were made to maximize survival—which required avoiding both predators and starvation—and he used dynamic programming (Mangel and Clark 1988) to calculate the strategy used to make attack decisions, relative to the current estimate of ϕ, and the amount of food reserves (fig. 9.7b). Sensibly, the model forager was more cautious when ϕ was high, and the forager took greater chances when its energy reserves were low.

9.5 CONCLUSIONS

In this chapter, I examined models of foraging and antipredator behavior to provide a basic framework that can be integrated into building the new disci-

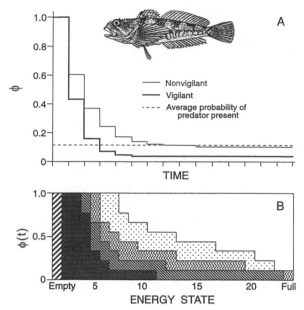

Figure 9.7. (*a*) Change in φ after a tide pool sculpin has detected a predator at time 0. Heavy solid line labeled "vigilant" represents the calculation in the text. Light solid line labeled "non-vigilant" represents the same calculation, except the forager did not use the third updating step (φ″ to φ‴). Horizontal dotted line represents the habitat average probability that a predator was present. (*b*) The survival-maximizing foraging strategy that governed prey-attack decisions depended on the energy state and the estimate that a predator was present [φ(*t*)]. In the hatched region, the forager died of starvation; in the clear region, the forager remained motionless without attacking prey. In the darkest shaded region, prey were attacked at the longest distance; in the lightest shaded region, prey were attacked at the shortest distance (from Houtman 1995).

pline of cognitive ecology. In the terminology used here, the alternative behaviors or options that a forager has in a particular situation are tactics. The choice among the tactics is made with a decision mechanism. I assume natural selection acts on the structure of the decision mechanism and favors variants that perform most proficiently. "Proficient" foraging best attains an objective, often termed a strategy, such as "maximize the net daily gain" or "minimize the foraging time to attain the requirement." Scientists measure the performance of foragers with a currency and often employ the procedure of optimization to predict the most efficient tactic. More careful use of these terms by foraging theorists will help resolve some of the difficulties that many ecologists have with optimal-foraging theory.

In this chapter, I distinguished two basic foraging processes, feeding and provisioning, and explored how time and energy limits affect strategies. In most theoretical work, rate (energy gain per unit time) currencies have been

investigated; however, I concluded that there are many situations in which tactics that maximize the currency called efficiency (energy gain per unit energy expenditure) should be observed in feeding and provisioning situations. A review of the available empirical tests supported this conclusion, but much more careful quantitative work is required. Even in the well-studied area of foraging, this theory remains rudimentary.

A few foraging theorists have worked on the "problem" of information since Oaten (1977) published his article shortly after the publication of Charnov's (1976) marginal value paper. Despite its importance, Oaten's central point is not widely appreciated because perhaps of its apparent difficulty. In trying to give the essence of the problem, I have portrayed the basic idea in its most simple and broadest terms. Any theory of cognitive ecology will have to recognize the importance of information use in foraging behavior to a much greater extent than has been the case during the past twenty years.

In contrast to the reluctant adoption by researchers in foraging of information ideas, ecologists during the past decade have embraced quickly the idea that predation risk is important in foraging behavior. In this chapter, I stressed the points that even very small risks can be important and risks often trade off with foraging gains so that tactics with the highest gains are usually those with the greatest risk. This fact has general, fundamental implications in behavioral ecology and deserves more consideration. Because risk is pervasive, foragers presumably always behave as though a predator is present. Nevertheless, foragers can adjust their behavior to the perceived risk on the basis of information acquired. I closed the chapter by outlining one of the few models that considers the process of information use.

9.6 SUMMARY

In this chapter, I provided an introduction to models of foraging and antipredator behavior. I reviewed some issues that are currently relevant to optimality models of behavior and focused on general properties of these models (and especially the way "currency" is used). I analyzed feeding and provisioning situations and showed how the currency of efficiency (energy gain per unit energy expenditure) is related to the currency of rate (energy gain per unit time) and when each currency should occur. A review of the literature showed that rate and efficiency have been observed. I concluded that much more work must be done before the foundation of a good foraging theory is complete.

Foraging theory has concerned ultimate instead of proximate features of foraging behavior, and I discussed how foraging theory may contribute to the development of cognitive ecology, which concerns decision mechanisms. The analysis of information problems is likely to be central. Unfortunately, few ecologists have given much attention to this important area, and our understanding is such that even simple experiments can still be very instructive.

By contrast, over the last decade much attention has been focused on investigating ways that foragers deal with hazards posed by predators. I provided a brief overview of some current issues and closed by considering a model of how a forager may combine several sources of information to form an estimate of the likelihood that a predator is present and how this estimate may be incorporated into foraging decisions.

ACKNOWLEDGMENTS

Reuven Dukas, Peter Bednekoff, and Mark Abrahams provided valuable comments that improved greatly an earlier version of this chapter. Yoh Iwasa discussed the information experiments with me on a visit to Vancouver in 1984. Students in my graduate seminar, "Survival Strategies" (Spring 1996), enthusiastically discussed information aspects of foraging theory, and Liz Hui in that class developed the presentation of the grasshopper sparrow articles I used here. I thank all of these people for their help.

APPENDIX A: FEEDING MODELS

The time budget is composed of feeding and resting so total time, T, equals $t_f + t_r$. The forager has behavioral options $i = 1, 2, 3, \ldots n$. Energy expenditure during feeding is c_i and gives a rate of intake of b_i (fig. 9.3), and energy expenditure at rest is r. The maximum daily intake is K. Which behavior (choice of i) is best?

Energy Limitation

In energy limitation, the time spent feeding, t_f, is the time required to reach the intake capacity K at rate of intake b_i. If K is reached before T expires, $T - t_f$ must be spent resting. This is called energy limitation. The *total net gain while foraging*, G_f, is then $(b_i - c_i) t_f$. By substituting t_f with K/b_i,

$$G_f = K(1 - c_i/b_i). \tag{A1}$$

This equation corresponds to equation 1 in Ydenberg et al. (1994) and, as explained, is maximized by choosing the most efficient (i.e. highest b_i/c_i or, equivalently, lowest c_i/b_i) feeding option. The *total net daily gain*, G_d, includes the time spent resting. Therefore, we must subtract from G_f the energy spent resting $(t_r \cdot r)$. Then, $G_d = t_f(b_i - c_r) - (t_r \cdot r)$, which yields

$$G_d = K(1 - c_i/b_i + r/b_i) - Tr. \tag{A2}$$

An identical result is derived with equations 1 and 2a in Houston (1995), who showed further that G_d is maximized with the feeding option that provides the highest "modified efficiency," $b_i/(c_i - r)$.

Table 9A.1
Best Feeding Tactic Under Different Strategies and Constraints

	Feeding Strategy	
Constraints	Maximize Net Gain While Foraging (G_f)	Maximize Total Net Daily Gain (G_d)
No limits	Rate	Rate
Energy limitation	Efficiency	Modified efficiency
Time limitation	Rate	Rate

Time Limitation

As explained in the text, feeding is considered time limited when the available feeding time, t_L is less than t_f, so that K is not reached before t_L expires. With a time limit, the *total net gain while foraging* is

$$G_f = t_L(b_i - c_i). \qquad (A3)$$

Taking resting time ($t_r = T - T_L$) into account, the *total net daily gain* is

$$G_d = t_L(b_i - c_i + r) - Tr. \qquad (A4)$$

In both these conditions, the greatest total net daily gain is given with behavioral choice i that corresponds to the rate maximum.

The basic results are summarized in table A1.

APPENDIX B: PROVISIONING MODELS

A provisioner's time budget is composed of time spent in delivery, self-feeding, and resting. Therefore, total time, T, equals $t_d + t_s + t_r$. The time allocated to self-feeding, t_s, must be great enough to maintain positive energy balance. Energy intake and expenditure during self-feeding are b_s and c_s (so the net self-feeding rate is $b_s - c_s$), and energy expenditure at rest is r. The provisioner has behavioral options for delivery $i = 1, 2, 3, \ldots n$. Energy expenditure during delivery is c_i and gives rate of delivery d_i. The energy balance equation is $t_d \cdot c_i + t_s \cdot c_s + t_r \cdot r = b_s \cdot t_s$. The maximum daily expenditure that permits energy balance is limited by the maximum daily intake, K. I assume that the provisioning strategy maximizes the total daily delivery, D_i, while maintaining energy balance. Which behavior (choice of i) is best?

Time Limitation

If the K limit is not reached, no time needs to be spent resting ($T = t_d + t_s$) because the forager is able to "finance" delivery by self-feeding. The day's

energy expenditure is recovered by self-feeding at rate b_s for time t_s, so that $b_s \cdot t_s = t_d \cdot c_i + t_s \cdot c_s$. Solving for t_d yields

$$t_d = \frac{t_s(b_s - c_s)}{c_i}. \qquad \text{(B1)}$$

Equation B1 shows that the time available for delivery increases with the net self-feeding rate ($b_s - c_s$) and declines as delivery becomes more expensive (higher c_i). Total daily delivery $D_i = d_i t_d$. Substituting from equation B1,

$$D_i = \frac{d_i t_s(b_s - c_s)}{c_i}. \qquad \text{(B2)}$$

The term d_i/c_i indicates the importance of efficiency. Behavioral choices with a higher rate of energy expenditure increase the delivery rate, but also increase the amount of time required for self feeding. Hence, the attainable self-feeding rate determines the behavior that maximizes total daily delivery, which lies between the highest-efficiency and the highest-rate options (Ydenberg et al. 1994). Behavior changes from the most efficient option when the self-feeding rate is very low to the highest rate option when the self-feeding rate is high.

Energy Limitation

When K is reached, some time must be spent resting. Therefore, the energy balance equation is $t_d \cdot c_i + t_s \cdot c_s + t_r \cdot r = b_s \cdot t_s$. Solving for t_d and substituting into $D_i = d_i t_d$, we obtain

$$D_i = \frac{d_i[t_s(b_s - c_s) - t_r r]}{c_i}. \qquad \text{(B3)}$$

Houston (1995) showed that under these conditions the tactic with highest "modified efficiency," $d_i/(c_i - r)$, gives the maximum delivery while maintaining energy balance.

LITERATURE CITED

Alexander, R. M. 1982. *Optima for Animals*. London: Edward Arnold.

Beachly, W. M., D. W. Stephens, and K. B. Toyer. 1995. On the economics of sit-and-wait foraging: Site selection and assessment. *Behavioral Ecology* 6:258–268.

Bouskila, A., and D. T. Blumstein. 1992. Rules of thumb for predation hazard assessment: Predictions from a dynamic model. *American Naturalist* 139:161–176.

Charnov, E. L. 1976. Optimal foraging: The marginal value theorem. *Theoretical Population Biology* 9:129–136.

Cheverton, J. 1983. Bumblebees may use a suboptimal arbitrary handedness to solve difficult foraging decisions. *Animal Behaviour* 30:934–935.

Clark, C. W., and D. A. Levy. 1988. Diel vertical migrations by juvenile sockeye salmon and the antipredation window. *American Naturalist* 131:271–290.

Dehn, M. M. 1994. Optimal reproduction under predation risk: Consequences for life history and population dynamics in microtine rodents. Ph.D. diss., Simon Fraser University, Burnaby, British Columbia.

Demas, G. E., and M. F. Brown. 1995. Honeybees are predisposed to win-shift but can learn to win-stay. *Animal Behaviour* 50:1041–1045.

Dill, L. M., and A. H. G. Fraser. 1984. Risk of predation and the feeding behavior of juvenile coho salmon (*Oncorhynchus kisutch*). *Behavioral Ecology and Sociobiology* 16:65–71.

Dill, L. M., and R. Houtman. 1989. The influence of distance to refuge on flight initiation distance in the grey squirrel (*Sciurus carolinensis*). *Canadian Journal of Zoology* 67:233–235.

Dill, L. M., and J. F. Gillett. 1991. The economic logic of barnacle *Balanus glandula* (Darwin) hiding behavior. *Journal of Experimental Marine Biology and Ecology* 153:115–127.

Dinsmoor, J. A. 1983. Observing and conditioned reinforcement. *The Brain and Behavioral Sciences* 6:693–728.

Ens, B. J. 1992. The social prisoner: Causes of natural variation in reproductive success of the Oystercatcher. Ph.D. diss., Rijksuniversiteit Groningen, the Netherlands.

Green, R. F. 1980. Bayesian birds: A simple example of Oaten's stochastic model of optimal foraging. *Theoretical Population Biology* 18:244–256.

Gould, S. J., and R. C. Lewontin. 1979. The spandrels of San Marco and the Panglossian paradigm: A critique of the adaptationist programme. *Proceedings of the Royal Society of London,* ser. B 205:581–598.

Harfenist, A., and R. C. Ydenberg. 1995. Parental provisioning and predation risk in the rhinoceros auklet (*Cerorhinca monocerata*): Effects on nestling growth and fledging. *Behavioral Ecology* 6:82–86.

Hedenström, A., and T. Alerstam. 1995. Optimal flight speeds of birds. *Philosophical Transactions of the Royal Society of London,* ser. B 348:471–487.

Heinrich, B. 1978. *Bumblebee Economics.* Boston, Mass.: Belknap.

Houston, A. I. 1987. Optimal foraging by parent birds feeding their young. *Journal of Theoretical Biology* 124:251–274.

———. 1995. Energetic constraints and foraging efficiency. *Behavioral Ecology* 6: 393–396.

Houtman, R. 1995. The influence of predation risk on within-patch foraging decisions of cryptic animals. Ph.D. diss., Simon Fraser University, Burnaby, British Columbia.

Houtman, R., L. R. Paul, R. V. Ungemach, and R. C. Ydenberg. 1997. Feeding and predator avoidance in the rose anemone *Tealia piscivora*. *Marine Biology* 128:225–229.

Iwasa, Y., M. Higashsi, and N. Yamamura. Prey distribution as a factor determining the choice of optimal foraging strategy. *American Naturalist* 117:710–723.

Juanes, F. 1992. Why do decapod crustaceans prefer small-sized prey? *Marine Ecology Progress Series* 87:239–249.

Juanes, F., and E. B. Hartwick. 1990. Prey size selection in the Dungeness crab: The effect of claw damage. *Ecology* 71:744–758.

Kacelnik, A. 1984. Central place foraging in starlings (*Sturnus vulgaris*). I. Patch residence time. *Journal of Animal Ecology* 53:283–299.

Kamil, A. C., J. R. Krebs, and H. R. Pulliam, eds. 1987. *Foraging Behavior.* New York: Plenum.

Kamil, A. C., R. L. Misthal, and D. W. Stephens. 1993. Failure of optimal foraging models to predict residence time when patch quality is uncertain. *Behavioral Ecology* 4:350–363.

Kaspari, M. 1990. Prey preparation and the determinants of handling time. *Animal Behaviour* 40:118–126.

———. 1991. Prey preparation as a way that grasshopper sparrows (*Ammodramus savannarum*) increase the nutrient concentration of their prey. *Behavioral Ecology* 2:234–241.

Kasuya, E. 1982. Central place water collection in a Japanese paper wasp (*Polistes chinensis antennalis*). *Animal Behaviour* 30:1010–1014.

Krebs, J. R., and A. Kacelnik. 1991. Decision making. In J. R. Krebs and N. B. Davies, eds., *Behavioral Ecology: An Evolutionary Approach,* 105–136. Oxford: Blackwell Scientific.

Kühnholz, S. 1994. Regulation der wassersammelaktiviteit bei honigbienen (*Apis mellifera*). Diplomarbeit, Julius-Maximilians-Universität, Wurzbürg, Germany.

Lima, S. L. 1983. Downy woodpecker foraging behavior: Efficient sampling in simple stochastic environments. *Ecology* 65:166–174.

———. 1986. Predation risk and unpredictable feeding conditions: Determinants of body mass in birds. *Ecology* 67:377–385.

———. 1987a. Clutch size in birds: A predation perspective. *Ecology* 68:1062–1070.

———. 1987b. Vigilance while feeding and its relation to the risk of predation. *Journal of Theoretical Biology* 124:303–316.

Lima, S. L., and L. M. Dill. 1990. Behavioral decisions made under the risk of predation: A review and prospectus. *Canadian Journal of Zoology* 68:619–640.

Mangel, M. 1990. Dynamic information in uncertain and unchanging worlds. *Journal of Theoretical Biology* 146:181–189.

Mangel, M., and C. W. Clark. 1988. *Dynamic Programming in Behavioral Ecology.* Princeton, N.J.: Princeton University Press.

Marrow, P., J. M. McNamara, A. I. Houston, I. R. Stevenson, and T. H. Clutton-Brock. 1996. State-dependent life history evolution in Soay sheep: Dynamic modeling of reproductive scheduling. *Philosophical Transactions of the Royal Society of London,* ser. B 351:17–32.

McNamara, J. M., and A. I. Houston. 1987a. Foraging in patches: There's more to life than the marginal value theorem. In M. L. Commons, A. Kacelnik, and S. J. Shettleworth, eds., *Quantitative Analyses of Behavior,* Vol. 6, 23–39. Hillsdale, N.J.: Erlbaum.

———. 1987b. A general framework for understanding the effects of variability and interruptions on foraging behaviour. *Acta Biotheoretica* 36:3–22.

McLaughlin, R. L., and R. D. Montgomerie. 1990. Flight speeds of parental birds feeding dependent nestlings: Maximizing foraging efficiency or food delivery rate? *Canadian Journal of Zoology* 68:2269–2274.

Montgomerie, R. D., J. M. Eadie, and L. D. Harder. 1984. What do foraging humming-birds maximize? *Oecologia* 63:357–363.

Myers, J. P. 1983. Commentary. In A. H. Brush and G. A. Clark, Jr., eds., *Perspectives in Ornithology*, 216–221. New York: Cambridge University Press.

Mylius, S. D., and O. Diekmann. 1995. On evolutionarily stable life histories and the need to be specific about density dependence. *Oikos* 74:218–224.

Norrdahl, K., and E. Korpimäki. 1996. Do nomadic avian predators synchronize popu-lation fluctuations of small mammals?: A field experiment. *Oecologia* 107(4):478–483.

Oaten, A. 1997. Optimal foraging in patches: A case for stochasticity. *Theoretical Population Biology* 12:263–285.

Orians, G. H., and N. E. Pearson. 1979. On the theory of central place foraging. In D. J. Horn, R. D. Mitchell, and R. D. Stairs, eds., *Analysis of Ecological Systems*, 154–177. Columbus: Ohio State University Press.

Palmer, A. R. 1985. Adaptive value of shell variation in *Thais lamellosa:* Effect of thick shells on vulnerability to and preference by crabs. *Veliger* 27:349–356.

Peckarsky, B. L., C. A. Cowan, M. A. Penton, and C. Anderson. 1993. Sublethal conse-quences of stream-dwelling predatory stoneflies on mayfly growth and fecundity. *Ecology* 74:1836–1846.

Piersma, T., R. Hoekstra, A. Dekinga, A. Koolhaas, P. Wolf, P. Battley, and P. Wiersma. 1993. Scale and intensity of intertidal habitat use by knots *Calidris canuta* in the western Wadden Sea in relation to food, friends, and foes. *Netherlands Journal of Sea Research* 31:331–357.

Price, K., and R. C. Ydenberg. 1995. Begging and provisioning in broods of asynchro-nously-hatched yellow-headed blackbird nestlings. *Behavioral Ecology and Socio-biology* 37:201–208.

Prins, H. H. T. 1989. Condition change and choice of social environment in African buffalo bulls. *Behavior* 108:297–324.

Pyke, G. H. 1981. Hummingbird foraging on artificial inflorescences. *Behaviour Analy-sis Letters* 1:11–15.

———. 1982. Optimal foraging in bumblebees: Rule of departure from an inflores-cence. *Canadian Journal of Zoology* 60:417–428.

Rapport, D. J. 1991. Myths in the foundations of economics and ecology. *Biological Journal of the Linnean Society* 44:185–202.

Real, L. A. 1993. Toward a cognitive ecology. *Trends in Ecology and Evolution* 8:413–417.

Roberts, G. 1996. Why individual vigilance declines as group size increases. *Animal Behaviour* 51:1077–1086.

Robles, C., D. A. Sweetnam, and D. Dittman. 1989. Diel variation of intertidal foraging by *Cancer productus* L. in British Columbia. *Journal of Natural History* 23:1041–1049.

Rosenzweig, M. L. 1974. On the optimal aboveground activity of bannertail kangaroo rats. *Journal of Mammology* 55:193–199.

Rowe, L., and D. Ludwig. 1991. Size and timing of metamorphosis in complex life cycles: Time constraints and variation. *Ecology* 72:413–427.

Salant, S. W., K. L. Kalat, and A. Wheatcroft. 1996. Deducing fitness implications of fitness maximization when a trade-off exists among alternate currencies. *Behavioral Ecology* 6:424–434.

Schmid-Hempel, P. 1987. Efficient nectar collection by honeybees. I. Economic models. *Journal of Animal Ecology* 56:209–218.

Schmid-Hempel, P., A. Kacelnik, and A. I. Houston. 1985. Honeybees maximize efficiency by not filling their crop. *Behavioral Ecology and Sociobiology* 17:61–66.

Schaffner, F. E. 1990. Food provisioning by white-tailed tropicbirds: Effects on the developmental pattern of chicks. *Ecology* 71:375–390.

Sih, A. 1992. Prey uncertainty and the balancing of antipredator and feeding needs. *American Naturalist* 139:1052–1069.

Smith, J. M. N. 1974. The food searching behaviour of two European thrushes. II. The adaptiveness of the search patterns. *Behaviour* 49:1–61.

Soler, M., J. J. Soler, A. P. Møller, J. Moreno, and M. Lindén. 1996. The functional significance of sexual display: Stone carrying in the black wheatear. *Animal Behaviour* 51:247–254.

Stephens, D. W. 1987. On economically tracking a variable environment. *Theoretical Population Biology* 32:15–25.

Stephens, D. W. 1989. Variance and the value of information. *American Naturalist* 134:128–140.

Stephens, D. W., and J. R. Krebs. 1986. *Foraging Theory.* Princeton, N.J.: Princeton University Press.

Sutherland, G. D., and C. L. Gass. 1995. Learning and remembering of spatial patterns by hummingbirds. *Animal Behaviour* 50:1273–1286.

Swennen, C., M. F. Leopold, L. L. M. de Bruijn. 1989. Time-stressed oystercatchers, *Haematopus ostralegus,* can increase their intake rates. *Animal Behaviour* 38:8–22.

Systad, G. H. 1996. Effects of reduced daylength on the activity patterns of wintering seaducks. Candidate scientist thesis, University of Tromsø, Norway.

Taghon, G. L., R. F. L. Self, and P. A. Jumars. 1978. Predicting particle selection by deposit feeders: A model and its implications. *Limnology and Oceanography* 23: 752–759.

Thorpe, W. H. 1979. *The Origins and Rise of Ethology.* New York: Praeger.

Tooze, Z. J., and C. L. Gass. 1985. Responses of rufous hummingbirds to midday fasts. *Canadian Journal of Zoology* 63:2249–2253.

Waage, J. K. 1979. Foraging for patchily distributed hosts by the parasitoid *Nemeritis canescens. Journal of Animal Ecology* 48:353–371.

Waite, T. A., and R. C. Ydenberg. 1994a. What currency do scatter-hoarding grey jays maximize? *Behavioral Ecology and Sociobiology* 34:43–49.

———. 1994b. Shift towards efficiency maximizing by grey jays hoarding in winter. *Animal Behaviour* 48:1466–1468.

———. 1996. Foraging currencies and the load size decision of scatter-hoarding grey jays. *Animal Behaviour* 51:903–916.

Weiner, J. 1992. Physiological limits to sustainable energy budgets in birds and mammals: Ecological implications. *Trends in Ecology and Evolution* 7:384–388.

Welham, C. V. J., and R. C. Ydenberg. 1988. Net energy versus efficiency maximizing by foraging ring-billed gulls. *Behavioural Ecology and Sociobiology* 23:75–82.

————. 1993. Efficiency maximizing flight speeds in parent black terns. *Ecology* 74: 1893–1901.

Wolf, T., and P. Schmid-Hempel. 1990. On the integration of individual foraging strategies with colony ergonomics in social insects: Nectar collection in honeybees. *Behavioural Ecology and Sociobiology* 27:103–111.

Ydenberg, R. C. 1984. Great tits and giving-up times: Decision rules for leaving patches. *Behaviour* 90:1–24.

————. 1994. The behavioral ecology of provisioning in birds. *Ecoscience* 1:1–14.

Ydenberg, R. C., and L. M. Dill. 1986. The economics of fleeing from predators. *Advances in the Study of Behavior* 16:229–249.

Ydenberg, R. C., C. V. J. Welham, R. Schmid-Hempel, P. Schmid-Hempel, and G. Beauchamp. 1994. Time and energy constraints and the relationships between currencies in foraging theory. *Behavioral Ecology* 5:28–34.

Ydenberg, R. C., and P. Hurd. 1998. Simple feeding models with time and energy constraints. *Behavioral Ecology* (in press).

Zach, R., and J. B. Falls. 1977. Influence of capturing a prey on subsequent search in the ovenbird (Aves:Parulidae). *Canadian Journal of Zoology* 55:1958–1969.

Zaklas, S., and R. C. Ydenberg. 1997. The body size–burial depth relationship in the infaunal clam *Mya arenaria*. *Journal of Experimental Marine Biology and Ecology* 215:1–17.

Evolutionary Ecology of Partner Choice

LEE A. DUGATKIN AND ANDREW SIH

10.1 INTRODUCTION

If we were to plot out virtually any animal's time budget, one thing would become strikingly obvious. Animals are constantly faced with choices—what to eat, where to live, with what individuals to live, with what individuals to associate, and what individual to choose as a mate. The list is almost endless. Many of these decisions concern *choice of partners* (i.e. other individuals with which animals interact) for various activities. How such choices are made can have an obvious effect on an individual's fitness. To the extent that choice behavior is cognitive, investigation of partner choice falls under the rubric of cognitive ecology, and we expect that natural selection has shaped partner choice behavior.

Even a cursory scan of the behavioral ecology literature demonstrates that mate choice, particularly female mate choice, is an area of great interest. Hardly an issue of any major journal in the field is published without at least one article on female mate choice. Andersson's (1994) monograph on sexual selection cites 243 studies on female mate choice (versus 30 references on male mate choice) (see Table 6.2.2; Andersson 1994, 128). Why the fascination with female mate choice? There are no doubt many answers to this question. On one level, female mate choice is important because it clearly influences the fitness of preferred and unpreferred males and could affect the fitness of the female. In particular, from an evolutionary perspective, the dynamics of female mate choice may explain the evolution of bizarre male sexual ornaments and behavior; thus, there is considerable interest in the coevolution of female preference and male traits.

Choice of mates, however, is only one of a number of decisions regarding association patterns that animals make on a regular basis. With regard to time budgets, mate choice may only account for a small portion of the total time that an animal spends on partner choice. Animals associate with other conspecifics and choose partners for a wide array of activities besides mating, such as foraging, antipredator activities, sharing territories, and dividing various labors. Depending on the associated costs and benefits, partner choice in these contexts may be more or less important than mate choice.

Despite the likely importance of partner choice, very little attention has been paid to how individuals choose partners other than mating partners. Why partner choice has received so little attention is difficult to explain. One possibility is that researchers simply have not started with the premise that animals are capable of complex behaviors such as partner choice (except in the limited sense of female choice). Once data began to accrue that animals are indeed capable of such actions, numerous follow-up studies were inevitable. Another possibility, before the emergence of game-theoretical thinking (which is based on the notion that an individual's fitness is contingent on its actions and those of others) is that behavioral researchers did not focus on how others affect one's fitness. Regardless of the reason that partner choice received little attention until lately, the subject is interesting because of its behavioral, evolutionary, and cognitive aspects, and the area of partner choice is replete with conceptually intriguing issues of general interest. In this chapter, we will examine some of these issues: (1) the definition of partner choice; (2) examples of partner choice; (3) different types of partner choice; (4) atomistic approaches to the study of partner choice; (5) the cost or benefit perspective of partner choice; and (6) cognitive ecology and partner choice. A fair share of the work on partner choice has been undertaken in the lower vertebrates; because this work is particularly interesting from a cognitive perspective, we will concentrate on this group of animals. This is not to say that partner choice has not been documented many times in mammals and birds (e.g., see the volume of Harcourt and de Waal 1992 on coalitions in animals); however, to tackle the questions we wish to address in a single chapter, we have opted to focus on lower vertebrates (particularly fish) and include discussion of the occasional invertebrate study.

10.2 What Is Partner Choice?

The term "choice" is somewhat amorphous, and so we begin with a brief discussion of definitions (see Bateson 1990 for further discussion). In its most stringent sense, choice implies a decision made among alternative options (Hutto 1985). For example, in the context of habitat choice, Rosenzweig (1990) suggested that choice means nonrandom behavior that is guided by the reception and processing of information by the nervous system. Although we agree that information processing is part of the process of choice, we define choice independently of the neural mechanisms that govern it (see Byers and Bekoff 1986 for more discussion on recognition, nonrandom behavior, and the nervous system). We define partner choice as a nonrandom tendency for an individual—the chooser—to interact with some individuals (or types of individuals) instead of other encountered individuals (or types of individuals).

Continuing with our discussion of definitions, we think it is worthwhile to distinguish between partner choice and apparent partner choice. Apparent part-

ner choice occurs when an individual interacts with a particular partner at a higher-than-expected frequency simply because it encounters that potential partner with greater frequency than that of random occurrence. Apparent partner choice does not mean interaction at a higher than random probability with that partner given an encounter. For example, size-assortative mate choice—the tendency for like-sized individuals to mate—can be due to true size-assortative mate choice by both males and females or size-assortative microhabitat use (Crespi 1989). The former possibility is mate choice; the latter possibility may be apparent mate choice. The existence of size-biased microhabitat use, however, does not rule out true partner choice. Microhabitat choice itself may reflect mate choice. For example, during the mating season, large individuals may share the same microhabitat because they prefer to encounter and mate with each other (see Hutto 1985 for a discussion of apparent habitat selection).

We distinguish a hierarchy of levels of decision making and partner choice. On one level, organisms choose activity patterns in space and time (i.e. they choose when and where to be active and a set of potential activities, such as foraging, antipredator, and mating activities). While active, organisms encounter and choose among potential partners. After selecting a partner, individuals choose particular behaviors that are often in response to a partner's past or current actions. We will focus on the middle step—partner choice.

This hierarchical view is analogous to that used in studies of foraging and antipredator behavior (Chesson 1983; Lima and Dill 1990; Ydenberg, this vol. section 9.4). For example, suppose that a forager displays a preference to feed on prey type 1 over prey type 2. A hierarchical perspective suggests three reasons why such a preference may be found: (1) Preference is determined by the forager's search mode. Does the forager ambush or actively search for prey? If the forager ambushes its prey and prey type 1 is more active and thus encountered more frequently by the ambush predator, then these conditions may result in an apparent preference for prey type 1. (2) The forager may exhibit a preference for a particular patch choice or a particular diurnal foraging habit, which may include prey 1 but not prey 2. (3) The forager experiences both prey types but displays an active choice for prey type 1. Active diet choice for type 1 occurs when a forager has a higher probability of attacking 1 than 2, given equal probability of an encounter with each.

If we now consider partner choice in the context of foraging, a similar scenario unfolds. Suppose that while foraging, individual X tends to be in the vicinity of individual Y but not in that of individual Z. This situation may occur because X and Y share a common preference for some type of prey and Z does not. Alternatively, all three share the same food preference, but X and Y are active at the same time and place and Z is active at a different time or place. Finally, X may be equally likely to encounter Y or Z; however, given an encounter, X prefers to forage with Y instead of Z. This last situation clearly

involves partner choice. The other two situations result in a tendency for X to forage near Y (but not Z) because there are more encounters between X and Y than between X and Z.

Most laboratory experiments on partner choice are designed to force X to encounter Y and Z; thus, some of the difficulties inherent in studying partner choice in the field are avoided. Nonetheless, laboratory experiments can be constructed to examine the possible complexities associated with the hierarchical view outlined. To study partner choice within the hierarchical framework, we suggest the following methodology. First, quantify nonrandom associations (e.g. X interacts with Y more frequently than X interacts with other individuals) with use of statistics developed for foraging experiments (Chesson 1983; Van der Meer 1992). Then examine activity patterns: Does X simply encounter Y more often than X encounters other individuals? If X and Y interact with greater frequency than that expected at random, remove Y to see if X's activity pattern is caused primarily by partner choice. Finally, directly observe encounters to see if X preferentially chooses to interact with Y (over others) when X and Y are near each other.

10.3 EXAMPLES OF PARTNER CHOICE

To be a truly interesting subject to cognitive and behavioral ecologists, partner choice needs to be a general phenomenon (i.e. one that takes place in a wide array of contexts). The evidence on most types of partner choice in lower vertebrates is still relatively scanty; however, we argue in this section that partner choice may be found in many different social milieus.

10.3.1 Imitation and Female Mate Choice

While there have been literally hundreds of studies on how females choose their mates (Andersson 1994), most of these studies, although interesting in their own right, say little about cognitive ecology. Recent work on imitation and female mate choice, however, directly addresses cognitive and evolutionary aspects of partner choice (Dugatkin 1996a).

Using the guppy (*Poecilia reticulata*), Dugatkin (1992) performed the first controlled experiments that examined female mate copying. A "focal" female observed another "model" female near one of two males, and the focal female was subsequently given the choice to spend time near either male. A significant proportion of the focal females preferred to associate with the male that was near the model female. In five control experiments, alternative hypotheses were examined regarding group size, position effects, male behavior, and partner choice outside the context of mating. These control experiments ruled out alternative explanations and strongly supported the hypothesis that the focal female remembered the identity of the male near the model and preferred that

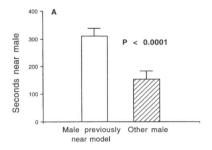

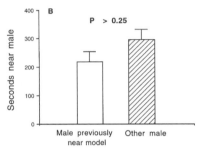

Figure 10.1. (*a*) Mean number of seconds (±standard error [SE]) younger focal females spent near each male when one male was observed near an older model female. (*b*) Mean number of seconds (±SE) older focal females spent near each male when one male was observed near a younger model female (adapted from Dugatkin and Godin 1993).

male in mate-choice tests. Subsequent work established that a female's choice of mates could be reversed with social cues (Dugatkin and Godin 1992a) and that young females were more likely to imitate older females than vice versa (Dugatkin and Godin 1993) (fig. 10.1). Furthermore, female guppies with a heritable preference for orange body color in males preferred less orange males if (1) the focal female observed the less colorful male near a model female; and (2) the difference in male coloration was small or moderate. If, however, the focal female observed the less orange male near a model but the difference in male color was very large, the focal female preferred the more orange male (Dugatkin 1996a).

10.3.2 Antipredator Behavior and Partner Choice

Because of the interest predator-inspection behavior has drawn as a possible case of Tit-for-Tat cooperation (see Dugatkin 1997 for a review), some of the most direct evidence for partner choice comes from studies on Tit-for-Tat cooperation in fish. During predator inspections, fish break away from their school and approach a putative predator in a slow, directed, saltatory manner;

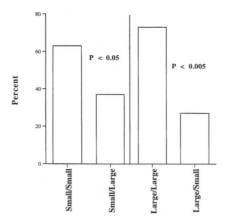

Figure 10.2. Two bars on the left show the percentage of time small sticklebacks spent near schools composed of small or large conspecifics. Two bars on the right represent the results when large fish were tested in a similar manner (adapted from Ranta and Lindstrom 1990).

fish appear to attempt to gain information about this potential danger (Pitcher 1993; Dugatkin and Godin 1992b). Dugatkin (1992) found that predator inspectors suffer relatively high rates of predation; therefore we may expect natural selection to select for "trustworthy" partners during this dangerous task (Milinski et al. 1990; Dugatkin and Alfieri 1991). As such, we might predict that inspectors tend to associate with others that have shown a tendency to inspect in the recent past. The effect of this type of partner choice would presumably decrease the risk of death because of the dilution effect. Recent work in guppies (*Poecilia reticulata*) and sticklebacks (*Gasterosteus aculeatus*) supports this notion; inspectors preferred co-inspectors that had, during prior inspection sorties, stayed by the inspector's side and approached a predator (Milinski et al. 1990; Dugatkin and Alfieri 1991). Experience, however, is not the only factor that influences how one chooses partners for inspecting a predator. Kulling and Milinski (1992) found that inspecting sticklebacks also seem to prefer large individuals as coinspectors.

One emergent effect of partner choice is the formation of groups that are segregated with the criteria used in such a choice. A widely discussed hypothesis for the production of such size-assorted groups is the oddity effect (Ohguchi 1981), which occurs when individuals sort into groups according to size because odd-sized individuals are most apparent to predators (Landeau and Terborgh 1986; Theodorakis 1989). For example, Ranta and Lindstrom (1990) and Ranta et al. (1992) found that large sticklebacks preferred to associate with schools composed of large instead of small fish, although large fish foraged more effectively when associating with smaller conspecifics (fig. 10.2). Apparently for larger sticklebacks, the decreased predation pressure experi-

enced in same-sized groups outweighs any foraging benefits accrued in the presence of smaller conspecifics.

10.3.3 Partner Choice and Foraging

When food is scarce, individuals may prefer foraging partners that enhance their feeding rates. For example, bluegill sunfish (*Lepomis macrochirus*) appeared to choose partners on the basis of long-term expected foraging returns associated with those partners instead of on aggressive history or relative size (Dugatkin and Wilson 1992). In addition, Metcalfe and Thomson (1995) found that European minnows (*Phoxinus phoxinus*) preferred to associate with groups composed of poor food competitors over groups consisting of good competitors (fig. 10.3). The most intriguing aspect of this study was that minnows were capable of making this distinction even when they had no experience foraging with fish in the groups from which they chose! In other words, minnows were able to use other (nonforaging related) cues to determine the foraging abilities of conspecifics.

In the wasp *Cerceris arenaria,* relative size (and not experience) seems to guide the choices of foraging (and more generally nesting) partners (Willmer 1985). Large wasps prefer small individuals as nest mates and vice versa. This mutual preference is likely to benefit both parties because large and small wasps have complementary foraging specializations. Large individuals forage well when temperatures are not extremely hot (and overheating is not a prob-

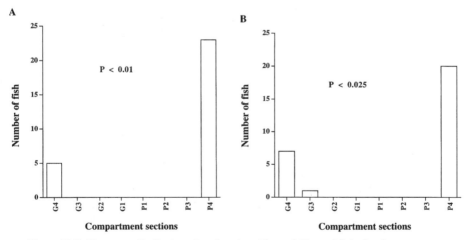

Figure 10.3. Frequency distribution of preferred positions of 28 test fish in the absence (*a*) and presence (*b*) of food. The preferred position was defined as the most frequently occupied zone in the compartment. Section G4 was nearest the shoal of fish with good competitors, and section P4 was closest to the shoal of poor competitors (adapted from Metcalfe and Thomson 1995).

lem), and small individuals forage more efficiently during very hot times of day. Large, territorial striped parrotfish (*Scarus iserti*) also display a preference for smaller nonterritorial conspecifics (Clifton 1991).

10.3.4 Alternative Reproductive Strategies and Partner Choice

Given that males typically compete directly or indirectly with one another for females, one might expect males to display partner-choice rules that increase their probability of mating with a female. The particular rule used, however, may depend critically on the ecology of the species being studied. For example, in natterjack toads (*Bufo calamita*), satellite males prefer to associate with other males that attract the most females to their territory (Arak 1988); this association increases the satellite's encounter rate with females. By contrast, male guppies prefer to associate with less attractive males (Dugatkin and Sargent 1994) (figs. 10.4 and 10.5). This rule may be favored because male

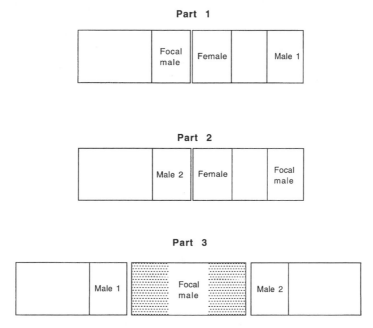

Figure 10.4. Experimental apparatus used by Dugatkin and Sargent (1994) in winner/loser experiment. In parts 1 and 2 of a trial, female proximity to a male was staged by placing the female next to one of two males (with use of clear Plexiglas divider). (*a*) Male 1 was a "loser" with respect to the focal male because the female was nearer to the focal male. (*b*) Male 2, however, was a "winner" with respect to the focal male because the female was closer to male 2 than the focal male. (*c*) In the third part of a trial, the focal male chose between the loser male in part 1 and the winner male in part 2. Results of control experiments ruled out any side preferences (adapted from Dugatkin and Sargent 1994).

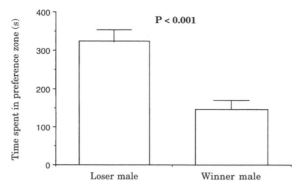

Figure 10.5. Mean number of seconds focal males spent near winner and loser males (adapted from Dugatkin and Sargent 1994).

guppies are not territorial, and females do not mate numerous times in a given male's territory. Thus for guppies, associating with high-quality males would probably decrease another male guppy's chance of copulating.

10.3.5 Familiarity and Partner Choice

Even when one can experimentally document partner choice, the precise rules used may remain a mystery (see section 10.7); (the mechanisms are somewhat better understood for partner choice among kin; Fletcher and Mitchner 1987; Waldman 1987; Hepper 1991). For example, a week after being captured, bluegill sunfish (*Lepomis macrochirus*), preferred to associate with individuals that were caught in the same trap as they were (Brown and Colgan 1986). Familiarity may be what guides partner choice in this case, but other alternatives must be ruled out. The familiarity hypothesis is, however, supported with work on adult bluegill sunfish. Dugatkin and Wilson (1992) found that when two groups of six bluegill sunfish were kept in separate communal tanks for three months and then given choice tests, the sunfish preferred fish from their own tank in 35 of 36 trials!

10.4 TYPES OF PARTNER CHOICE

Partner choice has been studied in numerous contexts (see section 10.3). To help organize and understand similarities and differences among these contexts, we distinguish several types of partner choice. From a functional view, we characterize choice by asking the following questions: (1) Is choice one-sided or reciprocal? (2) Do both sides or does only one side benefit from the interaction? (3) Will potential partners have one, a few, or many interactions? From a cognitive view, we ask the following: (4) Do individuals remember

Table 10.1
Scenarios of Partner Choice

Scenarios	Characteristics	Examples
I	+/−, one-sided	Producer/scrounger, satellite males
II	+/+, one-sided	Female mate choice
III	+/+, two-sided	Two-sided mate choice, predator, inspection, cooperative foraging

the actions of others and choose on the basis of previous experience or are partner-choice rules innate? (5) Do individuals choose partners on the basis of individual differences or do they divide potential partners into simple categories and choose on the basis of a category? We will discuss these types of partner choice in greater detail.

By combining questions 1 and 2, we can identify three main scenarios (table 10.1). In scenario I, choice is strictly one-sided and the chooser alone benefits from the interaction; the chosen partner suffers (i.e. scenario I is a positive/negative [+/−] interaction). Scenario I depicts the well-known producer/scrounger interaction; examples include dominants parasitizing the foraging efforts of subordinates (e.g. Barnard 1984; Hockey and Steele 1990), subordinate satellite males sneaking copulations in the territories of dominant males (Arak 1988; Gross and Charnov 1980), and brood parasitism of parental care (Rothstein 1990; Davies 1992). The +/− nature of this type of interaction creates a conflict that is absent from interactions in which both individuals benefit.

In scenario II, partner choice is still one-sided, but both individuals benefit (positive/positive [+/+]). The most obvious example of this scenario is female mate choice. In many systems, males are generally not choosy because they benefit from mating with any female (i.e. males are almost always willing to be chosen), but females are choosy about their mating partners. A large literature exists on the evolution and adaptive significance of single-sided mate choice (Andersson 1994; Møller 1994).

Finally, in scenario III, both individuals potentially choose their partners. Examples of +/+ two-sided choices include simultaneous male and female mate choice and partner choice for cooperative foraging (Dugatkin and Wilson, 1992), cooperative predator inspection (Milinski 1987; Milinski et al. 1990; Dugatkin and Alfieri 1991, 1992), and the formation of various coalitions (Harcourt and de Waal 1992). The dynamics of the three scenarios depend on the extent of individuals' interactions; repeated interactions tend to favor stable pair bonds and cooperation among partners (Trivers 1971; Axelrod and Hamilton 1981; Mesterton-Gibbons and Dugatkin 1992; Dugatkin 1997). Two-sided +/− partner choice should be relatively rare because the

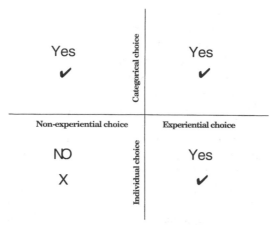

Figure 10.6. Cognitive axes for partner choice. A nonexperiential, individual choice is not possible under the schema devised.

individual that suffers should try to avoid the interaction entirely. Of course, if one defines avoiding a partner as a choice (and it seems reasonable to do so at times), then two-sided $+/-$ partner choices may be more common than stated. Such avoidance may even cause the partner that suffers to move to less preferred areas (e.g. more dangerous spots) to avoid the partner that benefits. In addition, if this partner is making the "best of a bad job," then the frequency of $+/-$ interactions may increase.

From a cognitive view, we distinguish two axes of partner choice—experiential versus nonexperiential and individual versus categorical (fig. 10.6). Experiential choice can be individual or categorical, but nonexperiential choice must be categorical (see the following). When invoking nonexperiential choice, individuals do not base their decision on experience with potential partners; instead, a decision is made on the basis of the categorization of potential partners. For example, a category may be size, and sizes may be large and small. Individuals that prefer to forage in the company of large conspecifics or females that prefer males on the basis of tail length may be displaying categorical partner choice. A correlate of nonexperiential categorical partner choice (or for that matter, categorical choice in general) is that if choice is based on n categories, then all individuals that have the same characteristic in each of these n categories are identical in the eyes of the chooser (i.e. when choosing between two of these individuals, the chooser should be indifferent). On the surface, nonexperiential choice appears equivalent to genetically encoded choice; however, this need not be the case. Partner-choice rules can, in theory, be "inherited" by means of cultural transmission (Boyd and Richerson 1985).

In experiential choice, the chooser uses its own experience to guide partner

choice. For example, an individual may prefer a partner that has been proved to be adept at finding profitable food patches in the past (e.g. Dugatkin and Wilson 1992). Such a choice may be indicative of individual recognition, but need not be. Experiential partner choice can also be categorical (e.g. if an individual has consistently foraged successfully when paired with large partners, its experiential rule may be "choose larger individuals as foraging partners").

Experiential choice may be represented best with points on a continuum instead of a true dichotomy because precise, narrowly defined categories can result in few or even only one individual per category. If individuals have a partner-choice rule such as "choose big blue male individuals that have found profitable food patches in prior foraging bouts," then categorical choice occurs (the categories are "size," "color," "sex," and "foraging history"); however, the composite of these categories may be so narrow that categorization essentially yields individual recognition (Barnard and Burk 1979; also see Barlow et al. 1975 for more on this issue in the context of kin recognition).

Partner choice may also entail a combination of experiential and nonexperiential criteria. For instance, Kulling and Milinski (1992) showed that sticklebacks prefer larger conspecifics as partners during predator inspection. This preference suggests that inspectors classify potential partners on the basis of categories (e.g. large versus small). On the other hand, individual recognition can also occur in the choice of coinspectors; sticklebacks prefer to inspect with partners that have stayed by their side during prior inspection visits (Milinski et al. 1990). More generally, the experiential component of partner choice may dictate "choose a partner that did x and not y the last time you interacted," and the nonexperiential component may be "choose individuals that fall in bin 1, not 2." If the chooser has no prior experience with potential partners, it should simply choose the largest partner. If two potential partners are of equal size, the chooser should select a partner on the basis of prior experience. If, however, one potential partner falls in bin 2, but did x and the other falls in bin 1, but did y, partner choice necessitates use of an algorithm that balances the relative importances of experiential and nonexperiential criteria. Experiments that address these sorts of questions should be easy enough to construct and would provide insight into the decision rules that underlie partner-choice behavior.

10.5 The Atomistic Approach to Studying Partner Choice

Partner choice has been studied in only a very limited context; focal individuals have almost always been given a choice between particular partners who differed in only a single trait (e.g. foraging abilities or antipredator qualities) (see section 10.3 for specific examples). Furthermore, tests of partner choice typically have been done in a single context—foraging only or antipredator

qualities only (see section 10.5 for specific examples). In studies in other areas (e.g. patch choice or activity patterns), animals often appear to use multiple cues to guide behavior. For example, Sih and Krupa (1992) found that predation and hunger level affected mating patterns in *Aquarius remigis* in complex ways that would have remained hidden if an atomistic approach had been taken. We need to move away from this atomistic approach and examine multiple traits and multiple fitness demands in the context of partner choice in general (Sih and Krupa 1992; Sih 1994).

Use of multiple cues appears to allow animals to balance multiple demands (e.g. foraging and mating) that often conflict (Sih 1987; Abrahams and Dill 1989; Lindstrom and Ranta 1993). For example, consider two partner-choice scenarios: (1) Females prefer to forage with males that have been successful at finding profitable food patches despite unusually aggressive behavior in males; or (2) females choose to forage and then mate with males that share food discovered during foraging bouts. In the first case, partner choice requires a balancing of the benefits of foraging against the costs of encountering aggression. In the second case, the same partner may be beneficial in two contexts. Thus, it is difficult (if not impossible), in the second case to delineate the proximate reason females choose particular males (e.g. female choice may depend on their energy intake or the food requirements of future offspring). Single-trait, atomistic partner-choice experiments may be a necessary starting point, but these experiments clearly only initially address the scenarios described.

How may experiments be constructed so that the effect of multiple cues on partner choice are elucidated? One possibility is a titration experiment in which the strength of a given cue is raised or lowered while the other cue remains constant. Such tests may provide evidence for the relative importance of different cues in relation to one another. Different cues may even provide contrasting information. For example, female guppies from the Paria River prefer to mate with more orange males; however, Dugatkin (1996b) found that if an observer female sees another female prefer the less orange of two males, the observer female will, under certain conditions, switch her preference to less orange males. Furthermore, the difference in male orange content can be titrated to examine the relative importance of color and social cues. Similar experiments could easily be constructed so that multiple cues in various partner-choice contexts can be examined.

10.6 THE COSTS AND BENEFITS OF PARTNER CHOICE

10.6.1 Variation in Partner Choice within a Given Context

Three interrelated questions about partner choice that can be analyzed by a cost/benefit approach are the following: (1) Should an individual, in a given situation have a partner or not? (2) If an individual interacts with a partner,

should the individual invoke some sort of partner choice? (i.e. Should the individual prefer to interact with some potential partners over others?) (3) If an individual shows partner choice, what criteria should the individual use to guide its choice? For each question, we can also ask how environmental factors or individual states ought to affect partner choice. Our primary focus is on question 2—Should an individual show partner choice?

In some contexts, an individual must have a partner; in other words, the individual cannot perform a particular task without a partner. In most contexts, however (e.g. foraging or antipredator behavior), one option is no partner. There has been some theoretical work on conditions that favor solitary action over performance of the same action with a partner, particularly in producer/scrounger scenarios (Barnard 1984; Vickery et al. 1991; Caraco and Giraldeau 1991) and during predator inspection (Lima 1989); however, more theoretical and empirical work on this issue is needed in most contexts.

To organize our thinking on adaptive partner choice, we return to the three main types of partner choice (see section 10.5). The best studied scenario is the one-sided $+/+$ interaction (i.e. single-sided mate choice in which both individuals benefit). By following Parker (1978) and Janetos (1980), Real (1990) used a theory that is analogous to optimal diet-choice theory to predict when mate choice (as opposed to random mating) is more likely. Real (1990) argued that mate choice should be relatively common when (1) the benefit of potential partners varies more to the chooser (i.e. there is a greater benefit to partner choice); (2) there is a higher density of high-value partners (i.e. there is a lower time cost of rejecting low-value partners to search for better options); and (3) there are decreased costs per unit time of searching for or choosing partners. These basic predictions should be true in other scenarios (e.g. $+/-$ scenarios or two-sided choices); however, there may be some added complexities (see Real 1991 and Weigmann et al. 1996 for more).

For producer/scrounger scenarios, the $+/-$ nature of the interaction introduces an inherent conflict. Scroungers choose the best producers, and producers presumably attempt to avoid or resist being chosen. Nonetheless, the basic predictions listed for $+/+$ interactions should guide partner choice by scroungers. The value of each potential partner (producer) should depend not only on the partner's inherent quality as a producer but on the probability that the scrounger is able to parasitize that partner (Giraldeau and Lefebrve 1987) and bear the costs of overcoming the partner's resistance/avoidance. Furthermore, if producers can modulate the amount of effort used to resist scroungers, then the interaction can be analyzed as a game (Maynard Smith 1982). Existing theory, however, on adaptive behavior by scroungers focuses not on partner choice among potential partners but on the first question in partner choice: Does an individual scrounge or act alone? Explicit theories (including game theory) and tests of adaptive partner choice and behavioral responses by potential partners in $+/-$ interactions should prove rewarding.

In other scenarios, individuals show reciprocal (two-sided) choice. Game theory on male/female, simultaneous mate choice (Parker 1983; Crowley et al. 1991) predicts that partner choice should depend on an individual's quality relative to other members of its sex. Higher-quality individuals should display the basic predictions listed for single-sided, $+/+$ mate choice. Lower-quality individuals, however, must account for the possible rejection by their favorite partners. For example, mate choice by lower-quality males should depend on the availability of high-quality females, which depends on the abundance of high-quality females and the likelihood that high-quality females will accept lower-quality males as mates. In turn, mate choice by high-quality females should depend on the availability of high-quality males, which depends on mate choice by high-quality males. Obviously, adaptive partner choice in reciprocal games can be very complex.

Both $+/-$ and $+/+$ games become even more interesting if individuals can recognize one another and remember the actions that were taken by particular individuals during prior interactions. In general, theory suggests that, with repeated interactions, individuals should be more likely to cooperate (Trivers 1971; Axelrod and Hamilton 1981; Mesterton-Gibbons and Dugatkin 1992; Dugatkin 1997). In producer/scrounger scenarios, with repeated interactions, it can be beneficial for scroungers to give some benefits to producers to reduce resistance by producers. For example, dominant individuals may allow subordinates to enjoy some feeding or mating opportunities in return for greater loyalty in the producer/scrounger interaction (Stacey 1982; Reeve 1989; Keller and Reeve 1994).

To date, theory on adaptive behavior in repeated reciprocal games has focused on the cooperative or uncooperative behavior of individuals (i.e. on the balance between cooperation and cheating/deception) and not on the partner chosen. Clearly, individuals should prefer partners that cooperate over ones that cheat; however, explicit theory must address more subtle partner-choice decisions that involve partners with variable inherent qualities (e.g. foraging abilities) and traits such as "honesty," "gullibility," or "forgiveness."

10.6.2 Comparisons of Partner Choice across Contexts

We have considered aspects of adaptive partner choice within a given context (e.g. foraging or mating). A more global view would compare partner choice across contexts. Does an adaptationist view help us understand which contexts (e.g., mating, antipredator, feeding) are more likely to feature partner choice?

In the absence of obvious constraints, we expect partner choice to be more likely to occur in situations in which the identity of one's partner has a large effect on fitness. For example, if all else is the same, partner choice for antipredator activities should be highly likely to occur (i.e. one mistake can result in death); choice of mating partners should also be common, but choice of

foraging partners should be less common—especially when food is abundant. This ranking of contexts is based on the supposition that predation and mating are most often multiplicative in terms of selection analyses (Caswell 1989; Lande and Arnold 1983); foraging rate is less tightly related to fitness and more likely additive in nature (we recognize that our ranking system is debatable). Indeed, when food is not limiting, foraging rate (and thus choice of foraging partner) may have little or no measurable effect on fitness. One should not always expect partner choice to be more common in anti-predator activities than in foraging. For example, suppose a physically strong partner is needed to bring down potential prey items, but most potential partners in the context of antipredator activities can warn of oncoming dangers. In such a case, partner choice would be more likely in the context of foraging than antipredator activities. Our argument regarding the occurrence of partner choice can be extended to address how much is invested in partner choice (a more continuous version of the "be choosy" versus "don't be choosy" argument outlined).

We may also expect partner choice to be more likely when it is associated with a larger future commitment in time and resources. In theory, individuals should continuously reevaluate partners and contrast their values against apparent values of potential partners (Peck 1993); however, the costs of switching partners may often force individuals into relatively large, long-term commitments (Lima 1989; Peck 1993).

Finally, $+/+$ interactions should be more likely to include partner choice than $+/-$ interactions. In antagonistic producer/scrounger interactions ($+/-$), a scrounger's encounter rate with available producers may be low because the producer should avoid or resist being chosen by a scrounger. As a result, scroungers may not be choosy about producers; scroungers may "parasitize" any producer they find. By contrast, $+/+$ interactions should result in a greater availability of potential partners for a chooser because both sides benefit; thus, choosers can be choosier. Also, partner choice should be more likely in situations with a one-sided choice versus a two-sided choice. If both sides choose, then most individuals face the risk of being rejected by some fraction of their potential, desirable partners. This risk of rejection, in effect, reduces the availability of potential partners for all but the most valuable individuals and thus reduces the likelihood of nonrandom partner choice.

10.6.3 New Horizons for the Study of Adaptive Partner Choice

Two relatively recent approaches within the optimality framework hold promise for expanding our understanding of partner choice: dynamic optimization (Mangel and Clark 1988; Houston et al. 1988) and the function of uncertainty and information processing in governing behavior (Stephens and Krebs 1986;

Sih and Krupa 1992; Abrams 1994; Bouskila et al. 1995). These approaches have been admirably reviewed elsewhere; we will discuss the sorts of major insights that could emerge from the integration of these approaches into analyses of partner choice.

Dynamic optimization incorporates several major elements of reality that are missing from static models including (1) the role of variation in individual state (e.g. hunger level, developmental stage, reproductive value); (2) the existence of time horizons (i.e. organisms face a finite end for each bout, day, season, or lifetime); and (3) explicit assumptions about the relationship between behavior, state, and fitness. These assumptions are required to express the effects of conflicting demands (e.g. foraging, antipredator, or mating needs) in the common currency, fitness. Some attempts have been made to use dynamic optimization techniques to understand mate choice (Crowley et al. 1991); to our knowledge, however, these techniques have not yet been applied to other aspects of partner choice. Given that variation in individual state, time horizons, and conflicting demands are probably important factors in many partner choice situations, the application of dynamic optimization to partner choice should prove insightful.

Uncertainty is another ubiquitous aspect of reality that is ignored in most analyses of partner choice. Adaptive partner choice requires estimates of the value of each potential partner, of the costs and benefits associated with not having a partner or searching for a partner (e.g. energy costs or predation risk), and assessments of relevant aspects of individual state. In addition, when games are involved, subjects must know not only their own conditions but the options and conditions experienced by other individuals to predict the behavior of perspective partners. Finally, in a variable environment, organisms must assess changes in all of these conditions in time and space. (See Bateson and Kacelnik, this vol. chap. 8; Ydenberg, this vol. chap. 9.)

Analyses of behavior in other contexts suggest that uncertainty serves an important function in shaping foraging and antipredator behavior (Stephens and Krebs 1986; Lima 1989; Sih and Krupa 1992). At a minimum, animals must sample their environment (both potential partners and surrounding conditions) to generate estimates of initial and changing conditions. Sampling usually implies suboptimal behavior in the short-term in exchange for information that allows a closer approach to an optima in the long term. To use information, organisms must obviously remember their past experiences. How should organisms weigh the relative importance of various past experiences? Depending on the pattern of change in conditions in space and time, some memories can be useless or even counterproductive. In addition, memory itself may have neural costs (Dukas, this vol. section 3.5.3). These trade-offs can be balanced to yield an optimal pattern of memory (Healey 1992). In some situations, the cost of sampling can be prohibitively high (e.g. uncertainty about predation

risk) (Sih and Krupa 1992). If organisms cannot afford to gather the information necessary to respond to changing conditions, then organisms may be forced to show inflexible use of an option that is, on average, satisfactory—even if, at times, the option is suboptimal. Some studies on the cognitive aspects of partner choice have shown that prior experience can influence choice (see section 10.5). To our knowledge, however, partner choice studies have not addressed explicitly optimal-sampling regimes or other adaptive responses to uncertainty (see Bekoff et al. 1989 for a discussion in the context of habitat choice). To understand how information processing affects partner choice, future studies should integrate cognitive and adaptationist approaches.

10.7 COGNITIVE ECOLOGY AND PARTNER CHOICE

Some of the most interesting unexplored issues in the field of partner choice concern the new discipline of cognitive ecology, in which the adaptive value of memory and cognition, from proximate and ultimate perspectives is studied (see Sherry this vol. chap. 7).

One issue addressed by cognitive psychologists concerns "domains of learning"—i.e. Do animals have a single, all-purpose learning "algorithm" or do various, separate (but not necessarily unconnected) domains exist in the brain? In terms of partner choice, we may ask if an animal uses categorical-choice criteria in some contexts but individual recognition in others. For example, Dugatkin and Wilson (1992) found that bluegill sunfish use experiential choice on the basis of individual recognition when choosing foraging partners. The question then arises whether sunfish use experiential choice on the basis of individual recognition when choosing partners in other contexts such as antipredator activities or mating. With the domain-general perspective it is suggested that bluegills should use the same type of partner choice across contexts. The domain-specific view allows for the possibility of employing different types of choices in different contexts. Domain specificity, however, does not necessarily predict the use of different types of choices. If natural selection favors different types of partner choices in different contexts and the species has the cognitive prerequisites to perform different types of choices, the domain-specific perspective predicts variation in types of choices across domains. If selection favors the same type of choice across domains, however, the domain-specific view predicts no variation across domains.

With the cognitive view of partner choice, the possibility of "crossover" effects between domains is also suggested. By a crossover effect, we mean the possibility that choices made in one domain (e.g. the foraging domain) affect choices made in a different domain (e.g. the antipredator domain). Imagine an experiment in which individuals use an experiential, individually-based partner choice in one domain (domain 1). With another group of subjects, however, the experiment uncovers that no partner choice is used in a second domain (individuals choose randomly between potential partners in domain-

2 related trials). To test for the possibility of crossover effects, the experiment can be repeated with a single set of subjects, tested first in the domain-1 task and then in the domain-2 task. A given individual chooses between two potential partners in a domain-1 test; then the individual chooses between the same two potential partners in a domain-2 test. Crossover effects are indicated if individuals prefer the same partner in the domain-2 task as in the domain-1 task. Of course, appropriate controls should be run to test for various confounding factors.

A particularly exciting aspect of cognitive ecology is its potential for identifying cognitive constraints on adaptive partner choice (see Dukas, this vol. section 3.2). The ability to make adaptive decisions in a complex, uncertain world can obviously be limited by memory constraints. For example, even if optimality theory shows that an omniscient organism should base its partner choices on the outcome of its last 10 interactions with each of 50 potential partners, the organism cannot if it can only remember the last two interactions with five players. Experiments in other contexts have indeed indicated that some animals base their decisions primarily on their most recent experiences (Logue 1988; Real 1994; Kacelnik and Bateson, this vol. section 9.4.3). If this represents a memory constraint (as opposed to an adaptive decision to ignore information from the more distant past), then this constraint could certainly limit adaptive partner choice.

Another possible constraint arises if individuals are domain general, even when it is adaptive to be domain specific. For example, in some situations it may be beneficial to use categorical, nonexperiential criteria for mate choice (e.g. prefer larger males) but use experience to choose partners for predator inspection (i.e. prefer individuals that have demonstrated that they are cooperative coinspectors). A domain-general individual that always used categorical, nonexperiential criteria to choose partners may then be incapable of adaptive choice of coinspectors. As discussed, the opposite situation does not pose a constraint; a domain-specific individual can, in theory, use the same partner-choice rules across domains if use of these rules is optimal.

Finally, crossover effects (which presumably reflect the organism's cognitive architecture) (compare Real 1994) can also result in nonadaptive partner choice. Any correlation between decisions in different contexts implies a potential constraint on independent adaptive choice in different contexts (Sih 1994). If a correlation (a crossover effect) does not match the optimal pattern of choice across contexts, then the correlation causes suboptimal behavior. For example, if different partners are best in different contexts (mating versus foraging versus predator inspection), then it may not be beneficial to show a tendency to prefer to forage or inspect predators with a favorite mating partner.

Conventional wisdom (no doubt reflecting our natural, unavoidable anthropocentric biases) suggests that organisms with more highly developed brains should be less limited by cognitive constraints (e.g. Harcourt, 1992; Seyfarth

and Cheny, 1994). Most of the extant studies on cognition, however, have concerned several model systems (e.g. rats, mice, pigeons, jays, bees, and primates). A broader comparative survey, with use of modern phylogenetic methods (e.g. Harvey and Pagel 1991), should help identify phylogenetic patterns of cognitive architecture. (See Dukas, this vol. section 4.5.1. Sherry, this vol. section 7.4.4.)

At present, few studies have melded methods in behavioral ecology, evolutionary biology, and cognitive ecology to address the possibility of cognitive constraints on adaptive behavior in any context (but see Real 1994; Kamil 1994; chap. in this vol.). Further work blending ideas in these fields in the study of partner choice should prove rewarding.

10.8 SUMMARY

Choice of mates is only one of a number of decisions regarding partner choice that animals make on a regular basis. Despite its likely importance, until recently, very little attention has been paid to how individuals choose partners outside the context of mating partners. Regardless of the reason that partner choice has received little attention until lately, the subject is interesting in its own regard from behavioral, evolutionary, and cognitive perspectives, and the study of partner choice is replete with conceptually intriguing issues that are of very general interest. In this chapter, we put forth the following ideas, definitions, and challenges:

1. Partner choice is a nonrandom tendency for an individual to associate with some individuals or categories of individuals over other *encountered* potential partners.

2. To date, most investigators of partner choice have focused on female mate choice; however, several studies have documented partner choice in other contexts (e.g. choice of foraging partner). More studies are required to determine the generality of partner choice in nonmating contexts.

3. To examine the adaptive importance of partner choice, it is useful to distinguish four categories of interactions on the basis of whether choice is one-sided or reciprocal and whether both sides $(+/+)$ or only one side $(+/-)$ benefits from the interaction. Female mate choice is an example of a one-sided, $+/+$ interaction. Reciprocal $+/+$ games include reciprocal mate choice and various cooperative interactions. Some models exist on mate choice; however, for other types of partner choice, existing models address primarily whether animals should engage in partner choice at all and not the adaptive consequences of such a choice. To further test the adaptive importance of partner choice, we need more empirical studies that document the fitness consequences of interacting with different potential partners. In the future, optimality-based studies of partner choice should incorporate dynamic opti-

mization, game theory, and the function of uncertainty in shaping partner choice.

4. From a cognitive view, it is useful to distinguish between partner choice on the basis of individual recognition versus categories of individuals (e.g. large versus small) and investigate the role of experience and memory in governing partner choice. More detailed cognitive issues that should prove informative include studies on the domain specificity of partner choice (e.g. Does a given organism use similar rules in different partner choice contexts?) and the possibility of crossover effects. Limited memory, domain-general rules, and crossover effects may serve to generate cognitive constraints that limit the potential for optimal partner choice.

5. Both cognitive and optimality views of partner choice should become less atomistic; they should account more for the possibility that partner choice may be based on multiple traits that balance multiple fitness demands. With both views, comparative methods should also eventually be used to identify phylogenetic patterns of partner choice.

ACKNOWLEDGMENTS

We wish to thank D. Blumstein, A. Dugatkin, D. Dugatkin, R. Dukas, L. Sih, and M. Sih.

LITERATURE CITED

Abrahams, M., and L. M. Dill. 1989. A determination of the energetic equivalence of the risk of predation. *Ecology* 70:999–1007.

Abrams, P. A. 1994. Should prey overestimate the risk of predation? *American Naturalist* 144:317–328.

Andersson, M. 1994. *Sexual Selection.* Princeton, N.J.: Princeton University Press.

Arak, A. 1988. Callers and satellites in the natterjack toad: Evolutionarily stable decision rules. *Animal Behaviour* 36:416–432.

Axelrod, R., and W. D. Hamilton. 1981. The evolution of cooperation. *Science* 211:1390–1396.

Bateson, P. 1990. Choice, preference, and selection. In M. Bekoff and D. Jamieson, eds., *Interpretation and Explanation in the Study of Animal Behaviour,* 149–156. Boulder, Colo: Westview.

Barnard, C. J., ed. 1984. *Producers and Scroungers.* London: Croom Helm/Chapman Hall.

Barnard, C. J., and T. Burk. 1979. Dominance hierarchies and the evolution of individual recognition. *Journal Theoretical Biology* 81:65–73.

Bekoff, M., A. Scott, and D. Conner. 1989. Ecological analyses of nesting success in evening grosbeaks. *Oecologia* 81:647–674.

Bouskila, A., D. T. Blumstein, and M. Mangel. 1995. Prey under stochastic conditions should probably overestimate predation risk: A reply to Abrams. *American Naturalist* 145:1015–1019.

Boyd, R., and P. J. Richerson. 1985. *Culture and the Evolutionary Process.* Chicago: University of Chicago Press.

Brown, J., and P. Colgan. 1986. Individual and species recognition in centrachid fishes: Evidence and hypotheses. *Behav. Ecol. Sociobiol.* 19:373–379.

Byers, J. A., and M. Bekoff. 1986. What does "kin recognition" mean? *Ethology* 72: 342–345.

Caraco, T., and L.-A. Giraldeau. 1991. Social foraging: Producing and scrounging in a stochastic environment. *Journal Theoretical Biology* 153:559–583.

Caswell, H. 1989. *Matrix Population Models.* Sunderland, Mass.: Sinauer.

Chesson, J. 1983. The estimation and analysis of preference and its relationship to foraging models. *Ecology* 64:1297–1304.

Clifton, K. 1991. Subordinate group members act as food-finders within striped parrotfish territories. *Journal of Experimental Marine Biology and Ecology* 145:141–148.

Crespi, B. J. 1989. Causes of assortative mating in arthropods. *Animal Behaviour* 38: 980–1000.

Crowley, P. H., S. Travers, M. Linton, A. Sih, and R. C. Sargent. 1991. Mate density, predation risk, and seasonal sequence of mate choices: A dynamic game. *American Naturalist* 137:567–596.

Davies, N. B. 1992. *Dunnock Behavior and Social Evolution.* Oxford: Oxford University Press.

Dugatkin, L. A. 1992. Sexual selection and imitation: Females copy the mate choice of others. *American Naturalist* 139:1384–1389.

———. 1996a. Imitation and female mate choice. In G. Galef and C. Heyes, eds., *Social Learning in Animals: The Roots of Culture,* 85–106. New York: Academic.

———. 1996b. The interface between culturally-based preferences and genetic preferences: female mate choice in *Poecilia reticulata. Proceedings of the National Academy of Sciences,* U.S.A. 93:2770–2773.

———. 1997. *Cooperation among Animals: An Evolutionary Perspective.* Oxford: Oxford University Press.

Dugatkin, L. A., and M. Alfieri. 1991. Guppies and the TIT FOR TAT strategy: Preference based on past interaction. *Behavioral Ecology and Sociobiology* 28:243–246.

———. 1992. Interpopulational differences in the use of the Tit for Tat strategy during predator inspection in the guppy. *Evolutionary Ecology* 6:519–526.

Dugatkin, L. A., and J.-G. Godin. 1992a. Reversal of female mate choice by copying. *Proceedings of the Royal Society of London,* ser. B 249:179–184.

———. 1992b. Prey approaching predators: A cost-benefit perspective. *Annales Zoologica Fennici* 29:233–252.

———. 1993. Female mate copying in the guppy, *Poecilia reticulata:* Age dependent effects. *Behavioral Ecology* 4:289–292.

Dugatkin, L. A., and R. C. Sargent. 1994. Male-male association patterns and female proximity in the guppy, *Poecilia reticulata. Behavioral Ecology and Sociobiology* 35:141–145.

Dugatkin, L. A., and D. S. Wilson. 1992. The prerequisites of strategic behavior in the bluegill sunfish. *Animal Behaviour* 44:223–230.

Fletcher, D. J., and C. D. Mitchner, eds. 1987. *Kin Recognition in Animals.* New York: Wiley.

Giraldeau, L. A., and L. Lefebrve. 1987. Scrounging prevents cultural transmission of food-finding in pigeons. *Animal Behaviour* 35:387–394.

Gross, M., and R. Charnov. 1980. Alternative male life histories in bluegill sunfish. *Proceedings of the National Academy of Sciences, U.S.A.* 77:6937–6940.

Harcourt, A. H. 1992. Coalitions and alliances: are primates more complex than non-primates? In A. H. Harcourt, and F. B. M. de Waal, eds., *Coalitions and Alliances in Humans and Other Animals,* 445–472. Oxford: Oxford University.

Harcourt, A. H., and F. B. M. de Waal, eds. 1992. *Coalitions and Alliances in Humans and Other Animals.* Oxford: Oxford University.

Harvey, P. H., and M. D. Pagel. 1991. *The Comparative Method in Evolutionary Biology.* Oxford: Oxford University Press.

Healey, S. 1992. Optimal memory: Toward an evolutionary ecology of animal cognition. *Trends in Ecology and Evolution* 8:399–400.

Hepper, P. G., ed. 1991. *Kin Recognition.* Cambridge: Cambridge University Press.

Hockey, P. A. R., and W. K. Steele. 1990. Intraspecific kleptoparasitism and foraging efficiency as constraints on food selection by kelp gulls *Larus dominicanus.* In R. N. Hughes, ed., *Behavioural Mechanisms of Food Selection,* 679–706. Berlin: Springer-Verlag.

Houston, A. I., C. Clark, J. M. McNamara, and M. Mangel. 1988. Dynamic models in behavioral ecology. *Nature* 332:29–34.

Hutto, R. L. 1985. Habitat selection by nonbreeding: Migratory land birds. In M. L. Cody, ed., *Habitat Selection in Birds,* 455–476. Orlando, Florida: Academic.

Janetos, A. C. 1980. Strategies of female choice: A theoretical analysis. *Behavioral Ecology and Sociobiology* 7:107–112.

Kamil, A. 1994. A synthetic approach to the study of animal intelligence. In L. A. Real, ed., *Behavioral Mechanisms in Evolutionary Ecology,* 11–45. Chicago: University of Chicago Press.

Keller, L., and H. K. Reeve. 1994. Partitioning of reproduction in animal societies. *Trends in Ecology and Evolution* 9:98–102.

Kulling, D., and M. Milinski. 1992. Size-dependent predation risk and partner quality for predator inspection in sticklebacks. *Animal Behaviour* 44:949–955.

Lande, R., and S. J. Arnold. 1983. The measurement of selection on correlated characters. *Evolution* 37:1210–1226.

Landeau, L., and J. Terborgh. 1986. Oddity and the "confusion effect"—in predation. *Animal Behaviour* 34:1372–1380.

Lima, S. 1989. Iterated Prisoner's Dilemma: An approach to evolutionarily stable cooperation. *American Naturalist* 134:828–834.

Lima, S., and L. Dill. 1990. Behavioral decisions made under the risk of predation: a review and prospectus. *Canadian Journal of Zoology* 68:619–640.

Lindstrom, K., and E. Ranta. 1993. Social preferences by male guppies, *Poecilia reticulata* based on shoal size and sex. *Animal Behaviour* 46:1029–1031.

Logue, A. W. 1988. Research on self-control: An integrating framework. *Behavioral and Brain Science* 11:665–709.

Mangel, M., and C. Clark. 1988. *Dynamic Modeling in Behavioral Ecology,* Princeton, N.J.: Princeton University Press.

Maynard Smith, J. 1982. *Evolution and the Theory of Games.* Cambridge: Cambridge University Press.

Mesterton-Gibbons, M., and L. A. Dugatkin. 1992. Cooperation among unrelated individuals: Evolutionary factors. *Quarterly Review of Biology* 67:267–281.

Metcalfe, N. B., and B. C. Thomson. 1995. Fish recognize and prefer to shoal with poor competitors. *Proceedings of the Royal Society of London,* ser. B 259:207–210.

Milinski, M. 1987. TIT FOR TAT and the evolution of cooperation in sticklebacks. *Nature* 325:433–435.

Milinski, M., D. Kulling, and R. Kettler. 1990. Tit for Tat: Sticklebacks "trusting" a cooperating partner. *Behavioral Ecology* 1:7–12.

Møller, A. P. 1994. *Sexual Selection and the Barn Swallow.* Oxford: Oxford University Press.

Ohguchi, O. 1981. Prey density and selection against oddity by three-spined sticklebacks. *Zeitschrift für Tierpsychologie* 23 (suppl.).

Parker, G. A. 1978. Searching for mates. In J. R. Krebs and N. B. Davies, eds., *Behavioral Ecology,* 214–244. Sunderland, Mass.: Sinauer.

———. 1983. Mate quality and mating decisions. In P. Bateson, ed., *Mate Choice,* 141–166. Cambridge: Cambridge University Press.

Peck, J. R. 1993. Friendship and the evolution of cooperation. *Journal of Theoretical Biology* 162:195–228.

Pitcher, T. 1993. Who dares wins: The function and evolution of predator inspection behaviour in shoaling fish. *Netherlands Journal of Zoology* 42:371–391.

Ranta, E., and K. Lindstrom. 1990. Assortative schooling in three-spined sticklebacks? *Annales Zoologica Fennici* 27:67–75.

Ranta, E., K. Lindstrom, and N. Peuhkuri. 1992. Size matters when three-spined stickleback go to school. *Animal Behaviour* 43:160–162.

Real, L. 1990. Search theory and mate choice. I. Models of single-sex discrimination. *American Naturalist* 136:376–404.

———. 1991. Search theory and mate choice. II. Mutual interaction, assortative mating, and equilibrium variation in male and female fitness. *American Naturalist* 139:901–917.

———. 1994. Information processing and the evolutionary ecology of cognitive architecture. In L. A. Real, ed., *Behavioral Mechanisms in Evolutionary Ecology,* 99–132. Chicago: University of Chicago Press.

Reeve, H. K. 1989. The evolution of conspecific acceptance thresholds. *American Naturalist* 133:407–435.

Rosenzweig, M. 1990. Do animals choose habitats? In M. Bekoff and D. Jamieson, eds., *Interpretation and Explanation in the Study of Animal Behaviour,* 157–179. Boulder, Colo.: Westview.

Rothstein, S. I. 1990. A model system for coevolution: Avian brood parasitism. *Annual Review of Ecology and Systematics* 21:481–508.

Seyfarth, R. M., and D. L. Cheny. 1994. The evolution of social cognition in primates. In L. Real, ed., *Behavioral Mechanisms in Evolutionary Ecology,* 371–389. Chicago: University of Chicago Press.

Sih, A. 1987. Predators and prey lifestyles: An evolutionary and ecological overview. In W. C. Kerfoot and A. Sih, eds., *Predation: Direct and Indirect Impacts on Aquatic Communities,* 203–224. Hanover, N.H.: University Press of New England.

———. 1994. Predation risk and the evolutionary ecology of reproductive behavior. *Journal Fish Biology* 45:111–130.

Sih, A., and J. J. Krupa. 1992. Predation risk, food deprivation, and non-random mating by size in the stream water strider, *Aquaris remigis. Behavioral Ecology and Sociobiology* 31:51–56.

Stacey, P. B. 1982. Female promiscuity and male reproductive success in social birds and mammals. *American Naturalist* 120:51–64.

Stephens, D., and J. Krebs. 1986. *Foraging Theory.* Princeton, N.J.: Princeton University Press.

Theodorakis, C. 1989. Size segregation and the effects of oddity on predation risk in minnows. *Animal Behaviour* 38:496–502.

Trivers, R. L. 1971. The evolution of reciprocal altruism. *Quarterly Review of Biology* 46:189–226.

Van der Meer, J. 1992. Statistical analysis of the dichotomous preference test. *Animal Behaviour* 44:1101–1106.

Vickery, W. L., L. A. Giraldeau, J. J. Templeton, D. L. Kramer, and C. C. Chapman. 1991. Producers, scroungers, and group foraging. *American Naturalist* 137:847–863.

Waldman, B. 1987. Mechanisms of kin recognition. *Journal Theoretical Biology* 128:159–185.

Weigmann, D. D., L. Real, T. A. Capone, and S. Ellner. 1996. Some distinguishing features of models of search behavior and mate choice. *American Naturalist* 147:188–204.

Willmer, C. 1985. Thermal biology, size effects, and the origin of communal behaviour in Cerceris wasps. *Behavioral Ecology and Sociobiology* 17:151–160.

Cognitive Ecology: Prospects

REUVEN DUKAS

All contributors to this volume express the central philosophy of cognitive ecology namely, that cognition must be studied with regard to an animal's ecology and evolutionary history, and that knowledge of cognitive mechanisms can help us explain behavioral, ecological, and evolutionary phenomena. In various chapters, however, the depth of analysis of cognitive and evolutionary-ecological mechanisms differs. This variation reflects the need for further cognitive-ecological research in ways I will discuss.

11.1 NEURONS AND BEHAVIOR

The building blocks of all cognitive systems are neurons. Hence, a comprehensive theory of cognitive ecology should explain how natural selection has acted on individual neurons and neural networks to produce various cognitive capacities. Research on the way networks of neurons mediate information processing and behavior is still in its infancy. The major theoretical tool presently is simulation of hypothetical or real neural networks (e.g. Rumelhart et al. 1986; Schwartz 1990; Gardner 1993). It is sometimes tempting to criticize a first generation of models for being unrealistic. For example, in artificial neural networks such as the ones described in chapter 2, there are very few neuronal components, and various known properties of biological neurons are not considered. All models, however, are somewhat simplistic because they are supposed to capture essential properties and omit numerous details. Thus, a simple theoretical neural network can be instructive *because* it is simplistic. As Enquist and Arak (chap. 2) showed, one can use theoretical models of neural networks to illuminate important behavioral and ecological phenomena such as the design of signals and the choice of mates.

One measure of the success of a theoretical tool, such as neural-network simulation, is its capacity to generate novel testable predictions. Neural-network models have indeed inspired exciting neurobiological research (e.g. Zipser and Anderson 1988; Gardner 1993); however, it is too early to evaluate the models' contributions to behavioral ecology and related disciplines. Nevertheless, it is likely that neural-network simulations can guide behavioral research by identifying (1) what networks of neurons can and cannot do; and

(2) what neuronal characteristics must be included in order to generate realistic models of certain cognitive functions and behaviors. Perhaps, however, neural-network simulations will inspire the generation of new analytic or simulation tools for network modeling. Such models should capture more of the fundamental properties of individual neurons, synapses, and neurotransmitters than the first generations of neural-network simulations (see Gerstein and Turner 1990; Gardner 1993).

11.2 CONSTRAINTS

In many chapters of this volume, various cognitive constraints are referred to implicitly or explicitly. In chapter 2, Enquist and Arak suggest that the basic design of neural networks creates some perceptual biases that affect signal design. In chapter 3, I discuss limits on the amount of information that the brain can process simultaneously (attention) and over short periods of time (working memory), constraints on long-term memory, and an inability to sustain vigilance indefinitely. In chapter 4, I raise the issue of learning rate limits, which may prevent animals from learning tasks that are crucial for survival quickly enough. In chapter 6, Dyer mentions computational limitations that may have shaped navigational capacities of animals with little brains. Finally, perceptual and computational limitations are also invoked in chapter 8 to explain animal sensitivities to variable rewards.

One can readily accept the notion of constraints on design if their only effects are some perceptual biases, which may have little or no effect on fitness. However, when constraints seem to influence survival and reproduction, a thorough analysis is required to determine the fitness costs and benefits and the fundamental system design that determine a certain cognitive capacity (sections 3.2, 3.6). For example, we all know that it takes time for animals (including humans) to learn certain tasks. Does this learning rate represent some optimal value, or is there a basic neuronal limit to learning rate? To answer these and similar questions, we need to know more about the way neurons and networks generate various cognitive capacities. The pursuit of such knowledge may be enhanced by integrating neurobiological knowledge with evolutionary-ecological considerations and with use of theoretical tools such as optimality analyses and refined models of neural networks.

11.3 COMPUTATION

Many animals must acquire knowledge about their location in space and time and the relative qualities of alternative resources such as food patches, shelters, and social partners. To these ends, mere acquisition of raw information is insufficient because this information must be somehow filtered and analyzed to evaluate environmental variables and compare available alternatives. Al-

though some of the analyses may require little or no computation, it seems that information processing typically involves, or at least can be described with, various algorithms. For example, to evaluate the relative qualities of various food sources, one can consider a few factors such as net energy content, handling time, and associated risk of injury or mortality caused by predation or other hazards. What algorithm should an animal use when considering these factors? In chapters 8 and 9, it is suggested that the answer is not obvious even if risks of injury and mortality are ignored. Currently, behavioral ecologists conduct behavioral experiments to test what algorithms animals may use to make foraging decisions. This somewhat indirect method can be augmented by direct measurement of neuronal activity, which can tell us how computation is indeed carried out in the brain.

Hatsopoulos et al. (1995) nicely demonstrated the feasibility of such an approach (section 1.4). First, predictions of the feasible algorithms that the locust *could* use to recognize objects on a collision course were tested and these predictions were rejected on the basis of observed neuronal activity. Second, they constructed a new algorithm that agreed with their neurobiological data. Thus, by considering feasible algorithms and testing them directly against neuronal activity, Hatsopoulos et al. (1995) gained more insight than that achieved with behavioral experimentation alone. Of course, to measure neuronal computation, one must first identify the neurons and networks involved. Although much of the relevant neuronal information is yet unknown, the rapid pace of neurobiological research provides an increasing number of model systems for integrative analyses of neuronal computations and the behavioral decisions they control (e.g. Hammer 1993; Ferrus and Canal 1994; Hall 1994; Montague et al. 1995).

11.4 The Natural Environment

A principal message in this volume is that knowledge of proximate cognitive mechanisms can help us understand behavior of individuals, populations, and ecological communities. However, research on cognitive mechanisms, as it is practiced by many neurobiologists and psychologists, cannot be an end to itself. Not only it is important to consider how these mechanisms determine an individual's fitness in its natural settings; studies on cognitive mechanisms must also be relevant to an animal's environment in the wild. Otherwise, conclusions about mechanisms that are reached in highly artificial laboratory settings can simply be wrong. For example, patterns of song learning by song sparrows in the field are different from the patterns observed in laboratory experiments with taped tutors (chapter 5). For another example, in most cognitive psychology texts, it is asserted that working memory has a very limited capacity. When tested with random information, humans indeed show a limited memory

capacity; however, when experts are tested in their area of expertise, they demonstrate a much greater working-memory capacity (section 3.5). Hence, these examples demonstrate that the empirical search for mechanisms must remain within boundaries determined with the animals' relevant tasks as they are experienced in the natural environment.

11.5 HOW DO BRAINS WORK?

Despite the outpouring of new information about brain functioning, we still do not understand how brains work. The central message in this volume is that insights from evolutionary biologists and behavioral ecologists can significantly contribute to the solution of this biological puzzle. After all, "nothing in biology makes sense except in the light of evolution" (Dobzhansky 1973). The central reasoning of ecological and evolutionary analyses is that a biological trait usually has some costs and benefits, which can be expressed in units of fitness (section 1.3). This rational is mostly absent in many neurobiological and psychological studies. As discussed in the chapters of this volume, such a functional approach for studying cognition provides fresh understanding and novel testable predictions. This volume cannot yet answer how the brain works; however, in this volume is indicated the way for a broader interdisciplinary field of cognitive science, which considers cognition an evolved characteristic that is shaped by numerous ecological factors that determine survival and reproduction of animals in their natural settings. The quest for understanding the brain's workings should proceed along two interconnected paths of investigation; in one, the focus on evolutionary-ecological questions must include fundamental neurobiological knowledge, and in the other, neurobiological mechanisms must be sought with use of established evolutionary-ecological principles.

LITERATURE CITED

Dobzhansky, T. 1973. Nothing in biology makes sense except in the light of evolution. *American Biology Teacher* 35:125–129.

Ferrus, A., and I. Canal. 1994. The behaving brain of a fly. *Trends in Neuroscience* 17:479–485.

Gardner, A., ed. 1993. *The Neurobiology of Neural Networks,* Cambridge: MIT Press.

Gerstein, G. L., and M. R. Turner. 1990. Neural assemblies as building blocks of cortical computation. In E. L. Schwartz, ed. *Computational Neuroscience,* 179–191. Cambridge: MIT Press.

Hall, J. C. 1994. The mating of a fly. *Science* 264:1702–1714.

Hammer, M. 1993. An identified neuron mediates the unconditioned stimulus in associative olfactory learning in honeybees. *Nature* (London) 366:59–63.

Hatsopoulos, N., F. Gabbiani, and G. Laurent. 1995. Elementary computation of object approach by a wide-field visual neuron. *Science* 270:1000–1003.

Montague, P. R., P. Dayan, C. Person, and T. J. Sejnowski. 1995. Bee foraging in uncertain environments using predictive hebbian learning. *Nature* (London) 377: 725–728.

Rumelhart, D. E., G. E. Hinton, and R. J. Williams. 1986. Learning internal representations by back-propagating errors. *Nature* (London) 323:533–536.

Schwartz, E. L., ed. 1990. *Computational Neuroscience.* Cambridge: MIT Press.

Zipser, D., and R. A. Anderson. 1988. A back-propagation programmed network that simulates response properties of a subset of posterior parietal neurons. *Nature* (London) 331:679–684.

CONTRIBUTORS

Anthony Arak
Archway Engineering (UK) Ltd.
Ainleys Industrial Estate
Elland, HX5 9JP
U.K.

Melissa Bateson
Department of Zoology
University of Oxford
South Parks Road
Oxford OX1 3PS
U.K.
and
Department of Psychology:
Experimental
Duke University
Durham, NC 27708
U.S.A.

Michael D. Beecher
Box 351525
Animal Behavior Program
Departments of Psychology and
Zoology
University of Washington
Seattle, Washington 98195
U.S.A.

S. Elizabeth Campbell
Box 351525
Animal Behavior Program
Departments of Psychology and
Zoology
University of Washington
Seattle, Washington 98195
U.S.A.

Lee Alan Dugatkin
Department of Biology
University of Louisville
Louisville, KY 40292
U.S.A.

Reuven Dukas
Nebraska Behavioral Biology Group
School of Biological Sciences
University of Nebraska
Lincoln, NE 68588
U.S.A.

Fred C. Dyer
Department of Zoology
Michigan State University
East Lansing, MI 48824
U.S.A.

Magnus Enquist
Department of Zoology
University of Stockholm
S-106 91
Stockholm
Sweden

Alex Kacelnik
Department of Zoology
University of Oxford
South Parks Road
Oxford OX1 3PS
U.K.

J. Cully Nordby
Box 351525
Animal Behavior Program
Departments of Psychology and
Zoology
University of Washington
Seattle, Washington 98195
U.S.A.

David F. Sherry
Department of Psychology
University of Western Ontario
London, Ontario N6A 5C2
Canada

Andrew Sih
Department of Biology
University of Kentucky
Lexington, KY 40506
U.S.A.

R. C. Ydenberg
Behavioral Ecology Research Group
Department of Biological Sciences
Simon Fraser University
Burnaby BC
Canada

INDEX

Please remember that this is a library book,
and that it belongs only temporarily to each
person who uses it. Be considerate. Do
not write in this, or any, library book.

Date Due

JE 18 '0

SE 15 '07

OC 18 '07

WITHDRAWN

BRODART, CO.   Cat. No. 23-233-003   Printed in U.S.A.

Please remember that this is a library book,
and that it belongs only temporarily to each
person who uses it. Be considerate. Do
not write in this, or any, library book.

The text of this book was
set on a Berthold Computer Typesetter in
a face called Garamond. Patrick Reagh Printers
of Glendale, California handset the type for the
front cover and the spine in a typeface known as
Perpetua. Composed, Printed and Bound by the
Castle Press of Pasadena, California.